A BETTER PLACE

A Novel of Early New Zealand

Enid Meyer

Published by Fraser Books,
Chamberlain Road, RD8, Masterton
First published November 2011
Second Edition February 2012

ISBN: 978-0-9864593-7-5

General Editor: Diane Grant
Editor: Audrey Adams
Formatting: Peter Watson, Printcraft, Masterton
Printed by Printcraft Limited, Queen Street, Masterton

Cover illustration: Watercolour by Enid Meyer

Dedication

I would like to dedicate this book to the pioneer families of the Small Farm Associations of the Wairarapa who, over one hundred and fifty years ago, worked tirelessly to clear the land of bush and swamp, allowing their descendants to enjoy a comfortable living here today. They suffered from fire, flood, earthquakes and early deaths, but made the best of what they had. They deserve our gratitude.

Author's Note

I would like to thank my daughters Jill, Pam and Shirley, my friend Lorraine McDonald, and David and Jacqui Scadden, for their love, help and encouragement. My grateful thanks to Beryl Cotter, Anna Bradley, Joan Dickens and Carol Fisher for reading the early drafts and urging me on; to Bryan Butler for keeping my computer working; and to Audrey Adams for giving the manuscript such a careful first edit.
And a huge thank-you to Diane and Ian Grant for making my dream become a reality.

While every effort has been made, through extensive research, to faithfully reproduce life in Greytown in the late 1860s, there will be errors and for these I apologise. The characters are all fictitious and have no connection to settlers living in Greytown or the wider Wairarapa at that time.

Enid Meyer

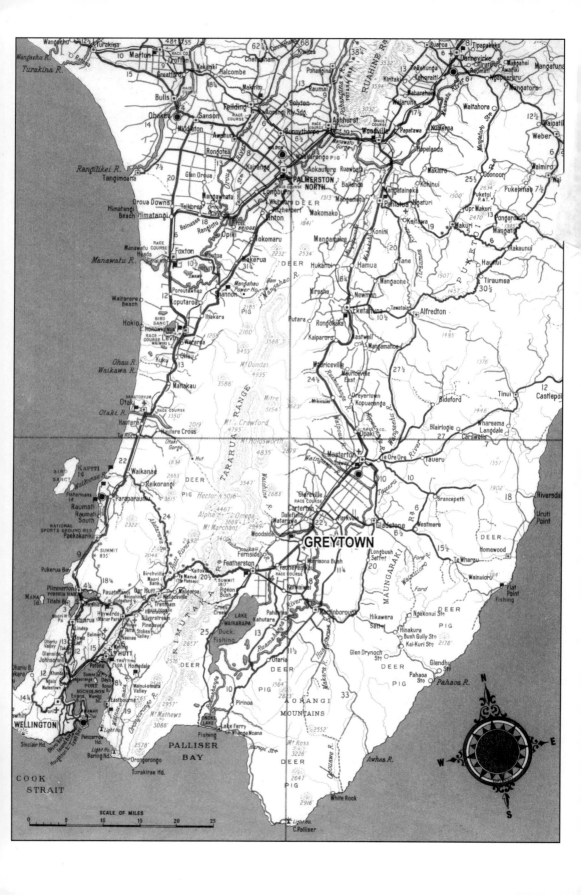

CHAPTER 1 The Reunion

Bright sunlight poured through the porthole as Kate woke the children. "Come on, up you get. The call to go ashore won't be long so we need to be ready. Look at the blue sky - it's going to be a lovely day."

The two children stirred and yawned, then quickly sat up. "Are we really there, Mother?" asked Jake as Cathy rubbed her eyes.

Kate looked at her young ones, wondering what the day would bring. "Yes, my dear. We docked during the night. So come on - get dressed and then we'll go up on deck."

Some time later the call came to disembark and they made their way down the gangway with the rest of the passengers, all a bit unsteady on their feet after three months at sea.

However, the surge of delight Kate had expected to feel at this moment didn't happen. Instead she felt close to tears as she and the children stood on the busy wharf with their trunks and bundles while other passengers were being greeted excitedly by friends and family. All seemed to be noise and confusion as eager hands gathered boxes, sea chests and luggage and loaded them onto carriages and drays. Where was John? He'd promised in his last letter to meet her and the children and he knew the approximate date of their arrival. But that letter was six months ago. It was two years since he had gone to New Zealand to set up a new home for them after learning of a small farm settlement scheme in the Wairarapa and, even though they had exchanged letters as often as they were able, something could have gone wrong.

As Kate looked around her, uncertain as to her next move, she became aware that someone was calling her name. It seemed to be a roughly dressed man sporting a gingery beard riding a roan mare. The rider drew nearer, waving and shouting until, leaping off his horse and throwing the reins to a worker on the wharf, he enveloped Kate in an embrace and lifted her off her feet. Shock and disbelief filled her as she raised her eyes to meet the gaze of her adoring husband. This was not the immaculate John she'd waved goodbye to in England, but a hard rough John she had never seen before. Nevertheless, as he cuddled her to him and crooned her name she was suddenly filled with happiness.

Kate coaxed the children to meet the father they'd not seen for two years and hardly remembered. Shyly young Jake, a sturdy ten year old, put out his hand and said a polite "How do you do?" Pert nine year old Cathy who was normally very friendly would have nothing to do with the rough man. He looked like the sailors on the ship she'd been told to keep away from.

John swung Jake and Cathy up onto his horse and then organised a carter to take the family's boxes and other luggage to an address in the town. "We'll be staying in Wellington for a day or two to give you time to recover from the voyage, and I've some business to carry out while I'm here," he explained to Kate as they walked away from the wharves. "We're going to stay with friends of mine, Mr and Mrs Parker. They've been helpful with advice as they've been out here a while. Mr Parker has a small blacksmith's shop."

"Oh John, I thought we'd be going straight to the farm," Kate said wistfully. "You said it was not far away. I'd like to settle in and begin to make our home. After living out of cases and putting up with the bad food on the boat, I can't wait to get there."

"It's not as easy as that my dear. As I wrote to you, between here and the Wairarapa is a mountain range called the Rimutukas. It's quite a feat getting supplies over that but the road is improving all the time. I need to buy a wagon for the trip and more supplies. You'll enjoy the company of the women here. There are only a few where you are going, some settlers' wives and Maori women at the pa. People here love to see a new face. You'll be made welcome. Anyway, here we are, this is the Parkers' home." Kate looked at the Parkers' house, one of a number of cottages lining the road. Like the others, it had pretty curtains and ornaments in the windows and flowers and shrubs in the neat garden. Suddenly the front door opened and a young woman about Kate's age greeted them with outstretched hands, a welcoming smile on her pretty face.

"Come and get settled. It will be lovely to have a woman to talk to and our little ones will enjoy each other's company for a while."

―――∞∞∞―――

After a refreshing meal of cold mutton, cheese, bread and pickles washed down with copious cups of tea, and lemonade for the children, the men went to the blacksmith's shop. John wanted to find out about a wagon Mr Parker knew of. It was a strong four-wheeled one but needed repairing. John had brought two horses with him. He arranged to buy two more half-drafts to pull the wagon over the hill, though most of the transport was done by bullock teams as the road was steep and dangerous.

"I'll need to get a driver to help with the wagon. Do you know of anyone?" asked John.

Mr Parker thought for a few seconds. "Yes. I believe I've just the man for you. He asked me the other day if I heard of a job to let him know. Donald McGee. Good man. I'll introduce you."

Meanwhile, Kate and Mrs Parker were fast becoming friends with Kate quickly becoming acquainted with the town and the way of life there. She was surprised at how many large homes and shops and different businesses there were in Wellington as well as hotels and boarding establishments. She was also interested to know several schools had been established, but women teachers were in short supply as they so often married soon after their arrival in the colony.

"You know, there was a governess on board our ship who was good with the children. The little charge she minded died on the way out," Kate said. "He was a very weak little boy though his mother was very careful of him. The journey was just too much and he was buried at sea."

"How sad, we hear of so many children dying on the way out."

"I don't think the poor girl knows what she's going to do. She said she would look for a place here, or - as a last resort - a settler who is looking for a wife. I know she is staying in Wellington for a time and I have an address for her so perhaps I can get a message to her before we leave so you can meet her."

After a couple of days rest, all was ready for the trip home. Excitedly, the children said goodbye to their new friends. Tears were not far away though when Mrs Parker and Kate farewelled each other and they vowed to write when possible.

CHAPTER 2 The Road Home

The whole family was excited to be on the road to the Wairarapa even though John told them it would be a long journey. After travelling the road on the narrow strip of land between the sea and the rocky hillside they reached Petone, the settlement around the bay from Wellington where the earliest settlers had come ashore nearly thirty years before. John told Kate how Maori had helped the settlers at that time.

"Are there many Maoris in the Wairarapa?" asked Kate.

"There are some. I've two men working for me on the farm. They're very reliable and good workers. They're looking after the farm for this week while I'm away."

"I know you've written about the farm, John, but remind me - how big is it?"

"We have forty acres and another acre in the village - you remember it's part of the Small Farm Settlement plan that Mr Grey developed. But now I think we should stop and have that lunch that Mrs Parker kindly made for us."

As they sat in the shade of some trees growing alongside the Hutt River, John explained that, even though the river looked quite small and peaceful it could rise quickly and flood, especially when there was rain in the hills. "There are floods every year, sometimes two. Nine years ago, in 1858, was the worst. I have heard stories about the whole valley being flooded and a number of people were drowned."

"I can hardly believe it," said Kate. "It looks so beautiful and inviting I think we could refresh ourselves with a paddle."

"We'd better not stop for that, my dear. We've a long way to go before nightfall. I want us to get to Barton's house before dark."

So they plodded on through the afternoon and early evening until, with sighs of relief, they arrived at the roadhouse. A good meal and a night's rest worked wonders, however, and next morning they set off again, with Donald McGee in charge of the wagon. John followed with the packhorse and with Jake and Cathy on his mount, while Kate walked with him. Climbing the rough road over the Mangaroa hill was tiring for all. Then they passed through swamplands before stopping for lunch.

"We won't get over the Rimutakas tonight Kate," John said. "But we'll go as far as we can. There's another hotel of sorts before the main range - we'll stay there the night."

"I must admit I never thought the journey would take this long," Kate said. Secretly she wanted it to end. 'It seems forever since we left Rosie Parker's.'

Another night spent on the road took its toll on the party. Next morning there were not so many smiles as they started out. Even Donald McGee looked weary as he fitted the halters and trace chains to his charges.

The wagon creaked and groaned up the hillside where rocks the size of chairs and tables littered the roadway. The ruts were deep enough to hide a wheelbarrow in and swallow it for good. Kate pushed hair from her eyes and stumbled on. It surely could not last for much longer. The sheer drop over the side made her feel ill and the grizzles of the children who often asked "How much further?" upset her.

After about three hours they were still only half-way up the main part of the mountain. John was walking on ahead, leading one of the pack horses and picking his way carefully around each corner. It had rained in the hills overnight. Large waterfalls had gouged out the road in places, making it difficult and slippery.

"We'll stop for lunch soon," called John as he disappeared around a bend. In a minute he was back, signalling them to halt. "There's a big slip down," he said. "I don't think we can get past without a lot of shovelling so we'll boil the billy here first."

The children lay in the shade, happy to be stopped for a while. After a quick meal from the provisions Mrs Parker had supplied and a thirst quenching drink from the waterfall, John unpacked a shovel and pick from the back of the wagon. He started pushing some of the rocks over the bank where they crashed onto the bushes below.

Kate watched for a while then took a spade from the wagon and moved some of the smaller rocks over the edge. John looked at her with admiration and astonishment. How different she was from the sweet-faced girl he'd left behind in England where her parents were fairly well off and her time had been taken up with embroidery and piano lessons. He'd do his best to build a home for her in this new land. He'd promised her father to take care of her, and he would.

With the help of Mr McGee a track was soon made around the slip. First, one of the pack horses was led carefully across and safely tethered to a tree on the bank. Kate and the children followed, picking their way slowly through the mud and debris foot by foot. Once through she hurried them past the pack horse to wait for the wagon.

John and McGee took the wagon horses by their halters and eased them slowly forward. Even after hours of work clearing the slip, the track was far from easy and very narrow at this point as part of the bank had fallen away with the rush of water. Kate held her breath as slowly the wheels turned. Most of what they owned was on the wagon. One slip sideways would see it descend down the bank to the valley floor far below.

Gently talking to the big brown mare, John coaxed her forward. "A bit further now, a bit further girl, you can do it." Suddenly there was a crunching noise from behind the wagon as a large piece of road crashed down the bank, flattening bushes as it went. The men hung onto the frightened horses as the wagon swayed and the horses struggled for a footing. Kate gathered the children to her and prayed that all would be well with even more fervour than she'd felt during the storms on the voyage out.

Slowly, surely, with super effort, the great beasts struggled forward, forcing the wagon back on to an even keel. Kate felt it augured well for the future. The little cavalcade marshalled together and continued on their way. It had been frightening, but Kate had faith in John and admired the way he'd been able to steady and encourage the animals.

About a mile further on they came across a road gang cleaning up rock falls and widening the track where they could. These men, who camped out on the job for weeks at a time, were pleased to see some fresh faces, and they exchanged news. John told them about the rock fall and track damage and they said they'd look at it the next day. In turn, they were able to give John some useful information about the road ahead as it was constantly changing. "There's talk that a railway will be built across these hills if a suitable route can be found," said one of the men. "But I don't know how it'll go with the wind we get up here."

"Watch out for the wind around the top of the last rise," said another of the men, after observing that Kate was far enough away not to hear. "A man and his horse were blown over the edge a few months ago. His companion was able to go down and shoot the horse but the man was dead when he reached him."

From then on the going was a little easier. All was calm as they passed the windy point with care. Although it was a weary party that made their way along the road they were heartened by their first view of the vast plains of the Wairarapa through a gap in the hills. "Look!" called John, "see the hills away to the east. Isn't that a wonderful sight?"

After they'd travelled down the far side of the mountain John decided to camp for the night. There were still some miles to travel in the morning. As they settled down on their straw mattresses, Kate looked with wonder at the star-filled sky with the moon rising above the distant hills to the east. She'd never seen anything so beautiful. Away to the right she saw a group of stars in the form of a cross. When she pointed it out to John he told her it was 'the Southern Cross' and was used by sailors for navigation.

Kate gazed at the surrounding hills so much higher than those at home and thought of the downs there. It all seemed so far away now. She smiled as she looked at the sleeping children and snuggled closer to John thinking, 'This is to be our home now.'

When she woke, the men already had a fire going. The horses were feeding on some of the hay John had brought. Kate stretched and thought, 'How can I walk another yard let alone twenty miles?' A grey fog covered the valley and she could hardly see the wagon just a few yards away. "What an awful day," she said.

"Don't worry, it will clear by mid-morning and be a lovely day," John assured her. "Come and have breakfast."

Kate watched as the children tucked into bread and cheese and drank water. "Better than ship's biscuits," young Jake joked as he chewed the crusty bread. Salt meat and hard biscuits had been the mainstay of the fare on board with ship's limejuice to drink.

"Wash your hands in the stream and we'll be off," said Kate as she packed the remains of the meal into the wagon. John rolled up the mattresses, placing them in the little gap he'd made at the back of the load. He looked thoughtfully at Kate, then with a little swoop he picked her up and placed her on top of the mattresses with instructions to hold on until she was used to the motion. He explained that the road was easier going from now on and the horses could cope with the extra weight. Cathy was soon hoisted up behind her mother and very cosy they felt.

Jake was sitting on the packhorse talking gaily to Mr McGee about all he could see. Tall kahikateas, totara and beech trees filled the hillsides with their sturdy trunks. Deep green pongas unfurled their fronds and gave shade to the smaller plants beneath. Green spongy moss and lichen clung to the rocks. Cabbage trees cluttered the sides of the stream, while smaller bushes sheltered flocks of birds which rose into the air as they passed. Large native pigeons came quite close. The whirr of their wings fascinated Kate as she watched them feeding on the berries of smaller shrubs. Bellbirds and tuis could also be heard singing a welcome.

Not long after they left the foot of the hill where they had camped, they had glimpses of water. At first, the children thought it was the ocean, but their father told them it was a very big lake and and much of the land around it had been taken up by large run-holders who farmed sheep and cattle on thousands of acres. In the early days, the first animals had to be been taken around the narrow strip of land on the coast route from Wellington, a hazardous journey and not undertaken lightly.

On the little group went until they reached the village of Featherston. Kate was surprised to see a number of cottages were built along the roadway with pretty gardens. There were even some grand looking two-storey houses, two hotels with their names prominent, the 'Featherston Hotel' and the 'Royal', a surveyor's office and a small school. There were also stables and yards for the horses and bullocks used to pull heavy loads over the Rimutakas, a blacksmith's shop and a store where supplies could be bought.

Now the going was easier, John lifted Kate and Cathy down from the wagon to stretch their legs and they walked along together as John told her of the fine soil he'd found in the clearings he'd made in the bush. After a while they came to a wide river which Mr McGee told them was called the Tauherenikau. Kate couldn't believe how different the New Zealand rivers, with streams interspersed with wide areas of shingle, were to those she was used to in England. John pointed to the sides of the riverbank which showed the height the river could reach when it flooded, and explained that men had been lost trying to cross at such times. Everyone was pleased that it wasn't such a time now and they crossed safely through a shallow ford.

The land was quite flat now. Large burnt areas could be seen and cottages were dotted at intervals along the road with cows grazing in little paddocks with post and rail ring fences. On some properties Kate was intrigued to see a few pigs grunting here and there in undergrowth. "They make short work of surplus whey and buttermilk," John told his family. And when they saw large red hens scratching about in the dirt with little chickens learning the art of survival at their feet, Kate reminded them, "They are just like Mother's at home."

As they passed by, a woman came out of one of the cottages with her two young sons to see the little cavalcade and called to them, offering refreshments which they gratefully accepted. Mrs Scott was obviously also grateful for their company, even for a short time. Her husband was working on the hill road while she and the boys had the responsibility of looking after their land and animals. "It's the children's job to round the cows up for milking and feed the pigs," she explained. "There's a ready sale for fresh milk, cheese and butter, so churning butter or settling cheese keeps me busy as well as all the other jobs that have to be done."

After a short stay they were ready to continue their journey, keen to reach their farm now not far away. As they walked John told Kate about a place up north that one of his Maori workers had been to. "It's called Rotorua, and it's on a volcanic plateau where boiling water gurgles out of the earth. The tribe who live there cook their food in kits or flax bags hung in the water. Mud plops and bubbles like porridge in a pot and geysers send columns of scalding water high into the sky. There's a lake there and hot springs too. I'd love to take you there one day."

"I hope you won't be disappointed in the cottage, Kate," John said as they walked along. "I've made it as comfortable as I could, but it's not a mansion."

"I don't want a mansion. I'm sure I'll manage very well. Seeing the way Rosie Parker and other women are living I would be ashamed not to do the same."

"Even though the farm is only forty acres it will provide all we need. I've felled a lot of the bush with the help of the men. There's also the town acre - perhaps we can build a house or shop there later on. I'll show you where that is as we go through the village. And there it is!" They were approaching what appeared to be a small settlement and, before long, they were in the main street which was also the road they had been travelling on. "See!" said John. "There are some fine buildings here." And he pointed out two hotels, as well as a store, a blacksmith's, a butcher's, a shoemaker's and other businesses. Kate was quite impressed, especially when a number of people acknowledged her husband as they passed.

CHAPTER 3 Home at last

It was late in the afternoon when John pointed to a distant clearing in the bush saying this was the beginning of their land. Soon a cottage came into view and before long they were all standing in front of their new home.

It was made of pit-sawn logs and slab timber with the smoother side forming the inside, and the rougher bark on the outside walls. The door creaked as it was opened but swung tightly shut again once they were inside. Chinks were packed with clay and windows gave light. There was a table and seats which John had made of pit-sawn timber and at the door there was a barrel that held water carried up from the stream, while through a doorway Kate could see a big iron bedstead that took up most of a second room. Against the wall were two bunks with sacking stretched firmly to make a comfortable bed for each of the children. Kate looked longingly at the bed but she knew it would be a while before she could crawl into it.

The children were dancing wildly around the wagon, keen to begin unloading the supplies while McGee attended to the horses and gave them food and water. Jake wanted to help but was warned to be careful as they could be flighty once released from their duties.

Meanwhile, Kate looked at her new home, thinking of all the tasks needing her attention and hoping she could learn to manage as well as Mrs Parker seemed to. How she wished she was here to give her some advice. Giving herself a shake, Kate picked up the kettle to fill it as John and Cathy came in, John with an armful of wood and Cathy with a bunch of leaves and grasses in her hand.

Kate took the bouquet from her grubby fingers and placed them in a glass of water in the centre of the table. "Don't they look lovely Mother?" asked Cathy.

"Yes indeed they do. They add a nice touch to the room, darling. Thank you." Soon John had a fire going and it wasn't long before the kettle was boiling merrily. Kate filled the teapot to the brim and the family, with their first guest, Mr McGee, was ready to enjoy their first meal in their new home, a large pie filled with bacon, eggs and sausages which Mrs Parker had given them.

"Let us give thanks to the Lord for our safe journey, for the meal, and for our friends and our family back home. May God protect us all," prayed John, and they all joined in with feeling, "Amen."

After the meal the children made no protest about bedding down for the night and were soon fast asleep. Kate and John talked for a while after McGee left to sleep in the shelter of a shed near the horses, but soon they too were ready for sleep on their first night together in their new home. As they lay together in the big bed, John told Kate of his plans for the real home he wanted to build on a small hill nearby, using their own trees. It would be a few years before it could be built but he was sure his dreams of a fine home would come true.

As she settled down to sleep, Kate's thoughts were of home and her family, especially her mother, and her eyes filled with tears even though she didn't regret the choices she'd made.

———— ✦✦✦ ————

Next morning, after Mr McGee joined them for breakfast before leaving again for Wellington, Kate gave the children some boxes to unpack and spent the day getting the house in order. She'd brought some linen and china with her but that could stay packed up where it was safe from breakage. She'd labelled the packages carefully and only opened those needed now. John said he'd soon start building a lean-to on the back of the house where goods could be safely stored, but first he wanted to build a sty and buy or barter for a pig or two. He had already milked the cows and returned with a bucket of fresh milk even though two young calves were still with their mothers.

The days passed in a flurry of activity. Kate was too busy to be lonely. John taught Kate, who had never cared for any livestock, to milk and to tend the hens, and Cathy and Jake helped dig an area near the house so Kate could start a garden with the seeds she'd brought from home. 'Home. Now there's a word,' she thought. She tried not to think of the place she'd known as 'home'. This was home now. But she missed the lovely Setter dogs her father owned that she and the children had played with on the lawn Perhaps one day they could have a dog of their own. The children would love that.

Each day Kate found time to tend her garden. Soon green shoots were pushing their way up through the fine soil and before long peas, beans and carrots were well up through the ground. Everyone looked forward to when they could enjoy fresh vegetables, Kate especially. As a child, she'd followed the gardener around at home and seen first-hand the way to grow a variety of plants. Meat was no problem as John kept a few sheep but vegetables were hard to come by. They had some Maori potatoes which had a distinctive flavour and a good string of onions were keeping well. Before long the first of the flowers she had planted were showing bud.

Kate even had some fruit stones and apple pips to grow and selected a sheltered place to start them off. It would be a challenge, but with some hard work they might one day have a good orchard.

The garden had a fence around the outside to protect it against the cattle and Jake had pushed thin branches of manuka tightly all around to keep the hens out. They were devils for scratching! Even though in New Zealand there were no foxes to attack hens as they did in England, another of Jake's jobs was to shut the hens in their pen for the night.

So the days and weeks passed as Kate settled down as the wife of a settler.

CHAPTER 4 An Accident

Late one afternoon Kate decided to take a walk in the bush. The scent of the tall trees reminded her of the park near her home where she played as a child. It was very pleasant, but was nearly time for tea. 'Better go home,' she thought, and began to retrace her steps. It had been a nice change to be away from the house, alone, even for a short period.

Suddenly, as Kate approached the cottage, Rangi, one of John's Maori workers, came running towards her calling. "Oh Missy! Oh Missy Kate, come, come quick!"

"What on earth's the matter Rangi?" she asked as a tight feeling of fear gripped her. Cathy was running behind him.

"Oh, Missy. Oh Missy. It's the boss."

Kate stopped in her tracks. "What's happened Rangi? What's wrong? Tell me, tell me!"

"A big tree, Missy. A big totara. I told the boss it was tapu, but he said it had to come down and so it did when we were cutting it. He's caught by the legs Missy Johnson. You go and get Mr Best from the shed, Cathy. Lucky he's still here. Tell him to come down to the titoki paddock."

As Cathy ran to obey, Kate called to Jake, "We need to take some sacks to make a stretcher. Look in the shed and bring them down. Bring the biggest you can find." The custom of naming the paddocks by the trees that grew there had been useful many times. Bush, cabbage, totara, and kahikatea, were simple ways to say where the men would be working each day. This made it easier for Kate to take food and drink to them as they worked. Now she was grateful as she knew where to run in the darkening light, taking care not to trip as she ran. It was lucky George Best was still helping John with the shed.

Rangi and Kate soon reached the place where John lay, his legs pinned by a branch of the totara tree. Thank goodness, the weight of the tree was supported by this branch but, if they cut it, the tree could fall and crush him. A young Maori lad, Ru, was sitting by John, comforting him, saying he'd soon be free.

Kate quickly tore a strip off her petticoat and dipped it into the stream to gently wipe John's face. He was conscious and his leg was not bleeding too badly, but she didn't want to risk making it worse by trying to see how hurt he was. She held John's hand and kissed him on the forehead, thinking about the tapu Rangi had mentioned. John dismissed such things as piffle though he was aware that Maoris were quite superstitious and were very careful not to offend the tree God.

Very soon George Best arrived and he and Rangi discussed the best way to proceed.

"We need to prop the trunk of the tree with logs to take the weight before we cut the branch away," said George Best. "Ru, you and the children gather some branches together and we'll make a fire to give us some light to work by and some warmth for John."

Rangi agreed. "That's right - we need a fire, and we should cut some rounds of logs to shore the tree up. It'll take time but it's the best we can do." He and George Best took hold of the crosscut saws and began work. Soon large pieces of logs were placed in position and secured with smaller off-cuts.

As soon as the men were satisfied the tree couldn't roll, they built up the fire to get as much light as possible. Then, taking a spade, George Best dug a hole under John's leg, to see if the props were holding. As everything seemed to be safe, they took a smaller saw and began cutting away twigs to get better access to the bough. It would be necessary to make two cuts but, as the branch was only three inches thick, they'd soon make short work of it.

Kate removed her coat and used it to shelter John's face from the sawdust. The first cut went well and if they could bend the piece even a few inches they'd soon have John out of danger.

However, totara doesn't bend easily. They began the second cut and were about halfway through when there was a loud crack. Rangi and George dropped their saw and grabbed lengths of totara, shoving them under the bowl of the tree and yelling to Kate and Jake to finish the cut. Jake had sometimes helped his father on one end of a saw and quickly gave Kate the instructions she needed, "Pull on the down stroke and coast on the rise."

As soon as they made the cut George Best shouted at them to pull John free as they couldn't hold on much longer. Without waiting they grabbed him by his clothes and pulled while John stoically muffled a cry of pain, then rolled clear themselves in case the props gave way.

Very quickly, everyone was crowding around, looking at John's damaged legs. The right one had a deep hole above the knee while the other was purple where bruises had already appeared. George Best, who described himself as "a bit of a vet cum bush doctor", felt the bones to see if anything was broken. Then Kate bound up the leg with more of her petticoat to prevent any more bleeding on the way home.

Two long manuka branches were threaded through the sacks that Jake had fetched and had been placed side by side to make a stretcher. With George and Rangi in front and Jake and Ru at the rear, they made their way home. The moon had emerged from behind the clouds to give some light. It wasn't far but with hazards such as fallen trees and stumps to negotiate, it took nearly an hour.

Although she didn't know who would feel like eating, Kate hurried to make up the fire and boil the kettle. The men laid John on the bed and Kate made him as comfortable as possible, bathing the wound with Condy's Crystals, a good all-round antiseptic. Then she gave him a cup of strong tea with some medicinal brandy and sugar, and he soon relaxed into a deep sleep.

Meanwhile, Cathy started setting out the meal her mother had prepared for the family that afternoon, little knowing the events that would see it being eaten so late in the evening by good Samaritans.

Outside washing their hands, the men chatted about the unexpected events of the night. "I told him, I told him," said Ru. "I told him it was sacred, that it was a king totara but he wanted it for posts as it was so straight and would be easy to split."

"These pakehas can be stubborn eh?" growled Rangi as he lit a smoke. "Lucky George Best was still here helping to build the lean-to."

'It's been a long day,' Kate thought later as she crept carefully into bed without disturbing her husband, 'Recovery will be slow, but John's healthy.' Though the work would be delayed, the men had things that needed doing and wouldn't waste any time. John had been talking about digging a new hole for the pit-sawing operations. That would take a few days.

When she woke, after spending a restless night, Kate was pleased to see John was already awake and seemed rested.

"How does your leg feel dear? Can you move it a bit?"

"It's stiff and bruised but the bleeding seems to have stopped. I guess I'll just have to rest it for a few days and see how it goes. It's not bad considering the size of the gash," replied John heroically.

Kate went to the kitchen and brought him some cold water which he drank thirstily while she told him about the events of the night before. John remembered little of the journey back to the house. He was eager to hear the details and praised everyone for their courage, realising he was lucky not to have been killed.

"I'll have to look at this tapu thing," he said. "It was just coincidence I know but I'll never forget the look on Rangi's and Ru's faces when the tree turned on us. It was falling perfectly, then swung around and caught me just as I heard their warning. I'm glad they never tried to get me out without help."

Kate asked John about the things the men could be doing. Digging the new pit for sawing the logs was one thing. Fencing the cleared land with the posts and rails that had already been split would also keep them busy. Kate went to prepare breakfast for the children as Rangi and Ru came to the door.

"How's the boss, Missy?" asked Rangi. "Did he sleep at all?"

Kate nodded. "Yes and he seems rested. He's really pleased with the way you managed to get him out from under that tree. He's truly grateful and so am I."

"Can we see him please? Just for a few minutes," Ru said. "I want to see for myself."

"Of course you can, come into the bedroom. My husband will want to thank you himself and tell you what jobs need doing," and she waved them through the door.

John was propped up on pillows and managed a smile as he greeted the men. Ru went up and pressed his nose to John's as he grasped his hand. John knew this was a normal way of greeting friends among the Maori people, and felt honoured. Rangi also gave this greeting, and said "A hongi from Rangi, eh boss?" and laughed his deep laugh.

George Best knocked at the door. In his hand was a walking stick made of supplejack. "I thought you might need something to lean on. This stick was my father's. It's very old but trusty." He grinned at John. "You have a good rest. We'll finish the shed later."

While the days passed slowly for John, Kate was busy. Every moment was taken up with milking and looking after the animals and hens, while trying to spend time with the children, teaching them to read and write.

One day, to while away the time, John asked Jake for a few pages from his exercise book and a pencil and began drawing plans of the house he hoped to build in a year or two. He knew exactly where he wished to place it and just how it would look. Two storeys, with an imposing entrance. He imagined a long driveway up to the house lined on both sides with English oaks, chestnuts and elm trees. The irony of planning to plant trees on land they were in the midst of clearing struck him as amusing but he wished to create a small piece of England for Kate. Beneath the trees there would be daffodils, crocus, snowdrops and bluebells growing in profusion. He could hear the clatter of horse's hooves and the rattle of carriages arriving at the entrance, as Kate and Cathy waited at the door to greet their guests.

John chuckled as he drew and made notes. He'd better not let Kate know just how ambitious his plans were

CHAPTER 5 Good News

The days went by. Soon John was able to move around with the help of George Best's stick - he even managed to make his way to the long-drop with care. He looked at the garden Kate was so proud of. The shoots from the fruit stones were growing strongly in their pots - they would soon need a safe place where Kate could establish an orchard. He'd tell the men to clear the branches and stumps from the paddock near the house so Kate could plant the young trees during the winter.

Kate came to the door with scraps for the fowls. They were looking settled and having a good scratch about in the run he'd built for them.

"They look happy," she said. "You look better too. The rest has done you good."

"Yes, maybe so, but I think I'll see if I can ride down to the men and see how they are. Jake, go and saddle my horse."

"Oh John, do you think you should? I think it's too soon. Please don't do it." Kate knew that John wanted to see how the men were managing, but also knew how risky it could be. "Just wait another day. Please?"

John laughed. He wasn't sure he could sit on the horse but was going to try. "Don't worry," he said. "I'll be very careful and go slowly. I promise. Jake, you can come with me. I can't go fast if you have to run to keep up."

"Put a coat on Jake, there's a cold wind blowing, you too John. I know I can't stop you, but think of what would happen to us if anything went wrong. We'd be on our own in the wilds of the Wairarapa. How on earth would we survive?"

"Nothing will go wrong. I just need to get outside for a while. Old Bess will take care of me." He put on the coat Jake had brought and led the horse over to a stump where he was able to mount without too much difficulty.

"Well I hope you're right, said Kate. " Remember, if anything should happen there'll be four of us left behind."

John looked puzzled, "Four of you?" He counted on his fingers. "You, Jake and Cathy. That's three by my reckoning. Is there something you haven't told me my love?"

Kate smiled a knowing smile and nodded."I didn't want to worry you while you were ill but if you're so much better and can go to work, you have the right to know I'm expecting again. Our baby will be born in the spring."

"Oh my dear, that's wonderful," John replied. "I'd get down and hug you but perhaps not. That can wait until I come back. I don't intend to stay out long so get inside, wench, and prepare a meal for my return." He picked up the reins, ready to leave.

"Yes my lord and master. I shall," Kate laughed and curtsied. Then, returning to the kitchen where Cathy was reading a book she said, "I do miss Mother. She'd know if your father is getting on that leg too soon."

"You could write to her," said Cathy "I'm going to write a letter to Grandmother today. I love to hear from her. I'm trying to be a tidy writer but it's very hard."

"You're right, Cathy. I'll write today and give it to Father to take to town next time he goes in, when he's better. It's easier to send a letter to England now than it used to be. Do you know that mail used to be taken to Masterton to be taken out to the boats off Castlepoint?" said Kate.

"Where's that Mother?" asked Cathy.

"It's a small seaside settlement where the wool clip is loaded onto barges out in the bay. The sea is too shallow for a proper port. There are hotels and staging places at intervals all the way out there," said Kate. "About every ten miles I think. As far as the horses can travel before they need a rest or changing."

As the sun rose higher in the sky Kate decided there would be no schoolwork today. Jake had gone with John so Cathy could help her in the garden. The carrots needed thinning and potatoes should be earthed up. There was plenty to do. Weeding was always a chore to fill in the time.

Ru and Rangi saw the boss coming long before he reached them and called a greeting with smiles of pleasure. "You must be better, boss," Ru said, helping him down from the saddle.

"I think the worst is over now, but I'm a bit sore from the ride." John looked at the site of the new pit Ru and Rangi had dug for cutting up the logs. It was a neat hole in the ground with sturdy sides, and steps made of short logs for access. "Looks great, Rangi, you've done a good job."

John looked at the stream running along the bank. How much better it would be if there was a bridge over it to give access to the rest of his land. It was not really a river, but when a flood came it was hard to cross. He'd give it some thought.

"Now I had better get home to my wife or she'll send out a search party. Just carry on as you are. I don't want you to take any chances cutting trees until I'm back at work. Just clean up the branches and burn them around the stumps."

"Yes boss," said Rangi as he helped him mount. "We'll be careful. See your father home Jake. You should take the cows back as you go, save you another trip, eh?"

"Yes, that's good thinking Ru. Just call them, Jake. They'll follow you home," said John. "They know what is what."

"I wish we had a dog, Father. I'd really love to have a dog." said Jake hopefully as they went along slowly. He watched his father for a reaction.

"Well, it wouldn't be a pet you know. Pet dogs are useless. A real working dog could help with the cows and sheep."

Jake pulled a face. He remembered the dogs they had left behind in Devon, two beautiful Red Setters. How he missed them. They followed him everywhere he went in the grounds of his grandfather's house, bounding ahead of him through the trees as they looked for rabbits or squirrels and giving him a merry chase.

John felt sorry for the boy. As he rode home he worried about his lonely lad, and thought perhaps he'd find a puppy on one of his trips to town. For the moment, though, he was anxious to get home to Kate and celebrate her news.

Kate looked up from the plot she was weeding, and called to them as they approached. "Are you all right? Is your leg bleeding again? Were the men working?"

Laughing, John replied "Yes, no and yes. They've made a good job of the pit. We'll be able to start using it soon."

Kate told Cathy to go in and put some wood on the fire and fill the kettle. "Father will be hungry," she said as she helped John to gingerly dismount.

"That's better," he said grasping the walking stick and taking a step or two. "I'm glad to be home."

Jake arrived after shutting the cows in the little yard ready for milking. "You're a bit early bringing them up Jake. They need all the grass they can find. It's so dry," said Kate reprovingly.

"Father said it would be all right, to save having to go all the way back again. Now if we had a dog," said Jake wistfully.

"Are you still on about the dog, Jake?" said John sharply. "He thinks we need a dog, Kate. I don't know what's got into him."

"He misses the Setters. They were his constant companions after you left. He spent day after day in the woods at home," said Kate. 'Home', that word again. A pang of nostalgia swept through her. 'Not now,' she told herself firmly, 'no thinking about home.' "Let's have a drink of tea and some food. You must be hungry after the ride."

CHAPTER 6 Living Off the Land

As winter approached, the family's basic stores were getting low although most of their food was produced on the farm. John had bought some young pigs which were being fattened up on scraps and some meal he'd bought, and a sheep was killed occasionally with part cured as a mutton ham. Hens would be put to good use when their laying days were over. Old fowls made excellent soup. Sometimes Ru and Rangi arrived with some Maori food, kumikumi and kumara. John knew Maori were good gardeners and had supplied the first settlers with potatoes and produce grown from seeds given to them by the whalers.

In late autumn there was often a bright shining morning to lift the spirits after a hard frost. Early, on such a day, John saddled the pack horse for a trip to Greytown. In his pocket he had a list of stores to buy from the well-stocked shop next to the hotel. Flour, sugar and dried fruits for Kate, some sweets for the children, grain for the chooks, a new axe for Rangi, plus two canvas covers for the horses that would have no shelter in the winter.

When he arrived there a group of men standing near the shop invited him to visit the hotel with them. "Not today, thanks. I'm a bit unsteady on my feet already," he joked.

"We heard about your accident," said one of the men. "You were lucky Rangi and Ru were there to help. It was all around the pa what heroes they were!" They looked at John's leg as if they expected to see blood.

John lifted his trouser leg to show his wounds and said, "Indeed they were. I could've died or lost a leg. They were great. My wife was wonderful too. I was lucky all right. By the way do you know of anyone with a good heading dog or puppy for sale? My boy has got his heart set on a dog of his own."

One of the men scratched his head. "I saw some pups the other day out near the pa. I don't know the breed, but there are always a few dogs around the whares out there. Be worth a look anyway."

"Thanks," said John "I'll keep a look out. Better get on I suppose."

As he went to load his purchases on the pack horse standing patiently nearby one of the men went to help him. He suggested it would be better to ask around for a puppy with a bit of breeding. "If you're not in a hurry, I know of a farmer who has brought some Blue Merle bitches and a dog over from Australia and would have pups available in the spring. They make good sheep dogs you know."

Thanking him for the tip, John asked for the man's name then said, "Good of you to tell me," as he rode off, leading the pack horse towards home.

'Home.' thought John. Kate was always upset if he talked about this country as home, but perhaps when the new baby arrived she'd be happy with her first little New Zealander, and be happy in New Zealand too.

Deep in thought he rode on, thinking how beautiful the countryside was in the valley. The hills rose up gently on the eastern side and rolled away in waves until stopped by the sea. John had learnt the name 'Wairarapa' meant 'Glistening Waters'. He could see more and more farms were being settled. 'One day there'll be many farms and maybe cities here as well.'

When he reached home the children watched excitedly as John unloaded the pack horse and passed them items to take inside. Soon they were finished. When he handed Kate a bundle of mail she was happy to see among the letters were some from home. They'd been written more than three months ago and could wait a little longer until she'd fed the family and could read them in peace. If it was not too cold, she'd take them out into the garden, to the little bench John had made for her.

John was full of the news heard in the village. "Some people want to set up a creamery near the township; when they do they'll be looking for suppliers. Wouldn't that be a boon? Just take the milk into town and bring home the whey for the pigs. We could get a few more cows then too." John watched Kate's face as he said this, wondering if she wanted more cows to milk, but she looked happy enough. "I also heard about a farmer who brought some dogs from Australia to breed from. I'll find out where he lives and next time I'm in the village I'll see if I can buy one of the pups when they're ready. The man I was talking to said Blue Merle is a good breed for sheep."

"Oh John," said Kate, looking pleased, "Jake will be thrilled. I know it'll be a working dog but he can have some fun with it as well. A dog is such good company."

After the meal, Kate made her way to the garden with her letters. John told the children to leave her be so she could read in peace. There were two. Deciding to read her mother's last, she held it up to read the post-stamp. 'Torquay, oh, what holidays we enjoyed there!'

The other letter was from Mary Smith, a school friend, who wanted to know all about life in New Zealand. She and her husband Jim were thinking of emigrating. Cheap fares were available on some boats and they'd read the advertisements about the 'Small Farm Settlement Scheme'. What did Kate and John advise? 'Oh how wonderful it would be to have a real friend here, living close at hand,' thought Kate. 'I'll write straight away. But first I'll ask John what he thinks.' She wasn't sure what he thought about Mary's husband Jim.

Kate lifted the last letter to her nose to see if the scent of home lingered on it. How dearly she loved her mother, and how sad had been their parting. Eagerly she opened the envelope and took out the folded sheets of blue paper. Her mother's fine writing filled the pages with news of home. The garden was a favourite subject and Kate could almost see the fruit on the trees in the orchard, the buds on the roses and bountiful crops of vegetables as she read the descriptions.

Towards the end of the last page, Kate found the words she'd been expecting, but didn't want to read. Her father was not expected to live much longer. He had congestion of the lungs and had suffered two bouts of pleurisy during the last winter. The doctor had warned her mother that another bout or attack of pneumonia would surely be the last. Oh, how Kate wished she could be transported home on a magic carpet to see him one last time. As the letter was written over three months ago he could already be at rest. Slowly she replaced the pages in the envelope and made her way to the house.

Noticing her downcast look as she entered John asked, "How are things at home?" Immediately, Kate burst into tears and he took her into his arms. As Cathy and Jake looked bewildered he told them not to worry and to go outside and play for a while. "Mother's missing home," he said, "she'll be fine soon."

By the time the children returned, Kate, busy preparing the evening meal, had recovered her composure and asked Cathy to fetch the milk in from the cooler. The cooler was a deep hole in the earth lined with bricks, on the shadiest side of the cottage. Milk for kitchen use was placed there with a wet cloth over the jug. It was several degrees colder than the kitchen and had proved a real boon for the family over the hottest part of the summer. Butter and cheese also kept longer when placed there.

After dinner, John fed the fire with a large backlog and they settled down for the evening. The flames sent shadows around the room, lighting up the sparse contents. "We'll have to build on another room before the spring," he said, "or we won't be able to move in here. With the new baby's things, we'll be too crowded, don't you think?"

"Yes I've been thinking the same," said Kate, "and I've sketched some ideas for an extension. I'll show you tomorrow. Right now I'm too tired."

After breakfast the next morning John said to Kate, "Well, where are your plans?"

Kate unfolded the page she'd taken from one of Jake's exercise books. "I thought as we've already put a lean-to on the back of the house, it would be better to build a fairly large room across the front, with a new door and a veranda over it.

"It'll take a fair amount of timber, but I can see the sense of your idea," John said enthusiastically. "I'd been thinking of extending sideways with a passage between the old and the new, but I like this plan better. We'll talk about it later - I'd better get to work now. Trees won't fell themselves."

John rode away to the back of the farm where the men were busy preparing logs for pit-sawing. The smell of the bush came to him as he rode. It seemed a pity to have to destroy such luxurious growth full of birdlife. He must decide on which patch he would leave undisturbed. Ideally, it would have to have some of each type of tree. Kowhai, kahikitea, rimu, totara, matai, karaka were all plentiful, and down near the river there was a stand of cabbage trees which should be saved from the axe.

He rode up to where Ru and Rangi had dug the new pit. It was wide enough to allow easy access for the men to get down, but narrow enough to support the tree being sawn up. The steady rhythmic beat of the work in progress had muffled the sound of his approach and he watched quietly, not wishing to startle them.

Ru was down in the pit and Rangi was standing on the log at the centre. The firm pull of his arms was making short work of the job. Down below, Ru had to put up with the sawdust created by the sawing but there was little that could be done about that. They changed places often and never complained about it.

When they paused in the work John called to them, "Time for a break boys, you're doing a great job."

Ru pulled himself out of the pit and took a long drink of water from the demijohn standing nearby. Sweat was pouring off his brow. "It is very hot work, boss," he said.

"We're going to have to work harder," John told them. "My wife wants a room built onto the house. She's going to have a baby in the spring and we'll be full to the rooftop," laughed John.

"You are a lucky fella, boss. You must build a fine room for her. She 's a lovely lady, we'll be glad to help," said Rangi, smiling.

"You're right Rangi. I'm very lucky. Some women are unhappy in the bush, but my wife never complains. Well, we'd better get on with this work eh? I'll give you a spell down below Ru, and you can go and bring another log over. Those horses are earning their keep now we're using them to pull the logs over the pit", John said as he climbed down and took up his position with the saw.

Ru went to where the big half-draft horse was tied to a tree and led it to a large totara log where he fastened the swingle-bar and chains. Then, going to the horse's head, he led him nearer the pit ready to pull the log into position once John and Rangi had sawn the one being worked on into slabs. It was a tricky business but was working well.

Rangi had heard about a new sawmill starting up near the village. That would be a good way to cut the timber for the new room. His brother had told him about how fast the saw ripped through the wood. Yes, the pakehas were bringing in new ways all right.

The men worked solidly all day, and soon there was a heap of sawn timber ready for transporting near to the house where it would be sorted and stacked for drying. While they were packing up their gear, Rangi asked John what he knew about the saw-mill being built near the village, how the saws worked, and what drove them.

John explained that a traction-engine provided the power with a belt drive. He'd seen one in the Hutt Valley that made short work of the logs. It would be a marvellous asset to the Wairarapa settlers.

"Rangi, you go up to the house paddock and bring the wagon back with Bessie. You can bring Jake back with you too. He can lend a hand to load, then take the cows up for milking," said John.

"Right ho, boss," Rangi said.

'I'm lucky to have such a great couple of workers,' thought John as Rangi went cheerfully up the track. The Maori were becoming a real help breaking in the country, but Rangi had told him there had been rumblings of unrest up north from some of the tribes with a native leader named Te Kooti. He wanted to push the settlers out of the country, by trying to make the tribes fight them. There were reports of raids in Taranaki where settlers had been killed and others had been forced to go to stockades for shelter. Some Maori also died. It was a real worry for the settlers in that region. When John had said he hoped there wouldn't be risings like that in the Wairarapa Rangi had laughed, saying there would be no trouble here in the valley. The settlers were well respected and treated the Maoris well, paying for their labour at nearly the same rate as Europeans. Many of the local Maori men had found work in the bush and on the big stations shearing sheep and as general hands, and there were negotiations going on with the chiefs for the purchase of more land for the settlers.

After the evening meal, John discussed with Kate what he had heard about the trouble further north. Kate was happy to leave the matter alone for the time being but, as she drifted into sleep the new baby made her aware of his presence with a firm bout of movement and she decided to put away a few stores and pack a box with spare clothes just in case things changed and the local tribes listened to the words of Te Kooti.

When John rose early the next day he looked out at the area around the house which had been cleared of bush. There'd soon be enough ground ready to plant a crop of wheat. He'd bought a plough from Bill Allen, a farmer who'd decided a settler's life was too tough for his family and intended to move to Australia. He told John, according to paper reports he'd read, there was not a problem with the natives there. They just shot them.

He also sold John his two bullocks, telling him to treat them roughly. "That's what they're used to. They'll work till they drop if you swear at them and crack the whip."

"I'll keep that in mind," John replied. He'd always had a way with animals, and it wasn't brutality that got results for him.

That day there was to be a meeting of the settlers to discuss the security of the women and children and the progress of the village which was fast becoming a town. John decided to take the dray. There was also to be an auction of some of Mr Allen's chattels. He wanted to look at the furniture to see if anything was worth buying.

As he rode towards the village he could see more new cottages dotted on cleared land. Then, as he turned onto the main road to the north he noted there were more buildings being erected along it, not far from the bridge over the treacherous Waiohine River. John thought about what he'd heard about earlier times when the only crossing of the river was by the ford. The river was a constant danger as the catchment area in the steep bush-clad hills had frequent heavy rainfall. Even recently a man had been swept away and drowned as the river rose quickly with little warning, and became what everyone was calling a 'banker' even when there'd been no rain on the plains. All the creeks in the area were the same.

John rode to the stables in the village where he chatted to the stable hands waiting for the coach to arrive from Masterton and looked at a couple of ponies in the stalls. They were nice little things. Perhaps he should think about getting a horse or pony for the children. There had been a proposal to start a school. If it went ahead they'd need to ride. They could double up on a horse, but a pony each would be better. 'I must find out how much they want for them,' he thought.

The men already gathered at the hotel greeted John as he entered. "Have a beer Johnson, come and join us," said a tall bearded man dressed in riding jacket and jodhpurs. "You don't come to town often, too busy getting the trees down eh?"

"Yes you're right," replied John. "I want to go to the auction of Allen's stuff and the meeting in the hall. Have you heard any more about the troubles up north?"

"Not a lot," said the bearded man as he sipped his drink. "The local Maoris think it's the Kingites as they call them. They're coming down through the bush from Napier to the pa here to try and get support. I can see why they're unhappy. They'll have no land left soon and they're fighting among themselves too. We'll just have to watch carefully for any signs of unrest. I've bought a block by the lake. They want to be able to keep on using the lake for gathering their food. That's fine by me; I've always been fair, but any nonsense and I'll block the access."

"I'm sure you have been fair," John agreed noncommittally. He'd heard stories of the deals the man had made with the Maoris as he increased his holdings. John hated to see these people cheated.

The auction had already started when he arrived. On offer were a table and some chairs. They'd been brought from Wellington by boat and unloaded at Castlepoint by barge, then carried to Masterton by bullock dray. Despite the rough journey they were in fair condition. The bids were quite low and John was pleased when he won them for two pounds. The next item was a Dutch dresser John knew Kate would love. He watched the proceedings and, after offering a bid of two pounds five shillings, had it knocked down to him as well. He'd have it stored here in town until the new room was ready and take it home then as a surprise.

The implements were more sought after and the bidding brisk, but two crowbars, a maul and wedges were soon added to John's account, along with a buggy.

CHAPTER 7 Things Look Up

Leaving the auction, John walked along the road towards a storage building owned by a general storekeeper where two men were loading sacks of grain off a wagon. John asked for the boss and on learning he was at the shop made his way there. Finding two others already waiting to talk to the storekeeper, he looked around the shop for any new items he might need.

Every day a great variety of goods arrived and the shop's contents rivalled those at Masterton, or so he'd been told. The trip to Masterton was not a journey to be taken lightly, but there was a coach most days. He thought of the little buggy he'd bought, and what would be needed in the way of gear to make it safe for Kate to use. She'd driven and ridden horses in England so it wouldn't be a problem for her.

"Now Mr Johnson, what can I do for you?" Henry Dickson the storekeeper asked as he came over to where John was looking at some horse tackle.

"I'd like you to store a Dutch dresser I bought from the Allen sale," explained

John. "I'm going to build a room on the front of the house as soon as I can. Until it's done I've nowhere to put it."

"That's no trouble. How about sixpence a week storage fee? Sound reasonable?" asked the storekeeper..

"That'll be excellent. I bought a buggy too. Can I leave it here by your shop for safe keeping until tomorrow? I can collect it then."

"Of course you can Mr Johnson. I'm happy to be able to help," Dickson said generously. He'd no problem with the settlers. They were good honest people trying to make a living off the land just as he was from his shop. He was sorry the Allens were off to Australia. Their eldest daughter was a pretty girl who'd caught his eye but he'd dallied too long. Oh well, there would be others, he thought ruefully. But maybe it wasn't too late to approach her now?

"Mr Johnson," he said tentatively, "there's something I'd like to ask your opinion about." He looked at John uncertainly as he spoke.

"Go ahead, if you think I can be of help."

"You know the Allens are leaving soon, maybe even today?"

"Yes I've just been to the clearing sale. What about it?" John looked at the man as he hesitated.

"The daughter is a pretty little thing, don't you think? I've thought about asking her to marry me but I didn't think they would be leaving so soon. Have I left it too late?"

"Never too late Mr Dickson," John said with a smile. "You can only be turned down. Have you asked the girl? Have you been seeing her? Does she like you?"

"I've seen her in the shop and she's always pleasant. We've been for a walk a couple of times, but never without her mother nearby. Do you think I should ask her?"

John was considering the question and wondering what to say when suddenly Dickson looked around at the few customers in the shop and, without waiting for a reply, said, "Mr Johnson, will you keep an eye on things here for a few minutes? I'll be right back." Grabbing a pretty scarf from a display he ran out the door.

John looked at the customers with a grin but didn't enlighten them. They were keen to buy their goods and go. John took details of the purchases and said they should pay for them next time they were in then sat on a chair near the counter and waited.

It wasn't long before happy voices could be heard approaching and the excited couple came in. It was easy to see that a proposal had been accepted as Henry Dickson was holding Miss Allen's hand tightly as if he'd never let go. She was looking demure with the scarf over her head. "All went well?" asked John, but needed no answer. The evidence was before his eyes.

The couple looked at each other as John offered his heartfelt congratulations. 'Things certainly move with speed in this new land', he thought. He learnt that Mr Allen had been supportive of the proposal, knowing his daughter hoped it would happen before they left for Australia, but not believing it would.

After he had explained the customers' purchases that had been made, the big clock above the counter indicated to John he needed to get to the meeting of settlers where he intended to have his say.

There was quite an agenda of items for discussion at the meeting. Finally it was agreed that a school was badly needed, also a house or board for the teacher. A building for church services would be welcomed too. While commercial buildings were going up rapidly and would be made available for the district's use in emergencies, somewhere for church services would be welcomed. Presently church members made their own arrangements, as and where they could. Services were already being held by the Catholics in a house at Greytown. Other denominations might follow this example.

Concern was expressed that the newly arrived doctor needed somewhere to treat patients but this was allayed when it was learnt he'd purchased a house on the main road recently vacated by a widow. She and her children were returning to Wellington as her husband had died after an accident. A moment's silence was held in the poor fellow's memory. Then the meeting resumed.

After much discussion, permission was given for a Mrs Thompson who had references from England to begin classes in her home for children from the age of five.

Then the question of absent land-holders was raised. After much discussion it was decided a letter would be written to the government in Wellington explaining that development was being held up by the lack of road works and bush clearing on unoccupied lots. "They should be forfeited and reallocated to the township in a trust to be set up for the purpose," said one speaker.

"The settlement can not progress if there are so many vacant sections," said another who went on to suggest that letters be sent to erring landowners advising them they must tidy up their sections and repair the road bordering their properties or forfeit them. This idea met with general approval and was carried.

After he returned to the stables for the dray and started on his way home, John thought about all that had passed at the meeting. He'd like more land and would make inquiries about any lots for sale. Now that the saw-mill was up and running, the hardest part of clearing land would be felling the trees. He had heard some wooden tramlines, that had been laid in the bush near Carterton, were proving invaluable in moving huge logs to the mill. Bullocks were able to move the trees over the ground to where the tramlines were laid, and as a result, the clearing process was really speeding up.

As John neared the house Cathy and Jake ran to greet him, full of curiosity about the goods in the dray. After helping carry the boxes into the house, they were rewarded with a bag of toffee each. "Don't eat too much before tea or your mother will have something to say," laughed John, as he turned to Kate to tell her of the happenings in the village.

She stood in the doorway, dressed in a long grey skirt and white blouse with an apron covering her midriff. John thought how lovely she looked in spite of the hard work she did each day. Her soft brown hair was coiled in a bun at the back of her head. A few curls had escaped forming a frame around her pretty face. He thanked God for the day they had met and fallen in love. 'It must have been true love', he thought, 'for her to have agreed to leave her family behind and come here.' Thinking this brought to mind Dickson and Miss Allen. He must tell Kate more often how much he loved her and the children.

Over dinner John told Kate of some of the day's happenings, beginning with the news about Dickson and his love. "What a good thing you were there to encourage him," she said. "Imagine all that love going begging. We'll have to help with the wedding. When do the family leave for Australia?"

"In a week or two," replied John. "They've sold all they own here and are staying with friends in town until they leave. If a vicar can be found they'll be married on Saturday. Everyone in the district is invited and are asked to contribute what they can to make it a happy occasion. It'll be a farewell to the Allen family as well. Mrs Allen is delighted but will miss her daughter."

Kate smiled. "It's just wonderful and I am so glad Mr Dickson trusted your judgement. I'll look for something I can find to give them. I have a box of embroidery somewhere. Perhaps a tablecloth and napkins, I can't see myself using them in the near future, can you?"

After the children were in bed John told Kate about the meeting. "The question of a school came up. It was agreed a woman will open a room in her house for a classroom. It'll be a start and I think she'll be an asset to the village. By the by, I looked at two nice little ponies for the children but don't know if we can afford them. Otherwise the children will have to ride Bessie together. It's time they got to school and were given some discipline."

"I do what I can to teach them their letters and sums," said Kate, slightly hurt by John's words. "It's the time it takes to get the chores done that holds up their learning. School will be a good thing even if we have to do their work ourselves. I know they'd love a pony each."

"Tomorrow," said John, "you are going to get something that you will love - a buggy!"

Kate threw her arms around John and hugged him. With a buggy she could get the supplies from town and perhaps visit some of the other families in nearby houses. Things were looking up.

❦

Early the next morning John and Jake set off to bring the buggy home. Jake drove Bessie in the dray as John wanted to pick up some sacks of seed. She was a docile animal that would do whatever was asked of her from moving the logs in line for sawing, or pulling the plough through the soil.

Although it was well into March there was no sign of rain yet. The ground was brick hard. Ploughing would have to wait until rain came. At present any brief showers only dampened the top layer and were soon dried up by the wind.

As they went along, Jake noticed smoke rising behind a group of trees not far from the road and called his father's attention to it. John stopped and dismounted for a better look. "Stay here with the horses Jake, I'll go and see if someone's burning rubbish or if it's a grass fire."

He soon came running back and grabbed a sack from the dray, telling Jake to run to a nearby house for help. The fire was spreading and needed to be put out as soon as possible. Then he ran back towards the smoke which was increasing.

Fortunately, it wasn't long before a stocky bearded man and his family and Jake, armed with wet sacks, joined John, hitting the flames which were now at their feet, stamping and banging the wet sacks until the flames died. Before long all that remained was blackened grass, and there was time for introductions.

Mr Paddy Kelly, for that was the man's name, was most grateful to John and Jake for their vigilance, thanking them over and over again. He'd been burning rubbish from the bush clearing, and hadn't realised how quickly dry grass could catch fire and spread.

Afterwards, Jake lay on his stomach by the stream where, after taking a long drink, he wiped the ashes and dust from his face. Fire fighting was hard work. What a tale he'd have to tell Mother and Cathy when he got home. Looking at the younger Kelly children who had worked just as hard, he wondered if he'd see them at school.

When they arrived at the store John asked Dickson if the arrangements for his wedding were organised and was told everything was going well. The Magistrate had the papers needed and the vicar was arriving from Masterton on Friday. He'd been coming to take a service on Sunday anyway and was pleased to oblige.

When John asked if he and Kate could do anything to help, Dickson gave a wry smile saying, "Well there is something I'd like you to do. Will you stand with me as my 'best man'?"

"Top hat and tails, is it?" said John with a grin.

"No, indeed it's not. We don't want that sort of carry-on out here. Just wear what you like. Miss Allen's sister is to be maid of honour or whatever they have these days. We're just ordinary folk and it will be a simple ceremony. Following the wedding there'll be a gathering of friends. I believe there's to be a couple of babies christened at the end of the service so Rev Porter will be earning his keep that day."

"What time should we be here? Is there anything else I can do?"

Henry Dickson looked thoughtful as he scratched his head. "No, can't think of anything else, thanks. Just be there at 10am to hold my hand."

"My wife is going to bring some food and drink for the guests. I know everyone is looking forward to the day. We'll all join in the celebration. Don't be nervous. You'll see, it will all go well."

John turned to go, then said, "Oh by the way, we've had our excitement for the day. Young Jake spotted some smoke on the way here and we helped put out a fire. Just grass burning, but it could've got into the trees. It was at the Kellys' farm. They're a bit happy-go-lucky. It could just as easily have been our place. Ru and Rangi do their best, but there have been times when they had to act quickly."

John and Jake took their leave, promising to be early on Sunday and soon had the horses in their places pulling the dray and buggy. It was quite a little caravan as they made their way home. Jake sat proudly in the driver's seat on the dray, urging Bessie on ahead of his father driving the lighter buggy.

Kate met them as they rounded the bend near the house, where she'd been feeding hens and collecting eggs. John helped her up into the buggy and gave her the reins. 'This is heaven', she thought as she drove the little buggy around the paddock a few times, 'Heaven'.

Later John told Kate that Dickson had asked him to stand with him for the wedding ceremony as best man.

"That's an honour John. Mr Dickson is well thought of. He must have lots of friends in the district now his shop is established. I know you'll do him proud."

"I realise it's an honour. I think it's because I gave him 'the push' so to speak. He would've been saying goodbye to Miss Allen if he 'd not spoken to me of his feelings."

"What about the other things you spoke of last night, the school and the ponies? How did you get on with those?"

"The school is to go ahead. Just in the mornings to begin with. The teacher seems quite well able to manage the children. There'll be about ten including ours."

Kate smiled. It would be good to have the children taught properly. "Well, that's a relief. What about the ponies?"

"The ponies belong to a big station owner and are not for sale so the children will have to make do with Bessie. The bullocks I bought from Allen will be able to help get the logs ready for the mill and that will leave my horse here for you on the days I don't need him. He's easy to catch and harness and pulled the buggy with ease today. I was really pleased with Jake too. He did a great job driving old Bessie with the dray."

CHAPTER 8 A Wedding

As the wedding day drew near, Kate looked over the clothes they might wear. There'd be nothing new of course. Even if there had been a place to purchase some wedding finery, there was no money to spare.

She'd just have to make do with what they had. A good brushing of John's suit, then applying the old Mother Potts iron would make his shirt presentable. Her good clothes, worn for the last time the day she arrived in Wellington, were still safe in her cabin trunk out in the lean-to. She'd noticed that the women in the village were wearing their skirts shorter. It helped to keep them out of the mud. 'Perhaps I can shorten mine,' she thought.

The children sat at their lessons at the slab table. Kate was doing a revision of their work in preparation for their entry back into school. They could write well enough but were slower at reading. Times tables were learnt by rote. They all chanted them when doing other chores like milking and weeding. Jake was a little ahead of Cathy but she was catching up fast.

Jake would be eleven on his next birthday and Cathy ten. The difference in their ages seemed smaller now than when they were in England. Kate spared some of her precious writing paper for them to practise their letters though John had brought home some slates for them to use. While the scratching of the slate pencils set teeth on edge, being able to clean them for reuse was a bonus.

"Six sixes are thirty six, six sevens are forty two, six eights are forty eight, six nines are fifty four, six tens are sixty," chanted the children.

"Don't stop, keep going to twelve times twelve." said Kate.

"Why twelve Mother?" asked Jake.

"Because there are twelve pennies in a shilling and twenty shillings in a pound - you have to be able to count your money you know," she said laughing, "or you might get robbed."

Everyone rose early to do their chores on the Sunday, rushing to get the milking done and the animals seen to. After a quick breakfast they dressed in their best and were off to the village. Kate and John travelled in the buggy while the children rode together on Bessie. It would be good practice for them before they started school. They soon covered the distance to town and were greeted by people who had arrived before them. There were looks of envy when people saw Kate in her smart clothes but most were friendly enough.

The service was to be held in a room on the ground floor of a house being built near Dickson's shop. While it was not yet completed, there was shelter from the wind, a roof over the heads of those attending and room for all who wished to help celebrate the wedding. Reverend Porter came up to John who introduced him to Kate.

"I'm pleased to meet you, my dear," he said, taking her hand. "I hope you're not finding life here too difficult."

"Not at all," Kate replied. "We're all enjoying our new life."

"I'm happy to hear that. I know it can get a bit lonely out on the farms. But almost daily new people arrive to settle here. It will be a proper town soon, you'll see," he said as he moved away to greet other folk.

After Jake and Cathy had tied Bessie to a kowhai tree they stood shyly observing other children standing quietly with the adults. Then Jake saw one of the Kelly boys and went to talk to him. When Kate wondered who the boy was as she watched Jake walking towards the older boy, John told her they had met the family when they put out the fire.

"They're an Irish family who've been here for a couple of years," he said. "There's quite a few in the family. Irish you see! Mr Kelly seems a good sort of bloke though. His kids respect him." John thought of the way they'd worked to put out the flames - the girls as well as the boys. "They'll be going to school with Jake and Cathy, so it'll be good if they get to know each other."

"If you say so John," said Kate thoughtfully. She was being careful not to show John she had reservations. The boy looked like a bit of a tearaway.

When it was time to begin, people entered the large room where hastily gathered seating was arranged. Chairs of many designs were evident. Cane, bentwood, some kitchen chairs, with stools placed at the front for the children. A small table draped with a white cloth served as the altar. Reverend Porter greeted the congregation then told them the order of service. "First we'll l have the wedding ceremony, then a short service and time of prayer, finishing with the baptisms. I hope this will suit everyone."

Murmurs of agreement were heard then the wedding party were invited to come forward. John and Henry Dickson stood up together and moved to the front of the room where they were soon joined by the bride and her sister. Both women carried bunches of daises picked from their mother's garden.

"Who gives this woman in marriage?" asked Reverend Porter. A quiet answer was heard from Bill Allen, "I do," while Mrs Allen stifled sobs at the prospect of soon being parted from her eldest daughter. Then, after the vows had been exchanged, John handed over the ring that had been put into his safe keeping. After pronouncing the couple to be man and wife the groom was told he could kiss his wife. This he did, drawing shouts of delight from those present. A short passage from the Bible was read, and prayers were offered for the happy couple.

The rest of the service was quickly over then two babies were brought to the front by their proud mothers. They cried loudly as they were baptised. Their names were read from a card held by their sponsors, and blessed by the vicar. The god-parents vowed to keep watch over them and ask God to protect them. It was a simple ceremony but everyone left the room feeling uplifted by what they'd been privileged to witness.

Tables had been set up in the shade with sheets used as tablecloths. All kinds of food had been prepared by the women who were watchful that everyone had their share. There was ginger beer for the children and homebrew for the men, while the ladies preferred tea poured from the large enamel teapot.

Soon the bride and groom came out from signing their marriage lines and were quickly surrounded by their friends. Kate gave the new Mrs Dickson a kiss and wished her well. "I do hope we can be friends," she said. "If I can help you in anyway be sure to tell me."

"Oh thank you Mrs Johnson. Everybody has been so kind. I just know we'll be friends."

Soon the celebrations were over and people began making their way home. Cows needed milking and animals feeding. As John helped Cathy sit in front of Jake on Bessie, he pointed to the house which was to become their school in a week's time. He'd introduced the children to Mrs Thompson after the service, explaining they'd been to school in Devon for three years and that Kate had tried to keep them up to date with their lessons. However, he suspected they'd find being indoors hard for a while. He'd been reassured by her pleasant manner and the kindly way she responded to the children's questions. "Yes, there'll be a place for you to put Bessie for the morning. The men have fenced off a paddock next to my house so she'll be no trouble at all."

As the buggy rolled along the dry pot-holed road, raising clouds of dust, John kept behind Bessie so as not to cover the children with dirt. If only it would rain, he'd be able to plant a crop to help with the problem of feeding the cattle. Some of the men said barley was a good choice and that chaff was a good stand-by. Others said wheat was a better bet. Growing grain was a new thing for John but he was ready to learn.

Kate was also deep in thought, thinking of the people she'd met and how just being together for a few hours made it seem they were a real community. It had been a wonderful day. There was an air of comradeship among the settlers, as if they'd passed a milestone. People seemed to have high hopes for the years ahead. It could be difficult in these first years of a new settlement but together they would make a better life for the children yet to be born here in the Wairarapa Valley.

CHAPTER 9 First Day at School

Soon it was time to prepare for the trip to school on Monday morning. After an early night, with their clothes hung ready behind the door, the children washed carefully in the cold water left ready in the china jug and basin and dressed quickly. John told them they could leave the milking to him that morning, "Tomorrow though," he said, "you'll have to get up earlier and milk two cows each before school."

Kate had packed some bread and cheese for their lunch. John caught Bessie and placed a horse blanket on her back as it would be more comfortable than a saddle for the two of them. He gave Jake instructions on putting Bessie safely in the horse paddock next to the school then helped them up on the placid old mare. As he and Kate stood together, waving as the children made their way down the dusty road, John looked hopefully at the clouds gathering to the south. Rain perhaps?

The journey to school took half an hour. There were no rivers to cross or hazards in their way even though the road was little more than a dusty track, and the horse went on at a steady rate. As they passed the Kellys' place Mr Kelly waved out. "The children have gone on ahead. You'll soon catch them up. You behave yourselves now. Don't let those terrors of mine lead you into trouble."

When the school was reached Bessie was pleased to be relieved of her load and cropped the grass in the horse paddock. She'd been on short rations lately, so this field that had not been used for a while was a bonus. The grass was long and lush. A small stream flowed across one corner, and Bessie drank thirstily from it as she took in the surroundings.

Mrs Thompson told the children to wait in the yard until she counted them and checked her list of the pupils she expected. She told them to answer "Yes Ma'am" when she called their names, then go into the classroom and wait quietly until they had all answered. Soon they were all seated on stools at the makeshift tables.

Calling the children to attention, she asked how many of them could read. Six pairs of hands went high in the air. Taking a book from the pile on her desk, she called the two older children to come forward and show their skills. Jake took the book and read a page from *Aesop's Fables*, the story of 'The Hare and the Tortoise', then gave the book to Patrick Kelly who stumbled over the first few words but soon became confident and read the next page.

"Now give the book to Cathy," said Mrs Thompson. Cathy took the book and read how the slow tortoise was able to beat the swifter hare.

"Thank you Cathy, pass the book to the next child. Yes, you Jane. Start on the next story please."

When all the children had had a turn, she said, "Now tell me what you have learnt from the first story about the hare and the tortoise?"

Jane raised her hand. "Even if you are slower at things you can still get there if you try."

Mrs Thompson smiled at her, pleased that the lesson had been understood.

"That's right Jane. Now you older ones can write down the words on the blackboard in your books and learn them. I'll test you later."

The teacher went to see how the younger ones were doing with their pictures, and spent some time finding out what stage each had reached in their lessons. Polly, the youngest Kelly girl, had just turned five and had no writing skills at all. Taking her hand, Mrs Thompson guided it to make a row of the letter O. Round and round they went until Polly could make a big round O on her own.

Deciding it was time for a break, Mrs Thompson told all the children to go outside and stretch their legs. They went eagerly and, once outside, chased one another around the yard, breaking down any shyness in the process. Jane and Cathy soon became friends and so did Jake and Patrick. When Polly, who was standing on her own, started to cry, Cathy and Jane went to see what the matter was and found she'd had " an accident" and her knickers were wet.

Jane took Polly back to Mrs Thompson who removed the britches, then produced some clean ones before rinsing the other ones out, leaving them to dry in the sun. Very gently she said, "There's nothing to cry about dear, I should have told you where the lavatory was. You tell me when you want to go but I'll show you where it is now." Taking Polly by the hand, she led her to a small building. "See here," she said, "at the back of the house, this little shed. We'll call it 'The Little Room'. You'll find some newspaper cut up ready to use if you need it."

After Mrs Thompson blew a whistle to call the children back inside she said, "Now I want you all to draw your family and name them, like this," as she held up a sheet with sketches of her own family. "This is my father," she pointed to a drawing of a tall stick figure with 'Father' written underneath, then to a shorter stick figure beside it. "This is my mother and this one is my sister Maud. Now you do the same. I want to get to know your family. Do them as best you can."

Time passed quickly and, before long, the children were asked to show the class what they'd drawn on their slates. One by one they held up their pictures and told the class about their families. Patrick's description took the longest. There were seven in the family. Polly, his sister, was the youngest in the class but she had only been able to mark the page with seven long lines with Os for the heads and bars for the arms. Mrs Thompson carefully wrote names down as Polly told them to her.

After lunch, the children packed away their school books and waved a cheery goodbye to Mrs Thompson. Patrick and Jake went to catch Bessie. Patrick wanted to ride him. Although Jake wasn't sure this was a good idea, Patrick scrambled on to the old horse's back while Cathy and Jane began walking home together, with Polly close by with the other two Kelly children, James and Dennis, trailing behind. After about a mile, Jake asked a reluctant Patrick to get off the horse then he and Cathy mounted Bessie. Off they went, waving and calling to the others, "See you tomorrow!"

At home, Kate was all questions as she watched them change into their work clothes. "Did you enjoy it? Do you like Mrs Thompson? Did you make friends with the other children?" She wanted every detail. It had been a long day without them.

Kate had made a cake in the morning and cut them a large slice before they went off to do the milking. As they ate the cake and drank the milk she'd poured for them, they told her how their day had been. "We have some spelling to learn," said Cathy. "Mrs Thompson's nice and kind, I like her. She was nice to Polly." Cathy explained about the accident. The fact that Mrs Thompson had spare bloomers impressed Kate a lot.

A little later Jake brought the cows in and soon they were all sitting on their stools in the cow-bails. As they pulled on the teats, squirting streams of creamy milk into the buckets which were foaming with the froth Jake worried about Patrick wanting to ride old Bess. He hoped it would soon stop being a novelty.

That evening, after the meal, Jake and Cathy took out the page of words they had to learn, "We have to know them by tomorrow," Jake said. It was not a long list and after a few mistakes with 'ie's' and 'ei's' they were word perfect and ready for sleep.

Meanwhile, John had high hopes of rain as clouds had been gathering overhead late in the afternoon. He woke sometime in the night and listened intently, but all he could hear was the wind. Even so, it sounded as if a change was coming so perhaps the drought would soon be over. The wind shook the house and rattled the branches of trees nearby. Hopeful signs, perhaps the drought would break today. Men at the wedding had told him that normally rain arrived in March but March was ending and none had fallen.

CHAPTER 10 War Clouds?

Next morning John gathered a water bottle and what was needed for a day in the bush. The rain hadn't arrived so it would be another day of chopping down trees and clearing the land. Ru and Rangi were hard at work when he reached the stand of totara they were clearing. The logs were being cut into shorter lengths for splitting for post and rail fences. Totara split cleanly and was useful for shingles too. However, John had heard the new material called corrugated iron made roofing buildings much easier. Corrugated iron was being made in six-foot long sheets and could be nailed to the timber to make a waterproof roof for a building. He had read that it had been used for the roof of the parliament building in Auckland. He decided to find out more about it.

Quite a pile of sawn timber was stacked ready to be taken up to the house to begin building the extension. When he tried splitting totara in longer lengths of narrower width to use for the scantlings in the wall framing he found this worked very well.

Rangi looked up from sawing a log. "You know boss, there's a bit of trouble up in the Taranaki and the Waikato. That King fella's making trouble for the pakehas."

"So I hear. There've been a few more scraps near Napier and New Plymouth. I've also heard a stockade's been built in Masterton by Mr Boys, the builder in Greytown. One man said it's like a fort with a moat round the outside and two rows of solid walls about eight feet apart. There's a building in the middle for women and children to shelter in if trouble starts. They're ready for trouble but

I hope it never comes to that. Have you heard anything?"

"We heard that a party of Hauhau are on their way down to the Wairarapa, but no one here wants trouble. It's still the same as it was earlier in the year. We're peaceful friendly people. We don't want to fight," said Rangi.

The men continued to discuss the situation while they went on with their work. John told them he'd learnt he had to join the other farmers for drill in the evenings with the militia which had been established.

That evening John set off for the drill session. He didn't like having to go after a hard day on the farm, but everyone had to do their bit. While he didn't really think there was any danger he needed to do all he could to keep Kate and the children safe.

After he left, Kate talked to the children about their day at school as they all made ready for bed. She'd just gone to sleep when there was an urgent knocking at the door and she heard Ru calling. "Wake up, wake up Missy, please wake up. Oh quick Missy, wake up the children. We must go and hide in the bush."

As Kate quickly dressed she roused the sleeping children, telling them to hurry and dress warmly and then went to the door where Ru was anxiously waiting. "The Hauhau are on the road and will pass your house soon," he said hurriedly. "They know the men are away in the village with the soldiers. We heard they're going to make a raid on one of the settlers' homes tonight. So quick, get the children up and dressed and we'll go into the bush."

Quickly Kate picked up the bag she'd prepared weeks before and they left the house as quietly as they could, Ru holding the children's hands to guide them in the dark.

There was not a lot of shelter left near the house, but a nearby stand of native trees and flax bushes, which would be dry and warm in their centre, would give them a place to hide. Ru told the children to keep silent as they crept along through the bush towards the flax. This was the best place he could think of as he hurried them past the bullocks standing in the paddock, the moon lighting the way ahead.

Kate didn't argue with Ru about where to go. Carrying the bag, she walked quickly, silently praying over and over, 'Dear God, please let us be safe,' until Ru suddenly whispered, "This is far enough I think. You can lie down here on the old dry flax leaves and try to get some sleep."

Too frightened and excited to sleep, Jake wanted to know what was happening. He had an idea it was Maori trouble. The teacher had told the class about the uprising in the Waikato.

As Cathy clung to her mother Kate wondered if they had done the right thing in coming to this struggling colony but, not wanting to pass her fears onto her child, she whispered, "Don't worry Cathy. Look at the beautiful stars overhead. They're very bright tonight. Look, there is the Southern Cross, and Orion, The Seven Sisters and just look at the moon. It will be setting soon, on its way to brighten the skies of Australia and then England. God will keep us safe tonight and we'll find it's all a big mistake."

Suddenly, Ru held up his hand for silence. He was listening intently with his hand up to his ear. Soon they could hear the sound of running feet as a party of

Maori passed close by, hurrying through the bush.

Ru couldn't see them clearly, but could hear the rustle of their clothes as they brushed against the branches of overhanging trees. He was sure they hadn't been seen and, after a time with no more activity, he decided they could go home. but he was glad he had kept his friends safe, even if it had been a false alarm.

It was a harder journey going home as clouds blocked the moonlight and branches and stumps lurked everywhere to trip them up. Jake and Cathy were told to keep quiet in case another party of warriors came along. The very thought made Kate shudder.

John had told her of the murders which had taken place on both sides of the conflict. Pakeha and Maori alike had been killed in the fighting in other parts of the country. Oh, how she longed for her beloved Devon. Oh, for a magic carpet to take her there, even for a little while. They stumbled on through the gloomy night, wanting only to be back safely in their beds.

―――⚬⚬⚬―――

Meanwhile, John had ridden home on sure-footed Bessie as quickly as he could along the rutted road. The house was dark as he approached it which surprised him - Kate usually left a lantern alight when he was away. He supposed she'd gone to bed. He unsaddled Bessie, gave her an extra ration of chaff and made his way to the house.

How he longed to build the house of his dreams for his darling wife, or at least make a start on the new room. His thoughts occupied with plans for the future, he opened the door quietly, not wishing to disturb his sleeping family.

After lighting the lamp, he drank from the jug of water standing ready for breakfast, washing down the road-dust which had made him thirsty before tip-toeing into the bedroom. Dear God! The bed was empty. Where was she? He rushed to look at the children's beds but they too were empty. What had happened? Were they all right? Had they been kidnapped, or killed?

Horrible things had been hinted at in the newspaper he'd bought at the store. There were stories of massacres of both Maori people and settlers, with tales of heroism on both sides. Maori women had sheltered white women and children from their own Maori relatives and, after a battle, had carried water to dying combatants from both sides.

'Please let nothing happen to Kate and my children,' John prayed as he searched the house for clues as to where they could have gone. Taking up the lamp, he looked for the bag he knew Kate kept ready and found it gone. He shone the lamp through the doorway, out into the night. 'I don't know what to do. Will I ride back into town and get help for a search or should I wait until morning?' he agonised as he shone the little light into the darkness, praying for their safe return.

Through the clouds he could see the sky was growing lighter in the east. Dawn was not far away. Should he just wait? Could he bear to do nothing? Overcome with tiredness he sat on the bed and stroked the pillow Kate used. Taking it up, he hugged it to him as tears ran down his cheeks while he tried to forget the things he'd read. His Maori friends had said there was no likelihood of trouble here, but with the Kingites stirring up matters and the young bloods ready for a fight, he wasn't certain this was the case. He rested his head on the pillow and waited, finally lying down on the bed.

————— ⊗⊗⊗ —————

Kate and Ru guided the children over the rough ground and were soon on the flatter fields nearer the house. Shafts of light lit the sky now, causing the clouds to turn a brilliant orange.

"I can't wait to get home, Ru, and I can't thank you enough," said Kate. "God only knows what would have happened if you hadn't come to warn us."

Back at the house, John decided there was nothing to do but wait until morning. His heavy eyes closed in sleep as weariness overtook him and he dozed fitfully; his mind couldn't relax enough for him to really rest.

This is how Kate found him when they entered the cottage on this eventful night. She woke him gently and he gathered her into his arms, tears wet on his cheeks. Cathy and Jake, who were not used to shows of affection between their parents, stood back watching for a moment or two then they too were gathered into the arms of Kate and John and hugged.

Ru stood watching. How he loved these people, and how much they meant to him as he tried to learn their new ways. Surely this country was big enough for both races to live together happily. While he knew that all immigrants were not as fair-minded as the boss and his wife, he wanted the pakehas to do well and help his people. The missionaries had told him this would happen, when they'd taught him English, and about Jesus Christ, and the big wide world.

Still with his arms round his family, John spoke to Ru. "I can't thank you enough Ru, for what you've done tonight. It was only a false alarm but it's better to be safe than sorry." He took Ru's hands in his own, thanking him over and over again. "I don't think we should work today. We need time to collect ourselves." John looked at the children. "No school for you two either. You can have a quiet day at home."

"I think I should go and see my people at the pa," said Ru. "See if there are any signs of trouble, eh? I think it's all talk. When those big mouths don't get anywhere with us they'll go back home. I'll call into the school and tell Mrs Thompson the children are having the day off if you like, Missy."

"That would be helpful Ru," said Kate gratefully. "I know she worries if the children don't arrive at school. She thinks they've fallen off the horse or drowned in the stream."

"Well, I'll get the fire going and we can all have some food. I'm so hungry I could eat a horse and chase the rider," said John.

Kate wasn't sure this was a good expression, knowing that the Maoris had been known to do just that. 'Well perhaps not the horse, but the rider was definitely on the menu in the past.' The thought made her smile, but she decided not to tell John just what she'd been thinking. His sense of humour was likely to be a bit dented this morning after the fright they'd had in the night.

As the family had their early breakfast, John said, "I'll ride into town later and see what news there is of the war party, if that's what it was. Will you be all right here with the children?"

"Of course, dear," said Kate "we'll be fine, unlike the weather. I think it might rain today. There's only one cow to milk. We'll use most of that for the house so thankfully we can have a bit of a spell and get over the fright we've had."

Later, as John rode up to the store, he saw men gathered around the doorway, deep in conversation. "I hear you had a close call last night," said one. "Ru told us what happened."

"Well it was a bit of a false alarm, thank God," replied John. "I'm grateful though that Ru took it into his head to take the family to a safe place. It could have gone the other way. The blokes in that war-party are an unstable lot, so I've been told. I believe a meeting's being held at the pa, but these Kingites have a lot to say and are not popular with the kaumatua. I believe they'll get their marching orders."

"That's good, Johnson," said one of the men. "I'm sure we'll hear more as the day goes on. I don't think we're in any danger, but it's good to have the rifles and ammunition sent up from Wellington. They came up by dray last night. Very hush, hush the deal was too. Just stowed under a load of goods and although the dray was stopped by Maoris in Featherston, they never looked under the piles of provisions."

The men continued their discussions as John made his way into the store where Dickson gave him a hearty handshake and his wife also greeted John warmly, saying, as she took his hand in hers, "Oh Mr Johnson. It's good to see you. I heard about the trouble you had. Ru came into the shop this morning and told us what a lucky escape it was. Is your wife all right? You must have been so worried when there was no-one at home!"

"Yes it was awful," said John, remembering how he felt the previous night. "I was beside myself with the frightening possibilities, but it's over now. I don't think they will try anything again. They'll be told to go home to Napier. I'm waiting to hear what the news is from the pa. But my wife is well and I let the children stay home today. It was terrible for them being dragged out of their beds in the middle of the night. Ru was a true friend. I don't want to think what would have happened if the Hauhau had meant to kill someone as a warning. Ru would have been in danger too."

"Yes that's right," Henry Dickson said. "I know there have been instances when the tribe have turned on anyone who helped the enemy, even when it was Maori against Maori. Taking utu, they call it."

"I don't know how you can be so calm about it," said Mrs Dickson. "Is your wife home alone? How could you bear to leave her? I'd be terrified to stay out there in the bush on my own. She's very brave."

"She has the children with her. I gave them the day off school to get over the trauma. There was only a rumour that the Hauhau would try something. Besides, we have the government guns here and a band of men ready to fight if things go bad. I believe the local Maori don't speak of war and would come to our aid if needed, as Ru's actions proved. I've heard that a stockade and a house for shelter have been built in Masterton just in case. I don't expect they will want to use it."

"The women of Masterton will be glad of the shelter provided after hearing of the troubles. I'd feel safer if we had some sort of fort here. My husband says not to worry but that's easier to say than to do."

John was anxious to get home to Kate, so didn't pursue the conversation further, other than to agree he thought people were quite safe in the settlement, now that more people were moving to the village and more houses were being built.

"You're right Johnson," said Henry Dickson. "There seems to be another home started every day, more businesses too. Another shoe maker has opened up - that will make three - and he's going to make shoes to order as well as repair them. That will be a godsend in the winter." Dickson stopped speaking and listened. "Do I hear rain on the roof? I believe I do. The drought may be over at last. Johanna, my dear, will you get Mr Johnson his mail? We're getting busier every day. I must say having my wife to help has made my life much happier. You can't beat good meals and good company can you?"

"Is that what I am, just a good cook and listener?" Mrs Dickson sounded a little put out, but there was a smile on her face as she passed the mail packet to John. "Do ask your wife to come in and see me if she's in the village."

Placing the mail in his saddlebag John mounted Bessie. The rain was coming down faster now and he was going to get wet. Then he saw Dickson come out of the shop with an oilskin shoulder cover. It looked like an apron but was worn on the back and secured in front by ties. "Try one of these. It'll keep the water off your back and keep your arms free to hold the reins, good for work too."

"That's good of you. I'll fix you up next time I'm in town. The rain's really set in. I'll be glad to get home."

CHAPTER 11 Kate has News From 'Home'

The journey, although uncomfortable, was soon over. Kate laughed as he removed his oilskin covering. "You look as if you're wearing a cow cover. You're quite dry on the back but your trousers are saturated. Come in by the fire and get warm."

Handing Kate the mail, John said, "It's not cold yet but the rain's very heavy. I think a storm is on the way. The clouds are looking dark towards the south." Taking the towel proffered by Kate he dried his face. "Well, what news from home?"

Kate opened the packet and sorted the letters. There were some for John from his sister and two for her, one from her mother plus a letter from her old school friend Mary, but that could wait. Sadly, among the newspaper cuttings from her mother was the obituary for her father. Kate turned to John with tears in her eyes. "Father died in January. He went quite quickly in the end. Mother said it was peaceful."

Kate said a silent prayer for him and for her mother. Mother would be missing him dreadfully after thirty years of marriage. 'Poor Mother, what will she do now?'

She was sure her mother would know what her daughter would be feeling when she heard the news, even when it was over three months old.

"My poor Kate." John put his arms around her in a comforting hug. "That's sad news, but at least he's at rest. He was a wonderful man and a good friend to me Kate. I'll miss him too. I'll tell the children and they can write a letter to Grandmother. I know she'd like that."

"Yes, she would, but I just wish I could be there." Kate turned to John for comfort again. He hugged her to him as she wept. When she calmed down Kate took the rest of her mother's letter and sat near the fire to read it. She could feel the sorrow in her mother's words and, as she read, she could see some smudged writing, perhaps from tears. 'Would Mother consider coming out to New Zealand? But how would she take to living in the primitive conditions? Better wait for a while before I suggest such a move.'

Looking at the envelope for the date stamp, Kate made out Jan 30th. It had only taken ten weeks to get here, quicker than ever before! As a wave of home sickness passed through her, Kate thought, 'If I could fly like a bird and visit home, how wonderful that would be.'

The letter from Mary was next. It was only a couple of pages long but held exciting news. The family was on its way to New Zealand. They'd sailed from Portsmouth on February the twentieth. If all went to plan they were expected to land in Wellington on May the tenth.

'Goodness! John will have to go to Wellington to meet them, or send word to friends down there to go in his place. The road's not much better than when we came over,' thought Kate. Even though gangs of workers were going up the Rimutaka hill each day to make improvements, it was still very rough

Rising quickly, she called John, who had gone out to do some work on the building they called the stables, although it was only a rough shelter. "John, Mary and her husband are on their way over here to New Zealand. They land about the tenth of May in Wellington, or maybe even earlier. Do you think they expect to come here?" Kate asked excitedly.

"As I don't know what you've said in your letters to them about the conditions here, I've no idea what their plans are," John replied. "I'll have to give it some thought. We've nothing to offer them here. I suppose I could get George Parker to make some preparation for them in Wellington if I wrote and sent him the information about their ship. He's a good man. I'd trust him to do all he can." John looked thoughtful as he pulled his ginger beard. "I could also see if there is any way a section could be made available for them to buy into the Small Farms Scheme. If they have any money! I was never sure about Mary's husband, as you know, but if you think we can help, I'm prepared to do what we can. We're too far from Wellington to do much, but can try. Mrs Parker might help too. She was good to us when you arrived. I'm sure she'll help all she can."

"Oh thank you John. I never thought they'd come so soon. I told Mary how things are here but it hasn't put her off. We'll just have to do what we can and they will have to do the rest." Kate looked at John for his reaction. "I'd love her to live close by, but I don't want to make a lot of extra work for you."

"Not at all. I'll do what I can and they'll, as you say, have to do the rest. What's for tea?" asked John smiling at her.

Kate laughed and said, "You men and your stomachs."

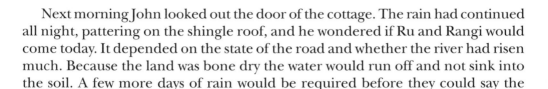

Next morning John looked out the door of the cottage. The rain had continued all night, pattering on the shingle roof, and he wondered if Ru and Rangi would come today. It depended on the state of the road and whether the river had risen much. Because the land was bone dry the water would run off and not sink into the soil. A few more days of rain would be required before they could say the drought had broken.

"I'll write my letter to Mrs Parker," said John. "Then I'll take a look at the river. I know it'll be up, but whether it's a banker or just a high, I can't tell from here."

"Do be careful," said Kate. "More bridges are what we need. There was another drowning last week. So many have been lost trying to cross streams and rivers, but at least it's better than the old days when they called it the 'New Zealand Disease'."

The storm was moving north and thunder was rumbling along the Tararuas in the west as John settled at the slab table to write his letter to Mrs Parker. He'd write in general terms, asking her to see them and help them find somewhere to stay. He wished he knew exactly what promises Kate had made to Mary.

Suddenly, there was an explosion as lightning struck a tall kahikatea tree at the edge of the bush and the children came running in fright. "What was that?" asked Cathy. "Whatever was that bang?"

"It was just a flash of lightning," John reassured her. "Don't worry my dear."

Seeing his own children, John remembered that Mary and Jim had two children themselves so they'd need to find a home quickly. "How old are Mary's children?" he called to Kate, who was tidying up beds.

"I think Peter is nearly six and Marie is four, if I remember rightly," Kate said.

"And Jim, how old is Jim?"

"He was thirty when we left and Mary must be twenty six now. I'm two years older than she is and you're four years older than Jim. We're all getting older. Cathy will be ten in June and Jake will be twelve in August. I'll be twenty-nine in October and you'll be an old man of thirty-five in July, poor old you."

John chased Kate around the kitchen and grabbed her around the waist. "I'm not that old that I can't catch you," he said, and went back to his letter. The children watched with interest and amusement. It took their minds off the lightning.

"Jim's a strange man in some ways," said Kate as she realised she knew very little about him and the sort of person he was. Through Mary she knew he was a good father but not a good provider. However, Kate didn't want to say too much, thinking he might have changed.

Finishing his letter, John stood up and took his oilskin cape off the hook by the door. "I'm going to see how the river is, and yes, I'll be careful," he told Kate. But as he went down the path he could hear rushing water in the distance. The thud of water-borne logs barging into the trees growing on the banks gave an early indication of the ferocity of the Waiohine River.

It was high, but not yet flooding the flat paddock near the house. The sheep were waterlogged and bedraggled while the cows seemed to be enjoying munching on grass washed clean of dust but, studying the scene, John could see no cause for alarm. Then he heard a horse approaching and looked up to see Ru and Rangi riding toward him through the bush. "Good day!" he called.

"This old river's pretty high, boss," said Rangi, "but I think the rain will stop now and she'll go down pretty quick too."

"I think you're right Rangi. How are things in town? No flooding there?"

"No, not really," Rangi replied. "There's a bit of water through the street but it's just run-off from the rain. The stream is high and so is the water at the ford. There won't be much movement on that road today. Some fellas come up from Tauherenikau on horses. They're sitting in the Rising Sun drinking beer while they're waiting for the rain to stop."

"Let's get in out of the rain," said John. "Come over to the stables. We can work there. It's a bit wet to go down to the bush. How did the meeting at the pa go? Have the King supporters gone home?"

"Not yet boss," Rangi said, "but they'll be off soon. We told them we didn't want any trouble. They had their say and we didn't agree. They'll try the Maoris at Akura, I think. But they won't get far with them or the Manaia Maoris either. The feeling at the meeting was that pakehas are all right and as long as they pay us their rents we've no quarrel with them."

"Not as long as they stick to their bargains," added Ru. "They've bought a lot of land. They should be able to clear it and work it without any wars."

"Well put!" said John. "Now let's get those holes dug for the posts."

CHAPTER 12 Tragedy Strikes

Some time later the men were glad to down their tools when Kate arrived with a welcome jug of tea. "Where's Jake?" she asked, looking around the shed.

John looked surprised. "He's not here. I thought he was home with you."

"He put his coat on when the rain stopped. I thought he'd gone to see you," said Kate. "He might be home again by now. I'll ask Cathy if he said where he was going," and, with a worried look on her face, she ran back to the house.

"I'm sure he'll be all right," said John, and the men drank their tea without concern. Boys were able to look after themselves out here. There were no ferocious animals or snakes, and he'd been told to keep away from the water,

However, Kate returned looking anxious. "Cathy says he was going to see Patrick Kelly. Evidently they found an old canoe on the riverbank the other day and wanted to try it out."

"Dear God!" cried John and he ran to get the horse's bridle and saddle while Ru and Rangi jumped on their horses and rode away to the river. John was saddling Bessie as Cathy came rushing out of the house. "Where was the canoe lying?" he called to her. "Was it the creek or the riverbed?"

"He said the riverbed, up by the Kellys'. I told him it was dangerous and to ask you."

Angry and terribly worried at the same time, John turned Bessie and galloped off, making for the Kellys'. Ru and Rangi were far ahead of him, but he could see them going through the trees and caught up with them outside the house just as Mr Kelly came out to see what the fuss was. "What's going on?" he asked.

"Is Patrick home? Have you seen Jake?" John asked.

"He called in for a while and then he and Patrick went off for a walk."

"Did they say anything about a canoe to you?"

"Oh, the old canoe down by the river? No, they never said anything about that. Damn thing should have been scuttled before this. It still floats you know. I never thought they'd be so stupid as to try it out in this flood. I'll flay him alive if he has."

With dread in his heart, John was soon racing through the bush towards the river with Ru and Rangi following him. Ru called to him as he caught up. "I thought I could see them through the trees, but it was only a calf that's been swept downstream. I'll ride along the bank and see if there's any sign. The river turns sharply around the next bend. They might have been driven nearer the bank."

"I'll ride back upstream and have another look there, boss." Rangi said and he rode away into the bush.

John sat on Bessie wondering what to do next. It would take Ru a while to search the bank. 'Maybe I should go straight down to the bridge and see if anyone has seen them in the canoe, or in the water. Stupid young sods!' he thought. As he rode along he looked closely at all the growth along the bank. Suddenly, a speck of colour in the willows caught his eye and, tying his horse to a branch, he went for a closer look.

The scrap of material caught by a thread on a branch was part of the jersey Jake had been wearing. John's heart sank. Was his son dead?

Frantically remounting, John rode towards the bridge. As he got nearer he could see a few people gathered there. He hurried to join them and they parted to let him through. There, lying on the ground, was his son. Someone was bending over him pushing on his back, trying to make him breathe.

When, after a moment or two, Jake coughed and a stream of dirty water gushed from his mouth, John gathered his son to him and hugged him to his chest. He held him tightly and wiped Jake's face with his sleeve, brushing away the sand and leaves that clung there.

"That was a close shave, young fella!" said one of those standing on the bank. "Now the rain's stopped we were on way to Carterton and were just about to cross the bridge when this young fool came along hanging on to a log. That bloke there walked into the river and pulled him out just as you arrived."

He pointed to a good-looking man with a full beard, a well-built young chap of about twenty years, and said, "Johnson, I'd like you to meet Patrick O'Brien, newly arrived from Ireland. Just in the nick of time, wouldn't you say?"

Near to tears, John took the outstretched hand. "I'm pleased to meet you. Thank you for saving my son."

"T'was nothing, Mr Johnson, just lucky I was here," said the young man with a smile. "Only too happy to oblige."

Suddenly, Jake struggled to sit up, gasping, "Where's Patrick? Did you see him in the canoe?"

"No boy, we didn't see anyone else. For God's sake, how many of you were playing around like idiots in the flood?" asked an older man.

"Just me and Patrick. We got into the canoe and were just sitting in it by the side of the bank, when this big rush of water came down the river and the canoe took off. We didn't have any paddles but were fine until the canoe tipped over. I grabbed the log. I don't know what happened to Patrick."

"What have you got to say to Mr O'Brien, Jake?" asked John.

"Thank you for saving me sir, but can we please look for Patrick?" He looked up at the men with tears in his eyes. He realised what had nearly happened to him. Patrick might not have been so lucky.

When two horsemen arrived at a gallop, John looked to see Ru and Rangi with, hanging over the front of Rangi's saddle, the limp body of Patrick.

"We found him caught in the branches of a tree about half a mile away," Rangi said. "We've tried to revive him but had no luck." He looked at Jake as he spoke. "I'm sorry young fella. This is what happens when you take chances with nature. This river is so strong and so fast; he'd have had no chance. What should we do now boss? Take him home to his family?" asked Rangi.

"Yes, yes, that would be the thing to do. I'll come with you. I'll need to talk with Mr and Mrs Kelly. They'll be devastated," said John. "Look Ru, you take Jake home to his mother, she's been so worried."

As they rode through the trees towards the Kellys' they could see Mr Kelly and his children - they had obviously been out in force searching. John was not looking forward to his mission. As they approached, Mr Kelly saw at once the burden the horse was carrying and let out a high-pitched scream of anguish.

John dismounted and put an arm around Mr Kelly's shoulders. "I'm so sorry. The men found him caught in the trees down river. Jake was pulled from the water at the ford by some young Irish fellow in the nick of time. He's alive, thank God."

"What will his mother say?" cried Kelly in anguish. "She's been ready to give up and return to the old country. Now this - it will just about kill her." He looked at Rangi holding the body of his son on the horse. "We'd better get him home to her I guess, though how she'll take the news, God only knows."

As the sad party made their way through the bush towards the rough cottage Patrick had called home, Jane and Polly, sobbing, ran ahead to where their mother was standing in the doorway. She pulled them to her as she asked, "Have they found Patrick then?" Then, as the procession came closer and she could see her son's body over the saddle, she screamed. "Mother of God! My poor darlin' boy."

As John lifted the boy from the horse she fell on her knees and took her son into her arms. "Whatever happened?" she asked, looking from one to the other of the men. "My poor, poor boy. You always were a mischievous one. Tell me, tell me what happened, please," she implored.

John looked at Kelly, wondering where to start. "The boys," he began, "Patrick and Jake, found an old canoe down by the river. They were just sitting in it, when the flood swept them away and overturned the canoe. Jake managed to grab a log and hung on until he was taken round the bend to where the bridge is. Luckily a young chap was able to pull him from the grip of the river and people down there revived him. It was nearly death for him too."

"But what about my son? Where did you find him?" asked the stricken mother, as tears streamed down her cheeks.

Rangi stepped forward to speak. "I found him on the river bank caught in the branches of the willows. I brought him down to the bridge. We tried to revive him but it was too late. I'm very sorry for you and the family Mrs Kelly. It's very hard to lose a son, I know."

"Dear Jesus have mercy on us," Mrs Kelly prayed. "Christ have mercy on us," intoned her husband, and Jane and Polly joined in. "Lord have mercy on us. Hail Mary full of grace, the Lord is with thee, blessed art thou amongst women and blessed is the fruit of thy womb Jesus. Holy Mary Mother of God, Pray for us sinners now and at the hour of our death Amen..." and saying the rosary together, they all watched as Rangi and John carried the boy who had been so loved, into the house and laid him gently on his bed.

Thinking it best to leave the family in their grief, John shook Mr Kelly by the hand, thanked Rangi again, said goodbye to O'Brien and set out for home.

When Kate and Cathy heard the horse arriving they ran out to meet John. "I think you should go and see Mrs Kelly, Kate. She's broken-hearted. You might be a comfort to her. She has no-one here except her husband and the children."

"Do you think so John? She might be angry that her son died and mine lived. He's asleep now but it took a while to settle him down. Poor Jake, he'll miss Patrick. He knows how stupid they were, but it's too late for regrets."

"But it's not too late for sympathy Kate. Yes, I think you could help, perhaps with laying him out. The family were saying the rosary when we left, but it hasn't sunk in yet," said John. "I'll get the buggy and you can drive over. If you feel you're not welcome you can come home."

"I'll take them some food. I cooked some bread this morning and I'll take them a loaf and a few things from the garden. I'll get changed while you harness up Bessie. Jake should sleep for a while. I gave him a drop of brandy in hot water as he was shaking like a leaf when he got home. He was so frozen, Ru had to carry him inside."

CHAPTER 13 Life Without Patrick

The Kellys' house was quiet as Kate approached, but the murmur of responses was audible as she walked up the path. She stood by the door quietly listening. She'd no idea whether to enter or not while the family were at prayer, so decided to wait. However, Jane had heard the approach of the buggy and came to the door to invite her in.

"Mama, this is Mrs Johnson, Jake's mother," she said, showing Kate to a chair.

Kate sat down thankfully. "I just came to say how sorry I am about the accident. I don't know what they were thinking, getting into that old canoe. I saw it once when John and I went for a walk along the bank but never ever thought it could do so much harm."

"I know. It could have been both of them. Thank you for your sympathy," said Mrs Kelly, wringing her hands. "I thought we were coming to a land of plenty. That it would be Heaven, in a way, after the potato famine and nearly starving to death. But you can't avoid sorrow, it follows you everywhere." She began to weep.

Kate took her in her arms and held her until the sobs subsided. "It's so sad, just when you are getting settled. A real tragedy," Kate said, then turned to Jane. "There are some things out in the buggy, Jane; would you like to go and bring them in please? It's not much but might be a help. Just some bread and a shoulder of mutton I cooked yesterday. There are a few vegetables from the garden as well."

"That's good of you Mrs Johnson. Very thoughtful," said Mrs Kelly. "We shall have to report the accident and arrange a funeral. My husband's not so good with things like that. I had to make all the arrangements for my father's funeral just before we left home."

"Would you like me to help you wash and dress Patrick and lay him out? I've had some experience in nursing, and I wouldn't mind doing it, if it would be a help."

Mrs Kelly smiled a wry smile and said quietly to Kate, "I helped lay out lots of people in the old country, but I'd welcome your help. T'would be a lonely task to lay out my own son on my own."

"First I'll make you a cup of tea. That's what you need, with a drop of brandy perhaps."

"Oh, no! I don't take strong drink, Mrs Johnson. I've seen too much misery caused by the drink back in Ireland. Men who couldn't find a penny for their wives could always find tuppence for their pots of Porter."

Kate could see that she was in earnest so said no more. After the tea was made, Jane went in search of her father. She found him sitting on a stump near the door, deep in thought as he puffed on his pipe.

"Will you come in for a cup of tea Dada?" said Jane as she took hold of his arm.

"Aye child I will. I suppose I have to face your mother sooner or later. She'll never forgive me for not taking the axe to that canoe." Paddy's eyes filled with tears. "Oh Jane, why couldn't it have been me?"

"No, no, Dada we need you even more now. Please come in." Jane helped him stand then steady himself for a moment or two. "Mama needs you to help her too you know," said Jane.

Paddy Kelly walked the few paces to the door holding on to Jane's hand, then with a shrug of his shoulders entered. His son's body lay on the bed covered with a blanket. The two women were filling a basin with water from the kettle.

"Sit here," his wife said as she poured tea into a large cup, adding a good dollop of sugar. "Drink this. You'll soon warm up a bit by the fire. What's done is done and can't be undone. We have things that must be attended to so drink this down and set about deciding what to do. Mrs Johnson and I are going to look to the body and do what must be done."

She put her arm around Paddy's shoulder and pulled him close before saying, "We'll dress him in his best clothes. You must go to town and report the events to the police. Try to find out when the priest will be this way next. We'll need to have a grave dug too. I suppose we could bury our boy here on the farm but you must find out if that is legal. Find out about the cemetery. I'll write you a list. And no going to the pub to drown your sorrows either," Mrs Kelly said firmly as her husband kissed her goodbye.

As Paddy saddled his horse he thought of the last time he'd ridden to town. He usually avoided the place. Pubs were too much temptation. There'd been many a time in Ireland when no hotel would be passed by, but he'd not had a drink for three years now. Ever since he left home he'd avoided it for his family's sake. He'd given his wife a hard time in the old country, but they'd come a long way since then. 'Dear God don't let me fall now,' he thought as he took the road to the village.

A group of men chatting at the door of the store parted to let him through as Henry Dickson came out to shake his hand. "We're so sorry to hear about Patrick. It's a terrible thing to lose a son like that. He was a good lad. I had a lot of time for Patrick, you know. He kept the little ones in order when they came in here after school to spend their farthings. Aye, he was a good lad. Would you let me buy you a drink?"

"Thank you Dickson, it's good of you to say so. No lad, I'll say no to the drink if you don't mind. I've things to attend to. Would you have heard if the priest's about the area, or where the policeman is at the moment?"

"Well the priest rode through here yesterday, on his way somewhere. Johanna love, where was the Father going? Do you know?"

"I think he was going to Featherston to say Mass down there. He should be back through the town today," she replied. "The policeman's just new in town and is down the road at a house near the doctor's. Someone will point you to him, Mr Kelly." She put her hand on Paddy's shoulder. "I'm so sorry."

The group of men gathered around the door were talking about the tragedy, but became quiet as Paddy Kelly left the shop. "Come and have a beer with us," one offered.

"No, thank you," replied Paddy. "I've things I must do so I'd better be on my way." He shook hands, promising to catch up with them another day and rode away to find the policeman.

Constable O'Reilly who had already heard of the accident, invited Mr Kelly into the small room that served as office and lockup, if one was ever required. It wasn't long before he had all the details needed. It was a sad case, a boy so young. 'Such a waste', he thought.

Once more, Paddy went to the store and sought out Mr Dickson. "Would you mind asking Father Brady to come out and see us when he comes in? I don't want to stay in town any longer than necessary. I've no idea where the cemetery is. I'm wondering if we could bury him on the farm? Do you know?"

"You'd better ask the magistrate," Henry replied. "He should be at the new courthouse, setting up shop. I think he'd know. I guess you'd like to have the boy home, but the priest would have to consecrate the ground, wouldn't he?"

Fortunately, as Paddy was about to ride away the priest rode up on his bay pony. He was only a small man in height but made up for it in girth. The pony was similar. Short and stocky, built just right for the job of taking Father Brady around the large district he was in charge of. "God be with you Mr Kelly," said Father Brady as he dismounted. "Tis a terrible time for you my son, I came back as soon as I heard what had happened. You'll be wantin' a Requiem Mass, no doubt? For the poor boy. God bless his poor mother, a terrible t'ing it 'tis."

"When could you say the Mass, Father? Are you staying round here for a day or so? We don't have any relatives here but I've a few friends in Greytown who'll come to see him laid to rest."

"Yes, Paddy," said the priest as he patted Paddy Kelly's shoulder. "I'll see what the best time for the funeral will be and tell you when I come out to visit tomorrow. We can make the arrangements then. Oh, and Paddy keep up the good work in staying away from the drink. Perhaps God has sent this trial to test your resolve. Now go carefully and God be with you."

"Thank you Father, I'll be careful to stay sober. It would only take one drink to set me off again. I don't want to slip into the old ways, you can be sure of that."

Turning his horse for home, Paddy set off at a smart canter towards the river. How he wished he could undo the events of the day, for it to be Friday again and the nightmare to be just that, a bad dream to wake up from.

Approaching their home, he could see a lamp was lit and inside, candles were glowing on both sides of the bed where Patrick lay peacefully. 'Oh my dear son,' he thought.

Jane ran to her father as he entered the room and hugged him. Polly looked up from the book she was trying to read as his wife, Tessa, came forward to take his coat and hat.

"Well it's been a long day Mother," he said. "A long, long day, but it will be a longer one tomorrow, I think. You've laid him out I see. He looks as if he's sleeping. Father Brady said he'll come to see us tomorrow after he's found out when and where we should bury the lad."

His wife moved close and held him to her. "Yes it will be another long day, but I know we'll get through it if we pray for God's help. Did you find out where you need to report the accident and death?"

"Oh yes I've done that. I saw the new policeman and he said he'd fill in the forms and I'll just have to sign them after the funeral, or was it before? I can't remember."

"You've done well Paddy." Tessa gave a great sigh. "We'd best get the children to bed, but I think I'll sit up with Patrick tonight," said Tessa.

Polly and Jane went to the corner of the room where they slept together on a stretcher and prepared for bed, but Dennis refused to go to the room where he'd slept with Patrick and his younger brother James. He looked at them pleadingly. "Please can't I stay here for a while?" he said as tears welled in his eyes. "I just want to be here with you. James is asleep and won't know I'm not in the bed with him. Please?"

"Well, for a little while. Your mother and I want time together to sort out the details of the funeral and say a rosary or two for Patrick, but you must be off to bed when I tell you next time, all right?" said Paddy. The boys would miss their big brother, for sure.

"Yes I will. I promise." Dennis sat back down on the stool again, folding his arms and resting them on the bed near his brother.

The candles glowed in the room, casting a shadow as they flickered in the breeze blowing through the cracks in the wall. Outside the wind whistled a sad song in the trees and the house creaked and groaned a lament. Soon Dennis was fast asleep, his head resting on the bed. "Just leave him be," said Paddy.

With the prayers said, Tessa felt like a cup of tea. She built the fire up again and waited for the kettle to boil. "Want a drink Paddy?"

"Aye that would be nice. You know, I had a hard time turning down the offers of a drink in town. You would have been proud of me Tess," said Paddy, pulling at his beard.

"I know Paddy, you've done so well. We must be strong for each other and our children. We've started a better life and mustn't let this accident throw us off our goals."

"You know Tess, I told Johnson how worried I was about you, that you would have a broken heart, might even want to go home. Now I see you're the strong one. I'll need all the help you can give me to get me through."

"Oh Paddy, I do have a broken heart but I know Patrick would want us to go ahead with our plans for the farm. We're not the first to lose a child to such a tragedy. For the sake of the others we must pray for help to continue with what life sends us."

"You're a brave women Tessa. Let's drink our tea and watch over our boy with love as we wait for the dawn."

The candles guttered and Tessa rose to replace them. Much later, as tiredness gradually overcame her, she shook Paddy awake and, as the clock showed three o'clock, they finally made their way to bed and settled down into restless sleep.

CHAPTER 14 Help for the Kellys

John and Kate also had a restless night with the wind whistling through the trees and making the house shake and rattle, so they both rose early. Deciding it would be best for the children to attend school as usual Kate woke them tenderly by caressing their heads as she pulled off the covers. "Time to get ready for school. The children will want to see you Jake, to be sure you're safe, but I don't suppose the Kelly children will be there. Up you get and have your breakfast."

John came in after checking on the weather. "Looks like it will be a good day after the rain. We might be able to start ploughing for the crops," he told Kate, "but first I suppose I should see Kelly in case there's something I can help with. When he arrives I'll get Rangi to harness the horse and be back as soon as I can."

"Good, John, I guess that's the right thing to do. I found Mrs Kelly much stronger than I imagined she would be. She told me her husband used to drink a lot, but hasn't touched a drop since they arrived here. I hope no-one starts him off again. Maybe you should say something on the quiet to Henry Dickson and his friends."

"I'll keep it in mind. If I get a chance, without saying too much, I'll let the men know. It would be too bad to get him drunk at the wake. I'll get the publican to put aside a bottle or two of dark ginger ale and tell Kelly if he gives me the chance. I don't think he'll want to know we've been discussing his faults."

"Of course not, that's not what I meant, but I thought you should know. You'd be the first one to offer him a drink, it's traditional."

John looked up as Rangi came to the door looking sad. "How are you today Rangi?"

"I'm fine boss, but it was hard you know. My wife and I lost a little boy. He drowned in the creek. It was years ago and we have three more now, but it's still hard. He was a cute little fella."

"I'm sorry about that Rangi," said John. "I never knew. It must be hard to get over a thing like that. I'm sorry for the Kelly family. It'll make their life harder. Patrick was becoming a good help."

"You know that chap that pulled Jake out of the river?" said Rangi. "He's looking for work with a farmer here, or in Masterton. I wondered if he would be any good to the Kellys since he's Irish too."

"That's a good idea Rangi," said John. "I'll sound Kelly out when I see him, but they may not have the money. Today I think we can start on the ploughing since the ground's not so hard."

Jake and Cathy came to the door ready for school with their books in sacking bags over their shoulders and, after saying goodbye, they went to catch Bessie. It would be a hard journey without the Kelly family to go with them, but the sooner they went, the sooner they'd be past the house and the memories it brought.

John ate his breakfast in silence as he thought about what nearly had been a tragedy for them as well. He went out to the pen where Kate was feeding the fowls grain. "Kate, I'm going to try out the new mare I bought last week. I'll ride over to Kellys, and then we'll get on with the ploughing."

Kate was not listening. She was deep in thought as she collected the eggs, worrying about Mrs Kelly and how she was coping. It could so easily have been Jake, the poor woman. However would she get over it? 'Dear Lord, please watch over her', she prayed.

When Jake and Cathy reached the schoolroom, they were greeted by Mrs Thompson and the other children. One of the older boys took the reins from Jake saying, "I'll put her in the paddock for you, Jake, if you like." Jake thanked him, and took the hand offered by Mrs Thompson. She put a hand on Cathy's shoulder and led them inside.

"It must have been dreadful for you, Jake. Poor Patrick and his poor mother." She let them go to their places then said to the children, "Now let's stay quiet for a moment and remember Patrick and his family in our prayers. I hope you know now that the river is dangerous, always very, very dangerous." Mrs Thompson looked at the children's faces. "Right, now let's begin with the 2x2 table. Altogether now 2x2 is 4..."

John found Paddy Kelly sitting on the stump by the door. "Good morning. How is your wife? It must have been a hard night for you all."

"It was Johnson, it was. I'm just waiting for Father Brady to come by. I milked the cows and Mother is dealing with the hens. Patrick would have done them if he'd been here. Well he is here in a way I guess." He laughed ruefully. "The Lord giveth and the Lord taketh away. What are we to do? How are we to manage without my boy?"

"That's one thing I wanted to ask you about. You know the man who pulled Jake out of the water? Well he wants a job on a farm. He's Irish and perhaps he could fit in well with you. I don't know about wages, but I was told he's desperate to get some farming experience."

"I don't know, to be sure, I can't think at the moment. Perhaps I'll ask my wife. She'll know what's best. Here's Father Brady coming down the path on that poor little pony."

"Right, well I'll get back to the ploughing. Good morning Father," said John as he went to leave.

"No, no, you stay a while, Johnson. I'll get my wife. Mother!" Paddy called as he went to the hen house. "Father Brady's here. Come along in Father, you too Johnson. Jane, get the kettle boilin' girl, then take the little ones outside to give us some room."

As Father Brady sat down he looked at the bed where Patrick was lying, then rose and laid his hand on the dead boy's head in a blessing. "Poor lad, 'tis a terrible shame so it is. When would you like the funeral Paddy? Would tomorrow be suitable? About 2pm? That would suit me as I'd have time to return to Masterton afterwards. With travel so slow I have to think about these things you see," the old priest said as he shook his head sadly.

"Where can he be buried Father?" Paddy asked him. "Is there a place in a cemetery?"

"There's a place set aside for Catholics down the road a bit; a plot there doesn't cost much. It's part of the whole cemetery but nearer the road. But you said you might want to bury him here at home. Is that right?"

"We did think it might be nice to lay him to rest here, on our land, but is it legal?" asked Paddy. "I couldn't find the Magistrate yesterday but...?"

"It would perhaps be better to see what your wife has to say," said John. "Thank you Jane, there's nothing like a good cup of tea."

Just then, Tessa came into the room and greeted the priest and John before taking the tea from Jane and sitting by the fire.

" My dear, I was asking Father Brady where we should lay our boy to rest," said her husband. "Here at home or in the Town Cemetery, in the Catholic block?"

"I suppose I'd like him to be here but I don't think that's best," she said. "After all, we will be able to go to the grave if it's not far from the Mass house, but to have the funeral out here? I don't think people will be able to travel all the way out here. No, I think in town. When do you think Father?"

Father Brady looked thoughtful, then he said, "About 2 pm tomorrow, and now I must be away further north. Some new folk just arrived from Poland, to stay I hear; Would you believe they're in Carterton?" said the priest. "Twill be a good thing for the parish. They're very devout. I give you all my blessings." Father made the sign of the cross. "In the name of the Father and of the Son and of the Holy Ghost Amen. God be with you 'til tomorrow." With that he was away on his pony.

John gathered his thoughts back to the present, and made to leave as well. "What have you done about a coffin, Kelly? When do you want to take your lad into town?" asked John.

"The men from the carpenters' shop have kindly built one and are coming out today with it. We don't want him to be alone so we'll keep him here tonight then take him in to town tomorrow on the dray in good time for the service."

"Would you like Jake and me to come by and help you?" John offered. "When should we come?"

"About eleven o'clock would you say? That will give people time to say goodbye if we're in town by noon? Is that right Mother?" said Paddy.

"Yes thank you Mr Johnson. It would be good of you to give Paddy a hand. We'll have to go in with the dray I suppose," answered Tessa.

"Well now," John replied, "let's think about that. How about you ride with my wife in the buggy and she'll drive. The children can go in the dray. Your husband will drive the dray and I'll ride my mare. My two can ride in on Bessie."

"Oh thank you Mr Johnson. That's very kind of you."

As John was riding away, he met the dray with the coffin coming down the road and reined in his horse to speak to the two men with it.

"Good-day to you," he said "That's a good thing you're doing. Kelly was so pleased Patrick would have some dignity at his funeral. The poor man is taking it hard and Mrs Kelly too."

"We're pleased enough to do it, Johnson. These things are not able to be foreseen and our turn may be next," said one of the men.

When John reached the paddock that was to be ploughed he found Rangi and Ru had the two horses ready to begin the task. Rangi held on to the handles of the plough to guide it through the soil to cut the furrows while Ru walked at the head of the horses, urging them on, with a whip handy in case they jibbed at the load.

Gradually, a long solitary scar the length of the field appeared. The soil looked rich and when John raised a handful to his nose he breathed in its earthy scent. He watched Ru and Rangi turning the furrow on the way back down the paddock. They'd marked out the area and divided it evenly to ensure all the ground was turned over to a good depth. There were many stump holes to be filled in, so shovelling dirt in from the sides to smooth out the dips and hollows kept John busy.

John thought of the times he'd watched the ploughman on his grandfather's farm turning the good soil of Devon. Sometimes old Roman coins and pieces of broken pottery were turned up, telling the story of previous occupiers. Here the soil had never before been ploughed. If traces of fires or bones were uncovered it meant that Maori had been here many years ago.

They continued working until the sun was low in the sky when John called a halt; the draft horses were set free to graze on the unploughed areas and the men set off for their homes.

As John rode up to his door, Kate came out to look at the mare he was riding. "Where did this beauty come from John? Have you bought another horse?" she asked with a slight edge to her voice.

"Now Kate, you know we needed another one. When the children are at school we've no means of travel except by foot. I'm always waiting for them to return home before I can do any business in town. I was offered her on trial last week, but with the things that have happened since I forgot about her. She's been out in the paddock by the kowhais eating her share of the fresh grass the rain brought. She's called Beauty. I'm sorry I forgot to tell you."

"Well I suppose you've done the sums. We'll just have to be careful and save in other ways. Can I ask what she's worth?" Kate patted the mare's nose and offered her a carrot from the bunch she'd pulled from the garden.

"The owner wants ten pounds for her, with the saddle, so she's a good bargain, don't you think?" He looked pleased with himself. Kate had to agree that another horse would be handy and together they made their way to the house, more than ready to eat and sleep after the trauma of the last few days.

CHAPTER 15 The Requiem

Next morning Kate went to milk the cow, leaving the children to sleep a little longer. The events of the weekend had been a shock to all of them, but Kate found comfort in leaning her head on the side of the cow as she rhythmically stripped the last of the milk from the udder.

As they ate breakfast John told the children what would be expected of them today. "No running around chasing the little ones," he said. Cathy and Jake looked at each other as if to say, 'As if we would'. "You'll be riding Bessie, Jake. Mother is going to take Mrs Kelly with her in the buggy. Mr Kelly will take Patrick in the dray with the other children. Cathy, you might be needed to ride in the dray to keep the Kelly girls company. Could you do that? Or would you rather go with Jake on Bessie?"

"I don't know Father, I don't want to look at Patrick when he's dead. Couldn't I go with Mother in the buggy?" Cathy wept as she spoke.

"We'll see when we get to the Kellys'," said John kindly as Cathy dried her eyes. "The coffin will be closed by then."

Everyone was very quiet as they made themselves ready for the day and, when they arrived at the Kellys', they found the family were all lined up, silently waiting for them. When the coffin was lifted onto the dray a stool was placed along one side and the Kelly children were helped up, Jane calling to Cathy where she sat beside her mother in the buggy. "Come and sit by me Cathy."

Cathy clung to her mother and did not respond until Kate said, "She'd love your company dear. Do you think you could do that for her?"

Cathy nodded and was lifted up on to the dray to join the Kelly children. She looked at the coffin holding Patrick and wondered where he was now. She'd heard of Heaven but the idea was a mystery. Angels were things one sang songs about. They were not real friends, not real people. She took the hand Jane held out gratefully and settled down for the ride.

The little cavalcade was soon underway along the bumpy road. It was muddy now after the rain and the dray bumped in and out of the puddles. What a sad picture it made. All the hopes and dreams the parents had for their children in this new land had been crushed with the accidental death of their eldest son.

Kate watched as Cathy put her arm around little Polly, who sat next to her in the dray. She was proud of her daughter, but this tragedy had hit everyone hard and she wondered about the new life she was carrying, 'Would life be better here than it would have been in Devon?'

Kate turned her attention to Mrs Kelly sitting beside her, stoic in her grief. The poor woman. It was a terrible thing to face, but Kate could see she was much stronger than people thought. Would her husband be able to curb the urge to drink, especially with townsfolk trying to help him drown his sorrows? Kate certainly hoped he would.

A welcoming group of people were waiting near the Mass house and helped the women down from the buggy. John rode up and soon the dray appeared around the corner. Some men helped carry the coffin into the house where a room had been prepared. The lady who owned the house welcomed them in and lit candles around the coffin, two on each side.

She left Mr and Mrs Kelly alone for a few minutes before offering them some refreshments, but they declined. They wished to go to communion and had fasted since midnight. Not the children though, they were being given some food at a table in the kitchen. The Kelly children had been too upset to eat at home, but they were hungry after the ride in the cart and the strangeness of the occasion soon had them helping themselves.

Jake, who had been putting the horses away in the school paddock, came up to where his parents were waiting. "Mother, Mrs Thompson wants us children to stand outside the doorway, lined up on either side of the path, when they bring Patrick's body out after the Mass to say goodbye to him. Will that be all right?"

"Of course dear, I'll leave it to you to tell the other children. Look, here is Father Brady coming on his pony. Go and offer to put it with the other horses, Jake. That would be polite."

Jake wasn't frightened of the priest, but he didn't like talking to strangers and had never spoken to a priest before. Nevertheless, he walked slowly over and offered to take the priest's horse.

"That's good of you, young fellow." said Father Brady. "And what is your name?"

"I'm Jake Johnson, sir," he said shyly.

"Ah." said Father Brady, "You're the one that got saved, are you not?"

"Yes, sir, I was lucky that Mr O'Brien reached me and the men there revived me, or I'd be dead too," said Jake.

"Well, I know you won't do anything like that again, but you know, boy, you must not let this accident spoil your life. It was a silly thing to do, but you might just have had a good ride on the canoe and no harm done. God works in mysterious ways. So put it behind you and be a good son to your mother, do you hear me boy?" asked the priest.

"Yes, Father, thank you," said Jake as he held out his hands for the reins and took the pony away to the other horses, calling to the children to tell them they were going to line up as Patrick's coffin was carried out of the building.

Inside, a small bunch of flowers and leaves from the bush had been placed on the coffin, their scent adding to that of the burning candles and incense Father Brady had placed ready for the service. Soon, the Kellys came and sat in the front with their children, followed by so many settlers and their families that very quickly no seats were left and a good number had to gather around the doorway.

Suddenly, as he was about to start the service, Father Brady looked at the young boy sitting by Mrs Kelly, and said, "I'd like you to come and be my altar boy; you're Dennis aren't you?"

"Yes, Father, he's my next boy in age to Patrick, he's eight," said Tessa. "He hasn't served at Mass before Father. Will he be all right?"

"I'm sure he will be, my dear. Now, have you made your First Holy Communion Dennis?" asked Father Brady.

"No, Father. Not yet. But I have been learning my catechism."

"Well, would you like to make it today? I'm sure your dear mother has taught you well," asked Father Brady as he took stock of the young lad.

"Whatever you think is best Father," said Tessa Kelly. She looked at her husband, and he nodded.

"I don't get this way often so I'll make an exception. I know he isn't fasting but I think God will understand," said Father Brady. "Now come up here Dennis and tap this gong to tell the people Mass is starting." When Dennis did as he'd been bid a loud musical sound filled the room and echoed around the walls.

"In nomine Patris, et Filii et Spiritus Sancti," said Father Brady, as he blessed himself.

"Amen," answered the congregation.

"Introibo ad altare Dei," said the priest.

"Ad Deum,qui latificat juventutem meam," answered the people. Dennis watched closely for instructions from Father Brady about what he should do. He hadn't attended Mass very often and had always wondered who picked the altar boys. The prayer book his mother used had pictures of the Mass, with each part shown in detail, and he loved looking at them. Father Brady held the host on high, indicating to Dennis to hit the gong to show people this was a very special time.

"Sanctus Sanctus," continued Father as he consecrated the bread and wine. Then Dennis was given a silver tray to hold under the chin of each communicant as Father Brady placed the wafer, the symbol of Our Lord's body, on their tongue. Finally, he whispered that Dennis should kneel and receive the sacrament too. Father Brady finished the service with prayers for Patrick and his family and gave all present his blessing.

As people left the room to mingle with those outside they expressed sympathy for the Kellys and said how sad it was for there to have been another victim of the river. For many of the Catholics present the service had been a reminder of similar sad occasions in their childhood in the 'Old Country', while for the non-Catholics, it had seemed a bit long but interesting and, even though the service had been in Latin most could easily follow the meaning of the priest's actions and prayers.

As the coffin was being brought out to the dray and carried through the little honour guard, some of the children wept, but all stood straight and tall. Then, the dray made the journey to the cemetery, a little distance out of town, with most of those present walking slowly behind it. When all had gathered around the grave that had been prepared that morning, Father Brady gave Dennis the prayer book to hold as he intoned the words of the burial dedication, "Kyrie eleison."

"Kyrie eleison," answered Dennis.

"Christe eleison," said Father.

"Christe eleison," said Dennis,

"Lord have Mercy," said Father

"Christ have mercy," said those present.

"Dominus vobiscum," said Father "Et cum spiritu tuo, the Lord be with you."

"And also with you," said the people, turning to each other for comfort, as the body of twelve year old Patrick was lowered into the grave. As Father Brady said, "It is from dust that you have come and unto dust you shall return, Amen," some people picked up a small handful of soil and threw it gently on to the coffin.

As most of the mourners made their way back to the village, the Johnson family stayed by the grave with the Kellys to say a final goodbye while two men with shovels ready to fill in the grave stood patiently aside, being careful not to intrude. Suddenly, Tessa Kelly said, "We should go, Paddy, people will be waiting for us. We must go now."

"Aye, you're right, Mother." said Paddy and turned to John. "Will you come to the bar with me Johnson? I can't face the men on my own."

"Of course, I'll be pleased to. I'll see you in there," he said as he waved to Kate.

As the two women walked to the buggy Kate took her new friend's arm. "It was a good service Mrs Kelly; you'd think that Dennis had been there before, the way he said the responses. I thought he was so solemn and watchful."

"I know, I'm so proud of him, but he's going to miss Patrick."

While they were helping the children on to the dray Kate said, "You'll come and see me if you need anything Mrs Kelly, I'm always home these days. I'm getting so large, it's too much trouble to go out, and not 'seemly' as they say."

Mrs Kelly laughed her first laugh of the day. "Sure and begorra you're hardly as big as a house now are you? I don't think anyone would have guessed your secret by looking at you Mrs Johnson. You look as slim and pretty as ever."

Back at the Mass house a cup of tea was on offer, and quite a few people were still there with Tessa and the Johnsons when Mr Kelly and the children arrived on the dray. "I'll have to go to the bar, Tessa," said Paddy. "I'll have to buy a few drinks for the men who've helped so much. You know that don't you dear?"

"I do, I do Paddy, but for my sake stay sober. I couldn't stay with you if you went back to your old ways. You know that, don't you?"

As Kate listened, wondering what Mrs Kelly might have gone through in her earlier married life, she whispered to John, "Watch him carefully, John. You know the men will think it's the right thing to do to get him drunk."

"I do my dear. I'll watch his glass very carefully," said John and, taking Mr Kelly by the arm, they went off together like old friends instead of having met only a short time before. 'It's funny how trouble cements people together,' John thought as they went along.

It was all 'Hail fellow well met' when they reached the door of the nearest hotel. "Come in boys," said Mr Fuller, the publican. "I'll get you something. What would you like?"

"A nip of whisky for me and a beer for Mr Kelly."

"Yes," said Paddy, "That would be fine. I'm keeping away from the hard stuff."

The publican poured the drink, using the bottle John had asked him to have ready. The colour was nearly the same as beer and men who'd had a few drinks were not likely to notice it was only ginger beer. Paddy sipped his drink slowly, trying not to show his dislike of the substitute liquid.

As the afternoon progressed and the men became rowdier John thought it would be wise to get away home. He touched Kelly's arm to give a hint that they should go and they were soon homeward bound none the worse for wear.

John thought it could have turned out so differently if the publican had not co-operated. He was a good chap. After all, ginger beer was much cheaper than real beer, so he'd not make much from Paddy's drinking. But that hadn't worried him. 'Yes, he was a good man.'

Kate was in the garden pulling carrots for dinner as he rode up the path. "Well, that's over," he said. "I'm glad I went with Kelly. He was offered gallons of grog but stuck to his guns and just drank ginger beer with no-one any the wiser. Then he shouted for the bar. That would have cost him a bit but not as much as if he had been drinking the real thing. Can I help you? You've had a big day too."

"No I've got enough now, thank you dear. I could do with some wood for the fire though. Some small stuff to make it get a move on would be good. Poor Mrs Kelly, she was so worried her husband would come home drunk, and bring company with him."

"I quietly told some of the blokes about his problem and I don't think they'll try to make him drown his sorrows while the family is in mourning, or after either. Most of them were very sympathetic. One or two thought it a pity if a man can't hold his liquor, but they agreed it was his business and not theirs."

The children were sitting on their stools gazing at the glowing fire and looking very thoughtful as their parents entered the cottage. "Mother, do you think Patrick's in Heaven?" Cathy asked.

"I don't know Cathy," replied Kate, "but if he's not who will be? He was just a child and God will be happy to see him. That is what the Kellys believe, and what I believe too. It was a nice service. I was proud of you today. How was Jane when you left her?"

"She was sad but not too bad. She'll miss Patrick. They were so close, and they were always doing things together. Polly made us laugh on the way home. She asked Dennis what the bread had tasted like when Father Brady put it on his tongue, and he said, 'Like bread'", then he said to Polly, 'Do you think God doesn't want me?' and Polly said, 'Well he can't have you. He's got Patrick, and that's enough for God', and she poked out her tongue."

John chuckled. "It's not a wise thing to do, to poke out your tongue at God, but I know how she feels." He sat back in his chair and surveyed his family. 'How lucky I am,' he thought. 'Kate is blooming. I must start on the extra room or the baby will be here before we know it'. "You know Kate," he said, "I think I'll start on the extension tomorrow. The saw-mill is up and running and the timber is good quality rimu. It'll last for years. I believe we could re-use it in the new house when the time comes to build that."

"That would be wonderful, we are a bit cramped in here. It would be good to have it done before the winter sets in," replied Kate as she stirred the fire.

"That's it then. Rangi and Ru have done a great job with the ploughing. The field is ready for sowing. We'll do that tomorrow. Now off to bed you two," said John. "It's been a hard day for all of us."

The Kellys were also tired after the emotions of the day. Patrick's bed lay empty, a grim reminder. The blankets he'd used to shield him from the cold still lay crumpled on top, and his favourite book was by his pillow.

"Let's go to bed Mother, leave all that 'til tomorrow. I'll help you in the morning," said Paddy. "Off to bed now Jane and Polly, it's been a long day, so it has. You too young Dennis, I was real proud of you today me boy. Really proud, but don't wake James." Paddy patted both his daughters' shoulders and kissed them as they said goodnight.

"And I was really proud of you too Paddy. It must have been a hard thing to sit through that wake with never a drop to wet your lips. But you did it. God bless you Paddy." Tessa put her arms around him and together they cried for their lost boy. As they made their way to bed Paddy turned to Tessa.

"Twas Johnson who kept me sober Tessa," he said. "I got tired of pretending but when he saw how I was going he brought me home away from the temptation. T'is a terrible thing, drink. It lures you with the promise of a good time. You forget the misery you'll find in the end."

CHAPTER 16 Back to Work

Next morning Cathy woke early to the sound of birds singing. Fantails were flitting around the bushes of manuka Kate had planted near the house because she liked the scent of the leaves. A tui was singing its beautiful song high up in the branches of the kahikatea and sparrows were sitting on the rope clothesline. 'Have sparrows always been here in New Zealand? Or have they been brought in like the rabbits Father growled about,' she wondered. 'I must ask Mrs Thompson.'

Then her mind turned to the events of the last few days. She would never forget Patrick. He'd been like another brother. They'd had fun together on the way home from school. He was always showing her a new bird's egg he had found, and once, a beautiful little grey warbler's nest, shaped like an oval ball with the little opening halfway down one side. So pretty the way it was made with lichen and moss.

Now, two wood pigeons flew noisily past the window, their wings wide as they swooped to land on trees not far from the house. The sound of their flight made them easily identified. 'Don't stay there too long,' thought Cathy 'or you'll be pigeon pie.'

"Cathy, are you up? You'll be late for school. Jake has milked the cow and fed the pigs, so come on lazy-bones, out of bed," called Kate. "Quickly, have your breakfast or Jake will be gone without you."

A little later, as they rode Bessie along the bush track towards the Kellys' house, Jake asked Cathy if she would miss Patrick as much as he would.

"Of course I will," Cathy said. "He was just like a brother even though we've only known him since the fire and school starting. I know you'll miss him more. You were the same age almost and there aren't any other boys near here to have fun with."

"Well, we're nearly at the Kellys'. Do you want to stop and wait for them? Or shall we just go on?" asked Jake.

"I want to go with Jane, Jake; you ride off if you want to, but I think we should wait for them. After all, it will be strange for them to go without Patrick."

"Yes, all right, don't get excited. I just thought you'd find it hard to see them, that's all." Jake shrugged his shoulders. He really didn't want to have to look at Jane and see the hurt in her eyes. He knew she thought it had been his idea to go in the canoe. But, as they neared the house, Jake could see the children waiting for them, and they all walked along the road together with Jake giving Polly and James turns on Bessie, much to their delight. No one talked much though.

After the school bell was rung the children filed into the schoolroom and stood by their stools, ready to sit when Mrs Thompson gave them permission. She was teaching the children some manners as well as their sums. They'd been told to rise if anyone came into the room, and be quiet if anyone was at the door. No fighting in the playground, and no bad language, were high on the list of 'don'ts'. She was pleased with their progress since the school had begun; she was also pleased that, after a good report from a government official who had visited, the school was being allowed to continue. There was even a hint of a purpose-built school in the years to come.

"I want to say how pleased I was with your behaviour yesterday," said MrsThompson. "No one caused any bother at all. Well done, children. I'm very very sorry about Patrick, Jane; it was an awful thing to happen to your family. Your faith in God will help you through I know. Wasn't it good to see Dennis helping Father Brady at Mass?" She smiled at him. He hung his head but was pleased.

"Now for some work; children, practise your printing or writing. I've put a sentence on the blackboard. Write it out three times then write a short sentence about what you think it means."

Jane looked at the words, wondering what they meant. MANY HANDS MAKE LIGHT WORK. 'Oh well, I suppose the more people to help the easier it gets. That's what I'll say.'

"Very good, Jane, you have understood the lesson well," Mrs Thompson said later as the children read out their sentences.

Meanwhile, when Rangi and Ru arrived for work John told them they'd begin work on the addition to the house. A dray load of his timber was ready at the mill and he expected it to arrive later that day.

Studying the plans Kate had sketched out weeks ago, he pondered the best way to begin then stepped out the area in front of the cottage. 'Perhaps,' he thought, 'We could put in piles for a wooden floor; perhaps we could put a floor in the cottage too. It would make Kate's job of keeping the place clean easier - and it would be less cold and healthier too.'

After Rangi had cut some short branches to use as markers John hammered the first one into the soil where he was standing near the doorway of the cottage. Then taking a length of rope, he stepped out the measurements of the area which was to become the new room. It looked larger now. John wondered if he was taking on too much. 'Oh well, we'll see.'

Holes were dug for the piles which had been cut from young totara trees. They worked hard all morning and were pleased to stop for a welcome cup of tea when the timber from the mill was delivered.

Ru and Rangi were excited as they watched the building grow, especially after the floor was laid, using pit sawn planks. Now the walls were starting to take shape. The roof would take some thought though. John remembered again the new method of keeping the rain out he'd heard about using corrugated iron. 'That would be much better than shingles and totara bark, especially if you could paint it. It could last for years.' He regretted he'd not thought to make inquiries about it before now, but would make it a priority the next time he went to the village.

Kate came out to inspect the proceedings. "That looks well John," she said. "I think I'll go and get the mail and groceries. I'll bring the children home if they've finished school. They'll love a ride in the buggy. Jake can ride Bessie, and I'll bring the Kelly girls home too."

"That's a good idea. Give my regards to the Dicksons."

The trip into town didn't take long as the new mare went along at a fine clip. Henry Dickson greeted her warmly saying "There's mail for you. I know you'll want that. It's so good to hear from home even if the news is three months old. My wife's out the back making up five-pound bags of flour from the fifty-pound bags." He called out, "Mrs Johnson is here Johanna. Go through. I'm sure you've lots to talk about."

Johanna Dickson dusted flour off her hands and rubbed her back as she greeted Kate and asked about her health.

"I'm very well Mrs Dickson, really I am," said Kate. "I came to town in style. My husband's new mare is quite happy in the buggy, and I can take the children home when they're done with school for the day. And how are you faring?"

"I'm so enjoying being able to help Henry," said Johanna. "We're so busy he's thinking of employing someone else to help. So many new people are moving here. Greytown's getting to be a real township now."

The two women continued to chat over a cup of tea then it was time for Kate to look at her list of requirements. There was such a variety of new products she was hard pressed to decide on her needs. She was tempted to buy some of the tinned goods on offer to give a change to their usual diet but instead ordered a large tin of golden syrup, a large bag of dried peas, beans and lentils for soup, and a bag of flour.

"If you rub lard on the advertisement on the flour bag and leave it for a while it will all come off in the wash," said Johanna as she totted up the cost of the goods and entered the amount into the ledger. "You'll have nice white cloth for the children's pants, and they won't be branded on the bottom. Well, that's what I've heard. I've yet to try it myself."

Mr Dickson helped Kate take the goods to where Beauty was tied up to the hitching post outside the shop. "She's a fine looking girl, Mrs Johnson," he said, admiring the mare. "I intend to look around for a conveyance of some sort to take orders around the houses. A lot of folk are asking if I'll deliver their groceries and mail to save them coming into town. I can see a nice little opening there. I might get someone to help my wife with the shop and do it myself. What do you think of the idea?"

"It sounds a really good idea, Mr Dickson. You are a clever fellow. I know I'd be happy to pay a little more to have the things brought out to the farm, say once a week."

"Well, I'll give it some thought. Please tell your husband about the idea, he often hears of horses for sale. I'd be a real gypsy. I saw a swagger along the road the other day, I wouldn't like to live like that, but a life out on the road would suit me fine, as long as I was home at night to see my wife."

Kate drove the buggy to the school, climbed down and tied the reins to the hitching post. The children came running out, glad to be free after the day's work. Kate wanted to see how they were getting on so left Jake in charge of Beauty while she went to talk with Mrs Thompson.

"Your children are doing well Mrs Johnson," said the teacher. "They're ahead of the others in their group. Jake has almost reached the limit of what I can teach him, but I've ordered some text books from Wellington. I think they'll challenge him. Cathy has a good grasp of Arithmetic and English, but her writing needs lots of practice. I'm thinking of keeping the children longer each day, perhaps until two. What do you think? Would that make things hard at home?"

"I'll have to check with my husband," said Kate, "but I'm sure it will be fine. Perhaps in the summer when we're busy on the farm it wouldn't be so good, but during the winter I'm sure he will agree." Thanking Mrs Thompson for her work, Kate said goodbye and went outside. However, to her consternation, she found the buggy gone. She asked some people who were passing if they'd seen the buggy or the children, but they hadn't. "I believe my son has taken it into his head to go for a drive while I was talking to the teacher," she told them, but she was worried. 'Where had they gone? Has someone taken the buggy and the children?' Kate thought this most unlikely and went back to the school-room to tell Mrs Thompson of this latest escapade.

"I think you're right Mrs Johnson," Mrs Thompson said. "Jake is good with the horses, but he should have asked. No doubt they'll soon come back. Come and have a cup of tea. I've just made one. Listen, isn't that the buggy I hear?"

They rushed out the doorway, all thought of tea forgotten, as Jake brought the buggy to a neat stop at the school-house door. Kate's eyes shone darkly as she looked at him. "What do you think you're doing Jake?" she demanded. "I've been worried sick. You haven't driven Beauty before. Your father will have a lot to say about this. It's too bad of you. You could have had an accident."

"I'm really sorry Mother. We were just going to go down the street a little way and come back but Beauty thought we were going home and took off at a trot. It took quite a while before I could get her to turn around and come back. We didn't mean to worry you."

"You did worry me. Never do that again. Do you hear me? Now get on Bessie and away home with you. Now, how are the rest of you going to travel? You sit beside me Cathy? No, Dennis! You sit beside me and the girls can sit in the luggage bay. All aboard. Goodbye Mrs Thompson," she called as they scrambled up.

As they went along Kate turned to Dennis. "How are you Dennis? Are you all right?"

"I suppose so, but I miss Patrick. I can't believe I'll never see him again." So saying, the little chap folded his arms and didn't speak another word on the way.

On reaching home Kate passed the mail to Cathy to carry in then waited for Jake to arrive on Bessie before unloading the buggy. She was feeling the weight of her pregnancy now and wouldn't lift anything heavy if she didn't have to. Filling her arms with a few small articles she went inside.

John came down from the rough scaffolding to help her. She wondered if she should mention the little trip Jake had taken but decided to say nothing at the moment. No good putting father and son offside with each other. No harm came to anybody. She would have loved to have seen Jake show off his skills. 'Ah, that would have been a sight.'

"Mr Dickson has an idea he asked me to tell you about it," said Kate, after they had finished unloading. "He wants to start a service, delivering groceries to houses in town and around the district. He'd buy a dray and a couple of horses and employ someone to help his wife in the shop. What do you think?"

"Sounds like a good idea to me."

"He does value your opinion John. You think about it. You'll be able to discuss it with him next time you're in the village," Kate replied as she took up the pile of letters and sorted them. "Here are yours. I've one each from Mother and Mary. Did you write to Mrs Parker about them arriving in May?"

"Yes I wrote to Mr Parker, just before the river trouble. There's a reply here." John opened the envelope, took out the thin sheet of paper and scanned the contents. "He says he'll be able to meet them off the boat. He's not sure about accommodation but will ask around the Hutt and Petone area. They have their hands full with people at the moment."

"Well, we've done all we can for the Smiths, haven't we?"

"We have indeed, Kate," John said with feeling, "but we'll see a lot more of them I think. It takes courage to pack up and come out here. I believe that Mary's the one behind the move, more than Jim, but this country has the challenge to be the makings of him if he gives it a fair go."

Kate took her mail out to the garden seat, to read in peace. "People were so good", Kate's mother wrote. "Some people I hardly knew came to your dear father's service, and then asked me out afterwards for a meal or to join in some activity. I must say the freedom is welcome after so many years of being at home."

It was reassuring to know Mother was coming to terms with widowhood. She'd joined in some church activities, even helping out at the church bazaar selling cakes. This was a great relief, as her mother's life had been taken up caring for her father for the last few years and it would've been hard to fill the space his death had left.

The minutes passed as Kate thought of her parents and the wrench it had been to leave them to follow John to New Zealand, with nothing but faith to see her through. 'Ah well, I'm happy aren't I?' she told herself and she patted her apron, thinking of the new life growing under it.

As they lay in bed that night Kate asked John if he thought it would be a good thing to have the Smiths come to the Wairarapa or did he think they should stay in the Wellington area and find work there?

Mary Smith's letter to Kate had been posted from Capetown where the ship had gone for repairs after a violent storm at sea. She had been pleased to get off the ship and had liked Capetown but the heat had been hard to take in the tropics. They were looking forward to seeing New Zealand soon.

John said they should make up their own minds. They knew what skills they had and he suggested she tell them to look for a position on the Wellington side of the hill until they had decided what they wanted to do. "Jim could get a job as a labourer on a farm, or as a jobbing tradesman. There are plenty of opportunities for a willing worker. Tell them to try around the farms on the road to Porirua, save some money then come over here later when the weather gets warmer. I know that you're longing to see her, but don't let your heart get in the way of your head. Be practical, eh? After all, there is no chance of them staying with us. Even when the room is finished it will be cramped enough."

CHAPTER 17 Eeling and a Fire

Some days later an excited Jake came running into the cottage, wanting to go eeling with Rangi's two boys who'd ridden over on an old nag. "Please Mother," he said. "We'll be very careful."

"I don't know about that. I haven't told your Father about last week's little episode; I don't know if I can trust you but I hope you've learnt your lesson around water. Just to the creek boys," she said. "No going near the river, you hear."

"Yes, Mrs Johnson. We can't go near the river, because of Patrick. It's tapu," said Hemi, the smaller of the boys. "Only to the creek. That's where the best eels are anyway."

"Well all right, but tell your father where you're off to and what time you'll be back," Kate instructed them.

A little later she went outside to look at the progress on the building. "It's looking very well John," she said. "I can see the whole thing better now. It'll be lovely to have a nice place to eat and sleep again. Bush life is fine but a good firm floor under my feet will be very welcome."

"I've ordered some new windows too. They're the latest thing. Double hung with weights to help with raising and lowering them. That should make life easier. You'll be able to let the breeze run through the house in the heat of the summer."

He climbed back up the scaffolding, calling to Ru to pass up some more timber to finish off the roof ready for the corrugated iron, which was ordered but yet to arrive. A stack of newly planed timber was drying out ready for cladding the outside walls. Rusticating was the best option available to keep out the cold winter winds, as each length fitted securely on top of the one below in overlapping layers. As the light was fading John called an end to work and said, "You send that boy of mine home when you see him Rangi, it's getting dark now and we don't want any more trouble, do we?"

"No boss, you're right. The creek's easy going though. You lookin' forward to a good feed of eel boss?" asked Rangi.

"No, I've eaten jellied eel at home at the seaside, but never the real thing here," John laughed. "Perhaps you might tell my wife how to cook it"

"They're great boss. You should try them smoked. Good kai eh, Ru?" said Rangi.

"Kai pai," agreed Ru, and they left for home.

Just along the road, they met the boys on their way back to Jake's house. "You fellas get away home now, and don't hang around the boss's place," Ru said. "Here, give me the bag to carry. You get home now Jake. Your father's looking for you."

"We got three beauties. Be good for smoking, not too big eh?"said Kingi, the older of the boys, as Jake left them. "They were cunning Papa, but we beat them in the end. Jake had a good laugh when I nearly fell in. We're gunna take the net next time. Some big hungry beggers down there, eh Hemi?"

"Got a mouth this big," said Hemi, holding his hands in a wide circle. "It was this long too," he said stretching his arms as wide as he could, "Big enough to eat a horse."

"Longer than that," Kingi scoffed. His eyes were shining as he remembered the fun they'd had.

"Well, get away home now. Your Mama will be worrying," said Rangi as he turned his horse around to ride into the village. He needed tobacco from the store.

As Rangi rounded the bend into the village there was a great commotion going on. Black smoke was coming from the ruins of one of the newer buildings and people were standing around the burnt-out remains of the blacksmith's shop. Rangi went to see if he could help. "Whatever happened?" he asked the people standing near. "I could smell smoke, but thought the blacksmith was working late."

"No idea," said one of the men. "By the time it was noticed the fire had too great a hold and the house next door was burnt too. It may be able to be rebuilt, but the blacksmith's shop is a write-off."

"Lucky for Dickson his place didn't catch fire too," said another. "It could've been a lot worse. There's a bit of room between the blacksmith's and the store, and the wind was blowing the fire the other way, but we still couldn't save the house. We need a brigade. I say we should demand the village gets some protection." The speaker looked around him for agreement.

"The new council should be able to do something," said another. "The village will never grow if fires take the buildings almost as soon as they're erected. I think we should go to the next meeting and put it to them, to go to the government for help. I'd be happy to join a fire brigade."

Rangi looked at the ruins, amazed at how quickly things could change. The new house had only been occupied for a month and now it was a heap of ashes and rubble. "Was anyone hurt?" he asked.

"No, they all got out. They managed to save a few of their clothes but everything else was lost," said one man. "There were quite a few children of all ages in there, so they were very lucky. We'll have to have a collection to help them out."

"Nothing else we can do today but we'll be back tomorrow to give them a hand if they need it. Where have they gone to?" asked one of the bystanders, trying to brush soot from his clothing.

"They're in the schoolhouse. Mrs Thompson is looking after them."

Rangi rode home, thinking of the trouble the new settlers had. At least he had a home to go to and eels for supper.

Back at home Jake washed his hands and face and brushed the dirt off his clothes before he went in. He was still excited about the catch. He would have liked to bring an eel home but Kingi said he'd bring some over tomorrow. Hemi told him that his mother would be glad to have them as they all loved eels to eat, and dried them for the winter.

John was sitting at the table writing a letter to and looked up as Jake entered. "Have a good time Jake? No trouble?"

"No Father. Kingi and Hemi know all about catching eels. It was fun. There was a great big one. It came up for the bait but the boys said it was too big to handle."

"One day you'll have to show me. Some jellied eel would go down a treat. Remind me of home," said John, smiling at his son.

"Not for me," said Kate as she brought in a pot of Irish stew to the table. "I'll stick to mutton or beef. Now eat up quickly and off to bed," she said as she filled plates and passed them around. "This is all our own food, our carrots, onions, potatoes and our own meat and herbs. The garden has done well, don't you think? Of course it's the soil. It's really fertile."

"Yes, and you are a champion gardener Mother," said John as he looked with pride at his family. "This is a great meal and a great tribute to you. You should be proud of yourself. The soil is good but the work you put in made it happen. Vegetables don't grow without help."

"Thank you John. Now, who wants ginger pudding and cream?"

CHAPTER 18 A New Start for O'bie

Patrick O'Brien walked the last few yards to the Kellys' door. He badly wanted a job on the farm. He'd left Erin's shores with the hopes of a new start in a new country. Bad company and the poverty of his family had driven him to do some stupid things in his young life. When little ones are starving you'll do anything for a crust of bread to feed them. They'd died anyway, his two young sisters, of diphtheria and starvation. But now he was here and had made a good start by rescuing the lad. He hoped he would not prove to be a constant reminder of the loss of their child whose name had been Patrick too. Perhaps he should assume some other name. 'What was it that his mates at school called him? 'O'bie' short for O'Brien.'

Patrick was truly amazed that he'd saved Jake. It had been an impulsive action, walking into the freezing water to clutch the boy as he went past, but now he felt as if the tide of his life had turned. He stood quietly at the door then knocked.

"Good morning," he said as Paddy opened the door. "I believe Mr Johnson talked to you about giving me a job."

"Come in," said Paddy, moving aside to let him enter. "We do need someone, now that Patrick has gone to a better place, God rest his soul. Have you worked on a farm before?"

"Not really," said Patrick, "but I spent time on my uncle's farm in Clare, and helped with whatever they were doing. I'll give anything a go. I can milk and use an axe and saw."

"I'll give you the going rate of ten shillings a week and you can sleep in the whare and have your meals with us. Do you have any bedding?"

"No I don't but I can get some in the village. I think Mr Dickson has some in his shop, doesn't he?"

"Yes he does, but we'll find enough for you to go on with." Paddy looked at Tessa for agreement. She looked uncertain.

"I'll find you some blankets for tonight," Tessa said, "but I want your promise that you'll not bring any strong drink onto the property while you work here. Is that a promise?" She watched as Patrick nodded his head.

"Well that's settled," said Paddy. "Put your swag in the whare and come and have a cup of tea and a bite of loaf, then we'll be off down the paddock."

"Thank you very much, you too, Mrs Kelly. I won't let you down. By the way you can call me O'bie if you like. That's what my friends at home called me, short for O'Brien."

"I'm pleased about that," said Tessa, "just hearing my son's name makes me weep." Wiping her eyes on her apron she left the men to get them another cup of tea.

Before too long the men were down at the back of the farm where the work of clearing the bush of stumps and branches went on daily. Supplejack, lawyer and five-finger undergrowth made the work arduous. While Paddy didn't have any bullocks, he did have one draft horse to help pull logs.

It was slow going but with two of them it seemed easier. Paddy enjoyed the company of the younger man and they soon settled into a routine of hacking away the rubbish and sawing it into manageable lengths. The best of the trees had already gone to the mill. What was left was rubbish that could be burnt or used for firewood for the house.

The Kelly household was finding life difficult after losing Patrick. He'd been a helpful boy and had taken care of most of the animals. Each morning, before he went to school, he'd milk six of the cows and feed the pigs with the skim milk from the butter churning. Now Paddy had to do more himself before he tackled the stumps and trees in the bush. "I've packed your lunches and a bottle of cold tea each," Tessa told Paddy next day as he pulled on his boots. "I won't have time to take the food down the paddock today. I've so much to catch up on."

"That's all right Mother, we'll be just fine," said Paddy. "The bush is not as thick now the mill has been through. We'll have the land ready for ploughing before you know it. O'bie is a fine hand with the saw. Have a good day Mother. I'll see you at dusk." He picked up the bag and went to harness the horse for the day's work. O'bie met him by the shed. "All set then?" Paddy asked the young man.

"Yes, I'm all set for a day in the bush. I sharpened the crosscut and honed the axes. It shouldn't take long to finish that section."

"I want to get on to sowing the new grass seed and a patch of turnips for the cattle after we finish the bush felling," Paddy told O'bie, "then get a fire going to burn the branches up out of the way." He was feeling more optimistic now that he had someone to talk to while he worked. "Thanks for doing the saws," he said. "I meant to do them but somehow I don't have the energy when I get home."

"That's all right. This old bloke showed me how to do a good job on the saw when I was over in Porirua at a mill there," said O'bie. "It was no trouble at all."

The two men made their way to the cart that Paddy had borrowed from a neighbouring farmer, and backed the horse into the shafts. He wanted to load some of the split posts and take them up to fence the house paddock to keep the cattle out of the garden. 'Tessa seems to have taken to growing things after seeing Mrs Johnson's fine efforts. T'would be a shame for the cattle to reap the benefits.'

They were just about ready to move when Rangi and John Johnson came down the track at a trot. "Did you hear about the fire?" John shouted as they came near. "We're off to give a hand to clean up. Do you want to come?"

"No, we hadn't heard. I guess we should. You never know when it will be your turn, do you?" answered Paddy. "Shall I bring the cart? Would it be a help do you think?"

"I do indeed," said John. "If we can shift the burnt timber and dump it down the road away from the village, the smell will soon go away."

They set off at a good pace, covering the miles quickly. As they approached the village the dank smell of burnt wood hung in the air. Several men were standing in a circle, with the brawny blacksmith in the centre.

"How can we help?" asked John as he came up to the group.

"We're trying to decide the best way to clean up the site," said a man. "Have you any idea, Johnson?"

"Kelly is bringing his cart along and will be here in a minute or two. Patrick O'Brien has come too. We could load the stuff on and take it down by the river. I think the further away it goes the better. It could start a fire again if we just leave it to rot away." The men nodded in agreement as Paddy and O'Bie drove up.

"Got yourself a cart Kelly?" asked a bystander.

"No, I borrowed it for the day to cart wood, but your need is greater than mine," he said, looking at Fairman the blacksmith. "I'm very sorry you lost your building."

"Well, let's get started then," said one of the group.

"I'll look for any tools that can be salvaged," John said.

"I'll help you," said the blacksmith as he picked up a hammer with a burnt handle. "Some of the metal tools will be all right and the horseshoe blanks I have on hand, and the anvil. No fire could destroy that." Feeling a bit more optimistic they set to work.

Next door, a group of women were looking at the remains of the house that had been a home for a family of six the day before.

"Do you think there's much good looking inside for anything not burnt?" asked Johanna Dickson.

"We might find some china and kitchenware perhaps. Let's go inside the front part, where the fire was not so fierce," Mrs Thompson suggested. "All the children came to school as usual, not knowing about the fire. I told them to go and play until the family find somewhere else to shelter and we can have the school back. They were happy enough to go into the bush for a while. The smell was making them sick. Jake is minding them and showing off his knowledge of the trees."

"Well here we go," said a woman holding a handkerchief to her nose. She pushed open the door. "Phew, what a smell! It looks pretty bad in here, I'll go into the main room as the roof looks safer there. The cupboards are all open and stuff is lying on the floor so walk carefully as you come in. Ah, here are some saucepans and plates that are all right. They just need a good soak and a rub with sand soap."

The other women made their way carefully into the room and looked at the shambles around them. "Poor woman," said one, "but if we can salvage some of her things that will help."

"Let's form a chain and pass anything that's still in one piece outside," suggested Mrs Dickson. "Mrs Browne will be grateful for anything we find."

The women worked all morning, rescuing crockery, pots and pans and anything else usable, and washing clothing that was dirty but undamaged. By the time they had finished, the family had arrived to survey their burnt-out home and exclaimed with pleasure at treasures that had been saved.

"Everyone has been so good to us and we hardly know you," said Mrs Browne. "I can't believe it." She wiped tears from her eyes and picked up a china teapot, rubbing away the dirt. "This was a wedding present."

Meanwhile, the men had cleared much of the section and were looking at the house to see if repairing was an option. "It's the shingles that are the problem. It's like having kindling on the roof, all ready for fire to take hold if a stray sparks gets blown there by the wind," one of the younger men remarked.

"You're right," said John. "I hope to use some of that new corrugated iron on the room I'm building at home. It won't be so dangerous."

"Any ideas about where the family can stay while the house is rebuilt?" asked Henry Dickson.

"I've nearly finished building a woolshed out on the road to Masterton. Perhaps they could stay there," said one of the helpers, a wealthy land owner. "It's big and roomy. It'll be a bit cold for the winter, but the husband has been working out our way, chopping logs for the mill, so it won't be too far for him to go to work. At the moment he only gets home a day or two a week. It'll be hard on him when he sees what's happened. I'm off home now so I'll tell him the bad news. But if the family are safe and the house can be repaired no doubt he'll think himself lucky."

"I hope so," said Paddy Kelly. "It's a hard old world, so it is," as his eyes filled with tears.

"Now now Kelly, it's just the way life is." John patted Paddy's arm. "You've done a great job here today. There's not a lot more that we can do. I think we should make our way home and get on with our own chores, don't you?" Paddy nodded. "I'm sure that others will see about setting them up in the woolshed. That was nice of the fellow to offer. These cockys are not so bad when you get to know them. They don't consider they're the 'landed gentry' like they do back home. Someone said we should set up a fund to help the family, and I think we should give the blacksmith a hand too. After all, he won't be able to start work again for a while will he?"

"You're right," said Dickson. "I'm all for that. The men were talking about putting up a shelter where he could work out of the weather, just three sides and a roof if they can use the remnants of the old shop. It could go on the same site. The forge is still all right. Well, we'll see, won't we? I'd better get back to the shop or I'll be in trouble. Oh, what did you think of my doing a delivery service around the district?"

"I think it's a great idea," said John.

CHAPTER 19 Trouble at the Kellys'

Paddy and O'bie did not go straight back to the farm as planned. As they were passing the hotel O'bie asked, "Do you feel like a beer, Mr Kelly? Have we got time to wet our whistle?"

Paddy passed a hand over his forehead and shook his head. "No, no O'bie, we've wasted enough time as it is. Let's get home."

"Oh come on boss, we deserve a pint or two."

Paddy didn't need much persuading. It had been a hard day and he'd only have one drink. "Well, not for long O'bie, we've work to catch up on."

They made their way into the bar where most of the men who had worked on clearing the fire debris were already imbibing. They greeted Paddy and O'bie warmly. O'bie was still a hero and Paddy had done great work with the horse and cart.

Offers of free drinks were made all around. Unfortunately, the barman on duty didn't know about the ginger-ale trick, and served Paddy the real thing. The first drink slid down his throat like an oyster, never touching the sides. After that, Paddy kept drinking.

O'bie, too, soon became the worse for wear and, by the time the barman called for the last drinks, neither he nor Paddy could hardly stand. However, the publican was not troubled. "We'll put them in the cart and the horse will take them home for us. It'll be a great joke when they wake up," and he and some of the other men loaded the two onto the cart, then sent the horse on its way.

As the men slept, the old horse plodded along the track, glad to be headed for home. Meanwhile, his owner, a light sleeper, had heard the rattle of the cart and met it at his gate, where he silently woke the men and pointed the way home.

Tessa heard them coming down the track singing Irish songs as loudly as they could, and giggling like children. She'd been waiting all evening for Paddy and O'bie to come home and had even walked down to the paddock where they'd been working the day before. She'd known nothing of the events in the village until the children came home from school full of the tale and, even before they finished talking, she'd had a foreboding.

Now it was nearly ten o'clock at night and her worst fears were being realised. The sound of their voices turned her heart to stone. Had it started all over again? All Paddy's promises to stay sober were gone down the drain. 'That O'bie!' she fumed. 'Why did I not send him on his way?'

As they came nearer, still shouting bawdy songs, she went outside, closing the door behind her, and waited till they stood, wavering in front of her. "So you're home then." She glared at them. "You needn't think you're coming in here in that state."

"What do you mean woman?" yelled Paddy. "This is my home and I want my bed. So get out of my way, wifey darlin' and let me in."

"You can sleep outside with the pigs for all I care but you're not coming in here." And, going inside, she shut the door and fastened the bolts that had been added at the time of the Maori troubles.

"Oh please Tessa, it's cold out here. I'm sorry, you know that," Paddy wheedled in his best Irish brogue. "It was O'bie's fault. He's off to bed and I'm begging you to let me come in. Please."

But Tessa was resolute. "I'm not the silly lovesick girl who put up with your drunken ways in Ireland. I told you I'd pack up and leave if you went down that path again. So get yourself away from my door and let me get to sleep. Go and bunk down with O'bie and he'd better be gone by the morning too."

Knowing that Tessa's mind was made up, Paddy slunk off to the stable and bedded down in the hay. His dog came and cuddled up to him, licking his face. Paddy sighed, closed his eyes and slept.

—⚬⚬⚬—

That night the plight of the family who lost their home occupied Kate's thoughts as she tried to sleep, and next morning she told John she wanted to go to town to visit the Dicksons to check they were all right after the fright they'd had. "It must be terrible to stand and watch a house near your property burn down and not be able to do anything about it. Poor Mrs Dickson, I can't imagine how she must be feeling. You'll be all right working on the room, won't you?"

"Sure, we'll get to work as soon as Rangi and Ru arrive. We'll try to finish the walls today ready for the iron when it comes up from Wellington. It should be here before long. I've heard that wagon-loads are going back and forth to Wellington several times a week now, taking timber and produce down and bringing back supplies. Jake," he called, "go and harness Beauty for your mother."

Jake came from the house, "Yes Father, I will straight away. I was wondering, can I go down to the creek with Rangi's boys after I get my jobs done, to catch some more eels?"

"As long as you're careful." John looked at Jake, thinking how much he'd grown up since he lost his friend Patrick. He was much more accepting of having to help around the farm.

Jake and Patrick had had a lot in common. Both were facing a new life in this country, so different from the one left behind. Both were more inclined to practical things and were not academic. Rangi's boys were a good substitute, and would show Jake another way of facing life. 'The Maori Way.' Nothing seemed to worry them; they took life as it came along, accepting everything and not looking for or making trouble.

After Jake returned with the horse and buggy his father said, "Yes, you can go down to the creek but don't go near the river."

"Of course not, Father There's a tapu on the river. It hasn't been lifted yet."

Kate placed a basket of food in the buggy. "I'm taking Cathy to spend some time with Jane and Polly, I'll pick her up on the way back," she said as she took up the reins and tapped Beauty's rump with the whip.

When they were nearing the Kellys' Kate and Cathy could see Paddy and Tessa standing outside by the stump near the door of their cottage, obviously arguing. Polly and Jane were holding each other, crying, and Dennis was hanging on to his mother's arm.

Kate wondered if she should drive on but, thinking she might be able to help, she gave the reins to Cathy and got down from the buggy.

"Whatever's the matter?" she asked as she went to put her arms around Polly and Jane.

"Well you may ask," said Tessa. "You should have seen the state of this one when he arrived home last night. I told him any more drinking binges and I was off, and taking the children. After all the goings-on yesterday, O'bie and himself here came home drunk. We think the horse and cart brought them as far as the owner's place then these two stumbled home singing, as rotten as two-year-old eggs. At least the horse knew where home was," said Tessa.

"Oh Mr Kelly, how could you? Poor Mrs Kelly, what will you do? How would you manage on your own?"

"I don't know Mrs Johnson," said Tessa. "I said I'd never ever again go through what we went through in Ireland. We came here to get away from the drinking and abuse I suffered at this man's hands for several years. Since we came here it's been wonderful, that is until Patrick died."

Paddy looked down at his feet as he spoke, "I'm sorry girl, I really am. We only went to have one pint but the men were pushing glass after glass on to us, both of us. They were trying to say sorry about Patrick and thanks for the work we'd done all day with the fire cleanup. Then the booze took over and we were sunk. As God is my witness I'll never go into a pub again."

Tessa looked at the children who were tearful and upset. They'd been through these arguments before, but it had been so long ago they'd almost forgotten.

Kate went to Mrs Kelly and put her arm around her shoulder. "I'm so sorry this has happened," she said. "I can't believe that you'd do such a thing, Mr Kelly. You're a fool. You know that, don't you. I guess O'bie had a bit of a hand in going to the hotel, but you can only blame yourself if your wife leaves you."

O'bie came out of the barn, looking sheepish and the worse for wear. His head ached and his mouth was dry. He looked at Tessa and saw pure anger on her face.

"I told you no booze, O'bie and this is what you bring my husband to. A drunken fool again. You wouldn't know what he was like before he gave up the drink, but I remember only too well. You can't stay here working if I can't trust you."

"I'm truly sorry Mrs Kelly. Johnson told me the boss was not going to drink after the funeral, but I never thought he had a problem with the drink. Oh God, I'm truly sorry. Will I pack my things?"

Kate looked at Mrs Kelly, wondering what she'd say. O'bie had been stupid, and Paddy had been weak, but the farm work had to go on. There was only so much one man could do.

"Look, why don't I take the young ones into town with me? Cathy can stay with Jane. They can help inside, while you and your husband sit down and talk about the best thing to do. I think O'bie should get on with the milking and keep out of the way until you've come to a decision about him. What do you think?" Kate asked.

"Thank you Mrs Johnson, I think that would be best if it's not too much trouble." Tessa looked at the tearful faces of her children, and said, "You'd better behave yourselves. No nonsense. Go and wash your faces and get tidy, while I talk to Mrs Johnson." She took Kate's arm and led her to the back of the house out of earshot.

"Mrs Johnson, I really don't know what to do. He's been so good since we came out here, but now to give in to the drink and come home in that state! I'll never be able to show my face in town again. What do you think? You're so sensible, advise me what to do. Please."

"Nonsense Mrs Kelly," exclaimed Kate. "Everyone will treat you just the same as always. You've done nothing wrong. Paddy made a big mistake drinking with O'bie. They were tired and thirsty. He's truly sorry, you can see that."

"So you think I should ignore this fall and give him another chance?" Tessa said through her tears.

"I don't know what it's like to be the wife of a drunkard, thank God, but trying to make it on your own out here would be far from easy. What could you do if you took the children back to Wellington or even Ireland? Do you have any experience of working for anyone? Or would you be left to take in washing and ironing? It's a hard world for a woman without a man. I don't think you have an option and neither does your husband. He must swear off the drink from now on."

"I expect you're right, Mrs Johnson. It will be hard to forgive and forget but perhaps I should, for the sake of the children." Tessa breathed a huge sigh that shook the whole of her body. Kate put her arms around her friend, thinking how close they'd become since the tragedy. Funny how some people had so much bad luck, while others sailed through their lives.

"What about O'bie?" Kate asked."Do you think you can forgive him too? Your husband depends on him now."

"I'll wait until I can talk to Paddy and see how much he had to do with going to the pub. Was it mostly his idea? Or was Paddy just as much to blame? Look, I'm holding up your trip to town. You've been a great help and I thank you. Let's go back to Paddy and the children."

"All ready then?" Kate asked the three children. "Well hop up then," she said as Tessa came out with a farthing each for them to spend at Dickson's store.

Kate shook the reins and Beauty moved off smoothly. "You look nice in that dress Polly," said Kate, smiling at the child. "You mustn't worry about your parents having a fight now and again. They'll no doubt be happy with each other when you get home."

Unconvinced, Dennis shook his head. He remembered much more than Polly about the way things had been before his father had given up the drink, the fights and the quarrels. Worst of all was the noise his mother's body had made when she was thrown against the kitchen wall. Those times had faded in his memory, but now they were all coming back. He didn't say anything though as he respected his mother's wishes to forget all about it. But was it going to start all over again?

Kate noticed how quiet he had become and tried to cheer him up. "Come on Dennis, give us a smile," but the young boy only lifted his eyes to heaven in a plea for peace and quiet. He didn't want to talk about the fight and wished Mrs Johnson would just leave him alone. Polly, feeling the tension in her brother's body as he sat still and lost in his thoughts, began to worry too. She wished things could go back to the time before Patrick was drowned. There! She had said it. The dreaded word, drowned. How sad it sounded. She looked at Mrs Johnson and wondered if her mother would ever be as happy.

Kate saw her look and tried to think of something to cheer them up. "What are you going to spend your money on?" she asked. "The store has lots of sweets, and things to eat.What are your favourites?"

"I love toffees," said Polly, licking her lips. "And jellies and marshmallows."

"I like bullseyes," said Dennis, coming out of his reverie with a ghost of a smile on his face. "But I want to get something for Mother, something special."

"Well Dennis, if you help me with the shopping, we'll see."

"Oh yes, I will Mrs Johnson, I will," replied Dennis with his eyes shining. Polly, not to be out done, said that she too would help.

Kate wondered just what she'd started. 'What would it matter if it cost a three pence or two to see the smiles back on their faces?'

As Kate tied Beauty up near the store, she told the three children they could go and play with their friends for a while. As the school was closed until Monday some of their friends were in the grass area near the shop. She watched as they ran happily to join them, then entered the store.

Mr Dickson had seen her arrive and came to greet her. "It's so good to see you Mrs Johnson. You certainly find out who your friends are when you strike trouble. Your husband and the other men were wonderful yesterday. They worked until dark to clear the section. The mill has donated some timber for the rebuilding of the house and let me have some quite cheap as well. I need to fix up the wall that got scorched. Some of the builders in town are volunteering time to fix up the house, and the blacksmith's. It's great how well everyone worked together, isn't it?"

"Yes, my husband was really impressed with how everyone got on with the task. I'll go and see your wife if I may. I was so worried about you both." Kate walked through to the store-room.

"Oh Mrs Johnson it's so good to see you. I've never been so scared in all my life. That house burnt in a few minutes. The roof must have been smouldering for a while, then up it went with a whoosh and embers fell into our room below. Fortunately men were able to save the store but I feel so sorry for the mother who lost her home. She and her husband 'll have a big job on their hands to start again."

"It must have been awful for her," said Kate.

"We've started a fund to help them. The men are going to take her and the children up to the wool-shed tomorrow. Some of them are there fixing it up now. What about you? Were you worried when your husband was late home?"

"I was. I walked down to the field where they were supposed to be working. There was no-one there so I thought he'd changed his plans. Not long after that he came home and told me about the fire. Poor Mr Fairman, the blacksmith's place looks so desolate. He may be a giant of a man but it still hit him hard. My husband said that men are going to put up a bit of a shelter for him to work in. After all, the horses will still need their shoes, won't they?"

"That's right Mrs Johnson, but things will start to return to normal when the house and blacksmith's are rebuilt. The town will look as if nothing happened but we'll always remember won't we?"

Kate looked at the young woman as she spoke, wondering if she missed her family as much as she missed her own. She seemed very happy and contented and much in love with her husband. 'Is there a great plan that we can't see?' she wondered.

"What else has been happening?" asked Mrs Dickson as she put the kettle on the fire. "How are the Kellys? Have you seen them?"

"Yes I called in to them on the way here. Things are not as good as they could be. I'm sure Mrs Kelly won't mind me telling you what happened; after all, the men who were at the hotel must have seen the state that her husband and O'bie were in last night," said Kate.

"Oh don't tell me Mr Kelly started drinking again," gasped Johanna. "Not after getting through the funeral and all."

"According to Mrs Kelly, the men were both rotten drunk and were put in the cart for the horse to take them home." Kate paused, then went on to tell what Mrs Kelly had said about leaving him. "I brought the little ones into town with me to give them a break and to let their parents talk things through."

"Poor woman, that must have been a big blow for her," Mrs Dickson said as she poured the tea. "I'll just take my husband a cup."

Kate picked up her cup and wondered how much she should say. 'The Kellys were customers of the Dicksons and news travels fast. I'll just tell her nothing is decided yet.'

"So?" said Mrs Dickson as she picked up her teaspoon and sugared her tea. "What will she do if she doesn't take him back?"

"I don't know. Mrs Kelly's much stronger than I thought she would be and seems very capable. She's coping with Patrick's death much better than her husband. I suggested she think very carefully."

"She's lucky to have you to confide in, as I am too. I won't say anything to anyone. I feel sorry for her and cross with O'bie, the stupid man. Didn't your husband warn him of the danger at the wake?" asked Johanna, as Kate rose to leave.

"Yes he did. My husband doesn't know about the goings-on yet, but he'll have something to say to O'bie, you can be sure of that. I'd better go and see where the children have got to. They want to earn some money to buy their mother a present. I'll let them carry the groceries out to the buggy, then find some little thing they can buy."

After Kate went to the front of the shop to give Mr Dickson a list of the stores she needed she went to find the children, who came running towards her.

"Look what I've got!" said Dennis, holding out his hand. There was a bright three pence in it.

"Is that the one your mother gave you?" asked Kate.

"No it's another one," replied Dennis, looking very satisfied with himself. "I held a horse for a man while he went to the hotel, and he gave me three pence, so now I'm rich."

Kate could see this had opened up a new world to Dennis. Patrick had been the one to do the odd chores and pick up the pennies; now it was his turn.

"Well, let's get the groceries and then you can have fun spending it," she said as they went back into the store. She handed Dennis a bag of wheat and watched as he manfully carried it to the buggy. It was quite heavy for the lad. He just made it to the backboard where a passerby lifted it on for him. Soon everything was on board.

"Come and see what you want to buy," Kate said to the children. They went very importantly around the shop looking at the display Mrs Dickson had made of anything that could be seen as a useful gift. Polly was sad she didn't have as much to spend as Dennis, but Kate whispered to Mrs Dickson and a pretty hanky was wrapped up. Dennis bought one pennyworth of sweets and a nice cake of scented soap.

"Your mother will love that Dennis," Kate said as it was wrapped up nicely for him. James spent his farthing on some lollies and was happy. After Kate bought some sweets for the girls and tobacco for John they went on their way with Beauty glad to be turned for home.

As they trotted past Kellys' boundary Paddy and O'bie could be seen working on the stumps. 'So they must have come to a decision, or perhaps Tessa wanted more time to consider things,' Kate thought as she pulled into the gateway.

Jane and Cathy came running to greet her, smiles on their faces. They'd had a lovely time together. After tidying up the bedrooms and washing the dishes, they'd spent the time looking at Jane's treasures. Mrs Kelly had been so pleased with their efforts she had let them make pikelets for lunch.

Tessa had been surprised at how well the girls had gone about their tasks without being told. It had been Cathy's idea to wash up the dishes, and work is so much easier when there are two to do it, so when Jane asked if Cathy could come again her mother smiled. "You'll always be welcome Cathy. It was lovely of you to help Jane. Thank you," she said turning to Kate. "I've decided to give him another chance. I believe that he didn't mean to start drinking again."

"I know you've thought about this carefully but what if he falls again?" asked Kate.

"I don't think he will, Mrs Johnson. I think he's learnt his lesson. He knows I'll be watching for any signs of him drinking, and he's truly sorry. I'll talk to O'bie and tell him about the way things were at home. I try to forget the misery we went through. The men could only find peace when they were in a drunken stupor. Paddy would come home from the pub and demand his dinner and threaten me and the children if I'd nothing left to give him. I never want to go through that again," said Tessa as she drew a deep breath and shuddered.

"Oh my God, my dear, was it really that bad?" exclaimed Kate. "I'd no idea you'd been through so much. We heard things were bad in Ireland, but thought that the reports were being exaggerated."

"I know Mrs Johnson. People in England have no idea the way things were. Even in the Houses of Parliament, they said we were a lazy lot who could feed ourselves if we tried. Folk said we were living a life of luxury because we spent three months a year growing potatoes and then no more work for the rest of the year. What they didn't realise is most of the food grown was sent to England. Or that landlords demanded most of the crops raised by the tenants as their right. Then they shipped it off for better prices while we starved. Anyway, I don't want to think about those times." Tessa wiped her eyes with the tea-towel, and smiled at Kate.

"I'm so sorry for what you have been through. Father would read things out to us from the *Times*, but we had no idea of the reality of life in Ireland," said Kate.

"Oh well, thank God we are here in a better country, with people in government who put the good of the people first," Tessa Kelly said. "That's why I've decided to overlook Paddy's behaviour. I'll pray to Our Lady to help me keep my belief that he'll come through this trial. I know that Patrick's death has almost crippled him."

"Oh, Mrs Kelly, you poor soul," Kate moved closer to Tessa and took her hands in her own. "If there is anything I can do, at any time, you must tell me. I'll be here for you." Then she smiled at Dennis and Polly who'd been waiting excitedly for a gap in the conversation.

"Mother, Mother, look what I have for you," said Polly holding out her gift.

Tessa took the little parcel and carefully unwrapped it. "Oh Polly, that's lovely. It's so pretty."

"Mine too Mother," said Dennis "Look what I've got." Tessa took the parcel from the outstretched hand and undid the string.

"What a lovely cake of soap. I'll smell so nice, wont I? You shouldn't have spent your money on me." She smiled at her children, and bent to kiss them. She had so much to be thankful for. If only Paddy could think so too. "Thank you Mrs Johnson for giving them the outing, I'm not sure how they managed to stretch their money so far but they had a lovely time. Will you have a cup of tea before you go?"

"I'd love to, but I must get home. Come along Cathy let's get away home."

"Bye everyone, bye Jane," called Cathy as she climbed up onto the buggy. "Thank you for letting me come and visit Jane, Mrs Kelly."

CHAPTER 20 Kate Goes Visiting

When Kate arrived home Jake took Beauty from the buggy to give her a rub down, water and a feed of grain. He loved taking care of both horses but Beauty was special. Bessie was an old hack compared with Beauty.

Jake had had a good day. Hemi and Kingi, though younger than himself, were good company. Their being Maori didn't seem to make any difference to their friendship and they were so smart about things in the bush and could teach him a lot. Together they'd caught seven eels which Rangi had taken to smoke.

Catching sight of Jake by the barn, John called him over to give a hand with a piece of timber he was lifting on to the roof. It was long and heavy but they soon had it in place. John hammered in some of the long handmade nails he was using to fasten the runners for the iron. As he climbed back down the ladder he was well pleased with the progress made. The scaffolding was getting a bit rickety - 'I must re-tie the places where the long thin branches of manuka touched each other, with flax, before we do any more work.' He couldn't afford holdups through accidents.

Indoors, John asked Kate how things were in town.

"The men are moving the family tomorrow, with the bedding and goods that have been collected. I think she'll be all right." While she set about preparing a meal she could hear Jake telling John about the fun they'd had at the creek. The boys had cooked some crawlies in an old tin and found them very tasty.

With the meal over, and the children in bed, Kate told John the bad news about Mr Kelly, but John was quite philosophical about it, saying he was sure Kelly would do his best to stay sober. "With help he'll do it."

The next morning, after the children left for school, Kate had time to look at the bundle of mail given to her the day before. There were letters from her mother and one from Mary too, sent from Capetown. It wouldn't be long now until they arrived in Wellington. Kate hoped the arrangements John had made for them in Wellington were in hand. In her mother's letter, she read all the usual chit-chat about her friends, but also she'd begun singing in the choir. There was a rather animated description of an evening at the Repertory Theatre, with a friend from the choir. Her mother didn't say if the friend was a man or a woman but, reading between the lines, Kate suspected it was a man. Surprised but not alarmed, she realised it was time for the men's 'smoko'.

John was telling Ru to fix the places where the flax ties were loose on the scaffolding. "We don't want any holdups do we? You'd break a leg, falling from there, even if it is only a few feet above the ground," he said as he pulled on the manuka stakes to test the ties.

"Fine boss, I'll do it now," replied Ru, adding, "Hey, your boy's a good hunter, boss. Them boys caught a fine feed of eels yesterday and some kereru too. Good tucker eh, boss?"

"I know the pigeon are tasty, but it seems a shame to eat anything so pretty," remarked John as he got ready to start work again.

"There's hundreds of them, boss. They're so slow moving and stupid, they deserve to get caught," said Rangi as he climbed up to the roof on the shaky manuka poles.

Then, a loud shout alerted John and he ran to find Rangi sitting on the ground nursing his knee.

"Plurry fool! Eh boss," said Rangi. "I didn't fall far but I've twisted my knee. It's not bad though. Give us a hand to stand up boss." As John helped him to sit down on a log, Kate, who'd heard the shout, came running.

"I knew this would happen. I thought you'd have trouble using those thin branches John," she said.

"Calm down Kate. Rangi's all right and Ru has gone to cut some more ties. It's really very strong. Anyway it's all we have to use. Don't worry."

"Not worry!" Kate's eyes blazed. "You could have been killed, Rangi, and then what would we do?"

"I'm all right Missy, really. It's going better already. See, I can stand on it now." Rangi bravely stood up but winced in pain as he took a step before quickly sitting down again. He turned to Ru who had arrived with a large bundle of flax to strip down to make the ties and didn't know what had happened.

"I fell off the roof, Ru. You were too late fixing the thing. Eh boss? It's not your fault Ru though, I'm the silly joker that fell."

John wondered if Rangi would be able to help again today or if he'd be better to rest the knee. "Look, you just cut the ties," he said. "Ru and I will put the rest of the scantlings on the roof. You can get the flax ready while you're resting your leg. We'll finish tieing the poles when we're done up there. The scaffold will need to be strong when we put the iron in place; it's heavier than shingles or totara bark."

Rangi was grateful for John's consideration. His knee was throbbing but he could sit and strip the long sticky strands of flax just as well sitting down as he could standing up.

Kate came out of the house with a chair for him. "This will be more comfortable, Rangi," and she placed it close to where he was sitting on the log.

"Thanks Missy, that's good. You and the boss are really good to us Missy."

"We're lucky to have you Rangi. We need each other," she replied as she went inside to prepare lunch.

After lunch Kate told John she wanted to visit Mrs Kelly to see how she was doing. "I won't be long," she said. "I'll walk over. I don't feel up to riding, or catching Beauty. I'll be back when the children get back from school." Kate went back into the house to pick up a basket of food she'd packed to take. In it were vegetables and a jar of pickles but also a cake she'd made that morning, thinking it might help cheer them up. "Bye," she called as she went down the path, "and be careful."

The walk didn't take long and soon she and Mrs Kelly were drinking tea and sampling the cake together.

"Tell me how you and your husband are getting on. Are you going to keep O'bie or give him his marching orders?" asked Kate. "He must know how upset you are."

"I told him how things used to be in Ireland, and that I'd rather leave Paddy than live like that again. He was very sorry and I believe he was, coming from a broken home himself. I don't think he'll take Paddy drinking again or bring drink here. I guess I can only trust the pair of them to get on with the work," said Tessa. "They have done such a lot of cleaning up down the far end of the farm and are ready to plough and sow the crop. It's getting so late because the drought went on so long. Now I expect it will rain too much too soon. I sound like a real farmer's wife don't I?"

"And how are the children? They had a lovely time in town and took such care over their presents."

"Thank you for taking them Mrs Johnson. It was good to be able to talk to my husband without them hearing and getting upset. I gave him the ultimatum in no uncertain terms. He just folded up. No argument at all. In the old days I would've feared for my life and would have had to hide until he cooled down."

"Well, I guess you'll have to wait and see. I'm glad you didn't tell O'bie to go. I think Mr Kelly needs the company. It's a hard job felling trees and stumping on your own. It's lucky John has Rangi and Ru. Oh, I haven't told you Rangi fell off the scaffolding and hurt his knee this morning. I don't think it's bad but he'll have to rest. I hate those little manuka poles they put up. They look so flimsy, and as for the flax ties..."

"Well, they all use them. There's quite an industry cutting flax and selling it for twine now. Mills have been built to make use of the flax in the swamplands. The Maoris have long known the value of it for clothing and covers and decoration. They really are clever, you know. Now tell me how the new room is coming on."

"Oh it will be lovely. My husband has bought a new sort of stove for me too," answered Kate. "It looks quite big but he says it will fit."

"How much longer have you got to go Mrs Johnson? You're due sometime in September aren't you?"

"Yes, I think about the end. I haven't seen a doctor but I'm fairly sure I'm right," said Kate as she gathered up her things. "I'd better get back; the children will be home soon. I'm glad I came. I'll not be so worried now. You're very strong; I don't think I could be as forgiving as you."

'Strong?' Tessa asked herself as she waved goodbye. 'Well I suppose I am but he'd better stick to the bargain, or I'll be done for murder.' She looked into the mirror on the wall and wondered who the woman reflected in it really was. Her reverie was broken moments later as the children burst into the kitchen, tossing their sugar-bag school holdalls in a heap on the floor.

"Pick those up, and put them away," said Tessa as a greeting.

"Can we have some cake?" asked Dennis and Polly together.

"Whatever happened to please?" said Tessa with a smile.

"Mama," said Dennis as he helped himself to another slice of cake, "are you going to let Father stay with us?" He watched his mother's face, trying to read her reaction. Usually he was told to mind his own business and just wait and see when he asked questions.

"Well that's a fine question for you to be askin' your Mam, Dennis. Where did you get the idea I'd toss your father out on his ear?" said Tessa, wondering how much Dennis remembered.

"I heard Jane and Cathy talking," said Dennis, swallowing hard to keep tears away.

"Well, since you asked," said Tessa, "I can say that I intend to keep everyone here with me, to work as hard as they can together. Your father has promised on the Bible that he won't slip back into his old ways. I'm sorry Dennis love, that you've been worried. I'll have something to say to Jane when she gets home. Where is she anyway?"

"She's walking home with Cathy," said Polly. "They were kept in for a while to help Mrs Thompson with the desks that have been made for us. They'll be better than the benches. We said goodbye to the Brownes today, they're going to their new home in the woolshed."

"Yes, poor souls, I hope they can manage up there on the road to Masterton. Remember them in your prayers tonight, Polly, that's a good girl." Tessa watched as the children took their bags up and began their homework.

"Where did the desks come from, Dennis?" she asked.

"One of the men working in Greytown made them for us. I think he likes Mrs Thompson. He gave us a school bell too."

"You see too much for your own good, my boy," said Tessa with a chuckle. "Now get on with your homework and then your chores. Be sure to give water to the fowls, Dennis; their bowl was empty when I got the eggs today. If they can't drink they won't lay you a nice egg for your tea." Tessa looked at Dennis with love. James watched his mother for a word of praise. "You're a good boy too James."

Kate made her way home, thinking about the Kellys and their problems. Jake and Cathy came trotting up beside her and they talked about school as they made their way along the road through the bush. What it would be like when winter really struck Kate didn't know. Drains had been dug along the sides of the road so the water should run off freely, and not turn the road into a bog.

She thought of their arrival on that cart and wondered where the months had gone. So much had happened and so many friends had been made. She hardly ever thought about 'home' now, unless there was a letter to remind her. No, this was home now and she would learn to love this country with her whole heart as she knew John did. She looked at the children and gave a prayer of thanks they were so healthy and happy.

Back at the cottage Kate walked around the back of the house to see how the men were getting on. Rangi was up on the roof nailing sheets of corrugated iron down while Ru was waiting to pass up another sheet.

"How is your knee Rangi?" she called, watching that she did not startle him.

He turned towards her and grinned. "Good now Missy, it don't hurt no more now. boss gave me some ointment to rub on it."

"That's good Rangi, don't do too much moving around, will you. Where's my husband?"

"He's gone down the paddock to get some more of the timber we sawed up. He said I'd be better to stay here and not move about too much. He took the dray. He'll be back soon, Missy," said Rangi as he took another sheet of iron from Ru.

Kate looked down towards the bush-line at the end of the farm. She could just see John in the distance through the trees. She wondered if she should send Jake down to help then thought not. He'd most likely be finished loading by now.

CHAPTER 21 The Family has a Fright

As Kate went indoors to prepare the evening meal, she suddenly felt quite tired - the walk had been further than she thought. There was enough cold meat left, and with some boiled potatoes and some carrots that would have to do. 'Perhaps a jar of fruit and some cream would go down well later.' Calling to Cathy to peel some potatoes, Kate sank into a chair near the fire.

"Are you all right Mother?" asked Cathy.

"Just a bit tired Cathy. I'll just sit here and rest for a bit."

"Oh Mother, I hope you're all right. Do you want me to get Father?"

"No, no, I'll be fine. Just do those potatoes. Your father will be hungry after his day's work. Put some wood on the fire and add half a teaspoon of salt in the potatoes. There's a good girl," said Kate as, with a sigh, she closed her eyes.

Cathy went quickly about the task, calling to Jake to bring some more wood for the fire as she filled the pot with water and began washing the potatoes. She'd never seen her mother sitting down while there was work to be done. It didn't seem right. Going to the doorway to take the wood from Jake's arms, she quietly told him to run and get their father as Kate slept on, oblivious to the world.

John came running. "What's happened Cathy? How long has she been like this?"

"She sat down saying she felt tired and told me to help with dinner. Then she went to sleep." Cathy was frightened by her father's worried look. "What do you think can be the matter?"

"I don't know. I'll carry her to bed so she keeps warm. Don't worry too much, she may just be tired. There have been so many things to think about lately and she's been overdoing it." 'But,' he thought, 'I might try and find the doctor.' He picked up his sleeping wife and carried her to the bed where he laid her gently down and pulled the blankets up. Kate only stirred a little.

Cathy stood by the door, wondering what could be the matter. "Do you think you should get the doctor Father?"

"Did she seem normal when you came home? When she sat down did she seem worried?"

"No Father, she was all right when I came home," said Cathy. "She said she felt tired, that's all, then she sat in the chair."

When Jake came in carrying more wood, John told him to saddle up Beauty as quickly as he could. "I'm going to town to find the doctor. You children watch your Mother. I'll be back as soon as I can."

John made his way to the village, as fast as Beauty could go. Thankfully, the little daylight left made the trip easier and soon he was able to see the first homes. John went quickly to the doctor's house and knocked loudly at the door. It was opened by his housekeeper and John quickly told her what the matter was.

As the doctor was eating his evening meal, John was shown to the parlour and asked to wait. Agitated and unable to sit still, he paced the floor praying, 'Dear Lord, don't let anything happen to Kate,' as he walked the length of the room again and again.

Finally the doctor appeared. "Sit down man. Tell me what the trouble is."

"It's my wife, Doctor. She walked over to see a friend and collapsed into a chair when she came home. She's pregnant."

"She was well this morning?" asked the doctor.

"Yes she was fine. She went to see the neighbour after lunch. It's not a long walk, but my daughter Cathy said she was tired when she came home and just sat in a chair and went to sleep. When I carried her to bed she stirred a little but didn't wake."

"Your wife is expecting," said the doctor. "How long has she got to go?"

"I believe she's due in September, about the end. I'm so worried about her. She's never sick."

"Well, I'll come and see for myself. I'll ride over with you. Just wait till I get my bag." He left the room, calling his housekeeper to bring his bag to the door while he struggled on with his coat.

"Don't worry too much, Mr Johnson," said the doctor as they rode along. "It may be that she's a bit anaemic and needs red meat."

"Oh, I do hope you can find out why she fell asleep like that. It's so out of character. She's always so busy and happy. I can't believe this has happened," John said as they reached the house and gave the horses to Jake to take care of.

"Well, we'll soon see," said the doctor. "By the way, I'm Alex McDonald, from bonny Scotland," and he held out his hand.

John took the hand and shook it warmly. "I'm very glad to meet you Doctor McDonald," he said. "Come through please. My wife's in here."

Dr McDonald walked through to the bedroom and looked at Kate who was still soundly asleep. He took her pulse, noting that it was a little slower than usual, but steady. When he felt her head to see if she had a temperature she seemed cool enough. He put his stethoscope on her stomach, listening for the baby's heartbeat and found it strong.

Dr McDonald turned to John, "I think she's all right and should wake up soon. Her vital signs are all good and the baby is fine. I think her body is telling her to slow down and take things quietly for the next few months. She might need something that will give her more iron. Any red meat is good. I think that's the trouble. The baby is leaving her short of what she needs."

Suddenly, Kate turned onto her side, opened her eyes and stretched. "What am I doing in bed? Did I faint?"

"Hello Mrs Johnson. You gave your husband quite a fright and he fetched me. I'm Dr McDonald. You've been asleep for a couple of hours. Your body is telling you to slow down and you should listen. I think you may be short of iron, but I'll examine you properly at the surgery if your husband brings you in tomorrow."

"Surely I can take myself in, Doctor," said Kate, "If I'm very careful. My husband has enough to do."

"No, I don't think so, not until I have a better look at you."

Cathy came to the bedroom door. "Are you all right Mother?"

"Yes I'm fine darling, don't worry." said Kate with a brightness she was far from feeling. "The doctor says I need to watch what I eat, to build my blood up."

"Oh, I hope you'll get better Mother, I'll help."

"That's a good girl, Cathy, you look after your mother, and I'll do my best too," said the doctor as he went to leave.

"Would you like a spot, before you go, Doctor?" asked John.

"I'd not say no to that! It's a cold night out there. Winter is not far away now. I see that you're doing a bit of building Mr Johnson," he remarked as he took the glass of whisky. "It's good to see a man get on in this new country. There's nothing like a piece of land to give one a sense of belonging, is there?"

"No, indeed you're right," said John as he sipped his wee dram, and reached for the bottle. "Another?"

"Not for me, I don't want to fall off the horse, now do I?"

"We don't want that. I must thank you for coming out. Will you be able to see to go home? It's quite dark now."

"Don't worry about me. My old grey mare will know the way home even though she hasn't been this far from town before. I'll be on my way." With a wave of his hand, he was off, cantering home, he hoped, to bed.

John returned to the bedroom to see how Kate was feeling and, as she was asleep again, he set about organising some food for the children. Cathy had laid out the cold meat, and the potatoes were boiling merrily on the fire with the steam lifting the lid on the pot. John wondered what else he could give them. He looked in the cupboards. "Did Mother plan having any pudding Cathy?" There were a few jars of preserves left.

"No, but we could have pancakes, I know how to make them," said Cathy.

Thinking it might help take her mind off worrying about her mother, John said, "All right, if you think you can."

Cathy set about making the batter and left it to stand while they ate their first course. Jake made the fire up while John stood at the door of the bedroom watching Kate, but she was back in a sound sleep. Cathy was soon frying pancakes with a will. When spread with plum jam and cream they were judged a great success.

"You're a great little cook, Cathy love," said John, "but that's enough for now. Save one or two for Mother. Jake, you've had enough. Have you done your homework, both of you?"

"No, there hasn't been enough time. Will you write us a note for Mrs Thompson, Father?" asked Cathy. "She can be quite angry when we don't do it."

John agreed then went to look at his wife again. He was so worried about her. It was all right for the doctor to say it was a lack of iron, but did he really know?

Kate opened her eyes and sat up. "Heavens, have I been asleep again? I must get up and get your tea." she said, as she struggled to stand up.

"It's all taken care of, love. We've just finished a delicious meal. I'm sorry that you missed it," teased John as Kate leaned on him and walked through to the table. Cathy had made a cup of tea and was placing the pot, covered with a cosy, on the stand.

"Have a cup of tea Kate," said John, as he helped her sit down.

"Thank you dear, that would be lovely. What did you eat then?" she asked as she surveyed the table. "Have you had enough?" The remains of the meat and potatoes were on the table, but it was the pot of jam and the lingering smell of the pancakes which made her feel hungry.

Cathy produced the last of the pancakes from where they'd been kept warm. "I made these," she said. "We've eaten all the rest, but I saved you these." Cathy picked up the teapot and poured tea for her father and mother, taking care with the old china pot Kate loved. It had belonged to her grandmother and survived the journey from 'home'.

"These are delicious, Cathy; suddenly I'm really hungry. It's been hours since I had some cake at Mrs Kelly's," said Kate. "It seems I'll have to be more careful about eating from now on."

CHAPTER 22 To Town and the Doctor

John woke early next morning. After bringing in the house cow for Jake to milk before he left for school, he sat at the table and wrote a note for Mrs Thompson explaining the lack of homework. It would be done by tomorrow he assured her.

He checked on Kate who was getting dressed, brought in some wood for the fire, and filled the kettle from the water-butt at the door. This would have to be relocated, he thought, as he looked over the work they'd done the previous day. The big wooden barrel served its purpose, but there must be a better system of supplying the house with water. Once the iron roof was finished, it should be easy to catch rainfall and store it. He'd find out about that. The room was taking shape but the boards he'd used for the veranda would need protection from the weather and paint was expensive. He decided to ask Dickson for advice when he took Kate to town. "What time did the doctor say to come in Kate?" he asked, as he sat up to the table. "I'd rather go this morning because Ru and Rangi have enough to keep them busy until lunch time.

"That's fine with me," said Kate as she ladled oatmeal into the dishes Cathy had set out. "I want to see Mrs Dickson and that'll give you time to see her husband too. Shall we go straight after breakfast?"

"That suits me well," said John as he heaped brown sugar on to his plate, and poured the cream. "There's nothing finer than a plate of porridge on a cold morning. My grandfather used to eat it sprinkled with salt. Can you imagine that?" he asked Cathy, who had come to the table.

"Ugh. That's horrible," said Cathy, her face screwed up.

"Mine used to dip his spoon into a cup of milk before he put it in his mouth," said Kate as she thought fondly of the old man who had jogged her on his knee, singing 'Too ra li oo ra li addy', and 'Ta ra ra boom de ay'. "He had a lovely beard, white as snow. I loved him and never knew why we didn't see him anymore until one day, when I was about ten, Mother told me he had died years ago. They never told me because they didn't want to upset me. Well...that upset me more."

"Poor Mother, did you let them know? That you were upset I mean?" asked Cathy, with a mouth full of porridge.

"I did. I did. Now off to school with you. No more questions."

John and Kate left for town soon after Rangi and Ru had been given their work for the day. John did not want them working on the building while he was away, so sent them down to the bush to remove more of the debris left from the tree felling. There were quite a lot of thick branches which could be used for the stove if they were cut into short lengths and stored near the house.

John looked anxiously at the sky, hoping for some rain. It'd been weeks since they'd had a good downpour. He noticed dark clouds coming up from the south. That was a good sign. He looked at Kate as they drove along, thinking, 'Please let there be a simple reason for her tiredness'.

He'd never forgive himself if anything happened to her. He shouldn't let her to do so much, but she was so willing. All the milking and churning and feeding animals were taking a toll. 'I'll have to do better,' he told himself as they neared the village. "I'll take you straight to Dr McDonald's, Kate," he said as they reached the first houses. "Then come back and get you in an hour. Will that be all right?"

"Yes dear. It's just a check-up. I'm sure I'll be ready by then, but I want to see Mrs Dickson as well so don't go to the shop until we're together, or else you'll get impatient waiting for us to stop talking. We have a lot to say."

Kate looked at John for his reaction, but he just smiled. She could have asked for the moon at that moment and he would have given it to her if he could. Kate walked up the path to the doctor's door and knocked. It was quickly opened by a woman wearing an apron who showed her into the room the doctor used for a surgery.

"Doctor will be with you in a minute, Mrs Johnson," she said. "I'm Mrs McDougal, his housekeeper."

"Thank you. Have you known the doctor long?"

"Oh aye, I have indeed. I came out from Scotland with him two years ago. I was his housekeeper there too. He lost his wife a few years ago and came out here to start again. Ah, here he is now."

"Well, you're here Mrs Johnson. Now let's have a look at you." He sat Kate in a chair and began to study her eyes, before moving on to an examination of her body, noting on his pad anything of interest.

"Have you been feeling tired for long?" he asked as she dressed.

"Just the last few weeks," said Kate. "I was happy and looking forward to the baby coming, but what with Patrick's drowning, and all that has gone on since then, I just feel worn out."

"I can't find much wrong with you my dear; I'll give you a tonic to take and remember to eat lots of red meat, not cooked too long. A bit rare is better, maybe some liver too and silver beet, and lots of rest."

Rising from his chair, he took a bottle of dark brown liquid from a cupboard and handed it to Kate. "Take this twice a day in half a glass of hot water. One tablespoon should be enough. It has no hurtful properties in it, no opium or anything like that. It's just a tonic."

Kate opened her purse to pay for the visit, looking for the right money. "What do I owe you Doctor? For today and for your help yesterday?" she asked looking at the coins in her hand.

"Five shillings for both will do, I enjoyed the ride out with your husband. Goodbye and be sure to rest." He opened the door and called to the housekeeper. "Mrs McDougal, will you see Mrs Johnson to her buggy, please?"

As soon as he saw Kate emerge John jumped down to assist her. "So what did he say?" he asked. "Did he find anything wrong with you or the baby?"

"Of course not John, he just gave me a tonic and told me to rest."

As Kate entered Dickson's store she could see Mrs Dickson was serving a customer. "Go through to the back, and put the kettle on Mrs Johnson. I'm ready for a good cup of tea. We've been very busy this morning. Running on the spot I call it," said Mrs Dickson, looking quite flustered and not like her usual meek and mild self.

Kate did as she was bid, then sat on the stool by the table until, noticing dishes in the sink, she prepared to wash them. Just then Johanna came through the curtained doorway. "Oh Mrs Johnson" she said. "I'll do those. Please don't bother."

"No bother at all my dear. Now here we are. A nice hot cup of tea," said Kate cheerfully as she stirred the brew.

"You shouldn't be doing that. Here let me. I'm a bit behind this morning. It seems to get busier and busier each day."

"Don't worry, it's your living. The customers must come first. I had to come in and see the doctor. John got him to come out home last night. I gave him a bit of a fright. I was so tired I went to sleep and didn't wake up when John carried me to bed. Can you believe that?"

"Oh, that's awful. Whatever was the matter?" asked Johanna. "Now here you are waiting on me."

"I'd just walked over to see Mrs Kelly and back, but could hardly move when it was time to get the evening meal. I feel much better this morning, so please don't worry. Dr McDonald has given me a tonic."

"How is Mrs Kelly anyway? Have they resolved their problems?"

"Yes, I think she's realised her husband is truly sorry. They're going to see how things work out, and they're keeping O'bie on as well - Mr Kelly needs the help now Patrick is no longer with us. Poor Patrick." Kate bent her head as tears began to fill her eyes. "I can't help thinking how I'd feel if it was Jake who died and not Patrick. I get quite upset so easily now. I must start taking the tonic the doctor gave me."

"Yes, you must, Mrs Johnson. You must build your strength up. It's all the things that have happened, your husband's accident, those Hawke's Bay Maoris stirring things up at the pa, the tragedy in the river. Just take things a bit easier from now on," said Mrs Dickson in a motherly way.

"Well, look at the way you're coping. You're a real brick. Your husband must be really glad he found the courage to ask you to marry him. Look how much you do around the store. You're never still."

"But I'm not pregnant," replied Johanna with a smile. "Well, I don't think I am. I'm just a bit late."

"Oh that would be lovely, if you are. I hope it's true," said Kate, excited by the possibility.

"Speaking of work, I'd better go and do some. Have you got all you want? Oh, there's some mail for you, I'll go and get it."

Kate went from the store-room through to the shop where Mr Dickson was dealing with some customers. She waited until they'd left before asking if he'd thought more about starting a delivery service. It would save such a lot of people's time if he'd call, say once a week, with the basics.

"I've decided to buy a dray and cover it in like a caravan, to keep everything dry. I'll have some lines available all the time, basics like flour and sugar. I think that would work well. What do you think of that for a start?"

"I think that sounds quite feasible. You have been putting thought into it, haven't you?" said Kate. "Will you get help for your wife while you're away delivering? She won't be able to cope on her own."

"I'm on the look-out for a lad or girl to help her. I'd only do it if I think she can manage. I'd go in the afternoons, say twice a week. I could drop mail off too. The mails are getting more reliable now that it comes up from Wellington on the coach three times a week."

"That sounds excellent. My husband will be in to see you soon. He's gone to see someone but didn't say much about what he was up to."

'Where has he got to? I thought he would have been back by now,' Kate wondered as she waited on the seat placed outside the shop for weary travellers. Ah, at last the buggy was approaching. "Where have you been?" asked Kate as John jumped down from the buggy. She knew from the silly smile on his face that he'd been up to something.

"I've been to see the men at the stables and found that the owner of those ponies is willing to sell them after all," he said, laughing at Kate's worried face. "He had a change of heart. When his two daughters arrived from England he found they are young ladies, not children any more. They've grown so much they need larger mounts. He sent word with one of the grooms to tell me I could take them off his hands."

"But what will you pay for them with John? Can we afford them?"

"Don't worry your pretty head about that lass. I've done a deal with him to exchange timber for the ponies. He'll get his men to come and take some trees to the mill by bullock dray. So we both win," said John. "His land is almost cleared and he wants to build a fine new homestead. He wants rimu and matai. I'm very pleased with the morning's work."

Kate relaxed as she heard John's words. Barter was becoming a normal way of doing business these days. Even the women were swapping things they'd brought from 'home' for more practical things. It made sense that John had made this deal though it was sad to see the lovely trees being cut down. However, he intended to keep a piece of thick bush intact, forever.

"So we now have two more horses, do we? When do they arrive"?

"I don't know how quiet they are. I'll get Ru to bring them out to us tomorrow. I'll just have a quick word with Dickson and then get you home."

The shop was free of customers so John wasted no time in asking if he had decided to have the delivery run. The two men chatted about the idea for some minutes.

"If I can get the mail contract for the area it would pay some of the cost. What do you think of that?"

"It sounds great. I think you're onto a winner. My wife had a bit of a turn last night and I had to get Doctor McDonald out to see her. I got a terrible fright. He said she'll get better, but I still feel as if maybe I ask too much. Just be careful of your lass."

"Thank you. You know how much I value your opinion, don't you?"

"I do, Dickson, just as I value yours. We're able to sound out ideas on each other, and that's a good thing. Bye for now."

"Did you ask about the paint for the veranda?" asked Kate as they drove home. "Did you talk about the delivery service?"

"Yes, and yes," replied John. "I think that he'll do well with the travelling store, and he's going to get some sort of stain in for the veranda."

"Are you going to tell the children about the ponies tonight? Or do you want to keep it a secret? You really are a dark horse. How long have you been negotiating with the big wig?"

"He's not a bad chap at all and he's pleased we came to an agreement which helped both of us. I won't tell the children until the ponies are home. Saddles and bridles will come with them."

On reaching home John ordered Kate to rest while he built up the fire and made her a cup of tea. "I'll go and see how Ru and Rangi are getting along. You have a rest until the children come home. There's no need to do anything. I'll help Cathy with feeding the animals. You've had a big day already."

"I hear, I hear," laughed Kate. And to tell the truth she was quite happy for once to do as she was told. She moved to bring more wood in but John forestalled her and steered her towards the big bed, lifted her on to it and placed a blanket over her. "Rest," he said and left the house to ride down to the men.

Ru and Rangi saw him approaching through the trees and called a welcome. "How's Missy?" asked Rangi. "Is she feeling better?"

"I think so. The doctor gave her some medicine. She seems stronger this afternoon. I won't stay long. I just wanted to see how you were doing."

"We done all right boss," said Rangi. "We gonna burn that heap of branches there before we go home then bring the dray up to the house with the wood."

"Sounds fine to me. Don't let the fire get into the bracken though. It could go up like a bomb, it's so dry. I thought we might have had some rain but the clouds have gone away again. It's halfway through May and still as dry as a desert."

"There was a shower a while ago but stopped now. Don't worry, it will rain soon," said Rangi.

"Ru, I want you to bring home a couple of young ponies from the stables tomorrow. The men will tell you which ones, so go there before you come to work. Be sure to go carefully. I don't know much about them but they look quiet."

"Yes boss, whatever you say." said Ru. "You got them for the children? They'll be happy, eh boss?"

CHAPTER 23 Burning Off

As John made his way back to the house it grew darker. He could see heavy clouds gathering around the ranges. Bull Hill to the south was almost obscured and a strong breeze was blowing tree branches about. He wondered if he should return to Rangi and Ru to tell them not to burn the rubbish after all, then decided not to, thinking it would go up very quickly and soon be just a pile of embers. He didn't want to leave Kate too long either so put it out of his mind.

Rangi looked at Ru as John left, saying, "I think we should get the rubbish burnt up before we go."

"Whatever you say Rangi, I want to get home before the rain comes. Let's do it." Ru pulled some wax matches from the little tin box in his hand and coaxed some flames from a bunch of dry grass and twigs. Catching quickly, the fire was soon consuming everything it could reach. Ru and Rangi watched as it tore through the mountain of branches and leaves they'd heaped up around an old stump in the middle of the clearing where John wished to plant a crop of wheat.

"She's got a good hold now, eh Rangi?" laughed Ru.

Suddenly, the wind changed direction. Hot ashes blew about. Fronds of bracken at the edge of the bush caught fire as flames spread rapidly through the undergrowth. Manuka bushes glowed like Christmas trees as they caught alight, the oil in their branches aiding the fire in its efforts to burn everything it could reach. As Ru rushed to move the horses to a safer place Rangi tried to stamp out the flames near the good trees John wished to leave untouched.

"I don't like the way it's going Rangi," said Ru. "We should have waited until tomorrow. boss won't be pleased."

"Well, he told us to burn it so I don't think he'll blame us. I hope it dies out soon, so we can go home," answered Rangi, as he looked ruefully at the flames that were now leaping from the top of a tall totara tree. Suddenly a flash of lightning lit the sky. Deep thunder followed and soon huge drops of rain were quelling the flames as steam rose from the parched ground.

"I'm getting wet, Rangi, let's get home. The rain will put the fire out. It's dying out already. Do you think we should go and tell boss what's happened?"

"Yes, that would be the best thing. Then if it flares up again he'll be prepared," Rangi said as he turned his horse away from the fire, now a heap of sizzling embers, and rode towards the house.

More claps of thunder were heard, nearer now, rattling up the valley then through the ranges to the west. Bright electrical charges filled the air with eerie flashes, lighting up the scene of burning stumps and smouldering logs, all that was left of a once proud stand of bush. They rode up to the house. Rangi called as he went to the door. "Hey boss. Can we see you?"

"Hello boys, have you had trouble with the fire? I nearly came back and told you to leave it. Good rain now though."

"Yes boss," said Rangi. "We would have been in big trouble without the rain. The fire took hold so quickly. It would've been away through the bush right up to the ranges if the rain hadn't come." said Rangi. "I was real scared for a while. Some of those totara trees you wanted to keep have been burnt boss, I'm real sorry."

"Don't worry about that. You're safe and the fire is under control. I'll have another look before I go to bed, in case it starts up again. You boys get home. You've got no coat Ru? Put this thing around your shoulders." John took his oiled canvas cape from behind the door and showed Ru how to put it on. "It will keep most of you dry. Bring it back tomorrow," he said.

"Thanks, boss. I'll look after it. Thanks."

"Just listen to that rain," said Kate as John closed the door. "It makes me feel so secure wrapped up in here with the tempest going on around us. Just like something out of the Bible. Remember the picture your mother had on the wall of the children with their protective guardian angel standing behind them. I loved that picture."

"Yes, I know the one you mean. It was a favourite of mine too. Now, speaking about children, I'm wondering if we might tell them about the ponies now."

"They're well asleep now. Why don't we wait until after school tomorrow? They're not going to have time to ride them before school even if Ru arrives early. So let's keep it a secret."

"Off you go to bed then," said John. "I'm going to have a look at the bush to see if the fire has come back to life. I doubt it will because of the rain but I want to be sure. Hark at the thunder. It's rolling along the hills away to the north. Goodness, that was a beauty," he exclaimed as lightning lit the sky.

John scanned the area where the fire had been set. There was nothing but a low glow of embers to be seen. It was a God-send, this rain. The rivers would be up but should be able to contain all the water coming from the streams up in the hills.

Next morning Kate woke early, feeling refreshed and ready for the day. The doctor's tonic must be working. She looked at the calendar Cathy had made for her at school and thought of the Smiths who would be landing any day now. It would be lovely to go to Wellington to see them, but that was out of the question. 'They may decide to come up here even if we can't put them up', thought Kate, as she prepared the porridge. "Come on sleepyheads," she called to the children. "Cathy, come and make the toast, please. Out of bed Jake, there's a cow to milk. You'd better get a move on. Here you are Cathy," she said passing her some thick slices of home-baked bread. Don't let it fall off the fork into the fire and don't burn your fingers."

Cathy wrapped a handkerchief around her hand to protect it from the heat then raked the coals until they were just glowing embers and held the bread out on the long fork made of wire. Soon the tempting smell of toast filled the room.

John emerged from the bedroom. "That smells good. Can I have the first piece?" Soon he was munching away on hot buttered toast and jam as Kate passed him a cup of strong tea. "And I'll have some porridge too please Kate," as she stirred the pot over the fire.

"Don't talk with your mouth full Father, that's what you always say to us," Cathy rebuked him with a laugh.

Jake came in carrying a billy-can of milk. "You can see the burnt trees down the end of the farm. It looks as if quite a lot of bush is gone."

"I'm going to see it as soon as I've had breakfast. I hope the rimu and matai are still there," John said. "I've already sold them to one of the big landowners down in the lower valley."

"I couldn't see from here, but it didn't look too good," said Jake. "I put the cow in the night paddock. I didn't think she would get much grass in the day paddock from the look of the burnt ground."

"I'd better go and see. You be careful Kate. I won't be long."

"Don't be long coming home from school today," said Kate as she wrapped up the children's lunches. "I might have a surprise for you,"

"What? What? What is it? Oh please Mother, please tell us," the children shouted together.

Kate just laughed, and said firmly, "It wouldn't be a surprise if I told you. Just come straight home. You hear." And she shooed them off to school.

Rangi arrived soon after they had left. He knew Ru was not far away and hoped he would hear the children coming and hide in the bush off the path until they'd ridden by.

Rangi went to the stable where John was making a place for the new ponies' gear. He helped shift some sacks of feed and put up a rail for the saddles to hang on, then asked John if the ponies would have to stay outside in the paddock or would he build a bigger stable for them?

"Well, they've been out in a paddock most of their lives," said John. "They should be good as gold there."

"I could see the fire damage from the road, as I came along," said Rangi. "It doesn't look too bad. I was amazed how fast it took hold. The bracken and dry grass just exploded when the wind turned. That was a lucky thunderstorm, eh boss."

"We'd better go and have a look. I just hope there are enough trees left to pay for the ponies. Here's Ru now," he said as the trio of horses came into view. The ponies were trotting along on either side of Ru's horse and seemed to be enjoying the outing.

Ru came up to John and Rangi, smiling. "I heard Bessie coming along so I took the horses off the path but Bessie neighed to them. Cathy thought she was just talking to the horse on the next property! They never saw me or the ponies," laughed Ru. "What a surprise they will have tonight!" He passed John the cape he'd borrowed. "That's a real good coat, boss. My back was dry and warm. I might get one from the store."

John and Ru unsaddled the ponies. "We'll leave the bridles on for now until we find out how hard they are to catch. Just let them go in the little house paddock Ru, then we'd better get going and see the damage from the fire."

Kate came out to see the new arrivals. "They look lovely John. They seem very quiet. Were they ridden much at the livery stables?"

"I don't think so," John replied. "I'll find out next time I'm in town. Now we're off to work, dear. We'll be back to go on with the room if all's well down there. I just want to see what damage the fire has done."

The ponies were chasing each other around the paddock, jumping and leaping high in the air. 'They must be happy to be outside after being shut up in a stall' thought Kate, as she went to look at her garden. It was doing nicely and there was a good selection of vegetables ready to harvest and preserve, potatoes to dig and some onions to hang in the rafters for the winter. Kate was happy with what she saw even if it did mean a lot of work. I'll just take a look at the fruit trees I've planted then I'll get to work.

The pips and stones she'd brought out from Devon, now young apple and peach trees, were growing well behind the house in a sheltered place. They were about two feet high and showed good growth. Kate had no idea what varieties they were. She began saving seeds when John told her they were to emigrate. 'By planting them I've transferred a bit of home here,' she thought. Satisfied, she went in to take her tonic and do the day's chores.

Meanwhile, the men were studying the results of the fire and finding that some of the bush on the next door property had been burnt as well.

"Oh, it's a real mess," said John, "but I guess it could've been worse. At least the stumps have burnt away and won't be much trouble when we plough."

"Yes boss, I guess you're right. It won't take long to move some of the logs around, and clean up the fences. Some have burnt away altogether. Totara burns too good eh boss?"

"Yes, it's a real pity so much good timber burnt," said John. Through the bush, on land not yet taken up, he could see a good stand of rimu and matai. Then an idea struck him. 'Perhaps, if I could get hold of that next piece of land, I could extend my farm by another forty acres or I could buy it for Jim and Mary. Then I could take the trees needed for pony barter and sell others to repay the deposit.' He looked at the boundary of the next farm. He might have to move fast. Land was being taken up quickly. 'I'll see what Kate thinks,' he decided.

CHAPTER 24 A Surprise

Deciding there was no danger from the fire as the ground was saturated, John was eager to get into town to find out how to obtain the rights to the farm next door. "I need to go to town Rangi. I want to see the 'town fathers'. Can you spend the time repairing the fences? You may need to split some more posts to replace any that burnt so we can keep the stock in. They'll be looking for feed over the fence line now their paddock is burnt out. It's not so bad up by the house, so drive them up there, and shut them in."

"Yes boss. We'll chop away any of the fire left on the trees too. It must have gone past quickly as some are only scorched," Rangi replied as he picked up his axe and spade. "You go boss. I'll watch things here."

John rode up to the house, his mind full of the possibilities of getting more land. Kate wanted Jim and Mary Smith to come and live near her, so he did not foresee her being against the idea. It would be a way of solving two problems at once. Catching sight of the ponies trotting around full of life he wondered what the children would say when they discovered them. He would love to see their faces. He slipped off Beauty's back, took off his hat, and went in search of Kate.

"So there you are," he said as he caught sight of her hanging clothes out on the line. He picked up the basket and held it at waist height to save her bending. "I've had an idea," he said. "The fire has burnt the trees I was swapping for the ponies, but it made me think about purchasing that land next door - you know there's a very good stand of rimu and matai there - and I even wondered about putting the Smiths on it. What do you think?"

"I don't know John. We don't want to owe a lot of money, do we? Do you think we can afford it? You know it's ten shillings an acre."

John followed Kate into the house, looking at the cramped space they called home. Although it was cosy enough, it was a far cry from the house he hoped to build for her in the future.

"I've given the idea a lot of thought, Kate. No, to tell the truth, I only thought of it this morning when I saw the trees were gone. But wouldn't it be good to have Mary close by when the baby is due?"

"I suppose you can go and find out if it's possible to put their name down for that block. You need to find out the reality before you get your hopes up. While I'd love to have Mary living close to us, I do wonder whether Jim will settle here."

"I know what you mean. I had reservations about him when they married but they've made the choice to join us so I guess we should do our best for them. I'll go into town and see what the situation is."

John lost no time getting to town where the man in charge of land sales could see no reason why he couldn't pay the deposit in Jim's name, and drew the papers up. John explained that the family were arriving in Wellington very soon. He assured the official he'd be able to pay for the land himself if that was necessary and promised to carry out any clearing work and property improvements as required by law.

As he made his way to Dickson's store he felt pleased with the way he'd dealt with the matter. Many of the lots had been taken up since he'd last looked at the plans of the district. This meant there would be more work done on the roads as each owner was responsible for the maintenance of the length of road which passed their farms.

Henry Dickson greeted John with the news that there was a lot of mail for him and for the Kellys too. "Looks official Johnson, I suppose it's to do with the death of Patrick. Will you drop it off on your way?"

"That's no bother. I'll be glad to. I want to see how Kelly is doing anyway."

Meanwhile, the children were on their way home from school, coming down the road as fast as Bessie would go, eager to see what their surprise could be. It was nearly time for their birthdays. Perhaps they were going to get an early present. Jake had let Polly ride with Cathy as far as her gate but now he was up on the old mare's back urging her on as fast as she could go. As they neared their gate, they saw the new additions in the house paddock.

"It's ponies," said Jake with delight. "Cathy. Look! Ponies! Look at them go."

"Oh, aren't they beautiful. Look at how excited they are at seeing Bessie. You'll be good to them Bessie won't you?" said Cathy as she and Jake slipped off Bessie's back, and approached the ponies carefully. They were not so small after all. One was taller than the other by about six inches. "This is my one," said Cathy as she took hold of the bridle of the smaller one. "I wonder what her name is? I might have to give her a new one. What do you think Bessie?" she asked as she took the bridle from the old horse's mouth. Bessie snorted, as if to say, "I don't care."

John came cantering up on Beauty, sorry he'd missed the event. "So you've found them?" he said as he led Beauty to the trough for water. "What do you think?"

"They're lovely Father, thank you so much. This one is mine isn't it? She's the smallest so must be mine. I love her already," said Cathy as she hugged her father.

Kate came out to see what all the shouting was about and said, "You're very lucky children. You'll have to look after them. Be careful about leaving gates open. They may take one look at you and head for home. Be careful at school too. Don't let the children ride them until you get used to their ways."

Cathy and Jake listened impatiently. They were keen to try the ponies out so John went and got the saddles, made sure they were tight, and helped them up. 'The ponies must have been used to having children riding them,' thought Kate as she watched the way they quietly trotted around the house paddock.

"Can we go as far as Kellys'?" asked Jake, looking hopefully at his father. We can see how they go on the road."

"What do you think, John? Will they be all right?" asked Kate.

"If you're careful, I suppose, but just for a little while. You still have your jobs to do. Half an hour should be enough," he said as he went to open the gate to the road. "No racing. You hear."

"Yes Father. We'll be careful," they said in unison and cantered away down the track, keen to show off their new mounts to their friends. Jake wished Patrick was here to share his happiness.

Mr Kelly was sitting on the stump outside the house smoking a pipe, as usual. 'He never seems to be working these days', thought Jake as he dismounted.

"What have you got there may I inquire?" Paddy asked as he drew on his pipe. "Where did you steal them two from?" he said, teasing Cathy who looked scandalised at the idea.

"Father got them from the stables so we can ride to school. Poor old Bessie is getting past her best." Cathy turned her pert nose up at the smell of the pipe. "Can we go and see Jane and Polly please?" she asked.

"T'is fine with me girl. I guess you'll want to show Dennis too? He's down with his mother milking the cows."

Paddy took a slow draw on his pipe and sighed. It took him a long time to get around to anything these days. O'bie and he were working on the stumps and rubbish, but really, days went past when he didn't know what he'd done. He'd have to take a pull on himself and get the crop in or there'd be no feed for the cattle or pigs. The pleasure had gone from the everyday chores he'd enjoyed in the company of his eldest son. But if Dennis were to take the place of Patrick he knew he must make more effort.

"Here they come now," he said as Tessa and Dennis came through the back gate carrying buckets of milk ready to set for the next morning's churning. Now the cows were nearly dry they were only milked once a day and would soon be put out to rest before calving in August. Then the whole cycle would start again.

Polly and Jane came running from the house when told they had visitors. Their faces flushed with excitement as they saw their friend's new ponies. They went to hold the bridle as Cathy dismounted, and were soon patting the noses and whispering affectionately in the ponies' ears.

"Can I have a ride?" asked Polly, looking hopefully at Cathy.

"I'm sorry Polly, Father said we're not to let you ride them until we are used to them and they're used to us, but that shouldn't be long. We can't stay long either; we just wanted to show them to you. There'll be plenty of times when we'll let you have a turn, just as we did with Bessie."

"Oh I wish I could have a pony just like this one," said Jane as she patted the head of Jake's mount. "He smells wonderful, sort of deep and earthy."

"Well they've been galloping around the paddock all day, so Mother said, rolling in whatever was there," laughed Cathy. "We'd better get home, Jake. We don't want to make Father angry."

"What are their names?" asked Jane, looking at Jake. "Have you thought of any yet?"

"No, not yet," said Jake as he swung himself into the saddle. "I'll wait to find out what they've been called up to now. Don't want to confuse them," he called as they rode away towards home.

John was watching for their return and was relieved to hear them coming down the track. Horses were often an unknown quantity when put in a new situation. These two seemed well trained and docile, but he'd watch them carefully for a while.

"Give them a rub down, before you turn them out Jake," John said as he went into the house. "You too, Cathy." He looked at the children to make sure they had heard him then went to sort through the mail he'd collected that morning. He'd taken the official looking envelope to Kelly as he came home, and spent a few minutes talking farming with him.

John was worried about Kelly, but it seemed as if he was beginning to get over the worst of his loss at last. He was glad he'd spent a few minutes with him, even when his own work was beckoning. A problem shared is a problem halved, so he'd been told. He looked through the mail and opened one from George Parker. It had been sent three days ago. That was faster than usual.

John read the short note and was happy to learn that all the necessary arrangements for the Smiths had been made. There were only a few days to go before their ship docked.

He decided he must write quickly, to ask George Parker to get them a place on a coach to come over the hill to the Wairarapa. There were regular services, but the travel was slow and could be dangerous. While the road had improved a little since he and Kate made the journey half a year ago, there were accidents and hold-ups every day. Large wagons, laden with timber were making the road journey on a daily basis. Teams of twelve bullocks were used to drag the great loads. The locals called it a 'hill' but the newcomers called it a mountain. Once winter arrived, John knew the road would become a muddy swamp.

When Kate called him for tea he noted her wan look and decided he'd have to make sure Cathy did her share about the house. 'It wouldn't hurt Jake and myself to help with a few things either,' he thought as he took his place at the slab table and thanked the Lord for the food.

As Cathy cleared away the dishes, filled the enamel basin with water from the kettle, then shook the soap shaker with its ration of hard yellow soap briskly through the water, her thoughts were on the pony. It had felt wonderful sitting up on her back. "What is my pony called?" she asked her father, as she slid the plates into the rack on the wall.

John found the papers he'd been given. "They were meant for the landowners' children but they'd grown too big for them. Here we go," he said, unrolling a bundle of papers. "The little one is called Bonny, Cathy, the other is Blueboy. How do you like those names?" he asked.

"Bonny's a good name for mine," said Cathy "I'll keep it."

"Blueboy's a good name too Father. He is a bit blue when you look at his dark coat. Blueboy will do me," said Jake happily.

"They're not pedigree, you know, so it doesn't matter if you want to change their names, but it's better to keep the ones they are used to. They'll know their names when you call them," said John as he went to put more wood in the stove. "Go and bring in some more wood Jake please. I'll put in enough to keep it going overnight. It's getting cold in the mornings. Chop some more for your mother before you go to school. Have you both done all your jobs tonight? Well, get your homework done, then off to bed with you."

John settled at the table and passed some letters to Kate, sitting in the chair opposite him. "Now, I've a lot to tell you about the new piece of land. I had no trouble with the Small Farms Association. The block was still unclaimed and they were pleased I've put Jim's name down for it. Now I need to write to George Parker and tell him about the change of plans. I must write to the Smiths too, and get them down to Wellington as soon as I can. The Smiths can stay in Wellington for a few days then come over here. We'll find somewhere for them to stay in the village until we get a whare built for them. I don't know how Mary will take to living in the bush but you've had no trouble fitting in with the life, have you?"

Kate gave a rueful smile. "No, it's been no problem. It's been hard but I love it here. Mary is a different sort of person though. She may not take kindly to bush life. Jim should be able to adjust. Look at you, you never saw yourself working so hard at bush felling and looking after animals did you?"

"No, I didn't know what to expect. I'd been told about the way we'd have to clear the bush, but had no idea of what that meant or of the hours we'd have to put in. I'm so lucky to have Rangi and Ru. They're such good workers and quick learners too."

Kate looked through the mail. There was one from her mother. Reading the contents quickly it seemed as if her mother had a new lease of life. She'd been to the opera and to plays by the local repertory company, with her new friend met at choir practice. 'Well that's a good thing, isn't it?' she thought pleased her mother was enjoying life and had a friend to share outings with. There was also one from Rosie Parker which she decided to read later.

As they sat together at the table their thoughts were miles apart. John was thinking of the challenge of the extra land. Kate was filled with a mixture of happiness for her mother and loneliness because she was twelve thousand miles away and wished she could see her in person. She patted John's hand in a loving gesture. "I'm too tired to do any more tonight. Do you want another drink? If not, I'm off to bed." she said with a yawn.

"I'm coming too," said John as he sealed his envelope. "I'll have a wee tot to celebrate. Will you join me?"

"Yes I will," answered Kate as she came to the door in her nightgown, "Mix mine with a little hot water, please. It might help me sleep."

"So good luck, good health, and God bless us all," said John.

"I'll drink to that." Kate lifted her glass, sipped the whisky, then pulled a face. "I need a bit more water and some sugar in mine. You must have a cast iron stomach, to drink it neat."

"What's wrong with you girl? It's just the thing you need to set you up for the night. You'll sleep like a baby, you'll see," laughed John.

"No more for me. I'm off to bed. I hope the baby doesn't kick all night after his tot of John-barley-corn. You know, I do think you're very clever, but don't take on too much too soon. I don't want you working yourself to death. I'm happy with what we have here."

John put the letters in a prominent place so the children could take them into Dickson's shop on their way to school. He thought of their faces when they went off to Kellys' on their new mounts. 'Kate's right. There was enough to do here, so he must make sure that Jim pulled his weight on the new property.' As he drifted off to sleep he thought he heard rain on the roof of the new room. He surely hoped so. The rain from the thunderstorm had disappeared into the ground which was looking dry again. He felt the warmth of Kate's body as he stretched out his full length in the bed and thought, 'Life is good'.

———— ∞∞∞ ————

When the family woke in the morning rain was still falling. John wondered if this meant the drought had finally broken. It was a softer gentler rain than that which put out the fire. It would sink deep into the soil. There was plenty to go on with inside the new room so they wouldn't have to be out in the weather. Cathy and Jake would need to wrap up warmly for the ride into the school. He woke them gently, hoping not to disturb Kate, but she was already opening her eyes. "How did you sleep?" he asked as he dressed in his work-day clothes. "Did the whisky help? Did you dream of me?"

"Why would I want to do that?" laughed Kate. "I have you in the flesh. I dreamt of Devon. I was home talking to Mother and her new friend. It was strange, and very real. I liked him a lot."

"I'm glad you had pleasant dreams. Don't forget to give the children those letters to take to the village. I'm off to see to the animals. Jake?" he called. "Are you up? You've a cow to milk, and the ponies might take longer than Bessie to catch. So up you get."

"Come on Jake, don't make your father angry," said Kate as she fed the fire. "Bring some more wood in for the stove before you go down to the bail, please," she added. "Come on Cathy, you need to get going too."

"It's so warm in bed, I don't want to get up," called Cathy. "I'll be up in a minute. Just another minute," she pleaded.

Kate smiled. She knew what it felt like when the bed was soft and warm and the temperature was freezing outside, but what needed doing had to be done. "Come on Cathy, get up and help. Please. Remember what you promised your father."

Reluctantly, Cathy made her way into the room and picked up the toasting fork to begin the task of 'burning bread' as her grandfather used to say when he was well enough to tease her.

Kate ladled the porridge into the bowls and set them to keep warm. "Be sure to dress warmly," she told Cathy. "You'll get wet on the pony."

"I will Mother, you know I will. I'm looking forward to seeing the other children's faces when we arrive with Bonny and Blueboy," said Cathy with a huge smile on her pretty face as she laid down the toasting fork. "Have I made enough toast for Father and Jake?"

"Yes, plenty. Now eat your breakfast and get away to catch the ponies. Don't forget to take these letters to the shop. They're important," said Kate.

John came in through the door, shaking his head free of drops of rain clinging to his hair. "It's not cold but it's a very wetting rain. You'll need a coat, Jake. Eat up your breakfast and we'll go and catch these ponies. I hope they don't get up to any tricks."

Jake ate quickly and went out with a piece of toast in his hands. 'Whatever happened to table manners?' thought Kate, but bit her tongue thinking, 'Oh well it doesn't matter that much.'

Cathy called her pony and held out the bridle so she'd understand why she was calling her, but Bonny took one look and ran away to the other end of the field.

Meanwhile, John took a sugar lump from his pocket and called softly to Blueboy who came close to see what was in his hand. John caught his mane, slipped the bridle on then gave him to Jake to hold. "One down and one to go," he said.

Disappointed that Jake's pony was caught first, Cathy wanted one more try to catch Bonny herself. She held out her hand to Bonny again, speaking gently as she approached her. Soon she had her hand on Bonny's mane.

Trotting along at a fast pace, they soon passed the Kellys' but there was no sign of their friends.

"They must've gone earlier than usual," said Jake as he looked up the empty road. "Do you think they're jealous?"

"They might be. I know I would be if they had ponies and we didn't," answered Cathy as they rode along.

"Have you got those letters safe?" Jake asked. "Father said they're important. Don't lose them."

"Of course not!" said Cathy as she tapped her pocket. " I'll take them to the shop as soon as we get to the village."

Just then, they heard someone calling and, looking back, Jake saw the Kellys coming down the road, picking their way through the mud. Jane called to Jake as they came close. "Why didn't you wait for us? Are you too smart now for your old friends?" she laughed.

"We thought you'd gone on earlier," Jake explained. "When we passed there was no sign of anyone."

"We had to wait for Mam to make a list of groceries for Mr Dickson to deliver. But look what I've got." She held up two rather muddy letters tied together with string. "You must have dropped them on the way. Just as well we were behind you. Looks like the horse walked on them but you can still read the addresses." Jake put out his hand for them, but Jane pulled them back. "Say please," she said.

"Oh come on Jane, let me have them. Cathy said they were safe and sound in her pocket and all the time they'd fallen out. I hope Mr Dickson won't mind the mud."

" I'm sure he won't," said Jane. "Here they are, and could you give him Mam's list as well please?" She called her brothers and sister. "We'd better get in to school or Mrs Thompson will give us the cane for being late," and off they ran.

Jake and Cathy put their ponies in the paddock then took the letters to the shop where Mrs Dickson assured them she could make them respectable. 'New envelopes', she thought. Then she put Mrs Kelly's list on the spike file for later attention. Henry's idea was working well. They were adding things all the time to the items people wanted stocked in the caravan, as Henry called his mobile shop.

Mrs Thompson was not at all pleased that half her pupils were late. She'd given them a good lecture on the need for punctuality at all times only last week and here they were late again. She heard their excuses, but held her cane in her hand for all to see that she was going to use it, if they, the tardy ones, didn't make more effort to be on time. "After all you expect me to be here when you arrive, don't you?" she asked. "Cathy, you'll have to stay after school and do your writing test. You may be able to go up a class. The instructions I have from Wellington are quite adamant that I should grade you all by ability, not age."

CHAPTER 25 A Near Miss

At home, Kate was surveying her garden. Now the weather had turned cold she would have to hurry and gather in more of the produce before frost ruined it. There were still root vegetables in the ground. They wouldn't come to any harm. A good frost on parsnips and swedes would improve the flavour. She'd grown some pumpkins that were now stored in the stable. She'd never eaten them in England, but had tried them at the Parkers' when they landed in Wellington, and was surprised at how good they were when roasted like potatoes. The potatoes were all out of the ground and they too were stored in the stable.

Kate thought of the letter she'd received from Rosie Parker asking if there were any positions going begging. She mentioned the young woman Kate had met on board their ship, the governess who'd lost her pupil because of his unfortunate death at sea. It seems she'd been working for a family in the Hutt, but wanted to come up to the Wairarapa.

While Kate knew of the bigger landowners in the Lower Valley, she did not know them well enough to ask them to take on a governess she knew little about. The school roll was growing; perhaps Mrs Thompson may need a helper. 'I'll ask next time I'm in town', she thought, as she went to check on the men's progress with the room.

"Well, dear, what do you think?" asked John as he finished nailing in the windows. The light from them filled the room and even the rain outside could not dull his pride. "Don't they look great? All we need are some curtains to guard against the cold." He watched Kate's eyes light up. The room was nearly finished. She could hardly believe it.

"It's beautiful, John, a real credit to you and you too, Rangi and Ru. You're master builders now. But you're going to have to prove yourselves again, building something for the Smith family. They'll be here next week, so don't rest on your laurels yet. I've just learnt another person wants to move over here too, the governess we met on the ship."

"Really?" asked John, with a worried look on his face. "I hope she doesn't want to stay here. It'll be hard enough to find some place for the Smiths to stay for a few weeks, without having someone else to worry about."

"I thought I'd ask Mrs Thompson if she needs help with the school, or you might be able to ask some of your rich friends down south if they need a governess. There's no need to get agitated yet. Let's just enjoy moving into the room before we squabble about other people's problems."

"Keep your shirt on," said John, laughing at Kate.

"What you mean boss? Keep your shirt on? Do you want the missus to change her clothes?" asked Ru, looking bemused.

"No, it means don't get angry. That's all. Men take off their shirts before they fight. So 'keep your shirt on' means keep cool," said John. "Let's have some lunch and then we'll go back down to the bush now the rain's gone. The room may be finished but the rest of the work is still there."

"There's plenty of soup in the pot," said Kate. "Come in."

The three men ate a good warming bowl of soup with a few slices of Kate's newly baked bread, before going back out to work. The rain had stopped and the clouds were lifting as they made their way out to the barn to collect their horses.

"We'll need more shelter for the ponies if the weather gets really cold," John told them as they made their way down to the bush. "We'll save as many of the burnt trees as we can then have them sawn up for use in the new stables and sheds. A few burnt patches won't spoil the look too much. So let's fell those ones first and see what they look like when we take all the burnt parts away."

"Good idea boss. See the big totara there, he still got a lotta good wood in him, eh boss?" said Ru.

"Then that's where we'll start today," said John picking up his axe to scarf the tree.

"You be careful boss, that tree's got a mind of its own. Just go slow. It may be burnt worse than you think on the other side," said Rangi as he went around the foot of the huge totara to knock a few pieces of burnt bark and wood away from the base. "It's not so bad on this side. You'll be right boss. Ru and I will start sawing as soon as you have that piece out of the way. She should fall over there by the matai if we get it right."

They positioned themselves either side of the tree, pulling the saw taut between them as they started the long rhythmic movement that would sever the tree from the earth where it had stood safe and unmolested for hundreds of years. Rangi asked the tree god to forgive him as he pulled the saw to and fro. In a few minutes the job was done.

John looked at the bole to see if the fire had got into the heart of the tree but the main part of the log was as firm as ever. Higher up past the place the fire had reached, the timber would be good enough for the stables and barn. It was a big tree. He'd get it milled at the new sawmill. He went looking for others to send at the same time, and soon had several trees that could be salvaged. John went on with the task of cleaning the bases up to allow Ru and Rangi to fell them when they were ready. He'd take a turn at the sawing when the boys started the next tree.

Suddenly he heard a shout from Ru. "Look out boss! It's coming your way!" John looked behind him and saw a big rimu totter on the stump, then fall with a huge crash right where he'd been.

It had been a close thing and John's heart went bang, bang high in his chest as he sat down on the bole of the tree, realising how close he'd been to certain death. "Thanks Ru. I nearly met my maker, didn't I?"

"You all right boss?" asked Rangi.

"I'm a bit shaken up," said John as a big shudder coursed through his body. "I never thought you were so far through that tree. I was going to give one of you a turn from the saw. That's why I was there."

"That's all right boss. You be sure to keep back out of the way when we're cutting these fellas down. Your wife would kill us if anything happened to you."

But John knew that he'd been more than lucky. It had been a miracle. No doubt about it. "What say we don't tell her?" he laughed.

Back at the school the children were getting ready for the trip home. The ponies had been much admired, but Jake and Cathy had explained they were not allowed to offer rides on them yet until they were used to riding them themselves. Eventually they were able to get away from the petting hands of the children and trotted off home. Jane and Dennis were well on the way down the road but Polly, dawdling a long way behind on the muddy road, looked longingly at Cathy as she passed, hoping that she might stretch a point and give her a ride.

"Sorry Polly," said Cathy. "It was different with Bessie; she was used to having two on her back. I'll give you a ride soon when Father says I can."

Although she understood what Cathy had said, Polly pulled a face at her back. Then she had a thought: perhaps her father would buy Bessie for her and Jane to ride to school. Dennis was a good runner, he could run to school. He beat everyone when they had running races in the paddock. 'Patrick was a good runner too', she thought and began to cry. 'Why did Patrick have to drown? I do miss him, even though he played tricks on me.'

"Whatever's the matter?" Tessa asked when she saw the tearful face of her younger daughter. "Did you get into trouble at school?" She helped Polly out of her coat and hung it to dry, "Tell me what's wrong. It can't be that bad surely."

"Cathy wouldn't give me a ride on her pony. She's mean and I hate her," said Polly, wiping her eyes on her sleeve.

"Now dear, be fair," said Tessa. "The Johnson children have only just got the ponies. They were good to you all summer giving you rides on Bessie." Tessa offered her handkerchief to Polly, and took her hand in her own. "There'll be plenty of rides for you soon. I know how generous those children are. You'll just have to be patient and wait."

Polly dried her eyes "Mam? Do you think Dada could buy Bessie for us to ride to school? It's a long way, and they don't need her now do they?"

"I don't think Mr Johnson will sell her, they'll still use her around the farm, but I'll ask your Dada what he thinks."

That evening after tea, Tessa told Paddy what Polly had said. He was scornful about the long walk to school. He'd had very little schooling available to him in Ireland, and would have been glad if he'd only to walk a few miles for an education."

"I'll ask Johnson, and see what he says," Paddy told Tessa. "I don't think for a minute that he'll want to sell, but I can ask."

CHAPTER 26 John Meets the Harveys

With the change of seasons, cold weather made getting up harder each morning. John lay in bed, musing about the farm now winter was here. The chooks had gone off the lay and the cow was nearly dry and not worth milking. She'd not been in calf when the other cows were checked, so he'd taken her for a late visit to the neighbour's bull. All going well she should be handy after the main herd had dried off next autumn and carry on the supply of milk for the family again next winter.

John recalled the promise he'd made to Jake to find him a dog for use on the farm. With the extra land one would be needed to move stock about. He'd ride into town and see if the deeds had come through for the new land, and check on the puppy he'd ordered from the man with the Blue Merle pups. It should be ready soon. 'But now, I'd better get on with the day,' he thought as he rose and dressed.

Later in the morning John farewelled Ru and Rangi who were helping transport the logs over to the mill. It took a lot of man and bullock power to move the heavy timber and the poor animals strained as they pulled the logs through the muddy tracks, with the bullocky shouting obscenities as he whipped their hides.

Beauty travelled the miles with an easy gait as John made his way to see about the puppy for Jake. They cantered past the marae at Papawai with its school for Maori pupils, and headed out to where the farmer lived with his wife. The cottage, built of pit-sawn timber with a thatched roof, was very basic. Smoke drifted from a brick chimney. Small windows on each side of the door gave some light to the interior.

Macrocapa trees had been planted as hedges to break the wind that whistled across the fields. It seemed odd planting trees when so many had been cut down but John knew good shelter for cattle was a necessity when they stayed outside all the winter.

He pulled Beauty to a halt at the farm gate where the farmer greeted him. "Good day! It's good to see a new face. We don't see a lot of people out this way. The name's Jock Harvey."

"I'm John Johnson," said John, taking the man's hand and shaking it warmly. "I heard about some puppies from a friend of yours in the village. He was going to ask you to save me one. Did he?"

"Yes, Bill Brown told me you were interested in one. There are six pups, three of each, so you'll have plenty to choose from. I give them a good drink of milk twice a day so they're not too much drain on the mother. They're about a month old now and very playful and boisterous. They'll be weaned soon - they're eating meat already."

John noticed an accent, an unusual drawl he couldn't place, and wondered where the fellow was from. "Have you been here long?" he asked as they walked towards the barn. "Did you live in Australia for a while, or just pass through on your way here?"

"No, I was there for two years working on a cattle station in Queensland. It was hard going," said Jock. "Just miles and miles of country filled with sand and gum trees and not a lot else. I worked as crew on a boat that came down to Australia from Scotland then tried the stations. That's where I saw the dogs. I heard New Zealand was a better bet, so came over here two years ago. I've been on this place for most of that time. I'd just landed off the boat when I met a man in a hotel who needed someone to look after this property. He'd business to do in Wellington and couldn't stay up here himself so offered me the job. He's a bit of a toff but treats me very well."

"I thought I could hear an accent. Perhaps the years in Australia knocked the edge off your burr, I'd never have thought of Scotland."

"That's all right, I fool a lot of people when I meet them, but my wife says it was the sound of my speech that attracted her to me. I'm very glad it did. She was a passenger on the boat when I came to New Zealand. We married before we came over to the Wairarapa. Life moves fast around here."

"Yes, I've found that to be true," said John, thinking of the Dicksons. They reached the barn where frisky puppies were chasing each other around the hay strewn floor. "When will they be able to leave their mother? They look big enough already, but I don't know much about dogs."

"I'd rather they stayed here for another month. I want to make them learn a few commands before they leave. Now what do you think? Aren't they a bonny lot?"

All the puppies were a dark blue-grey colour with a good coat of wiry hair. One came to say hello to John and he was immediately taken with its bright face and eyes.

"Is this one available?" he asked, patting the puppy's head.

"Yes, I've had enquiries for three of them but none are spoken for yet." He laughed as he watched the big man cuddling the little puppy. "She can be yours Johnson; I'll look up the papers for you. They're pedigree dogs. You could breed from her when she is old enough."

"How much will she cost?" asked John as he looked over the dogs. He'd no idea what a fair price was.

"Tell you what, you can have her for ten shillings, and pay me when you come to pick her up in a month's time, how does that sound?"

John was considering the offer when the puppy suddenly licked his face. "That will be fine," he said, and they shook on the deal.

"Now come and meet the wife. She'll be getting a cup of tea ready, you can be sure of that. She's a bit lonely, and hardly ever comes to town with me. She just potters around in the flower garden."

"It's a very pretty sight," said John, "My wife gardens too. She mostly grows our vegetables."

As Jock Harvey opened the door a nice-looking woman was setting a teapot on the table. "This is John Johnson, Ellen. I've just sold him one of the puppies. Do sit down, Johnson."

John looked around the room with interest. It was larger than the one he was building at home but had little in the way of furniture. An easy chair stood near the hearth, and a sofa was covered with a patchwork cover. The table they sat at was made of slabs of timber much the same as the one at home. He accepted the cup of tea, and slice of cake from Mrs Harvey who sat down at the table with them.

"You have a lovely garden Mrs Harvey," said John as a way of breaking the silence that had descended.

She looked at her husband before answering. "Thank you for saying so, I love flowers. They remind me of home in Kent."

"I've never been there, but I know it's supposed to be the garden of England," John replied.

"Pity my wife doesn't grow a few vegetables like yours, Johnson. You can't eat flowers, can you?" Harvey said.

"No, you can't eat flowers but they do brighten up the day for the women who put up with so much out here in the bush. Perhaps you could help grow the vegetables, Harvey. I do the hard digging for my wife, and she does the rest."

Soon it was time for John to leave. "It was nice to meet you Mrs Harvey. You must take a drive out to our place one day, and meet my wife. I'm sure you'd enjoy each other's company." John turned to her husband. "If you leave word at Dickson's store about when I should come and pick the pup up, he'll let me know. It's good to do business with you." And he mounted Beauty.

As he rode home John thought there was something odd about the atmosphere in that kitchen, some undertone that didn't seem healthy. 'I might get Kate to drive out there one day and call on her. Harvey seemed a nice enough fellow but there was something about that couple that I'm not sure about.'

CHAPTER 27 More Room

Once at the village John dropped into Dickson's to pick up a few items and tell him he'd asked Harvey to leave a message there when the pup was ready.

"You've been out there, have you?" asked Henry. "What did you make of him?"

"It's hard to say. He was nice as pie until we had a cup of tea. His wife was quiet, nervous almost, as if she was expecting trouble. When she said she came from Kent and loved flowers Harvey said it was a pity she didn't grow vegetables. I told him he should help grow them himself. Well, help with the hard digging as I do for my wife. It didn't go down too well at all."

"I know. I take the groceries out there once a week and she'll hardly say a word, even though she only has him to talk to day after day. You'd think she'd be glad of a chance for some company."

"I'll get Kate to go and see her on a visit without telling them she's coming. There's no reason to think badly of this man but something felt odd. He was great with the mother and her puppies and is obviously a good farmer. The cattle looked well cared for. I can't put my finger on it. Just the sad look in her eyes."

"Perhaps she's just homesick," said Henry. "Now, did you hear that the Browne family are about to return to their house? It's all been fixed up. The wagon is fetching their goods tomorrow. The carpenters are well on the way with the blacksmith's shop too. And there's to be a meeting about getting some sort of fire fighting body in the village."

"That sounds sensible, but now I'll be off. Better go and earn my keep. It's further out to Harvey's than I realised. My wife will be wondering where I've got to."

As John passed the blacksmith's shop he could hear the steady sound of the hammer striking iron and waved to Peter Fairman, receiving a cheery wave in return. As he rode on, his thoughts were on the near miss he'd had the day before. He hoped Rangi had not told Kate about it. She didn't need any more anxiety and no harm had been done. In the future he'd be more careful when timber was being felled.

Ru and Rangi were busy clearing up the mess left after loading trees for the mill and he stopped to talk to them when he reached the farm boundary. "How did it go then?" he asked Rangi, "Did they get all the logs we wanted on the skids?"

"Yes boss, they good, those blokes, they know their stuff," said Rangi with a grin. "We got all loaded up by lunch time and they're probably at the mill now. We're just clearing up here, and then we'll get on with the barn."

"Good, thanks for that. I'll be there to help as soon as I've talked to my wife."

"Where have you been? I've been so worried," said Kate as she helped him off with his coat, "I expected you home long ago. I was frightened you'd had an accident."

"No chance of that," laughed John, but thinking of the close shave with the tree. "It was further than I thought to the Harveys. A rum set up there. He's good with the dogs and animals but his wife looks as if she thinks he'll beat her. She hardly said a word."

"Poor thing, there are some mean brutes out in the world. I wonder if I can do anything to help. Does she come in to town?"

"Not often. I admired her flower garden and instead of agreeing with me that it's beautiful, he said she'd be better off growing vegetables," said John. "I told him that I help with the digging, but he was dismissive of her work. She looked cowed."

Kate looked lovingly at him. "I wouldn't like you to behave like that. I wonder what the trouble is."

"Dickson thought she might be homesick. He sees her when he delivers the groceries. Always very quiet he said. Well, I'd better go and give the men a hand or they'll sack me."

"When can we use the new room John? I can hardly wait."

"We'll move everything in tomorrow when the children are here to give a hand. I've been thinking that some of the things we aren't using can go in to the back of the barn. Trunks and stuff still packed up will be quite safe from the rain there. I've made it water-tight. That'll give us more room when the Smiths visit. They must be in Wellington by now. When you get word about the time they're arriving, we'll meet them and get them settled into the boarding house. I'll bring them out here maybe a day later. They'll need a day to recover from the journey."

"Oh thank you John, you're so good to me," said Kate and she gave him a big kiss.

"Enough of that, wench. The children will be home soon," John laughed as he left to help with the extension to the stables.

Kate thought about Jim and Mary's arrival, hoping it would all work out and they'd be happy with the land John had secured. She knew full well that while the holdings were not large a lot of work was needed to make them productive.

Hearing the sounds of the children coming closer on their ponies, Kate wondered if they had too many horses. Bessie was not ridden as much now and the two half-draft horses were only used occasionally now the bulk of the land was cleared, but of course they'd be used again when John and Jim took over the next block.

"Had a good day?" Kate asked as the children came through the door. "No school tomorrow, so we're going to move into the new room. Won't that be great?"

"Wonderful," said Cathy as she took the bag from her back. "It was dusty on the road. I'm so thirsty."

"We're going to store a lot of things in the back of the barn to give us more room here. It'll be a bit of work, but worth it." Kate smiled at Jake as he made a face. "It'll mean more room for you too. Your father is going to put a partition in the back room so you can each have your own space. You'll have to put up with the stores in there but I'm sure it will be nicer for you."

"The Brownes are coming home tomorrow," said Cathy with her mouth full. "I'll be glad to have them back. Mrs Thompson thinks I can look after the little ones when she's busy, but then I miss what she's teaching the others. I ask Jake what she said and he won't tell me."

"That's not very nice, Jake. Why's that necessary?"

"She's not supposed to be doing the same work as me. She's nearly two years younger. Just because she's smart, she thinks she can do it," Jake said grumpily.

"Well I can. I can beat you at addition. Ha!"

'Is it really ten years since this daughter of ours was born back home in Devon?' Kate thought. 'Where has the time gone?' Then, "That's enough you two, she said. "Your father will be in here in a minute and he won't want to hear you fighting."

Kate went into the new room and looked around. It was nearly twice as big as the old living area. Hopefully, later, she'd get John to help her hang the new curtains she's sewn for the windows. "How's the building going?" she asked as John came in. "You've been hammering away all day. Did you have enough timber?"

"Not quite. However, I've thought of another improvement so I'll need to order some more boards and scantlings for that." He took a folded piece of paper from his pocket and showed Kate a sketch. "See where the wall meets the back of the old shed. I think we should be able to extend the store room past that to make more room for storage. Then we could use the old store room for tools and tackle for the horses. What do you think?"

"I'd have to see the place with my eyes but I'll come and have a look after tea perhaps. You know best. I just can't wait to move the things tomorrow."

"It won't make any difference to our shifting the things out of here. I'll have to make sure I can make the changes anyway. We'll begin the move as soon as we've had breakfast. So what's for tea?" And he scooped a basin full of water from the barrel at the door. Rubbing his hands with the hard yellow soap that lay ready for use, he thought, 'I'll have to find a good water supply.' The nearby creek was used by cattle and maybe there was a chance of disease. 'It's a real problem to work on,' he thought.

Kate put a boiled ham on the table ready for John to carve and distribute. Dishes of vegetables from her garden supplemented the meal. She was proud of the way they were able to make ends meet. It seemed as if they were living on the fat of the land, but she knew it was hard work that made the difference. There was no lack of that, here in the Wairarapa. Hard work was the order of the day.

Suddenly, John rose from the table and rummaged in the pockets of his coat which he'd hung by the door. "I'm sorry Kate, I forgot these letters that Dickson had for us. There's a letter for you too, Cathy," and he passed it over to her. "It's from your grandmother but leave it until you've eaten your tea, or your mother will be on your tail."

"Oh it's all right Cathy, you can open it. I think you've had enough to keep you alive until your pudding comes," said Kate as she looked at her letters from her mother and Rosie Parker. "You two can do the dishes then do your homework without fighting. Father wants to show me something at the barn. We won't be long." Hearing what she had said about fighting, John sent a questioning look at the two children. "It was just a tiff about school work," said Kate and gave the children a smile.

"Well, I don't want to hear you've been fighting. You're the eldest Jake, and should know better," said John sternly.

"It's just that Cathy always wants to do what I do. I hate it," said Jake as he stacked the dirty plates.

"Do not," said Cathy. "I don't want to mind the children for Mrs Thompson when she's busy. I want to do the work Jake does and he doesn't like that."

"You have to help Mrs Thompson if she asks Cathy; she has a big job with all the new ones. It doesn't mean you won't learn as much as Jake," said Kate.

Kate walked arm in arm with John as they made their way to the barn and stables. It was only a little way from the house and had the bonus of providing shelter from the southerly winds that could occasionally blow with some vengeance.

"See where the shed ends, we can make another wall there," said John, indicating the place. "Then if I put a back on that part we'll have another room almost built. It will be more accessible too, being at the side, instead of the back of the stables. Do you agree?"

"You seem to know what you're doing John, but you'll have the farm covered with buildings if you go on this way," said Kate as she took in the number already there. "Don't forget you have to do something for Mary and Jim."

"I know," said John, "but, with Ru and Rangi, we'll have that whare up in no time. Jim can do something to help as soon as he arrives. That could be next week, if they can get a ride on the coach. Look how far we've come in just a few months. It's hard to remember what the place I brought you to looked like, without your gardens."

"Don't forget the additions you've made John, and don't forget your accident and how long that took for you to get over."

John looked up sharply, wondering if Kate had heard of the close shave he'd had a day or two ago, but soon realised she was thinking of the one he'd had soon after she arrived. That was a tree felling accident too. 'I'll have to be more careful,' he thought.

"So you approve?" he asked, as they walked back to the house.

"If you think we can afford it, go ahead," Kate replied.

CHAPTER 28 Moving Day

Eager to get the move done, John roused everyone earlier than usual the next morning. He'd put together a wooden wheelbarrow with a flat top and wooden wheel, to be used to take most of what wasn't needed over to the stables. After a couple of trips he left Kate and the children to finish the work, saying there was something he needed to do in town.

Kate watched as he drove away with the horse and wagon, thinking he was probably going to get more wood for the shed or iron for the roof.

"What's in this?" asked Cathy, as she struggled to carry a box that had remained unopened since they left Devon. "It's quite heavy," she said as she laid it on the ground with a thud.

"Be careful Cathy," growled Kate, and she looked at the paper stuck to the side of the box. "It's full of books from our old home. Goodness knows when we'll get time to read them."

"Oh good," said Cathy, "It'll be lovely to have new ones to read."

"Well, it's work you need to be doing now," said Kate as Jake came out from the cottage with another tin trunk. Once he'd placed it on the wheelbarrow, it took him a moment to gather the strength to lift the handles and push it.

Kate came forward to help carry the trunk inside. "This is full of good clothes but I don't think they'll fit you anymore. You two are growing so fast. You know it's Cathy's birthday next week," she whispered to Jake. "I want to make a cake for her, but don't tell her in case it doesn't turn out. I wish we had a proper oven."

"It'll be great, Mother, you're a really good cook," Jake said as he went back inside.

They'd toiled all morning and Kate decided to take a break. "Bring some more wood in please, Jake," she called. "I need a cup of tea, then I'll start a meal. I don't know how long your father will be though."

Meanwhile, John had gone straight to Dickson's store to collect the dresser he'd left in storage. He'd also found a better type of stove advertised in a newspaper from Wellington and had ordered one to be brought over the hill. Mrs Dickson said it had arrived and was down in the shed together with the dresser and a table and chairs. "My husband will come down and help you load it all onto the wagon as soon as he gets back from delivering the groceries and mail. He'll be at least another half hour. In the meantime I have a job you could help with if you don't mind. I need some barrels of paraffin oil lifted into place, and some sacks of dry goods lifted down to where I can manage them. My husband is so busy with the cart, he's never where he's needed and the boy I have to help is not very strong. Would you mind?"

"Not at all," said John. The job was soon done with rice, flour and sugar all placed in convenient places in the shop.

"Come and have a cup of tea," said Mrs Dickson, "You deserve one."

While they were drinking their tea Henry Dickson joined them.

"You're doing well with the cart?" asked John as he helped himself to another piece of cake.

"Yes, very well indeed. I don't get time to help my wife as much as I'd like to though. The lad is not able to do as much heavy lifting as I'd hoped."

"I asked Mr Johnson to give me a hand while you were away; all those jobs have been done. You don't mind?" asked Johanna.

"Not at all, I'm glad you thought to put him to use. Thank you, Johnson. That's a big help."

"Well, you can repay me with a bit of help yourself. I've come to pick up the dresser as well as a stove that will take a bit of lifting. There's also the table and chairs down in your shed. I need to pay you for storage. Let me know how much I owe you."

"Johnson, you don't owe me anything. I'm only too pleased to help."

"That's good of you, but a deal is a deal. This is your living, and I must pay you. Now you can come and help me so I can get home to my wife. I hope she'll get a big surprise," said John as he stood up ready to leave.

"Right sir, your wish is my command."

Away they went and loaded the dray with John's purchases. The stove, however, proved a real challenge so they called on Peter Fairman, who was working in his blacksmith's shop, to give them a hand. "How are you getting on in the new shop?" asked John. "Is everything back in place?"

"Yes. It's better than the old one. There's more room. I've sorted out, and got rid of a lot of old equipment past its best. There are all sorts of new ways of doing things. Look at the way the sawmills have updated their methods. It's quite amazing to go and watch the way they put through hundreds of feet of timber a day with a precision that can hardly be believed," said the blacksmith.

Once the wagon was loaded to John's satisfaction, he thanked both men and set old Bessie on the road for home. It was a heavy load for her but one she accepted willingly. As he passed the Kelly farm he could see Kelly and O'bie working and waved a greeting. He was anxious to see Kate's face when she saw the dresser. Having furniture in the new room would make a real difference to their comfort.When he pulled into the yard as near to the house as he could take the wagon, the family came running to greet him.

"What on earth have you got there John?" asked Kate as she saw the covered load. John carefully lifted a corner to reveal the table and four chairs. "Oh my goodness!" Kate could hardly believe her eyes. "What a man you are for secrets and what a lovely surprise!"

The children helped unload the furniture and soon it was indoors. Kate thought the dresser looked lovely and was keen to get some of her embroidery out of the stored boxes to show the children how civilized they were becoming. "You have been busy, John. I wonder what else you have hidden." Kate pointed to the last mound of items on the wagon.

"All in good time, woman," said John. As he lifted the cover Kate could see a cast-iron stove. "This is heavy, so I'll wait till Monday for Rangi and Ru to help me. I'll have to find out where it should be placed. It will need a chimney. I'll have to find out how to build one. So, what do you think?"

"I'm delighted John. You've really spoilt me," said Kate as she admired the stove. "What about a cup of tea? We can sit at our new table on our new chairs. How lovely that will be."

"I'll get some more wood Mother, and I'll chop some kindling too," said Jake, looking at the wood-box in the corner.

"What does he want?" asked John. "He doesn't usually do anything without being asked."

"I think he wants to ride over tomorrow to see Rangi's boys now that he's got the pony," said Kate, smiling. "It's Sunday, after all. I'd like to go to church. The Catholics will have Mass but perhaps Reverend Porter will be holding a service in the village. What do you think?"

"I don't mind at all. We should give thanks for our blessings, I agree. I'm sure we would be welcome at either," said John.

"I know that Catholics have some restraints about going into other churches, but the Protestants seem to mix freely in whatever churches are holding a service," mused Kate. "What say we go to the village in the morning and hope there's a service we can attend? After that Jake can visit Hemi and Kingi and I might drive out to meet Mrs Harvey."

"Sounds good to me," said John. "I want to see Fairman and Dickson to ask about the chimney. They're sure to know someone who'll know what to do. I should have gone into the details before I ordered it from Wellington but it will work out."

CHAPTER 29 Giving Thanks

After a good night's sleep, and with all the chores done, the family set off for the village. John was driving Beauty in the buggy, with Kate at his side, while Cathy and Jake followed on their ponies. The day had been planned carefully. Cathy was to ride back to the Kellys' to spend time with Jane and Polly, Jake would ride over to meet Hemi and Kingi, John would stay in the village while Kate drove out to see Mrs Harvey.

"Well, here we are," said John as they reached the village. "I'll see if Mrs Dickson knows where the service is to be today. Just sit tight. I don't want you hurting yourself getting down."

"Oh I'll be fine John. Don't fuss so," protested Kate, though secretly pleased at his thoughtfulness. "I'm fine now, really. The doctor's tonic has done the trick."

"Good morning," said John as he entered the store. "We've come in, to go to church. Do you know where it's being held this morning?"

"So what are you today?" asked Henry Dickson, "Micks or Proddys?"

"We don't mind. We just want to thank the Lord as we're feeling very blessed. Everything is going well at the moment. We thought a few words of thanks wouldn't go astray."

"I know the Catholics are holding a Mass in the house down the road as they usually do. There's talk of a church being built soon on ground given to the church by the Small Farms Association," said Henry, as he moved over to a notice board. "Here you are. Mass is at ten am and there's a service for the Anglicans at 5pm. "

"I'll go and tell Kate. I don't want to stay in town all day but I do want to ask you about a chimney for that stove I bought. Kate wants to drive out to see Mrs Harvey after church, so I'll see you while she's away."

"We're just in time for Mass. The Anglican service is not until five," John told Kate as he got up into the buggy and took the reins. As they went along the road, now bordered on both sides by new houses and shops, Kate was surprised to see that so much building had taken place since she'd come in to see Doctor McDonald.

Father Brady, who was standing outside the house greeting his flock, welcomed Kate, John and the children with pleasure. "I remember you from the Kelly boy's funeral," he said. "It's nice to see you again. Come on in. There are not a lot of us today. We're always pleased to have some new people."

"We're not Catholic," said Kate, "but we do want to thank God for our lives out here. I went to church every week at home and really miss it."

"That's fine with me," said the priest. "I can't give you communion, but you're welcome at Mass. Everyone is free to thank God in his own way."

As they made their way into the room which they'd last visited for Patrick's funeral, Kate watched Cathy and Jake to see if they were upset as they remembered, but they seemed to be taking it all in without any problem. Father Brady began the Mass in Latin, but read a considerable part of it from the English translation, and they were able to follow the rest of the congregation as to when to stand, kneel or sit.

As Cathy rubbed her knees when she rose from kneeling Kate smiled, thinking of her days at home when she and her mother had gone to High Anglican services. When her mother had made them little kneeling pads to use at church her grandmother had been scandalized and refused to use one. Then, as her attention returned to the service Kate realised Father Brady was giving the blessing. "In nomine Patris, et Filii et Spiritus Sancti," he intoned.

To which Kate said a fervent "Amen." Afterwards they shook hands with the other folk there and chatted briefly, aware the children, although politely quiet, were anxious to be gone.

"You be careful on the way back to Jane's, Cathy," warned Kate as she waved her good- bye.

"I will Mother," replied Cathy, riding away at a fast trot.

Jake was already making his way out of the paddock with his pony. It was not far to Rangi's where Jake knew he'd get a warm welcome from Rangi and May, his wife. He had been to the pa before and enjoyed trying to play stick games with the other children and watching the women weaving mats and kits from flax. Rangi and May were also introducing him to the protocol for approaching the meeting house, and the people. As well, he was picking up a good deal of Maori language from Hemi and Kingi.

Kingi came running as Jake approached. "Can I have a ride, can I have a ride?" he yelled as soon as Jake was close enough.

"Well, just around here. Father said I had to get used to him first, but I guess it won't hurt," said Jake as he dismounted.

Kingi swung himself up into the saddle and rode around the grounds, drawing looks of envy from other children gathered there. "He's beaut, Jake. Can I take him out the gate just a little way?"

"I suppose if you're careful you can, not too far though," said Jake as Kingi cantered out the gate and away up the road. He was not away long and soon the other children wanted rides. One older boy, Wiremu, was most insistent. Finally, when Jake gave in, the boy was up and away, heading out the gate really fast while Jake, suddenly worried, watched.

Rangi, though, had heard the noise of the pony's galloping hooves, and came running, calling, "Where's the pony gone?" When he heard what had happened, he mounted his horse and galloped off.

He didn't have to go far. He found the boy standing on the roadside clutching his arm which hung limply at his side. The pony was nowhere to be seen. Rangi didn't want to leave the boy but didn't want to let the pony run wild. "I'd better go and find the pony. Wiremu, you're always in trouble," he growled. "Now, you walk back home and see May. She'll know what to do."

'What a way to spend Sunday looking for a lost pony,' he thought. He didn't blame Jake for letting Wiremu have a turn - that boy was getting too big for his boots. He needed a good hiding. He'd have to see his father.

Eventually, as he'd expected, he found the pony at the gate to the property where it had been born, neighing to its old friends and, catching the bridle he turned for home with the pony following.

Meanwhile, Wiremu had trudged back to the meeting house at the pa feeling very sorry for himself. May wasn't there, so he started off for Rangi's house, just as Jake came along. "I'm sorry, Jake," he said, I didn't know he'd take off like that."

"What have you done to your arm?" asked Jake, noticing Wiremu was in pain. "Did you fall off?"

"Yes, I came off on the road. My arm is so sore. I'm looking for May to fix it."

"What about Blueboy? Is he all right?" said Jake as he went to help Wiremu.

"I don't know. Rangi's gone off after him, and told me to see May. Where is she? Oh my arm's sore," cried Wiremu, bending over in pain. "Can you find her?"

"I will, but I won't let you ride the pony again. Father will be mad at me." Jake looked up as Rangi came through the gate leading Blueboy. "Oh you found him! Thank you Rangi. I'm looking for May, for Wiremu."

Rangi gave the reins to Jake and told him to tie the pony up to the fence. "Now run for May, Jake. She'll be in the wharekai. Let's have a look at your arm, Wiremu." 'Might be a case for the doctor,' he thought as he felt the top of the arm. "I think it's come out of the shoulder socket."

About then, Kate, who had stayed longer than she meant talking to Mrs Dickson, was driving past the pa on her way to see Mrs Harvey, when she saw some children around Blueboy near the fence, and stopped to speak to them, worried that the pony might lash out if they got too close and rowdy.

The children were shy but, when one girl plucked up courage and told her

Wiremu had fallen off the pony and hurt himself, Kate drove the buggy into the grounds past the tall carvings like totem poles that marked the area.

May came to greet her. "You have heard about Wiremu, Mrs Johnson? I think he should see Dr McDonald. Rangi could take him on his horse but it would be painful."

Kate thought for a moment, "I can take him in the buggy. I was going to see Mrs Harvey but she doesn't know that. Is Jake here? Or has he gone off to hide? He was told not to let the children have rides yet. I have some things here that I was taking to Mrs Harvey; would you like them, May? They won't be so good tomorrow and I don't know when I will get another chance to go out to the Harveys'."

"Oh no, I can't do that. You take them home again," May protested vigorously.

"It's only some vegetables and a jar or two of jam. We have plenty at home, so you enjoy them, May."

As she lifted the basket down to May, Rangi arrived with Wiremu. "Thank you Mrs Johnson," he said as he helped the boy onto the buggy. "I'll follow you in. I think that after he's seen the doctor he should be able to come home with me on the horse. Jake can stay here for a while with my boys. May will send him home in good time. No-one else will ride the pony today." And he looked hard at the children gathered around watching proceedings.

Kate turned the buggy around and started back for the village. "I hope this has taught you a lesson Wiremu," she said, looking at the boy holding his arm, but he was silent.

The doctor answered the door himself, as it was Mrs McDougal's day off. "How are you Mrs Johnson?" he asked. "Not more trouble for you?"

"No indeed Doctor," said Kate. She pointed to Wiremu sitting in the buggy. "He fell from Jake's pony, and hurt his arm. It's dislocated I believe."

"Well let's have a look. Bring him in," the doctor said just as Rangi rode up. "We might need you, Rangi. Please come in as well."

In the surgery, Doctor McDonald asked more about what had happened and examined the boy's arm. "Well now, let's see what we can do," he said. "Rangi. you'll have to hold him tight while I apply pressure on the joint. It's going to hurt, young man. Mrs Johnson can hold your other hand while we work on this one. Lie down on the bed and grit your teeth. Now a quick tug while you hold hard against me Rangi, and it'll be back in place in no time. That was easy, wasn't it?" he said as Wiremu yelled in pain. "Now lift up your arm - higher, - all right?" he asked as he moved the joint about gingerly and Wiremu winced. "Don't use it much for a few days, my boy."

Wiremu murmured a word of thanks. He wasn't keen on these pakeha folk. But his shoulder felt better, still painful, but better.

"You're lucky it wasn't broken," the doctor said as he washed his hands. Rangi and Kate both thanked him for his help and Kate asked how much they owed. It had been good of him to see Wiremu; some doctors were not keen on treating Maori.

"Don't worry about it Mrs Johnson. You and Rangi did as much work as I did so we'll just put it down to experience. I've found a bit of give and take is the way to make a good life here," he replied.

As Rangi and Wiremu set off for home Kate returned to the store to meet John. "You didn't stay long, dear," he said when he saw Kate. "Were the Harveys out?"

"No, I didn't get as far as the Harveys'. There was an accident at the pa. A boy went for a ride on Blueboy and came off. I brought him in to see Doctor McDonald. Jake is still out at the pa with Rangi's boys. He'll be home before dark. May is going to see to that," explained Kate in a rush.

"What did Jake mean by letting the boy on Blueboy? He was told no-one was to ride until we know the pony is safe with strangers. Wait till he comes home." John was not pleased.

"Apparently Jake said he could only ride in the yard, but he took off and this was the result," said Kate. "Luckily Rangi found the pony out where it used to live."

"Wait until I see Jake," said John angrily as they drove home. "Young fool."

"You should get Jake's side of the story. Listen to what he has to say, please John," said Kate, with a frown.

"Whatever you say, dear," John said. "Do I give him a medal too?"

"Just be careful to listen, that's all. Let's change the subject now. Did you know there was a letter from Mary at the shop? They're coming up on the coach tomorrow so we'll need to find them a place to stay until the whare is built."

"You'll have to go and meet them, Kate. I'd planned to make a start on the hut tomorrow with Rangi and Ru. I might get O'bie to come and give a hand too."

As they drove past the Kellys' house, John spotted O'bie smoking a pipe out near the gate. "I've got a job for you tomorrow if Kelly can spare you. We're going to knock up a hut for some friends arriving tomorrow. They're just off the boat."

"I'll see Kelly, there's not much doing here at the moment," replied O'bie.

"Come about eight, to the new block by the river near the old cabbage trees. You know where I mean? Kelly might come too. It would do him good to have some company, don't you think?"

"I do indeed Mr Johnson. We'll meet you there in the morning."

CHAPTER 30 A Good Shake-Up

That night the family took a long time to settle. The children found it strange to have their own place in the storage area after being in the bunks. Cathy missed Jake's wriggling as he turned over in the bunk below her, or the way he tried to push her out of the bunk by pushing his feet up from underneath. 'It's nice though, to have a little piece of room all to myself,' she thought.

She could hear her mother and father moving around in the new bedroom they'd partitioned off at one end of the living room. Mother had told her that Aunty Mary, Uncle Jim and their children, Peter and Marie, were arriving on the coach. It would be lovely to see them. Cathy drifted off to sleep and was dreaming of being on a boat when her bed shook. "Go away Jake, leave me alone," she instinctively shouted. The shaking stopped as suddenly as it had begun.

"What on earth was that?" Kate asked. "John, can you see to the children? Are they all right? Stay in bed you two!" she called out.

"It was an earthquake. Don't get up. There may be broken glass on the floor. That was a beauty," he said after he had lit the lamp. "That was a real beauty."

"Not to me it wasn't. It was terrifying. Do they happen often?" asked Kate as she pulled her wrap around her.

"There was a huge one a few years back. It raised the bed of the Ruamahunga River and made it unusable for boat traffic and tipped some cliffs on their sides down by Lake Ferry. You can see the layers of clay and stones raised up at an angle of thirty degrees. But most earthquakes I've felt are soon forgotten. It's over now."

"Do you think there might be another one?" asked Kate. "I hope there isn't."

"I don't know but it was quite a good shake," said John. "Often there are several, one after another. Sometimes we get a few for a day or two. We'll just have to wait and see. We can't look for damage till the morning, so we may as well try and get some sleep." And he climbed back in to bed.

"I wonder how bad it was elsewhere. Oh, I hope we don't get anymore."

John cuddled Kate telling her not to worry. "The house is secure and strong because it's made of wood. I hope you didn't lose many of your treasures though. We'll see in the morning."

As they were going back to sleep, there was another gentle shake lasting only a few seconds, but John held Kate close and they were dead to the world when some time later the whole house shook and creaked. As jars of preserves on the shelves in the storeroom fell to the floor with a mighty crash, and the children began screaming John leapt out of bed. "It's all right my dear. I'll check on the children."

"Oh John, I'm so scared." Kate sat up in the bed, her face pale. "I hate earthquakes. They make you feel so insignificant, of no worth, just like an ant."

"I don't think ants would like you saying that," laughed John as he lit the lamp. "I'll just look at the children and I'll be back before you can say earthquake."

John took the lamp into the back room and saw the children had stayed in bed as they'd been told to. There were bits of broken crockery on the floor, and a real mess near the shelves. "Stay where you are until it's light. Don't try to get up at all."

"Do you think there'll be anymore?" asked Jake. "Will they go on all night?"

"Nobody knows, Jake, but we hope not. Your mother is frightened so I'll go back to her. You're safe here in bed, just stay there." As John got into bed Kate took his hands and held them to her chest, taking strength from them as she snuggled up seeking his warmth.

When it was light John dressed and went into the children. He surveyed the damage with worried eyes as he saw some of Kate's treasures smashed on the floor. 'She's not going to like this,' he thought, 'but we're all safe so have a lot to be thankful for.' The area around Cathy's bed was free of china and glass fragments but near Jake's bed, a mess of glass bottles and sticky fruit covered the floor. Jake went to get out of bed but John held him back. "No, don't move until I clear a pathway through this mess.

"All that jolly work!" Kate exclaimed as she joined him, a wrap around her shoulders. "I don't think it's fair. I could cry."

John took her in his arms and said quietly as he stroked her shoulder, "We're all safe Kate. That's what matters. It's only things that are broken. They can be replaced. It's sad but it doesn't really matter."

Kate dried her eyes. "Yes, John, you're quite right. Do you think we could light the fire? I'd love a cup of tea."

"I don't see why not. There's nothing wrong with it as far as I can tell. I'll clear a place by Jake's bed so he can come and help. He can check the stock and ride over to the Kellys' to see if they're in any trouble. Light the fire and I'll be back in a minute or two."

John got the milking buckets and a fire shovel and made a start on the cleanup. Jake soon had room to dress and went out to get wood, chopping it like kindling so it'd burn faster and boil the kettle quickly. He could see by his mother's face that she was upset. 'It was a shame about all the preserves,' he thought as he carried the wood inside. Then he checked on the stock before riding to the Kellys'.

<hr />

When Jake arrived at the Kellys he was surprised to see Mr and Mrs Kelly standing in their yard. Mr Kelly had his arm around Mrs Kelly who was crying.

"Are you all right?" Jake called out. "We were lucky. Mother lost a lot of preserves but that's about all."

"We lost a lot more than that, Jake." Mr Kelly looked very worried. "We think young James has a broken leg and Polly is lucky to be alive. The wardrobe fell over and caught James's leg and hit Polly on the head. The doctor will be too busy to come out here. There'll be more casualties in town, you can be sure of that. Whatever shall we do?"

"I'll go and get Mother, she'll know what to do," said Jake. He ran to his pony and rode home as fast as he could, feeling very sorry for the Kellys.

"Mother!" he yelled as he ran towards the cottage. "The Kellys have got troubles. Polly has a hurt head and they think James has a broken leg. They don't know what to do, so I said I'd come and get you. I'll go and catch Beauty for you."

"John, did you hear that? I need to go over to the Kellys'," called Kate. "Poor things - that's all they need."

"You do what's best Kate. Don't you worry about what's going on here. I'll follow if it's necessary." John looked at Cathy as he spoke. She was sweeping up broken plates, and picking up those that had survived. "We'll just carry on. It isn't what I had planned for today but needs must when the devil drives, so they say. You get on over there."

Hoping things wouldn't be as bad as Jake thought, Kate shook the reins and set off at a good pace. She was puzzled about why the parents had seemed so helpless. 'Perhaps they've been through so much they can't face any more.' As she halted the buggy, the parents appeared to be just where Jake had left them. Mrs Kelly, obviously distraught, was clinging to her husband like a limpet.

"Thank goodness you're here," cried Mr Kelly. "I've been unable to do anything. My wife won't leave my side or come indoors. It's all been too much for her. Jane is in there with them."

"On her own?" asked Kate, hardly believing what she heard as she hurried into the house to the bedroom. Both James and Polly were lying on their beds with the wardrobe still lying where it had fallen across the boy's left leg. Although he looked pale he was alert and claimed his leg wasn't feeling very painful. 'The leg may not be broken after all,' thought Kate. 'But it must be at least four hours since the quake' and she worried that its circulation had been cut off. "What a brave lad you are," she said. "Don't worry. We'll soon have you out of there."

Turning her attention to Polly's injury, Kate took a cloth from Jane who had been holding it to Polly's head. There was some blood on the cloth but the bleeding seemed to have stopped so Kate told Jane to take Polly out to her mother then to fetch O'bie to come and help.

Just as Kate was wondering about the best way to lift the wardrobe, O'bie came into the room at a run, followed by Mr Kelly.

"What do you think Mrs Johnson? Can we hold it up while you get James out?" asked O'bie.

"We'll have to be careful not to break the leg as we lift," said Kate. "Jane, you sit on the bed and hold onto James's leg above the knee. When we lift see if you can pull him out."

"I don't think there's enough room between the side of the wardrobe and the runner on the bed," said O'bie. "Maybe we should chop away some of the wardrobe to make more room. It's a pity but not worth as much as the boy's leg. What do you think Mr Kelly?"

"I don't know to be sure," said Paddy. "Earlier I tried to push the wardrobe hard against the other bed and make more room, but couldn't manage on my own."

"Why don't you turn Polly's bed on its side, or take it out? Then you can move the wardrobe into the space that's left," suggested Jane.

"What a good idea! Yes, take Polly's bed out altogether," said Kate. "Just slide it out without moving the wardrobe and then it will be easy to push it sideways, away from James's leg."

"It's a tight fit but might work," agreed Mr Kelly. He and O'bie pulled the bed out into the room and were then able to slide the wardrobe away from the little boy's leg. "I'll nail the bloody thing to the wall, so I will, so I will," said Paddy as he and O'bie heaved it upright again. "Thank you Mrs Johnson. What would we have done without you?"

"It's Jane you should thank. She was the one who found the solution," Kate replied as she gently examined the leg, thankful it didn't seem to be broken although a large bruise had developed. After they cautiously got James to his feet Kate rubbed his leg to help with circulation then helped him walk from the room to his mother. Tessa was sitting at the table and clasped James in her arms. " My poor boy," she said. "How does it feel now?"

"I'm all right, I think," said James. "It's sore when I walk. There's a huge bruise but I'm glad to be free at last. I thought I might have been trapped forever," then he added manfully, "It was a good shake wasn't it?"

"If you say so," said Kate. "I didn't like it. You should see the mess in my kitchen and storeroom. All my jars of fruit and a lot of the preserves are gone. No, I don't think it was a good shake at all, but at least you and Polly are fine and that's the most important thing. Where is Polly?"

"Sitting outside with Jane," Mrs Kelly replied as she poured tea for them both. "I gave her head a wash and found it was just grazed. I put some ointment on it. That seems to have made it better, as far as she's concerned. Mrs Johnson, thank you, you're so good to us. We were so afraid."

"So was I. I've never felt an earthquake before. I was terrified. The first one wasn't so bad but the big one was awful. I hope we don't get many more. I thought the end of the world had come, but now it's over, the sun's come out and all's well with the world again, except for the mess at home. Still, my husband and Cathy will have righted that as much as possible by the time I get back. Did you lose much?"

"I've been too scared to look; I was so worried about James and Polly I didn't care about anything else. I should have a look around. But you must go home Mrs Johnson before they begin to worry about you."

"I will. I've friends and their two children just arrived from England coming over the hill today by coach if the road's all right. They'll think it bad, but I remember when it was a lot worse. John was going to get O'bie and your husband to help him and the boys build a whare for them to sleep in on the new block. That will have to wait now. They can stay at the Rising Sun for a bit longer than was planned, but I must drive in to greet them," said Kate.

"You'll be pleased to have friends here; it can be a bit lonely. I miss my mother so much."

"I know how you feel Mrs Kelly. I miss mine too. I'll just see how the children are then I'll get off home."

Mr Kelly was waiting by the buggy. He shook her by the hand. "'Tis a fine woman you are Mrs Johnson," he said. "I can't thank you enough for the way you helped us out. I feel stupid for not being able to think how to get poor James out from the fix he was in. Stupid."

"Don't worry," said Kate, smiling at him and taking the reins up. "James is from hardy stock and he'll bounce back. By the way, my husband wants you and O'bie to come and give a hand to put up a shelter for friends who are arriving today. He'll start tomorrow if all goes well."

Meanwhile Dennis had arived and was patting the horse, "Can I come for a ride up the road a bit, Mrs Johnson?" he asked as Kate gave the horse the signal to go.

"Whoa there, Beauty," she said. "Of course you can. Hop up." Dennis was soon seated beside Kate, chirpy as a sparrow. He waved to his father.

"Would you like to hold the reins?" Kate asked him.

"Oh yes please," said Dennis, remembering his manners for once. Soon they were trotting along as Dennis guided Beauty around the bends and ruts in the road.

"You're a born coachman, Dennis," said Kate. "You'll have to get down soon, or it'll take you a long time to walk home."

"Just a little longer, please?" pleaded Dennis.

"Well, just to the next bend. Then it's home for you." The short distance was soon covered and Kate stopped Beauty.

"Thank you for the ride," said Dennis as he jumped down. "That was tops."

And he went away whistling happily. 'A coachman! That's what I want to be,' he thought as he plodded his way home.

"You sound cheerful, Dennis, me boy," said Paddy as the boy reached home. "What's put you in such a good mood?"

"Mrs Johnson said I was a born coachman," said Dennis and he went to tell his mother.

⸎

Jake was tending to Blueboy when Kate arrived home. "How are the Kellys, Mother?" he asked as he took charge of Beauty and the buggy.

"They're all fine, thank goodness. How are things here?" asked Kate.

"We took out all the broken glass and china to bury." replied Jake. "Did the Kellys lose much?"

"They haven't looked yet. They're still shocked by it all," said Kate, and she went to see how John and Cathy were getting on. Everything was neat and clean and she was pleased to see her remaining jars of plum preserves were now held safely by rails that John had attached. The fruit had been sent over the hill by Rosie Parker and Kate had made jam and sauce from them as well as bottling some. "What a great job you've done," she exclaimed, then told John of all that had happened at the Kellys'.

"So all's well that ends well," John smiled. "Well, we're all finished here. Next I want to mark out the spot for the whare. Jake can help me. That'll give us a good start for tomorrow."

"I'll need to go to town about four o'clock," said Kate. "Before then I'll make a start on tonight's meal. If the coach has been delayed I could be late getting back."

Kate busied herself getting bread, cheese and pickles on the table for a meal. "That will have to do today, I'm afraid," she said. "I'd open a jar of fruit if there weren't so few left."

"This is plenty dear," said John. "Think of the starving in Ireland."

"Who's starving in Ireland?" asked Jake as he came through the door.

"A lot of people, if you believe what Mr Kelly told us," said Cathy. "He said the potatoes weren't any good and people had nothing to eat. That's how they came to be here. They were given the fare."

"Things are bad over there," said John, reaching for another slice of bread. "In the papers that come over from England, they tell you things are bad but often blame the Irish themselves."

"I don't believe that at all," said Kate. "They've wanted to rule their own lands for centuries, and so have the Scots. I don't approve of all Mother England does. There are far too many lords and ladies getting rent from land that should belong to the Irish people. We can't do much from here though can we?"

"We surely can't my dear. I think we'd better just worry about our own problem, which is finding a home for the Smiths. I'll get away now, and then I'll be here when you go to the village." Suddenly the cottage shuddered as another after-shock struck. "That makes four I've felt this morning. That might mean the coach is late if there have been any slips on the hill. If it is late just come home and let Dickson see to them. You can go back tomorrow."

"All right John. It's just that I haven't seen Mary for over two years. I'm so excited. Go and get started on the whare." said Kate firmly, "I'll be fine."

"I don't like leaving you when quakes are still happening but it will make it easier in the morning if I've had a good look at the place I've mapped out in my mind. We'll need to dig a long drop somewhere near, and find a place for a shed. I don't suppose they'll have much with them, but there'll need to be room for it when it does arrive." John kissed Kate and he and Jake hurried to where Bessie was dozing the day away. "I've a job for you old girl," he said as he patted her nose and placed the collar over her neck. "We're going to take the things we're going to need in the wagon."

<hr>

Kate looked at the cuckoo clock still hanging on the wall. It was two o'clock. 'Thank goodness the clock didn't fall in the quake. I'd have had to tell the time by the sun,' she thought. She called to Cathy to come and peel the vegetables for the evening meal and started to brown some pieces of beef. Soon the smell of hot meat filled the room. After adding the vegetables Cathy had prepared with some garden herbs and water she put the lid on the pot.

"Now keep the fire in Cathy, and stir the pot a few times. Don't let Jake put too much wood on the fire when he gets back or it will boil dry. Now I must get away to the village," Kate instructed Cathy as she changed into a fresh skirt and blouse, brushed her long hair and wound it up in a bun, and put on her button-up boots.

"I'll be careful Mother," said Cathy. "I'm going to read my book. I'll lie on the bed and if there's another quake I'll stay there."

As Kate drove along, lots of thoughts about the events of the day and what was still to come danced in her head. 'It's just as well we don't know what lies ahead,' she thought. 'Now I must think about Mary and Jim. I hope the coach got through without any trouble. What will Mary think of me? And what will she and Jim think of our valley?'

CHAPTER 31 Meeting Jim and Mary

On reaching the stables Kate drew up close to where a hard layer of cobblestones had been laid to make an area free of mud for passengers alighting from the coach. A small group of men were chatting together and Kate asked if they had any news of the coach from Wellington.

"It's just a matter of waiting, Mrs Johnson," one said, then asked, "How did you like the shake?"

"Not at all," Kate said then told them about her experiences. The men were full of stories of past quakes and near misses. Some remembered the Palliser Bay quake in '55 that raised the coastline and told of some terrible times they'd been through.

"Please," Kate said, "I don't want to hear any more earthquake tales. Do you think the coach will get through tonight?" she asked. "It's getting darker by the minute."

Just then the sound of horses could be heard in the distance and before long, with a clatter and rattle and a "Whoa there!" the coach pulled up. As male passengers climbed down and assisted some ladies, there were smiles and sighs of relief from them all. The Smiths were the last to alight.

Kate rushed forward to greet them. "You're here at last!" she cried as she hugged her friend.

"Oh it was a terrible journey, just awful. I'm so pleased we left the children with Mrs Parker in the meantime," said Mary as she brushed tears from her eyes. She kissed Kate and turned to Jim. "Can you get our cases? I'm so eager to get to where it is we're to stay in this terrible place."

'Not a good start,' thought Kate as Jim went to do his wife's bidding, but smiled at Mary. "I've got the buggy here, we can take the cases with us, but Jim will have to walk. It's not far."

"Oh Kate, we've brought someone with us who you already know. She was governess to the boy that died on your way out here. Remember her?" Mary turned to point at a lonely figure standing to one side.

"Oh Miss Goode, how lovely to see you. Was the trip really so bad?" said Kate as she greeted the new arrival.

"I never want to go through that again Mrs Johnson," said Elizabeth Goode. "The road had slipped away in parts and we had to get down off the coach and walk past the very narrow places, but it's lovely to see you and be here at last."

"Can we go, please?" interrupted Mary, "I need a bath and a meal."

"I'm not sure you'll get a bath but a meal will be waiting for you at the Rising Sun, and a bed," said Kate, wondering again how Mary would cope with being a settler. "I'm sorry I can't take you straight to our farm. We just don't have enough room. I'll explain later."

"Will there be room for me at the hotel?" asked Miss Goode.

"There should be. I heard from Mrs Parker that you might be on the coach so I booked rooms tonight for you all," said Kate.

"So let's go then," said Jim huffily. "I want a wash and a change of clothes."

Kate gave Beauty the signal and they moved off down Main Street towards the hotel - a two storied wooden building that provided basic shelter and meals to travellers at reasonable cost. As they approached the Rising Sun, Miss Goode asked Kate if there might be work for her anywhere as she needed an income.

"Oh you'll be in great demand Miss Smith. Young pretty women don't stay idle for long. I'll ask Mrs Thompson if she needs help at the school. There are a lot more pupils now. You may be just what she's looking for."

When they arrived at the hotel, Kate explained she'd come to town in the morning to take them out to the farm. Jim could help John, then drive them back into the village in the evening. By the next day the whare would be ready. "Well, as ready as it can be," said Kate with a laugh. "You'll be surprised how good a builder John has become. We have two Maori boys, well, men really, Rangi and Ru, who help."

"Aren't you frightened of them?" asked Mary. "They look so fierce with all those tattoos on their faces. I don't know how you can go near them."

"Not at all, they're very gentle. Rangi has tattoos on his arms but not his face. Ru who is younger, saved our lives. One night he hid us from a marauding tribe who were visiting the area. They may have been harmless but Ru wouldn't take the chance," said Kate, with more than a touch of pride. "Oh, here's mine host, Mr Evans. He'll look after you. I do hope you will all sleep well. I'll see you tomorrow."

It was quite dark as Kate approached the cottage and she was glad to give the reins to Jake who came out to meet her, and to see that the table was set ready for tea. John was sitting by the stove smoking his pipe. Cathy was having another look at the stew and stirring it for the umpteenth time. She'd added some water when it seemed likely to burn dry and had cooked a pot of potatoes.

"Well, how were they?" asked John, tapping out the bowl of his pipe on to the hearth. "What was the journey like?"

"Not so good John, they were terrified. The road was so narrow in places they had to get out and walk. Jim didn't look impressed with the place at all and Mary is frightened of the Maoris. They felt the earthquake in Wellington. That scared them too. I told them I'll pick them up tomorrow and then they can see for themselves how well we're doing."

"Well, if they're not going to be happy here there's no point in trying to make them stay is there?" said John. "I know you'd be disappointed not to have them close by, but you have your new friends now. Not lonely are you?"

"No, I'm not lonely." replied Kate as she dished up the meal. "Everything looks just right Cathy," she said as she mashed the potatoes with some butter, and ladled the stew on to the plates. "You found enough plates? I didn't check how many had broken."

"Yes Mother, only a few had fallen and smashed. Father and Jake took such a lot of broken china and rubbish to the pit they dug outside the fence. I packed all the books back into the bookcase after Father nailed it to the wall."

"I think we should count ourselves lucky, Cathy; some of the people in town lost a lot more than we did. I believe it was a bad shake in Wellington too. You can have a rest from doing the dishes after taking such good care of the meal. Get off to bed and no reading by candle-light. I don't want a fire to deal with as well."

As Kate washed the dishes John dried them. Kate was going to tell him it was not his job but it was companionable just standing together exchanging stories of the day. "I don't know about the Smiths," said Kate, "Coming out here I mean. It's so different to what they were used to at home. He's been spoon-fed all his life, and will find life here a challenge I fear."

"Never mind dear, we'll soon see what stuff he's made of. He'll have to knuckle down to some hard work, and his wife will have to rough it for a while, but look at the way you've adapted. Your life was never like this at home," said John as he looked at her proudly.

"No, but we weren't spoilt by our parents were we? We had to help around the house and garden and learn to look after things properly. I love it here. I wouldn't change anything, except perhaps the chance to see my mother again," said Kate.

"Have you had any more letters? Was there mail today?" asked John as he hung the tea towel up on a peg.

"You'll find it hard to believe that I didn't even go and see Mrs Dickson today, I was so worried about meeting the coach that I never left the stable-yard. The men there were telling awful stories about other earthquakes they'd experienced. It's quite amazing that they lived through some of them but I think they might have added a few things for my benefit."

"Ah well, we'll have a big day tomorrow and we need our sleep. Are you still taking your tonic?" asked John with concern.

"Yes of course. I feel much better and I'm sure the baby knows it's bed-time; it's moving such a lot," replied Kate.

CHAPTER 32 Will the Smiths Stay?

Next morning Kate drove the buggy into town to collect the newcomers, with the children cantering along beside her until they reached the school.

At the Rising Sun Kate was warmly greeted by the proprietor and shown into a sitting-room and, before long, the Smiths appeared, looking happier than they had the previous evening. After assuring Kate they had slept well and that Miss Goode was going to have a quiet day in the village, they all squeezed into the buggy. Kate made a short stop at the store for mail then they set off. It was a heavier load than usual for Beauty, but she didn't seem to mind, and Jim was soon admiring the large areas of bush on both sides of the road.

"You might change your mind about 'beautiful trees' when you start removing stumps from the ground," laughed Kate. "There are sawmills working all round the valley. The timber is in high demand to build houses and shops in Wellington. A lot is being used locally, too. New houses are going up everywhere."

John had heard the buggy approaching and was waiting outside to greet them as they drew up. After putting Beauty into her paddock he followed Kate and the newcomers inside.

"You're getting well set up here John," said Jim. "You're lucky to have found such a nice farm."

Kate was nervously making a cup of tea. While she looked at her home with pride, she wondered what the Smiths were thinking but she quickly interrupted. "Luck has little to do with it. It's been jolly hard work all the way. John has been working here for nearly three years now and never had a minute's rest in all that time."

"And none to be had now. We should get going after we've had our tea," said John. "Ru and Rangi have been digging postholes for the foundations of your whare. I mapped it all out yesterday, and showed them what to do."

"Will they be all right, doing jobs like that with no proper supervision?" asked Jim. "After all, they're only natives."

"They're quite capable. They helped build here and Rangi has built a whare for his family too. They're fine fellows who, by the way, we don't treat any differently to the way we treat each other. There is none of the old slave and master stuff here.

"I don't know about that. I don't like the idea of people owning other people, but to say they are equal to us is a bit much."

"You'll have to change your ideas or you'll find yourself an outsider. The Maoris are a very proud people, and will fight for their rights. Be very careful to treat Rangi and Ru with respect. That's all I ask," said John, finishing off his tea. "Now let's get going. Have you brought some old gear to wear? The gum from the trees is sticky and won't come off clothes easily, so something old is better."

The two men made their way to where Rangi and Ru were working. John made the introductions and, shaking hands, the three men eyed each other up and down. Rangi was quite happy to meet a friend of the boss's, but Ru, who'd not always been treated well by pakehas, had some reservations.

As there was no time to waste they set to work. Jim was put to ramming the dirt around the posts that had been cut from young totara trees then placed in the holes already dug along each side, marking where walls would stand. Timber scantlings from the mill would be nailed to these horizontally at two foot intervals, then a vertical layer of flat-sided pit-sawn boards nailed on, overlapping an inch or two to make a solid wall with few gaps. Soon the shape of the hut was easy to see.

They were well underway when the women arrived with lunch. Kate had put Bessie in the buggy and driven through the trees watching for stumps hidden in the grass and toetoe. "I know I'll never be able to do that," said Mary as they got down from the buggy. "Never in a hundred years."

"Yes you will Mary. I learnt to drive a trap at home and the buggy is not much different. You'll soon pick it up," said Kate as they set about laying out the food.

"I very much doubt it Kate. I've something I want to talk to you about. The reason I left the children in the Hutt with Mrs Parker is because I don't think Jim wants to stay here. He wants to return to Australia. He met some men from Melbourne in a bar who'd been to the goldfields in Ballarat. They're sure gold is still to be found there. He says he'll go on his own if I won't go too."

"That's not good news," said Kate with a sigh. "I was so looking forward to having a friend close by but, if Jim wants to try something else, there's not a lot you can do. Do you think you'll be all right in Australia? We read about the terrible things that went on in Ballarat and the Eureka Stockade, back in England. The poor miners, to get shot down like mad dogs, how dreadful."

"Kate, the men are coming for their tea," Mary said quickly, an anxious look on her face. "Please don't say anything about what I've told you. He may still decide to stay after all."

"How's the job going dear?" asked Kate, looking at John. "I can see the whare is going up well. It looks quite big."

"It's the same size as our store room was before we extended it," John explained. "That was big enough for us for the first few months, wasn't it?"

"Yes, it was quite cosy. We were happy there." Kate looked at John, wondering how he would take the news if Jim's decided not to stay. 'Perhaps it will never come to that,' she thought.

Jim looked at his wife's friends, wondering how they could stand to live like this, sitting on a tree stump drinking black tea out of battered cups and seeming to enjoy it. "I'm not sure this is the life for me, John," he said, draining his cup. "I've been considering returning to Australia. Would it make much difference to you if I don't take up this block of land?" he asked, as he picked up some bread and cheese.

"Well, it would make it a bit harder, but I guess we'd manage. We have to make some improvement to the holding in the first year according to the agreement I signed on your behalf. Building the whare will cover that."

Jim sat silently, waiting for John to say more. Both were thinking of the future and what problems it might bring.

"What draws you to Australia?" John asked after a long pause.

"I met these men from Melbourne who've been prospecting in Ballarat. They believe there's still gold to be had there. Its years since the Eureka Rebellion and the authorities have sorted out all that trouble."

"You'll find it hard going. And what about your family?" John asked. "You can't expect your wife to fend alone with the children while you go off hunting elusive nuggets. Have you thought about what they are going to do while you're away?"

"I know it's what I want to do," Jim said confidently. "They'll be all right in Melbourne. These men have contacts and a house in the city. They assured me that it would be a safe thing to do. I only have to find a few hundred to buy a share of their claim."

"I think you're mad and have been hypnotised by the sight of a few grains of gold dust. I say God help you, and your family if that's all you have to go on," said John, making his feelings known as he got up from the log to return to work. "I think you're foolish, but it will make no difference to us if that's what you want. We'll manage both blocks and are quite in our rights to do so. This land is where the future lies, better than any gold." John looked over to where Rangi and Ru were working already. "I'm sorry if you think we misled you about conditions here," he said, "but you know you'd never have thought of gold prospecting if you hadn't met those men. I'd be very careful about buying into their claim. They could just be after your money."

"I'm sure they are what they say," Jim said with a slight edge to his voice. "I don't get taken in easily you know."

After packing up the remains of the meal the two women went for a walk in the bush. Sunlight filtered through the trees and sparkled in the water of a stream gurgling happily on its way to the river. Mary was entranced by the sight of a pair of fantails darting here and there as they fed on insects. All about them the scent of the bush filled the air with a heady aroma, fresh and earthy. Kate and Mary were quiet as they enjoyed this respite from the everyday world and its concerns.

Finally, Mary broke the silence. "It's lovely here Kate, I'm sure we would be happy if Jim didn't have this mad idea to go looking for gold. I fear John is right. The men may be fraudsters. I wonder if I should say what I think."

"A wife is meant to be subject to her husband's wishes." Kate took her friend's hand. "But it's such an important decision I think you should discuss it wih him. Now I think we'd better be getting back home. The children won't be long coming from school, and I want to show you the clothes I've made for the baby."

The two friends spent a happy hour looking over the items Kate had ready for the coming babe. Among them were clothes Kate had brought from home and some she'd knitted in her few hours of spare time. A beautiful shawl of fine wool made by Kate's grandmother was the finest piece of knitting Mary had ever seen.

"They're just lovely," said Mary enviously. "I'd love to have another baby, but Jim's not keen. He's happy with our two - not that he spends a lot of time with them. He's always off doing some business with his cronies. I thought that would stop when we left England."

"I'm sure he'll change when he finds what he's looking for," said Kate with a smile she hoped hid her real thoughts. "He just hasn't found his place in the world."

"He's had plenty of time as far as I am concerned," said Mary with a quiver in her voice. "I'm sick of chasing after his ideas. I thought that coming here would give him a real reason to settle down. Instead, we'll be off again on some new scheme."

"Give him time to make up his mind. John will no doubt have a good long talk to him, and try to show him the danger of following some wild goose chase after gold. I'm afaid I think that gold that's buried in vaults as ingots is such a waste of energy, and with the loss of so many lives too," said Kate.

Just then the sound of horses could be heard and the children were soon trotting into the yard. Mary ran out to greet them as they dismounted, kissing them firmly on the cheek as she held their hands in hers. "Do you remember me? It seems such a long time ago since we saw you in England just before you left."

Jake pulled away, but said politely, "Yes, Aunt Mary, I remember you from home. Did you have a good trip over in the boat?"

"Yes, thank you Jake. My, you've grown so tall. You must be nearly as tall as your father, and you Cathy? How are you? Do you like school? Have you got a nice teacher?" Mary's questions went on with no chance of reply.

Kate could see Mary was near to tears. "Put the ponies away Jake, and come inside. I'll make a nice cup of tea, we could all do with one of those."

"Where are the children, Aunty Mary?" asked Cathy.

"They're still in Wellington. I don't know if you will be able to see them this time. We don't know what Uncle Jim is going to do yet. He wants to return to Australia for a while," Mary said, giving Cathy another hug.

"Oh why?" said Cathy, "I've been so looking forward to seeing them."

"It's not for us to reason why, just for us to do or die," said Mary. Kate smiled, recognising the poem they'd learnt together at school. "Now let me look at you. My, you've grown too."

Cathy thought it would have been funny if she hadn't grown. It was a year since she'd seen Aunt Mary. Adults say silly things. "I'm going to be ten next week," she said proudly.

"Oh happy birthday, Cathy," said Mary and kissed her again "What would you like for your birthday?"

"I'm going to have a cake and my friend Jane is coming to tea. We want to look at the books in the shed and find some we haven't read," said Cathy. "Her family doesn't have many books, so I'm lending Jane some of mine. Ours," she amended.

"Well, make sure that you write down the titles of all you lend, Cathy. Lending books is the surest way to lose friends. She may love them too and not want to give them back," said Kate as she poured the tea. "I had some arguments with girls at my school about the ownership of a book."

"Oh Jane is not like that," scoffed Cathy. "She'd never do anything like that."

"I hope you're right," said Kate, passing a plate of biscuits around. "Remember, they're my books too. I brought them halfway round the world, you know."

Just then the men came through the gate to the yard and stood talking for a while at the stables, seemingly comfortable with each other. Kate watched as they continued to look at the buildings John had put up at the side of the house. The new room was nearly complete.

"You've done a fine job," said Jim, as they came into the house. "I'll think things over tonight and let you know tomorrow. Are you sure you're allowed to take up another section of land under this small farms scheme if I decide not to stay?"

"Yes I checked on that. We can say I'm looking after it for you until your return. Half the blocks still await ownership, so there's no shortage of land."

"It's wonderful here, don't you think Jim?" asked Kate. "Can't you feel the spell the place casts on you?"

"Not for me Kate, I only see a lot of hard work. If today's toil was a taste of what's to come, I don't think it's what I'm cut out for," said Jim as he stretched his arms high in the air. "It was tough on my back. I may never be able to stand straight again." He made faces as he raised his shoulders up and down, and ran his hands over his hips. "We should get going back to the hotel Mary," he said, thinking of the good Scotch whisky he had seen in the bar. "We need to be there by dark. I didn't like the look of some of the types I saw in town this morning."

"I wouldn't worry about the folk you'll meet in town. They're a law abiding lot, and very helpful to each other. You wouldn't get a better lot of people anywhere in the world," said Kate.

"She's right Jim," said John. "Everyone's had lots of troubles these past two years, but have still supported anyone else who needed help."

Jake went to get the buggy ready for Jim and Mary to return to town. "Bessie or Beauty, Father?"

John thought for a moment about what he wanted to do the next day. "Bessie, I think Jake. She's used to staying in the schoolyard so won't mind being shut in the paddock at the Rising Sun. I want to go into town tomorrow so I'll need Beauty,"

Kate gave Mary a hug before she was helped into the buggy by John. "Goodbye, goodbye," she called as they drove away. "Tell me what you think." Kate turned to John. "Will he ever get the gold out of his head?"

"I don't think so, but I don't believe he's cut out to be a farmer either. It takes a different type of man to put up with the upsets and the seasons. I think he'll head for Australia. It makes me worry for Mary though."

"Yes I worry too. I know she'll follow him anywhere, but how she'll manage with the children, I really don't know," said Kate.

CHAPTER 33 New Beginnings

The next morning John set out for Greytown to see if Jim had made a decision and also to check again the conditions for buying the extra block of land so he could be sure he'd attended to all that was needed. Reaching town, he went to the Rising Sun where he found Mary, mopping tears from her eyes, in the sitting-room with Miss Goode. 'Oh my, this doesn't look good', he thought as he went to greet them. "So where's the great prospector?" he asked.

"Gone!" said Miss Goode. "He left on the coach this morning. Mrs Smith is beside herself with worry. What on earth will she do?" She placed her arms around Mary who was sobbing her heart out.

"I was afraid of this when I first knew of your plan to come out. Jim has never looked reality in the face, has he Mary?" John said. "Did he say what you are to live on while he gets the gold out of his system?"

"He left me enough money to go back to Wellington for the children and said he'll send more when he gets to Melbourne. But he doesn't have a lot. There won't be much left after he buys a ticket. Whatever will we do?" sobbed Mary.

"I guess it's better he left now and didn't pretend he was going to be an asset to the district. You're better without him," said John. "It's a hard lesson but one you need to learn. Think of the mess you left behind in England. Jim was lucky not to be taken to court by people wanting to get their money back from his get rich quick schemes."

Mary lifted her head from Beth Goode's shoulder and shrugged her shoulders. She hated hearing John say all those things but, "I suppose you're right," she admitted. "I did so hope he would change, but it seems it wasn't to be. But what do I do now?"

"You'll find a way, here, or over the hill. I'm sure there are plenty of shops looking for honest people to help run them in the Hutt and Wellington. I think I'll take you home to Kate. I've a few things I need to see to, but I'll be back to pick you, and the buggy, up as soon as I can."

John went to settle the bill for the room Jim and Mary had used, thinking of ways to make ends meet. He'd been going to ride out and pick up the puppy for Jake, but that would have to wait now. After paying the bill he walked down the street to the store. He'd never had much faith in Jim and was glad he'd never given in to Mary's pleading to advance Jim some capital. Friends and business were better kept apart,

"Morning, Mrs Dickson. Is your husband around?" asked John. "Did you lose much in the earthquake?"

"Indeed we did. How about you? I heard that your partner arrived with his wife so you will have been busy."

"It was all to no avail Mrs Dickson. He caught the coach back over the hill this morning. He wants to search for gold in Australia. I think he's mad. He's left his wife and children behind and gone off chasing his dream, dream for him, nightmare for the rest of us," John shook his head as he spoke. "But just keep it to yourself in the meantime."

Johanna agreed that the least said the better. "Your wife's friend. What's she like, trustworthy and a good worker?"

"Oh yes, I'd say you could bank on her. Why?" asked John.

"We need someone to help. Things are getting a bit much for me. I've got a boy but he's not much good in the shop. If I could get someone trustworthy to help I would. I've talked to my husband about it and he agrees."

"I'm to get her from the Rising Sun very soon. She's there with Miss Goode at the moment and was in a real state of shock when I saw her. I'll bring her round to meet you," said John.

———— ∞∞∞ ————

When John returned to the Rising Sun Mary was sitting with Miss Goode in the sitting-room with her cases ready beside her. Her eyes were dry and, although she wasn't smiling, she seemed easier than when he'd seen her earlier.

"Now Mary," he said, "I want you to come and meet some people I know. They have a store here in town and are very busy. I told Mrs Dickson that I'd introduce you before I took you back to Kate. And, Miss Goode, Kate wants you to go and see Mrs Thompson at the school. It's possible there could be work for you. She sent Mrs Thompson a letter with our son this morning and she'll have it by now. So why not pop over to the school, to see if she has need of you?"

"I will, thank you Mr Johnson. Your wife is very kind. I'll pluck up my courage and go right away," Miss Goode said as she hurried off.

When they reached the store Johanna took Mary's hand. "I'm glad to meet a friend of Mrs Johnson's. I hear you've been left in a tricky situation."

"Yes, my husband has this mad idea of finding gold and wants to try his luck. It was my idea to come out here, but I thought he'd come to like farming. I hadn't expected one day to be enough," said Mary, beginning to cry again.

"Mr Johnson said you could need a position as a shop assistant or such like, to give you something to live on. Is that right?" asked Mrs Dickson.

"I've two children. They're in Wellington with a friend of the Johnsons. I need to find some way to support myself, and them," Mary replied. "I'm used to hard work."

"I'm expecting our first baby," said Johanna. "It's not due for a while but I'm tired after a long day. I'd be happy to give you a trial."

"That would be wonderful. I was going to see if I could get work over the hill, but here, near the Johnsons, would be so much better," said Mary, looking at John for confirmation that he thought it the right decision.

"So let's say you start next Monday. That'll give you time to go and get the children. Is that all right with you? We'll talk about wages and things later on. We'll have to find you somewhere to live too," mused Johanna, as they shook hands.

Just then, Miss Goode hurried into the store looking excited and happier than she had since coming off the coach. Then she'd looked forlorn and lonely, now she was beaming.

John thought he knew why. "How did it go with Mrs Thompson?" he asked.

"She received me with open arms and will be happy to give me a trial teaching the infants. The school was getting too much for one person to manage. She was thinking of advertising for an assistant. I was the answer to her prayer and she's the answer to mine. The children just love her; you could see that from the way they went on with their work while we spoke, quiet as mice."

"That's wonderful," said Mary. "I've found work as well. Now we'll both need a place to live. Perhaps we could share a house, or part of a house together? What do you think of that idea?"

'How lucky we all have been,' Johanna thought. "It's all thanks to the Johnsons," she said to the two women. "I think this calls for a little celebration, something different. Tea doesn't seem to be the right choice does it?" And she fetched a small bottle of fruit wine from off a shelf. "Let's drink to our successes," she said and they all raised their glasses.

"So this is how you carry on when I'm away," said Henry Dickson as he entered. "What are you celebrating?"

"Oh it's a long story. I'll tell you tonight," said Johanna, as she poured him a glass. "But now we must get on with some work."

"Yes indeed," replied Henry, "too much drinking can be the ruin of you. I'm surprised at you Johnson, the sun's not over the yard-arm yet you know."

"Quite right," said John with a laugh. "It's lucky you don't rely on me for your income from liquor isn't it?"

He turned to the women to ask whether they wanted to go back with him or stay in town and make their arrangements for the future. "When do you think you could face the journey over the hill to get the children, Mary?" he asked.

"I'll see if I can get on the coach tomorrow, then I might see Jim before he leaves as he'll have to wait for a passage. I'd like him to not have to worry about us while he's away."

"You're too good to be true," laughed Johanna.

"So what's it to be then?" asked John, realising they'd need time to think over what had happened this morning. "Look, I need to speak to the Small Farms Association people, so I'll do that and return in an hour."

"That sounds excellent," said Mary. "We'll ask Mrs Dickson if she knows of any rooms that we might be able to rent. I think I should stay in town."

"I'd like to see Mrs Johnson too, but as Mrs Smith says, the need to find a home is the most important thing at the moment," said Miss Goode.

Out in the street once more, John made his way to the lawyer who was responsible for looking after matters relating to land sales. A little later, happy with some new information about land purchases, John looked into the blacksmith's to chat with Fairman for a moment or two. There he found the station-owner who had bartered the ponies for timber, watching his horse being shod.

"Ah, Johnson," he said. "I wanted a word with you. I saw one of my ponies out our way the other day, being ridden by a native boy. Have you sold them to the Maoris?"

"No of course not," said John. "My boy was out visiting a friend and one of the friend's brothers took the pony for a gallop."

"Well, I don't think you should get too friendly with the Maoris, Johnson. Only a few years ago they were cannibals, you know. I don't trust them," said the land-owner.

"I treat them as I wish to be treated," said John. "The pony is mine now, not yours, but thank you for your concern."

"Of course. Quite right too. Ahem, I wonder if you have any more timber available. I've decided to add a bit more to the house."

"I'll see what there is that would suit you. I'm using quite a bit myself building some sheds and a room on the house but I'll certainly look to see what's to spare," John said and went to take his leave. They shook hands. John was pleased that he'd stood his ground. 'Cheeky beggar,' he thought, 'you're not in Mother England now.' And he made his way back to the store.

"So have you decided?" John asked the women waiting there.

"Yes, we're going to look at a house that belongs to a widow. She may let us have a room there, to share. It will be a bit of a squeeze with the children but will do in the meantime," said Mary. Beth Goode nodded in agreement.

"Well I'll be on my way," said John. "I'll take the buggy home with me, Mary. The men will have finished what I gave them to do on the whare. So I had better get back."

"Well now you have a new start and so do I," said Mary as the two women walked to the address Mrs Dickson had provided.

"Isn't it strange how things sometimes work out?" said Beth Goode. "I nearly stayed in the Hutt to look for work there, but I'm glad I didn't. I feel safe with the Johnsons to give support. I'm sure Mrs Thompson gave me the job because she trusts their judgement."

"That's right; I feel this is a new beginning for me too. My husband is so stubborn, maybe it's something he has to get out of his system." said Mary. "I shall have to pray for him."

"Well here we are," said Beth as they reached a cottage with lace curtains in the windows and a white picket fence. It looked neat and tidy. There were a few flowers in the front garden, even though it was nearly winter. They walked through to knock at the front door. "I hope she's home. I do like this place, don't you?"

"Oh yes, it's like something out of a picture book," replied Mary.

"Can I help you?" asked the little lady who answered the door. She had a sweet face and a kindly smile.

"We hope so," said Mary. "We saw the notice at the store, that you wanted to let a room. We need somewhere to live while we get settled, both of us. I'm Mrs Smith, and this is Miss Goode."

"Pleased to meet you. Are you new in town? I don't remember seeing you around. I'm Biddy O'Toole." said the little lady and held out her hand. "It's not a very big room, but has two beds. Come and have a look." She pushed the door open wider and showed them into a narrow passage. "Through here," she said, as she opened a door.

The room was square with beds against the walls either side, a wardrobe at one end and a dressing table at the other. Bedside cabinets for chamber pots completed the furnishings.

"It's five shillings a week, but as there are two of you I'll let you have the room for nine shillings, that's four shillings and sixpence each. What do you think?" she asked. "Meals will be extra if you want them, or you can do for yourselves."

"I think it's splendid but I need to tell you that I have two children down in Wellington. I'm going tomorrow to bring them here. They are four and six," explained Mary. "I'll be working at Dickson's store during the day, and I hope they can go to school. I'll get a house of my own as soon as I can afford it, but in the meantime this would do very well."

"I don't want children under my feet all day. I'm past all that," said Mrs O'Toole, "but if you can keep them quiet, and your friend doesn't mind, you can have the room."

"I don't know how we'll all fit in, but I'm happy to try," said Miss Goode. "I just need to have a home. Can I move in this afternoon?"

"Of course my dear, but I need two weeks money in advance. I've been taken down a few times just lately."

The women agreed this was fair and looked in their bags for the money. After counting the coins Mrs O'Toole wrote them a receipt. "I'll show you the kitchen and sitting room," she said.

Mary and Miss Goode felt well pleased to have a home. It was not furnished expensively but had all that one needed. The kitchen had an oven so cooking simple meals would not be a problem. It was very clean. Mrs O'Toole had her rooms in the back part of the house. She explained she had one other boarder, a surveyor, who was mapping the district and only stayed a night or two once a week. The women left feeling as if God was on their side. As they made their way back to the hotel to pick up their cases, they stopped at the stableyard for Mary to book the coach for tomorrow.

———— ✿✿✿ ————

When John reached home, he got busy showing Rangi and Ru how to lay and secure the shingles on to the roof of the whare to give a firm waterproof layer over the boards put up earlier. It was a slow job, as the shingles had to be laid evenly from the lower edge of the roof, rising in overlapping layers until they reached the highest point of the building where even more care was needed to get a good seal to prevent the wind from lifting them. Because the dry totara pieces could easily split, the work was slow and tedious.

"You should've got more sheets of iron, boss. This job's no plurry good," said Ru. "We'd be finished by now eh?"

"It's the cost, Ru. The iron costs a lot more than shingles," said John as he stretched his back. Much of the work could be done from a ladder, but the last two feet on each side of the peak needed to be done on the roof. "Never mind, we're nearly there for today. We'll finish it tomorrow. Let's get away home now."

They looked at the whare proudly. "She's a pretty good job, boss. You make a good builder," Rangi said.

"Well, I have to thank you two for doing a good job too," said John as he mounted Beauty for the ride home. "We'll finish tomorrow if we don't get a storm. I don't know who's going to live here now. Mr Smith has gone to seek his fortune in Australia and I don't think his wife could live here on her own with her children. So now we have a home ready for a couple and no-one to live in it."

"Don't worry boss, something will come along and the house will be here, ready and waiting," said Rangi.

"It's good to know you have faith Rangi. Get away home before it starts to rain. It looks very dark down south." John looked at the clouds gathered around Bull Hill. Big spots of rain began hitting his face as he rode home, and he hoped the men got back to the pa before it really set in. They were a great help. 'I must tell them so more often,' he thought.

"You've been a long time John," remarked Kate when he reached home. "How did everything go?"

"It went very well. Miss Goode has taken a position with Mrs Thompson and Mary has a job helping at Dickson's shop. They're both going to stay at Mrs O'Toole's boarding house. Mary plans to go to the Hutt tomorrow to get the children. I hope they have a lot better journey than the last one," said John as he sat down at the table.

"Cathy," called Kate, "go and call Jake for tea, please dear. And shut the fowl pen door as well, while you're out there. I think something might have been worrying them. Do you think someone's pet ferret has got loose? People shouldn't be allowed to bring pests like that into the country."

"Oh I don't know dear, I had a pet ferret when I was young. They're dear little things. We used to go out hunting rabbits and hares," John added, as he thought of his boyhood home.

"Not when they slay our chooks. We don't need things like that over here, or stoats or weasels either," said Kate grumpily.

Once the meal was over, and the children were in bed, Kate turned her attention to the mail John had fetched home. It had been some time since she'd heard from her mother, and she was anxious to hear how the friendship was going with the man she'd met at the choral group.

Kate read quickly, scanning the pages for news. Sure enough, near the end, was an account of a show they'd been to together and enjoyed. A surprise awaited her though. "I'm writing to let you know that we are to marry," her mother wrote. Kate could hear her Mother's voice as she read the words. 'Oh no, that can't be right' she thought, so she read them again. But no, it was quite clear; there in black and white, she read, 'We are to marry.'

"John, John," she called. "You'll never guess who is to be married."

"Don't tell me it's your mother," John laughed. "It's not a year since your father died is it?"

"No, it's not but, as Mother says, they have a lot in common. Evidently he's Welsh and his name is Rhys Jones. She wants our blessing."

"I think it's wonderful. She'd such a hard time before your father died. She deserves every happiness."

"You're right. Mother is no fool. If she's happy, who are we to try to change her mind?"

"Write and give your mother our best wishes. I'm off to bed. You never know what tomorrow will bring. I hope Mary gets down to the Hutt and back without too much trouble. The thing will be if she sees Jim, and he wants her to go with him. That would make it hard for her."

"John, thank you for your part in getting things settled for Mary. I married a good man and I hope Mother is doing the same," said Kate as she shook up the pillows. She sipped at the glass of tonic as she watched John settle into a deep sleep.

'Yes,' she thought, 'I'm very lucky. Good night Mother. Rest in peace, Father. I hope Miss Goode will be all right and that Mary will be able to help the Dicksons. God bless my family and all my friends,' and she fell asleep to the sound of rain on the roof.

CHAPTER 34 Miss Goode Goes to School

The next morning, the rain had cleared and, as the sun came up, Mary and Beth made their way to the coaching stables. Already several people were waiting for the stable-boys to harness up the four strong horses which would pull the coach over the ranges to the Hutt Valley. It would be a long and arduous trip, as Mary knew from the journey over. This time it might be even harder because the earthquake had dislodged rocks that road gangs were probably still working hard to clear away.

Mary had no way of knowing if Jim had already caught a boat for the gold fields of Australia, but she hoped that, in time, he'd return, and they could take up their lives again together as a family. 'Dear God, let that be true,' she prayed as the team of horses started on their journey.

After Beth had farewelled Mary she made her way to the school, ready to begin helping Mrs Thompson. She knocked on the door of the schoolroom, heard the call "Enter" and went in to be greeted warmly.

"Ah there you are. How are you this morning? I suppose Mrs Smith has caught the coach. She's lucky they're going over the hill nearly every second or third day. They used to only travel once a fortnight but now they have the mail to carry they go as often as they can. I was just going to read the younger ones a story, then hear their reading, but you can do that. Take them outside into the sun. There are stools by the wall they can sit on. This is the book I was going to use but you may want to choose another."

"I like the look of this one. This will be fine," said Beth.

"Now children, you go out with Miss Goode. She's to be your teacher from now on. Just you primers, I mean. The rest of you get out your sum books. Today we're doing halves and quarters." Going to the blackboard she wrote several sums on it.

"Copy out these, do them and show your working out. Like this." She did the first one to show what she meant, then added some wood to the fire and hung the kettle over the flame on the large black hook which hung in the centre of the fireplace. It would be good to have someone to talk to that was not a child, or a parent with some complaint. 'Not that there's many of those around, thank the Lord,' she thought. Soon all she could hear was the singing of the kettle and the scratch of slate pencils on slates.

Outside, Beth Goode had a happy morning getting to know the children and their names, reading to them and hearing them read. Before she knew it the bell rang and it was lunchtime.

"Come and have a seat, Miss Goode," said Mrs Thompson as she poured a large cup of tea and offered her sugar and milk. "And do try one of my biscuits. It was a recipe of my mother's. Now, you must tell me about yourself. What have you been doing while you were in the Hutt?"

"I had some work minding children for a family, but they decided to return to Australia and I didn't want to go with them. I've been waiting for an opportunity to come over to visit the Johnsons. Mrs Johnson was so good to me on the boat. So when I found the Smiths were coming over here, I took the chance of finding work and came too."

"I'm glad you did. The school has grown and I was feeling I needed an assistant."

At the end of the school day, as the children made their way home, Cathy said Polly could ride Bonny for part of the way, so she and Jane could talk about the birthday tea on Saturday. Jake was a little ahead on Blueboy with Dennis running to keep up with him when suddenly, a hawk flew up and Bonny reared.

"Help me!" screamed Polly, hanging on for dear life and crying, as the pony gathered speed and set off up the road.

Luckily, Jake heard Polly and saw what was happening and turned Blueboy so he was able to catch the reins as Bonny cantered past, but it was a close thing. Cathy came running and talked quietly to Bonny to calm her down while Dennis dried Polly's eyes with a rather grubby handkerchief. "You're all right," he said. "You didn't even fall off."

"Don't cry, Polly," Cathy said. "Bonny didn't mean to frighten you. She didn't really. It was the silly hawk. How would you like to come to my house on Saturday with Jane?"

"Yes, that's a good idea - if it's all right with your mother," said Jane. "Now don't cry when you see Mam and Dada, Polly, or you won't get to ride Bonny ever again."

"Home already?" asked Kate, as Cathy and Jake came through the door. "Had a good day?"

Like the Kelly children, Jake and Cathy had decided it was best not to say anything about Bonny taking fright at the hawk - it had turned out all right, thanks to Jake's quick response, and Polly had come to no harm. "Yes Mother, Miss Goode came to teach the little ones. I didn't see much of her but the babies seem to like her," said Cathy. "Some of the little ones need a lot of help to read and write." Cathy gave her mother a winning smile. "Mother, can Polly come on Saturday with Jane? She could help you. Would that be all right?"

"Just what I need, a little helper in the kitchen," laughed Kate. "That's fine by me. I don't think she gets much fun these days. Now, about this special tea, what do you think we can make?"

"I don't know Mother; you're always making nice things to eat so I don't mind at all but I would like a cake," said Cathy.

"Oh I don't think we'll starve," said Kate. "I'll find something. You'll just have to wait and see."

After a long day working with Rangi and Ru, John came back to the house for the evening meal. He gave a sigh of relief as he removed his boots on the veranda, and sat in one of the chairs there. He was worried about wasting time building the home for the Smiths when he should've been working on the tree stumps left in the ground. He'd heard about some men using explosives to blow the stumps up, but didn't know enough about it to do so himself. 'I'll look into it,' he thought just as Kate called, "Dinner's nearly ready. And bring some more wood in for the fire, please Jake. You could cut some more kindling too. The box is getting empty. Have you locked the fowls away Cathy? You'd better do it before it gets dark. It looks as if it might rain again."

Later, John lay awake listening to the rain and wondering if the shingles on the whare roof would keep the water out. They'd made as good a job as they could, but they weren't experts by any means. He thought about his trip to town to read again the regulations regarding his purchase of the block he'd bought in Jim's name. He'd learnt that so long as he was living on his land and was not an absentee owner he could buy a block for his son. It was an option he hadn't realized was available, but could be the answer if Jim Smith didn't return within a reasonable time.

CHAPTER 35 Floods

Rain fell throughout the night. When John woke to a dismal dawn he thought it wise to look at the river to see if there was a likelihood of flooding. He soon saw it had become a raging torrent but not yet so high it was breaching its banks. 'I'd better shift the stock up to higher ground,' he thought, and returned to the house to wake Jake. "Saddle the horses while I tell your mother where we're going."

"Goodness, you're up early." Kate sat up, rubbing her eyes. "What's the matter?"

"It's the river. There's been so much rain up in the hills it's running a banker so we're moving the stock to higher ground. Don't worry. We won't be long."

"Oh I couldn't rest while you and Jake are out there in the rain. I'll get dressed and come out too," said Kate.

"No you won't," said John. "You'll do what I say for once. I don't want you falling over in the water while we're away down the other end of the farm coping with the cattle. You hear me?"

"Yes my lord and master," said Kate. "I suppose you're right. I'll start on breakfast and have a hot drink for you when you return."

"Do you think it'll be a bad flood?" asked Jake as he ran to get the horses ready for the muster. "If we had a dog it would be easier."

"We won't worry about that now, Jake. It won't take long to round up the cattle but sheep are silly things and can be hard to shift."

Their few head of cattle were lying down among the trees, but were very quickly hurried through the creek from the low-lying half of the farm to the higher ground which, in John's time on the property, had never been flooded. However, by the time they returned, the hoggets were up to their knees in the floodwater now pouring through a gap in the bank. From just a ripple of water when they started to move the stock, there was now a wide, fast-running stream. It was as if the river was cutting a new channel for itself.

"We'll have to walk the sheep the long way around the boundary," said John, dismounting. "They'll never be able to swim across the stream. You get down too, Jake and keep them moving along." Waving his arms and flapping his cape he shouted, "Ho, ho, ho!" until the sheep began to move with John and Jake urging them on until they were safely on the higher ground. "Throw some hay to the cattle, Jake; they'll be hungry."

<hr />

"So all's well?" a relieved Kate asked as they came through the door.

"So far," said John. "But I think the river's higher now than I've ever seen it."

"Goodness," said Kate. "I hope it doesn't reach the house. I've just got used to having a proper floor to walk on. I'd hate to see it covered in mud."

"It'll do whatever it pleases. That river has a mind of its own," said John as he sat down to eat. "I wonder if a stopbank will ever be built. There's talk of it but it would be a huge job. I'm not sure you children should go to school today. I'll decide when I have another look at the river and see if it's reached its peak."

After a hurried breakfast John left to inspect the river again. "School's out for you today," he said to the children as he returned to the house. "It looks as if the water's still rising. I'm going to put the sheep into the house paddock. The water has reached their bellies."

"What about my garden?" Kate was alarmed. "You know how the sheep love fruit trees. I don't want them chewed to pieces."

"I know dear. I'll put some branches around them for protection but I can't promise they'll survive. We'll have to put the dry goods in the store-room up high in case the river rises. Cathy, you'll have to move the books and stores in the barn if the water gets any higher. Put them anywhere you can. I'm going back to keep an eye on the water-level."

As he watched the rising water John became increasingly worried. He'd never seen it this high before in any of the three floods there'd been since he took up the land. Usually, when there was a deluge in the ranges, the river rose and fell in a few hours as a torrent of water rushed to join the Ruamahunga River on its way to the sea. This time though the water was steadily creeping over land he'd never seen covered before. He wondered how the new whare was faring in the flood. 'It should be all right' he thought. 'I picked the highest site available, but you can never tell what a river will do.'

Taking his knife, he marked a branch with the height of the water and made another a foot higher so he could see how much the water had risen in an hour's time.

Riding home again, he saw Kelly and O'bie coming towards him, driving their cattle to a higher part of their land. "What's the bank like over your way?" he called as they came near. "Is it going to hold?"

"No idea, Johnson. It's hard to say what the river's up to this time," Paddy called back and, as he came nearer, "I don't like the way it keeps rising. There's water all around our house and a foot deep in the sheds. There must have been a devil of a deluge in the ranges. How are you faring?"

"Not good at all. The sheep are standing in water a foot deep poor things. I've put them in the house paddock much to Kate's disgust, but there was nowhere else for them to go. I've never seen a flood reach those paddocks before. It must be a once in a hundred years flood," John said, lighting his pipe. "What about you and your family?"

"We've been through a few of these floods before, but the trouble starts when the water goes down and the paddocks are covered with silt. It's a lot worse now that so much of the bush has gone from the hillsides. The water can flow faster and it brings more soil with it as it tears along - and branches and rubbish left after the sawmill has been through. Then we'll have it all over the cleared areas we've just sown down. It's a trial," said Paddy.

"I don't know why we bother," said O'bie. "We must be mad to think we can make farms out of these blocks of land while the river runs wild."

"Oh, it's just another set-back," said John. "It's not the end of the world. Come over and we'll see if the water is still rising."

When the three men studied the rough gauge John had marked it was obvious the river was still on the way up. There was only about two inches of spare branch between the mark and the level of the water. "Thank goodness it's stopped raining, but my god!" John exclaimed. "It's risen about nine inches in less than half an hour. We'd better get back to the women."

"I'll keep a watch on the bank. If it shows any sign of breaking I'll let you know," said Kelly and he and O'bie continued on their way.

Meanwhile, Beauty had been standing quietly nibbling at titoki branches within her reach. John patted her neck but, before mounting, decided to have another look at his 'water-gauge' and was pleased to see the water-level had dropped a little.

As he approached the house a bedraggled Jake came to meet him, sloshing his way through foot-deep water. "I'm leaving the saddle on for now, son; I might need to ride out again in a hurry," John told him, tying the horse to a tree near the door. "But whatever have you been doing?"

"Keeping the sheep away from the fruit trees." Jake shook his coat and stamped his feet on the veranda to rid himself of water. "Mother said they'd ruin the young trees if they ate them so I had to keep them away. It wasn't so bad. They were happy to eat the cabbages instead. The water's going down isn't it?"

"Yes I think it is. How did you get on shifting the dry goods in the back room?"

"Fine father, we managed to move everything. We put things up on the beds."

Cathy came back from the barn where she had been stacking things out of the flood's reach. Like her brother she was a strange sight. She'd rolled her skirt up around her waist, exposing bare legs and feet covered with mud. Her hair was a wild thatch, like a bird's nest, with straw and seeds tangled in it.

"Whatever have you been doing Cathy?" asked John. "You look a sight."

"My dress was getting wet so I rolled it up to make it easier. I had to clean the rubbish off the shelves before I could put the books up on them. That's why I'm covered with dust. Now I'm cold," and Cathy shivered. "But I had to get the books up. Jane is coming over on Saturday and we're going to make a library with them so they can be borrowed. It's a special day for my birthday, remember," said Cathy. "I've been looking forward to it for weeks."

Laughing, John waded to the barn to see if things were up high enough. Cathy was a game little thing but she was only little and not able to reach up very high, but she'd done a good job and things seemed secure. Then he went to see how the sheep were doing and was pleased to see that the water was lower around them now. The peak must have passed. The saturated sheep were looking poor and miserable though. 'I'll put them back out into the main paddock. They'll be all right there now.'

Kate looked up as Jake came into the house. "What about the fruit trees? Did they eat any?"

"No. Father's shifting them out again into the other paddock so the trees will be fine now. I'm frozen," Jake said as he moved closer to the fire.

"Get your wet clothes off and I'll make you a drink. I've made a pot of soup too," Kate said. "I know I'm silly about the trees but it'd set my plans for our orchard back years if they're eaten to the ground. I'm really proud of them. They might even have fruit in a year or two. Won't it be lovely to pick peaches off our own trees?"

"I didn't mind Mother. It was funny watching the sheep trying to walk through the water, with their short little legs and the water pushing them around. They chewed on the cabbages though," said Jake as he removed his clothing. Just then his father and Cathy came in.

"Come on, sit down and have some hot soup," said Kate

"The water's nearly gone from the store-room now but the floor is very muddy and slippery." Cathy took her place at the table and warmed her hands around the mug of soup Kate placed in front of her. "Smells good," she said. "Better than the store-room does."

"It will take a while to dry out," her father said, "seeing it's just a dirt floor."

They sat around the table in companionable silence, sipping their soup. It was good to be together in warmth and shelter knowing the flood was receding and the worst was over.

After lunch John and Jake went out to look at the damage the flood had done. Logs and branches were stacked up against the post and rail fences, driven there by the force of the water. Debris was strewn over acres of land. It would take a lot of effort to clear the ground. It was heartbreaking.

"Well, we can't do anything here now," John decided. "We should go and see what can be done in the barn. I'd like to ride over and see how the Kellys are but I don't think I should put Beauty at risk of a broken leg. Those stump holes are treacherous. Go and unsaddle her and give her some hay, please Jake."

"Right, I will. I think the rain has finished for a while. I'll go and see if the harness and tackle is dry. I put it up as far as I could. I hope Mother's trees survive. They mean so much to her."

"It's a link with home for her; you know how she is. It's hard for her to be so far away from her family," said John.

⸺⸺⸻∞⸻⸺⸺

Next morning, with the children still home from school, John and Jake were surveying the paddocks close to the house when they heard horses approaching. Soon Rangi and Ru rode into the yard. "Good-day, boss," said Rangi. "Plurry bad flood, eh?"

"It was indeed Rangi," said John. "You shouldn't have tried to come out today. I thought you'd have had enough to keep you busy at the pa."

"No that's all right boss. We're not too bad, eh Ru? The stream came up and flooded the road but then it went down pretty quick. Not like you've had here," said Rangi.

"It'll take days to shift all the rubbish off the paddocks. I wish we had a sledge," John said. "It would make the job much quicker."

"You could make one boss," Ru said eagerly. "I've seen one at the neighbour's next to the pa, just a couple of lengths of wood for runners with some boards to make a deck. We could do that. It would go good in the mud too."

John laughed. "What are we waiting for?" And the three men went to the barn.

There they selected two long pieces of strong timber to build a frame to hold the deck, as well as devising a way of attaching chains to the runners. It didn't take Jake long to see what they were doing and he added his ideas as they went along.

Before long John told Jake to harness Bessie and bring her to the barn and they all proceeded to the paddock near the house to try loading some of the heaviest branches brought down by the flood onto the sledge. Soon they had quite a load which Bessie hauled to an area where the wood could dry out. They found if they kept the timber away from the front of the sledge it would ride over the muddy ground better. As the smaller rubbish would be better put in the wagon when the ground was drier they concentrated their efforts on moving the biggest branches away from the fences and repairing rails where they had come down. The sun came out warming their backs as they worked. "This is a good idea boss," said Rangi, heaving another big branch onto the sledge. "Plurry good idea."

⸺⸺⸻∞⸻⸺⸺

In the house Cathy was still worried about her birthday. "I wish we hadn't had the flood. It has spoilt everything. It will be all mucky in the barn now. We won't be able have a good look in the book boxes."

"Cathy," said Kate. "Why don't you wait and see? It might be a nice day. Then you can use a table outside and they'll all be out of harm's way. Tell you what, why don't we make the cake? Mrs Kelly gave me a new recipe, and I want to try it out."

"I suppose so," Cathy answered. "But I hate the rotten river."

"It's a lovely river Cathy. It's just doing what rivers are supposed to do. It has made a mess of the land but it can be cleaned up. Poor Waiohine, please don't blame her. Think of how you like to swim in her in the summertime. Now, for the cake we need some eggs. I hope we've got enough - we need three."

"Here you are," said Cathy. "I'm sorry Mother, I do love the river in the summer. What else do we need?"

"Just build the fire up and then I'll tell you," said Kate.

Outside, the men worked all afternoon and were glad when knock-off time came. John was pleased the sledge had gone so well and once again was glad he'd Ru and Rangi to work with. Jake had done well too, leading Bessie around the muddy paddock as the sledge slid easily over the silt, and avoiding stump-holes as much as possible.

Father and son made their way back to the house with Bessie. John told Jake to rub her down and give her a feed of oats. She'd done a great job this afternoon but there were four more paddocks to clear. 'Oh well, all in good time. The water's hardly off the ground and we've made good progress,' thought John as he went through the door. "That smells good," he said, sniffing the air.

"Well, you can't eat it Father," said Cathy. "It's my birthday cake."

"What a shame," said John. "Not even a little piece?"

"No," said Cathy and Kate together.

"How did the sledge go? Did it work?" asked Kate.

"Yes, very well. We shifted a lot of the biggest wood off the paddock. Ru and Rangi were a great help, and Jake too," said John.

"Tea's ready, so have a wash and I'll dish up. I wonder how Mary got on in Wellington, and when they'll get back. I'm so worried about her."

"She'll be all right. Mrs Parker will take good care of her. She might get seats for her and the children tomorrow or the next day," replied John.

"I hope she gets back soon," said Kate. "Meanwhile, set the table Cathy, and we'll have an early tea. I'm ready for bed."

In Greytown, people were counting their losses as they looked at where the river had cut through the road, turning the main street into a mess of gravel and mud. Large logs and branches lay strewn around gardens and empty sections. There would be weeks of work to get the town back to its tidy self. Talk of a stopbank to contain the river was on everybody's lips as they looked at the damage and tried to look on the bright side. It was hard to feel positive even when the sun came out.

"I've had enough, Johanna," said Henry as he looked at the floor of the stockroom which was deep in silt. "It's more than a man can stand."

"It's only dirt Henry. It'll dry out, be swept away and you'll forget about it."

"No Johanna. Not this time. I'm determined to build a new store well away from the bed of the stream and not get caught out again. I'll see the Town Board about getting a section up the other end of town. You wait and see."

"Wait until you've slept on the idea." Johanna Dickson undressed slowly and got into bed. She said her prayers for her mother and the rest of the family, wishing she knew how they were getting along in Australia. She never let Henry know how she missed them in case he thought she was sorry she'd married him. She wasn't, she loved him dearly, but building another store? Where would they get the money? Johanna was a good book-keeper and knew they didn't have a lot extra.

By nine o'clock next morning the sun was shining and Henry was feeling better even though there was flood debris and mud all around the village. He went along the street to talk to the blacksmith who was already shoeing a Clydesdale mare. "What have you got there? A blooming elephant?" asked Henry.

Fairman looked up as Henry came near, and let go of the horse's huge foot.

"She's a beauty all right. One of the station-owners down the valley brought her up to be serviced and thought he'd get her re-shod while she was here. She's a big girl isn't she?"

"You wouldn't want her to stand on your foot. That's for sure." said Henry. "Have you heard how people further down the valley got on in the flood?"

"Covered in water still I believe. The Ruamahanga was over the banks all down that way. Some stock losses, but it's going down," the blacksmith said as he lifted another of the great hooves to fit the next horseshoe on. "I feel sorry for them but I guess that's what happens when you live on a river bank. We could do with some protection around here though. The roads are a mess."

"What about the hill? Have you heard anything about how the coach got over to Wellington in the storm?" asked Henry. "I'm expecting Mrs Smith and her children back soon. She's going to help my wife in the store. Will you let me know if you hear any news of the coach?"

"I will Dickson, I will. Sooner or later someone will ride in from down Featherston way and fill me in on what's happening. It's great how fast news travels."

CHAPTER 36 Mrs Smith Returns

Early the next day Mrs Parker waved good-bye to Mary and the children as they left the Hutt on the Wairarapa coach, snuggled up in coats, rugs and scarves to keep them warm on the journey. Mary had resolved, now she knew her husband had a place on a ship and was working his passage to Australia, to concentrate on the future. She'd not been able to see Jim before he left Wellington but he had left a letter for her with the Parkers, along with the last of his money. Although she was now on her own, in a way she felt free. Free of the worry about Jim's next get rich scheme. She was satisfied she was doing the right thing. With a job to go to, a new friend in Miss Goode, and Kate and John to advise her, she felt things could only improve.

Most of the passengers were sitting close to each other to stop being thrown from side to side as they lurched along, and when one of the ladies said to Mary, "I'll come and sit by your little girl if you like. That will make her feel more secure," Mary gratefully accepted her kind offer.

The motion of the coach soon had the children asleep, and Mary was pleased to see that Marie's 'carer' had her arm around her, making sure she was safe.

The road wound its way across the boggy flats of Pakuratahi and, although the way was hard going, the coach soon reached the Mangaroas, the foothills of the Rimutakas.

Through the window could be seen bush-covered hillsides, lush and green. Pongas spread their fronds wide, with new growth curling up black and beautiful from the centre. Tall trees grew from the bottom of the valleys and pigeons could be seen feeding on berries, seemingly not at all worried by the passing traffic.

At the summit the driver stopped to speak with the men working at widening the road. Most of the road was one way so travellers had to watch carefully for places where they could safely pass each other. After he was assured there were no new hazards on the road ahead, the coachman started the descent.

At Featherston some of the travellers alighted, then the coach was soon on the way to Greytown. The river was subsiding after the flood so the ford was easily crossed.

Waiting at the stableyard, Miss Goode heard the clatter of the horses on the cobblestones as the coach approached, and soon the passengers began to climb down, stretching and yawning.

"I'm so pleased to see you," Mary called to Beth. "Could I pass Peter down to you? He was awake in Featherston but went back to sleep after we were across the river." Beth took hold of the sleepy boy and stood him up beside her, then she reached up to take Marie. Finally Mary was able to step down. "I'm so glad that's over," she said. "Thank you for meeting us."

"I'm pleased I could help - and we have some more help. Mrs Dickson has sent the shop cart to carry your luggage." Soon it and the children were loaded onto the cart drawn by a sturdy lad. The women walked alongside as they made their way to the boarding house.

"Be sure to thank Mrs Dickson for sending you to help." Mary turned to the boy as they reached the boarding house. "It has made things easier than I thought possible. And thank you too. What's your name?"

"Thank you Mrs Smith, my name is Billy Broome. Mr Dickson calls me Billy-the-broom for a joke as I have to sweep the floor several times a day," said Billy as he carried the bags to the door where Mrs O'Toole waited, then went to leave.

"Wait a minute," said Mary, feeling in her bag for a coin. But he didn't wait. Instead he jumped onto the cart and was away. "Fancy that!" she said. "Not waiting to get paid."

Once they had all eaten, Mary washed the yawning children then dressed them in their night clothes, a long night-shirt for Peter and an embroidered nightie for Marie. Soon they were settled, top and tail, in a small bed which Mrs O'Toole and Beth had brought from another room. Then the two women began to tidy their belongings, carefully storing them in the small amount of room available.

When she came across a flannelette nightgown, Mary shook it out. "I made this especially for when Jim and I were together in our new home here," she whispered, the tears running down her cheeks.

Watching Mary gave Beth a feeling of how a mother must feel when things take over and there is nothing that can be done for a child. "I think it's time for bed - you've had a difficult few days. It'll be better tomorrow," she said kindly.

"But first I have a suggestion. I hope it won't upset you. I've been thinking that if we are to live as closely as sisters, maybe we should, in private at least, address each other as sisters would. What do you think?"

"It's a splendid idea! And you can be 'Aunt' to the children, except of course at school." Mary smiled. "Oh, I feel so much more 'at home' now we are a family of sorts."

CHAPTER 37 Birthday Girl

Cathy's birthday had arrived at last but it couldn't be the day she'd planned. The flood had made such a mess in the stable there could be no looking in the boxes of books as she had planned.

Kate put bowls of porridge on the table as Jake fetched more wood for the fire. "We'll have to bring up some more logs for the stove," he told his father. "I've chopped most of the last lot and now there are only scraps left."

"Good lad," said John. "We'll bring more back tonight. Where's our birthday girl?"

"She's late getting up," said Kate as she sat down to eat.

"She's already up," said Jake. "I heard her get up quite early and go outside."

"What do you mean? Where can she be?" said Kate, rising from the table. "She said she wanted to go and meet Jane and Polly, but I didn't know she meant this early."

"I'll have a look outside," said John. "Jake, you go and see if Bonny is there."

"Yes Father. I'll go as soon as I've eaten my breakfast."

"No," said John. "You'll go now."

Reluctantly, Jake got up from the table and went out the door. "I can only see Blueboy from here, but I'll go and look," he called, jumping off the steps and running towards the barn. He was soon back. "Bonny's not in the paddock or stall."

"You'd better saddle up Beauty and Blueboy. We'll have to go and look for her. Silly girl," said John. "Don't worry Kate, we'll find her. She's most likely gone to the Kellys'. Just couldn't wait for them to arrive."

"Oh John I hope so, Bonny is very quiet but things can go wrong," Kate said, a worried look on her face. "She's a good little rider, but she's always had Jake there beside her, or very close."

Father and son were soon trotting along the road, looking for a sign of the pony or the girls. There was no sign of either. "I don't know, Jake," said John. "Do you think she would have gone through the bush the back way? That's the shortest route."

"We can go through the gate up there by the kowhais and have a look. She might just be at Kellys' waiting for the girls to get ready," replied Jake, scanning the bush for any movement.

"Let's go to the Kellys' before we panic," said John, and the two started along the road.

Suddenly, Jake thought about the near thing with Polly. "Father, the other day," he said in a sheepish voice, "when Polly was having a ride, a hawk flew out of the trees. Bonny bolted, but I caught her before she got very far. Polly wasn't hurt, so we didn't tell you. I'm sorry."

"I'm sorry that you didn't think to tell me, because I heard that Bonny's last owner's daughter was thrown and hurt. I need to know how the pony is behaving. You mustn't keep things like that to yourself."

Very soon they were at the Kellys'. Mr Kelly met them at the door. "Hello. Nice to see you. Got over the flood? Come in, come in."

"I'm looking for Cathy. She went out on the pony. I thought she might have come to meet the girls as they're coming over today. Has she been here?"

"Not as far as I know. I've been doing the milking. I'll ask. Jane," he called, "have you seen Cathy this morning?"

"No Dada, not yet," said Jane. "We're going there later on. Why?"

Paddy looked into the bedroom where the boys slept. Tessa was making the beds. "Have you seen Cathy this morning ?" he asked, but she shook her head as she came into the kitchen.

"Not yet. Why?" she looked at John for an answer. "Did she say she was coming over this early?" she asked.

"We're not sure Mrs Kelly. She's not in her bed and the pony's gone too. We thought she might have come over here already. I think we'd better go and look in the bush between our farms," said John.

"We'll come with you if you wait a moment," said Mr Kelly and he called to Dennis. "Young Cathy is missing, we need to go and look for her."

Where the farms met the bush was still thick on both sides of the boundary fence.

Jake rode on ahead, making for a stand of totara near the banks of the stream. Suddenly, he glimpsed something and, pulling Blueboy to a halt, he slid off to the soft ground, still boggy from the flood, and pushed his way through the undergrowth. Bonny was standing beside a big white pine. Near her, lying still on the ground, was Cathy.

Jake ran to her, shouting he had found her.

The two men and Dennis were soon there, and John knelt down by Cathy, feeling for a pulse. Oh the relief when he found it, faint but there. Cathy's eyes were closed and her face was white. "Jake, ride into town and ask Doctor McDonald to come out to the farm," ordered John. "Go quickly."

Jake was immediately up and off, racing through the bush and away up the road as fast as Blueboy could go, while Paddy looked at John, wondering what he could do to help. They had no way of knowing how badly the girl was hurt. John had taken off his coat and laid it over the still little body, thinking 'How can I get her home safely?' but suddenly he said, "I have it. We'll get the sledge we made to move the timber. If we put some blankets on it we can take her home that way."

"I don't know," said Paddy. "Maybe we shouldn't move her."

"She can't just lie here on the wet ground. She could catch her death of cold while we make up our minds. No, I know I'm right. Dennis, you go and get your mother to stay with her while I get the sledge harnessed up. Kelly, will you come and give me a hand as soon as your wife gets here?" He mounted Beauty and rode through the trees as quickly as he could, praying, 'Please God, keep Cathy safe'.

"Kate, Kate!" he shouted as he reached the yard. "We've found Cathy but she's been thrown from the pony."

Kate came out to the doorway wiping her hands on a cloth. "Oh John! Is she all right?"

"I've sent Jake for Doctor McDonald. We're going to try and bring her up to the house. On the sledge. Kelly's helping - he's sent Dennis to get Tessa to stay with Cathy while we get the sledge. She was unconscious when I left. I'm going to get Beauty hitched up. Can you fetch some blankets, love?"

Just then Paddy arrived and the two men quickly harnessed Beauty to the sledge. Kate came out with a bundle of rugs and a pillow. She laid some sacks down first then quickly made a bed. "I hope it's the right thing to do," she said to John. "Perhaps you should wait for the doctor. I'll put some wood on the fire to keep the house warm and then I'll be down."

"No, don't come down Kate. Wait here. We'll be back as soon as we can. You're not in any condition to come down there."

Kate returned to the house to feed the fire, anxious thoughts racing through her mind. This was not the birthday she'd planned for Cathy. 'What had possessed the girl to go off like that so early?' she wondered as she paced the floor and peered from the window.

The men were soon back to where Cathy lay, watched over by Mrs Kelly. Jane was there too. John saw she'd been crying and patted her arm in a comforting way. "We may need your help Jane," he said. "We'll have to lift Cathy very gently onto the sledge. It'll take all of us. We mustn't jolt her. If we slide a blanket underneath her by raising her a little, then once she is on it, if we each take a corner we can carefully lift her onto the sledge with as little movement as possible. Understand?"

He looked around the group to see if they realised how crucial it was to be steady and sure with the task. They all nodded and then began to lay the blanket out on the ground. Cathy never moved as they watched John feeling again for a pulse.

Taking a grip on Cathy's clothing, at the count of three, they raised her slightly off the ground. Dennis quickly arranged the blanket under Cathy's body then she was gently lowered on to it.

"Now take a corner each and we'll lift her onto the sledge, again at the count of three," said John. "One, two, three." They took the strain evenly and moved a little at a time until they were over the improvised bed. "Right, slowly down. Good. Kelly, can you guide the horse? Mrs Kelly, you and Jane can walk alongside and hold her hands. I'll walk behind and keep her head from moving any more than necessary. With luck the doctor will be at the house by the time we get there. All ready? Good, let's go."

Paddy took the the bridle, telling Beauty it was time to move. She looked at him with her big brown eyes as if she understood that a lot of patience was required of her, and went forward carefully.

Because the ground was still very damp the sledge moved over the ground easily, but it was a slow journey. John was almost bent double as he walked along, keeping Cathy's head steady. Bonny seemed to know she was in disgrace and followed at a distance.

As they neared the house they could hear the sound of hooves on the gravel road and reached the yard at the same time as Jake and Dr McDonald. Jake took charge of the horses as the doctor greeted John and Kate and studied Cathy. "Let's get her inside," he said. "Can you lift her off the sledge the same way you put her on please?"

Everyone took their places and they carried Cathy to her bedroom and placed her on the bed. There Dr McDonald examined Cathy thoroughly. Apart from bruises, only her left arm seemed to be broken, near the wrist. It was her head that gave him the most worry and he carefully felt it, looking for signs of fractures but there was nothing obvious.

"I'll sit with her," he said. "I want to wait till she comes around. When did this happen do you think?" Kate and John looked at each other. It was a mystery.

"I heard her get up early," Jake said. "But I don't know the time for sure. It must have been about seven o'clock."

"So she might have been unconscious from about seven-thirty or thereabout?"

"Yes, about that time," said Jake. "It would have taken her a while to catch Bonny and saddle her, so that's about right."

Jake and the Kelly children were gathered about the doorway to the kitchen where Tessa was making a cup of tea for the doctor. James, who had hobbled all the way from their house with Polly after their mother had gone to help, wanted to know what had happened.

"It's Cathy," said Jane. "Bonny threw her off. She hasn't woken up yet. The doctor is with her now."

"Will she be all right? It's her birthday today," said Polly "Will she still have her special tea?"

"Not today, Polly," said Jane, putting her arm around her little sister. "Let's just wait and pray she gets better."

James was listening to what all the children were saying. "Do you think she'll die?" he asked. "Like Patrick?" He balled his fists and rubbed his eyes, trying to stop the tears. He missed his big brother so much.

"We just have to wait and see. I'll ask Mam what she thinks," said Jane and went into the kitchen. "How is she Mam? Will she get better?"

"We don't know yet. Doctor McDonald is hopeful she'll come round soon and then he can assess her better. The brain is a funny thing, but while she's asleep it's mending. Well, we hope so anyway. You'll have to pray very hard that she'll wake up and be fine."

"That's what I told the others," said Jane. "Jake said he was lucky the doctor was in. He'd just come back from delivering twins out in the country and his horse was still saddled up. He came straight away."

Just then the men came back from the stables where they'd been unhitching the sledge. The kitchen was full of worried people, all sitting quietly, hoping for the best. Mrs Kelly put her arm around Kate as the doctor came into the room.

"She's still unconscious, but I think you should sit and talk to her. Some doctors believe people can hear even when they are unconscious. Read her a story or sing to her; you can all take turns. Keep her warm and if there's any change send Jake to get me."

The five children watched as he disappeared down the track to the road.

"I think he should have stayed a bit longer," said Jake. "He didn't really do anything for Cathy at all."

"I think he should have stayed too," said Dennis. He kicked a stone along the path where they were standing. "It's not fair. Cathy was only going for a ride like she does every day to school." Polly and James started to cry, but just then Kate came outside with a jug of milk and some biscuits.

"I suppose you missed breakfast with all the goings-on," she said, handing around the food. "There, there Polly, I'm sure Cathy will recover. Your mother is reading to Cathy from one of her favourite books right now. So just go and play. We can't all be miserable can we?" Her voice didn't sound real, even to herself. Just then the sun came out from behind a cloud. "See, even the sun thinks she'll be all right."

Suddenly, John's voice could be heard from the bedroom where he had been stroking Cathy's hair while Mrs Kelly was reading. "Kate, Kate, Cathy's awake, she's back."

Kate ran to see for herself. "How are you darling?" she asked, bending to kiss Cathy's cheek. "You gave us a fright. How are you feeling?"

"I'm thirsty Mother," whispered Cathy. "And my head's sore." She sank back on to the pillow. "I remember Bonny running fast. I thought she was going to try and jump the rails. I don't remember anymore."

"I'll get you a drink, dear, and Jane can bring it to you. You must just stay in bed and rest," said Kate while John looked at his little girl and prayed she wouldn't have any lasting injuries.

When Jane came into the room with a drink of warm milk she knelt by the side of the bed. "Happy birthday Cathy," she said. "How do you feel now?" She looked at her friend's bruised face, "I see you've spoilt your beauty for a while, does it hurt?"

"I thought Bonny was going to jump the rails. I was scared." Cathy drank thirstily then gave a little smile and shivered as she lay back on the pillows and closed her eyes.

"I think we should leave her to sleep, Jane," said John. "Doctor McDonald is coming back this evening to see to her arm. I think sleep is what she needs. Thank you so much for all your help."

Kate looked around the kitchen at their friends. "I don't know what we would have done without you. Now children, I want you all to come back another day, and we'll have a cake to celebrate."

"Come on you lot, let's get you all home," said Mr Kelly as he looked at the sad faces of his children. "I'll find some jobs for you to cheer you up."

"Thank you Mrs Johnson," said Tessa. "We'll come by tomorrow to see how she is." They walked slowly away, thinking what a long morning it had been. At dinner that evening Paddy gave thanks for the family he had, and offered a prayer for Patrick, his poor lost boy.

CHAPTER 38 Visitors

Rangi made his way to the farm with a heavy heart. He knew what it was to lose a child and he prayed to his old people to ask God to protect this child from harm. As he rode past the Kellys', he saw Kelly and called to him. "Doctor McDonald said Cathy'd fallen off her horse and hit her head. He only told me because he knew that I work for Mr Johnson. Have you heard how she is today?" he asked, reining in his horse.

Paddy shook his head. "No, we're going over there later on, but we've heard nothing since yesterday."

"I'm going out there to see if there is anything I can do," said Rangi. "I know it's Sunday but the boss may need a hand with the animals. I quite like looking after stock. I'd like to farm myself one day," said Rangi.

"Good on you Rangi. No reason why you shouldn't. A big strong bloke like you could do well." 'Maori or not,' thought Paddy, 'we should all get a fair deal.'

John was sitting on the veranda as Rangi rode up. "Morning Rangi, you shouldn't have come all the way out here today. It's Sunday," he said.

"We all want to know how Cathy is. How is she boss? Is there any change?"

"Yes, she woke up last night then went into a deep sleep. She's a better colour this morning. I'm waiting for her to wake up so I can see her then get about my chores."

"That's why I came out boss, so I can look after the animals for you. I know Jake is capable, but I thought I might be able to help," said Rangi as he tied his horse to the old titoki tree. "Now, what is there that needs doing?"

"First come and see Cathy for yourself," said John.

"Good morning Missy," Rangi greeted Kate. "How is Cathy?"

"We don't know yet. She seems to be asleep. The doctor will come again this morning. While she sleeps the body is repairing itself isn't it? We're trying not to wake her," said Kate.

After John told Jake to go with Rangi and move the stock into a new paddock where there might be more grass free of the silt from the flood, he returned inside to hear Kate talking to Cathy. So she was awake. That was marvellous! He hurried to the bedroom and hugged her. She looked very pale and frail. "How are you?" he asked, looking at the large bruise on her forehead. "Do you know how lucky you are?"

Cathy smiled faintly and patted John's shoulder, with her right arm. The left arm still hung at an angle though. The doctor had put a temporary splint on it but not very tightly as it was swollen. "Is it very sore, dear?" he asked, pointing to her arm.

"It aches but it's not too bad," she said and tried to raise it. "Ouch," she said, lowering it back to the pillow.

"Doctor McDonald will be here soon. He'll fix it up for you." said John. "You just stay in bed until he's seen you. Do you want some breakfast?"

"I'm hungry," replied Cathy, "but I'm more thirsty."

"I'll get Mother to see to you," said John. "I have to go and do some work. Rangi came to say hello. He's out helping Jake with the cattle. He'll call in before he goes home."

As John went to see where Rangi and Jake had got to he heard an approaching horseman and Doctor McDonald appeared on the pathway from the road.

"How's the lass?" he asked. "Awake?"

"Yes, thank God," said John. "She's looking better and she's thirsty."

"I'm glad to hear that. Sometimes in these cases there is bleeding in the brain that can cause big problems. I'll take a look to see what I can do for the arm."

Kate led him to Cathy. "How are you this morning?" he asked her. "How's the arm?"

"It's a bit sore if I move it," replied Cathy. "It just aches."

"I've brought a wooden splint I'll put on your arm. It's there to help the bone grow back around the break. No riding for a while for you. You'll have to walk to school when you're well enough to go back. Understand, my dear? Mrs Johnson, I'll need you to hold her arm steady." He brought a roll of plaster from his bag, and the wooden splint. It would need to go right over her hand as well as the lower part of the arm and was in two parts. He carefully laid her wrist on one piece of the splint, which had a soft layer of cotton wool to shield the muscles, then held her arm in position to make a good fit. With the top of the splint in place, he wrapped plaster around and around to make a tight sheath to provide protection and stop movement.

"Can you move your fingers?" he asked. Cathy wriggled her fingers slightly. "That's good," he said. "Just watch it in case it's too tight. It might need to come off. It's hard to tell how tight to make it when it's still swollen. It could be sore for a while."

"I'll make you a cup of tea, doctor," said Kate.

"I'd love a cup of tea. How are you?' he asked. "This must have been a real ordeal."

"I'm fine," said Kate as she made the tea. "I'm just glad she's going to be all right."

"Well don't overdo it. You know you had that turn a while ago. Are you still taking the tonic?"

"Yes. I feel much better now and John is so helpful even when he has so much to do. He just gets on with what needs doing as and when he can. Rangi came out this morning to give him a hand. He's such a good help."

"I know Mrs Johnson, that's why I told him about Cathy's accident. I knew he'd be worried." The doctor looked at the sky through the doorway and said, "Well I must get on, I have one other visit to make while I'm out this way. Oh, by the way, I thought you'd like to know that Mrs Smith and the children are back from Wellington. They're staying with Miss Goode at Mrs O'Toole's."

"Oh, I'm so pleased! I've been worried about how things were going for them. Thank you Doctor!"

As Kate farewelled the doctor she saw the Kelly family approaching in the distance and hurried inside to tidy up a little. 'Bother,' she thought. 'I could've done with a little time with just Cathy.' She went to welcome them. "She's better," she said. "I'm just boiling her an egg. Do come in."

Mr and Mrs Kelly came into the kitchen but told the children to stay outside. "We're not here for long. We just wanted to see how Cathy is. I thought we'd call early then we're going to church," said Tessa. "We've bought a horse and wagon from the O'Malleys and we're going to pick it up on the way. Jane was wondering if she could stay with Cathy, but I'm not sure that's a good idea."

"Doctor McDonald has been and set the break in her arm. He's very pleased with her but said she needs plenty of rest," said Kate. "It was so good of you to help yesterday. Do come and see Cathy."

As Kate ushered them through the doorway into the back room, Cathy opened her eyes and smiled. "Hello," she said. "Is Jane here too?"

"Yes, she's waiting to see you. You gave us a nasty scare, but you look so much better today. Don't you agree Paddy?" asked Tessa.

"Yes she does. Thanks be to God and his Blessed Mother Mary," said Paddy. "Now, let Jane have a go at seeing the invalid then we'll be off."

Kate gave the tray she had prepared to Cathy. "What do you think? Would you like Jane to stay with you for a while?"

"Oh yes please Mother. It's so boring lying here. We can read a few books and talk. If I get tired she can help you while I have a rest," said Cathy, looking pleadingly at her mother.

"All right then," said Kate. "But no high jinks. Just read quietly. Now have this egg before it gets cold."

Kate offered the Kellys some tea but Paddy said, "No thank you, we must get over to pick up the wagon. It will be so good to have transport again. The poor man who sold it to us had an accident and hurt his leg and it's been slow to heal so he can't work for a while. He has a buggy and the wagon, so sold us one as he's a bit short of the readies. Thank goodness, he has an older boy who's helping so they're just keeping on trying to make a living. I feel sorry for him but that's the way things go, isn't it?"

James and Dennis and Polly were waiting outside so Kate let them go to the door of Cathy's room to see her. "Happy birthday for yesterday," said Dennis.

"Yes, yes. Happy birthday Cathy," echoed James and Polly. Then they were all gone, walking quickly towards the farm where they'd become the proud owners of a wagon and a nag to pull it.

———— ✺ ————

"It's not much of a wagon but we'll all fit on it," said Paddy as they neared the O'Malleys'. Paddy introduced his wife to the settler who was sitting in a chair outside the door resting his leg on a stool. "How's the leg?" he asked. "Getting better?" The man winced as he tried to get up.

"Don't get up," Tessa protested, and walked over to shake his hand.

"I'm pleased to meet you," he said. "I've seen Paddy around but never knew he had such a pretty wife."

"That's enough blarney from you," said Paddy. "Here's the cash I promised you. I hope I got the best of the bargain. I sold a couple of young steers to the butcher for this."

"That's fine. I'll manage with the buggy for a while. You'll be kind to the old mare, won't you? She's quiet and reliable but old by horse standards. I wouldn't have sold her if I had the choice. Good doing business with you Kelly."

"You too," replied Paddy as he motioned to the family to get on the wagon and settle themselves for the ride into town. Church was to be at eleven and it was ten o'clock already. He clicked his tongue and they moved off along the road, with a rattle of the wagon's backboard and a swish of the horse's tail. Dennis and James sat on the seat next to Paddy while Polly was sitting moodily with her mother at the back.

"What's the matter with you?" asked Tessa, looking at the scowl on Polly's face.

"I wanted to stay with Jane and Cathy. It's not fair," said Polly.

"You know very well that I only let Jane stay because Cathy wanted her too. You'll see her soon enough, don't worry."

The ride into town was uneventful. The old horse plodded along at an easy gait. She was used to the journey and hardly noticed the change of driver. Dennis begged to have the reins, but Paddy erred on the side of caution and told him to wait for another occasion.

A few people outside the church-house greeted them with smiles and the new resident priest greeted them. Dennis and James went to talk to their friends, but Polly hung around her mother and wouldn't let go of her long skirt. Tessa couldn't understand her shyness. Polly had always been an out-going girl. "What's the matter with you Polly?" she asked. "Go and see your friends."

"Don't want to," said Polly, as two little girls came up to speak to her. She hid her head and wouldn't even say hello.

"I'm sorry girls," said Tessa, "I don't know what's wrong with her. Well, no, I think I do. She wanted to stay with Jane and Cathy, but I thought Cathy shouldn't have too much company after her accident."

"What accident?" asked the older of the two. Tessa proceeded to fill them in on the details. "The poor girl is lucky to be alive," she said.

"Poor Cathy. Will she be all right?" they asked in unison.

"We hope so. Look, Father Brady is ready, we'd better go in." Tessa went to sit with Paddy and the boys. Polly looked at her mother then walked back and sat down beside the other girls with a scowl on her pretty face.

The chatter after Mass was full of Cathy's fall. Everyone hoped she'd fully recover. Paddy fielded many questions about the accident and their shifting Cathy on the sledge.

As it was Sunday, the Dicksons' store was closed, but Tessa wanted to see Mrs Dickson and tell her about Cathy. Paddy stopped the horse outside their door and jumped down from the wagon. "You children can run and play for a little while," he said. "Listen for my whistle when we're ready to leave."

Johanna Dickson was shocked to hear about Cathy. "I can hardly believe it. Mrs Johnson must have been sick with worry."

"She was, but this morning she looked more relaxed. Cathy is resting. Jane stayed there as company for her."

"I'm glad to hear that," said Johanna. "Now, did you know that Miss Goode starts officially at the school tomorrow? The trustees approved her position last night. The school roll has grown so quickly with all the new people in town. And we're so busy in the store - I'm looking forward to Mrs Smith coming to help me."

Just then Henry came in. "I've just seen your new wagon. You're not setting up in opposition are you?" he said with a laugh.

"Not at all," said Paddy. "We'll be pleased to have you call anytime. I don't know what we'd have done without your delivering our supplies the last while. Thank you again. Now, if you're ready Mrs Kelly we'll be off." And he gave a deafening whistle to call the children.

"You'll wake the dead, Paddy," Tessa said. When the children came running, calling goodbyes to their friends, Polly was smiling. Tessa was pleased to see she was over her grumps. "Did you have a good time?" she asked as they climbed aboard.

"Oh yes," said Polly. "There's a new family with a girl just the same age as me and her birthday is only a week after mine. I think we'll be best friends."

"That's nice," said Tessa, relieved that her daughter was back to her old smiling self. "What's her name?"

"Olga Peterson. She's from another country, Sweden, wherever that is."

"You'll have to ask Mrs Thompson to show you on the map. It's above Ireland," said Tessa. "In Scandinavia," she added as Paddy shook the reins and they set off.

"Will we ever go home to Ireland?" asked Dennis.

"I doubt it Dennis. Remember how long it took us to get out here. Well, I suppose you don't remember much about the journey. You were only about four."

"I remember Ireland," said Dennis. "We had a house, cows, pigs and everything."

"Perhaps when you get old enough to travel you might go back and see the old place, me boy," said Paddy. "I don't want to go back. I'm happy here, but it would be nice to see my friends again. To sit in the pub, have a drink of Porter and watch the sun go down over the sea, would be wonderful."

Paddy puffed on his pipe and urged the old horse along the road, thinking on the things that had driven them to leave their home where the family had lived for hundreds of years. However, as he neared the house he lifted his thoughts to the present day and thanked God for the life he'd found here. Patrick's death would haunt them forever but life must go on.

Jane and Cathy spent the morning quietly reading. Cathy was propped up with pillows and Jane sat in a chair next to her. They were talking about the accident as Kate came in with a drink for them. "How are you feeling?" she asked Cathy as she placed glasses of milk on the box by the bed.

"Not bad," said Cathy. "My head still hurts and my eyes are funny."

"I don't think you should be reading if your eyes are bad. Let Jane read to you or have a sleep when you've had your drink," said Kate. "What about your arm dear?"

"It just aches." said Cathy looking miserable.

Kate looked at Jane. "I think perhaps you should go home now Jane, and let Cathy rest. You've had a good morning together and your folk should be back from Mass now."

"Yes Mrs Johnson," replied Jane. "It's been good sitting here with Cathy but I know she's tired."

"Before you go we'll have a piece of birthday cake. I finally got it iced this morning." Kate brought the cake into the bedroom with one big candle burning on top. "Make a wish Cathy."

Rangi and John had been busy clearing the rubbish from around the fences so they could make good the flood damage. The ground was so wet and boggy that the cows needed to only push against a post for the rails to fall out of position onto the ground. They worked steadily, then when they were sure the cattle were secure they made their way back to the house. John arrived at the veranda just as Jane was leaving. "Going home Jane?" he asked as they passed.

"Yes Mr Johnson. Cathy is tired and is going to rest. I'll come and see her tomorrow after school if that's all right?"

"That's a good idea Jane," said John as he went inside. "Thank you for being here. I know Cathy wanted you to stay." 'She's a nice girl,' he thought as he went to see Cathy. He found her curled up fast asleep.

Kate made a fresh cup of tea and set down bread, cheese and pickles for lunch. "Where's Jake?" she asked.

"Out in the stable doing something, I guess. I'll call him." He went to the door, gave a whistle and waited.

"He's not a dog," laughed Kate, but within a minute or two Jake arrived at the door, taking off his muddy boots as he went.

"I'm starving," he said as he sat at the table.

"Don't talk too loud," said Kate, "Cathy's asleep."

"Poor Cathy, she didn't have much of a birthday, did she?" said Jake, as he helped himself to bread and butter, slices of mutton and pickle.

"We cut the cake while Jane was here," said Kate.

"Oh good," said Jake. "Can I have a piece?"

"Eat what's on your plate first," laughed Kate. She reached out and took a piece herself. "I'm hungry too. We hardly ate at all yesterday, so let's make up for it today."

The sun was shining like a brand new penny when Kate woke early next morning. As she walked out on to the veranda and stretched her arms up to the sky she felt the baby kicking a good morning greeting. 'Not long now,' she thought.

Three deep breaths of fresh morning air gave her the energy to begin preparing breakfast. A quick peep into the children's room showed they were still asleep. 'It's a blessing to have only the house cow to milk,' she thought. 'Winter is nearly over. The cows will be calving soon, and then the year's work will begin all over again. Ah well, that's the way of farming.'

John came out of the bedroom, dressed and ready for work. Going to the barrel outside the back door he washed in the ice-cold water. He looked closely at Kate who was stoking the fire, to see how she'd weathered the trials of the past few days and thought, 'Poor lass, she didn't need this.' "How's Cathy?" he asked.

"She's still asleep. I want her to stay that way if she can. I'll wake Jake up so he can go to school but Cathy won't be going for a while."

"Indeed not," said John. "That was a nasty fall. We're lucky she came out of it without more injuries. Not a good way to celebrate her birthday."

"I've bought her a new book. I'll give it to her when she wakes up. That will keep her entertained," said Kate.

"What about you?" asked John "How do you feel after all the excitement?"

"I'm fine love, don't worry about me. The babe has been doing his exercises today. Won't be long now," she said.

"I want you to go to the store after school and get the mailbag, Jake," his mother told him at breakfast-time. "You can tell Mrs Dickson how Cathy is this morning. Miss Goode will be at school today, so be nice to her, and Peter and Marie, the Smith children, should be there too. I'm counting on you." Kate looked at Jake to see if he had taken in the message. "Don't talk about them to the other children as it's not our business. You've heard things that have happened, like Jim leaving but I forbid you to say anything about it."

"Oh Mother, I know that! You don't need to lecture me. You told me that Aunt Mary will be at the shop, and her children might be at school but I won't say a thing." Jake was a bit upset that his mother would think she had to tell him not to gossip.

Cathy called from the bedroom as Jake was about to leave for school. He looked in the doorway and asked how she felt. She looked very pale as she tried to stand up. "I'm a bit shaky still," she said. "Tell them I'll be there tomorrow, I hope."

"We'll see about that," said Kate. " How are you feeling today?"

"I feel wobbly when I try to stand up," said Cathy.

"You've been in bed for two days hardly moving so that's to be expected," said Kate. "Now let's get you to the long-drop then find you something nice to eat." She put one arm around Cathy and helped her to stand. The arm in the splint was hanging heavily so Kate took a scarf from a drawer, tying it around Cathy's neck to make a sling.

"That's better, isn't it?" she asked. "That will take the weight off your hand and keep your arm steady."

"Yes Mother, thank you. That's a lot better."

"Now what would you like? Are you hungry?" asked Kate hopefully.

"Not really Mother. Just a drink will do," she said.

Kate poured Cathy a drink of milk, adding some sugar. Then she sat down to eat her own bowl of oatmeal.

"Mother, I've changed my mind. Can I have a piece of toast and honey, please?" Cathy smiled. "Father was so clever to find the hive, and brave too, with all those bees around him."

"Yes he was, but it's nearly all gone now. We'll have to get him to find some more for us." Kate spread the honey on to the toast and offered it to Cathy. "It's so good for you too. You know some people call New Zealand the 'Land of Milk and Honey' don't you?"

"I thought it was called the 'Land of the Long White Cloud'.

"Well it's that too. That's what the Maori name 'Aotearoa.' means. When the canoes first arrived the land was covered in cloud. Now what do you want to do today? Read your new book?" Cathy nodded.

"You can sit on the veranda in the sun and I'll get on with my work. Tomorrow I want to drive in to town so I might take you to school in the buggy, and call on Mrs Harvey. It's been weeks since I promised your father I'd call and see her."

"We're getting a dog from them aren't we?" asked Cathy.

"Yes that's right, a pup. It should be big enough now. I could pick that up couldn't I? Clever girl," said Kate. Cathy settled herself down to read and Kate went to hang out the washing. She looked around the garden which was beginning to show some bud movement on the little fruit trees. Snowdrops were happily flowering among the marigolds, and bright gold daffodils lifted their heads up. Kate felt good about the world. They'd been so lucky with Cathy. It could quite easily have been so different.

CHAPTER 39 Earning and Learning

In the village it was time for Mary and Beth to take up their new roles. They woke early and dressed the children in their tidiest clothes. Mary was not sure if Marie would be able to go to school too. She knew some men didn't hold with too much learning for girls. Most of the schools had more boys than girls. Several schools were starting up in outlying areas after the government made grants available. Families had to contribute money too. While this was quite a burden, most were keen for their boys to be taught.

As they trooped down to the school together, the children's eyes were everywhere, looking at the animals in the paddocks, and the sparks that could be seen coming from the blacksmith's anvil. They were fascinated by the huge man who stopped to greet them. When told Peter's name, he laughed a huge laugh and roared with delight as he shook Peter's hand. "Good luck to you lad," he said. Peter rubbed his hand down his trouser leg to remove the dirt left behind in the handshake, but he stood tall and proud to be sharing his name with this giant.

When they reached the schoolhouse Mary told Peter, "I'm coming in with you to see Mrs Thompson before I go to the store."

Peter just shrugged his shoulders. He didn't know why he had to go to school, he never had to before. He held tightly to his mother's hand as they entered the school. All the children were sitting quietly as Mrs Thompson called the roll, answering one by one as she looked around the room. Jake said that Cathy was away today but should be back tomorrow.

"How is she Jake?" asked Mrs Thompson. "I heard about the fall and that she broke her wrist. Is she getting better?"

"I think she is. I only saw her for a few minutes this morning so I don't really know," said Jake.

"You give her our best wishes Jake, won't you?" said Mrs Thompson.

Mary and Beth had been standing at the door waiting for Mrs Thompson to finish the roll. Now they came in to see what she thought about Marie staying in class.

"I don't know, Mrs Smith. The school board is told what to do by the government. They've passed such a lot of rules that the school boards have to be very careful or they'll not get the grant towards our wages. We're not allowed to hold any religious meetings in the building and yet that was one of the reasons it was built. I think it would be best if she didn't begin until she's five."

Marie pulled a face and Mary was quick to give her a frown as a warning not to make a fuss. "And this is Peter," said Mary, pulling Peter forward. "Peter, this is Mrs Thompson. She's to be your teacher. You're to do whatever she tells you."

Peter said a polite "How-do-you-do," but his face said it all. 'I don't want to be here.'

"I'm here too, Peter," said Beth. "So you'll be fine and able to read and write in no time. Now what would you like me to do Mrs Thompson?"

"We will divide the children up between us, Miss Goode. I'll take the older ones and you can have these littlies." Mrs Thompson pointed to five children sitting on a mat before the fire. "With Peter you'll have six. Tell Miss Goode how old you are children. She's to be your teacher now; be sure to do what she says. You start Polly." Polly stuck out her chest and said in a loud clear voice, "I'm Polly Kelly and I'm six."

"No you're not," said Dennis who was next. "You're five. I'm seven. I'm Dennis Kelly."

"I'll be six soon," said Polly who was not to be beaten.

Beth looked at the plump round face and thought this one will be a challenge. "Next please," she said.

"Olga Petersen, I am six yars of age."

"Years, not yars dear," said Beth. "We will have to work on your English."

"Please, what is, work on?" said Olga in a worried voice.

"I just meant that we will practise your pronunciation," said Beth. "You're doing very well to speak English at all."

Mrs Thompson then suggested that her new assistant could do some sums with the children. "Simple additions like counting blocks. Singing the alphabet is a good way to help them remember where the letters come, but you can do that outside where we don't have to listen," she laughed. "I'll get on with the older ones. Where did we get to with the story about Captain Cook finding New Zealand?" she asked. The children looked at the book and found the place. "Now you read please, Jane, from page four."

Soon all were engrossed in the story of the sailing ships that had travelled half way around the world and discovered the islands of the Pacific. Beautiful tropical islands with people just like our Maoris, she told them. After a while she asked them stories about the journeys they themselves had had on their way to New Zealand. Hardly any of them had been born here. Two were born on ships on the way out. They couldn't remember anything about the boat but did remember the time they'd spent in Wellington before coming over the hill.

Mrs Thompson told them about the journey she'd taken with her husband in 1858 from England to South Africa, where they had stayed some years before coming to New Zealand. They'd taken a trip into the hinterland of South Africa and had seen lots of wild animals from a 'hide,' a shelter that looked like a bushy tree, that did not let animals know they were there. They'd ridden out on horseback and then the horses were taken away to safety, before she and her husband spent the night in the bush. They were near a water hole where zebras and elephants came down to drink.

The children were very interested and asked lots of questions. None of them had seen any wild animals except in books and paintings. Mrs Thompson wanted to show them the size of the elephants, so she got the children to stand, then she placed them in groups, one for the trunk, two for the front legs and shoulders, two in the middle for the belly, standing on chairs, then four at the end for the back legs. She told them to imagine that they were the parts of the whole elephant.

"Now you know how big an elephant is," she said. Just then Miss Goode came through the door with the little ones. "I'm showing the children how big an elephant is. We were talking about when I was in South Africa. You can all go outside for your playtime now," she told the children.

"I'll make us some tea," said Beth, taking the kettle off the hook over the fire.

"Thank you Miss Goode. I got carried away with my memories. I can hardly ever bear to talk about that trip because that's where my husband caught a fever; he died soon after we came up here, but the children's enthusiasm took me by surprise. I could almost smell the bush. How did your morning go?"

"Very well I think. They're a bright lot. We talked about their families and each drew a picture of their house, as well as they were able to. Polly Kelly seems to have taken to Olga Petersen. I hope they'll be good friends. It must be strange to be in a new country with a new language to learn. Polly told us about losing her brother Patrick and how much she misses him."

⸺∞∞∞⸺

Down at the store, Marie was out of the way of customers behind the counter, building a tower with some blocks of wood. She loved the smell of the dry goods even though they made her want to sneeze. In big drums dates, sultanas, candied peel, brown sugar and raisins all added their aroma to the air.

"Leave that Mrs Smith and come and have a drink of tea," Mr Dickson said as he carried yet another box of groceries out to the wagon. "I want to get going soon, but we must get to know each other. Take a seat and tell me how you think you'll like living here."

"Everyone is so kind and helpful I'm sure I'll like it very well. It was good of you to send Billy Broome to help us with the luggage," said Mary. "It made things so much easier. The children were so tired I thought I'd have to carry them to Mrs O'Toole's, plus the bags and boxes. "I only knew the Johnsons when we came here, but now I've met lots of people. Even here in the store, people have been wishing me well." She placed her cup on the table and prepared to go back to work.

"Here, I've something for you," Henry said. "It came in the mail this morning." He held a letter out to her. Mary gasped as she saw that it was from Jim. A range of feelings raced through her. Happiness, sadness, fear and regret for what might have been filled her with apprehension. "Take some time if you like, I know you'll want to read it."

"Thank you but I'll wait until I get home, I can't face it yet. I don't suppose you can understand. I do want to know how he is so I can tell the children that he's happy and doing what he wants to do, but it can wait."

"Just as you like, my dear," said Mr Dickson, taking out his pipe and filling it ready for the journey to the country. "I'll be off then. Don't let them put anything over on you. Take good note of anyone who wants tick. Don't say no, but ask them for their addresses. Get them to sign if they can, or make their cross. Most of them are honourable, but you never know."

"I'll be very careful and ask your wife if I've any doubts," said Mary and she went to attend to a customer. "Good morning. What can I get you?"

The lady looked at Henry, wondering where Johanna was. "Is your wife not well?" she asked, without answering Mary's greeting.

"No, she's very well, Mrs Bell. This is Mrs Smith who's going to help from now on, and this is her daughter," he said pointing at Marie. "I'll leave you in Mrs Smith's good hands." And Henry Dickson left with a tuneful whistle on his lips.

Mary looked again at Mrs Bell. "Can I get anything for you?" she asked pleasantly.

"Yes, I've a list here," said Doris Bell. "I'd like you to get it filled for me to pick up when I return. I'm going to see a friend in the village and will be an hour or so. I believe you're a new arrival, just off the coach?".

"Yes I'm new here. I'm a friend of Kate and John Johnson."

"So you're to help Mrs Dickson. Have you worked in a shop before?"

Taken aback, Mary was thankful when Mrs Dickson come in from the back room. "Oh Mrs Bell," she said, "don't let us keep you. You'll be anxious to get to morning tea with your friends and tell them all the gossip - I mean news."

Doris Bell looked at Mary. "Have my order ready when I return please, and make sure Billy is around to deliver it," she said then left.

"What a charming lady she is," said Mary. "I tried to be as nice as I could and she was down-right rude."

"Oh don't let that one worry you. She can be as nice as pie if she wants something done. Billy carries her things home every week and I don't think she even offers him a sip of water on a hot day, but she's a regular customer. Henry keeps her under control. Shop keepers have to grow hard skins, thick as an elephant," Mrs Dickson laughed.

"When she never said hello or anything, I wondered if she'd heard about me. I felt as if I was an exhibit she'd trot out at her next gathering," said Mary.

"Oh don't let her bother you. You'll be a nine minute wonder for a few days, but people on the whole are very kind. You'll see." Mrs Dickson picked up the list of items Mrs Bell wanted. It wasn't long and together they got everything ready for her return.

The day passed quickly with, in between customers, the two women doing an impromptu spring-clean. Many items had been put back out of place after the earthquake and Johanna was anxious to tidy up and check the stock. There was never enough time when she was on her own.

When school was over Miss Goode arrived at the shop with Peter. He looked longingly at the jars of sweets behind the counter as his mother asked, "How did your first day go, dear?"

"I liked it better than I thought I would, Mother," he said. "I liked the other children. I kicked a ball around with them. They said it was really a pig's bladder, though. Ugh! Poor pig."

Johanna looked up from recording the goods she'd sold. "Thank you Mrs Smith, you've worked hard today. We will see you tomorrow."

"I enjoyed it," smiled Mary. "Marie was no bother?"

"No, not at all. I hardly knew she was there - it was a pleasure having you both here." Johanna took a jar from the shelf and held it out to the children who picked a hard round sweet each.

Back at Mrs O'Toole's Beth and Mary set about getting the evening meal started. The letter still waited to be read, and Mary realised she could no longer put the moment off. She took it from her pocket and held it up for Beth to see. "It's from my husband. I haven't read it yet. I'm afraid to. I want to know how he is, but I'm scared to open it."

"Oh Mary," Beth said. "If he's well enough to write to you it will be all right. You'll be better off, knowing how he's got on".

"I suppose so." Mary tore the envelope open and scanned the two pages with a wry smile. "He's lost the little money he had in the bank in Melbourne. Those two men were just what I thought they might be. Tricksters. I'm glad I didn't take the children over there."

"You poor thing, what will you do if he wants to come back? Will you send him money?" asked Beth.

"I don't have any. I could raise a loan I suppose but I don't want to get into debt. No, I won't do it. He can find his own way back." Mary had a determined look on her face. "I'll write and tell him so. He has a job in Sydney so he can save the fare or work his passage. We're just starting to feel secure now and I'm not going to give that up. I'm not going to say anything to the children."

"Well said my dear! I'm glad you can look at this realistically. Now we had better get on with peeling those vegetables."

CHAPTER 40 Kate Visits the Harveys

The day passed slowly for Cathy. She finished the new book then went back to one of her favourites but soon fell asleep. Kate covered her with a warm rug and let her sleep, before tackling the weeds in the garden. When John came in at lunch-time he brought some watercress he'd found in the stream.

"We'll have that with the meal this evening," Kate said as she prepared the lunch. "Now, tomorrow - I think Cathy could go to school if I take her, and I want to go and see Mary - and Mrs Harvey. I can pick up your puppy if you like. I've been going to go for the past month, but what with all the upsets..."

"I know Kate. Things have got behind everywhere. But do you think it's wise to go driving all the way out to Harveys?"

"I'll be fine John. Beauty is so easy to drive and it will do me good. Cathy is beside herself with boredom. I want to get some stores too. I might call on the doctor too if he's not too busy. So should I pick up the dog?" asked Kate. "Will it be ready?"

"Will SHE be ready?" said John. "Remember, I'm getting a bitch so I can breed from her. Make sure you get the right one. I'll give you the ten shillings I still have to pay."

"I'll make sure he gives me the right puppy, and I'll talk to Mrs Harvey if I get the chance. I'll be very discreet and ask her to come and see us when she can."

Once Kate and Cathy reached the school the next day children crowded around when the buggy stopped at the school gate. They wanted to know how Cathy had fallen off the pony, how sore was her arm, and did her head still hurt? On and on they went until Kate called for some peace and took Cathy inside the building.

Mrs Thompson looked up as they came through the doorway. "Why Mrs Johnson, how nice to see you, and Cathy! How are you?"

"I'm fine thank you, Mrs Thompson. But my arm's still sore," said Cathy and she went to sit at her desk.

"Oh Mrs Johnson, it's so good to see you," said Beth Goode. "Are you well?"

"I'm very well, thank you," said Kate. "I'm doing some calls and other things while I have the chance. But how are you and Mary and the children?"

"We're having a lot of fun finding our way. Marie is happy at the shop with her mother, and Mrs O'Toole is treating us like long-lost children. She brought us a meal last night fit for a king - a wonderful Irish stew. She said it was left-overs, but we knew better."

Kate saw it was time for school to begin. "I'll collect Cathy early so she doesn't get too tired," she said quietly to Mrs Thompson. "I'm going to see Mrs Harvey and to pick up a puppy for Jake."

"Do be careful Mrs Johnson," said Mrs Thompson, "I've heard a few strange stories about that gentleman. Their house is not far from the pa."

"That's right. But I'll be careful not to upset him," said Kate.

As Kate approached the Harveys' she observed that the stock looked well cared for. 'Funny how a man could be so good with animals and hard on his family,' she thought.

Jock Harvey met her at the door of his stables with a gruff greeting. "Are you Mrs Johnson? Have you come for the dog?"

Kate held out her hand which was ignored. "Yes, that's what I'm here for, but I'd love to meet your wife too. It must be lonely for her out here."

"She's a bit shy," he replied. "Doesn't like meeting people."

"I'm sure you're right," said Kate, "but I've looked forward to getting to know her ever since my husband said what a nice person she was. I'd only keep her for a minute or so." As Kate looked towards the house she saw the curtain move and felt eyes watching her. "I'm very thirsty. Would she give me a drink of tea, or water, do you think?"

"You can go and knock, but she won't answer," he said. "I'll go and get the dog."

"It's to be a bitch, my husband said. Here's the money he owes you." Kate walked through the gate to the house and knocked at the door.

It opened just a fraction, then, as if the woman had taken strength from seeing

Kate, she opened the door wide and pulled her into the kitchen.

"Does he know you're here?" Mrs Harvey asked in a frightened voice.

"Yes, he's gone to get the puppy my husband's buying. I'm Mrs Johnson. I told him I wanted a drink of water and he said you wouldn't open the door for me," said Kate. "Whatever is the matter? You look so afraid. Are you just shy as he said?"

"No it's not that. He won't let me out of the house. He says I'm not a good person and he doesn't want people to meet me because they'll think he was a fool to marry me. He's changed so much since we came over here. He used to be kind and loving but now…." Mrs Harvey began to weep. "I don't know what I should do." Kate could see bruises on her arm. "I'm afraid if I stay he'll kill me."

Kate wondered what she'd feel like if John changed from being a loving husband. "You must come into town with me," she said. "You don't have to put up with this any longer. Get a few things together and I'll tell your husband you're unwell and need to see a doctor," said Kate. She poured herself a cup of water from the jug on the table. She'd need to have a clear head as she put her case to Mr Harvey.

Mrs Harvey took a few things from the drying rack over the stove and stowed them in a bag. While she was clearly frightened about what her husband's reaction would be, this might be her only chance to escape.

The sound of heavy boots on the veranda announced Mr Harvey's return. "Are you there Missus?" he called as he dumped a sack on the boards. "I've put him in a sack so he won't trouble you as you're driving."

"Him? Don't you mean her?" laughed Kate. "John is expecting a bitch. He paid you the extra. I gave it to you today."

"Quite right Missus. It's a bitch. Just like another one I know." Jock Harvey looked at his wife.

"Your wife is coming into town with me Mr Harvey," said Kate in her best cajoling manner. "I'm going to take her with me to see Doctor McDonald. We have a woman's problems to sort out."

"My wife's not going anywhere!" said the man, grabbing his wife's arm. "What lies has she been telling you?" He shook his wife violently as he spoke.

"She's unwell and needs to see a doctor," said Kate firmly. "Please Mr Harvey, just let her go. She'll come home as soon as she's well. You wouldn't want her to die would you? Can't you see she is unhappy?"

"I'll give her unhappy!" he shouted and he hit his wife full in the face. As she fell she collided with Kate and both women fell to the floor.

Scrambling to her feet, Mrs Harvey grabbed a knife from the bench and held it in front of her as she helped Kate up from the floor. "You're nothing but a bully, Jock! I'm not frightened of you anymore. Move aside and let us go." She motioned Kate to go out the door and picked up her bag. "It's good-bye Jock. I'll never ever come back. The animals can have you." She dropped the knife on the veranda and picked up the puppy. "Don't annoy those girls at the pa either, or you'll have the tribe after you."

Her husband just stood where he was, making no movement towards the women as Mrs Harvey helped Kate into the buggy. He looked shocked, his face scarlet but, waving his arms in a threatening manner, he shouted, "Go then and good riddance! You're no bloody good to any man, see if I care. I won't have you back even if you come crawling on your hands and knees."

Kate shuddered as she and Mrs Harvey settled themselves on the buggy seat, placing the puppy in the sack between them. This had been far harder than she could have imagined. Mr Dickson had told her of the hard time Mrs Harvey was having, but Kate had never known anyone behave like that before. As Kate shook the reins she looked back at the house, but there was no further sign of Jock Harvey.

CHAPTER 41 Kuini to the Rescue

The fall had given Kate a nasty shock and she could feel the baby protesting at the rough treatment. 'Oh to have the birth over,' she thought. Once out on the open road, she looked at Mrs Harvey. "How are you? I'm sorry if you think I did the wrong thing. I just couldn't bear thinking of you being bullied like that."

"No, no, you were right. I shouldn't have stayed with him so long. He changed such a lot from the man I married. I was always hoping that person would come back to me if he could only see that he was behaving strangely, that I loved him, and did my best.

"I really was only going to get you to see Dr McDonald," said Kate.

"Don't worry Mrs Johnson. I'm glad it came to a head. Jock is a bit of a case, I think. 'Round the bend' as they say. I felt as if I was in danger of going to cuckoo land myself."

Suddenly Kate felt a sudden stab of pain shoot through her and gasped. Her waters had broken, puddling on the floor of the buggy. 'Dear God, no' she prayed. 'Not here in the countryside, with nobody around to help except this woman.' She looked at Ellen Harvey to see if she'd seen what had happened, but she was staring straight ahead, engrossed with her own thoughts. "Mrs Harvey," said Kate, "my waters have broken. I'm going to have my baby very soon. Is there anyone you know in a house near here?"

"Not really. The pa is nearest and I have a friend there. I think we should go there. Give me the reins." And Kate handed them over meekly.

As Mrs Harvey drove through the gate of the pa a number of children came running followed by some women. Mrs Harvey called to one of the women who, seeing Kate still sitting in the buggy obviously in pain, rushed to her.

"I know you, you're Rangi's wife, aren't you?" said Kate through the birth pangs. "You're May."

"That's right Mrs Johnson. I'm May. Now you come inside. I'll send one of the boys for the doctor." And she spoke in Maori to two of the older boys. Kate felt reassured when one of them ran to get his horse. 'He must be getting Dr McDonald,' she thought. 'But I wonder what the other boy is doing.' She was soon to find out.

Together, May and Mrs Harvey helped Kate into the house. There were mats on the floor with a table in the centre of the room. As she covered a sofa that had seen better days with a clean sheet and helped Kate on to it, May said, "I've sent for Kuini as well. She delivers our babies; she will be here very soon."

As May spoke, an elderly Maori lady dressed in black with a tattoo on her chin came into the room. Kuini's appearance was a shock to Kate, but her calm manner was reassuring as the woman examined her, giving instructions in Maori to May. Then May made some tea and the women sat on the floor, drinking tea together while they waited for the doctor or the baby to arrive.

"May came to help pick potatoes on the farm," explained Mrs Harvey. "I was allowed to talk to the girls who came to help, but not the men."

"May's husband Rangi works for my husband," said Kate and she gasped as another pain came.

Kuini spoke to May. "Kuini wants you to get up and squat down, Mrs Johnson," said May. "She said it will be easier for you to have the baby the Maori way."

"I'm not sure," said Kate. But when the old lady insisted, Kate reluctantly crouched down, holding onto the sofa for support. Mrs Harvey and May stood either side and before long Kate's new son slid into the world to be caught deftly by May.

Then Kuini took a shell from her pocket, as well as a strand of flax which she used to tie the umbilical cord in two places. With a flick of the shell the cord was cut and May helped Kate back onto the sofa while Kuini wrapped the baby in a clean piece of old sheet. "He's a lovely boy, Mrs Johnson," she said. "Your old man will be mighty pleased with you eh?"

"I'm not so sure about that," said Kate. "He didn't want me to come out here today. He said it was risky and I shouldn't do it."

Just then there was the sound of a horse on the road then voices outside told of the arrival of someone and the doctor came into the room, greeting Kuini and May as if they were old friends.

"I'm sorry you had to come all the way out here, doctor," said Kate.

"What did I tell you about being careful?" The doctor frowned at her as he examined the baby, then he and Kuini conversed in Maori while Kuini stroked her moko and May laughed. "Doctor McDonald is saying that Kuini has done a good job again and that she is better at childbirth than he is," she told Kate and Mrs Harvey. "And Kuini said she'd had a baby, well ten babies, and knew more than the doctor what it felt like. And Doctor McDonald said, "I can only imagine, Kuini, but I do my best."

"Now," said the doctor, turning again to Kate, "you've got a healthy boy there, and everything is as it should be but you must stay here for a while. How are we to let your husband know what's happened?"

"Would you mind calling into the school and tell Cathy to walk home with Jake and the Kellys. Perhaps you could give them a note for their father, but you can tell them what's happened, they'll know soon enough," she said then lay back on the sofa as Mrs Harvey brought her new son to her and the doctor farewelled the women, saying to Kate, "I want to see you at my rooms on your way home."

"You must get some rest now, Mrs Johnson," said May, and she, Kuini and Mrs

Harvey left the room. "We'll be close by if you want us."

May and Mrs Harvey sat outside in the afternoon sun, "I'm so glad you were home, May," said Mrs Harvey. "I don't know what I would have done if you'd had been out. The baby would have been born on the roadside. How awful that would have been."

"You look tired Mrs Harvey - and how did you hurt your face? How's that big man of yours?" asked May.

"Oh May, you don't know how hard it's been lately. I think my husband has gone mad. He won't let me out of the house. When Mrs Johnson told him I needed a doctor he hit me. I'm afraid it's not the first time." Ellen Harvey lifted her sleeve and showed May her bruised arm.

"That's no good," said May. "He's one rough fella. I thought he was a nice man when we picked the potatoes but if he does a thing like that, he need a good shake up. What are you going to do now?"

"I'm not going back. I have a cousin in Masterton. I tried to do everything he asked, and made the house nice and planted a garden, but he was unreasonable. He would want something done one day and berate me for doing it the next, and never say why. Only Mr Dickson was allowed to come near the house but I could tell he saw and heard enough to know what was happening." Mrs Harvey wiped her eyes. "I think Mr Johnson knew something was not quite right too when he came out to the farm," she said with a shiver. "I think it was probably what he and Mr Dickson told Mrs Johnson that made her come out here."

"Oh Mrs Harvey, if we'd known we would have helped you," exclaimed May.

"Thank you for listening to my troubles, May. I don't think I could have gone on much longer. I even looked at the river when it was in flood, and thought of throwing myself in. It's a sad end to the marriage I thought we had. My husband is so good with his animals. I don't know why he's acted so differently with me since we came up here. Perhaps the work was too hard. Acres of bush to fell and all the clearing up that went with that. I really don't know. I do wonder though if it was the big tree branch that caught him and laid him out. He was never the same again. I tried to get him to see the doctor but he refused."

"I think you've done the right thing. Just go on from here and make a new life for yourself." May stood up and went to look in on Kate.

Late that afternoon there was the sound of hoof-beats on the road followed by a clatter of pebbles against the wall of the house as John brought Bessie to a halt at the door. He must have ridden her hard because she was snorting foam from her nose and sweat covered her flanks. He bounded through the doorway, hardly pausing to greet May and Mrs Harvey, and gathered Kate into his arms. There were tears in his eyes as he asked how she was feeling.

"I'm fine John. Just glad it's all over. You have a nice little son waiting to meet you," said Kate. "Doctor McDonald has been, and he said I could go home when you came for me."

"Let me see him," said John moving the sheet away from the bundle in Kate's arms. "He's very small. I forgot how small babies are. What are we going to call him?"

"I don't know really but I like William. Do you?"

"That was your father's name, wasn't it? But we don't have to decide tonight. Let's get you home," said John and he helped Kate to stand. Then he took Beauty from the shafts and replaced her with Bessie before settling Kate in the buggy with the baby in her arms and the puppy, still in her sack, in the back.

It was not the time to explain to John the events of the morning but, when Kate said that Mrs Harvey would be coming with them to Greytown, John suggested Mrs Harvey drive. He'd ride Beauty if she could handle Bessie.

"I drove the other horse here, so I'm sure I won't have any trouble with this one," said Mrs Harvey and, with a final farewell and thanks to May they started for home.

"Now let us think about you Mrs Harvey," Kate said as they trotted along. "Where will you go? Have you any friends in Greytown?"

"I'll be all right; I've a cousin in Masterton. I might be able to travel up there on the coach and perhaps I can stay the night at the hotel. It won't be very expensive will it? I never took any money when I could have. Now I have none."

"Don't worry about that. My husband knows the publican and we'll make sure you're all right; after all, it's my fault that you're in this predicament," said Kate.

It took no time at all to reach the doctor's house. While Kate saw Doctor McDonald John heard about the events of the day from Mrs Harvey. "I need to go the hotel to see if I can get a bed for the night. Then I hope to go up to Masterton to my cousin's. I just hope my husband meant it when he told me not to come back. He won't come looking for me will he?"

"There's no knowing," said John, "but I doubt it. Perhaps he has learnt a lesson, but you stood up to him, and that won't go down well. I think your plan to go to your cousin is a good one."

Doctor McDonald and Kate came to the door. John took the doctor's hand and gave it a good firm shake as he thanked him for his help. "Your wife is fine Mr Johnson, you can take her home. Old Kuini knows her stuff. I've looked over the baby too. He's a nice little chap. Mrs Harvey, I'll see you while you're here as well." He helped Kate up into the buggy. Mrs Harvey passed up the baby. "I'll be out to see your wife soon. Now get her home."

John took some money from his coat pocket and passed it to Mrs Harvey. "This will see you through for a while," he said. "And I'll stop at the hotel and make sure there is a room for you. Don't worry about trying to pay us back either. What you did for my wife today is payment enough. You can write to us at the store. We want to know you're all right."

"You're sure this cousin will take you in?" Kate looked anxious.

"We've always been close. She runs a boarding house in Masterton. I'm sure I can make myself useful there, for a while anyway."

It was getting dark as John shook the reins and started for home. Kate watched the road ahead, thinking how differently the day had turned out. She hoped the children had done their usual tasks and would be on their best behaviour, ready to welcome them home.

As they reached the house, Kate could see the fire was burning. A good stack of wood was waiting in the wood-box on the veranda, and there were shrieks of delight as Jake and Cathy rushed to greet them. Jake put his arms up to take the baby, while Cathy, one arm in a sling, watched, a disappointed look on her face. Kate put her arms around her. "You can have a cuddle when you're sitting down. Now let's get inside."

CHAPTER 42 New Additions

Jake went to see to the horses after he was relieved of his baby brother. "They need a good rub down, a drink of water, and some oats," John told him as he went to take Bessie from the buggy. "There's a sack on the back of the buggy, Jake. Be careful of it." 'Yes, yes,' thought Jake as he walked away. 'What now?' He reached into the back of the buggy for the sack. It wriggled.

As Jake tore the sack open a little grey bundle started licking his face. The pup had arrived at last. He gave her a drink of water and wondered what he could give her to eat. He'd ask his mother for some meat. He laid the sack in an old box and coaxed the pup to lie down on it. 'Now the horses,' he thought.

He worked as fast as he could. Soon they were munching happily on oats. "I hope you'll be all right here," he said as he patted the pup's head. "I'll come back and see you when I've had tea." He ran inside and threw his arms around his father. "Thank you, thank you," he cried. "Thank you for the puppy."

John looked at Jake and said sternly. "It's a working dog, you know," but he had a twinkle in his eye.

Cathy was seated by the fire holding her new brother. She would rather have had a sister, but this baby was beautiful, even if his face was screwed up in a funny way. He started to cry again, so she gave him back to her mother with relief.

Everyone wanted to hear about the events of the day so, after Kate had put the baby into his cradle, over a scrappy meal of cold meat and boiled potatoes (that Jake had peeled with a butcher's knife), she began to tell them about how things had happened. She didn't mention the episode at the Harveys' though, just saying that Mrs Harvey was travelling to Greytown with her and how they had gone to the pa when the baby started to come.

"Dr McDonald told us you had had the baby. He told us it was a boy," said Jake. "What are we going to call him?"

John looked at Kate. "I was thinking about this on the way home," he said. "How does William George sound? William George Johnson. William, after your father, and George after Grandad. My father's father, I mean."

"I think that's just lovely. William George Johnson he is. What do you think Jake? Cathy? Does that sound right to you?" asked Kate.

When they all agreed, Jake asked what they were going to call the pup.

"You know it's a girl Jake, don't you?" his father said, laughing. "You need a good clear name she'll understand at a distance. Short and sharp,"

Next morning, when Cathy wanted to ride to school, her father was adamant that she should wait until at least next week. "You can ride again when we are sure the bone is mending. If it doesn't mend properly you'll have an ugly arm," he said. "It's not worth the risk."

Jake offered to walk with Cathy and to carry her bag of books and lunch to help her and they left for school full of the news about the baby. Jake was keen to see what Kingi and Hemi thought about the baby being born at their house. The Kelly family were all waiting for them when they reached their gate, wanting to know when they could visit. News had travelled fast.

The children arrived at the school just as the bell was rung and joined the other pupils in line, waiting for Mrs Thompson to give them the order to enter. She was trying to teach them to march in step. It was proving difficult. "Left right, left right, left..." she said as the children tried to keep in step. "Tommy, which is your right hand? And right leg? Remember you write with your right. You can all go out and come in again." Miss Goode began to clap time and soon all the children were clapping to the beat, and saying "Left right, left right" as they walked. It became a very noisy exercise.

"Thank you children, that's enough," said Mrs Thompson. "Now who has some news for us?" Hands flew up all over the room. She looked at the eager faces. "You, Kingi, what news have you?"

"Please Mrs Thompson, Mrs Johnson had her new baby at our house yesterday. It's a boy. My Great-aunt Kuini, she helped her."

"Thank you Kingi. What about you Hemi? What did you think of that happening at your house?"

"It was great, Mrs Thompson. We seed the baby. It was all screwed up." Hemi looked as pleased with himself as she'd ever seen him. She wanted to correct his English but decided to let it go. Cathy put up her good hand and was asked to speak next.

"We've called the baby, William George, after our two grandfathers," she said. "He woke up twice in the night."

"Well, babies do that. They need to be fed often. Jake, what news do you have?"

"I've got a new puppy as well as a new brother," said Jake.

"Thank you Jake. Now we must get on with our work. We may have some gentlemen from the school board come to see us today. If they do I must impress upon you to be very good and quiet and keep on working unless they tell you to stop. Understand?"

"Yes, Mrs Thompson," they replied almost together.

"Now take out your work books and copy these sentences out, then write in your own words what you think they mean."

When school was over for the day, all the children raced home, each of them keen to tell the story of the new baby to their mothers. Polly, Jane and Cathy walked together along the road as quickly as they could as Cathy had said Polly and Jane could come home to see William.

The Kelly boys were not interested in the baby. They were anxious to see the puppy. "What's its name?" asked James. "Is it a boy or a girl?"

"They're not boys and girls, stupid," said Dennis. "They're bitches or dogs.

Don't you know anything?"

"I haven't thought of a name yet. Father said it has to be short and sharp. I have to learn to whistle her up too," Jake added.

Tessa was watching from the window for the first signs of the children. They were good at coming home on time. She was keen to see Cathy to see how her arm was and to hear all about the new baby too. She'd heard a garbled account from Paddy who'd heard it from O'bie, who'd heard it from Mr Dickson, who'd been told by Miss Goode. Tessa thought she'd rather have the story from Mrs Johnson but wouldn't worry her for a while. She knew what it was like with a young baby. She patted her tummy, wondering if it was a sign of her age she was late, or was she having another, then walked out to greet the children. "How was school?"

"Good thanks," Jake said. "Can Dennis and James come over to see my new puppy?" Tessa laughed at his request. "Don't you mean new baby?"

"Oh the girls want to go and see him, but the boys want to see the dog I got yesterday as well. Will that be all right?"

"So long as you don't make a lot of noise and work for your mother," said Tessa. "Would you like a drink of lemonade?"

As soon as everybody had satisfied their thirst and eaten the cake put out for them they made their way to the Johnsons'. There Jake took the boys straight to the stable where his puppy was tied up, to get their opinion and see the envy in their eyes.

He'd thought a bit about a name, but nothing sounded right. The puppy bounded about, greeting each of the boys in turn. They ruffled her coat and patted her head as she jumped up and down around them. She'd spent a long lonely day on her own. Only John had been to talk to her. The cows had put their heads into the doorway and sniffed at her. This was much better.

Jake took off her collar and let her run free as they went into the yard. She dashed after some hens and ducks, then ran up to the cows and began to bark. Jake caught her and told her to be quiet.

This was her first lesson. Mr Harvey had taught her to bark at everything on the farm, even people if they came near the house. It was going to be hard to get her out of the habit. Jake looked at her with love, she was such a little dot. Dot! That was it. He'd call her Dot. He watched as she ran after James and called, "Here Dot. Come here girl," patting his leg so she'd understand. When she came running he gave her a warm welcome, "Good girl."

Kate was feeding the baby as the girls arrived and he protested when Kate pulled the shawl from around his face. "He's a good baby and likes his tucker," Kate explained to Jane and Polly.

The girls sat quietly while William finished his afternoon tea. It took a while.

"Now, if you sit down, you can hold him for a minute," and Kate placed him in Jane's arms when she was seated.

"He's lovely, Mrs Johnson. He's so little," said Jane.

"Now you Polly, and no jiggling him about," said Kate as the girls changed places. She gave William to Polly's waiting arms. Cathy was next in line. Kate was pleased she had been patient.

"Now you can come and see me put him to bed. Then you can go out and see the boys and the new puppy before you go home. Tell Jake he still has his jobs to do, Cathy."

"Mammy sends her love, Mrs Johnson," said Jane. "She'll come over and see you soon. She said to tell you she's pleased it's over for you, and that you are to give Mr Johnson her and Dada's congratulations. I think that's all I had to say."

"Thank your mother for me, Jane. I'd love to see her but I won't be going anywhere for a while. Baby's too small to travel even though he's already been quite a way," Kate said as she gave Jane and Polly a hug goodbye.

When Cathy walked out to the yard with the girls Jake was tying Dot up. She whimpered a bit as Jake filled her water bowl and gave her some scraps of meat. "You're a good girl," he said as the girls all patted her. "Did you know I've given her a name? It's Dot."

"That's nice." Cathy smiled then told Dennis and James, "You have to go home now and you have to do your jobs, Jake. Mother said."

When tea was over and William was settled, Kate turned her attention to the bag of mail Jake had brought home. She quickly sorted John's and laid them on the table ready for when he returned from the long drop. She hoped he noticed it was getting smelly. 'He needs to dig a new hole. It was probably the flooding that caused the trouble.' Kate walked outside to the garden to read her mail.

There was one letter from her mother. However, feeling the chill in the air, she returned inside and read by the light of the lamp. The opening paragraph was full of how much Kate was missed. 'I would love to see you and introduce you to Mr Rhys Jones,' her mother wrote, 'I'm very happy. We often go to a play and then have a late supper. He is always a gentleman and I like him very much.'

Kate read on, wondering if her mother would say if she still intended to marry this man. 'Would I mind very much if she did?' Kate wondered. She knew many years of loneliness stretched ahead for her mother if the match didn't go ahead.

News of the village, and some births and deaths were mentioned in the last pages. Kate was sorry to hear that several of her mother's friends had died. She thought of them each in turn, picturing them in her mind's eye as they'd looked when she'd last seen them. 'Poor Mother, I'll write her a nice long letter. She'll be pleased to hear about William and I know she'll be happy with his name. There he is waking now,' thought Kate, as she heard the baby's cry. 'Not to be denied, either, by the sound of it,' she chuckled as she went to feed him.

CHAPTER 43 Troubles for Ellen Harvey

Ellen Harvey had not slept very well. The hotel smelt of stale beer and was noisy until the small hours of the morning. She washed at the marble topped wash-stand where water had been left ready in a heavy china jug. She poured this into the ornate basin and washed her face. It was cold but she felt fresher now than she had for months.

Brushing the dust off her dark skirt and smoothing creases from her jacket, she wished she could get a message to her cousin, but knew if she wrote her a letter it would go on the same coach she was to travel on.

As she made her way to the dining room for breakfast, her host greeted her and asked how she had slept. Good manners forbade her from telling the truth. "Well enough," she said. "I'm catching the Masterton coach this morning."

"I'll get your breakfast," he said. "Martha has it cooked ready for you. I hope you're hungry. Name's Bill Evans," he said, and held out his hand. "I wasn't on duty last night when you came in. Are you from around here?"

"I was," she said and went to sit at a table in the dining room where she was given a large plate of chops, eggs and fried potatoes. Toast, butter and marmalade were placed on the table too. Two men sitting at a table across the way greeted her with a good morning and, relieved that they did not offer any further conversation, she began to enjoy the meal.

It seemed such a long time since she'd served porridge to Jock yesterday. What friends the Johnsons had turned out to be. While Mr Johnson had said not to worry about the debt she knew new farmers were having a hard time. Jock was always complaining about the price of things.

Martha came out of the kitchen with a large pot of tea and began to fill the cup sitting beside her plate. "Milk?" she asked.

"Yes please. Thank you for the breakfast."

"That's all right love," said Martha. "That's my job. Are you from around here?" she asked "We don't get many women on their own."

Once again Ellen was hard-put to answer. "I was," she said.

She walked slowly down to the coaching station to catch the service for Masterton. She'd paid the publican five shillings for the night's board, and thought that not too expensive. 'What will the coach cost?' she wondered. Mr Johnson had given her ten pounds. If her cousin didn't want her, she'd have to find work. What could she do? Not much, according to Jock.

Ellen shook her head. 'Don't think about him,' she told herself. 'I'll find something worth doing with my life.' She approached the stables and asked when the Masterton coach would leave.

"Nearly ready," said one of the grooms. He pointed to a shelter where she could sit and Ellen watched with interest the activity around the departure of the Wellington coach. Bags and hatboxes were loaded up on top and soon people began to climb inside. She didn't envy them at all. The road over the hill might have improved since her journey two years ago but she doubted it had become a more comfortable trip.

Soon the coach-driver whipped up the horses and they clattered off over the cobblestones towards the south and the Masterton coach took its place.

Other waiting passengers spoke kindly to Ellen. The two men who had breakfasted at the hotel were part of the group and they nodded to Ellen as she took her place in the coach and settled herself in the corner. Eight other people climbed aboard. Soon there was no room left inside.

The groom let go of the horse's heads and the driver urged them forward. 'Well,' thought Ellen, 'I wonder what will happen to me now? Perhaps this is a new beginning. I wonder how Jock is this morning. Is he missing me?' Her mind turned to the events of the day before - this way and that way they went, giving her no peace.

The coach journeyed on down the road towards the Waiohine River. Thanks to the settlers' hard work building a bridge some years before, it wasn't long before they reached Carterton and pulled into the stopping place where coaches from outlying areas met and exchanged passengers. One was just in from the small settlement of Te Wharau, east of Carterton. As the coach moved off again through the countryside Ellen closed her eyes and put the troubles of the day before behind her.

CHAPTER 44 Trouble At The Harveys'

Next morning Rangi and Ru arrived later than expected. "It's like this boss," Rangi said. "One of my kids said there was something wrong at the Harveys' so I rode over there to have a look. The cows were crowded around the gate and hadn't been milked, and the dogs were barking their heads off. I didn't want to poke around but it looked strange, not like him. Old Jock is usually the first to finish milking. Something's wrong."

John wondered whether he should tell Rangi about Mrs Harvey leaving her husband. He most likely knew anyway, May will have told him. "His wife's left him, Rangi. Perhaps he got drunk and just hasn't got up yet."

"He's a hard old bugger May said. I never thought he'd act like that. Do you think we should go and see if he's all right?"

"Yes, you're right. I'll just tell my wife what we're doing. Would you get Beauty saddled up for me while I tell her?" John went inside to see Kate but, not wanting to alarm her, said they needed to go to town on some business and wouldn't be long.

Kate gave John some letters to post and a list to drop into Dicksons'. She was a bit surprised at the unexpected trip but knew enough not to ask questions. John was a man's man and did not need her to pass judgment on his plans. Still, he usually told her what he intended to do each day. This trip was not planned yesterday, she was sure.

"Be careful," she said. "I don't know what you're up to but I'll be glad to see you home."

"I'm always careful Kate. You know me," John said, but thinking, 'It's funny that Kate sensed something was not quite right'.

The three men stopped first at the store where John explained to Dickson where they were going. "Funny bloke," he said. "That poor woman. Let me know what happens."

At Harvey's farm the cows were still gathered around the gate to the two-cow bail. Their udders were extended and obviously uncomfortable. John walked to the house and knocked at the door, but only a tabby cat came out to greet him, rubbing his head against his leg. John pushed the door open and looked in. There was no sign of Harvey in the house. John went outside to Rangi and Ru. "No one there," he said, "we'd better try the barn."

As the men walked to the barn, watching for any movement, John called out loudly as they approached. There was no reply, but chickens and hens fled as they walked into the dark interior where there were sacks of grain, implements and piles of boards and rubbish. The men paused, looking around, then suddenly Ru screamed and pointed to the loft. There, hanging from a rope, was the body of the Scotsman. Ru screamed again and ran from the barn.

"Ru don't like dead people, boss," said Rangi. "Poor boy. He's scared of spirits. What should we do?"

John was already on the ladder to the loft. "I'd say he is dead, but I must check - no, he's quite cold. He must have done this last night by the feel of his body. We'll need to go and tell Constable O'Reilly. Let him deal with it."

"What about the cows? We can't leave them like that," said Rangi. "Would it be better for you to go and report what's happened while Ru and I see to the animals?"

"Yes Rangi, you're right, that would be best. What a bloody waste of a life. His wife said he used to be so loving and kind. You'd wonder what would make a man change like that."

John made his way into town with a heavy heart. 'Mrs Harvey told Kate her husband had been hurt on the head by a falling tree, or branch. Perhaps that had something to do with the tragedy.'

The constable was drinking tea as John rode up, but was soon making notes. As he went over the details several times John felt as if he was being cross-examined.

"This Rangi," asked the policeman, "he works for you? That right? And the other boy? Is he a Maori too?"

"Yes that's right. They've been with me for two years now and they're very good workers," said John.

"You don't think they could've been involved then?"

"Of course not, they were worried about the animals. One of their boys saw the cows had not been milked and told Rangi," said John. "Do you think we should get Doctor McDonald to come and see to the body? Is that the right thing to do?"

"I'll need you to come back to the Harvey farm, Mr Johnson. I'll need to see the situation myself. Yes, I think you should go and see McDonald and ask him to come too," said the constable. "I'll see you there shortly."

Doctor McDonald was just finishing morning surgery when John arrived at his door. When he heard the news he agreed to come straight away. He told Mrs McDougal he'd been called out and went to get his buggy hitched up to bring the body back for an autopsy.

———— ⌾⌾⌾ ————

Back at the farm John explained to Rangi the need to state clearly what had made him think something was wrong.

"What's the matter boss? Does the policeman think someone killed him?" asked Rangi.

"No, I don't think so for a minute, we just need to be clear about what we have all seen," said John.

The clip-clop of horse's hooves told of the approach of the policeman. Doctor McDonald walked over to greet him.

"A nasty business, Doctor," said Constable O'Reilly. "I know his wife has left him and gone to Masterton. We keep an eye on who travels in and out of the area."

"I'm sure you do," replied the doctor. "But I'm also sure this is a straightforward case of a poor man losing his will to live."

"Well, I'll be checking everything very carefully. I've heard a few rumours, you know. Dickson seemed to be getting very friendly with Mrs Harvey from what I heard."

"Look here, don't try and make smoke where there's no fire. I'd stake my life on this being a case of suicide. Dickson just delivered their supplies. We'd better get the body down and see what's what," said the doctor, not so sure he could talk the policeman out of his strange ideas. "Mr Johnson, can you and Rangi help bring the body down?"

Rangi had none of the delicacy of feelings that had sent Ru running from the barn. He was quite happy to help. Soon the corpse lay on some sacks on the floor and the doctor had a cursory look at the body. "I need to get back to town, Constable," he said. "You can come and talk to me at home later. It's clearly death by strangulation. I want to have a look at the brain though, because his wife said his personality changed so much after an accident he'd had. Mr Johnson, if you and Rangi put Mr Harvey on the back of the buggy I'll get away."

Constable O'Reilly was not finished with questioning the three men left at the scene. He opened his notebook and waved his pencil about as he went over the events of the morning, what they could tell him about the day before, and what they knew about the wife.

John was getting impatient. He was losing a lot of the day's work. While he knew the circumstances were exceptional there was a limit. "I must go soon too," he said. "I can't tell you much more than I already have. Doctor McDonald is satisfied about the cause of death and so should you be."

"Yes, yes all in good time I just want to be sure there's been no foul play."

"What are you going to do about the animals?" asked John. "It won't be easy to get someone to caretake the farm. Shouldn't you be worrying about that?"

"You're right, I'll enquire at the village for help," the constable replied. "Just a few more questions Johnson, just to get the facts right. What do you know about Harvey? How long have you known him?"

"I met him a few months ago when I went to order a puppy, a Blue Merle. He brought a breeding pair over from Australia and I wanted a working dog for my son. My wife went out to pick it up and met Mrs Harvey. She could see she was unhappy and offered to bring her into town to see the doctor. Her husband was not pleased and they left with him saying not to come back. My wife had her baby at the pa on the way home. Mrs Harvey helped her," said John.

"Why did your wife think she was unhappy?" asked Constable O'Reilly.

"Dickson at the store told my wife the woman seemed terrified when he delivered the supplies. I myself heard Harvey speak to his wife in a most derogatory manner."

Constable O'Reilly looked thoughtful. "Do you think there was anything going on between them? Mrs Harvey and Dickson, I mean."

"Absolutely not," said John. "He's devoted to his wife."

"I believe the wife caught the coach to Masterton. Do you have her address?"

"I understand she was going to a cousin in Masterton who has a boarding house. She hoped to be able to help her for her keep, until she was able to find some other work. I only know this because she told my wife what she was going to do. She shouldn't be hard to find. I gave her some money to tide her over for a few days. She had no money of her own and my wife asked me to lend her some."

"It sounds very organised. Do you always help people out? Lame dogs and such like?"

"A helping hand never goes astray. I only went out to Harvey's place to see what the trouble was with the cows. I never thought of what we were to find. It's unbelievable."

"How much money did you give the wife?" asked Constable O'Reilly, smirking a little.

"Ten pounds. It was a kindly gesture and should not be misunderstood. Can you not understand that?"

"I'll not make up my mind one way or the other before I know all the facts, but it seems strange that everyone is so keen to help her all of a sudden. I might ask Dickson a few questions. He seems to be the one who has had the most to do with her. You can get home Johnson. Thanks for your help this morning. I'll write to the police in Masterton and ask them to inform Mrs Harvey of the events of the day. They'll advise her to return to Greytown as soon as she's able, to answer some questions, and to find out what is to happen to the farm."

Riding back to the village with Rangi and Ru, John decided to see Dickson and let him know the constable was not happy with some aspects of the matter. As far as John was concerned, it was straightforward but he could see how things could be misconstrued. Poor woman, this was something that no one could have seen coming. He'd only spent a short time with her but felt she was a good honest person, not deserving of the events of the past two days. 'It's hard to believe that it's all happened in such a short time.'

CHAPTER 44 Rumours and a Reunion

Henry Dickson was busy putting up a big new sign over the shop's door. Dickson's General Store was written on it in large red letters on a yellow background. It was most impressive. John laughed and said, "Everyone says go to 'Henry's'. Many don't even know your other name."

"Thank you sir. I've felt for some time that I needed to improve our image.

We're a company now - my wife and I are equal partners. That's why I've had the sign made to mark a new beginning. Come inside. What can I do for you?"

John asked Rangi and Ru to wait and went into the store. "I've just come from seeing our policeman friend. I think he has some strange idea that you and I had something to do with the goings-on at Harveys'. Goodness, you don't know do you? Jock Harvey hung himself last night."

"That's awful. The poor lass. The poor old beggar. I never thought he was suicidal. What do you mean about us having something to do with this? How could that be?"

"I'm not sure how the constable's mind works but he seems to think that you were very friendly with Mrs Harvey, and then Kate goes out there when she's nearly due to have the baby. He found that unusual since she'd never met Mrs Harvey. I gave Mrs Harvey money for the hotel and coach after she left home with none, and now her husband is found hanging in the barn."

"That's preposterous! I only delivered groceries and never talked to her for more than a minute or two. Harvey was always present. I could see if she'd been in his bad books just by watching her. I'll flatten that constable if he tries to make more of it than there was."

"Well I thought I should tell you to be careful of what you say. It seems if he gets his teeth into something he can be like a bulldog. Dr McDonald has taken the body back to his surgery. It's a bad business."

"What terrible news! I feel sorry for the poor man, and his wife. I must go and tell Johanna. She'll be very upset," said Henry.

Just as Henry expected, Johanna was shocked by the news about the Harveys. "Poor man," she gasped. "And his poor wife - she'll be devastated."

Henry put his arm around her shoulders. "When the police find Mrs Harvey and tell her what's happened, and then bring her back to Greytown we'll have to try to help her as much as we can. Mr Johnson said Constable O'Reilly has some idea that I've been involved with Ellen Harvey other than as her grocery boy. He's trying to make a big mystery out of it. Johanna, my dear, you know that I love you and only you so don't let this dreadful event upset us. I give you my word that I was only ever concerned for her safety."

"It's all right Henry, I believe you. I just feel so sorry for the woman. She was so good when Mrs Johnson was in trouble with the baby coming."

Happy that he'd squared things with Johanna, Henry saw it was time to get on with the deliveries. "Come on Billy, you can come with me today; that'll stop tongues wagging. I won't be seeing the ladies on my own if you're there beside me. You'll be all right Johanna, if Billy comes with me today?" called Henry as he put his head into the back store-room.

"Of course dear. I can manage with Mrs Smith. I've made you some lunch - I don't want you taking tea with the women out in the sticks and adding to your reputation. Don't lead Billy astray," laughed Johanna as she passed over a package and bottles of cold tea.

As they went along Billy sat up proud as punch beside Henry who thought it had been a moment of inspiration to include him in the day's deliveries. Billy was a good lad and a good worker so they'd be a lot quicker. And so it proved.

At the last stop Henry turned to the boy. "Now, Billy, you grab that sack of flour and I'll bring the rest. We'll be back on the road in a minute. There's a nice little lass here, about your age, but don't go making sheep's eyes at her."

Billy went a bright shade of red and kept his head low as he and Henry carried the supplies to the house but, as they approached, the door opened and a woman in a bag apron and a girl of about sixteen with a real crown of copper-coloured hair appeared and took the boxes and bags from them. When Billy heard the woman call the girl Milly. he decided to look on the order sheet to find out the rest of her name. He wouldn't risk asking Mr Dickson and being teased, but here was the prettiest girl he'd ever seen.

Henry took them back to Greytown by a different route with more farms along it. The roads were in better condition now that the weather was better and they made good time. Henry looked at the new houses being built on the farms. They were bigger than the first pioneer cottages. Some were real homesteads. 'Yes,' thought Henry, 'the district is expanding in all directions.'

Ellen Harvey arrived at her cousin's door about noon, carrying her small bag of possessions. The trip to Masterton had been uneventful and the coach-driver had pointed her to the street where her cousin lived, saying she'd easily see the boarding house as it was the largest.

As the door opened to her timid knock she was suddenly clasped in an embrace by a pair of floury arms. "Just look at you," said the woman. "I would have known you anywhere. But why are you so thin? Come in, come in. Is your husband here too? Having a little time off the farm are you?" She led Ellen into the sitting room of her establishment where two men were seated reading the daily news. "Now tell me. What brings you to Masterton?"

Ellen could not speak. Tears flowed from her eyes and she took a while to recover. "Oh Dora, you've no idea what I've been through. My husband changed so much these last few months, I had to leave him. He told me to get out and not come back. So I've come to you to see if I could help you in some way, for my board for a while. I've no one else to turn to." Ellen paused for breath. "It's such a story. Yesterday a lady called Mrs Johnson came to collect a puppy, but when she saw how miserable I was she wanted me to see the doctor but Jock went mad and raved at us and pushed me over. I fell against Mrs Johnson and knocked her over onto the floor. I believe that's why her baby started to come. We had to go to the pa, where she was delivered of a boy."

"Look, come and I'll make you some tea. Where did you stay last night? Have you just come off this morning's coach?" asked Dora.

"Yes, I stopped at the hotel in Greytown. Mrs Johnson's husband gave me enough money for the room and the coach fare. Kate and John Johnson are their names. They were very kind."

Dora took her hand and led her into the kitchen where the kettle was singing cheerfully on the stove. Soon they were seated at the scrubbed table drinking a welcome cup of tea.

"I could do with an extra pair of hands for a while Ellen. We're getting busier every day with people coming to work in town or out in the bush. I even have people here who are working on roads on the way to Castlepoint, Tinui and to the north too.

"I'd be so grateful Dora. I didn't know what to do. You were the only one I could think of."

"I can see that you've been through an ordeal, but it's over for now. Jock may come looking for you when he wakes up and sees what a mistake he's made. I think you should have a good hot bath and I'll find you some things you can use so I can wash your clothes. You don't seem to have much with you, or have you a case at the coaching stop?"

"No, I just grabbed a few things that were airing over the stove before Jock went berserk. I'd love a hot bath."

"After that maybe you should have a sleep. Come and I'll find a bedroom you can use." They went down the hall to a small room at the back where an iron bedstead stood ready for use. It was covered with a large patchwork quilt of many colours and looked very inviting. The walls were painted cream and lace curtains covered the small window. A washstand with basin and ewer ready for use, a bedside table complete with candle, lamp, and cupboard with a chamber pot completed the furnishings. "I'll fill the bath for you," said Dora as she left.

Half an hour later Ellen was lying back in a hip bath half filled with hot water. Steam was rising and misting the mirror on the wall and the water was warming and relaxing.

There was a tap at the door and Dora came in with some clothes, "Don't mind me." she said as she gathered Ellen's clothes together. "I'll brush the heavy things and wash the rest. Just wear some of these and go to bed. I'll get you something to eat when you wake up. You look exhausted."

"I am, and thank you Dora. You're a true friend."

John climbed the steps to the veranda. There was no sign of Kate in the kitchen or bedroom where William was sleeping peacefully in his crib. He went outside to see if she was hanging washing out, but no, she was not there either. Around the corner of the house he could hear someone digging the ground. There was a bang as the turf was broken up with the shovel.

"What do you think you're doing?" John asked as he took the shovel from her hands. "I told you I'd dig the garden for you, you silly woman. You shouldn't be doing this."

"It's just that I have some plants ready to put in. I thought I'd do a little bit while William was asleep."

"I'll do it soon, I promise. You must come and sit down. I've something to tell you. It's bad news, I'm afraid." John took Kate's arm and led her to the seat in the sheltered part of the garden.

"What is it? Rangi said there was something wrong, but that you'd be home soon and not to worry as you were well and not in any trouble. What is it John? What's happened?"

"Rangi's boy saw something was wrong at Harvey's place so we went out there to see what the trouble was. We hunted for Harvey and finally found him in the barn. The poor sod had hung himself. I checked that he was dead, left Ru to mind the place with Rangi, then went to Greytown to report it to Constable O'Reilly." John paused for breath. "I also went to see Doctor McDonald to tell him and he took the body back to his surgery. He said it's a straight case of suicide."

"That's terrible John. Why on earth would the man do that?" asked Kate. " His poor wife. Whatever will she do now?"

"The thing is Constable O'Reilly seems to think there was something going on between Dickson and Ellen Harvey and because I gave her that money for the hotel and coach, he's suspicious of me as well."

"Oh John this is a terrible thing to happen. It's my fault. I would never have encouraged Mrs Harvey to leave her husband if I'd thought this would happen. The poor thing! How can we find her to help her? Do you know where the cousin lives?"

"Only that she has a boarding house in Masterton. The constable was going to send word up to the police there to contact her and bring her back to Greytown."

Kate and John sat together on the garden seat thinking of the way things had turned out. John was going over in his mind, the last time he'd seen Jock Harvey. Nothing had seemed out of the ordinary. He'd taken the bitch out for John to inspect, was in a good humour, and agreed to keep a female pup for him. That was until they'd gone into the house for a cup of tea.

Kate was also thinking of her part in the saga. Never in her worst dreams would she have imagined her trip out to Harvey's farm would end in such a disaster. "I suppose Doctor McDonald will conduct a post mortem?" she asked.

"Yes, that will done today I believe. He'd dearly love to examine the man's brain to see if there was any reason for the change in character, but that won't happen unless he gets permission."

Kate could see John was worried about the situation, but there was nothing he could do about it. She felt responsible for trying to help Mrs Harvey. The things Mr Dickson had told her had made her try and find out just what was happening at the Harvey farm. She'd read of cases at home where women had been killed by their husbands, children too sometimes. Had she over-reacted and caused this tragedy? 'God help me,' she thought.

"I suppose you must get down to help Rangi," she said. "He'll be fixing the fences. I wish he'd told me what had happened this morning. Well, no perhaps it was better not to say anything. The poor woman, she was so good with me when William was born. She was facing her own problems, all the time she sat with me and May. I hope she found her cousin."

"Constable O'Reilly will want to talk to Mrs Harvey when she comes down on the coach. He'll be seeing the doctor about a post mortem and they'll ask her where she wants him buried. It could be in the church grounds, even when it's a suicide. Perhaps he could be buried on the farm. It's not his farm though. I remember him telling me that he was running it for a chap from Wellington, who he met when he got off the boat from Australia."

CHAPTER 45 The Police Find Ellen

When Ellen Harvey woke from her sleep, she momentarily wondered where she was. But memory soon came flooding back. She rose and crossed the room to look in the small mirror on the wall. She looked dishevelled to say the least. There was a brush and comb on a tray by the ewer and she tried to tidy herself up. The dress she wore was clean and warm but a few sizes too big. However, she was grateful to Dora for providing it. It would do until she received her own back. Making her way to the kitchen, Ellen was greeted by Dora. "Feeling better?" she asked.

"Yes thank you, I had a lovely sleep," said Ellen but, as she rolled up the too long sleeves of her dress, Dora gasped.

"Good heavens! What's been going on then?" she said, shocked to see the ugly bruises on her cousin's arms.

"Jock tried to stop me going with Mrs Johnson, that's all," she said.

"That's all?" asked Dora. "He's a bloody brute of a man. He'd better not turn up here or he'll get a piece of my mind. Now let's get you something to eat, my dear." Dora moved to the oven and lifted out a plate holding a hot meal of roast beef and vegetables.

Dora settled Ellen at the table and poured herself a cup of tea from the large pot that stood ready. Two spoons of sugar were added and stirred carefully as if Dora didn't want to start asking questions of Ellen until she'd eaten her fill. The food was delicious and Ellen did justice to it.

"Oh that was so good Dora. I had nothing much yesterday and couldn't eat last night at the hotel either. I was so worried about coming up here this morning, I only had a piece of toast, but you're so lovely I feel right at home."

"You're very welcome, my dear. I've often thought of our times together at Grandma's. We used to have such fun didn't we?" said Dora as she went to answer a knock at the door. "More guests I suppose."

However, on the doorstep was a large policeman with a paper in his hand. "I'm looking for Mrs Harvey, madam," said the constable. "Is she here? I've some bad news for her I'm afraid."

Hearing her name mentioned, Ellen had come into the hallway. "What is it? How did you find me? Did my husband send you? I'm not going back."

"I'm sorry madam but you must come back to Greytown with me on the coach that leaves here in an hour," said the policeman.

"What's this all about?" asked Dora, getting ready to defend Ellen. "Come into the kitchen where you can explain yourself."

In the kitchen the policeman stood nervously. " I can see you're reluctant to accompany me to Greytown, since you think your husband is waiting there to see you, madam. But I'm very sorry to inform you that your husband is dead. I believe he hung himself last night. I'm afraid I have to take you back to Greytown on the coach today."

"Hung himself? Surely that can't be true. Oh my God! Poor Jock," said Ellen, as she felt behind her for a chair and sat down.

"That's what we were informed of by letter. You're needed to decide where he should be buried and what will happen to the farm and stock. I'm sorry to have to tell you these things, but I think it's better you know how things stand."

"Oh Ellen, this is terrible!" exclaimed Dora. "What an awful thing to happen. You must go of course. I'm so sorry, but your husband must have been very unstable to do such a thing. I'm glad you were able to get away from him safely. Come and we'll find your clothes and get you ready." As she guided Ellen out of the kitchen she said to the policeman who was still standing by the table, "Pour yourself a cup of tea while you wait."

In the bedroom she helped Ellen to gather her things together and get dressed in her warm skirt and jacket and boots. Back in the kitchen Dora put her arms around her and hugged her tight. "Remember you're always welcome to come and help me here. I thought you were going to take a load off my shoulders. I was making plans while you were asleep. You must come back when everything is sorted out." And she kissed Ellen on the cheek.

"We'd better go, madam," said the policeman as he finished his tea, "I have to call at the station and see the Sergeant to tell him I've located you." After that they were soon on their way to the coaching stable to begin the journey on the afternoon coach.

It would be nearly dark when they arrived. Ellen wondered where she'd spend the night. She had a little money for the hotel, or could she go back to the farm? The coach was full again. The two men who'd been at the hotel the night before were travelling back with her. They nodded in recognition but offered no conversation. Ellen was relieved. She had no wish to talk to anybody. Even the policeman was quiet and thoughtful. The horses moved along at an easy pace and soon they were crossing the new wooden bridge over the Waingawa, and the plains of Taratahi.

Constable O'Reilly was waiting for the coach to arrive, and was relieved to see the constable alight and help a lady off who looked as if she might be Mrs Harvey. He moved forward to introduce himself. "I'm Constable O'Reilly. You are Mrs Harvey?" he asked.

"Yes, I'm Ellen Harvey. The constable told me what happened. Where is my husband? Will I be able to see him?"

"Not tonight, I'm afraid. The body is at the doctor's for a post mortem. We'll need to find you a place to stay tonight. I want to question you tomorrow morning and there are things that need to be decided. I believe you stayed at the hotel last night. Would that be the best place for you to stay again? Or do you have any friends you could stay with for company?"

"I'll go to the hotel. I know no-one in town except Mr Dickson. But why do you need to question me? I know nothing about what happened," said Ellen.

"I don't think you should see Dickson before I have questioned you Mrs Harvey. There are some things I need answers for. I'll see you early tomorrow before you go back to the farm. I've found a man to take care of the stock. He'll stay at the house tonight and longer if you need him. A young Maori boy, Ru Rewai who works for Mr Johnson looked after it today. It was Mr Johnson who found your husband. I'll fill in the details tomorrow."

"I'll accompany you to the hotel," said the Masterton constable. "I need to have a bed for the night too." And he ushered Ellen out the door. Though she wanted to hear more about Jock, she knew she must wait.

At the hotel Ellen was given the same room but the constable was told he would have to share with another guest. The two men off the coach were also staying. Ellen wondered who they were.

Ellen had a restless night. She'd never thought Jock would do such a terrible thing. She would never have left if she'd realised how it would affect him. 'But I couldn't have stayed after he showed such violence.' She dressed once more in the clothes she'd worn on her flight from the farm and went to have breakfast.

The two men who were on the coach were also at breakfast and this time they looked at her with interest. 'News must travel fast,' thought Ellen. 'They most likely know that I am the poor widow.' One of the men extended his hand to her and murmured some words, but Ellen just nodded, and sat down. Food was put before her but she could manage no more than a few bites. As she drank some tea the constable came into the room and sat with her. In a way it was comforting to have him at the table. She could begin to ask some of the questions that ran around in her brain.

"I'm Constable Burns," he said. "I should have introduced myself properly yesterday, but you weren't in the mood for small talk. How did you sleep?" And he helped himself to toast and marmalade.

Before Ellen could reply Constable O'Reilly came into the room. "Good morning," he said as he pulled out a chair and sat down. "I hope you slept well."

Constable Burns nodded but Ellen said, "No, not very well at all. I was just about to ask Constable Burns what he knew when you arrived."

"I know nothing at all about what happened," said Constable Burns. "Only that we were to find you and bring you back. I believe I need to catch the morning coach back to Masterton."

"Yes, that would be the best course of action," said Dan O'Reilly, who didn't want any interference from Masterton. "You go as soon as you're ready. I'll take Mrs Harvey to the station."

"Could you not stay Constable Burns?" asked Ellen. She didn't feel comfortable around Constable O'Reilly. He seemed to be against her in some way.

"Well, I could wait for this afternoon's coach I suppose - if you think I could help."

"If you must," said Dan O'Reilly. "Now we must go down to the doctor's where you can identify your husband Mrs Harvey." Ellen flinched at his words. "Then I want to go out to the farm, after you've told me what you know."

As they rose Ellen said, "I need to pack my things and pay for the room."

"Don't worry about that now. Pack your things by all means, but you might need to be back here tonight. The police will pay for the hotel."

At Doctor McDonald's house Annie McDougal opened the door and invited them into the sitting room to wait. The doctor came in a few minutes and, taking Mrs Harvey's hands in his own, told her how sorry he was. "I never thought to see you back here so soon and with such a tragedy to face."

"I need Mrs Harvey to see the body," said Constable O'Reilly. "I want to get to the station to ask her some questions, and then go out to the farm so it will be a busy morning Doctor."

"I appreciate that but Mrs Harvey has had a bad shock. We must take things slowly if we're not to cause her more grief."

The body lay on a bed in the surgery, covered with a white sheet. Doctor McDonald pulled the cover down and looked at Ellen. However, when Ellen merely nodded Constable O'Reilly told her to speak up. He had to hear what she said aloud, that the body was that of her husband, Jock Harvey.

At this, Constable Burns looked at his colleague sharply. This man was going to be strict in keeping to the letter of the law. 'The poor lady,' he thought, 'she's going to be put through a lot before this is finished.'

After Ellen said in a clear voice that this was indeed her husband, Doctor McDonald asked the men to wait outside while he talked to Mrs Harvey. "My dear," said Alex. "I'd like to examine your husband's brain to see if there is any visible damage from the accident with the tree, but I need to have your permission. Would you agree?"

"Of course," said Ellen. "I'd like to know there was some reason for the change in him. I loved him dearly in the first years of our marriage, you know. Yes, I give you permission."

They walked out to where the policemen were waiting. "I have permission from Mrs Harvey to perform an autopsy on Mr Harvey. I'll do it this morning," said Alex.

"Surely it's a straight case of suicide," said Constable Burns. "What do you hope to find?"

"I believe the man was under some stress from an injury he suffered about six months ago and that it caused the changes in his personality. I want to see if I can prove my theory," replied the doctor.

"We must go to the station Mrs Harvey, where I'll ask you to fill in some details and then we'll proceed to the farm. I'll hire a buggy from the stables for our journey," said Constable O'Reilly. "You'll catch the coach back to Masterton this afternoon Constable Burns?"

"I might stay around a little while longer. I'll send word to the Sergeant to let him know my plans."

"No need for that! I can handle it. You're probably needed in Masterton more than here," said Dan.

Constable Burns looked at Mrs Harvey. "No, I'll stay around," he said.

CHAPTER 46 The School Inspection

The two men at the hotel finished eating. After paying for their board they made their way to the school to examine the teachers and the children. They'd been sent up to the Wairarapa to check on the standard of teaching at the small, sole charge schools that were springing up.

Yesterday they'd been to two schools in the Masterton area and now it was Greytown's turn to be evaluated. From the outside the school house was tidy and the garden well kept. Some ponies were grazing in the paddock next to the house. Everything seemed to be as it should be.

When they knocked at the door it was opened by a girl of about twelve. She looked a little afraid when she saw them, but recovered enough to ask whom they wished to see, and ushered them into the sitting room. The taller of the two looked at his list, and saw that the teacher's name was Mrs Thompson, assisted by Miss Goode.

"Would you go and tell Mrs Thompson that we wish to see her please?" he said as he sat down.

Jane hurried to get Mrs Thompson. These must be the men she'd told the children she was expecting. Jane went to the schoolroom door, knocked and said, "Excuse me, Mrs Thompson; there are two men to see you."

"Please take over, Miss Goode, I'll bring them in here after they have talked to me. Children, remember to be on your best behaviour." She looked in the small mirror on the wall of the passage as she passed. Bother the school authorities and their big ideas. She pushed a lock of hair in place and went into the sitting room. The men stood up and extended their hands. "I'm Richard Milne," said the tall one. "I'm Clive Lea," said the other.

"Nice to meet you Mrs Thompson," said Mr Milne. "We have just a few questions to ask then we'd like to see the children and your assistant."

"I've been expecting you for a while," said Joan Thompson. "The children are learning well and are very settled."

"We should be the judge of that. Now how many have you on the roll? And what are the attendance rates?" asked Mr Milne.

Mrs Thompson reached for the school roll book and passed it to him. It was exactly up to date. "We have seventeen on the roll. They all come every day unless they are sick or have had an accident. One of the children fell off her horse about two weeks ago and broke her arm. She was away for a day or two, but was keen to get back."

"That's very good to hear, but why did you not reply to the questionnaire we sent you?" asked Mr Lea. "You did receive it I presume?"

"Yes, yes. It was in the mail last week, but we haven't had time to consider our reply. It only came with the mail on Friday. You'll appreciate that the mails are sometimes erratic," Mrs Thompson replied.

"Perhaps we could go through it now," said Mr Milne. "I have a copy here."

Mrs Thompson thought about what she'd read on the forms, something about the use of the building for religious meetings. What else was there? Where the money had come from to build the schoolhouse? Oh well, she'd do her best.

Mr Lea opened his case, took out a copy and laid it on the table. "Now let's see," he said. Mrs Thompson answered as well as she could but there were a few things she was unable to answer. "You were teaching on your own, in a room in your home, I believe, before this building was established?" asked Mr Lea.

"Yes that's right. After we moved here, things were much better and when there was an offer of another teacher to help, I was glad. Miss Goode is very capable with the little ones. Would you like a cup of tea?" she asked them as the bell rang for playtime. "We always have a break now for ten minutes. The children come back refreshed and ready for more learning."

"That sounds very sensible. Yes, tea would be very acceptable, thank you," said Mr Milne. He watched as Mr Lea folded up his papers and placed them in the case. "We'll just have a word with the other teacher and talk to the children when they come back inside. Then we'll be able to make our report. You'll get a copy in time, of course."

"We're catching the afternoon coach over the hill so we won't have a lot of time to talk to the children but we have been able to gauge the standards you set and I can say that we're quite happy you are doing your best for the children," said Mr Lea.

Just then Beth Goode arrived and Mrs Thompson introduced them. She made the tea and passed cups around to each in turn then opened a tin and offered them some biscuits. Perhaps it had gone well and perhaps not. You could never trust anyone in authority. After the two men had finished their tea Mr Milne said they would like to talk to Miss Goode alone.

"I believe you have no formal training Miss Goode. Is that right? What education have you had yourself?"

"I had a normal education at the school I attended in England and passed exams with above average marks. I've read widely and believe I'm qualified to teach the children Mrs Thompson has placed in my care. She's always present anyway and we discuss any matters that need attention. The school board approved my appointment after they'd questioned me, and have seen me since, to say they're happy with my work."

"Quite," said Mr Lea. "I'm sure you are doing your best, but I believe that children are better able to learn if taught by men. Don't worry about that in the meantime. We'll give you and Mrs Thompson a good report if we find the children are up to the standard set in Wellington. I'll talk to them now," said Mr Lea.

The two men went into the schoolroom where the children were waiting quietly. "Now who can tell me something about Queen Victoria?" asked Mr Milne.

Hands went up from the older pupils and Jane was asked to answer. "She is the Queen of England and New Zealand, sir," said Jane. "She was made Queen when she was only eighteen, in 1839."

Other hands went up. Quite a lot of time was spent on the young Queen. Then Mr Lea asked the children to open their work books and looked around the room to ask someone to read a passage. When he saw a young native boy sitting with his head down he picked him. Hemi stood. Mrs Thompson smiled encouragingly at him. He spoke quietly, but there was no hesitation in his voice as he read several lines on the page.

"Very good," said Mr Milne. "I'm glad to see you are willing to teach the Maori children as well, Mrs Thompson. There is a need to get them to speak English. The sooner they stop speaking their gibberish the better."

"I'm afraid I don't agree," said Beth. "They have a right to their language as we have a right to ours." She wondered how that would go down. 'Oh well, I'll soon see,' she thought as the men went to leave.

"It has been very nice to meet you," said Mr Lea. "We are quite happy with the standard of your teaching but we will make a recommendation that a male teacher be found to assist you. These children are having a one-sided education with both teachers being female. I have in mind a young fellow who has been to college in England."

"I would expect nothing else from you," said Mrs Thompson. "However, I don't know where you're going to find the funds to meet the cost, as families already find it hard to pay the weekly fee. The government will have to increase their contributions if they want the children taught."

"We'll let you know of our decision," said Mr Lea as they all shook hands. Then, picking up their bags they walked down the road to the stables to join the people waiting for the Wellington coach.

"I wondered if they would say something about having Maori children in the class," said Mrs Thompson. "But I think Hemi did very well."

"That Mr Lea is a prig. An opinionated prig," said Beth. "I'm going to lose my job. I can see that. I love it here, too."

"Don't worry yet. There's much water to flow under many bridges before they can put their plans in action. The school board will have something to say about them getting rid of us," said Mrs Thompson.

CHAPTER 47 Investigations Continue

Meanwhile, at the police station, Constable O'Reilly questioned Ellen about her husband's behaviour towards her and also what relationship she had with Mr Dickson.

"There's no relationship Constable," Ellen said, offended. "Mr Dickson saw the way Jock treated me and was kindness itself when he brought the supplies. I believe he talked to Mrs Johnson, and that's why she came to pick up the pup and pay a visit."

"Did your husband know she'd come to take you away? Was that why he pushed her?"

"He didn't push her at all. She suggested I should go and see the doctor as I looked ill. He objected fiercely, and pushed me. I fell against her and she fell to the floor. I believe that's why she had the baby so soon after the fall."

"Is there anyone else that can confirm your ill-treatment?"

"Only Mr Johnson. He came to order the puppy about three months ago," said Ellen. "I believe he told his wife he was surprised at the way Jock spoke to me."

"It was Johnson who paid the hotel and coach fare, wasn't it?" asked the constable. "How did that come about?"

"Mrs Johnson asked her husband to give me some money as a loan, because I had nothing except the clothes I wore, and a small bag of things I grabbed as I left. He said that I should not try to return the money because I'd looked after his wife and he was very grateful."

"Well I think we should leave it there now and think of what needs to be done.

Will you stay at the farm tonight?"

"I don't know yet. I'll have to think about the funeral, and where my husband is to be buried. The farm doesn't belong to us. I'll have to look through my husband's papers and find the name of the owner. It was a man he met in Wellington when he landed off the boat. He gave Jock the job of minding the farm and running it as if it was his own," said Ellen. She was feeling exhausted.

"How did you get the job in Masterton so quickly?"

"Dora is my cousin. We were close when we were children, but she came to New Zealand. I only knew where she lived because she wrote to me with her address and thought I might follow her here."

———— ⚬⚬⚬ ————

Doctor McDonald had been busy with surgery all morning. But now he had Mrs Harvey's permission to undertake the autopsy he was anxious to proceed so the funeral could be held. It was already two days since the death. Over lunch he told Mrs McDougal of his wish to examine Jock Harvey's brain. "I hope you get it over and done quickly," said Annie. "I don't fancy having a body in the house for days."

"Nonsense, my dear. I'll get it done as soon as possible, believe me," said Alex. "Do you fancy a drive in the country, Annie? I have to go out near the Harveys' farm to see a patient. If you'd like to come, I'll take the buggy."

They were soon bowling along the road at a good clip. It felt so good to be out in the open air. Sunshine, contented cattle in the fields, and acres of wheat newly planted. What more could a man ask for?

———— ⚬⚬⚬ ————

When the constable and Mrs Harvey reached the farm Ellen was surprised that it looked no different now than it had when she left. The events had made no visible dent in the landscape. Cows were happily grazing in the paddocks and the dog came to greet them as she always did. A man was fixing the fence near the road and the constable waved out to him, commenting to Ellen, "That's the fellow I arranged to mind the animals."

When Constable O'Reilly unlocked the door and they went into the house it felt cold and empty although everything looked the same. The knife still lay on the veranda where Ellen had dropped it as she left the house with Mrs Johnson. How she wished she could take those hours back and tell Mrs Johnson that she wouldn't go with her after all. Had she done that Jock would still be alive, and she wouldn't be in this position.

The constable asked if he could light the fire and make a hot drink. "Do whatever you like," said Ellen. She needed to find the papers about the owner of the farm. She'd never looked in the drawer of the small table that Jock had used as a desk, but she was sure they'd be there and walked over to it. There was a letter lying on it addressed to her, but when she picked it up the constable said, "What have you got there?"

"It's a letter addressed to me. I've the right to read it in private," said Ellen.

"It may be used in evidence," said the policeman and he took it from her.

"Rubbish," said Doctor McDonald, as he came through the door. "Looks like I was just in time, my dear." And he took the letter from the astonished policeman and returned it to Ellen.

"What are you doing here Doctor? Mrs Harvey and I came out to find the papers relating to the farm ownership, but why are you here?"

"I've been to visit a patient and thought I'd call in and see how Mrs Harvey is." Alex turned to Ellen. "Mrs McDougal is outside. Would you like to see her?"

"Oh I would. Thank you. I'm so glad to see you. I just found this letter from my husband, but haven't had time to read it. I feel so shaky and cold."

"Go outside and sit in the sun. We'll bring you out a drink. I want to talk to the constable. You go and let Mrs McDougal cheer you up. Now, what are you like at fire lighting constable?"

"Don't think you're fooling me. I can see a cover-up. You had no right to take the letter from me. No right at all."

Alex looked at the young constable with pity. "You're trying to make this unfortunate affair into a major event," he said. "Mrs Harvey is the victim in this situation. Jock Harvey took his life while in an unsound frame of mind, and that's all there is to it."

"Well, I'm not so sure. There seems to have been a lot going on here. I find it funny that Mrs Johnson came so far from her home when she was nearly due to have the baby. That's a most unusual thing for a woman of her standing to do. Also, we only have the word of Dickson, that Mrs Harvey was being ill-used. Then John Johnson gives her the money to escape from her husband after she helps to deliver his wife's baby at the pa. It all looks too pat I say."

"Well, don't say it too loud, or you'll be the one up on charges," the doctor warned. "Let's get the fire going." He placed some kindling on the paper and bark he'd put ready as he'd listened to the policeman. After he struck the flint a flame began eating away at the scraps of wood. "Keep it going,"he told Constable O'Reilly. "I'm going to have a talk with Mrs Harvey." And he went outside. "How are you now? Are you feeling warmer?"

She nodded her head as she held out the letter for him to read. "Jock says he's sorry for the way he treated me, and that he had headaches that drove him mad. He said that the papers for the farm are in the drawer and that he loved me. Poor Jock. Why didn't he tell me why he was so bad tempered? I tried to get him to see you but he always said he didn't have time."

Alex read the words Jock had written and felt sympathy with him for his decision. He'd seen other strong men broken by a blow to the head. Suddenly he was anxious to get home to open the brain. "What will you do tonight Mrs Harvey? Will you stay here?"

"I have nowhere else to go and I need to look for those papers. I expect the constable will be here for a while yet. I'll give him the letter to read and perhaps that will stop him looking for ulterior motives."

"I don't like to think of you out here on your own. I say Annie, what about you staying here for the night then you can both drive in tomorrow in Jock's buggy. The chap who is milking the cows will catch and harness the horse for you. I'll see him before I go. How about that?"

"What an excellent idea," said Annie McDougal. "I don't like you being here on your own either. Doctor McDonald can manage for himself for once."

When the constable came through the door with four cups of tea, as well as a small jug of milk and a bowl of sugar on a tray, Ellen stood up and went around the side of the house and came back with a knife and a lemon which she carefully sliced and offered to the others. They all sat quietly as they sipped their tea, wrapped in their own thoughts. Then Ellen passed the letter to the policeman. "This might explain why Jock did what he did," she said. "I'll go and look for the name of the owner of the farm and the contract Jock had with him."

"Mrs McDougal is going to stay here tonight with Mrs Harvey, and they'll come in to town tomorrow," the doctor told the constable firmly. "It's all arranged."

"I need to ask her some more questions before I go," said the constable.

"Go right ahead," said Alex. "The letter explains everything."

In the house Ellen carefully searched through the contents of the drawer, but could see no sign of a contract. Then she remembered the diary in which Jock used to write any special dates or events on the farm. Where was that?

Constable O'Reilly came into the room and looked at the pile of papers on the desk. "I won't trouble you anymore today. If you come into the station tomorrow I can check the details then," he said and left the house to return to the town. There was a different air about him. After the belligerent way he'd spoken that morning Ellen was relieved.

"I've just had a word with the cowman," said the doctor, appearing at the door. "He'll get the buggy ready in the morning if you tell him when you want to go."

"Are you sure you don't mind Mrs McDougal staying with me tonight?" asked Ellen. "I'll certainly feel better if she is here."

"It was my suggestion my dear. It won't be the first time I've looked after myself."

"Thank you both so much. I'd have been a bit afraid to stay on my own. But I'll have to get used to that won't I?"

"I hope you find the papers you're looking for," said the doctor. "I had a word with young O'Reilly, and I convinced him he had no reason to think it was more than a poor man with a touch of brain fever. I think you'll find him in a different frame of mind."

"Oh thank you Doctor. I was getting quite afraid to speak in case he found more things to question," said Ellen.

"Yes. The doctor gave him a piece of his mind," said Mrs McDougal. "It did him the world of good. Now let's find this diary. Where did your husband keep it usually? When did he write it up?"

Ellen thought for a while, before answering. "At night, before he got into bed. He'd sit at the table and call out to me to ask the name of a traveller who had called about the stock, or what time we'd done such and such. He had quite a poor memory lately."

"What did Doctor McDonald say to the constable? He seemed very quiet and polite just before he left," asked Ellen.

"I'd better not say. Just a few home truths about what he gets up to in his spare time, I believe. There are no secrets in a small town. People are always willing to spread a bit of gossip about," said Mrs McDougal with a smile. "Perhaps when this trouble is all over I'll enlighten you."

"I suppose he has to look at the facts and if they don't fit he has to look again," said Ellen. "He seems to be thoroughly convinced that Mr Dickson and I were more than just friends but we weren't. I swear."

"I believe you; now let's look for that paper. Is there a place in the bedroom where it might be?" Ellen opened a wardrobe door to reveal a box with string tied around it. She pulled it free and placed it on the bed then cut the ties and lifted the lid. There on top was the diary. Ellen opened it up and read a few of the entries that had been made in the last few days. "Well," asked Annie McDougal, "what does it say?"

"It's just his usual mention of things that should be done in the next few days. There's nothing about his intentions." Ellen turned the pages looking for clues, but there was no entry for the day she'd left.

"Well, let's look for the documents we need. Are they in the back of the diary?" asked Mrs McDougal. "Or in the box?" She lifted some of the papers out and read the headings. Most were accounts for things Jock had purchased. But finally they came to what seemed to be a contract. It was signed by Jock and the owner and gave the name of a bank in Wellington as a forwarding address for the man. However, his name was crossed out and over-written with the name of Jock Harvey!

"What do you think his idea was?" asked Mrs McDougal. "Did he think the courts would pass such a document?"

"I've no idea. I never saw the man and I never questioned Jock about the farm either. I just took his word that the man had told him to come up here and take charge. What do you think it means?" said Ellen. "I thought it strange that we never heard from the man after we arrived. Jock went straight into caring for the farm as if it was his own. What should we do now?"

"I think you should write to the bank and wait and see what eventuates. I'd just state that you want to contact the man on a private matter then wait to hear from him. We'll write tonight and post the letter tomorrow then wait and see. Now what's for tea?"

"Do you think I should tell the constable about this? Or wait to hear from the owner?"

"Never say more than necessary. Wait until you hear from the man. What about some boiled eggs? Are your hens laying?"

After they'd eaten, the two women set about writing the letter. It was short and to the point, only asking for the bank to contact the man and ask him to get in touch with Mrs Harvey. Jock's sad demise was not mentioned, as there was no easy way to put it. "There," said Annie, "that will have to do."

Ellen picked up the diary and turned to the pages Jock had written in the first few weeks after they arrived at the farm. It brought back many memories of the happy times they'd had. The first cattle he'd bought, and the first calves born. It was all carefully recorded. Realisation suddenly hit her that it had all been for nothing.

Later, desperately sad for Jock, Ellen lay in bed unable to sleep and mourned for her husband. She'd really not had time to think about what she'd lost but now, in the quiet stillness of the evening, with only the sound of Mrs McDougal's gentle breathing alongside her, she wondered again what was to become of her. Perhaps she should go to work for Dora at the boarding house, but then all Jock's plans for the farm would be wasted. It was not easy trying to bring bush-covered hills and flats into production, but that was the way of life they'd chosen. Thinking about it all, she finally fell asleep.

———∞∞∞———

Up early, and keen to get home, Annie McDougal asked the cowman if he'd catch the horse and harness him to the buggy as soon as he'd finished the milking. She returned to the house to find Ellen up and about.

"How did you sleep?" she asked. "You were dead to the world when I woke so I went to see about the buggy. I've started the fire so we can have some breakfast. Would you like some porridge? Or toast? The bread is a bit stale."

"Porridge I think. That should set me up for what's likely to be a bad day. I'll go over to the shed and get some fresh milk," said Ellen and she put on her boots and coat. The morning air was fresh but not too chilly.

Annie thought she looked more relaxed than she had last night. Fair haired, blue eyed with lovely skin, she was only a slip of a thing. Annie could see how easily Jock Harvey would have fallen for her on the boat from Australia.

CHAPTER 48 Funeral Arrangements

The women made their way to Greytown, keeping the buggy moving at a steady trot. Ellen said she should go and see the policeman as soon as possible, but Annie said she should see Doctor McDonald first. Plans would need to be made for the funeral. "Did your husband have any special church he attended?" Annie asked.

"No, he never said. But he did read the Bible sometimes if the weather made farm work impossible. There's no Presbyterian church here yet. I don't know if the Anglicans or Catholics would bury him, being a suicide victim. Do you know what they think?" asked Ellen.

"I don't think there is any need to worry about that out here. It might have been the practice at home but I've never heard of a case here in New Zealand. I don't know for sure. We'll ask the doctor," said Annie as she went into the house.

Alex came into the kitchen. "How are you both feeling?" he asked. "Did you find the contract?"

"Yes we did," said Ellen. "I've brought it for you to see what you make of it. Something doesn't seem quite right."

"Let me see." Alex took the document and studied it, especially the alteration Ellen thought had been made by Jock. He looked at it with a critical eye. "There's certainly something funny here. Did you ever see the owner of the farm yourself?"

"No, never. We were married on the boat by the captain. I had no family and Jock had nobody here either so we decided not to wait. Then, when he was out looking for work in Wellington, he met the man who had the farm and offered him the job of minding it. That was more than three years ago and we've not heard from the man since. I think Jock would write letters to him care of the bank, but I never saw any come to the farm. I never thought anything of it. What do you think it means?"

"I'm not sure my dear, but we'll try to find out."

"We've written to the bank asking for them to please get the owner to contact us, well me I mean. I seem to be dragging everybody into the mess," said Ellen.

"Not at all. I hope you'll let us assist you in any decisions you make. Life is hard on a woman on her own. Now I have some news for you. I examined the brain. Sure enough, there was damage on the left side that would have caused considerable pain and led to a change in his normal temperament. You'll be able to see him to say goodbye whenever you are ready. Have you decided where he should be buried?"

"I'm not sure who'll be willing to have his body in their churchyard. I'll need to see the priest and the vicar today. What do you think?" asked Ellen.

"I'm sure you'll find either of those gentlemen quite acceptable to holding the service. You need to see them as soon as possible. I'm sure there will be a good turnout of support for you by the people of the town."

"I have to see Constable O'Reilly too so I'd best hurry up."

"Now you're to have a cup of tea before you go and I'll walk down to the police station with you," said Annie as she came through the doorway with a tray. "The doctor will manage here for a while. He's quite right; you need to hold the service as soon as possible."

"When do they have church services here?" asked Ellen "I never went to church from the farm, but I heard clergy visited quite regularly. Who would know?"

"I go to the Anglican service. That's only once a month but the vicar calls every week or so. We'll go and see the Dicksons. They'll know," said Annie. "Now drink up and go to see Constable O'Reilly. He'll be very docile I think. Don't you Alex?"

The doctor chuckled as he agreed. "If you want to see your husband, I'll take you through before you go. Then you'll have something to add to your evidence for him."

Together they went to look at the remains of the husband she'd loved so well. The doctor removed the sheet covering her husband's face. Ellen could only see a line of stitches through the hair. He looked peaceful and she said a prayer for his soul and hoped he'd soon be laid to rest. "What do I do about a coffin?" she asked.

"I've seen the undertaker who does most of the work for the town. He has one ready if you want it. He understands the position and he's ready to come as soon as I give the word that you're agreeable."

"I can't thank you both enough," said Ellen. "Yes, tell him I'd like him to take charge of the body." She turned away.

Annie could see that she was crying, but she thought that no bad thing. Poor child, she'd had no time to grieve. After a while Annie said, "I think it's time to see the constable," took Ellen's arm and guided her out on to the road where the horse was waiting patiently.

"Oh goodness, I forgot the poor thing," said Ellen. "What shall I do about the buggy and the horse?"

"Let's ask the constable. He's sure to have a place available to leave the buggy and somewhere the horse can graze," said Annie.

The constable was standing outside his station talking to a couple of men when they drew up. "Good morning, Constable," said Annie. "Could you tell us what do we do with the horse and buggy? Mrs Harvey needs to see a priest or vicar to arrange the funeral."

"I'll have the horse taken care of, Mrs Harvey. The buggy can stay here on the road. If you decide to return to the farm it will be here waiting. We just need to clear up a few facts then you'll be able to find the vicar. Are you staying Mrs McDougal?"

"Yes, I'm here to see you don't bamboozle her. She's had a terrible shock. Two shocks, really."

"I've reviewed my assessment of the death," he said. "Come into my office and we'll straighten things out." It took only a few minutes for Dan O'Reilly to ask Ellen what he needed to finish his report, and then the women were free to go. They walked down the road of the small settlement looking at the new buildings.

"It seems to grow overnight," said Annie. "Even though I live right in the heart of the village, I'm surprised every time I walk along the main road, to see the new houses and shops."

Ellen was glad to have a new topic of conversation, and admired the new look of the town too. They reached the store where Mrs Dickson greeted them warmly. Mary Smith was there as well, busy restocking shelves. "I was so sorry to hear about your husband," she said. "What are you going to do?"

"Thank you. I don't know yet. We're here to see if Mrs Dickson knows how I can contact a vicar or priest. We need to have the funeral as soon as possible. Is there room for graves near the house where Mass is said?" asked Ellen.

"I expect he can be buried in the new cemetery set aside on the outskirts of town. I think a vicar will be here tomorrow on his way to Wellington."

"How can I speak to him?" asked Ellen.

"The best thing to do is write him a letter, take it to the stables where the coach departs from and ask them to give it to him. Reverend Porter is well known. He may even come down from Masterton today if he's to catch the Wellington coach tomorrow."

"That's what I'll do. We have to walk down there anyway as we have a letter to post."

"You could leave the letter here, if you like. My husband will be taking the mail down later."

Ellen wasn't sure if that was the best thing to do with the letter for the vicar. The one for the bank would all right, but the one for the vicar was urgent. "I think I'll walk down to the stables on my own. You'll want to get back to the surgery, Mrs McDougal. If I can't find a priest or vicar, should I try to get a J P to conduct a service at the farm? Is that legal?" asked Ellen.

"I really don't know," said Johanna. "We'll find out. You go home, Mrs McDougal. Surgery will start soon. I'll look after Mrs Harvey."

———∞∞∞———

Ellen Harvey decided to walk down to the stables and also call into the house where the priest said Mass to see if that would be an option. While Jock hadn't been at all religious, she felt the people who knew him would expect to have a service to attend.

The priest was away in Featherston but she had more luck at the stables. The Masterton coach was just in and when she asked the driver if he knew Reverend Porter she was introduced to a man waiting to collect his case.

"Well my dear, what can I do for you?" he asked.

Ellen asked if he had time to discuss a private matter. He agreed and together they walked a little way down the road to where they could sit together, on a fallen log, left there for just this purpose.

"Now my dear, what's the problem?" he asked.

"My husband died on Saturday evening or Sunday morning by his own hand. I'd left him alone. Some neighbours found him on Sunday morning. He'd hung himself," said Ellen.

"Oh my dear," said the vicar. "That must have been a terrible shock. How did this come about?" Reverend Porter listened attentively as she filled in the details and asked about the possibility of him conducting a service.

"I'm very sorry. I'm leaving for Wellington tomorrow morning on important business. I really can't delay my trip. There's also the question of burial in the Anglican part of the cemetery. We have a strict rule, you know. Well, not so much here in the Antipodes, I suppose, but...."

He stopped as Ellen stood up. "Thank you for your time. I've been told that my husband may be buried in the new cemetery just out of town. Thank you for listening," she said and walked away as quickly as she could before tears started. But back at the store there was good news - the priest had been into the store only half an hour ago and had said he would be happy to hold a service.

"Now," said Johanna. "Sit down, have a drink of tea and a rest. You're wearing yourself out with worry. My husband will take you to see the priest in a few minutes and it will all be settled quickly. You'll see."

Half an hour later Ellen and Henry were knocking on the door of the house used for Mass. Father Brady opened the door. "I hear you've been through a lot, my dear. Mrs Dickson told me about your loss. I'm very sorry. I've met your late husband and was very surprised to hear what he'd done but Doctor McDonald told me he's found the possible cause during the autopsy. I have no qualms about burying him in the Catholic part of the cemetery at all. The Bishop need not know all the details and I'm sure God has forgiven him. Now we need to lay him to rest."

"When could you hold the ceremony Father?" asked Ellen.

"Tomorrow? About ten a.m.? Or later if you like," said the priest. Ellen gave a sigh of relief, and burst into tears.

"I think perhaps it should be in the afternoon Father," said Mr Dickson, "to give people time to hear about it. What about two o'clock?"

"Yes, yes that will suit me fine. I'll say Mass as I usually do on Thursday morning. Mr Dickson will spread the word. I think a lot of people will want to attend the service for your husband. Not a Requiem Mass of course, but a good send off anyway," said Father Brady, in his cheerful Irish way. "With a bit of a wake afterwards," he added.

Ellen was so relieved. She thanked him warmly. "I'll go home now, and return tomorrow for the service."

"Do you need to go back to the farm?" asked Henry. "Will you be all right? You could stay with us," he offered.

"I will be, now that the funeral is settled. I'll tell the constable when I pick up the buggy. Will you put a notice in your window and tell people?"

It was getting late in the afternoon when Ellen reached the police station to collect the buggy. Constable O'Reilly was waiting for her and was very friendly. Ellen wished she knew what had caused the change in his attitude. She knew it was something the doctor had said to him. 'I must ask Mrs McDougal to tell me when things settle down,' she thought.

"I've sent a new man out to the farm to relieve the first one," the constable told her. "He's a young chap, but he's been working on a farm out by the Waiohine with Kelly. I think he'll be able to manage until you contact the owner."

"Thank you," said Ellen "We've sent a letter to the bank, and should hear back soon."

"We? Who are we?"

"Mrs McDougal and I," replied Ellen. "We wrote it last night, and I took it to the stables this morning. Oh, the funeral will be tomorrow at two p.m. At the Catholic Mass house down the end of town. Father Brady has agreed to do it."

As Ellen drove the buggy down the road through the small settlement, she saw Mary Smith and Beth Goode walking home with Marie and Peter and pulled the horse to a stop to greet them.

"We are so sorry to hear of your loss," Beth Goode said.

"How are you, Mrs Harvey?" Mary asked, thinking of how sad it was to lose your husband under such circumstances. At least she could still think of Jim as being alive, prospecting in the bad lands of Australia. What she'd feel like if she heard he was dead she could only imagine.

"I feel better now the funeral has been arranged. Father Brady will hold it tomorrow at two p.m. Will you tell the children to tell their parents if they go home for lunch? I think some won't come because of what happened, but I hope those who have a Christian outlook will support me," said Ellen.

"Of course," said Beth. "The Dicksons will spread the word. I'm sure there'll be morbid curiosity from some people, but many folk will want to show their respect."

"Mr Dickson is shutting the store so we can all come," said Mary. "So you'll have six friends there at least. The Johnsons are sure to be there. I told Rangi when he came into the store. No, I don't think you'll be short of mourners. Are you going home now? It's a bit late isn't it?"

"Yes I am, but I'll be fine. There's a new man looking after the farm so I won't be on my own. I'll see you tomorrow. Thank you for your sympathy," said Ellen.

CHAPTER 49 More Worries

Kate was putting the baby down for a sleep when Mrs Kelly arrived. She kissed Kate then settled herself into the chair by the fire. "How are you both doing?" she asked. "You must be thankful it's over. He looks a good strong baby."

"Yes, you can be sure I am. He's been so good. Four days old already, but it's been such a worrying time. I couldn't believe it about poor Jock Harvey. He was a big strong man, there must have been more wrong in his life than his wife leaving him. Mind you, I didn't blame her. He was very vicious when I suggested she needed to see a doctor, ordered her out of the house and told her not to return. The poor girl had bruises up her arm. But how are things with you and your husband now? Is he behaving?"

"Yes, but he's going to find it difficult to get all the work done on his own now that O'bie has found another place to work. Did you know he's gone to look after Harvey's farm?"

"No, we didn't know," said Kate. "That will be good for Mrs Harvey, having the place looked after. Your husband is a good farmer and I'm sure O'bie will have picked up enough to manage. But is he still fond of the bottle? I know you kept it under control when he was around your husband, but what will he be like when he's on his own?"

"I don't know. It seems he can be good for months and then he breaks out on a bender. I'm glad he's gone. He's a nice chap and worked well but I can't put up with that, even if he was a hero when he saved Jake."

"I expect young Dennis is getting to be a good help," said Kate. "Oh, I can hear Jake arriving from school. Cathy's still not allowed on her pony. She'll be walking along with Jane and Polly."

"I'll get off home. I don't get into town much, now Henry Dickson comes around, but we might go to church on Sunday. Will you let me know if you hear anything about the funeral for Jock Harvey?"

Kate waved good-bye. It was lovely to see her, but Kate was feeling the stress of the last few days. Visitors were good but sometimes she'd be just as happy on her own.

"Hullo, Mother. What's for tea?" asked Jake as he came through the gate and threw his bag onto the veranda.

"Bread and scrape," said Kate, laughing. Food, food, food, was all Jake thought about these days.

"Wha whee!" said Jake. "Bread and scrape. I can't wait," And he ran out the gate and over to the barn to let his dog off the chain.

Kate looked fondly after him. It was so sad that Patrick Kelly died. She was sure Jake missed him still. Jake came back with Dot before going to bring in the milkers. "I suppose you want something to eat now?" she asked.

Jake nodded enthusiastically and Dot barked. Kate went to the store cupboard and found some biscuits, and a bone from the last night's meal to give them, and reminded Jake he had things to attend to before he was free to play. They ran off happily just as Cathy arrived, walking slowly and holding her arm at her side. The scarf had come undone and Kate could see she was in pain.

"Cathy dear, what have you done to your arm?"

"I just banged it when we were playing chasing. It'll be all right."

"Let me have a look at it," said Kate. She picked up the arm and felt where the arm left the plaster bandage. It was very warm. "I hope it's not broken again. You were a silly girl to play chasing, now weren't you?" Kate said. "I gave you credit for more sense."

"I'm sorry," said Cathy, "The girls were having fun and I didn't know I'd get pushed over."

"If it continues to hurt you'll have to go and see Doctor McDonald. Now, what would you like to eat?"

"I don't feel like much, thank you," said Cathy. "I'd like a drink though. "Some ginger beer?"

Kate poured it, feeling sorry she'd growled at Cathy when she was in pain. "How was school?" she asked.

"Two men came to see Mrs Thompson and Miss Goode. Mrs Thompson said they're going around all the schools. She didn't look very happy when they went. Jane heard one of the men tell Miss Goode they didn't think women were good teachers. He said he had a young man in mind for the job, but Mrs Thompson told Miss Goode that there was no need to worry."

"What else did they say? Did they talk to you children?" Kate asked.

"Yes. They told us that we were doing well and asked us questions about Queen Victoria. We'd been looking at the royal family, how long she's ruled, and things like that so we were lucky."

Annie was glad the body had been removed from the surgery, and the house no longer smelt of death. She opened the doors, both back and front, to let the breeze blow down the passage, wondering as she did so what she could give the doctor for tea. He was looking very sad. She didn't ask what was bothering him as she understood that some things must be kept in confidence. His unhappiness seemed to deepen as the day wore on, however. Was it what he had found in Mr Harvey's brain or was it some other patient he was worried about? She thought if she hurried she would have time to reach the butcher before he closed so she could buy a nice piece of rump steak.

"How do you like it Mrs McDougal?" asked the butcher. "Fresh or ripe?"

"About halfway between," said Annie. "Not too fresh, but not too ripe."

"Some people are fussy!" laughed Joe Taylor. "Have you heard when they are going to bury Harvey? It's one of his beasts that I'm selling you now."

"I think it will be tomorrow. Dickson will be sure to know. Have a look in his window as you go home." When Annie arrived home she found Alex sitting in the darkened parlour deep in thought so she went to prepare the meal.

When they'd eaten she was pleased to see he'd done justice to his steak. She asked again what was troubling him, but he didn't reply, just sat there holding his dead pipe. Then he rose and made his way to his bedroom. Really worried,

Annie prepared for bed, wondering what she could do until she could bear it no longer and tiptoed down the hall to the doctor's room. He looked surprised to see her but turned back the blanket and she lay beside him on the bed as he embraced her. "Do tell me," she said. "What's the matter?"

"I lost another child today - one of the Halls' children; you remember, her sister died last week of diphtheria. The poor mother is broken-hearted. I did all I could to save her, but it was not to be."

"Oh my darling you've done all you could," She put her arms around Alex and he wept. "Once that disease takes hold it's almost impossible to cure."

"I just wished it hadn't happened to this woman. She's had such an unhappy life, and now to lose two of her children. I'm afraid for her sanity." He sank closer to Annie. It was comforting to feel her arms around him. They must set the date for the wedding and to hang with wagging tongues. When she went to leave he held her close and they went to sleep with their arms entwined.

When Annie woke she was pleased to see he was still asleep. She could slip away from the room and they'd say no more about it. He looked peaceful and she wasn't sorry for what she'd done. He took the troubles of the world on his shoulders. When she had made the porridge she called him and he came into the kitchen, sat down at the table, and said, "So when will we marry, my love?"

<hr />

Ellen admired the sunset as the horse plodded along the road back to the farm. Wisps of clouds, coloured red and gold by the setting sun, curled about the tops of the Rimutakas like party streamers and she thought of an old saying of her grandmother's. 'Always have enough clouds in your life to make a perfect sunset.' 'Well I've enough clouds in my life for now,' she thought. As she drove through the gateway to the farm a man came from the stable.

"I'm O'bie," he said as he helped her down from the buggy. "Patrick O'Brien, but my friends call me O'bie for short. The policeman gave me the job of looking after the place until you decide what to do with it." Ellen shook his hand. Not very old, he didn't look a bad sort. Perhaps they'd be able to manage the work between them until she heard from the owner.

"I have to go in to Greytown again tomorrow for my husband's funeral," said Ellen.

"I'll have the buggy ready for you, at what time?" asked O'bie.

"I suppose I should go and see the undertaker and decide on who should be pall bearers and things like that. Perhaps I'll go in at ten o'clock. Yes, have the buggy ready by then please," said Ellen.

"Right you are then," said O'bie. "Would you like me to light the fire for you?"

"Oh yes please. Have you had tea yet?" asked Ellen. Was she going to have to make his meals?

"No, not yet, but I can look after myself, Mrs Harvey. I've made a place in the loft of the barn where I can sleep, so as not to be a burden to you," said O'bie. "I'll have a hot meal with you at night if you're making one, otherwise I can take care of myself. I'll light the fire if you unlock the door."

"Come in and have some supper when you've taken care of the animals. I'm not sure what I can offer you, but it will be something."

The house felt cold and dark when Ellen and Obie went inside. She wished Annie McDougal was still there with her. She looked to see where the lamp was and lit it. It gave a good light and immediately the room didn't look so gloomy.

O'bie set the fire and went to finish his chores. Soon its warmth edged towards her while the flames lit the corners of the room, pushing away cold shadows, and an unexpected peace came upon her. She thought of the ordeal of the funeral which was to come tomorrow, but somehow she was not depressed. People were being so good to her and Dora had been so welcoming as well. Would she be wise to return to Dora? At least she had options to consider.

Now what could she give Mr O'Brien to eat? Ellen laid the table for the meal, thinking of the eggs she and Mrs McDougal had enjoyed. It seemed ages ago. She unwrapped the ham she'd bought from the butcher and sliced some of the loaf Mrs Dickson had pressed on her. With cheese and pickles, that would have to do. The kettle was singing a happy song and she made the tea then went to call O'bie.

CHAPTER 50 The Funeral

Next morning, when Rangi and Ru arrived at the Johnsons' farm, John came out to the veranda to give them their 'riding instructions' for the day. They were still working on clearing the bush in the lower paddocks of the farm that he had secured for Jim Smith. It had been a lot of work but was now starting to pay off as there was more feed for the cattle and sheep. The flood damage was nearly cleaned up and fresh grass was growing on the blocks of newly sown fields.

"We'd like to go to Mr Harvey's funeral, boss," said Rangi. "If that's all right? May wants to go too - she picked spuds for Mr Harvey and I want to be there with her."

"Of course, I expected you'd want to go," said John, putting on his boots. "What say we all work for the morning and go to town at noon? My wife wants to be there for Mrs Harvey too, so we'll go in the buggy. William will be quite happy with his mother. The children have gone to school, but will come to the service with us. I think it's important they're involved. It's a hard lesson to learn, about life and death, but the sooner they learn it the better."

Alex McDonald was discussing the funeral arrangements with Father Brady who'd come to see him about his aching knee. "It's getting harder and harder to get around," said Father as he rolled his trousers down over the offending knee. "I might have to get a trap and stop trying to climb on my horse,"

"Well that would make life safer for you. The roads are better now and driving is surely easier on the pins than galloping around on that mare of yours."

"I'll give it some thought," said the priest. "Now I must get away to prepare for the service. I want to give him a good send off for that poor girl's sake. It's a dreadful thing to happen, but it seems she has some friends who've gathered around her. What was O'Reilly going on about foul play or some such?"

"Oh don't you worry about that. I put a stop to that line of thought. I had a word to him and said that if he proceeded with that view of things, I'd tell a few husbands around town what he gets up to when they're out in the bush. Of course he said he was just keeping the ladies company. Doing his duty."

Father Brady chuckled to himself as he walked away home.

At the Harvey farm Ellen had woken early and lay there, the eiderdown up close around her shoulders, thinking about the events of the last few days. Father Brady had told her the undertaker would make all the arrangements for grave digging, but she needed to decide who would carry the coffin. Who could she ask that wouldn't be offended at the thought of assisting at the funeral of a suicide victim? She turned the names over in her mind. It will all work out, she thought. 'Wait and see who is there.'

Eventually she rolled the covers back and got out of bed. Should she go and help with the milking? She'd always helped Jock and it didn't seem right to lie in bed while someone else was working. Ellen dressed in warm things and made her way to the bails. "Good morning," she said to O'bie, who was busy emptying a bucket of creamy milk into the vat. "I've come to help. Who's next?"

"The jersey," said O'bie.

Ellen took her bucket, settled herself on the stool and pumped away at the udder of the old brown cow as if nothing had changed. It was a comfort in a way. Things change, but things stay the same. O'bie let the cow he'd milked out the door and replaced her with another one. Soon all that could be heard was the drum, drum. drumming of milk hitting the bottom of the bucket in a tuneful rhythm.

"I'll harness the horse for you as soon as I've had breakfast," said O'bie as he washed the buckets.

"I need to decide who'll carry the coffin and I'll have to ask them if they're happy to do it," said Ellen as she dried her hands. "Yes, I think that I'll go as soon as I can. Will you take the milk to the piggery in the dray first? That won't take long then you can put the horse in the buggy for me."

"I'll do that for you, Mrs Harvey," said O'bie. "It'll be better for you to have things settled before the service begins, won't it?"

At the school Mrs Thompson told the children it would be a half day because of the funeral. "All the children who are going to the service may play for a while after lunch and I'll ring the bell when it's time to go to the church. You can walk down together," she said. "Father Brady wants Dennis to be altar boy. Will you make sure he goes a bit earlier, Jane, so he can put on his surplice in time? Those who are not going to the service may go home after lunch, which will be eaten here in the school grounds. I don't want you walking down the road eating food in public. Understood?"

"Yes Mrs Thompson," they all replied. Beth, watching her class to see they understood, noticed Olga Petersen looked worried. "Do you know what your mother wants you to do?" she asked. "Is she going to the funeral?"

"I don't know. Please, what is funeral?" asked Olga.

"It is a service for a man who died and will be buried today," said Beth.

A little later in the morning Dennis approached Mrs Thompson with an anxious look on his face. "Mrs Thompson, can I ask you something?"

"Of course, Dennis." said Mrs Thompson, wondering what was coming.

"Why did the man hang himself? Would it hurt?" asked Dennis. Jane had told him how the man had died.

His teacher pondered the questions. "He was sick Dennis. That's all."

Ellen drove the few miles to town along the dusty road. It was strange how quickly the roads could turn from slushy mud to dry dust that rose in a cloud as you passed.

At Dickson's store Ellen was greeted affectionately by Mrs Dickson and Mary Smith. "How are you this morning?" asked Johanna.

"Not so bad but I'll be glad when this day is over. Is there any mail for the farm? I'm waiting to hear from the bank."

"No, nothing yet," said Johanna.

"I've been thinking about who'll carry the coffin," said Ellen. "Have you any idea about who I should approach?"

"Now let's see," said Johanna. "My husband, for sure, John Johnson will, and Rangi would be pleased to be asked. Mr Kelly might as it is in his church. I think the blacksmith Peter Fairman would want to, as he said how much he liked your husband. How far would they need to carry it?"

"Only from the dray into the church and back after the service. Then from the dray to the grave, so the undertaker explained to me," said Ellen. "Jock was a big man. I think we need six, don't we?"

"I think Dan O'Reilly might," said Mary Smith. "We were talking last night when we met in the street."

"You'd do well to watch him," said Johanna. "I was told a little piece of news by Annie McDougal. I won't say why, but I'd be careful around him."

"Oh tell us," said Ellen. "I know Doctor McDonald was able to make him change his mind about hounding me. Mrs McDougal said she'd explain later."

"He's a bit of a philanderer, it seems," said Johanna smugly.

Kate wrapped William warmly and laid him in a large wooden box for John to place in the buggy. It would keep him out of the wind and Kate wouldn't have to hold him on the journey. She'd prepared some food to take for the refreshments being organised by Johanna Dickson. Other ladies had also promised to help. But Rangi said that when he'd called in at the store that morning Mrs Dickson was annoyed. She'd asked Doris Bell to help and had been refused. "I don't believe he should be given a Christian burial at all," said Mrs Bell. "I certainly won't be attending."

Rangi was amused at how angry Mrs Dickson had been. Everyone knew what a nasty person Doris Bell was. May had once done housework for her but had been treated so badly she left. All sorts of rubbish had been put around town about May being dishonest, but no one believed the rumours when they found out who'd spread them.

❧

When John pulled the buggy up outside the store and helped Kate down the women there were quickly clustered around she and William. "He's a lovely baby," said Johanna. "I'm getting so excited about my baby. I felt the first kicks yesterday. They'll be great friends when they grow up, won't they."

"I hope so," said Kate. "There'll only be a few months between them. How are you Mrs Harvey? I was so sorry to hear of your husband's death."

"Thank you Mrs Johnson. I don't feel as if everyone is blaming me for Jock's death anymore, since the doctor found the cause of his misery. I'm so grateful to Doctor McDonald for his care," said Ellen. "We were just discussing who could be pallbearers when you arrived."

"John would be honoured, I'm sure. He didn't know your husband well but did admire him for his farm work and care of the animals."

Time was moving on. The women talked about the arrangements for the afternoon tea that would be served when the mourners came back from the cemetery. "The men will put up some tables under the trees and some chairs for those who need to sit. I'm sure it will be fine," said Johanna.

"I want to go and see Father Brady and the undertaker to see everything is ready," said Ellen. "He's bringing Jock's body to the church at ten to two. Will Mr Johnson be there by then, to help carry it in?"

"I'll see that he is and I'll see Peter Fairman too. I can leave William with you for a few minutes while I do that, can't I Mrs Dickson?" asked Kate.

"Of course," said Johanna. "It will be my pleasure."

❧

Ellen arrived at the church-house door at the same time as the undertaker. "Everything's ready Mrs Harvey," he said. "But can you tell me who will be the pall bearers?"

"Mr Johnson and three other gentlemen have been asked to do it," Ellen said. "I was going to see who else came."

"The men who found him, what about them?" he asked. "They did a good job looking out for their neighbour."

"I know, but they're Maoris, would they be happy to be asked? I was told Ru was upset when he saw my husband. How would he react now?" asked Ellen.

"I'm sure Rangi would be honoured to do this one last thing for his neighbour," said George Morris. "I hope Johnson and the others arrive early, or would you prefer to leave the coffin on the dray until everyone is in the house?"

"Oh, no, I think it'd be better to be inside before the people get seated," replied Ellen.

Just then Dennis Kelly arrived. "I'm going to help Father Brady," he said, and knocked at the door which was opened by the housekeeper.

"Good afternoon to you all," she said to them. "Father is just saying his office. He'll be out in a few minutes. You go inside Dennis. He'll tell you what to do."

Before long Father Brady came out of the house with Dennis, now in his surplice.

They walked together to the dray which held the coffin then paused as Kate and John, Henry Dickson and Peter Fairman and Mr and Mrs Kelly all arrived. Father began the welcoming prayers for the dead.

When it was time to move the coffin inside Father Brady walked ahead, then Dennis, who was making the responses, followed by the four men. There was a bit of difficulty negotiating the doorway but soon the coffin was safe on its stand.

Ellen, Kate and Tessa stood silently until the coffin was inside the house, then turned to greet the people who were arriving. Some came and shook Ellen's hand, or expressed their condolences, but most were keeping their distance. " I think we should go inside," said Kate, just as John appeared, and Rangi and Ru arrived.

"Is May not coming then?" John asked.

"No, one of the boys is sick," said Rangi.

"Mrs Harvey wants you to be pall bearers," said John.

"That's all right with me," said Rangi.

Ru nodded and said, "If you tell me what to do."

"Just follow us. You'll be fine," said John.

Soon the service began.

"In the name of the Father, and of the Son and of the Holy Ghost," Father Brady said. "We are come together to farewell Jock Harvey, and commend his soul to Heaven. Let's remember the happier times when he was a good husband to his wife and looked after his farm and the animals well. There has been some talk about the rights and wrongs of burying him in consecrated ground. I'm sure that the good Lord will call none of us to answer for affording this man a good send off. Let us pray.

"Oh Lord, receive the soul of your faithful servant and forgive him his sins as we lay his body to rest." Then he began the litany of the saints. Some of the people answered in Latin, "Ora pro nobis," others in English, "Pray for us," as he called upon all the saints in heaven to gather and accept the body of the deceased.

After the short service Father Brady walked in front with Dennis as the pall bearers made their way to the waiting dray. The six men made light work of the task. Soon, those who had horses to ride or buggies to drive followed the dray along the road to the cemetery. Quite a few townsfolk walked the mile to the field where the Catholic portion of the cemetery was marked out. The Anglicans were buried some distance away. Old habits die hard. Fighting between the church faithful was not as rife here, as it was in England, but still had some people willing to continue the battle at any opportunity.

Soon all were gathered around the newly dug grave where Ellen stood silently waiting for this last act in the life of the man she'd loved. The men took up the coffin and carried it to where she stood with tears running down her cheeks.

"Out of the depths to thee, O Lord, I cry," intoned Father Brady. "Lord graciously turn thy ear to hear our prayers for the soul of our friend John Stuart Harvey. If his sins offended you, we pray for your forgiveness. Grant thy servant eternal rest. May his soul rest in peace. Lord have mercy."

"Lord have mercy," the people replied.

"Lord have mercy. Christ have mercy," said Father.

"Christ have mercy," they replied.

"Christ have mercy. Let us now say the prayer Jesus taught us. Our Father who art in heaven, hallowed be thy name, Thy kingdom come. Thy will be done, on earth as it is in Heaven. Give us this day our daily bread, and forgive us our trespasses as we forgive those who trespass against us. Lead us not into temptation but deliver us from evil."

Father Brady took a handful of soil and scattered it on to the coffin. "Oh Lord we are but dust and unto dust we shall return." He turned to Ellen, offering her the pot of soil and she sprinkled a small handful on top of the posy of flowers she'd picked from her garden and laid on the coffin.

Afterwards people came and shook her hand and spoke words of encouragement, but it was as if she was somewhere else, looking down from a hillside at the age old ceremony. Not here at all. She stood silently until Kate took her by the arm. The men were waiting to fill in the grave.

"I'm all right Mrs Johnson, don't worry," said Ellen as she was helped in to the gig. "I nearly gave way to misery but now I'm ready to face whatever comes along."

Soon all were back at the church-house where tea and cold drinks were being served. Groups were discussing the funeral and their opinions of how Father Brady had conducted it. "Went very well," was the opinion of the majority. One or two disliked the 'who' in the Lord's Prayer instead of the Anglican 'which', but most agreed it had been a good send off. Many wondered what the lady would do now.

Among them was Doris Bell. Helping herself to another piece of cream sponge she said in a loud voice, "I hope she doesn't think she can stay out on the farm with that young man. I mean it's not right."

"What's not right?" asked Mrs Dickson as she came into earshot.

"That Mrs Harvey, staying out on the farm with only that young man for company," said Doris. "I mean..."

"What do you mean Mrs Bell? If I hear anymore of your sly remarks I shall ban you from my store. I thought you weren't coming to the funeral. That's what you said."

"Oh I never went to the church, I just waited for the tea to be served here," said Doris Bell smugly.

━━━━━∞━━━━━

Before long most of the people had left, the remains of the refreshments had been cleared away and some of the men were packing up the tables. "What about a pint or two to wet the baby's head?" they asked John, "and to say good bye to Harvey?" He agreed and whispered to Kate that he wanted to shout the men a pint or two.

"How will you get home?" she asked.

"Jake can ride with you and Cathy in the buggy and I'll ride Blueboy home. I won't be late," he promised. He told the men he'd meet them at the hotel shortly and all went away feeling glad they'd asked him. "Good bloke," one said.

"All right," said Kate, smiling, "but I'll send a search party out if you're not home by dark."

Kate was getting into the buggy with the children when Mr Kelly came by driving the dray and asked where John was. The ladies side-stepped the question by saying he had business to see too, but Paddy guessed what the 'business' was. He looked at Tessa. "I wouldn't mind a pint," he said. "I'd only have one." But Tessa shook her head determinedly.

As Kate and the children were soon bowling along the road towards home Jake asked his mother why Mrs Kelly wouldn't let Mr Kelly have a pint with the other men. He thought it was mean of her.

Kate thought of how to answer without tainting Jake's view of the man, but decided it was a good opportunity to tell him of the dangers of drink. "I'm afraid, Jake, that Mr Kelly likes his beer, but he has an illness that means he can't stop at one drink. If he has one drink, he has to go on drinking until he is drunk. He can never drink liquor again."

"Couldn't Doctor McDonald give him something to fix it?" asked Cathy who'd been listening.

"No my dear, there's no cure. Now here we are home safe and sound. Don't talk about what I've said but remember the lesson. Never drink to excess. Let's get William inside. He's had a big day."

Jake went to feed the puppy and do his other chores. He milked the two cows and fed the calves and pigs. He really wanted to go and play with Dot but as his father wasn't home he had a larger than ever list of things to do.

After Cathy checked their nests for eggs then fed scraps of food from the funeral to the fowls, laughing as she watched them fighting over the choicest morsels, Kate gave her William to hold while she got tea ready. Cathy sat in the big easy chair with him against her shoulder. He felt lovely and soft and smelled of the soft soap Kate had washed him with. His fuzzy hair tickled Cathy's nose. "What did you think of the funeral?" Kate asked. "Did you find it interesting?" She could remember sitting through church services at home, praying for them to be over.

"No, I liked Father Brady, but Dennis looked funny in a dress."

CHAPTER 51 The Wake

John and Doctor McDonald were relieved Kelly was missing from the group of men gathered around the bar with pint glasses in their hands. "Fill them up again Mr Evans," said John. "I want you all to drink young William's health." Soon the froth was rising up the glasses as the publican did his job. "And again," said John, "To say goodbye to our friend Jock Harvey. May he rest in peace."

"Not pieces," said some wag. Some of the men were recounting stories about Jock and of how careful he'd been about money. "A true Scot," said another.

At which point Alex McDonald said, "As another Scot, I have to tell you some news about me and Mrs McDougal. We are to be married."

"You are a sly old fox," said John while the other men crowded around to shake the doctor's hand. "Congratulations to you both. We're really pleased for you. When will the wedding be?"

"Thank you. You'll hear in due course. It will be a small affair with just a few friends. We don't want any fuss," said the doctor, then shouted another round.

Eventually Doctor McDonald said he'd had enough and would make his way home, "You'd better call it a day too, Johnson. You'll fall off the pony."

"Never," said John, "but you're right, I think I've had enough. My darling wife will be waiting for me." His voice was not as firm as usual. "One more drink, men," he said. "To Doctor Alex McDonald, who's going to tie the knot. Best wishes Doctor from all here. Drink up."

John said good-bye and started for home on Jake's pony, thinking about the events of the day. 'It's funny how funerals, even such an unusual one as today's, can make a man think about his own mortality.' Life was good. The baby was a healthy little chap and Kate was all a man could ask for. 'What would happen to her if I died? I must look at taking out some form of insurance to see she's well provided for.' A man had visited the farm a while ago selling policies for a few shillings a week. John had thought at the time that they couldn't afford it, but he'd reconsider it now. He rode along the ill-formed track at a trot. 'What will the widow do? It's not my job to worry but the women are concerned for her welfare. I suppose O'bie will be able to manage until she hears from the owner.'

Suddenly the loud cry of a ruru startled the pony and he took off at a gallop. Tree branches brushed John's head and he laid low in the saddle, his head down, trying to avoid them. But whack! A low branch hit him full on the forehead and toppled him off the horse. Blueboy didn't stop, but galloped away home as fast as he could. He pulled up at the gate with a flurry of pebbles beside Jake who was playing with Dot.

Jake caught him and soothed him as he called for his mother. Kate came running, wondering what the matter was. One look at Blueboy told her. She ran to the house for a blanket and told Cathy to mind William. "Go and saddle Beauty and Bessie, Jake; bring them, then ride to Kelly's for help." Jake ran to do as she said.

Soon Kate was riding Beauty along the track in search of her husband. Please God let him be all right, she prayed, watching out for John in the gathering dusk as she rode.

Meanwhile, Jake had ridden to the Kellys' as fast as he could. He could barely speak as he banged loudly on the door. "Whatever is the matter?" asked Tessa, as she opened it.

"My father has fallen off Blueboy," Jake panted. "Mother has gone looking for him and wants Mr Kelly to help."

Tessa called out for Paddy and Dennis to come quickly. "Jake's mother is looking for Mr Johnson. Get the lantern, Paddy, you must find him."

"I wonder where we should start." said Paddy. "He could've fallen off near town or closer to our house." He looked perplexed.

Dennis thought about the road he travelled each day to school. "I know a place," he said. "There's a broken branch hanging over the road just before you get to the stream. It broke off in the storm and is just hanging; Jake has to go around it carefully. We tried to pull it down but it was too strong for us. I'll bet that's what hit Mr Johnson."

"Come and show us lad," said Paddy. He took up the lantern and they walked into the night. Tessa watched them go, wondering what else could be sent to try them. 'What would Mrs Johnson do if something has happened to her husband? Please God, let him be safe.'

Kate was finding it hard to see the road, but called out as she went along. Beauty was sure footed, but the darkness and the ruts in the road made progress slow. Before long she saw a lantern bobbing behind her and pulled Beauty to a halt. "The pony came home without him. Whatever shall I do?" she said.

"Now, now, just wait and see. Young Dennis said he knows of a place where he may have received a hit on his head."

"Oh, let's go there," said Kate. "Where do you think he might be Dennis?"

"It's just around the next corner. There's a branch hanging down."

Kate urged Beauty to hurry and, rounding the bend, saw the broken branch, lit now by the rising full moon. There on the ground lay John, groaning with his face bloody. Kate jumped down and felt for a pulse just as Paddy and Dennis arrived.

"How is he?" asked Paddy. "It looks as though he's got a nasty gash on his head."

Kate looked up. "Where's Jake?" she asked Paddy.

"I thought it would be best for him to get Bessie and bring the buggy along in case John needs to go to see Dr McDonald."

John groaned again and tried to sit up - with little success. Just then Jake arrived with the buggy.

"You did well Jake," said Kate. "I'm going to try to see if Father can stand up."

"Really?" asked Paddy. "Is that wise?"

"You take one side Jake. You take the other please Mr Kelly. Dennis, you hold the lantern up as high as you can. Now we'll try to lift him up. John," she said, "we're going to see if you can walk." Soon they had him standing up and were able to walk him slowly towards the buggy where they managed to lay him on the floor. "What's a matter?" said John with a slurred voice.

"You're drunk!" said Kate. "Thank you so much Mr Kelly, and Dennis. I'm really grateful. We'll be all right now, I think," said Kate. "There's enough light from the moon to see our way. You go on home. And thank you again."

"That's all right. Glad we could help. It's not often I can say I have helped Johnson off the ground. He's done it for me a few times. Get him home and mind his head," said Paddy with a laugh.

Once home, Kate and Jake helped John into the house and onto the bed. Kate covered him with a blanket and left him to sleep, wondering if she should try and wash the blood off his head. She didn't want it to start bleeding again.

Anyway, William was hungry and restless. Cathy had done all she could think of to keep him happy, even letting him suck on her finger. She was glad to hand him back. "What's the matter with Father?" she asked as Kate took her seat in the comfortable chair and put William to her breast.

Kate was not sure whether to be happy or sad. "He went to the hotel to shout the men, as you know, but must have had one too many. It was a wake for Mr Harvey, and a shout to honour William as well. Never mind, it's only once in a month of Sundays that your father has one too many," said Kate.

"A month of Sundays?" asked Cathy. "What does that mean?"

"Sunday can be a slow uneventful day," replied Kate. "A month of nothing but days like that would be very trying indeed. It's just a saying, dear. Don't mind me. He'll be better in the morning."

"I hope so, I love my father," said Cathy, "and you."

John woke up with a sore head. Kate had crept into bed beside him, trying not to let the beery smell make her nauseous. Really, it was too much! She thought of the way Mrs Kelly had been firm and wished she'd made a stand with John. She didn't have anything to complain about really and she knew that, but after the tiring day they'd had she wished they hadn't had to go searching for him in the dark only to find he was drunk.

Next morning she rose and dressed early. She wanted to bathe John's face before the children woke. She stirred the ashes in the fire, put some kindling on to start a blaze then filled a basin of water.

John sat on the side of the bed as she washed the dirt and blood from his head. "I was good as gold at the pub," he said. "It was when I went to ride home that the cold air hit me. I remember going most of the way but then I must have fallen off. The next thing I knew you were helping me inside, here at home. Did something knock me off?" John spoke slowly, in short sentences, as if it hurt to talk.

"A tree branch hanging down across the path hit you. Dennis said Jake has to skirt it on the way to school. It was Dennis who said where you might be lying, after Blueboy came home without you. How's your head?"

"It's sore, but not too bad. Thank you for looking for me. It wouldn't have been too good being out in the cold all night. I'll have to go and cut that branch down. Bloody thing," said John.

"How did the wake go?" asked Kate, carefully washing the area around the gash. "Did many turn up for the shout?"

"Quite a few. O'bie didn't come and neither did Paddy Kelly, but there were about twenty drinking up as fast as their tongues allowed. We drank a toast to William. And did you know that Doctor McDonald and Mrs McDougal are getting wed? We drank a toast to them too."

"Oh, that's wonderful! exclaimed Kate as she finished sponging John's face."
"There, that's better. You're back to your beautiful self. You won't frighten the children now."

Despite his sore head John was keen to plough a bit more of the cleared land. The land was rich and fertile and he'd been planning to put in a crop of potatoes for some time. Some sacks of seed had been sent up from Wellington. Rangi had suggested it, telling John about the crops Harvey had grown on his land, and of how May and the other women were paid for helping to mound them then picking them up when they were dug.

It was quick money. Potatoes only took a few months to grow and there was a good market for them in the towns. Transport was expensive, but wagon drivers were pleased to have produce to take back over the hill after bringing goods across for the settlers.

Ru and Rangi were quick to chide John for his fall from grace. Word travels quickly in small communities and they had a good laugh at John's expense. He didn't mind and was pleased to be able to get on with some real work after the disruptions of the last few days. He called to Ru to harness the draft horses ready for work.

The men went ahead of the team, smoothing out bumps and hollows and, where needed, removing roots and branches left after the stumping. It was slow work, but with a lot of effort there'd be reward at the end. Not today, but in time they'd be able to look at the fine fields of good pasture they'd created - or an excellent crop of potatoes.

Kate was enjoying time with William. With Jake and Cathy at school there was no pressure from them wanting something, and John and the men had taken cold tea and sandwiches with them to save her the trouble at lunchtime. John's thoughtfulness was appreciated by Kate who forgave him his lapse but hoped it wouldn't happen too often.

She picked William out of his basket and carried him outside to sit on her favourite seat in the sunshine. It was bliss. 'I hope I get some mail from home,' she thought but, for once, the word did not bring the sharp stabs of longing that she used to feel with thoughts of her mother and family.

It was so comfortable in the sun. William sucked at the good milk as if he was starving and Kate moved him to the other breast. Kate smiled at his earnest little movements. Life was good, she thought as her eyes closed and she fell asleep in the chair, holding William safely in her arms.

Tessa Kelly looked at the scene as she approached the house and thought how lovely it was. She was just going to creep away when Kate woke up with a start. "Oh goodness, I must have been asleep."

"I just got here and was going to leave you alone to rest. It's been quite a week or two hasn't it? You must be worn out. How is your husband?"

"He's well. He's ploughing a paddock. He wants to grow potatoes of all things," said Kate.

"Reminds me of Ireland," said Tessa. "But they grow well and I haven't heard of the blight getting here."

"Lord, I hope it stays that way. Come, I'll make a cup of tea." Kate passed the baby to Tessa and went to rekindle the fire. It was nice to have a woman friend to talk to.

CHAPTER 52 Facing the Future

After the funeral Ellen drove back to the farm with a heavy heart. She'd hoped to be able to face the future without Jock in a true pioneering manner but the reality of her situation was suddenly overwhelming.

The months she had spent at home with no one to talk to except the cat and Jock, if he was willing to do more than grunt, had turned her into a recluse. Only Mr Dickson had been able to get through the shell she had drawn around herself. But now she had these new women friends. She'd heard what that nasty woman had said about her being out here alone with O'bie but, as Mrs Dickson had said, it was nobody's business but her own.

O'bie came to take care of the horse and said he'd got the fire going. "I was going to go back into town, but I've decided I won't bother. I don't want to get caught up in the wake."

"Go if you like," said Ellen, but he walked away without answering. She entered the house and looked around the room, seeking comfort from familiar things. She looked at Jock's empty chair with sorrow. 'I must decide whether to go back to Dora's, or stay here.' She fed the fire and looked at the box of food Mrs Dickson had given her from the afternoon tea. O'bie would be in soon for a meal. There was plenty for both of them, but Ellen didn't feel hungry, only empty.

O'bie knocked at the door. His large figure filled the room as he entered. "Everything's done. I put the herd down in the last paddock near the road as the feed's better there. The young heifer was quieter tonight. She must be getting used to me milking her."

"That's good O'bie," said Ellen "I'll be out to help you in the morning. There's not much for tea, just leftovers from this afternoon, but they're still fresh. I hope you're not too proud to eat them."

"Not too proud at all. I'm happy to eat anything - except artichokes. I think you did well today. It must have been an ordeal for you."

"Then you'll be happy to hear there are no artichokes in this box," said Ellen.

When O'bie left to return to the barn where he slept, Ellen lit another candle and turned her attention to the papers in the drawer of the table used as a desk. She picked up the diary and began to read it. Jock had been a man of few words yet she could sense loneliness in what he'd written. Leaving Scotland and his family were mentioned.

Ellen read on until the candle was low and decided that the rest could wait until tomorrow. She undressed slowly then washed with care, taking time to clean every part of her body. It was a ritual cleansing, washing away her past life with every movement of the flannel against her skin. Early in their marriage Jock had been a thoughtful lover who tried to please her but lately, love-making had been brutal in the extreme. Now there would be nothing. Ellen didn't care; she'd make a new life and begin again.

She turned back the bedclothes and was met with the scent of her late husband on the pillow and sheets. 'So sad an end to such promise,' she thought as she got in and pulled the covers over her. Sleep did not come easily.

When Alex arrived home (in a better state than John Johnson) Annie was waiting to help him, but he walked steadily through the doorway and sat down at the table.

"Johnson told the whole village that we are to marry." He looked at Annie fondly. "They all send their warmest congratulations to you Annie. So the secret's out. We'll have to decide on a date. When shall that be, my dear?"

"Just as soon as you like. I've been waiting for a long time. I thought you'd never go against the convention that doctors don't marry their housekeepers," replied Annie. "You know the old saying, 'A man chases a girl, until she captures him' "

"Don't you mean 'until he captures her'?"

"I said what I said."

"So how soon can it be arranged, my dear?" asked Alex.

"What about November the seventeenth? That's my birthday. You'd be a lovely present," Annie laughed.

As the new day began Ellen watched the sun rise over the eastern hills. She could hear the dog barking as it rounded up the cows for the morning's milking. 'I'll go and help O'bie, I'm still of some use around the place.' She thought of Jock lying still and cold in his grave, and said a prayer for his soul. 'I'll do all I can to preserve my memory of the good times we had and try to forget the last six months. They're over and gone.'

At the bails, O'bie had started on the old cow that took a long time to let her milk down. He'd found that if he milked her a little then left her alone until he had milked another cow, she'd relent and co-operate. "Good morning," he said to Ellen as she took her place on one of the stools, and began milking.

"Good morning to you too," she said. "How did you sleep? Were you cold?"

"No. I took good care to make myself a good shelter and I'm quite comfortable there, don't you worry," said O'bie.

"I'm relieved to hear that," said Ellen as she worked.

Ellen had breakfast ready by the time O'bie returned from feeding the pigs. "Theyre getting to be large animals," he said.

"It must be all the milk they're consuming," Kate replied. "There's bacon and eggs for you, and I'm just doing some toast."

"Thank you," O'bie said. "It smells good."

"When do you think we should sell the pigs to the butcher? They looked big enough when I last looked into the sty."

"I don't know much about them, really," O'bie replied. "Best ask Dickson or the butcher in town. I think there's a good trade in pork but you'd get more for a baconer."

"I'll do that. I'm going into town today to see if there's any news from the owner. I should see what has to be done about the inquest. Dr McDonald said there would have to be one because there was no doctor present when Jock died. I need to see how much the funeral has cost as well. I forgot to ask for a price."

"I'll get the buggy ready then I should look at the sheep. Some of them are getting dirty backsides so I'll need to crutch them. I found some shears in the tool-shed. Even though there's only twenty or so that'll keep me busy," said O'bie. . "Thank you for breakfast," and he pushed back his chair.

Ellen looked at him, thinking how well mannered he was. It was a change to be spoken to nicely after the months of grunts. "That's all right. I'm glad to have something to do," she said, feeling happier than she had for days.

The trip into town didn't take long. The road was dusty and a good rain would be welcome, but there were only a few clouds clinging to the hills to the south. She thought of the list of things she needed to attend to.

When she reached the store people were talking about a fire which had occurred overnight. A house had caught alight from hot ashes left on dry grass and it had become a raging fire. Half the house was badly burnt and, if it hadn't been for a passing late night reveller, the whole house would have been lost. He had run back to the hotel and called for men to help and they'd beaten out the flames with sacks. Then they'd chopped a lot of the wall away to prevent the fire starting again. A mother and her two children were lucky; they'd been woken up and helped out of the smoke-filled house. The husband was away working on the roads north of Masterton and only came home once a fortnight. Mary Smith said Mrs Dickson was looking after the woman and her children so Ellen decided to return later and went instead to see the doctor and Mrs McDougal about when the inquest would be held.

"Yes," said Alec. "It's to be Friday week. At eleven, I think. You'll need to attend and bring any papers of your husband's that you find. His birth certificate, marriage lines and things like that. If you have any correspondence from the owner of the farm, that would be good too."

"That's over a week away," Ellen said. "Does it have to take so long?"

"I'm afraid so my dear," Alex replied. "The area is too small to warrant a resident coroner. So what happens is that a panel of well thought of citizens acts as a coroner's jury with a chairman. He's a very busy man with his own farm to run plus he has to organise the panel to assist him. You'll just have to wait."

"Does the constable know when the inquest will be?" asked Ellen.

"Not yet, but I'll tell him. It's nothing to worry about. He's tame as can be now."

"I need your advice about something else," said Ellen. "Do you think it's wrong for me to stay at the farm while O'bie is out there?"

"Load of rubbish. I heard what that Doris Bell said. You've no need to take any notice of that gossipy old fool."

"Thank you so much for that - I must admit I have been worried about what people might think. Well, I'd better get on," said Ellen. "I need to see Mr Dickson and get some stores. It's awful about the fire, but it's so lucky the people were saved."

By the time Ellen returned to the store the crowd had lessened and Ellen was pleased to see that she had Mary Smith and Johanna Dickson to herself. "I've just been to see Doctor McDonald," she told them, "and the inquest will be on Friday week. It will give me time to go through all my husband's papers and find the ones that are needed."

"We just have to go day by day, don't we?" said Mary. " I know it's different for me, because my husband hasn't died, he's only away, but I feel the same as if he was dead, in some ways."

"Now, now," interrupted Johanna. "You must be thankful you're not the poor woman I've had here this morning. She'll have a hard time getting over the fire. Her husband doesn't know about it yet. She'll have a bit of explaining to do."

"Yes, I do feel sorry for that poor woman," said Ellen. "Now, let me think what I need to buy. O'bie is having his meals with me. Oh, do I owe you much for groceries? When did my husband last pay you?"

"There's a bit on the book," said Johanna. "He paid once a month, by cheque, so there should just be this month owing. Look, wait until the inquest is over and we'll have a balance-up then."

"That's very good of you. I thought of selling some of the pigs as porkers, but O'bie said they could be worth more as baconers. I want to ask your husband for his advice. Is he in?"

"He's helping the men demolish the burnt wall but he won't be long. They'll put up some sort of cover to keep the room dry. The mother and children have gone to see what they can salvage. I don't think the rest of the house is too bad. It was the boy who threw the ashes out on to the grass, so he's not popular. His father will give him a few stripes on the bottom, you can be sure of that. He's a fiery sort of individual. I'm sorry. I didn't mean to make a joke," said Johanna with a laugh.

When Henry Dickson arrived back at the store he suggested to Ellen she keep the pigs while there was plenty of food for them and look at them again in a few months' time. Then he sorted the mail. There was a letter for Ellen from the bank.

'Unfortuately,' the bank clerk wrote, 'we have no address for the owner other than that of the farm. He has not contacted us since Mr Harvey took over as manager and all the funds he sent down are still in the farm's account at the bank.' The letter finished, expressing gratitude if Ellen could find any other address for the owner.

Ellen showed Mr Dickson the letter. "I think you should ask Constable O'Reilly to look into this," he said as he read it. "Something could have happened to the man."

"Thank you. I'll ask him if the police can make inquiries. It's very strange. I'll go through Jock's papers again too."

CHAPTER 53 A Letter from Jock

Two days later Ellen began sorting through the papers Jock had put away in the drawer. There weren't many and were in orderly sections of accounts, receipts and such like.

Only one pile at the bottom contained personal items. Her marriage lines were there and both their birth certificates. There was a letter from the owner of the farm about a visit he wished to make when winter was over. Strange that Jock never told her of his visit. Perhaps he'd never come.

Ellen put the papers away and picked up the diary. She turned to the place she'd reached the last time. Again it was a record of tasks completed, or lists of things to do when the weather improved but, towards the end, there was an envelope. Inside was a sheet of paper folded tightly. It was Jock's writing. Whatever could this be? And why did it seem to be hidden away?

Ellen sat down on the bed before she unfolded the paper and read the letter.

"This is the confession of John Stuart Harvey, September 15th 1867. It is written while I am suffering pangs of guilt and remorse. I have killed the owner of the farm. He came to visit and we argued about the rent I was paying him. He struck me in anger and I hit back. He fell and hit his head on a stump. I tried to revive him but could not do so. He is buried in the bottom paddock, near the stream. I am truly sorry. I cannot tell my wife. She is so good and I am sad that I have treated her badly. My head is like a raging beast and I have no control of my actions. The wrong I have done lies heavy on my soul.

I intend to do away with myself but know it will take time to get the courage to do this. There are two posts planted together on the grave, about a foot apart. If this letter is discovered, I will have found the strength to do what I must. The owner's name is Major Maurice Martin. His address is 40 Bellevue Road, Lower Hutt, or care of the Bank of N.S.W.

I know nothing more about him. Please forgive me Ellen for the wrongs I have done you. I truly love you. Jock Harvey."

Weeping, Ellen put the paper down. Jock had loved her after all.

When she heard O'bie arriving at the cottage for lunch she pulled herself together. She'd not say anything about what she'd found and hoped he'd think she was feeling sad about Jock. 'That's true anyway,' she thought. 'Why hadn't he confided in her? The poor, poor man.' It was an accident. He'd had to face the future with the knowledge of what he'd done always in his mind. Sooner or later the bank would start wondering where Major Martin was and the truth would emerge. "I'll be out in a minute," she called, and splashed her face with water from the jug on the dressing-table.

Ellen set out bread and the usual selection of pickles, cold meat and cheese. She sat down, took some food and placed it on her plate. Could she force anything down? She mustn't let him see the turmoil inside her.

"How are things today?" she asked.

"Good. The pigs are looking fine and growing fast. When should we get the pigs to the sale? There'll be one soon."

"There's no hurry while the cows are milking so well, and I've a lot to think about at the moment. The inquest will be on Friday. Let's wait a while. What else needs looking at?" said Ellen.

"The post and rail fences took a bit of a hammering in the winds and flood so I'll patch them up before next door's cattle are eating our feed."

"You don't mind staying on as caretaker?" asked Ellen, thinking the farm would need looking after for a while yet if this mess was to be resolved.

"No, not at all. I'm getting good experience at being a manager. I was only the 'boy' where I worked before. I've found out a lot about myself when I've had to make my own decisions. Kelly was a good teacher but not modern enough for me. There's more to farming than just milking cows."

"I'm grateful O'bie," said Ellen. "I hope to have more idea of what will happen to the farm after the inquest."

When he'd gone Ellen collected her thoughts and wondered whether she should go to town and talk to Mr Dickson or Doctor McDonald. "Or should I stay quiet about the discovery until the inquest, and show the diary to the coroner then? Or should I say nothing at all?' Round and round went the options clogging her mind. Should she just let it simmer until she'd read more of the diary? 'No.' she decided, 'I'll just wait for the time being and work as if all is as usual.'

Ellen took the bucket of table scraps and went to see to her fowls. They were scratching happily in the dirt of their yard, their shiny black feathers and red combs glowing in the sun. Watching them made her feel more at peace.

Just as Henry was about to leave on his deliveries Mary Smith told him he was wanted by his wife. "She said she's worried about Mrs Harvey being at the farm on her own."

Henry jumped down from the wagon and went back into the store where Billy-the-broom was busy shifting dust from one side of the shop to the other. "Put a bit of water down for goodness sake, Billy, or you'll have the place covered in dust," he said. "Now what did you want me for my dear?"

"I've been thinking of Mrs Harvey out there on her own and wondered if we could find her a companion. What do you think?"

"She has O'bie. It seems he's calmed down a bit. I don't think we should interfere but I'll sound her out when I take the groceries today. I think it'll take her a long time to adjust. She may rather do it on her own."

"Well, have a good talk to her. See what she wants. I don't mean to interfere as you put it. I'm just worried about her, that's all," said Johanna as she kissed Henry good-bye.

When Henry reached the Harvey farm in the early afternoon, Ellen was in the garden weeding the flowerbeds. They were a riot of colour and he could not but admire them as he walked towards her. "They look lovely," he said. "My wife would love a garden but there's no time." Henry carried the box of goods in to the house. "Is there anything else I can help with?" he asked.

"Yes, there is, please take a seat. I'm in a quandary as to what to do. Something has happened and I'm not sure what to do." Ellen sat down opposite him and brought out the diary. "I've found a note written by Jock. The contents are disturbing to say the least."

"Do you want to tell me about it, or would you rather discuss it with Johnson or the Doctor?"

"I'd like to talk it over with you all before I make a decision."

"Why don't you come to town tomorrow? I'll get the others together so we can talk about it," said Henry. "Rangi always calls in on his way home from work and I'll tell him to ask Johnson to come in. What time do you think?"

"In the morning, say about eleven. I can help milk and get away by then. I'm sorry to put more on your shoulders when you've all been so good. Where will we met?" asked Ellen, already feeling relieved.

"Perhaps at the Doctor's? It will be quiet there. You look really worried so I suppose it is serious," said Henry.

"You can be sure it is. I need to decide what's best to do, before the inquest."

"Look here my girl, you've been through so much. I'm pleased we've been able to help. We need to stick together when troubles come along, don't we?"

———— ∞ ————

John was surprised when Rangi delivered the message. He hadn't wanted to make another trip before the inquest, but Kate said she'd go with him so she could spend a little time with Mrs Dickson. They set off soon after the children had left for school.

Johanna was pleased to see Kate. She only had three months to go and the baby seemed to be moving normally, but she felt something was not quite right. Kate advised her to see the doctor soon and get a check up as a precaution.

Mrs Smith was busy with customers so the two women were able to talk freely about the events of the past week, and speculate on the urgent meeting the men had been called to.

"I saw Mrs Harvey drive past in her buggy. She went straight to see Doctor McDonald, so Doris Bell said when she came in. She'd waited on the street to watch where Mrs Harvey was going."

"She's a nosey woman, but maybe she doesn't have a lot to think about since her daughter got married. I feel sorry for her in a way."

"You're too good to be true," said Johanna. "I think Mrs Harvey must have found out something when she read the diary. Rangi was to tell your husband to come in and Henry said he had to see the doctor this morning. Oh well, we'll know soon enough. Have one of these buns. I made them this morning. They're very tasty."

As the two women enjoyed their tea and buns Johanna drew Kate's attention to some advertisements in *The Independent*, the newspaper that came from Wellington. "Look at these new fashions - you can order them by mail. Look how short they are! You can see the ankles of the models. And look at the boots, buttoned all the way down. Aren't they smart? Wouldn't we look grand standing on the lawns at the Moroa Races?" asked Johanna.

"We would indeed, but I don't think our husbands would like paying for such modern wear, do you?" laughed Kate.

———— ∞ ————

Alex welcomed Ellen, asking how she was feeling and was she able to sleep. John arrived soon after and then Henry. "What's this all about, Mrs Harvey?" asked John. "Have you found out more about the owner?"

"I found a letter inside my husband's diary that's most upsetting. Look, here it is." Ellen pulled the diary from her bag and placed it on the table. The three men bent over it to read what was written there. Soon they were looking at each other with disbelief. This really was a serious matter.

"What are you going to do about it?" asked John, shocked. "Poor beggar," he said. "What a burden to carry."

"We need to find the best way to go forward. Can we say nothing? I don't think so. The body must be exhumed and given a decent burial. The bank must be informed, and the widow, if there is one, told," said Alex McDonald.

"Don't go so fast Doctor," said Dickson "Let's think it through. At the moment the only ones who know, are we four. Mrs Harvey might lose the farm if we're too hasty. Would you want that?"

"I don't want the farm really, I'd be happy to go and work for my cousin in Masterton," said Ellen quickly. "I think Doctor McDonald is right. We should go and see Constable O'Reilly and ask him to contact the police in Wellington to search for the widow. Don't you think so?"

"I'm not entirely convinced," said John, "but if you think that is the only way.... It must have been a terrible shock for you. I agree the man deserves a decent burial and his wife must be told. Will you go and see Constable O'Reilly or do you want one of us to do it for you?"

"I'd like you to come too, if you can spare the time. We can see the inquest chairman too and show him the letter. I hope he'll be able to make a decision about my husband and the letter in the diary without it becoming common knowledge. Do you think that's possible?" asked Ellen.

"I'll have a talk with the chairman before Friday," said Alex, looking thoughtful, "and I'll see Constable O'Reilly to tell him to start the police looking for the widow without saying anything about the letter, but say that the bank hasn't heard from the owner for months. That will start the process. We'll get the inquest over and then wait for a while before we let on about the body in the field. Then you won't have to face the entire trauma at once."

"Oh thank you Doctor, I couldn't face all the questions and probing as well as the inquest. In a little while I'll be ready to accept the outcome of the search for the widow and whatever happens after she is found. The man's name was Major Maurice Martin. She shouldn't be too hard to find."

The men were ready to leave when Annie came through the doorway with a tray of tea and cakes. "Did the doctor tell you we've set the date for the wedding?" she asked Ellen.

"NO! He did not. When is it to be?" asked Ellen.

"Seventeenth of November, and I'd like you to be my matron of honour," said Annie with a smile.

"I'd like that very much. It'll be good to have something nice to think about," said Ellen. "It will be an honour."

"And Mr Dickson, would be you be kind enough to give me away? It will only be a small affair."

"Just a few friends and a quiet lunch together at the hotel is what we have in mind," said Alex. "It'll be in the morning, about eleven o'clock where the Church of England holds services. I hope you'll all be willing to help us celebrate the occasion. Mr Johnson, will you be best man for me?"

"It sounds as if it will be a very happy event and we'll look forward to it," said

John smiling. "I'd love to be best man."

As Mrs McDougal went to see to something in the oven John said to the others, "I think the least we say about the matter until the inquest is over the better. I suggest we don't discuss it with the women, or O'bie. Do you all agree?" They all nodded. Henry said he'd have to have something to tell his wife in the meantime. She was not easily fooled, and had deduced that Mrs Harvey had seen something in the diary.

"Just say it was to do with the inquest," said John.

"How did the meeting go?" Johanna asked Ellen, back at the store. "Did you find something in the diary that would help at the inquest?"

"Yes, that's what we talked about." Ellen was selecting some extra stores. "Annie has asked me to be matron of honour at the wedding. Isn't that lovely?" she said, changing the subject. "John Johnson is to be best man and she asked your husband to give her away as well so we'll all be involved. But now I'd better get home and help with the cows."

When they reached home Kate quickly changed into her work clothes after putting the sleeping William in his cradle, then tipped the bag of mail she'd collected from the store on to the table. Amongst the letters were two from her mother, one from Rosie Parker, and one for John from George Parker.

She fed the fire and put the kettle on to boil then opened the first of her mother's letters. It was dated about three months ago and told of the many ways her mother kept busy and occupied. She'd been singing with the church choir, and with the Happy Circle Group with Mr Jones. "I enjoy it very much. Mr Jones has again asked me to marry him. I've agreed to, when the year of widowhood is up in February. I hope you will be happy for me."

Just then John came in to have a drink before he went down to see how the men were getting on with the ploughing. He could see by Kate's face that she was excited. "Mother and Mr Jones are to marry after Father's anniversary. What do you think about that?"

"I think that's great," he said. "Why should she live alone, when she can have some happiness? I must get away down the paddock. It'll take all of us to keep the horse moving and get a straight furrow. Rangi and Ru do their best, but it's better with three."

CHAPTER 54 The Inquest

Over the last few days the thought of the impending inquest had been constantly in everyone's mind. Now at last it was Friday. Kate and William drove into town with John. Ellen Harvey travelled alone. All the other witnesses made their way to the newly built courthouse in Kuratawhiti Street where they quietly greeted one another. It was a subdued little gathering. They all felt anxious at having to give evidence, especially Rangi and Ru who waited outside until John encouraged them indoors - just as Constable O'Reilly arrived with a policeman from Wellington.

It wasn't long before the clerk called for silence and the coroner's jury of four entered. The chairman explained the order of proceedings and the inquest was under way.

One by one all those who had played a part in the events that began when Rangi's son noticed the cows in distress, told their stories. Probing questions were put to them and gradually all the details were laid out before the jury. Ellen Harvey felt some relief when Constable O'Reilly described his inquiries and stated he had found no evidence of anyone else having been involved. He mentioned the rumours heard about visits from tradespeople but offered no names. Instead, he simply said they had been looked into and had been found to have no bearing on the matter.

Ellen was the final witness. Although she stood straight she was trembling as she was led gently through the story of her marriage, the changes in her husband's personality and of how she had fled with Mrs Johnson.

Satisfied eventually that all the evidence was before them, the chairman announced that they would give their judgement later in the day. He requested Mr Johnson, Mr Dickson, Doctor McDonald and Mrs Harvey stay behind, and then dismissed the rest of those present. Kate, Annie and Johanna waited outside, curious as to what the meeting could be about.

"I should think they'll tell us when they are able. I must get back. Mrs Smith will be run off her feet," said Johanna. "Do come and tell me if you hear what the verdict is."

"We will," said Annie. "Mrs Harvey is such a nice person. I hope she'll go up to Masterton to help her cousin and find peace."

"Look, here are the men now," said Kate as John appeared. "What was that about?" she asked him.

"It's something Ellen found in Jock's diary that needs attention. We've been told not to say what it is yet," said John.

"Surely you know we won't say anything," said Annie.

"We'll tell you as soon as things have been decided. It's nothing that concerns us directly," John replied.

"Is Mrs Harvey all right?" asked Kate.

"Yes. Doctor's talking to her. She'll be out in a minute or two. We should be getting home my dear. William will want feeding. He was very good though. You wouldn't have known there was a baby present," said John as Alex and Ellen came out.

"Mr Johnson, I know what the chairman said but I think we should tell the ladies. What do you think?" said Mrs Harvey.

"He asked us not to, but I suppose if they can promise not to discuss it among themselves so it stays with us it should be safe enough," said John. "It would be best if we each told our husband or wife when we are alone and no-one else. Not

O'bie, or Rangi or anyone else."

As they were driving home, John told Kate about the confession, impressing on her the need for secrecy. "The trouble is that it may all be a figment of Harvey's imagination. We'll have to wait and see if the police in Wellington can find the widow. We don't want to say anything about it until we're sure and can verify the facts, so not a word to anyone."

"I'm glad you have faith in my ability to stay quiet," Kate said. "I won't say a word. Did you read the letter?"

"Yes, we all read it, and it was very moving. Hopefully the police will find the Major's wife and if his body is unearthed then we'll give him a decent burial," said John. "It would be better not to discuss it even when we are on our own, or with the others. Just put it out of your head and forget it until the truth can be found."

Back at the farm, Rangi and Ru were stretching their backs after planting row after row of potatoes. "Well done!" John said. "They're all in now. Next we'll mound them up when the shoots show through the earth in about two weeks."

"Have you heard the jury's verdict about Mr Harvey?" asked Rangi.

"No, but it'll be public soon," said John. He turned the talk back to farming matters. "Is there going to be another drought this year?" he asked.

"Going to be a wet summer," said Rangi. "The cabbage trees were flowering early with lots of blossom."

"Is that a Maori sign?" asked John.

"Yes. That's a sure sign of a wet summer," said Ru.

After the inquest Ellen drove home slowly, wishing that the coroner's jury had given their verdict while she was there to hear it. The chairman had been very good about the letter and had sworn them to secrecy because of the effect the gossip would have on her. Mr Johnson was right. "I should put it out of my mind and wait until the police find the man's wife.' Ellen got down from the buggy and gave the reins to O'bie who'd been watching for her.

It was nearly milking time again. She changed into her work clothes and drank the tea O'bie had made. Jock had never been known to make a cup of tea. Ellen wondered if the idea of cooking and doing for himself had been a factor in his awful decision. 'Ah well, it was too late now. Let the rest of my life be peaceful.' As she walked to the bails to help O'bie, she prayed to her Lord for forgiveness for any actions that might have contributed to Jock's death. Seated on the stool, she laid her head against the cow's flank and let her tears flow as she squirted milk into the bucket.

If O'bie noticed the tears, he gave no sign as he let one cow out the door and replaced it with the next in line. "How did it go?" he asked later, as they finished sweeping down the yard.

"I don't know what the verdict is yet, but I think the jury was happy with what they heard."

On the farms it was time for cutting hay and making stacks of it to dry. The next day O'bie tried out a scythe for the first time. He soon mastered the technique and had a good few rows of sward laid out to dry when Ellen came down the paddock laden with baskets of food and drink for O'bie and the two men they'd employed to help.

She offered to do the evening milking on her own but O'bie said he'd be glad to stop scything at four o'clock. "I'll be ready to drop by then," he said as he sank to the ground and took the bottle of cold tea from Ellen.

Ellen looked over to the eastern hills and saw how brown they had become even though it was only early November. "Do you thing the drought will be as bad this year?" she asked the neighbours helping O'bie.

"It's hard to say missus," said one. "It usually goes season to season, one wet and the next dry. But there's no telling really. We'll see soon enough. I don't think it'll be as bad as last year. Then, we had no rain until April and that's unheard of."

That evening Kate sat in the cane chair feeding William, thinking of the frocks she'd seen in the paper at the store. 'Wouldn't it be lovely to have something new for Dr McDonald's wedding?' John seemed to be in a good mood so in a quiet moment she plucked up courage to ask him.

"John," she said, in her most loving voice. "I saw some pictures of frocks in the paper at Dickson's. They were so pretty and modern. I don't suppose we can afford for me to have something new for the wedding?" John had heard this voice before.

"Don't wheedle woman," he said. "If you want something, ask for it. One of those advertisements I suppose. How much?" said John in the grumpiest tone he could manage. It was lovely making Kate beg.

"They're not expensive... The one I liked was soft grey with a bustle. It was two pounds, five shillings. You can order by mail from one of the shops in Wellington," said Kate. "I'd love something new John."

"I believe we can afford that huge amount. It can be a thank-you for William, my darling," said John with a laugh.

CHAPTER 55 A Good Report

At the school the following day the mail brought welcome news for the teachers - their pay would be covered by the government, and they'd been approved in their positions for the next two years. There'd be a review if the roll increased to any great extent. As well, funds would be set aside for an extension to the building - good news indeed.

Meanwhile, Mrs Thompson had almost made up her mind to accept the offer of marriage she'd received from a widower with three children. She was tired of trying to make the school day exciting for the children, with scarcely any equipment. However, now she had a new admirer who was helping around the school.

"So you won't marry the widower?" asked Miss Goode who'd been watching the romance with interest.

"Not yet anyway - although he's very persistent. Perhaps in a year I might. I like Mr Jones better. He was so kind making the desks for us and giving us the school bell."

"That sounds very serious," said Beth.

"Perhaps I am," laughed Mrs Thompson as the children came into the room for the afternoon lesson. "And maybe you can marry the widower."

That afternoon Beth asked Olga to teach her class a little Danish song as a way for them to understand how hard it was for Olga to speak English if they also had to learn words from another language, and the children were soon singing away with Olga. Beth also had the Maori children teach the class their songs. Mrs Thompson said it was against the rules but Beth thought that unfair and encouraged it.

At the end of the school day Beth walked home with Mary's children. Peter was excited as he'd been put up a class. He'd been able to read a whole book on his own and didn't have to sit with the babies any longer.

Marie was still not allowed to go to school, but Johanna kept her amused with lots of paper, pencils and pictures to colour in as she played behind the counter. It was fun to have a child about the place. Johanna was looking forward to the birth of her own child, only three months away. Henry sometimes took Marie for a drive if he only had a short trip to make. He'd never had a lot to do with children but loved her chatter as she watched the animals in the paddocks as they drove by.

"What'll we have for dinner?" Beth asked as they neared the boarding house. Marie thought for a moment and said, "Let's have a picnic. Let's go down to the river when Mother comes home, and we can paddle in the water."

"That's a good idea. We can boil some eggs, make some sandwiches and we can take some of Mrs O'Toole's cakes."

"Oh yes, let's do that," said Peter. "Mother would love that."

Mary Smith was a little late coming home. The children ran to meet her, excited about the picnic. They'd been busy getting everything ready. Although Mary would rather have sat and rested after the morning she'd had in the store with only Billy to help she was pleased she didn't have to cook tea, as it was her turn.

Biddy came out to see them leave for the river with a bag of walnuts, a packet of raisins as a treat for them and a bottle of ginger ale. "You children be careful. Do what your mother says," she said as they waved goodbye.

The children ran ahead, bubbling with exuberance, and several times Mary had to call to them to slow down. Finally Mary said to Peter, in a stern voice, "Here, you carry the bag. That'll fix you my lad." Weighed down with the heavy bag he walked at the same pace as the adults. Marie had no such baggage to hold up her flight and was splashing in the water as they reached the stream.

"Watch out, Marie. There are big eels in the water," said Peter. Bigger boys had teased him like that when they'd gone on country rambles with their teachers. He was pleased to have a chance to catch someone else out, and frighten them, but Marie only laughed.

Mary plucked Marie from the water and wrapped her in a towel. "You were a naughty girl to get so far ahead. There could've been a big bull in the paddock you just came through. You must stay close to Mother," she said.

"I looked. He was away over the far side. I would've just talked to him anyway, and told him to go away," Marie said.

"Was there a bull in the paddock?" asked Mary, looking back anxiously at the way they'd come.

"Yes there is," said Peter. "See over there, by the tree." Mary looked at where Peter was pointing to a large dark bull calmly eating grass a few yards away. She blanched.

"Oh, he's not interested in us," said Beth. "We can come back here when we need to go home. It's a long way around if we can't take the short cut."

After they had all eaten Mary and Beth lay back in the grass chatting. "I wonder what Mrs Harvey will do now," Mary mused. "The farm will have lots of memories and she'll want to stay there if she can. But when you've been married to someone it's hard to carry on without them. I should know."

"Oh I'm sorry Mary, I should have asked. Is there still no word from your husband?" said Beth.

"No, I've been hoping for a letter but still nothing. Well, we'd better get the children home before they catch their death of cold. Come on. Now!" she called. They gathered up the remains of the picnic, and started for home.

The bull had moved to the other end of the paddock to talk to some cows over the fence. While he was busy they crept through the rails and walked quickly to the next fence and the road back to town.

As they walked Peter told his mother about the book he'd read on his own. It was about a little boy and a kite. "Can we make a kite, Mother?" he asked.

"I don't know. Did it say how to make one?" asked Mary. It was times like this that she missed Jim.

"It looked easy," said Peter. "I'll ask Mrs Thompson if I can bring the book home. Would you help with a kite, Beth?"

"Auntie Beth, please Peter, or Miss Goode," his mother corrected him. "All right, if you can get the plans we will try."

"Yipee!" shouted Peter and, as they walked past the blacksmiths' shop he called out to Peter Fairman, "I'm going to make a kite and fly to the moon."

Peter looked at the group of friends as he swung young Peter high up in the air. "Don't need a kite, I'll throw you up," he said. "I'll toss you up to the moon," and he turned round and round with little Peter flying out from his arms.

Mary had walked ahead with Marie, but Beth was watching, looking amused and very pretty. The blacksmith had seen the young school mistress going past his door every school morning, but she was always in a hurry. He would have stopped her on her way home but the children were always with her. Now he put Peter on the ground and said quietly, "Miss Goode, would you walk out with me?" She looked startled but not angry, so he continued, "I've admired you for weeks and have been trying to pluck up courage to ask you. What do you say? Please say you'll think about it."

Beth was speechless. She'd always admired the giant of a man who was so good with Mary's children but had never thought about whether he was married or not. Big Peter was looking at her. She had to say something. "Yes, thank you Mr Fairman. I'll think about it tonight and call in and tell you my answer tomorrow morning." And she walked away to join Mary. "You'll never guess what's happened."

"No, tell me," said Mary.

"Mr Fairman wants to walk out with me."

"Really?" said Mary. "How lovely. He's such a nice man. Do you like him? Will you agree?"

"I told him I'd think about it, and let him know in the morning," said Beth, blushing. "Yes, I have to admit I like him very much. I think I'll say yes." Beth looked thoughtful as if she was urging herself to take the chance. 'Will I, will I? Why not? I jolly well will.'

The blacksmith waited every morning for Miss Goode to pass by and give him his answer. So far she'd only waved as she rushed past in a hurry to get to school, but she was always happy and laughing when she looked at him. Finally, Peter thought he should be more forceful and decided he'd go and see her that evening to ask her to go for a walk with him.

He belted away at the hot metal with a new vigour. After all, she'd said she'd give him his answer the next morning and now it was several days since he'd spoken his mind. What could be holding her up?

That evening after tea Beth and Mary were sitting outside in front of the house when Peter Fairman appeared at the gate, then walked up the pathway. Mary stood up to go inside, but Beth stopped her, saying, "Don't go, what I decide will have an effect on your life too."

"Miss Goode,' said Peter, " Will you come for a walk with me and tell me your decision? I've been waiting for nearly a week and I can't keep my mind on my work. Please come."

"Oh Mr Fairman I'm sorry, I've been turning it over in my mind. I don't want to make a mistake, but I would like to walk with you," said Beth as she rose and took his hand and they walked together down the road. When they reached the stand of bush at the edge of the town where a small stream ran through ferns and flax, Peter took off his coat and laid it on the ground for Beth to sit on as she laughingly said, "Thank you Sir Galahad."

"Well have you thought about it?" asked Peter, not wanting to waste time with small talk. "I've been waiting to hear what you'll say. Please say yes."

"It's not that easy. You know I work with Mrs Thompson at the school and I want to help Mrs Smith with the children. Yes, I'd love to walk out with you, but we must wait a while, don't you see," said Beth, taking his hand in hers.

"That's all right, my darling. I'll wait, but not for ever," said Peter, as he slid his other arm under her shoulder and pulled her close. "We'll wait as long as you like. I'll need to build a new house. I live in a whare but want something better for you, my dear."

It was lovely there in the bush with the stream tinkling and the earthy scent of the ferns. Beth didn't want to leave but knew she must. "I'd better go home. Mrs Smith will have a search party out, trying to save my reputation," she said regretfully.

CHAPTER 56 Findings

The Wellington police had no trouble finding the widow of Major Maurice Martin. He'd been with the soldiers sent out from England to quell the Maori uprisings in Lower Hutt and Taranaki, and had retired four years ago. Then he'd decided to purchase land in the Wairarapa near Greytown. However, farming had not been to his liking, so after a time he returned to live in Lower Hutt but still retained his holding. When he met Jock Harvey and found he was looking for work, had just married and was used to running a farm he gave directions for him to travel to the Wairarapa and take up the position of manager.

His wife was glad to have him home with her instead of trying to run the farm himself. But in September he had travelled to Greytown to discuss the rent for the next year. He thought the farm should be doing better and Harvey should be able to pay more.

As the weeks passed Mrs Martin wondered if anything had happened to her husband on the road. She'd been going to go to the police and report him missing, but didn't want to appear foolish. 'After all, he's a trained soldier and should be able to cope with any danger he might face. Perhaps he's been drinking again? That was it. He's in prison somewhere. Do they have prisons over the hill?' she wondered.

The police officer, who went to ask Mrs Martin about her husband, didn't want to say anything about their fears for his safety. Instead he told her there was need of her presence in Greytown, adding that there had been an incident that needed looking into.

When he left, Mrs Martin sat for a long time, wishing she'd gone to the police when she first became worried. 'He could have written a letter. Even if he'd had to take over the running of the farm again he could have let me know,' she thought, deciding she'd have a good deal to say when she saw him.

The idea of travelling over the Rimutakas again did not give her any pleasure, even though she knew the roads were being improved all the time. Life as an army wife was not easy but she'd survived living in the Sudan, India and Australia, before coming here. Oh well, she'd just make the best of the circumstances, as she'd done for the last thirty years. She breathed a deep sigh - 'If only I had a close friend.'

The police report on Major Maurice Martin was sent up to the Masterton station by the coach that left next morning. It was received by the sergeant there with some reluctance. It all seemed very mysterious - he was not to act on it until he had word from the constable in Greytown, and was not to discuss the contents with anybody. Maybe it had something to do with the bloke that hung himself eh? 'Better obey the law. After all I am the law.' He was laughing at his little joke as a constable came in from checking the hotels.

"What are you looking so cheery about?" the constable asked.

"Oh nothing, how were the pubs?"

"Quiet. Funny business that hanging in Greytown," said the constable. "I heard that there was talk of murder and the hanging was just a cover-up."

"You mustn't believe rumours. The report on the inquest came through today and it was clearly suicide. So leave it there," said the sergeant. "Haven't you got work to do?"

After a letter was received saying they were to make arrangements for the exhumation of a body on the Harvey farm in Greytown, tension at the Masterton police station was putting pressure on the smooth running of the office, especially as there was to be complete secrecy about the matter until the body had been examined. "So who's to do this then?" asked one of the constables present when the letter was read.

"I suppose it could be the Greytown constable, but I don't know if he's up to it," said Sergeant Pringle. "Look, I'll go down and talk it over with him. There'll need to be an autopsy - the doctor down there can do that. The sooner the better I think. The widow is coming up to Greytown on the coach on Friday so it will have to be before then. She doesn't know what's happened. Well, neither do we until we have a look at the body. It won't be a very pleasant job. I'll go down tomorrow morning and get it done as soon as possible," said the sergeant.

The following day Ellen was surprised to have a wagon arrive while she was getting breakfast, and called to O'bie to see who it was. However, the policeman with Constable O'Reilly asked for Mrs Harvey and refused to tell him what their business was, only that they needed to see her alone. When it was explained to her, Ellen told the men to go ahead with what they were proposing to do, just as Doctor McDonald and Annie McDougal arrived in a buggy. "I've come to give you support," she said to Ellen as she gave her a hug.

"You both stay here," the doctor told them and went to talk to the policemen who were taking shovels from the back of the wagon. "You can drive down the paddock and get quite close to where the grave is thought to be."

"Good-oh, we'll do that then," said Constable O'Reilly and they drove off down the path through the fields, with the doctor following.

There were two posts in the ground close together where the trees had been cleared except for a few stumps and Dr McDonald said to try there first. The police hadn't seen the letter written by Jock Harvey, but Alex remembered well the site mentioned and he was sure this was where they'd find the body.

Within a short time they found some clothing that had been laid on the body to protect it from the earth shovelled over it. The body was well into a state of decay but Doctor McDonald studied the remains. "The jaw has been broken and there's a fracture of the skull. I'll have a better look at the surgery. You can have the pleasure of taking the body to the surgery - I have Mrs McDougal with me. Just put it on the wagon, cover it up and then fill in the grave. The women will have a drink ready for you at the house so leave the wagon at the gate and come back there. Wash up in the stream before you leave here."

O'bie wondered what was going on as he went about the business of feeding the pigs. It was all very strange. What was going to happen next he wondered? He was getting quite fond of Mrs Harvey and she was looking after him well. 'I'll stay here as long as she needs me, but something funny is going on,' he thought.

When the wagon returned he saw there was something covered up on the back and, even more curious, when the policemen and Doctor McDonald went into the house he crept up to the gate and looked under the blanket that covered whatever was there. Dear God! It was a decomposing body! 'What ever did that mean? Did Mrs Harvey kill him? Or Jock Harvey? That was it. Jock had killed him.'

O'bie wished he was down at the local with a pint or two under his belt. What a story he'd have to tell! But, no, he'd not be doing anything like that to Mrs Harvey. It had been kept very quiet. She'd not confided in him but she'd tell him when she could he was sure. She'd been looking so sad as she helped with the milking - as if there was a great weight on her shoulder. This must have been it.

When the policemen arrived at the surgery Doctor McDonald was waiting for them with a trolley ready at the gate. In the surgery Sergeant Pringle wrote a report, noting the items of clothing worn. A watch and chain were hanging from the jacket and he told the constable to remove them to see if there was a name engraved on the watch. Then it was time for the post mortem. "I'd like you both to stay for that," said Alex.

"I will if I have to. Will it take long?" asked Dan O'Reilly.

"No longer than necessary, you can be sure of that. I need to look at the head to see if I can decide which blows killed him. So let's get on." He went to the coffin and, wearing rubber gloves, took up the head to examine the break in the jaw and the skull fracture. The broken jaw would not have been enough to end a man's life, but the back of the skull had received a hard hit. It would have been fatal if help had not been received quickly. Perhaps the site where the body had been buried might provide the evidence. "We need to go back and look for anything the Major may have hit his head on when Harvey struck the blow that broke the jaw. We can go back today after lunch. I'll have a good look at the rest of the remains and then make a report. The widow arrives tomorrow. I want to have everything tidied up before she comes. The name on the watch establishes his identity so she won't have to see him. We'll arrange to have him buried here if she wishes."

Kate was looking forward with pleasure to the doctor's wedding. It was time there was something to celebrate. She decided to go into town after lunch to order the dress she'd seen advertised and to call on Mrs Kelly on the way as she might want to go too.

She dressed William warmly, even though the day was fine, left a note for John and was soon on her way. Mrs Kelly was pleased to see her and quickly decided to accompany her. Paddy was down at the end of their farm and they stopped to tell him their plans as they passed by.

At the store Johanna and Mary told them of the wagon driving past with Constable O'Reilly and another policeman on board, heading off in the direction of the Harvey farm. Kate and Johanna listened, careful not to speculate on what it might mean as Mary and Mrs Kelly discussed the possibilities until a customer came in. It was Doris Bell. "Did you see the policemen go out Harvey's way?" she asked, dying to hear any news.

"No, I was busy in here, Mrs Bell," said Mary. "What can I get you?"

"Just sugar, please. I'm going to make marmalade. Did you hear about the murder?"

"No," said Mary. "Has there been one?"

"That's what people are saying. I mean, that woman staying out on the farm with that young chap. It's not right."

"I wouldn't know anything about that, is there anything else?"

"No good will come of it. You can be sure of that," said Doris, as she picked up the sugar. "Did you weigh this properly? It has to be just the right amount for the jam."

"Yes. Three pounds is what you asked for and three pounds is what you've got. Will that be all?" asked Mary.

Doris glared and marched out of the store, saying, "You'd better watch your manners, girl, or I'll shop somewhere else."

"And where would that be, Mrs Bell?" Mary asked softly.

"Are you upsetting my customers again?" asked Johanna as Mary returned to the back room where the women were looking at the fashion advertisements in the Wellington papers. "Look at this one, Mrs Kelly. It would suit you. It's only three pounds. You are going to Doctor McDonald and Annie McDougal's wedding aren't you?"

"Yes, we've been asked. Is there time to order and have it here in time? I do like that one. Oh, why shouldn't I have something new if you're all going to," laughed Tessa.

Eventually, the ladies had all made their choices, helped by Johanna's willingness to order them immediately on the store's account and do all the necessary paperwork. "I hear that there might be more wedding bells ringing in Greytown soon," she added as the women enjoyed a cup of tea. "Peter Fairman is sweet on Beth Goode and Joan Thompson might say yes to Mr Jones"

"Do you really think Mrs Thompson will marry Mr Jones?" Kate asked Mary. "It would be good for them both. And Miss Goode and the blacksmith? That's a surprise."

"I believe they'll all marry soon," replied Mary. "And why not?"

"It seems as though we might have a number of occasions when we can wear our new finery," Kate said. "But now we should be on our way home. The children will finish school soon and they could have a ride in the buggy."

School had just closed for the day when Kate halted the buggy at the gate and soon they were all on their way home with the two ponies trotting along behind the buggy. At the Kellys' Kate declined a cup of tea. "No, I'd better get home and have a nice meal ready for my lord and master, after the money I'm planning to spend," she laughed.

———⚬⚬⚬———

The same afternoon, when the doctor, constable and the Sergeant made their way back to the farm, Ellen was surprised to see them, but Doctor McDonald explained the need to look again at the place where the Major had died. There, he feigned a hit to Constable O'Reilly and, when he slumped to the ground, missing a hard totara stump by inches, it was clear what had occurred. Even though the policemen had not seen the letter, Alex had no difficulty convincing them of the way things would have happened.

When all were in agreement they made their way back to town, the doctor pondering how he'd word his report.

"The widow is due on the coach this afternoon," said Constable O'Reilly. "Would you like to be there to meet her?"

"I'm sorry, but you'll have to do that on your own. I can't hold surgery until the body is removed."

"I'll take her to the hotel to stay the night," said Dan O'Reilly. "What about you Sergeant? Do you have to go back to Masterton?"

Donald Pringle thought about the work he should be doing. "I'll stay another night and talk to her with you. It's not an easy job, being a copper."

At four o'clock the two policemen made their way to the stables to meet the coach. The last person to alight was a tall lady dressed in grey, and when she saw the two policemen she put her hand out in greeting. "I'm Mrs Martin," she said. "I believe you have news of my husband. Has he been drinking again?"

"No madam, it's not that at all. We'd like you to come to the hotel with us. We can discuss the matter there," said the constable, picking up her suitcase.

Soon Mrs Martin was safely at the hotel drinking a cup of tea. "So you know where my husband is?" she enquired.

"I'm afraid we do. I'm sorry to tell you that he met with an accident and was killed."

"Oh, no!" said Mrs Martin. "Here I was telling myself that he'd been drinking again. Poor, poor man. Was he badly hurt? Can I see him?"

"No, I'm afraid that won't be possible," said the Sergeant kindly. "You see, he's been dead a good while. We can't say exactly when, but soon after he came over here in September, is what we think."

"What do you think happened?" asked Mrs Martin tearfully.

"He appears to have been in an argument with his farm manager. He received a blow on the jaw, fell and hit his head on a stump and died. We exhumed the body yesterday. It's at the doctor's for a post-mortem. I'm very sorry."

"And the man who did this? Is he in jail?"

"I'm afraid he's dead too. A tragic case," said the sergeant. "I'll tell you the details after you've had time to rest. It's a dreadful thing to hear about your loved one. We have his watch and chain, and the engraving tells us that it's his body."

"Thank you Sergeant, I'll go to my room now if you don't mind, I feel quite sick. You know, I was going to give him a piece of my mind. But now......."

———⁂———

Doctor McDonald dealt with the examination as quickly as he could. He was sure his finding of accidental death would be accepted. He told Annie he was going to see the undertaker and arrange for the body to be collected and, taking his hat from the stand by the door, he thankfully ventured out into the fresh air. It had been a nasty job but was nearly over. Then he'd be able to turn his mind to his wedding day which was fast approaching. The blacksmith was whistling a tune as he passed so he put his head in the doorway and offered his congratulations. "You're a dark horse. Just like the one you're shoeing. When's the big day?"

"Not for a while. Miss Goode wants to wait until next year and I need to build a house for her. I can't expect her to live in the shack I inhabit."

"Well, good luck to you anyway," said Alex. "You'll most probably hear on the grapevine that we went to Harvey's farm today and dug up the body of the farm's owner. I'm just going to get the undertaker to remove it from my house. The widow came up to Greytown today. I'll see her tomorrow and tell her what I think happened."

"Oh, the poor lady. That will be a shock."

"We kept it quiet until we could talk to her, but now we'll be able to tell the truth. Poor Mrs Harvey has had a rough time, but it should be over soon. I'll be glad when it's settled and we can get on with our real lives."

"I really liked Harvey," said Fairman. "I can hardly believe he was abusive to his wife, but you don't really know what a person is like until you live with them, do you?"

"Well, I'm lucky there. Annie's been looking after me for years, even in Bonny Scotland. We're so fond of each other I wouldn't want to be without her," said the doctor. "All very proper you understand. But now I really want her to love me as I love her."

"I wish you nothing but happiness Doctor. This trouble with the Harveys made me understand that you mustn't waste time. I hope you have a long life together."

———⁂———

That evening Ellen decided to tell O'bie why the policemen had come to the farm. She began saying, "I expect you've been wondering what was going on yesterday. I found a letter written by my husband hidden in his diary. It said that he'd killed the owner of the farm in an argument and where the body was buried."

"That's awful," said O'bie. "What else is going to happen? I'm so sorry for you."

"It'll all be over soon. Doctor McDonald said the widow has come up to Greytown. I expect there'll be a funeral as soon as the inquest and post mortem are done with," said Ellen.

"I have to confess that I saw the body," said O'bie. "I took a look when the police were in here talking to you. I was worried about what they wanted."

"I've been dreading telling you in case you thought I had something to do with it," said Ellen quietly.

"I'm glad you told me. I never thought you had anything to do with it but I knew something was worrying you."

"The result of the inquest on my husband is to be given tomorrow, and there'll have to be another one on the Major. Really it is all too much. I'm glad you're here," said Ellen. "I'm going into town to hear the result and get a copy of the death certificate from Doctor McDonald. I don't know what the widow will do with the property. Would you like to stay on?"

"I would. Would you like to stay here too?"

"I don't think that would be a good idea. I might go and work for my cousin Dora but I'll stay here until things are settled."

"Well, let's wait and see. The widow may want to see me too. Perhaps I should come in to town with you?" said O'bie.

"Yes, that's a good idea," said Ellen. "You can see her and tell her you're keen to stay on."

CHAPTER 57 Revelations and Arrangements

Widow Martin, as she thought of herself now, slept fitfully in the bed she was shown to after dinner. The room was sparsely furnished but adequate for her needs. She didn't intend to stay long here where everything was so very primitive. She thought of the time she and the Major had spent in India. There'd been servants galore, and all the time in the world to enjoy the company of the other army wives. No, she'd get back to Lower Hutt as soon as she could summon up the courage to face the journey back over the hill. Hill! It was a mountain.

The policemen were coming at nine o'clock, so she'd better eat. Maurice dead? Well, that was a turn up for the books. 'I'd better look the sorrowful widow,' she reminded herself as she toyed with her breakfast and buttered a piece of toast. The waitress was sympathetic as she poured the tea and asked how she'd slept.

"Not very well, dear," said the widow in a soft voice as she wiped her eyes with a lacy handkerchief, "but thank you for asking."

"The policemen are here to see you. They're waiting in the parlour, through the door there."

"Thank you. I'll go in as soon as I've drunk my tea." She sugared it and drank quickly, wanting the ordeal over.

"How did you sleep?" Constable O'Reilly asked. "Did the wind wake you?"

"No, but I was very restless, thinking of my husband. Now please tell me what happened."

"We don't know exactly. We've brought the body in for a post-mortem and there will be an inquest. A panel will conduct the inquiry. Do you know the date your husband came over the hill to see his manager?" asked Sergeant Pringle.

Dulcie Martin thought for a moment or two then said, "He came over by coach on September the tenth. Well, he left home that day and that was his plan.

Sometimes he stayed at the Club, but no, I'm sure he would have come over that day. He was intending to spend a few days here, seeing some of his friends. We lived here for a while when he bought the farm but I wasn't happy. So we bought a house in Lower Hutt."

"Were you not a little worried when he never returned?" asked the Sergeant.

"Not in the beginning. Then I just waited for him to come back. He'd been friendly with a Maori girl when we lived here. I thought he might have rekindled that flame."

"Did that thought upset you?" asked the Sergeant.

"We have gone our separate ways for years, Sergeant. You must know how it is in the forces, being a policeman."

"I wouldn't know about that," said the Sergeant sharply. Constable O'Reilly looked a little uncomfortable and smiled sheepishly, but no-one was looking at him. "We need to talk about the funeral for your husband, Madam," continued the Sergeant. "Where will that be?"

"It would be best if he was buried here," she replied. "As soon as possible. I'd like to return home as soon as I can. I'm sad that my husband has died in such a way, but I'd like to have the inquest over and the body buried as quickly as it can be arranged."

The Sergeant said he'd see the authorities and try to hurry things up. He went on to explain the events of the past week and of how they'd been able to exhume the body. As well he told her they were sure of the way things had occurred and what had happened to the farm manager. Mrs Martin was grateful for their help and said if they'd make all the arrangements for the funeral, she'd agree with whatever they decided.

"Which church would you prefer, madam? There's a Catholic priest in town and a visiting Anglican minister comes twice a month. I believe he'll be here at the weekend."

"My late husband was Church of England. So I think he should be buried by the vicar, don't you?"

"Mrs Martin," said Constable O'Reilly, "I think all the people who've been helping Mrs Harvey would like to pay their respects to your husband. They're very caring people and I'm sure would feel it was right to give your husband a suitable farewell. I'll see what I can do about finding the vicar."

"And I'll go and see about holding the inquest as soon as it can be arranged," said the Sergeant.

"I'll rest in my room and wait for your return. Thank you for your help and understanding. I hope I haven't shocked you by my attitude, but I'm tired of pretending that our marriage was all it should have been."

"I admire your honesty Mrs Martin," said Sergeant Pringle. "I have a happy marriage and expect everyone to be the same but I know there are some who live in misery, as Mrs Harvey was supposed to have been doing, for the last few months. We'd better get on with making the arrangements." He held out his hand to the widow and she shook it firmly as she said goodbye to them both.

As Constable O'Reilly walked down Main Street to Dickson's he thought of the widow's reaction to her husband's death. 'She'd expected to have to bail him out for drunkenness so it must have hit her hard to find out that he'd been killed in a brawl, well accident,' he mused as he reached the store.

"How did you get on with the exhumation?" Dickson asked. "Did you tell the widow about Harvey's letter?"

"Yes. We went into all the detail needed. I'm going to see the undertaker. Do you know when Reverend Porter is due back?"

"Yes, tomorrow. I hear the doctor asked him to marry them on the seventeenth, and it's the sixth today, so he's going to be busy," said Henry.

While the constable saw the undertaker and arranged for the grave to be dug the sergeant went to see the chairman of the panel about the inquest on the Major, and to see if a decision had been reached about Jock Harvey. "If you could find a way of combining the inquest for Major Martin with the result of the inquest on Harvey, it would make it easier on the people involved. They're all working folk and have given up a lot of time to these matters already. I'm asking for a favour I know, but I need to get back to Masterton."

"I'll do my best. However, we've reached our decision about Harvey and I've told the doctor to issue the death certificate. It will say 'self inflected death while of unsound mind because of a brain tumour. Happy with that?" he asked

"Yes, very happy sir. The Major's funeral will be as soon as we can get the post-mortem over and the death certificate issued for his body. The widow wants to return to Lower Hutt as soon as she can. She's a very attractive lady and won't find it had to remarry should she wish to do so."

"I should look her up, then?" said the chairman, in an odd burst of humour. "It's all right, I'm already married."

"I didn't mean to give the wrong impression, sir. I was thinking of the single men about town, always on the lookout for a wife."

"I know what you mean and you're quite right. There are too few single women coming to the colonies. Though there's a nice wee slip of a school teacher at the school now, isn't there?" asked the chairman.

"Too late for her, sir. She's to marry the blacksmith. So I've heard. Wedding bells are ringing everywhere around here."

"Be a change from the funeral toll anyway. I'll see you this afternoon at the hearing. If I can talk to the doctor before then it might be possible for us to decide on the Major today as well. See you at two p.m."

———— ∞∞∞ ————

John and Kate were driving into town in the buggy to the inquest, when Paddy Kelly hailed them from his front paddock where he was working. "Dickson told me about the Major and finding his body out at Harvey's farm. What do you know about it?

"We're just off to the inquest. We'll call in on the way home and tell you any news, said John. "But we'd better get on our way or we'll be late." He clicked his tongue and Beauty set off at a trot.

"I guess it will be all over the district now," said Kate. "It's a shame Mrs Harvey will have to put up with the gossip. Everybody will be out-doing one another with the lurid details. I'm not sure she should stay out on the farm. I'll have a talk to her and tell her what people are saying."

"I wouldn't bother, Kate," said John. "Just let it rest. It's all a five minute wonder."

"I suppose so," replied Kate, but she was still going to whisper a word of warning if she got the chance. 'Women have to be so careful, even in these modern times. It's so wrong. In a way she's being blamed for her husband's death. That's unfair.'

At the inquest the chairman waited for the court to settle down then said in a steady voice that a verdict had been reached regarding Mr Harvey. "We have determined that he died by self-inflicted strangulation while of unsound mind. No other person was responsible for the death. We offer our condolences to the widow."

Ellen sat back on the seat, clasping her hands together, her head lowered, unable to raise her eyes. The feeling of relief was so great she felt faint. Kate, sitting next to her, saw her distress and grasped her hand. "It's over Mrs Harvey," she whispered. "You can get on with your life now. Make a new start," said Kate.

"Thank you Mrs Johnson. I'll be all right in a minute. It's what I hoped he would say, but it still came as a shock."

"You're not to blame, you mustn't blame yourself. It's over, you hear? Go up to your cousin and start a new life," said Kate.

The chairman cleared his throat and began to speak again. "In the matter of the deceased Major Maurice Martin, we find that he died accidentally from a blow to the head during an altercation with his farm manager, Mr Harvey. A blow to the face was strong enough to break Major Martin's jaw, and knock him backwards where his head struck a tree stump and split open the skull. Death came quickly. The farm manager buried the body. I ask the widow to accept our condolences. The inquest is now concluded. Burial may now take place."

Doctor McDonald went to shake the chairman's hand. "I'm very pleased that your jury saw fit to make the decision to finish the cases together today."

"Oh well, I was heartily sick of the matter. First Constable O'Reilly wanted to turn Harvey's death into a murder. Then the diary turned up and there was foul play to consider. But all in all it was a straightforward case of suicide, and since the poor beggar was dead there was no point in looking for a suspect to hang in the case of the Major. The Major's widow doesn't look too concerned, and poor Mrs Harvey has seen enough of courts and misery to last her a lifetime."

Dr McDonald joined Ellen and O'bie who were standing with the Johnsons. "How are you now my dear?" he asked.

"Much easier in my mind now," said Ellen. "We're just going to see Mrs Martin to see what she wants to do with the farm."

They walked to where Dulcie Martin was talking to Henry and Johanna Dickson. She turned to the doctor and said, "Thank you for your help in this sad chain of events, thank you all."

"We were only doing what we could to help in a sad situation," Alex replied. "But may I ask what will you do with the farm? Will you put on another manager or will you sell it?"

"I don't know what provisions my husband made in his will. I'm happy to leave things as they are at the moment." Mrs Martin turned to O'bie. "Do you want to stay on the farm Mr O'Brien? And you Mrs Harvey, what do you want to do?"

"I'd very much like to stay on as manager," said O'bie. "And I'm hoping Mrs Harvey will stay there too. She does a lot of the work with me and advises on the running of the farm as I'm really only a novice," said O'bie.

"Well, that's settled then," Mrs Martin said. "The funeral should be held tomorrow and I can go home on the coach on Friday."

CHAPTER 58 Another Funeral

Reverend Porter rode into town late in the afternoon after holding a service in Carterton. His was a large parish. Moving from one group of Christians to the next kept him busy but he enjoyed his work. The population was steadily growing and it was pleasing to see young families growing strong and fervent in their religious lives as they carved out farms from the bush.

He made his way to the store to collect any messages the Dicksons had for him. It was very convenient to have a place for people to contact him for urgent needs. They kept a schedule of his visits, and he did his best to be on time at the next port of call. He was always ready to conduct a wedding or a funeral at a moment's notice, and often had to do just that. "So, Mr Dickson, "what have you for me today?"

"The funeral of Major Martin," said Henry. "Tomorrow." He went on to explain the circumstances and told him that Mrs Martin was at the Rising Sun, waiting for him to arrive. "She'll be glad you've been found."

"I was never lost," laughed Reverend Porter. "I knew exactly where I was. But I know what you mean. I'll visit her as soon as I've been to my lodgings and washed up a bit. It's quite dusty on the road now the weather is drier."

"Would you like a cup of tea?" asked Johanna as she came down from the upstairs living area over the store. "There's one just made."

"That would be welcome, thank you. You can tell me all the news," he said. "I hear you've had quite a time of it."

When he returned to his lodgings he shed his dusty clothes and put them ready for his landlady to launder them. She was a good little body and always had a meal ready on the days he stayed with her, but his lifestyle made the question of marriage an unlikely proposition.

It would be lovely to have a wife to come home to even if it was only for one or two days a week, but it wasn't going to happen. His life was rewarding in other ways though. He had a quick word with the Lord, thanking Him for a good week.

As he walked to the hotel, children home from school were playing in the street. They waved to him as he passed and he waved back. He sometimes went to the school to tell them some Bible stories so was a familiar figure to them.

Mrs Martin was waiting for his arrival. She'd received a message to say he'd been contacted and would call soon to see her.

"Good evening," he said. "I'm Reverend Porter. I believe you wish to see me. I was sorry to hear about your husband. It must have been a great shock to you."

"Yes, it was most unexpected. I feel guilty in a way. He'd been missing for over two months and I never told anybody. I should have gone to the police, I know, but I thought he may have taken up with a girl he was involved with when we were on the farm. That's about three years ago now. She was a young Maori girl from the pa."

"I wouldn't dwell on that aspect as you can do nothing about it. He'll face his Maker, and may have done so already. There's no point in torturing yourself. Now let's decide on where and when he'll receive a Christian burial."

"Tomorrow, as early as you like," said the widow. "I've asked the sergeant to arrange things with the undertaker, and it's just a matter of saying when. Is there a place where you hold services?"

"Yes, there's a house we use. Say eleven o'clock?"

"If that suits you, I'm happy to hold it then. I don't expect many people will be there."

The next morning the sun shone brightly. As Ellen and O'bie milked the cows she asked him if he would like to go to the Major's funeral. He thought it would be good to pay their respects and suggested they could drive in together as they had the previous day.

After breakfast Ellen dressed in her best skirt and jacket. She set a pretty little hat on her head and donned a pair of black gloves to finish her widow's outfit off. Dust would be a problem but she took a blanket and shawl to protect her clothes, and wrapped them around her as she sat beside O'bie in the buggy.

Doris Bell was in her front garden as they drove past. Not surprisingly, she looked disapprovingly at Ellen sitting alongside O'bie, and later said to her neighbour, "There's more to this murder than meets the eye. She'll be sorry she doesn't conform to what polite society expects."

"Oh I don't know. She's had a hard time," said the neighbour. "She's a pretty little thing, isn't she?"

The people attending the service were settled and waiting when the undertaker arrived. Reverend Porter met the coffin. Going before it, he said, "I am the resurrection and the life, saith the Lord..." It was a simple service following the precepts laid down in the 1662 Book of Common Prayer, held before a table covered with a white cloth on which stood a plain cross flanked on each side by a candlestick.

Afterwards the pall bearers carried the coffin back to the waiting dray to be taken to the cemetery, just down the road towards Featherston. While some of Mrs Martin's friends from the time she was on the farm offered their sympathy, a young Maori woman stood alone, weeping and wailing, distraught with grief. She carried some leaves and wore a garland on her head. The widow's pakeha friends clucked their tongues as they watched her. This was not the way one should behave. The natives made so much more of displaying grief than was seemly. Who was this girl anyway?

Kate led Mrs Martin away to a coach hired to take mourners to the cemetery. "Please don't be upset about the young woman," said Kate. "The Maori people are so much better at showing their grief than we are. Please don't let it upset you."

"Thank you Mrs Johnson. I'm not really upset. It's just unnerving to see that my husband was loved by this lady to such an extent that she would make a spectacle of herself when I can hardly shed a tear," said the widow as one of her friends took her hand and helped her into the coach.

A little time later, as she and John were trotting along behind the other mourners, Kate wondered about the scene they had witnessed. "I'm surprised that Mrs Martin wasn't upset by that young woman."

"I don't think we should get involved, my dear," said John. "If Mrs Martin is not going to make a fuss, why should we?"

"I'd no intention of making a fuss. I was just surprised she seemed so calm," said Kate as they drew up at the cemetery gates. The mourners gathered around the open grave as the men lifted the coffin down from the dray, and carried it to where Reverend Porter was waiting.

He began the graveside ritual with the familiar words, "Man that is born of woman hath but a short time to live..." When all the prayers were said he gave the blessing and the coffin was lowered into the grave. Mrs Martin bent to place a bunch of flowers she'd picked from the hotel garden on top of the wooden box holding the remains of the man she'd shared much of her life with. Then she sought out John who called on everyone to listen to Mrs Martin.

"I'm grateful that so many of you came to say good bye to my husband and for the kind way you have accepted me in your lives over these past three days. I was not sure of the circumstances I'd find here. I had no idea that my husband had died, that I'd never see him again." She wiped her eyes with her handkerchief. "I'm also grateful that the inquest was held so promptly and I thank all those who have supported me in any way at all. I know who the young woman who wailed and cried is. I hold no animosity towards her at all. Please let the matter rest there. Thank you."

"Well, what do you think about that?" Doris Bell asked her neighbour as they climbed aboard a coach to ride back into town.

"I think she was very brave to speak to people like that," said the neighbour.

CHAPTER 59 Unexpected Events

That afternoon, after lessons had finished, Paul Jones called into the school to find the teachers discussing ways to obtain new books for the children, and immediately suggested a sports day just before the Christmas break. "It could be like a fair day at home in England, with races and ball games and a bang up tea party for everybody. Perhaps there could be a dance at night in the woolshed, or one of the new halls, if one were finished in time. We could hold a raffle. Maybe one of the farmers would donate a pig or sheep."

His ideas were coming thick and fast when Mrs Thompson held up her hand. "It sounds wonderful, but it would be a lot of work. The school committee would have to be consulted, and it would have to be soon as there's only five more weeks until the end of the year. Next Saturday is the doctor's wedding; once that's over we can look at your idea Mr Jones. Thank you for thinking of us."

"I'm thinking of you all the time, you silly woman. When are you going to make up your mind to do the decent thing and marry me?"

Joan Thompson admitted to herself that he was right. She must decide. 'Soon? No, Now!' "Yes, I will marry you," she said.

Beth Goode looked on with disbelief. Mrs Thompson had said she would not take such a big step until she'd talked to the widower again and now here she was being kissed in a most masterful manner by Paul Jones. Beth embraced her. "Congratulations. I'm so happy for you. I hope you'll both be very happy. Gosh, the wedding bells are really going to be busy."

"Miss Goode, 'gosh' is a common expression," said Mrs Thompson, laughing. "Not suitable for a headmistress."

"Ah, but I'm not a headmistress yet. You won't give up teaching will you?"

"No, not for a while, but I don't think I can keep Mr Jones waiting forever either." She looked at him for a sign that he agreed. She wanted to stay working at the school even after she married. Would he mind?

"I won't want you to give up straight away, but perhaps in time, you might want to," he said. "We'll worry about that later."

Next morning Mrs Martin looked around the parlour at the hotel, thinking how lucky she'd been to find friends in such unfortunate circumstances. Everyone had been kind and caring, especially Reverend Porter. Now it was time to catch the coach for the journey back to Lower Hutt and to think of her future without her husband.

She had paid the undertaker and the hotel bill; the hire of the coach would be settled when she reached the stables. There was nothing more to do except gather her belongings and walk down to the coaching station.

Beth and Mary were walking down to the store and school as she left the hotel. They greeted her warmly and they walked together with Marie and Peter skipping ahead. "How will you live now you're on your own?" asked Beth. "Can you stay in your home?"

"I won't know until I see my solicitor. My husband was a good provider. He had a pension from the army. Please don't worry about me. I've been on my own for the last few months anyway. I should have reported him missing but I thought he'd gone back to his lady love. I never thought for a moment that he was dead."

"We heard about the girl at the church. Did you know her?" asked Mary.

"Yes I did. She helped my husband on the farm when we lived up here and I hoped he'd given her up when we left. I realise she was mourning him in the native way."

"I do hope you have a safe trip back to Lower Hutt, Mrs Martin," said Beth as they reached the schoolroom, while Mary Smith called to Peter and Marie.

"I have a surprise for you Marie dear. Mrs Thompson has said you may go to school for the last weeks of the year so you'll be familiar with the routine when you start properly after Christmas." As Marie jumped up and down with excitement, her mother explained that she had packed an extra lunch and instructed Peter to watch out for his little sister, then the children followed Beth into the school.

As Mrs Martin and Mary reached the store Johanna came downstairs, holding the banister for support. She was getting quite big and, with the baby nearly due, was careful not to take chances. "Good morning, Mrs Martin. So you're off then? I'm glad to have met you, even when it was an unhappy time. I do wish you well. Mrs Smith, we have some boxes to unpack."

The two women unpacked the boxes of clothes received from Wellington, and checked sizes against the order. "They do look very fashionable. They'd better be right, as there's no time to change them," Johanna said, thinking, 'Mine will be a tight fit,' as she lifted out the grey silk skirt and matching jacket she had ordered for herself. 'I'll wear my good blouse with the high collar, and leave it to hang over the skirt.' She picked up her outfit and carried it upstairs. She didn't want Henry to see it yet.

Several people were waiting to board the coach to Wellington when Dulcie Martin arrived. Some were going to Featherston and it would not be long before they were safely home. Others were bound for the bigger towns over the Rimutakas. Resigned to the ordeal ahead, she boarded the coach.

With all the passengers settled, the driver was about to whip up the horses when a rider cantered into the stable-yard, talked briefly to the driver, gave his horse to the stable-hand to care for and climbed in to sit alongside Mrs Martin. It was Reverend Porter.

"Mrs Martin, please don't look so surprised, but I couldn't let you go without telling you of my feelings," he said, taking her hand. "I'm going to Featherston with you so we can talk on the way. I'll hire a horse there to get back to Greytown."

Astonished, Dulcie Martin looked at the vicar, wondering at this unexpected declaration. She knew he was lonely but was she ready to enter into another marriage ? Was that what he meant? Or had he only wanted to ask for permission to dream that at some future time he might pay his respects and court her? She looked at the other passengers who were trying to pretend they weren't eavesdropping and took her hand away from Reverend Porter's grip.

The Reverend realised he had to explain. He'd plucked up courage to get this far and wasn't going to stop now. "I only want you to say I can hope to see you again. Please think about it."

The passengers were taken back by the fervour of the Reverend's plea and they listened expectantly to hear her reply. Mrs Martin pulled herself together. 'I must say something, but what?' "I really like you, sir," she finally said. "I know we've only just met, but I feel as if I've known you for a long time. Perhaps the events of the past week have speeded up the process of getting to know one another. I would like to get to know you better, so I'd be pleased to see you, if you are able to call on me in the future, at Lower Hutt. If you can see your way to visiting when you are there on business, yes please call." At which the passengers clapped and the Reverend beamed.

Before long they were in Featherston where the Reverend Porter climbed down from the coach with Mrs Martin's address safely in his pocket. The male passengers shook his hand while the two other ladies aboard took Mrs Martin's hand in a soft gentle clasp and wished her well.

———— ∞ ————

Back in Greytown, after receiving the school committee's approval of Mr Jones' idea, Mrs Thompson told the children about the treat in store. "We've decided to hold a special sports day in the paddock over the road. And I want you to think of some of the races and events we can have."

Hands shot up all over the room. Beth Goode went to the blackboard to write down the suggestions. "Sack races? Yes, and... three legged races, egg and spoon, and...? Hop, skip, and jump. Fastest runners? A backwards race. Highest jump and longest jump? What else can we have?" No more hands went up so she said, "Right! We 're going to go out into the paddock now for a little practice. I've cut some pieces of rope to tie two children's legs together in pairs. You have to move as one. I've some sacks ready too. Let's go and see how we get on."

The children went quickly over the road to the vacant paddock. It was high in weeds and grass. "We'll have to have something done about that," said Miss Goode. "A farmer might put some stock in to eat it down a bit but they leave their calling cards. I suppose all the tramping around will flatten it a bit."

"I'll ask Mr Jones what he thinks we can do," Mrs Thompson replied. "Let's have a go at a sack race." They helped the younger children into sacks and watched as they fell about, trying to run in the restrictive bags. Then, after they tied some children's legs together, they had three-legged races. The children were laughing and running and falling over and getting up to try again. It was such fun. Better than sitting in a school desk on a warm day.

CHAPTER 60 Another Wedding

Kate and John sat out on the veranda discussing the events of the past week or two. Tomorrow they'd join many of their friends at the wedding of Alex and Annie. Kate was looking forward to the occasion as she missed the social life she'd enjoyed at home. John was more worried about the potatoes that needed earthing up now they were through the ground and wondered if he could leave Rangi and Ru to get on with it without him.

"They should be all right," he said. "I think they know more about it than I do."

"He's married people before, John. I'm sure it will be just fine," said Kate.

John threw up his hands in exasperation. "I was talking about the boys doing the potatoes. Not the bloody wedding. Sorry, I'm looking forward to being there too, as I know you are. But we've lost so much time these last weeks I don't know when we'll catch up again."

"John, I've something to confess," said Kate. "I not only bought the dress we talked about; I bought a new pair of boots to go with it. Johanna has put them on our account at the store."

"You have earned them, my dear. I want you to be as beautiful as the bride. I'm sorry I snapped. I'll stand alongside the doctor and be proud to be there. To hang with the farm tomorrow. What'll you do with William though? Will Cathy be able to look after him now her wrist is mended?"

"She'll be fine with him. Biddy O'Toole kindly sent a note to school for me, saying that the little ones can stay at her house during the ceremony. Jane will be there too. I'll pack some food for them to take."

Annie McDougal was up early. She went into the garden to pick some flowers to carry. She didn't want a large bunch, just something that smelled nice and would add a bit of colour to her outfit. There were some pinks in the border; they had a lovely scent, as did the sweet-peas. They'd do with some fern fronds. As she gathered the flowers Annie thought about how much she and Alex wanted everything to go smoothly for their wedding. The doctor had talked to the publican to reassure himself that the luncheon he'd ordered for his guests would be ready on time and of suitable standard. The publican, Bill Evans, had hired a new cook to help Martha and was sure everything would be in hand for the great occasion. They'd set the menu and decided on the wine so there was no need for him to worry. The ceremony would be held in the house where the Major's funeral had been held.

Meanwhile, Alex was up looking for his breakfast. He called to her through the open door. "Is this any way to treat the prospective bridegroom?"

"I'm so sorry sir," said Annie with a smile. "And who is the bride may I ask?" Alex grabbed her in an embrace, but she wriggled out of it neatly. "Be careful or I might change my mind."

"What have you got for my breakfast, woman?"

"Just the usual dry bread and water, my lord."

Just then there was a knock at the door. There stood Bill Evans looking worried. "Whatever is the matter, Mr Evans?" asked Annie.

"There's been a bit of an upset at the hotel," said Bill. "Martha has taken exception to the new cook and refuses to let her help. I'm wondering if you can talk her around Mrs McDougal?"

Annie took off her apron and donned her walking shoes. "I won't be long."

"I don't know about that," said Bill. "They've had a real barney. Martha says she doesn't want the new cook to make the desserts, and Molly, that's the new girl, said she wasn't hired to only peel the potatoes."

"Oh come on. I'll soon sort them out," said Annie, with a certainty she was far from feeling. As they walked to the hotel she tried to think about how to fix the problem.

There was no sound from the kitchen as they entered the back door. Perhaps a truce had been reached. Martha looked up at them from where she was sitting. "It's not that I don't trust her cooking, it's just that I've been looking forward to making the éclairs myself," she said. "You need a really hot oven, and we have to be quick or there won't be time to cook the lamb. I would've made them during the week, but we've been so busy, what with all the goings on. I asked her to do the vegetables, and she hit the roof."

Molly sat across the table, with a sour look on her face. Annie sized the situation up with a practiced eye. "Why not just have trifles instead? Or apple pies?"

Jake and John had finished the milking, Cathy had fed the fowls with the scraps and Dot was safely on her chain. There had been some sheep worrying in the district and Jake didn't want to take any chances with his pet. The stray dogs at the pa were often the culprits and Constable O'Reilly had been to tell the kaumatua that the dogs must be controlled or they might get shot.

Kate dressed William in his pretty little long dress. He was nearly two months old. Cathy was very good with him and Jane was always coming over for a cuddle. They'd manage very well. Jake looked at his father to gauge his mood before asking if he could go to see Hemi and Kingi for the day. He might call in on Dennis as well. They could play cricket with some bats and wickets they had made if they could get enough children to join in.

"May I go and see Kingi and Hemi today?" he asked.

John looked at his expectant face. "If I'm having a day off, I suppose you think you deserve one too?" he said.

"I could help Rangi and Ru, I suppose, if you'd rather I did that," said Jake in a sly way. He knew how to get around his father. It was easy if you knew how to ask. John smiled; he understood Jake.

As Annie dressed in a soft silken gown she thought about how different it was from the dress she'd worn at her wedding to her first husband, Mac McDougal, twenty-five years ago. Poor Mac, it was a shame he'd died so suddenly after only five years of happiness. Then she'd taken the job of housekeeper for Alex. They were two very different men. Mac was quiet and reserved, not used to showing his feelings. Alex was a bluff, cheery fellow, who'd asked her to accompany him to New Zealand as his housekeeper. He'd never asked more of her all the time they'd been together, than to be company for him.

Although Annie had grown to love him she had never let herself hope that someday they would be more to each other. She thought of the night she'd found him weeping over the death of a baby, and had lain beside him to comfort him. Now today she was to be his wife. She was forty-two, past the child bearing age, more's the pity. She felt her childlessness keenly. 'Ah well, you can't have everything,' she thought.

The dress was a good fit. It came to her ankles and showed off the satin slippers and hose she wore. She hoped the cooks had come to their senses and wouldn't ruin the luncheon. Soon she was ready and waiting for Mr Johnson.

Ellen Harvey had dressed in her best and she and O'bie drove into town early enough for her to see Johanna Dickson and be reassured that she looked as a bridesmaid should. Johanna had some flowers for Ellen to carry and they all made their way to the house where the vows would be exchanged. There, Kate was waiting outside with Miss Goode and Mary Smith while Peter Fairman and Henry Dickson showed guests to their seats. Tessa and Paddy Kelly arrived in a cloud of dust as their wagon pulled up near the house and the children hopped down and went to where Cathy was waiting for them under a shady tree, with baby William safe in her arms.

Soon Doctor McDonald arrived, looking every inch the 'toff' in a morning suit with a stiff shirt, and entered the house to stand by the makeshift altar where two silver candelabrums, each holding six candles, gave a feeling of a religious occasion with their flickering light.

Meanwhile, John had driven down the road to the doctor's home to collect the bride. When they arrived at the house he helped her down from the buggy. Ellen Harvey was waiting for her and the little group proceeded into the house while a piper played a wedding march.

Reverend Amos Porter stood by the altar with the groom and his best man, ready to conduct the ceremony. As far as he knew, nobody here knew of his exploits yesterday and he hoped it would stay that way for as long as possible. He began the service. "Dearly beloved, we are gathered together to join this man and this woman in holy matrimony. Who gives this woman in marriage?"

"I do," said Henry Dickson.

"This is a serious state for a person to enter into, and must not be taken lightly. Does anyone know of any reason why these two people should not be married? Speak now or forever hold your peace." There was no sound from those gathered so he continued. "Dear friends, I am happy to unite these two fine people, whom we have come to admire, and we pray that God will bless them."

He looked at the bride and groom standing before him, and asked "Do you, Alex Robert McDonald, take this woman, Annie Heather McDougal, to be your wedded wife, to have and to hold from this day forward, for richer, for poorer, in sickness and in health, as long as you both shall live?"

"I do," replied Alex. Reverend Porter turned to Annie and asked her the same questions. "I do," answered Annie in a quiet voice.

"I now pronounce you man and wife. You may kiss the bride." The doctor gave Annie a smacking great kiss. This was followed by one from John, then Henry, and not to be outdone, the vicar also took time to kiss the bride. The couple knelt for a blessing and then went to sign the register in a room off the hallway.

The guests said all the right things as they admired the dress Ellen wore, and said how beautiful the bride looked while they waited for the bride and groom to return to the room. Then Ellen gave Annie back the bouquet she'd been holding for her, and walked alongside Mr Johnson behind the happy couple as they left to the music of the piper who was now playing a toe tapping reel.

As the guests made their way to the hotel where luncheon would be served,

Annie wondered what the outcome of the spat between the cooks would be. She'd not had time to tell Alex about the changes that might occur in the menu but did it really matter?

Meanwhile, the piper was playing a merry tune at a fast tempo, and it was a relief to reach the courtyard of the hotel. 'Perhaps the satin slippers had not been a good idea,' thought Annie as she leant on Alex's arm for support.

Bill Evans had left the ceremony a little early to return to the hotel to check on the situation and was waiting for them to arrive. He welcomed the bride and groom and their guests and ushered them into the parlour, offering them wine, beer or lemonade.

Annie would have preferred a good cup of tea, but had a glass of lemonade while Alex was offering a whisky all round. Tessa Kelly was quick to ask for lemonade for her husband and herself. She knew how hard it was for Paddy to resist the thirst he had for drink and was determined to keep her eye on him.

The smell of food from the kitchen was filtering through the open window and soon the guests made their way to the dining room which had been decorated with greenery and flowers for the occasion. Five round tables, each seating four people, were laid attractively with white cloths, silverware, and vases of flowers, in the bridal colours of pink and white. An iced cake sat on a small table ready to be cut when the meal was over. The guests found their places and sat down as soon as Alex and Annie had taken their seats.

After Reverend Porter said grace, Martha and Molly brought laden plates to each of the guests who tucked in with pleasure to the roast meal of lamb, chicken and ham, with a fine selection of vegetables, mint sauce and gravy. There was not a lot of chatter as eating took precedence over polite conversation.

When two young women, who'd been engaged to help, removed the empty plates, and Martha wheeled in a tea trolley with large bowls of fruit salad and trifle on it as well as small apple pies dusted with icing sugar, Alex, puzzled, looked at the selection and quietly said to Annie, "Where are the éclairs?"

But Annie just shook her head and mouthed the words, "I'll explain later."

After the dessert had been eaten, John Johnson called for quiet by tapping a wine glass and began his speech, speaking of how lovely Annie looked, and how fortunate Greytown was in having Doctor McDonald and his bride in the community. Finally he asked everyone to rise and drink a toast to the happy couple. "To Dr and Mrs McDonald."

Alex replied and thanked John, saying that he had never had such kind loving friends as those who were gathered together here today. "May we all live long, happy, safe and useful lives here in Greytown."

Then John rose again and asked everyone to drink a toast to Mrs Harvey, saying how beautiful she looked, and also to Mr Fairman and Miss Goode who would be marrying in the future. "You must all give Mr Fairman lots of work so he can build his house and join the rest of us in holy matrimony."

───────⊗∞⊗───────

Meanwhile, Jake had ridden out to the pa to meet Kingi and Hemi. There they tried to play cricket on the grass but the weeds were too long and the bats which Jake had brought were not very successful so they saddled their ponies and rode to the bush at the end of Main Street where they climbed some kahikateas so they could look into the bird nests. Jake and Kingi had no trouble at all scaling the large trunks but Hemi got stranded half way up and couldn't move. He was so frightened Jake decided to climb up and help him down. However, although there were knot holes and small branches, not many were strong enough to hold his weight so it took Jake a while to reach Hemi and try to make him move to where he could hold him. Meanwhile, Hemi was crying and Kingi wasn't helping by calling him a baby, especially when Jake was helping the younger boy down. Suddenly, Jake's foot slipped but he caught hold of Hemi's trousers as he was falling, pulling them both to a sudden descent from the tree.

Kingi was laughing fit to kill, rolling on the grass, but Jake and Hemi soon had him calling for mercy as they turned the occasion into a wrestling match. By the end of it, the trousers were torn from top to bottom, and a good deal of Hemi's backside was showing through the seat of his pants.

The boys were all were lying panting on the grass when a man came running from the bush looking upset and anxious. "Do you know where the doctor is, boys?" he shouted. "There's been an accident at the mill."

"He's at the hotel. He just got married," called Jake. The man started to run towards the hotel, but Jake, thinking quickly, overtook him on Blueboy and told the man he'd ride to tell the doctor. "I'll be quicker."

Soon he was sliding off Blueboy's back and running into the public house. Martha was waiting for the guests to leave so she could set the tables for the evening meal and stopped him at the dining room door. "Whatever are you doing here, lad?" she asked.

Jake could hardly speak but managed to say there had been an accident at the mill. "There's a man coming to explain. He needs the doctor."

Hearing Jake's voice, John came to the door. "What on earth are you doing here?" he asked his son.

Just then the man arrived at the door, panting and breathing hard from the exertion, and Martha went to get the doctor while John asked him for more details. "He's lost an arm," he said. "He fell onto the saw and has lost a lot of blood. We need the doctor to come now. He'll bleed to death." He staggered and looked as if he would fall but John caught his arm and sat him on a bench by the door just as Alex appeared. John quickly told him what had happened.

"Please go and tell Annie I'm away to a case," Alex said. "It's not the end to the day I imagined but I must do what I can." He'd been called several times to the mill to attend to severed fingers and broken bones. This sounded worse than that. He turned to Jake who was still at the door holding Blueboy. "I might borrow your mount, young fellow. Would you agree to that?"

"Yes of course," said Jake and John together.

"And Jake, will you go and get my horse and trap and bring them to the mill? I'll get my bag on the way."

Which is how the doctor came to be riding a pony through the streets of Greytown dressed in a morning suit on the afternoon of his wedding.

It wasn't far to the mill if he went through the bush, but Alex had to ride carefully, watching for low branches and fallen trees. There was an eerie silence as he approached the mill where the normally noisy engines were waiting to recommence their raucous wailing.

Mill staff were gathered around a figure lying on the ground, and someone reached up to take the reins from his hands and help him from the saddle.

One man had a tight grip on the stump of the left arm of the victim. The doctor moved quickly to the victim's side and took a cloth from his bag to make a tourniquet to stop the bleeding when the pressure was released. The man had done a good job and had most likely saved the poor fellow's life. Alex picked up a short piece of wood to use to tighten the hold and stem the flow of blood as he screwed the bandage as tightly as he could. The victim was slowly regaining consciousness, and though pale, still had a good colour.

As soon as Jake arrived, having driven the horse and trap the longer way by road, Doctor McDonald asked the men to lift the victim into the trap so he could take him back to the surgery for treatment. Then he thanked the men for the help they had given their workmate and advised the manager that he should see how the accident happened and what could be done to stop the same thing occurring again, before driving off.

The poor man moaned as the trap hit the potholes and big stones that lay about on the road but they were soon at the surgery where two men working nearby helped take the victim into the house.

Once inside, the doctor was able to have a closer look at the arm and assess the damage. It was a mangled stump with bone protruding from flesh. "There's no way I can repair this without causing you more pain," he told his patient. Then, taking a pad of gauze, he said, "Bite down on this. I'll be as quick and gentle as possible." Carefully he cut back jagged bone and trimmed torn flesh before removing the tourniquet to allow blood to flow from the artery to make sure it was free of obstructions like splinters of bone.

Taking needle and thread, he stitched the stump to make a compact end to the wound, leaving a short length of forearm that would allow better use of the stump when it healed.

Suddenly the surgery door quietly opened and Annie appeared, coming straight to the bed where she held the patient's hand and wiped his brow with cool cloths while Alex stitched away at the gruesome chore. He looked at her with admiration. What other woman would be prepared to give help with an operation on her wedding night? When it was over he prescribed a stiff whisky all round, to which Annie said, "Thank you but no, tea will be better for me." For the patient, however, it was a welcome solace and he drank it gratefully.

"How did it happen? What went wrong?" asked Doctor McDonald.

"I don't know really. I was standing watching the saw going through the wood when I must have tripped or fallen and put my hand out to save myself. This is the result," he said, looking at the bandaged stump. "I'll be no bloody use to anyone now," he said.

"Come on, man. That's no way to talk. Many men have lost their arms or legs and gone on to be as useful as ever. It's early days yet. Just wait until you've got used to being without your paw before you give up hope all together."

"I've six children to support. How, I ask, will I do that?" He looked as if he was going to cry. "First the house burns down while I'm working in the bush. The village people got together and rebuilt it for us. Now here I am unable to work."

Annie said that he should rest on the bed and try not to look too far ahead. "Do you have any education?" she asked. He nodded hesitantly. "You might get a job in the mill office then. Has anyone gone to tell your wife?"

"I don't know. How will I be able to face her?" As Eddie Browne looked at Annie with anxious eyes there was a knock at the door and Annie opened it. It was Mrs Browne.

"Can I see him?" she asked. "Is he all right?" and she pushed past Annie and ran to her husband. "For God's sake, what have you done?"

Doctor McDonald took the woman's hand in his and patted her shoulder. "I know you're upset," he said, "but there's no need to blaspheme."

"I'm sorry Doctor. I didn't mean to swear. It's just that we've had so much go wrong, I don't think I can take any more," said the distraught woman.

"I know how much you've been through, but I can assure you that life will go on. Your husband will find there are things he can do with just one hand. It's early days yet and you should both be grateful that he's alive thanks to the fast action of his workmates. In the meantime, I think he should stay here for a while longer. I hope we've done enough to stop any infection in the wound. It was a ragged cut but I've trimmed it as well as I could. Luckily there was enough skin left to cover the wound." He looked at Annie. "I think Mrs Browne could do with a cup of tea my dear, don't you?"

The woman looked at her husband's bandaged arm and put an arm around his shoulders. "We'll be all right," she said quietly.

———— ❧ ————

John had told the wedding guests what had happened as soon as the bridegroom had left on Blueboy. All were sorry that more misfortune had fallen on this family. Someone suggested that they should pass the hat around, and before too long a goodly sum was gathered to give to the man's wife.

The festivities were at an end. There was no point in waiting for the bride and groom to return so John called the gathering to order, thanked them on the doctor's behalf for attending and said they'd be able to taste the wedding cake at the couple's home when they called, as there had been no time to hold the cake cutting ceremony. "One last toast," he said "To the Browne family. May they survive this latest ordeal, with the help of the people of Greytown." All raised their glasses.

Martha was pleased to see they would soon have the room to themselves so they could get on with serving the meal she was preparing with the help of Molly, for their paying guests. 'It was too bad of the doctor to go off like he did, and then for the bride to go home. Really, this was the worst wedding reception I've ever had to cater for. Not that there have been many. Most girls only have a few friends around to their parents' home, not an event like this.'

Martha walked back into the kitchen. It had been a funny day. It was nice to have Molly to talk to but she was used to being queen of her realm and didn't like things being done any way but her way. "Will you not put the dirty dishes on that side of the sink?" she said. "I always wash from right to left. I can't work the other way."

"It doesn't bother me," said Molly. "I'll do them either way." She looked at the pile of plates and sweet dishes that still needed washing. As she went to move them they slipped out of her hands and hit the floor with a crashing thud. "Now look what you've made me do!"

Martha picked up the unbroken plates and swept up the remains of the others. "I'm going to have a rest," she said. "You can do what's left, yourself." She walked away with the air of a martyr.

CHAPTER 61 Back to Reality

It had been a long day for the wedding guests as they made their way home. Ellen and O'bie drove along the dusty road back to the farm in silence, lost in their thoughts of the last few weeks, the problems they had overcome, or had decided to ignore or forget.

O'bie was the first to speak as they came to the gateway. "I'll do the cows," he said. "It won't take long. You look tired."

"No, I love the cows. I'll be out as soon as I've got my old dress on," said Ellen.

"If you're sure, but I think you should have a rest. What did you think of the wedding ?" asked O'bie.

"It was a lovely wedding. They'll have a good life together. They know each other so well. Do you think I looked all right?" she asked.

O'bie paused. Should he tell her how he felt? "You looked lovely, and did a good job of looking after Mrs McDonald," he said gently. He turned away and went out the door to change for milking.

As Ellen hung her dress up carefully, she thought, 'This elegant gown may get another outing but not for a while.' She thought she knew what O'bie was feeling, and knew how tongues were wagging, but she would not give them any ammunition.

Kate and John made their way to the boarding house where Cathy and Jane were minding William. They were anxious to get home. Accidents were so hard to accept. The Browne family had gone through so many upsets already. It seemed unfair that the breadwinner should lose his arm. Cathy met them at the door.

"Where's Jake?" asked John. "Has he gone on home?"

"I think so," replied Cathy. "He came back with Blueboy, and said he was going to tell Kingi and Hemi to go home as he didn't feel like playing any more after seeing all the blood on the ground where the man had been lying."

"Oh the poor lad," said Kate. "Did he see the man's arm?"

"He didn't say. He just looked white. He waited until they put the man into the buggy then came here, a wee while ago. I think he'll be home by now," said Cathy. "Jane's gone home with her parents too."

When they reached home Jake had the fire alight and the cows up ready for milking. Cathy still had to churn the cream and feed the fowls. As she threw wheat to the pullets and chased the big black rooster away she worried about the Browne children's father. Jake said he had lost an arm. How could you lose an arm?

When she churned the thick rich cream it didn't take long to bring the butter up. It stuck to the paddles while the buttermilk ran into the bucket for the pigs and ducks. Soon she was able to wash the churn with water from the copper. Jake had lit that fire too. He was being unusually helpful. He had looked so upset when he came home. She'd ask him what he had seen. She wanted to know because Maggie Browne was one of her friends.

Once home, Kate had set about getting a meal for the children and John. She wasn't hungry as the luncheon had been plentiful and delicious. It was funny how one enjoyed someone else's cooking. Those apple tarts had something extra in the flavouring. I must ask Martha for the recipe. When the meal was ready she saw that John was dozing in his chair on the veranda. She'd just leave him to sleep. He'd been so busy lately and was doing too much. 'We need more help,' she thought.

As Cathy and Jake tucked into their cottage pie, Kate sat and nursed William, who'd woken up hungry and grizzly, and thought about the day. She guessed that being a doctor's wife or housekeeper was not easy, but knew Annie would be no different now than she'd been all the years she had helped Alex as nurse, housekeeper or confidante.

She thought Ellen Harvey had looked lovely and was glad they had bought the new outfits. Her feet were sore from the new boots she'd worn, but all in all it had been worth it to feel well dressed in front of the other guests, even though they were all friends.

She had observed O'bie had paid attention to Mrs Harvey as they walked to the hotel. Kate hoped he wasn't getting above his station. Mrs Harvey was really vulnerable after the turmoil of the past months. She wondered if she should warn her about O'bie's drinking. 'But then, he may be growing up.'

When John woke from his nap the sun had gone down and it was cooler. 'I must be getting old,' he thought, as he stretched his arms. 'Sleeping in the daytime. That's not good. But hat poor bloke Browne, how will he manage to provide for all those children? I should get up a deputation to go and see the mill owner. He shouldn't get away with this. It's not the first time there's been an accident.'

He thought of who could lend their weight to a meeting - Fairman, Dickson, Doctor McDonald and that friend of Joan Thompson's, Jones. He seemed a good chap. He'd been helping the teachers at the school house. He'd ask Dickson to organise it and for the owner to be ready to meet with them on Wednesday. When he went inside and saw Kate asleep in her chair with the baby still in her arms he gently picked him up and laid him in his cradle out of harm's way.

Kate woke with the movement. "I must have gone to sleep," she said, yawning. "Do you want any tea?"

"Just a cup of tea and a bite of cake. I'm still full from the luncheon," said John. "I've been thinking there should be a meeting with the owner of the mill. I know he thinks he's reasonable and tells the men to be careful, but from what I've heard, he's a slave driver and counts every second the men take to do a job. Anyone he thinks is shirking he sacks. I'll ask Dickson to get a party together for Wednesday, and we'll put the case for Eddie Browne to be given a job in the office or yard."

"I think you're right John," said Kate, "but can we just get to bed? This little man will be screaming for more food before we can say 'Jack Robinson'."

———— ∞∞ ————

Alex and Annie had drunk a welcome cup of tea after he had taken the Brownes to their home and given instructions about Mr Browne's care. It had been a long day. Not what they'd looked forward to at all. Alex watched as Annie brushed her long hair. It was wavy from being tied in two plaits that went around her head to form a coronet, but now it was flowing free and tumbled down around her shoulders in a silken cloud. "Leave it down like that," he said, as he moved to take her in his arms. "It looks lovely."

"You're not sorry you wed me, then?" asked Annie. She'd imagined this moment many times, since she had taken the position of housekeeper. All this time her love had grown stronger, and now at last, her dreams had come true.

"No, I'm not sorry at all, but do tell me what went wrong with the chocolate éclairs."

The romantic moment went out the window. "Do men always think of their stomachs?" asked Annie.

"No, but I want to know. You went rushing off to talk to Martha, then what happened?" asked Alex. He caught Annie's hand.

"I'll tell you tomorrow," said Annie.

CHAPTER 62 The Meeting at the Mill

On Wednesday John rode into town for the meeting with the mill owner. The deputation which Dickson had organised were waiting at his store and they spent a few minutes discussing how to go about the task without having an unpleasant confrontation.

"I think we should just tell him it's his duty to look after the poor chap," Fairman said. "It'll be hard going for him."

"You won't get far with words like 'duty'," said Paul Jones. "I think he should be asked to provide office work for the man as it would be a compassionate act. That will make him feel that he's a good employer."

"What education does the man have anyway?" asked John. "It's all right laying down the law but could Browne handle an office job? I think we should see Browne before we go to the meeting."

Henry looked quizzically at the men and said, "Well, let's get on with it," and they walked to where John had his horse tied to a hitching post and Henry's wagon was waiting.

When the men stopped at the Brownes' Mr Browne came to the door. "Please don't go the mill," he said when he discovered the reason for the visit. "You folk have done enough for us. I'll find something myself when the stump heals."

But his wife came to the door too, shushing the children clinging to her skirt. "If they can help you Eddie, don't be too proud to take their offer. You're a good book keeper. The mill is getting so busy, he might be glad to put you on to help the manager. I think you should go with them. See the owner yourself. Let him see the consequences of the lack of guards around the saws."

"Well, perhaps I will. The arm is sore but I'll be all right if I don't hit it on anything." He took his hat from a peg behind the door and joined the men in the wagon. John watched from his horse, glad Browne had recovered enough to come too. The little deputation set off again, going the long way round to the mill. The bush was too thick to take the short cut.

The saws were busy and the noise made it hard to hold a proper conversation. They went to the mill office and asked to see the owner who'd been sent a letter by the new lawyer in town, asking him to meet with them. He'd left word that they were to go to his house where he would receive them.

They tied the horses up as far away from the noisy saws as they could and walked through the remaining stand of bush near the owner's house. It was a large two-storied building, with a pleasant garden. There were several oaks, chestnuts, elms and other English trees making good growth, plus a scattering of natives.

"He's doing well," said Jones who hadn't been in the district long and was unaware of the wealth some people had made from felling the beautiful bush for timber. "He must be worth a fortune."

"He is that, all right," said Eddie Browne. "He imported a new sawmill from England, all ready to go. It cost him hundreds of pounds."

When John knocked at the front door of the house, a maid opened it and showed them in to the sitting room. "I'll get the master," she said.

Eventually the owner entered the room, a smile of welcome on his face. "Sit down, please, sit and tell me what it is you want to talk about, gentlemen. Is it money for the school, perhaps? I hear you all take an interest in it. Please make it brief, I'm a busy man. Ah Mr Browne! I'm truly sorry about your accident. How's the arm?"

"No," said Dickson "It's not the school we've come about, but a donation would be welcome. We are here on Mr Browne's behalf, to ask you to find him an office or yard position. We feel it would be a charitable thing to do. We also want to have a look at the state of the safety rails around the saws, not today, but soon, to see if there are improvements to be made. Doctor McDonald wasn't able to come today, but he'll be making a report when he has looked at the area more closely."

"I say," said the owner, "you can't come barging in here telling me what to do. I'll do something for the man, as and when I please. It's not for you to come here and lay down the law. I take every precaution I can. The men are lazy and take short cuts. I can't be blamed for what occurred, I wasn't even there."

"I'm sorry we upset you," said Paul, "but he needs help."

"The fact is that new laws are going through parliament to govern the use of dangerous machinery. I think we'd have a good case if we need to go to court," said Dickson. "I think you'll see the sense in hearing us out, if you listen."

John tried to appeal to the owner as a good Christian. "Mr Browne tells us that he can read, write, and do accounting so he could be a good help to the manager. We can see how much work you have on and we're only asking that you give him a trial when he's recovered enough to begin work. You should also pay him wages until then at the rate he was earning on the saw."

"Utter rubbish," said the owner. "I've had to build my way on my own. I never had a hand-out."

"I thought your father set you up in the business," said Dickson. "I read it in the paper. You were sent out to the colonies in disgrace, so I read, but we'll keep it to ourselves."

"I'm sorry to disappoint you. You're quite mistaken. That was a distant cousin of mine. However, I'm prepared to give Browne a position in the office for a trial period as soon as he's ready, and I'll give him twenty pounds as compensation, so gentlemen?" He indicated that the meeting was over by ringing the bell for the maid.

The men returned to the store well pleased with their morning's work. Not that they would ever say what had occurred or reveal the details of the newspaper item, unless the mill owner didn't come up with the offer of work. It was only by chance the copy of the London paper had reached the very place where the mill owner had made his home and started his business. And an even bigger chance that it was seen by someone who could read between the lines, and understand the meaning. Dickson had been scanning a three-year-old paper when the name had jumped up and caught his eye. Remittance men, was what they were called, paid to stay away from Britain and out of trouble. "Oh well, he's making work for the settlers and as long as he keeps his word, we'll say no more."

After the men agreed to say nothing to anyone else, John decided to see the doctor before he went back to the farm to tell him of the outcome of the meeting and encourage him to go and look at the accident site. More to annoy the mill owner than any thought that he could make much difference to the way the mill was run. The new Mrs McDonald came to the door and showed him to the parlour, saying, "The doctor is attending to a case of measles."

When the doctor came in he looked very anxious. "There's a lot of measles around. Some of the pakeha children are affected but I'm really worried about the Maori children. Up north they're dying from this disease, and tuberculosis is becoming a real problem. I don't know what I can do to help them. These are diseases they haven't been exposed to before and they have little resistance. I'm really worried about the little chap I've just seen - he's ten and Maori."

John could see the doctor was really affected by feelings of inadequacy. He patted him on the shoulder. "I'm sure you'll do all you can. No-one can ask for miracles. It's very sad that Maori people are so badly affected by our diseases but they'll build up some resistance in time. Causes will be found and cures discovered. You can only do your best."

"I suppose you're right Johnson, but it's sad when a young strong boy is struck down. I'm seeing him at home tonight - I just pray there'll be an improvement. Now tell me how it went at the mill."

John recounted all the details of the visit to the mill owner concluding with the moment when mention was made of the newspaper item.

"So what happened then?"

"The man denied it was him. Said it was a distant cousin, and then said he'd give Browne a job when he was recovered and twenty pounds compensation. We told him that you'd have a look at the site, to see if the accident could have been prevented, then we left," said John.

"So what was this deadly deed?" asked an amused Alex.

"We've decided to keep it quiet. It was a romantic escapade."

On his way home, when John stopped at Kelly's to tell him about the meeting, Paddy remarked on how well the potatoes were doing in John's field. He could see them through the fence next to his back paddock. They seemed to be growing inches every day. Some had even started flowering and they looked so healthy. The plot looked a real picture, just like a piece of Ireland.

Continuing on his way home, John stopped to deliver some mail he'd picked up from the store to the farms on the way. One delivery was to a settler who'd lost his leg to a tree falling, and John paused to consider how lucky he'd been when the tree fell on him not long after Kate and the children had arrived. He couldn't imagine how he would have managed.

CHAPTER 63 A Fright With William

Kate was busy weeding in the garden. Now the frosts had finished she wanted to plant out the marrows and squash plants she'd raised on the kitchen window-sill. The spring growth was rampant and John thought it looked very much like a real English garden but without the resident aged gardener standing by to do the work! Kate stretched her back as she stood up. It was really pleasant out here but William would be making his demands known soon. "How did it go?" she asked.

"Very well thanks to Dickson - he had some information that turned the tide our way. The owner agreed to everything. I won't go into details, but it was all good. I've brought you some letters from home. Are you interested?" And he laughed as Kate grabbed the bag and ran inside, anxious to read a letter from her mother. However, the letter was forgotten when, a little later, William woke up coughing and flushed.

Kate picked him up to nurse him, but he wasn't interested in her breast. That wasn't a good sign. She took a soft cloth and wrung it out in cold water to sponge his face. There were so many illnesses about. One of the neighbour's children had died of whooping cough. 'Please God, don't let it be that,' she prayed.

Kate was worried and thought they should get the doctor to see him. John thought he'd be all right but said he'd go after lunch if the baby was no better. Perhaps she was worrying too much. She felt William's head. He seemed hot and flushed so she wrung out the cloth in cold water again and gently washed his face and hands.

William started to cry so she put his mouth on her breast to see if he'd drink. After a few sucks he tired and began to cry again so she sat and rocked him back to sleep. Then, worried that he wasn't drinking, Kate washed out his feeding bottle, poured in some water from the kettle and waited for it to cool down. She was a great believer in boiled water to feed him. Not water straight from the creek.

William stirred again so she tried him with the water and he managed a few sucks. Then she undressed him to sponge him and her heart sank - he was covered in spots. So it was measles, or scarlet fever. She ran to the door, calling to John. "You'll need to get the doctor John. William has a rash, all over him."

When John came to see for himself he could see Kate had reason to be so concerned and it wasn't long before he was on Beauty and on his way back to town.

Doctor McDonald was relaxing in his easy chair drinking a cup of tea when John arrived to tell him he was needed. "William's off his food. My wife said he will only have a few sucks then cries. He's come out in a rash too."

"Well, what are we waiting for?" the doctor asked as he put his cup down and reached for his hat.

They travelled the few miles to the farm in silence, each busy with their own thoughts. Doctor McDonald was praying the Maori boy with the measles was improving and that the disease wouldn't spread. John was thinking of how grief-stricken the family would be if William died.

Kate was relieved to see them back so soon. Sometimes, if the doctor was away with a case out in the country, it might be hours before he could come. She lifted the garments away from William's hot little body so the rash could be examined.

"I'd say it's measles, my dear. He'll begin to recover now the rash has erupted. You must be sure to make him drink or he'll get dehydrated. I see you're giving him water. Boiled? Just keep him cool, but not in the light. He'll recover better in a dark room; we don't know why the light hurts their eyes but patients have told us it's true.

They're finding things out every day about medicine and illnesses. I could go back and study at medical school again and it would all be different to what we were taught only fifteen years ago."

"I'll be off," the doctor said as he prepared to leave. "I want to call in on a friend on the way, the man who lost a leg. What an inspiration he is. I never come out this way without visiting him, sometimes just for a minute or two. My spirits lift after talking with him. I hope Mr Browne will be the same. By the way I've had a look at the mill, Johnson. There's a lot needs to be done to make the saws safer."

CHAPTER 64 The Sports Day

Some days later the teachers were planning the last items for the sports day when Mr Jones called to see them. All the children had gone home except Marie and Peter who were playing outside, waiting for their mother to finish work at the store.

"How did you get on at the mill?" Joan asked. He'd told her of the deputation. "Did the owner agree to help?"

"Yes. After we put the case he said he'd give Browne a trial at keeping the books and twenty pounds compensation. It took a bit of hard talking, but he saw sense in the end."

"Well done. We've been making a list of the events for the sports day. I think we've got enough to keep everyone busy. The children are getting so excited. Some of the fathers have scythed the grass. The children were gathering it up to make haystacks; I was frightened they'd get in the way. We've promises of prizes; money is the easiest - a shilling for first, and sixpence for second. That will be a fortune for them and we've decided on eight events, so it won't cost too much. We'll have a picnic lunch too."

Mrs Thompson told him he'd be Master of Ceremonies. "It will be on Saturday from nine a.m. and over by lunchtime. Mr Dickson has a notice in the shop window and I've told all the children to tell their parents, but we'll just have to wait and see who comes along. The band has been asked to play a few tunes. They love to strut their stuff, and were more than willing to take part. The children can form up at the school then march to the big paddock over the road. There's plenty of room to park buggies and drays at the end of the paddock and they can tie the horses up in the shade. Now all we want is fine weather. Some of the children have nasty coughs and there are a lot of measles about. See, you didn't know what you were letting yourself in for."

"I'm glad to help. Until I decide what I want to do, I've time on my hands. I want to be part of this town. I feel at home here just as I did in Wales. I've only known people here for six months or so but they're like old friends. I think it's because we have to rely on each other, don't you?"

———— ∞ ————

Saturday came at last. Jake and Cathy were up early to finish their chores before they ate breakfast and rode into town. Kate said she wasn't going to the sports day. "I'd like to but I think it's too soon to take William out. No, I'll stay here and catch up on some work and letters. There are plenty of parents to help."

"I think you're wise, said John. "You'll be missed but they'll understand. The Dicksons will help. He's going to close the store for the morning." He went to kiss Kate goodbye, and placed his hand on his youngest son's head. "He looks better, doesn't he?"

"Yes, he's a lot better than yesterday. He's drinking now and quite hungry. I was only up to him twice last night. I'll have a good rest too." Kate waved goodbye to the family and breathed a sigh. It had been stressful, but she was sure William was on the mend.

⧭

The excitement around the school grew to fever pitch as the band tuned their instruments. Mrs Thompson was trying to keep control of the children and put them in line according to height. Marie was the youngest, and the shortest, but was firmly attached to Polly and Olga and wouldn't let go of their hands.

When all were ready Mr Jones waved to the drum major and the band marched off in step to the rousing music. The children tried to keep in time as they'd been practising, but Marie's legs were short and she had to run to keep up. There were only a few yards to walk across the road then the children stopped and waited while the band did a circuit of the field. Many of the band members had been in the army and they gave a fine display of marching and played several well known tunes, to the delight of the onlookers.

Now Paul Jones took control, thanked the band and announced the first race, 'the under seven boys fifty yards'. And so the sports day went on. Parents were called on to act as referees and lines-men to ensure fair play. Beth Goode sat at a table and wrote down the names of the place-getters. Mr Fairman was busy helping control children who were not ready to run yet.

The sack races were very popular with fathers helping the next group into their sacks while a race was going on. The big boys could jump well and were easily the winners.

Later, two posts were placed into the ground with a cross-bar showing the height to be jumped and the bar was raised again and again until the highest jumper was found. When Jake and Hemi were the finalists John was urging Jake to go higher, while Rangi and Ru were calling encouragement to Hemi. Jake knocked the pole off at four feet. Hemi cleared it easily, so won the prize.

When one of the Browne children won the long jump everybody was pleased. His father was there to cheer him on while his wife stood near talking to Mrs McDonald. "I'm glad he won," she said. "He's been so miserable since the accident. He didn't want to come today. Some of the children have been calling him nasty names, and saying that there's a jinx on the family."

"That's terrible. I didn't think anyone at the school would be so mean. I'll have a talk to Mrs Thompson."

The egg and spoon race for the little ones caused much merriment. Eggs were dropped and replaced on the spoons as the children ran their wobbling way to the finishing line. "It was just as well the eggs were hard boiled," Miss Goode said to Joan Thompson as they noted down the last names on the winner's sheet.

At lunch-time picnic baskets were lifted from the back of buggies and blankets were spread on the grass as families and friends settled down to the serious work of eating. Sandwiches of cold meat and pickles, bacon and egg pies, ginger bread and sultana cake were laid out to tempt the appetite, with bottles of lemonade and ginger ale.

Paul Jones, talking to Peter Fairman about the visit to the mill, suggested they should take the hat around the crowd to raise more funds for Eddie Browne.

Peter scratched his head. "I don't know about that. I think the family would be embarrassed. Let's just leave it alone for now. If the old bugger at the mill does as he says he will, they'll be all right. He seems to have come around to the idea of a desk job. Doctor McDonald looked at some of his book keeping of his own accounts and said he was neat and accurate. That's all you can ask. I say we just keep an eye on the situation."

The two men walked over to the teachers. "Time to stop for lunch, ladies. You can't work on an empty stomach," Paul Jones said. "It's gone very well but I think you should relax a bit. Come and eat."

"All right, if you insist," said Mrs Thompson. "Come over to the school. I'm dying for a cup of tea. I sent Jane over to build up the fire, so the kettle should be hot." They walked across the road to the school grounds and made themselves comfortable in the kitchen. Once lunch was over the teachers returned to the field, leaving the men to chat.

"Have you set the date yet?" Paul Jones asked as they finished their tea.

"Miss Goode wants to wait until the winter so I'll have time to build the house but there's no reason why you shouldn't marry early in the new year, is there?"

"Mrs Thompson wants to wait until the local board have made up their minds as to whether she'll get the position renewed even though the two inspectors from Wellington told her she'd be headmistress for two years. Things change all the time, don't they, when you're dealing with the authorities. The idea of a new education board and all their rules has set her teeth on edge. She does a good job and the school board should appreciate that. I think we'll wait until the winter too. We're not young, but still look forward to a happy life together. I'd tie the knot tomorrow, if I could."

"Things will sort out, Jones. You'll see."

"I guess you're right, but it's lonely out in the country. I heard that the vicar has been down to see the widow and got a good reception from all accounts. The coach driver was full of the tale. He gives a report on the situation as he sees it every time the vicar goes over the hill. Well, he's only been once since she went home, but you can see how the land lies."

"I did hear about the poor man catching up with her on the coach and asking her to consider him as a husband. So he's been down to 'plight his troth', so to speak. Did she say yes?"

"I believe she's thinking about it and might come over here to live. The vicar said he'd like to get a house in Masterton. He'd still travel around the district, but that would be his home. I hope it works out for him."

By now the two men were walking back to the sports field but, as they approached, they could see something was wrong. People were looking around the buggies and trees at the end of the field, searching for something and Mary Smith appeared to be distraught with worry. Peter Fairman ran to Miss Goode. "What's the matter? Is something wrong?"

"The three little ones are missing. Olga, Marie and Polly," Beth said. "We think they've wandered off into the bush. Jake and Hemi have been calling them but they haven't had any luck. The bush is quite thick there. They might have strayed off the track that the men use to get to the mill. If they don't turn up in a minute or two we'll have to get a search party up to comb the area although there's nothing to hurt them except the stream. Polly should know to keep them away from that."

Just then Henry Dickson came up. "They're most likely looking for frogs or bird nests," he said. "Children lose track of time when they are happy. I'm sure they'll turn up, but I think we should organise a group to search the bush." Soon a party was gathered together and instructions given about where to look.

The bush was thick with five-finger and lawyer and it was hard to see more than a few yards ahead. The men spread out across the open space at the end of the field and walked a few feet apart, calling to the children all the time as they entered the thickest part of the reserve. However, they'd not been searching long when Dennis and Kingi came running towards them, shouting that they'd found them.

"They won't come because they're frightened," Kingi said. "They think they're in big trouble. Olga fell into the water and is all wet. Marie and Polly pulled her out but she's scared she will get into trouble."

"Show me where they are, Kingi. I'll go and talk to them," and Henry followed the boys through the bush to where the three girls were huddled by some flax bushes, crying. Olga was wet and shivering so he took off his coat, wrapped it around the quivering little body and began carrying her back to her family while Polly and Marie were led by the boys, relieved that they weren't going to spend a night in the bush with the ruru calling their mournful cries. All the children and their families cheered as they emerged from the trees and there were cries of relief from Mary Smith and Tessa Kelly who received their children with open arms and hugs.

However, when Henry took Olga back to her father Mr Petersen grabbed Olga roughly and slapped her on the head with his open hand, saying angrily, "You are stupid brat!"

"Hey, hold on!" protested Henry Dickson. "You can't hit the child like that. What's she done to deserve that?"

"Is my child," Petersen said. "I do what I like. Her mother is too soft with her. I teach her lesson. What I do is my own business. She need good hiding."

"What she needs is a hug, from you or her mother. She's had a big fright. Don't you hit her or you'll be sorry."

Petersen let go of the child and faced Henry. "You want fight?"

"If you like. I don't believe in thrashing children when they've got into a bit of trouble and are too frightened to come home. What sort of a father does that make you?"

"You very clever. You not a father yet. Wait till you have young ones get up to mischief and you have to set them on the straight and narrow. Bible says spare rod spoil child," said Petersen as he rolled up his shirt sleeves and spat on his hands while the men standing near moved to make a ring.

Suddenly, before Henry Dickson had time to take off his hat, he was lying on the ground in a prone position with one arm up his back. Petersen was a very large man and, although Henry bucked him off, he knew he was not strong enough to wrestle him. Nevertheless, he had managed to take a fresh hold on

Petersen when Peter Fairman arrived on the scene. He yanked Petersen up from the ground and held him in an embrace where he couldn't do any more damage. "You big bully!" he said. "Wrestle me!"

Petersen looked at the blacksmith's strong arms, burnt brown from the sun and with bulging muscles from years of belting hot metal into subjection. He knew he'd be taking on a lot to try and wrestle him. He looked at his sobbing daughter who was being cuddled by Mrs Dickson, and scoffed. "Such a lot of fuss about a baby. No, I not fight you. I have great regard for you." He picked up Olga, gave her a hug, then put her on the ground, saying, "Now get away home."

She still looked afraid and was about to leave when Polly ran over and took her hand. She looked Mr Petersen in the eye. "You won't beat her at home will you? She didn't mean to fall in. She slipped on a boulder. Please don't hit her. She's my best friend." All the people around clapped as Polly made her plea for forgiveness.

Unexpectedly Petersen smiled. "No, I not do that. I'm glad she has such a loyal friend. I got a bit angry about them going into bush on their own and for causing problem." The big man looked at the men who were watching. "Hey, we forget it eh? You all come to pub, have a beer on me?"

"Thank you," said John Johnson. "I'd he'd be glad to share a drink with you soon, but I must get home as my wife is there alone with our baby and he's been ill."

Paddy Kelly looked uncomfortable. He glanced at his wife and knew he must refuse even though his throat was burning with thirst. "I'd better get along too, Petersen. I hope we'll see you around the township more often. I don't drink liquor anymore but these fellows here will join you with pleasure I'm sure." He looked around the crowd of mill workers who would be certain to take advantage of a free beer. They'd been disappointed that the fight had come to a sudden end and were glad at the offer of the coming shout. They nodded.

Petersen offered his hand to Paddy. "Not many men be willing to admit that. I shake your hand. So we go?" he said to those still hopefully waiting.

⸎

On their way home in the wagon the Kelly children were discussing who'd run the fastest race when their mother surprised them by saying, "I'm proud of all of you, whether you won a race or not. But I'm most proud of Polly and Dada. You, Dada, for facing your demon head on and you, Polly, for putting Mr Petersen in his place. That was wonderfully brave of you."

Polly went scarlet with pride. She didn't usually get much praise as she was mostly in trouble for silly deeds but she couldn't let that man hit Olga anymore. She'd seen the bruises on her friend's legs, and once Olga had shown the welts on her backside. "I just had to stop him Mam, he's hard on all the children, not just Olga."

"Weren't you frightened?" asked Tessa. "He's a big man."

"No, I had to say what I thought. She was so scared. If Dennis and Kingi hadn't found us we would've stayed out all night."

"Well thank goodness that didn't happen," said Paddy. "That would have meant no sleep for anybody. The sports-day would have ended on a bad note and we'd have been worried sick. I'm proud o' you too, Polly, my dear, very proud indeed."

The Kellys' wagon reached the farm gate and the boys leapt off to bring the cows in for milking. It had been a long tiring day, but full of good memories, as well as the moments of panic when the three young friends were thought to be lost. Tessa thanked God that Polly and her friends were safe.

———— ∞∞ ————

Kate was feeding William when Jake and Cathy arrived back on their ponies, full of news. Cathy said it had been a good day until the three young ones had gone missing. She'd won a prize in the fifty yard race, and come second in the one hundred yards. She told Kate about all the trouble when Olga was found and how Polly had spoken out about Mr Petersen's bad temper. "He'd have beaten Olga, right there," she said.

"Perhaps he was just glad to see her," her mother said. "Some men don't know how to react when they are worried. They just get in a rage."

John was not far behind the children but stopped to admire the potato field. The potatoes were all in flower and looked very healthy. John hoped the disease that took hold of the crops at home wouldn't travel here. It was a long way from the shores of Britain, but you could never be sure of being safe.

He saw that Jake was getting the cows in with Dot. She was a willing helper and barked at any animals that tried to stay behind, but was more of a nuisance than a help. John hoped she'd soon learn to listen to Jake's commands. He slipped off Beauty and walked beside Jake as he drove the six cows up to the bails. "You've had a good day, then?" he asked. "Did you see the fight?"

"I saw Mr Petersen wrestle Mr Dickson but it was over in a minute. I left to ride home with Cathy when Mr Fairman was stepping up. Did they have a go?"

"No, Fairman was too strong. Petersen gave in. Polly told him off. It was a real joy to see her."

CHAPTER 65 One Too Many

O'bie had gone home before Petersen made the offer of a beer or two, but rode back into town to join the men at the hotel as soon as he'd eaten. He told Ellen he was going and she was not concerned but hoped he wouldn't get drunk. She trusted him, although there were times when she wondered if she was wise staying at the farm. While O'Bie was always a gentleman when he was around her she noticed him looking at her with a longing she couldn't ignore.

She'd had a busy day but, before she went to bed she sat out on the veranda and watched the clouds forming around Bull Hill. It looked as if it might rain. The farm could do with it. She wondered how Reverend Porter was getting on with his courtship of Mrs Martin. It had been the talk of the village. A good few laughs had been heard as the tale grew in the re-telling. 'It would be nice if they were to marry and perhaps come to live at the farm. O'bie could stay on as manager, and I could go and help Dora in Masterton.'

It was nearly dawn when she woke, to hear someone in the kitchen. Fully awake, she listened to the sound of someone pushing a chair along the floor before it toppled over. Ellen pulled on her wrap, and crept to the kitchen door. There was O'bie looking in the pantry. "What are you doing?" she asked.

"I was hungry and thought I'd make a sandwich," he said in a slurred voice. Then, stumbling over to Ellen, he tried to put his arm around her and pull her into an embrace. The smell of whisky was almost overpowering. She wrenched free of him.

"What are you doing, O'bie? Let me go. You're drunk and don't know what you're doing. Please go to bed."

"I want to go to bed with you here. I love you Ellen. Please say you care for me." O'bie tried to take her arm.

"You don't know what you're saying, O'bie. I don't care for you in that way. Please just go and sleep it off and we'll say no more about it."

O'Bie shuffled his way towards the door. He looked as if he would cry. "I love you Ellen, s-sorry if I hurt you. Please don't turn me out." He looked at her hopefully but she wasn't moved at all.

Ellen tried to go back to sleep. She wasn't sure if O'bie would try to come back. 'He's just a silly infatuated boy,' she thought, 'but I can't stay here if he can't be trusted. Mrs Johnson warned me that this could happen.' They'd been getting on so well with the farm work. The animals were being cared for. The cows were milking so well that they might have to get another lot of pigs to fatten up. 'I thought I could trust O'bie with my life. Now what am I going to do?'

As the sun rose over the eastern hills and lit the room with bright light Ellen decided to get up. 'I'm not going to get any more sleep and I may need to milk by myself if O'bie doesn't wake up.' She pushed some chips into the fire box and soon had a fire going. A good strong cup of tea was what she needed. Ellen looked out the door and saw there were dark clouds rolling up from the south. A good downpour would clear the air, she thought.

Refreshed by the tea, Ellen walked to the bails to find that O'bie had begun to milk already. "Good morning," was all he said, as he hung his head against the cow's flank.

Ellen decided she wouldn't bring up the subject, and walked Daisy into the bail and put the rope around her leg. She was an easy cow to milk. Comfortable and easy going, not like some of the other ones who kicked and jumped about as they were chained up. She began to pull the teats in a steady rhythm and the milk made music on the bottom of the bucket - swish swish, swish swish. As the level rose it became quieter.

The milking over, Ellen washed up the buckets while O'bie went to feed the pigs. She was not going to mention the night before if O'bie didn't bring up the subject but if she was to stay at the farm there would have to be a firm understanding about behaviour and drinking. O'bie was a strong young man with natural desires. Ellen knew this but she didn't feel about him in that way. She was just not ready to marry again. He would have to accept that. She didn't really want to go to Masterton to work for her cousin, but if she had to, well, she would.

She prepared breakfast for them both and waited for O'bie to sit at the table before she placed the bacon and eggs before him. He looked at her with a shame-faced expression. "I'm sorry about last night. I don't know what came over me," he said. "Constable O'Reilly told me to go home when he thought I'd had enough to drink. I was lucky I never fell off the horse."

"We need to get some things clear, O'bie. I've never given you any cause for you to think I was in love with you. I'm sorry if you think I did. The show of bravado, riding into town together, was never meant to be anything but a snub to the likes of Doris Bell and her nasty tongue. I don't want to have to go up to live with my cousin, but I may have to if you persist in making more of our friendship than what it is, a working partnership." Ellen spoke with feeling as she cleared the breakfast things away. "We'll never speak of this again, if you agree. No more drunken nights."

"Oh Mrs Harvey I'm truly sorry. I agree to keep our friendship on a business footing. I'm such a fool when I've had a few. It will never happen again. I promise," said O'bie.

"All right then. What needs doing today?" asked Ellen, happy to have put the matter to rest. "It looks as if we might get some rain. The ground is very dry so it will be welcome. Did you see the butcher about the pigs?"

"He'll be out to see them this week. They'll come in handy for the trade at Christmas time. Hams are always popular because they keep so well. He'll give us a good price too," said O'bie.

CHAPTER 66 The Drought Ends

The rain was beating a tattoo on the roof when John woke early in the morning. It would hold up work on the farm, just when he was able to attend to it again. Still, there were always jobs to be done in the stable or barn. Now that summer was here and Jake home from school he really didn't need the two men as well although, if the weather had stayed dry they could have got on with the clearing of the farm he had secured for the Smiths.

The rain kept up a steady rhythm as John built up the fire for Kate. To everyone's relief William seemed to have recovered from the measles with no ill effects. Two children had died of scarlet fever or measles at the pa and Rangi had been very worried about his own children. Doctor McDonald had been very upset about one of the settler's children who had died of diphtheria. 'It's a hard life for many families but we've been lucky,' he thought as he filled the kettle and placed it on the stove.

A little later Rangi and Ru arrived at the farm gate and tied the horses up to the old titoki tree. "What do you think the boss will want us to do today eh?" Ru asked Rangi.

"Some more building in the barn, I hope. This rain's heavy. I don't want to be dragging logs around in this. There's been a lot of rain in the hills. I heard it thundering up in the tops last night. Some lightning too. The river's pretty high boss," said Rangi as John came to the door. "Plenty rain up the mountains last night."

"Yes, I heard it too. I think we'll just go on with the stalls for the ponies. I know it's summer now but they'll need shelter when the cold weather comes again. I'll be over shortly to show you what I want done."

"Yes boss," said Rangi. "Me and Ru will go on over and start clearing the space." John nodded and went inside to finish his breakfast. He was so lucky with his workers. These last few weeks had seen him having to be away from the farm day after day, leaving the work to them. They never said a word about being left on their own. 'I'm very lucky,' he thought again as he pushed his chair away and reached for his hat.

The rain continued all day and, at about four o'clock, John told the men to get away home before it got dark. It was already gloomy outside and had turned colder as well. It looked like being a real southerly and felt like the middle of winter even though it was November. Wind blew the branches of the trees about and rain lashed the side of the barn.

Rangi rode back to tell John that the river was running a banker and he might need to shift the stock from the paddocks near the river. The sheep had been hard hit in the last floods. It seemed prudent to take Rangi's advice and move them to the higher ground. He saddled Beauty and went with Rangi to drive them up nearer the house.

It didn't take long to have the sheep safe. John thanked Rangi then rode off down the back of the farm to find the cattle were standing with their legs in water. The river had eaten a hole in the bank and was pouring through the gap. The old river bed which ran through the farm was usually dry but was now filling up fast and the field with the potatoes was partly covered. The middle section was under at least a foot of water. While both ends of the field were still safe for the moment John scratched his head, wondering how he could stop the torrent, but there was nothing he could do.

He'd just have to pray that the river would go down as quickly as it had risen. The potatoes would be all right for a couple of hours, but days of lying in a foot of water would make them rot. John looked again at the gap in the bank. The breach was wider now but the water level had started to drop. The volume of water flowing through had slowed to a trickle.

If the river took a mind to change course it would cut his farm in half and make it worthless. Perhaps it would be all right. The cattle had walked to where they could eat some grass at the far end of the paddock, and were not in any danger. 'I should just go home and wait,' thought John.

Beauty was happy to trot along through the rain sodden grass and flax bushes but darkness was closing in as they went along the bush lined track. Wood pigeons swooped past as he rode along, making their way to their favourite tree for the night's rest. The whoosh whoosh of their flight broke the silence of the evening. Suddenly, something moved on the path ahead. A dark figure stepped out of the trees and Beauty came to a halt.

John slipped out of the saddle to confront the stranger who was dressed in a dirty old coat and had a bundle tied to a stick slung over his shoulder. "It's a raw night," said John. "What are you doing out on a night like this?"

"Do you not know me then John?" said the man.

"I don't believe I do, no," said John. He looked again at the tall, roughly dressed man. There was something familiar about him but John couldn't say what it was.

"It's me, Jim Smith, back from the diggings." He looked at John and laughed. "I'm back a sore and sorry man."

"You didn't find your pile of nuggets then?"

"Oh I did, I did. But then the seam ran out. It's been a hard road to hoe. The price of food took all I could make. It's a fool's game, that's for sure," said Jim. "I haven't seen Mary or the children. I couldn't let her see me like this. I need somewhere to stay while I get my life together."

"Well come back to the house and Kate will fix you something to eat. I've problems too you know. The river is threatening to cut my farm in half. The crops are under water and the sheep are here in the house paddock. If they get into Kate's garden I'll be in even more trouble. Look Kate," he said when they arrived at the house door. "Look what the cat's dragged in."

Kate studied the figure standing in the doorway dripping water from a shabby coat, wondering what else the day would bring.

"Take off your coat, and come on in Jim," she said. She passed him a towel to dry his face and hung his sodden coat on a nail on the veranda. "The children have gone to bed. Sit up to the table John and you too, Jim."

Kate took plates down from the Dutch dresser and filled them with good warm stew. "Now eat up while it's hot. You can tell us all about your travels later Jim." Jim would want to go over his experiences in great detail. He was never one for a short explanation if a long detailed one would do. She yawned. "Oh excuse me," she said. "It's been a long day." William stirred in his cradle and Kate picked him up to show off the latest offspring. "Meet our new son."

"He looks a bonny fellow, Kate, I congratulate you," said Jim. He could see she was really tired. "If I can sleep somewhere tonight, I'll get to bed too. I've been walking for three days to get here. I didn't have enough money to buy a ticket on the coach. I worked my passage over from Sydney. Once I had made up my mind to come back, I couldn't get here quickly enough."

"We're glad to see you're safe and sound, Jim, but there's only the loft above the stable. You're welcome to stay there. It's dry and there's some hay. Kate will find you a blanket. We'll have a nightcap to celebrate your return, and then I'm off to bed. I'll need to be up early in the morning to check where the river has broken through into the potato paddock. You can tell us about your exploits then," said John as he poured them each a stiff whisky.

Jim took the glass gratefully. He'd not known what to expect from these friends after the way he'd walked out on them. He'd almost gone to try and find Mary before walking out here, but was too frightened of what he would find. "And Mary?" he asked. "Is she all right?"

"I know she's missed you Jim," Kate said, "but yes, she's fine, happy and working at the store for the Dicksons. I'll tell you all about them tomorrow. Here's a blanket. John has lit a lamp for you. He'll see you over to the stable and please don't keep him talking. Goodnight Jim," she said firmly.

The men closed the door as William stirred in his sleep. Kate picked him up to feed and change him. 'Stupid man,' she thought. 'I'm glad he's safe but poor Mary will get such a shock to see him in such a state. We'll have to find him some better clothes before he sees her and the children.' She sank into the cosy chair and lifted her blouse. William sucked hungrily. He was back to his old self. He lifted his head and smiled at Kate.' A real smile,' she thought, 'not just wind.'

John came in, shutting out the wind and rain as he closed the door. "It's a foul night," he said "I suppose he'll be comfortable up there in the loft."

"Really John, I don't care. He treated us very badly, and Mary too. He'll have to get a better outlook on life if he wants to take over the farm you signed up for him," said Kate. She laid William in his bed and walked into the bedroom.

"I don't think he'll ever make a farmer," said John. "No, he won't want to come and live out here. He can get a job at the mill like the rest of the young fellows. I saw Browne a day or two ago and he's ready to start work in the office. The stump has healed, and he's looking forward to earning his keep. That's the sort of men we want."

"If he did that, Mary could still stay on at the store. Our children really like her. I think they're sad that school has finished for the year and they don't see her so much. It's funny how thing work out, isn't it. Now get to bed and let's get some sleep." Kate pulled her blouse off and put on her long nightdress with the high buttoned neck. John reached over and took her in his arms. "Just a kiss goodnight, dear," she said. "It's been a long day."

CHAPTER 67 The Wanderer Returned

Morning came quickly. Kate could hardly believe she'd been to bed at all. Jake was up and setting the fire. "Uncle Jim came back last night when you were asleep," she told him.

"Where did he sleep?" he asked.

"In the barn. Would you go and see if he's awake after you've brought in the cows?" These days, Jake usually rose early and went for a run with Dot before he brought in the cows. She'd chase a rabbit or two, offspring of some that had been liberated down the valley. They were becoming more and more of a nuisance as they were breeding prolifically. If Dot caught one Jake would skin and gut it and give it to his mother for the table. Rabbit pie made a nice change. But this morning he'd slept in longer and decided to light the fire for Kate instead.

John came out of the bedroom and looked out of the door to see what the weather was like. "I've had a thought. He turned to Kate. "What would you think about letting Ru and his wife have the log house we built for Jim and Mary. He wants to marry the girl who was crying at the Major's funeral. It would be handy to have him living on the property and there'll be plenty of work on both the farms. So what do you think?"

"I think that would be a very good idea. I know you trust Ru and it would be good to have someone living in the place. You all put in a lot of work building it. So yes, I agree."

"Good, I'll tell Ru. Now I'm off to see what the river is doing and how the potatoes are."

Cathy came out, rubbing her eyes. Kate sent her to fetch the milk and cream from the cooler. It was such a help to have the brick-lined hole sunk in the shady side of the house rather than in the dairy some distance away.

Jim walked in the door and greeted Kate with a smile. "That was the best night's sleep I've had since I left Ballarat two months ago," he said. "Now tell me about Mary and the children."

Kate placed a bowl of porridge in front of him and passed the jug of cream. "Later, please Jim. I'll tell you all about what has happened these last six months when breakfast is over and Jake and John have gone to do the milking. Mary is fine and working at the store, as I told you last night. Marie has been to school for the last few weeks with Peter."

"I want to see them as soon as I can, but I'm ashamed of my clothes. There are some nasty people out there. I had my bag stolen in Sydney. I've got some funds in the bank of New South Wales, but not a lot," Jim said between mouthfuls of porridge and brown sugar.

John came in from the stables. The ride to the back of the farm had been easy as the water had soaked into the soil and was not lying about in puddles. The crop of potatoes looked refreshed so perhaps the overflow from the river might not have done any harm after all. Time would tell. He sat at the table, nodding a greeting to Jim. "Sleep well?" he asked.

"Yes indeed I did, thank you John. I think it was the relief of being with friends again. I hope I can make up for the trouble I caused you," said Jim.

"Just find a job and look after Mary and the children. That's all any man can do. They're looking for labourers at the mill. It's hard work and the pay's not much but it'll see you over the hard patch if you're willing to give it a try."

"What about the farm you bought me?"

John caught his breath as he realised what Jim had said. He steadied himself before replying. "I'm sorry Jim but that 's no longer an option. One of my workers is to live in the log cabin we built. He's to marry soon. As well, I've changed the title into Jake's name as I was entitled to do under the Small Farms Act. We never knew when you'd return or if you wanted to try your hand at farming. You could've let us know how you were. Mary was beside herself with worry until she decided she had to face life without you. She's done just that. She and the children are living at a boarding house run by Biddy O'Toole with a friend called Miss Goode who teaches at the school. They're settled and happy."

"I suppose I couldn't expect you to hold it on my behalf. I understand that. I don't think I'd ever make a farmer anyway. There's too much to learn. I'll try and get a job at the mill and find a place in Greytown to live. Where is this boarding house? Can I go today to see them?" asked Jim.

Kate looked up at Jim. "Yes, if we find you something to wear. Dickson's store has a good stock of trousers and shirts but you need to have a bath and change before you go there. Mary will be working. Mrs Dickson is resting because she's expecting. I'll find you some clothes you can borrow. They won't be new but they'll be cleaner than what you have on now."

"You can take Bonny and the trap I suppose," said John. "But don't try to make her go too fast She's getting old and fat now the children don't ride her to school every day."

"I saw the ponies. You must be doing well," said Jim. "I bet they cost a pretty penny."

"No more than they should have," said John. He looked at Jake with a warning not to say that the ponies had been swapped for some timber in case Jim took exception to the deal. "Jake, go and get Bessie in the trap and light the copper for a bath for Uncle Jim." John turned to Jim. "Mary will be at the store. The children stay at the store most of the day during the holidays. They do small jobs and run messages. Their friends from school are all around the town or come in with their parents to shop so they have plenty to entertain them. I will see you later, Jim - I'm off to have another look at the river."

"Jake will have lit the copper for your bath in the wash-house," said Kate. "It's just a lean-to John built on earlier in the year. I find it a real help. I do the washing out there now. I used to use the creek when I first arrived. '

"Thank you Kate, I'll go and wash and change then go and face Mary and the children," said Jim. "I don't know how she'll receive me. I deserve her scorn, anyway."

"Oh, just get along and have your bath. There's a tin tub on the wall and no-one will disturb you. Here are some towels. And some clothes that John left for you. Jake will have Bessie harnessed for you when you're ready." She passed Jim a cake of hard yellow soap.

In the wash-house Jim stripped off his ragged shirt and trousers. The soiled underclothes were stinking and he was glad to throw them into the fire. The copper was full of hot water. He took down the tin bath, filled it to halfway and stepped in. He could only sit down with his knees drawn up to his chin but the water felt so good.

The soap lathered well. Soon the grime of the past weeks was gone. 'I've been a fool,' he thought.' I could have had my own farm and employed someone to do the chores, as John does. Well, I know he works too but I could've had it easy instead of chasing gold. I can't make any more mistakes. I'll try for a job at the mill or find something else to do. There must be some openings for a willing worker even though that's something I've never been before. But I intend to start now. I must try to regain John's respect, and Mary's love before it's too late.' He sponged the soap from his limbs and stood up. A quick rub with the towel around his back and he was ready to put on the clean clothes. First a singlet and long-johns, then the shirt. John was a much bigger man and its long sleeves dangled over his wrists. The trousers were too big around the waist, but could be held up with a piece of string.

He'd leave his dirty clothes soaking in the bath. Kate had told him she'd deal with them. 'But,' he thought, 'if I'm to make a new start?' He took the soap and began to wash the clothes, soaping the stains and rinsing them in clean water in a bucket. He had learnt a lot when he was living rough at the diggings. He thought of the old man who had befriended him and whose death had hit him hard. It was why he decided to return home.

A line was strung across the ground between two young totara trees and Jim hung his shirt and trousers over it and pegged them with dolly pegs from the basket. They'd soon dry in the fresh wind blowing from the south. Kate's garden was full of flowers. Jim could see how much she loved it. The vegetable patch was well tended too. 'They must live off the land,' and he went to say he was off. "Garden looks lovely Kate," he said. "I hope I can get some tips if we can get a house in town."

"You'll be welcome to cuttings of anything I have, Jim. After all, that's the way out here. Everyone shares," laughed Kate.

"I'll be off then. I'll bring back the buggy this afternoon. I might stay here in the loft again. It depends on the reception I get from Mary."

CHAPTER 68 Reunited

The road was hard underneath a layer of mud stirred up by the rain and the old mare plodded along at a steady pace towards the village. Jim could see new houses on farms near the road. Everything looked well cared for. A couple of mallard ducks swooped low across the pond. It was an idyllic scene of prosperity Jim was finally able to appreciate.

The road passed the school and, without being asked, Bessie stopped outside. Not realising Bessie knew the school because of her frequent trips to it, Jim was annoyed and just about to urge her on when he noticed a little girl sitting on the steps playing with a doll. Jim looked twice and when he was sure it was his daughter he stepped down from the trap and called to her softly. "Marie, Marie, my child. Let me look at you. You've grown so much taller." Startled, she looked up at the strange man, got up and ran into the schoolroom where Beth Goode was painting one of the walls a bright shade of yellow.

"What's wrong dear?" asked Beth. She was used to Marie being nervous of anything or anyone new. "What's the matter?"

"There's a man out there who called me Marie. But I don't know him," she said. Beth looked at the girl. She was not one to tell fibs. "Well let's go and see, shall we?" she said, taking Marie's hand. "If he knows your name, he must be a friend of your mother's."

"He's driving Johnsons' buggy," said Marie.

They walked outside and down the steps. Beth looked at the stranger and said to Marie with a smile. "You know who this is, don't you?" The little girl only hung her head and refused to look. Beth had only seen Jim Smith once when he and Mary first arrived, but she was sure it was him. "Look, Marie. It's your father."

Marie lifted her head a little to see more clearly the man standing in front of her. He looked nothing like the father she remembered. Six months is a long time in a child's life and his clothes were old and patched and too big for him. She shivered with fear. "No! No! It's not. My father is big and strong and tidy," she said, with finality, and clung to Beth's skirt.

"It's all right Marie. I know it's a shock to see me. I am your father. You stay here and I'll go and see your mother. I'm back to look after you all. I've come home."

Beth suggested that she and Marie walk down to the store in a little while after Mr Smith had been to see his wife and they agreed this was a good idea.

Jim shook the reins and set Bessie off again down Main Street to stop a short while later at the store. He sat looking at the building with its fine sign and selection of goods outside on the pavement. Dickson's General Store, read the sign. A young lad was sweeping the rubbish into the gutter and looked up at the man sitting in the trap.

"Can I help you sir?" he asked. He patted the horse. "T'is Bessie," he said, and rubbed her nose.

Jim looked at the lad. He had to get it over with. "I'm looking for my wife, Mrs Smith," he said.

Billy nearly dropped his broom with shock, but recovered enough to call into the doorway, "Excuse me Mrs Smith; there's a person here to see you." He walked inside to make sure she'd heard.

Mary was serving a customer. "Tell whoever it is to come in and wait. I'm busy, Billy." Billy put away his brush and shovel and went out to pass on the message. "Mrs Smith is busy, but will be with you in a minute or two." Jim tied the horse to the hitching post, hoping Mary wouldn't keep him waiting long.

The customer taking her time with her purchases was, nosey as ever, Doris Bell. Finally, when she could find no more faults in the service, Mrs Bell asked, "I need Billy to carry these home for me."

Mary looked at the woman standing laden with goods. "I'm very sorry Mrs Bell. Billy will need to mind the shop while I attend to my visitor. He can bring them later if you like."

"That will have to do then, but I'll have something to say to Mrs Dickson about this," she said and made her way down the street, muttering about the way things were going from bad to worse.

Meanwhile, the visitor had been standing in a darkened corner. Now, when she realised who it was, she gasped and ran to him. "Oh Jim!" she cried. "I thought I'd never see you again. Is it really you?" And she flung her arms around his neck

"Yes, my love. I've returned, sadder, wiser and broke." He clasped her around the waist and swung her around and around the room, nearly falling over the sacks of wheat and pollard on the floor.

Mrs Dickson came carefully down the stairs to see what all the commotion was. Her baby was due in just two weeks and Mary Smith was practically running the shop while she rested because of the pain in her legs. Doctor McDonald had told her to put her feet up for at least an hour after morning tea and again in the afternoon. Billy was proving to be a great salesman and was often taking the wagon out to the farms on his own.

Johanna looked at the figures still embracing and wondered who it could be. No, that was not quite true. She was afraid of who it might be, that scoundrel husband who'd gone off to the goldfields. That's who it was for sure.

"Look who's here, Mrs Dickson. My husband has turned up safe and well. Isn't that wonderful?" asked Mary, just as Beth and Marie arrived. "Look, Jim's come home." She took Marie's hand and drew her close to her father. "Here's your father, Marie. Father's come home." But when she picked her up and thrust her into Jim's arms, Marie wriggled out of his grasp and clung to Miss Goode.

"Leave her for a while," said Miss Goode. "It will take her time to get used to you again, Mr Smith. I'm glad you're safe and well."

Mary looked at Mrs Dickson and smiled. "I knew he'd come home," she said. "Now we can start our new life properly. My husband will find a job, and I'll work here if you still want me." She looked at Mrs Dickson hopefully. She'd enjoyed working in the store and living with Beth and the children. But she was sure they could find a place of their own and still be friends with all the people in town who'd been so supportive of her.

"Of course you'll stay on in the shop, Mrs Smith. Whatever would I do without you? They're looking for workers at the mill. It's hard work, but pays enough to live on. You should try there, Mr Smith," said Johanna.

"So I've been told. Mr Johnson said I should go and see the foreman this morning, so I will. Marie, my pet, you have grown so much I hardly know you. Come and give Father a hug," said Jim and Marie walked shyly towards him as he held out his arms.

She took his hand and stood near, still with one eye on her mother. "Don't be shy," he said, and pulled her to him in a rough hug, then began to tickle her as he used to. Marie laughed delightedly. Perhaps it would not be too bad to have her father back home.

"Let's have some tea. Then you can go away and talk, Mary. I'll be all right with Billy until lunchtime," said Mrs Dickson and she went to prepare it.

"Where's Peter?" asked Jim.

"Where else would a boy mad on machinery and horses be if not at the blacksmith's shop? He's been there every day since school broke up. He just loves helping the blacksmith, Peter Fairman. He's made a real pet of our Peter and is to marry Miss Goode. Young Peter needs a good scrub when he comes home but it's worth it. He'll be here soon for his lunch."

⸎

Eddie Browne was getting used to the office work at the mill. He was a good book-keeper but it was years since he'd had to use that part of his brain. The stump had healed but still throbbed. He badly wanted to scratch the missing part. It itched unmercifully.

He looked up as a man dressed tidily in a set of working clothes that looked brand new entered the office. 'Probably just off the boat,' thought Eddie. 'Out to make his fortune, perhaps.' "Looking for work?" he asked.

"Yes, are you the boss?" Jim looked at the man's sleeve tucked into the pocket of the jacket he was wearing. 'Poor beggar', he thought.

"No. I'm just the book-keeper and wages clerk. You'll need to see the foreman. He's over at the shed where the men are working on the big logs. There's been a new saw installed. Things are really buzzing now. Ask for Joe Brooks," Eddie told him, pointing to the building across the way.

Jim walked over to the shed where the noise and rhythm of the motor was deafening. 'Could I bear to work in a place like this?' he thought.

The man standing on a platform overlooking the work motioned for him to come on up. "Looking for a job?' he asked. Jim nodded. "There's a job going out in the forest bringing the logs into the railway line. It's just a wooden rail affair but works well enough. How are you with horses?"

"I'd be glad of anything," said Jim. "I've just come back from Australia, and have a wife and two children to provide for. My wife works for Henry Dickson at the store."

"Little dark haired lady?" asked the foreman. "I know who you mean. Boards with the schoolmarm at Biddy's."

"Yes, that's her. I was a bit of a fool. I could've had my own farm out next to John Johnson but went to seek my fortune as they say. I never found it."

"Well, you won't make your fortune here, but it's a living. Will we see you tomorrow?" asked the foreman. Many came looking for a job but some didn't bother to come back. "Where are you living?"

"I was out with Johnson last night but I'll have to find somewhere today. I'll have to walk everywhere," said Jim.

"The railway where you'd be working is just a short distance from the village," said the foreman. "And there's room at the boarding house an old lady runs for single men. She might take you for a while until you get settled. Or Biddy might have a room there. Look around and see what you can find, then be back here at seven o'clock tomorrow morning and I'll show you the ropes."

As Jim made his way back to the store he hoped he could handle the job. Mrs Dickson kindly had lunch ready in the back room but, as there were a lot of customers, Mary was busy so Jim went through - to find his son sitting at the table eating bread and cheese. He looked up as his father came in but didn't speak. "Hello Peter, how are you?" said Jim.

Peter picked up his glass of water and drank deeply. He looked at Jim as if he wasn't real. Just then, Marie came into the room, and sat up to the table with Peter.

Jim looked at his children and thought what a fool he'd been to leave them to look for gold. His gold was right here.

"That's Father, Peter," Marie said as she picked up a sandwich and began to eat. "He's come home to us."

"Well, I don't want him," said Peter. "I'd rather live with Auntie Beth and Big Peter. I'm going to when they get married. So there."

"Oh, Peter," said Jim, looking at his son with tears in his eyes. "I'm sorry I left you all. I know it must have been hard."

"We were all right without you." Peter scowled."Go back to Australia. Mother looks after us and Auntie Beth. We don't need you."

"Peter, don't talk to your father like that," said Mary as she came into the back room. "He's going to get a job and help look after us as he used to. We'll get a home of our own as soon as we can. Auntie Beth and Big Peter will always be our friends. Just wait for a while and you'll be glad Father is home again. I'm very glad." She turned to Jim. "How did you get on at the mill?"

He shrugged his shoulders. "I don't know. There's a job working the horses. I can do it I'm sure, but I haven't had much experience. I've asked the woman at the single men's quarters for a bed. She has room and will provide lunch and dinner if I want it. It'll take a bit of getting used to, but I'll give it a try. Peter will be glad I'm not moving in with you at the boarding house." Jim smiled at Peter as he spoke.

The boy looked stoically ahead at the wall and gave no response. It would take time to repair their relationship, but Jim was ready to do whatever he could to make it up to his family for the pain he'd caused them.

"I'd better get the buggy back to John. Then I'll walk back here. They said to be at the mill at seven in the morning so I'd better be on my way." He kissed Mary and Marie, and held out his hand to Peter. "Friends?" he asked.

Peter took the outstretched hand, but didn't look Jim in the eye. Jim could feel the tension in the boy's body as he shook the little fingers. 'Better leave it there,' he said to himself. It would take some time for Peter to relinquish his position as acting head of the family.

"Are you going back to the blacksmith's?" Mary said to Peter.

"Can I please?" Peter asked. "I'm helping him by passing things when he's shoeing the horses. I keep back out of the way though."

"Yes, go on," said Mary. "I know you love his company." She watched as Peter ran away towards the blacksmith's shop. "He'll come around in time Jim. You get away as soon as you can. Come and have tea with us tonight at Biddy's. What would you like? We'll have a celebration dinner."

"Anything you like my dear," said Jim. He was surprised at how easy it had been to meet and talk with Mary, after what he'd done. She was very forgiving. Miss Goode had not been as friendly, but Mrs Dickson had been very kind, letting him put the clothing he needed on an account. He'd pay them back as soon as he could.

—⧂⧂⧂—

Bessie plodded along the country road. She was getting too old for all this gallivanting about. She'd be glad to get back to her mates at the farm. A nice cold drink from the stream and a good feed of oats, that's what she needed.

John was down the back of the farm looking again at the flood damage to his potato crop when Bessie and Jim came along. 'If it would only rain a little,' he thought, 'it would wash the silt off the plants and they might be all right.' Jim got down, tied Bessie to the post and rail fence and walked over to where John was studying the ground. He'd pulled up a root of potatoes. Jim could see there was a heavy covering of mud on the plant but the tubers clinging to it were firm and plentiful.

"It looks like a good crop," said Jim. "Will they be all right?"

"Too hard to say yet; they look fine so far, but it's early days. The water has all drained away now. A good shower of rain to wash the dirt off would be the saviour of them. How did you get on at the mill?"

"All right so far. Joe Brooks told me that I'll be driving the horses taking the logs to the railway. How do you think I'll manage that?"

John scratched his head. He thought for a while and then said, "Well, I don't know and neither will you until you try."

"Can you give me any tips?"

"Only to treat the horses well. They'll be more used to the job than you for a while. Pay attention to their movements. Take it slowly and you'll be fine," offered John.

"I've got board at the single men's quarters. I have to be at the mill at seven in the morning, so I'll take the buggy back to the house and say good-bye to Kate and the children then walk back to town. Thanks for your help. I didn't deserve it."

"Say no more about it Jim. We all make mistakes at times." He held out his hand and Jim took it eagerly. "New start eh?" said John.

"I'm not getting on with Peter, John. He won't look me in the eye. Spends all his time with this blacksmith chap, and hasn't said a kind word to me. I'm having dinner with Mary and the children and Miss Goode tonight. He might have thawed out by then."

"Don't worry; he'll come round in his own good time. I'd be careful not to try and hurry things. Just take your time with Peter and the job. It'll all work out." John pulled the tubers off the potato plant and put them in his coat pocket. "For tea tonight," he said.

CHAPTER 69 Christmas

Father Brady was thinking about Christmas. It was hard to realise it was only three weeks away. It was so different here. Back in the old country there'd been snow on the ground, everyone singing carols and the big celebration of Midnight Mass.

Here it was summer, the weather was hot, and the traditional meals of roast goose or fowl seemed out of place, but his housekeeper was determined to have as much Christmas fare as she could. She'd been boiling puddings and baking cakes and had made sweets for him to give to the altar servers who'd helped through the year.

It was wonderful he'd found such a helpful woman to take care of his home. A widow, she was well thought of in town and had made a good fist of settling him into the house he'd found. He still made journeys to the outlying areas, but stayed in Greytown most of the time. There were other priests to take care of the faithful in Masterton now. The Anglican vicar had told him last time they met that he was thinking of marriage. 'Well that's out for me,' thought Father Brady. 'But I'm happier than I can remember, since Widow Miller took pity on me.'

The smell of Christmas cake cooling on the bench sent Father Brady's mind back to his mother's kitchen in Dublin. What happy times they'd had - ' peace and poverty' they'd called it. He and his brothers had spent hours taking baskets of food around the slum districts of Dublin to the families where the poor wretched children looked so hungry. His father had been on the council and they'd never been likely to starve, but there were times when he could've eaten more.

One of his reasons for joining the priesthood had been the needy children he'd seen. His old teachers were all in favour of his vocation and, if the truth be known, helped him to make the choice. It must be sharing a home with a lady housekeeper making him question his calling for the first time in his life. 'Fancy the Reverend Porter getting married. Well good luck to him. I'm happy as I am.'

"I've made a cup of tea, Father," said Widow Miller as she looked into the parlour where the priest had just finished saying his office. She walked over to open a window.

"I'll come directly," said Father Brady. "But I've something on my mind I want to ask you about. I want to do something for the children to impress upon them the true meaning of Christmas. That it's not just presents."

"What do you have in mind?"

"I know that the teachers have read them the Bible stories. I was wondering if we could hold a service for the children and do a little tableau of the Christmas story. There are the Kelly children, the Bourkes and others. Perhaps on a Sunday morning we could have a practice run. What do you think?"

"It sounds a good idea to me, but who would do the work of organising it? These things can get out of hand."

"I think it would have to be the teachers. They might be willing now that school's out. I'll go and see them today," said Father Brady. He drank his tea thoughtfully, wondering about the best way to approach the ladies.

"What about the Anglican children? Would they be able to come? I mean, they all go to school together and would feel left out if they couldn't take part." Mrs Miller gathered the tea things and went to carry them to the scullery. "I think it would be wonderful for the little ones. They could dress up as Mary and Joseph and then there are the three wise men. Mrs Johnson might lend you the baby for Jesus."

It didn't take long for Father Brady to walk to the school house to put the idea to the ladies. Beth Goode was painting the class room and Joan Thompson was doing some paper work. "So what do you think?" he asked. "I'd like the children to understand the story. By acting it out it might stay with them longer than if it's read to them."

"It sounds a lovely idea, but a lot of work. When would you do it and where?" asked Miss Goode. "There are only two Sundays left before Christmas."

"I think we could have it in Jones's barn after Mass. I'll talk to the vicar as well. We could combine our resources. Dickson will let us put up a notice in their window and we can also tell people about the idea."

"I have just the two children for Joseph and Mary - Dennis Kelly for Joseph and Cathy Johnson for Mary," said Joan Thompson.

"I know who I'd like to be one of the three wise men." said Beth Goode, "Hemi or Kingi, because one of them was dark-skinned. They would fit the bill perfectly. It would be good to include them as their families would come to see them too."

"I can see this growing at the rate of a mushroom," said Joan Thompson. But you're right. Hemi or Kingi or both would make wonderful wise men and then there are the shepherds and angels. We'll have to get the children together to practise. What a pity we didn't think about it before school broke up. Never mind - we'll write a script and have the bones of it ready for you tonight. It's a very simple story, but must be well told."

And so it was that on the Sunday before Christmas the people of Greytown came to see their children perform the town's first nativity play in Jones's barn. It was decorated for the occasion with greenery and toetoe. The excitement on the children's faces as they dressed in borrowed clothing with tea-towel turbans wound around their heads was a sight for weary eyes.

Rangi and May watched with pride as Kingi and Hemi made their way across the stage carrying gifts for the new-born baby who bore a distinct resemblance to William Johnson. The third wise man was taller than the others and answered to the name of Jake. He'd told his mother that on no condition would he take part in this children's play but somehow, when asked by his teacher, he never found the words to refuse her. He even offered his pony for Mary to ride as Joseph escorted her along the road to Bethlehem, and Blueboy behaved perfectly, surprising everyone when he stood quietly by the stable door then was led across the stage by Joseph for the departure of the holy family for Egypt after Joseph's dream. Mary climbed on; the baby, who was now crying lustily, was passed to her and, the audience clapping loudly, they exited out the side door where Kate collected her precious son. To more applause and cries of "Well done!" from the large crowd of parents and friends the cast made their bows in the age-old fashion.

All the mill workers with children had gone along to watch and enjoy it and stayed talking to the farmers and townsfolk and drinking tea with them. There were not many church goers among them, but all could recall Christmases in the old country. After the play a small group of Welshmen - all with beautiful voices - had led the audience in singing carols and the barn rang with music as the children looked amazed at their parents, some with tears in their eyes, singing the old songs.

"This might be the start of a theatrical career for some of the children," said Mrs Thompson afterwards. "Dennis and Kingi lapped up the attention didn't they?"

"They all did well. I can hardly believe it," said Beth Goode. "It's really made Christmas for me."

———— ∞∞∞ ————

Christmas day arrived, and Jim took the presents he'd made for the children to the boarding house where there was to be a gathering of friends at the midday meal. Big Peter Fairman would join them, as would Mrs Thompson and Paul Jones, and all were to eat together in the dining room. There were two other men staying at Biddy's who would be glad to be part of a friendly gathering rather than have just themselves for company. It was a happy group that sat down to the laden table.

Marie hugged her father when she opened her parcel. Jim had carved a wooden doll with movable arms and legs from a piece of pine, and Mary had made a dress for the doll out of scraps of material and ribbon. Marie was delighted. Jim gave Mary a bone carving on a leather thong, a delicate piece carved in a spiral that a Maori working at the mill had made for him.

Mary was very pleased that Jim had been so thoughtful. She'd knitted him a pullover in a neat cable pattern. It was thick and would be warm in the winter.

Big Peter had made presents for Mary and Beth from scrap iron. Mary's was a trivet to place on the stove to keep the heat from burning pots of food when the fire was too fierce. Beth's was a boot scraper, shaped like a frog and very decorative. Finally there was only Peter's parcel to open. Jim held it out to him, waiting to see how he'd like it.

It was a boat carved from a strong piece of totara with tall masts and ropes of flax and the rigging of a brigantine. The sails were furled but could be set and Peter could see he'd be able to sail it. Pleased, he happily thanked his father. But what could he give Father in return? He thought of what he had among his treasures but there was nothing good enough. He'd discussed the matter with Big Peter, who told him he'd find the perfect gift if he just looked around him. Peter had looked and looked, but found nothing. He thought of what Aunty Beth had told him at school.

"You have a flair for drawing Peter," she'd said, as she looked at his sketch book on the last day of school. Peter was pleased. He took his book everywhere and drew pictures of trees and plants as carefully as he could. Perhaps Father would like one of his drawings. He quietly left the room to look in the box where he kept his things away from Marie's nosey eyes.

One drawing he liked was of a tui sitting on a kowhai tree. He took it back into the dining room and shyly offered it to his father. "This is for you. You can put it on the wall by your bed at the hostel."

Jim looked at the drawing. He didn't know his son could draw like this. The kowhai had bright yellow flowers and the tui's white tuft of feathers at the throat, that gave it the nickname of 'Parson Bird,' were beautifully detailed. "Why, thank you son," Jim said. "I didn't know you had such a good hand." He held up the drawing then passed it around for all to admire. Peter smiled happily - Big Peter had been right.

Beth Goode was especially pleased Jim had taken the drawing seriously. If he'd brushed it off as a childish scribble, he could have done real damage. By not doing so he'd risen several notches on the mental ladder of worth she used to evaluate people. 'He's not so bad after all - so far,' she thought.

———∞∞∞———

Ellen and O'bie were spending a quiet Christmas. They had a mid-day meal together but she was still going through Jock's papers and the day was full of memories of the Christmases gone before. After the meal O'bie excused himself to have a sleep.

Ellen wondered if Mrs Martin had made up her mind to marry the vicar. She supposed they'd live in Masterton. It needn't make any difference to the arrangement we have now, she thought, as O'bie entered the room late in the afternoon, rubbing sleep from his eyes. "Have a good sleep?" she asked. He nodded and went to put the kettle on the hob.

"I'll do the milking a bit early then I might go into town - if you don't mind."

"No not at all," said Ellen. "I was just wondering about Mrs Martin and whether she will marry the vicar."

"Speaking of marriage, when do you think Fairman and Miss Goode will tie the knot?" asked O'bie as he poured the tea. "I saw him in town this week. He said the house is well on the way to being built."

"You know more than I do then. I don't suppose they'll want to wait long." Ellen drank her tea thoughtfully. 'O'bie was good company. We work well together.' "You go and celebrate. I suppose the hotel will be open tonight. You might meet a nice young woman," said Ellen.

"I don't need to. I already have," said O'bie with a knowing grin. "There's only one girl for me."

"Do I know the lady?" asked Ellen.

"Better than anyone else," said O'bie. "You know I love you. Will you marry me? Please say yes."

"I'm too old for you. You're only a lad. You'll find someone soon. If I tie you to me, you might live to regret it."

Obie put his arm around Ellen's waist, and held her close. "Rubbish," he said. "I'm only a few years younger. Please say yes." Ellen breathed deeply. She looked at O'bie and knew she could love him.

When they woke, John and Kate could hear Jake and Cathy exclaiming over their gifts while trying not to wake William. Kate had ordered some new clothes from advertisements in the newspapers and smuggled them into the house while the children and John were busy elsewhere. Jake had grown several inches and both he and his father were heavier now. Cathy was slim and tall for her age. Kate hoped the dresses she'd chosen would suit her. There were also two books for Cathy, as her love of reading had not diminished, and some tools for Jake. John had asked Kate to order an elaborate pocket knife for Jake.

'I'm so lucky to have John and the children,' Kate thought as she and John dressed. 'I hope Jim and Mary will be as happy as we are.'

In the kitchen Jake had the fire going and Cathy had already made the porridge. "Merry Christmas," they both said and gave their parents a hug as they thanked them for their presents.

"Merry Christmas to us all," their father said, laughing. "Now, the day! Jake and I will do the cows. Cathy, you can help Mother. She'll need you to help get dinner on the go."

"Let's have breakfast first," laughed Kate. "I've two chooks all ready for the oven. It won't take long for them to cook. I'm worried about Mrs Dickson. Do you think we could pay them a visit after lunch?"

"If you don't think they will be swamped with visitors. You know how popular they are. Dickson said he was looking forward to a quiet day with no customers."

Kate could see John didn't really want to go in to town. "You don't need to come. I'll just go and check. Mrs Dickson was having niggling pains when I was in town on Monday but Doctor McDonald said she still had a week or two to go. I'd feel happier if I saw her."

"Do what you think is best, my dear," said John and he passed her a small box from a jeweller in Wellington.

In it was a string of pearls on a satin bed. It was lovely. "Oh, thank you John!" And Kate threw her arms around John's neck. The pearls gleamed in the morning light as she lifted them from the box and held them to her throat.

John fastened them with the clasp and stood back to admire them. "They're just as pretty as you," he said.

"They're beautiful," said Kate, admiring them in the mirror on the dresser. "I'll wear them when we go to Miss Goode's wedding. Their house is coming on. It shouldn't be too long before they will marry."

John undid the catch and Kate placed the pearls back on their bed of satin. She looked at the clasp and saw it was decorated with tiny diamonds, a work of art in itself.

"Can I hold them Mother?" asked Cathy and Kate passed the box to her. Cathy lifted the string of pearls to her neck and looked at herself in the mirror. "Don't I look pretty?" she said.

"You do indeed my daughter," said John. "I'll buy you one just the same when you reach twenty-one." Cathy smiled at her reflection. She could hardly wait, but twenty-one was years away.

After Kate had given John his new set of clothes and the chores were done, Jake took Dot for a run down to the river to see if the bank had eroded any further, and found the water was just a quiet flowing stream confined to the middle of the river bed and behaving well. He looked over the fence at the potato patch and saw the water had dried up around most of the plants. They had pushed through the silt that had covered them, but were upright and looked to be growing well. He had helped with the earthing up of the plants - it had been a lot of work and he'd been promised some reward if the crop was good. Jake called Dot who'd been off chasing a rabbit. She'd already caught three this week.

They were breeding like flies, so Mr Kelly had said, and ate all the grass. "Seven rabbits can eat as much as a cow." Jake doubted that. They were pretty little things and looked harmless. Dot came bounding up with a tiny rabbit in her mouth. It was not dead and looked unharmed. Jake took it from her and put it into his pocket. He'd take it home.

Jake called to Cathy as he reached the veranda. "Come and see what I have." He lifted the rabbit from his pocket and put it into Cathy's hands. She stroked the fur and nuzzled it to her nose. "Dot caught it. I had to bring it home."

Kate and John came to see what the fuss was about and admired the tiny rabbit. "We had rabbits at home," she said. "Find a box and make it a bed. Then we'll find it some dandelion leaves. They like those."

"Can we keep it, Father?" asked Cathy.

"I don't see why not, but there are a lot about. I'll make you a cage, but not today. It'll be all right in the box. Now what about this Christmas dinner we've been waiting for?"

A little later Kate called that dinner was ready, and the family sat down to a table laden with poultry, dishes of roast potatoes, new potatoes sprinkled with chopped mint, carrots and parsnips, baked onions, squash pumpkin and a big bowl of fresh green peas, the first of the season. The smell was mouth wateringly inviting and, after the grace was said, soon there were only empty plates to be seen. Even William had a taste of gravy, which made him lick his lips. Plum pudding with custard and cream followed. "That was delicious Mother," said Jake. "I won't want another mouthful today." Kate laughed. She knew her son's appetite.

Later, after they had all done the dishes and had a rest Kate asked Jake to harness up Beauty for her trip to town.

"Do you think it's wise to go now?" asked John. "It's half two already, and you'll take half an hour to get there."

"I'll be all right, John. Don't worry. Cathy will be fine with William. Jane is coming over, isn't she Cathy?" asked Kate.

"Yes, she said she would. I can manage. You go and see Mrs Dickson, Mother."

CHAPTER 70 A Visit to Johanna

As she drove to the village, Kate thought of Christmases enjoyed at home. There'd never been much snow in Devon but sometimes they'd woken to a world covered with white patches in and around the bushes. No chance of that here. Well, not in the summer, but the recent flood showed that the season didn't control the weather.

What were her mother and Mr Jones doing at this moment? It was about three o'clock now so it would be early morning on Christmas day in Devon. They'd be sleeping. 'May God bless them, and the new life they are planning together.' As the miles slid past her thoughts turned to Johanna Dickson. 'I do hope she will be all right. She's so looking forward to this baby. It would break her heart if she were to lose it.'

Kate pulled the buggy up outside the store, tied Beauty to the hitching rail and knocked on the door. It was opened by Mary who put her finger to her lips. Kate crept quietly inside.

"Billy has gone for Doctor McDonald," whispered Mary. "Mr Dickson was really worried but didn't want to spoil the doctor's Christmas dinner, but Billy was worried too so he came and got me. I took one look at her and sent Billy for the doctor." Just then there was a quiet knock and Mary opened the door to admit the doctor and Billy.

Kate followed Doctor McDonald up to the bedroom and looked at the young woman lying there, very pale and quiet, while her husband held her hand, huge anxiety on his face. It was sad that her mother was so far away in Australia. While Kate knew they exchanged letters, this was the time she needed her mother most.

Doctor McDonald pulled back the covers and looked to see how the birth was proceeding. Looking at his patient's eyes he could see the misery she was going through. "It won't be long, now," he said, with more hope than he was feeling. "Give her water," he said to Kate. "We don't want her to get dehydrated. Then come outside. I want to talk to you."

Kate did as she was asked. The doctor was worried. "It's not looking good. I wish the old girl at the pa was here, the one who delivered William. She knew a trick or two."

"Why not get her?" asked Kate. "Could I go and see if she can come? It's not far to the pa and she's always there. We can try."

"I feel there's something I'm not seeing. It should be a straightforward birth. She's a strong woman, but it seems as if it's beyond her to push this baby out."

"I'll be back soon," said Kate and she rushed down the stairs where Billy was feeding the fire to make sure there was plenty of hot water. He remembered when his mother had her last baby his job was to keep the kettle boiling although he never did find out what they used it for, other than copious quantities of tea. Now, he untied the reins and Kate set off on her mission.

May was weeding her garden as Kate arrived at the pa. "Merry Christmas Mrs Johnson," she said. "What brings you out this way so late in the day?"

"We need the midwife that helped me deliver William - Auntie Kuini. Mrs Dickson's in trouble. Can she come?"

"Kingi, fetch Auntie!" said May. "Go quick and tell her to come." Calling for his Auntie Kuini, Kingi ran to the meeting house. Someone called to him to be quiet but he ran straight into the big room, calling again for his aunty. The old woman shuffled forward but, when she heard why she was needed she picked up her skirts and hurried to climb up onto the buggy. The folk at the pa were all fond of Mrs Dickson. Seeing Kate, she remembered delivering William and gave her hand a reassuring squeeze. Kate urged Beauty on and soon they were pulling up outside the store again where Billy was waiting to take hold of Beauty.

In the upstairs bedroom Aunty Kuini laid her hands on Johanna's head and murmured to her in Maori then gestured that Kate should hold Johanna's hand while she and the doctor felt for the position of the baby. Kuini then gently massaged her back and Johanna seemed to relax.

The doctor had heard stories of how Maori women gave birth. Now it seems he was to see for himself. When Kuini indicated that Mrs Dickson should get out of bed and walk around Johanna only lifted her head until the kuia helped her to a sitting position then to stand. "You walk," said Kuini. And Mrs Dickson took a few steps

Now it was Kate's turn. "Johanna," she said urgently but softly, "now you must crouch down. Squat." By now Johanna didn't care what she did as long it was over soon and in a short time the baby was born.

The doctor watched as Kuini took the shell from her pocket with the piece of flax, and tied then cut the cord just as she had done with William. She smiled a toothless smile at the new mother and everyone present. "Well done," said Doctor McDonald.

"You have a daughter." Kate smiled at Johanna. "She looks perfect to me,"

Mary was waiting outside the door and came into the room to see Mrs Dickson cuddling her baby who was now crying lustily. Henry too had heard the cry and he rushed upstairs and into the crowded room, relieved to see his wife looking tired but radiant. Peering at the bundle that had caused so much trouble, he was amazed by the intense feeling he experienced as he saw his daughter for the first time. 'If Mother could only have been here,' he thought. 'She'd have loved Johanna.' "We'll call her Catherine," he said.

Johanna swallowed her disappointment. She thought of her own mother who was named Agnes, wondering if that could do for a second name. Kate broke the silence. "Cathy will be pleased if you call the baby Catherine."

Kuini looked at the baby and the new mother. They were all right these pakeha whanau. This tamahine would be well loved. Her job done, she said goodbye and Doctor McDonald shook her by the hand saying, "Well done, Kuini."

"I'll drive you home Kuini," said Kate.

But Henry held up his hand. "No, Mrs Johnson. Billy can take Kuini home. You get home to your family. I can never thank you enough for coming."

Kate looked again at baby Catherine and said goodbye to the new mother.

"Thank you so much, Mrs Johnson," smiled Johanna. "Doctor McDonald didn't say much but I knew something wasn't right. I'm glad you fetched Kuini. She's a real marvel."

It was a cool pleasant drive back to the farm. Kate was pleased she'd been able to help. There was something about the old Maori lady that couldn't be easily explained. She had a spiritual touch that soothed a mother-to-be, a touch that led to calm and eased pain.

William was protesting loudly as Kate walked into the kitchen. Cathy was nursing him in the comfy chair and was only too glad to give him back to his Mother. "How is Mrs Dickson?" she asked as Kate sat and took William.

"They have a little girl. Her name is to be Catherine Agnes Dickson," said Kate with a smile. She knew the name would please her daughter. "She's small, but she seems to be healthy enough. Her father is delighted." Kate changed William to her other side and asked, "How has he been while I was away?"

"He was all right. He slept a lot of the time. Jane came over. She brought her new dress so we both tried on hers and mine. Dennis came over as well. He and Jake went eeling down the stream with James. They all went home about an hour ago. I feel tired now. I've had a sandwich. Is there anything you want me to do before I go to bed?" Cathy asked. "The rabbit seems happy."

"No thank you - you've done well, dear. Don't read too long," said Kate.

John came in from the barn where he had been building a small hutch for the rabbit. "How did you get on?" he asked.

Kate told John all the details of the birth she thought he'd want to know. "Kuini was amazing, John. She seems to have the right touch. I'm glad I went to fetch her."

"And Mrs Dickson, is she well?"

"She was asleep when I left. She'll be fine. Mary will mind the store while she gets her strength back. Billy is getting to be a good help too." She laid the sleeping baby in his bed, and looked up to see John looking at her fondly.

"It's been a good day, even if you had to go off to help Mrs Dickson," he said "The children seem pleased with their presents. It's strange to think that Christmas has been and gone again. All the excitement is over for another year. New Year will be upon us next week. I wonder what that will bring?"

"Who knows? Let's have a nightcap. I could do with a tot of whisky."

CHAPTER 71 Mrs Martin Moves On

Mrs Martin was bored. She'd been invited to the Officers' Club for dinner by another army wife. However, she had quickly tired of the unwanted attention from some of his old friends who obviously thought they were cheering up a poor lonely widow.

The wives of the officers were strange too. These women who had promised undying affection after Maurice died now seemed to regard her as competition. 'I don't want your silly husbands,' she thought as she finished a glass of wine and turned to her hostess. "It's been a lovely night, thank you, but I feel rather tired and think I should get away home now. I hope you don't mind."

"Not at all, my dear. George!" her hostess called. "Mrs Martin is ready to go home. Will you find her a cab?"

"Certainly my dear," said George, detaching himself from a pretty young lady.

"But do you think she'll be safe on her own? It's getting quite late. Perhaps I should go with her?" His wife nodded in placid agreement, and he followed Dulcie outside. She was used to her husband's ways. Also, the latest trouble in Taranaki with the Maori had made people fearful of travelling alone in the Hutt. There had been fighting there a few years before and the thought of a possible new uprising was never far from the pakehas' minds.

Several cabs were waiting for late night business, their drivers having a late night smoke together as they chatted. They knew that soon after dinner the officers would be ready to return to their homes. If they were available until midnight they could always add to their day's takings.

Mrs Martin climbed into a trap and settled down on to the leather seat when George appeared. "There's no need for you to accompany me. I'll be quite all right thank you."

"Now, now, my dear," he replied. "It's no trouble," and settled his large frame beside her. "I'm quite looking forward to our little journey." He told the driver the address then put his arm around Mrs Martin's shoulder in a most familiar manner and pressed her to him.

"Leave me alone. You've quite the wrong idea about me. I'm not some sad little widow in need of attention." Mrs Martin felt in her evening bag for a nail file, a short folded up one with a sharp point, and proceeded to prod George in the ribs with it to lower his ardour.

"No need for that. I thought you might be ready for a little fun."

"You may as well know I'm to marry a vicar from Masterton. I think the sooner the better. I'll be leaving in the new year as soon as my late husband's business matters are completed. Your attentions are most offensive and unwelcome. What would your wife have to say?"

"Oh I say, Mrs Martin. I never meant any harm," said George, finally understanding he'd been brushed aside like an unwanted insect. "Please don't take offence. Let's forget about it. Look, here we are at your address." The cabby pulled the horse to a stop at Mrs Martin's door.

She scrambled down without help and gave George a look of contempt as she took a coin from her bag and paid the driver. "Take him back to the club, please," she said. The driver who'd heard the whole exchange smirked as he took the money. He'd have something to tell the lads when he got back.

<hr>

Next day Mrs Martin went to see her lawyer. Everything was in order. She could now sell her house in Lower Hutt and use the money to buy one in Masterton if that was what Reverend Porter agreed to. She hoped he wouldn't be too proud to live in a house she had paid for. He only had the stipend from his parishioners. It was little enough to feed him, let alone buy a home.

While there wasn't a lot of sentimental value in the furnishings there were a few things she'd like to take to the Wairarapa. Perhaps she could find someone with a wagon and who knew the road to take what she kept over the hill for her.

She sat in her kitchen and thought of the events of last night. The odious George would not trouble her again. Thank goodness she had the nail file in her purse. That was one thing Maurice had taught her - to be prepared. It's not always brute strength that wins out.

'I'll walk into town and find a wagon driver,' she thought. The men who have cabs should be able to advise her. She'd always found them polite and helpful if she had needed to take a cab into Wellington on business. Putting on her walking shoes, she made ready for the trip into Lower Hutt.

The cabbies were most helpful, telling her of a carrying firm near her house. Then she went to her bank to inquire whether her business could be carried on from a branch in the Wairarapa. The bank manager was interested to hear about her High Street house being for sale and asked if he could inspect it as he was looking for a home. They arranged for the visit to take place that evening. At the carrying company she asked them to send someone to assess the load and give her a price. It all looked promising.

That evening she sold her house for cash at the price she was asking. Was she too cheap? 'No. Let go and begin a new life with Amos,' she told herself, and sat down to write to Amos and the Johnsons with the good news and to tell them of her plans. The folk in Greytown had treated her so well when she made the trip there after Maurice's body was found. 'I'm sure I'm doing the right thing,' she thought.

CHAPTER 72 More Arrivals

The week passed quickly. Celebrations for New Year were being discussed all around the town. Baby Catherine was much admired by the few privileged people Mary allowed to climb the stairs to visit Mrs Dickson. Beth Goode and Joan Thompson were among the first visitors. Mrs Dickson seemed to have recovered well. They could see that she glowed with pride as they listened to details of the birth and the unexpected visit of the old Maori midwife.

"She has healing hands, I'm sure. The pain just vanished. I couldn't have gone on much longer. I can't thank Mrs Johnson enough for bringing her to me."

"I think Maori people have a lot of common sense," Mrs Thompson said. "Rangi's boys are so quick at picking up pakeha ways but still keep their own customs. There are some things they won't do. If the river is made tapu, because of a drowning, they won't go near it until the time is up."

Miss Goode turned to Johanna. "It's been lovely to see you but I think we'd better go and let you rest. There's going to be a gathering at the hotel for New Year's night. It should be fun."

Rangi and Ru planned to take advantage of the holiday on New Year's Day to shift Ru and his wife into the cabin they'd helped build near the river on the second farm belonging to John. They would have help from some of the boys at the pa, and a loan of John's wagon. There should be no difficulties as the track across from John's house was now well defined. Jake asked his father if he could ride out to the pa and give them a hand preparing for the move. John agreed, but told him not to get in the way.

Kate said it would be good for Ru to have a home close by and was looking forward to meeting the girl he'd married, the girl who'd been looked down on at the Major's funeral for displaying her grief so openly. Ru must have known of this, but still married her. 'Perhaps we'll find out more one day,' thought Kate.

Cathy came in from the stables to say a tramp outside wanted to see her father. "He didn't say what it was he wanted. He's a bit grubby."

Kate didn't like strange men but went to the door to see for herself. The man was gray headed and bent. "Could I have a drink of water please?" he asked. He looked as if he would drop to the ground if he wasn't supported.

"Sit down here," said Kate, pointing to a chair on the veranda. "Get him a drink of water Cathy."

The man drank thirstily then brushed his hand across his beard. "I've walked all the way from Napier. There's some good country to be brought in, bush all the way. There's a bit of clearing done at Woodville and Mauriceville where the Scandies are, but mostly it's hard going with just a few roads or tracks." He rubbed his brow with a dirty cloth but Kate thought he had the air of a well educated man down on his luck. "I used to be a surveyor and worked on the land around Napier," he went on. "It was hard work on the hills though and I had to give it up. Now I'm just moving around looking for work here and there."

Just then John rode in on Beauty. He gave the horse to Jake to attend to and went to see who Kate was talking to. The man held out his hand to John, saying, "I'm Arthur Peat," he said. "I divine water."

John took the grimy hand and shook it, saying, "Where did you spring from?"

"I just walked down from Napier, through the bush. I've been on the road for a week," said the man.

"So what can I do for you?" asked John. "Why did you come out here, so far from town?"

"Yours was the first house I came to. I asked for a drink of water from your wife here. Now I can hear the river; I could've had a drink there." The man looked really worn out. No-one ever turned a tramp away with nothing.

"I'll get you something to eat," said Kate and went inside to put some left-over stew to heat on the stove. The kettle was nearly boiling. Kate cut some slices of bread and butter to take out to the man with a mug of tea. "The stew will be hot soon," she said. "Have this to go on with."

"Thank you, missus," he said as he tasted the food, the first he'd had for three days. "You're very kind."

John looked at the man with interest. "What did you mean about being a water diviner?" he asked.

"Just that, I can find water for you. If you need a well dug, I can find the most likely spot," he replied just as Kate came out with a tray holding a plate of stew and more bread. She placed it carefully on a small table and passed him a knife and fork.

"No more questions for now John, let the poor man eat," she said.

Arthur Peat tucked in to the meal with relish, pausing between mouthfuls to say how good it tasted. "Lovely, ma'am," he said. "You're a lucky man," he said to John.

"I know that," said John "Now tell us about the well."

"I've a gift for divining water. I don't know why but I can find water almost anywhere." He wiped his plate with some bread and sat back replete. Kate brought another mug of tea, and sat down to hear what the men were discussing.

"We could do with a well here near the house," said John, "but I don't know where the best place is. Perhaps you could tell us."

"I'd be only too pleased. If I can sleep in the barn I could have a go tomorrow."

"Yes, by all means," said John. " You'll want a wash too, so I'll get my son Jake to boil the copper and put the tin tub ready for you when he returns. My wife will find you a blanket and towel," said John. "We had a friend stay here a few weeks ago. He was in the same position as you in a way. He had tried the goldfields to no avail and came back to us."

Arthur Peat looked near to tears as he accepted the generosity of these strangers. Why the people of this land were so helpful and forgiving was a mystery. Perhaps it had something to do with their backgrounds. Working class people anxious to get ahead, but not too mean to share their luck with others. That must be it.

———— ❦ ————

Next morning the family were up bright and early. It was New Year's Day. It hardly seemed a whole week since they'd enjoyed Christmas and Mrs Dickson had her baby. Kate thought about how they could celebrate the day together. 'Perhaps a picnic? We could ask the Kellys and go down to the river for a swim. But would that be a good idea after Patrick was drowned?' " Cathy. What could we do to make the day special? It's a brand new year."

"We could have a picnic down by the river and go for a swim," said Cathy. "That would be lovely."

"Great minds think alike," laughed Kate. "I thought about that too. Do you think the Kellys would like to come with us?"

"I could go and ask them."

"I don't know what your father has in mind, so we'll wait before we decide."

John and Arthur Peat had been having a practice session near the barn. Arthur Peat had cut off a piece of green willow branch shaped like a wishbone with a short tail. He held the two longest pieces in his hands with the end pointing ahead of where he was walking and paced the earth, waiting for the bough to tell him of a stream of underground water.

"Any sign?" asked John. He watched the man doing something he had dismissed as witchery but could not fail to see how over one spot the willow turned down to the soil.

"There's a good strong stream here. About fourteen feet down I think. Here, you have a go."

John took the willow from the man's hands and walked over the spot. He felt nothing. Jake took the branch from his father and walked steadily over the place Mr Peat had said he felt the pull. Again nothing was felt. 'Load of rubbish,' he thought. John was not so sure. He'd heard of people with these special powers, and knew of wells that had been dug out on the Moroa plains as the result of divining.

Cathy came to call them for breakfast. "Here, you have a turn," her father said. Cathy took the wand of willow and walked forward. Suddenly a surge of power went through her arms from the willow, now pointing firmly to the ground even when she tried to stop it. "It's pulling my arms," she said. The man laughed. He knew that feeling well. "I can't hold it up," said Cathy. "It's funny."

"Mr Johnson, you have a gifted girl here. I don't know how many women can divine water, but this one certainly has the skill."

"Perhaps it's just power left over from you. Let's cut another wand and let her try on her own," said Jake. He was a bit put out that it didn't work for him.

Another piece was cut and given to Cathy. She walked around the field for a while keeping away from the place where they'd been. Then, with a cry, she stopped and held on to the branch as it tilted to the ground. "It's a funny feeling," she said. "A force that is strong, but not frightening. I quite like that feeling."

"Well, let's go and have breakfast. Your mother will be getting bothered. When we tell her that her daughter has special powers she'll be surprised," said John. "Or frightened," he added.

"It was a fluke," said Jake as he playfully hit Cathy's arm.

"Was not," said Cathy as she hit him back.

"Leave it off you two," said John, as he climbed the steps to the veranda. "Let's see what your mother has to say about it Cathy." They went inside and sat at the table. Kate ladled the porridge into bowls and John passed the jug of cream to Mr Peat. "Nothing like a good plate of oats to start the day," said John.

"You're so right Mr Johnson. I haven't felt so full since I left Bonny Scotland. There hasn't been much porridge on the menu lately," said Arthur. "It's been bread and scrape all the way since the job went."

Kate looked at the man. He looked so much cleaner but she didn't want to embarrass him by asking if he'd enjoyed his bath. "How did you sleep?" she asked. She could see he'd washed his clothes and thought he looked almost respectable.

"I slept very well missus." said Arthur. "The barn is quite cosy."

"How did the water divining go?" asked Kate.

"Your daughter did very well," laughed John, looking at Cathy.

Just then, there was a noise of a wagon on the road outside and Jake said, "Oh, that will be Rangi and Ru and his missus shifting into the cabin. Can I go and help?"

"Don't let me hear you call Ru's wife 'missus'," said Kate. She looked at John for support. "She'll have a name more suitable if you ask Ru. What is his name anyway? I always just say Ru."

"His name is Ru Rewai and his wife's name is Betty," said John. "Yes. You may go to help them as soon as you've had breakfast."

"We're thinking of going down to the river for a picnic at lunch time, Jake, so look there when you finish helping Ru. Ask them to come and join us. Then we can meet his wife," said Kate.

"I should get on my way," said Mr Peat. John had found some of his clothes would fit Arthur Peat's tall skinny frame with a bit of cord to hold them up, so he did not look quite so much like a man down on his luck. "Thank you for your hospitality."

"Surely you can stay a while? What's the hurry? I might want to put a bore down at the back of the farm. Cathy's power might have run out by then," laughed John.

Kate looked at John. She knew he loved to have a new friend to talk to. "Do stay," she said.

"Well, if you don't mind, I'd be glad of a bit of company." Arthur Peat looked around the group to see if they were really in earnest. He felt uncomfortable in his old clothes but this family didn't seem bothered. "All right then," he said. "A picnic it is."

Cathy looked pleased. She studied the man who had made so much of her divining ability. His hair was grey. He walked with a bit of a limp but he was cheerful enough. Father seemed to like him.

"Cathy," said Kate. "Will you ride over to Kellys' and see if the children want to join us down there at eleven o'clock? Ask Mr and Mrs Kelly too but make sure they know we won't mind if they'd rather not." Kate stretched and yawned. 'Goodness, I could easily go back to bed.'

John watched her with concern. Many nights of broken sleep with William had left their mark on her face. She was still as pretty and slim as ever but there was a tired look about her eyes. "What can I do to help?" he asked. "Will we take the buggy or push the wheelbarrow? We don't need a lot of food. Give me some jobs."

CHAPTER 73 An Outing

Johanna was sick of staying upstairs. It was, after all, New Year's Day. There must be something they could do to celebrate. Henry had been to the hotel the night before but returned at a respectable hour. She'd been awake and was regaled with some of the goings-on of the mill hands and townspeople who'd clashed briefly after they'd imbibed too freely. The constable had broken up the fight and three men had spent the rest of the night in the lock-up. "Was O'bie there?" she asked.

"No, I never saw him, or Paddy Kelly. There were a lot of people new to the town who I didn't know. One man played the piano, while a woman sang some music-hall songs. She was no beauty but had a strong voice that filled the hotel lounge. She went down well. There was a fiddler, and a bloke with a concertina as well, so a few people danced some of the new dances, but it was waltzes and jigs mostly. Then when the clock chimed the hour we all joined hands and sang Auld Lang Syne. Martha gave us a great supper. Old Bill Evans must have made a fortune."

"I'm glad it went well. I'd like to go somewhere today. I'm so much better. We could go and see the Johnsons. Catherine will be all right if we don't stay out too long."

"Whatever you say, my dear. When should we go?" Henry was pleased to see Johanna was feeling up to a jaunt away from the store. They'd shut the shop for the day as it was New Year.

"Why not now? I'll get a few things for Catherine and you can get the trap. We should take a bit of food too. You carry Catherine downstairs and I'll get dressed and be down in a minute or two," said Johanna.

They were soon bowling along the road out to the Johnsons' farm. The fresh air made Johanna's cheeks glow, and Henry looked at her lovingly. How lucky he'd been to mention to Johnson his desire to marry her. The consequent push had set things in motion. Now here he was with a wife and family. The store was doing well too. 'I must talk to Johnson about the new building I'm thinking about.'

John was filling the buggy with food and a box for William to sit in when Henry Dickson pulled the trap to a stop at the gate. He called a welcome to his visitors and explained they were off to a picnic by the river. "Come along," he said. "It's good to see you out here."

Soon the party of friends were headed down the bush track to the river that flowed peacefully past Ru and Betty's whare. Blankets were spread on the ground and the men were soon discussing the affairs of the world while the women laid out the meal. The Kelly children and Cathy, who had arrived first, jumped into the water, splashing one another and diving off large rocks that bordered the stream on one side. It was a good swimming spot but the river changed each time there was a flood. "You children be careful," said John. "Don't land on each other when you jump. You could do one another some harm."

Johanna and Kate were admiring each other's babies when Tessa and Paddy Kelly came through the trees. Kate rose to greet them. "It's so good to see you. I'm glad you came. Look at Mrs Dickson's baby. Isn't she sweet? And so tiny - William could make four of her."

"She's lovely," said Tessa Kelly. "How are you feeling?" She knelt down beside Johanna Dickson and took her hand in hers. "I wish you all the best my dear, but don't overdo it, will you?"

"I just needed to get out of the house. I've felt like a prisoner. Mrs Smith is so good, but she does worry about me. But when I saw this beautiful day I thought, 'Where can we go for a change?' And here we are. Who is the tall man with the baggy britches talking to Mr Johnson and my husband?"

"Arthur Peat. He called in yesterday and showed John where to dig a well. He can divine water, and so can Cathy, if I can believe what he said," explained Kate. "He's a bit down on his luck, but was a surveyor."

"How interesting," said Mrs Kelly. "He found a stream for you?"

"So they say. I think there's a lot of underground water here. Well, let's eat," said Kate, and she called to the children to come out of the water. They needed no second summons and soon all were tucking in to the good food laid out while the women exchanged recipes for cakes and biscuits, and the men talked of stock prices and improvements on the hill road.

After lunch Kate told the children they must not swim for at least an hour or they might get cramp and, with the sound of the river murmuring along the stony riverbed and lulled by the peaceful setting, the whole party sat or lay on the grass, talking quietly or drowsing.

A noise like distant thunder woke John from his reverie. "What was that?" he asked as everyone sat up, listening to the sound as it came closer. Suddenly, young trees close to them swayed and the grass rippled as the ground under their blankets moved in a wave. The younger children hung on to their mothers. "I'm frightened," said Polly to her mother. Cathy looked white as she clung to Kate.

"It was just an earthquake, silly. It's gone now," said Mrs Kelly, with a conviction she was far from feeling.

"It was a shallow one to move like that. I don't think there'll be anymore," said Arthur Peat, hoping he was right.

Jake finished a bottle of ginger beer off as he watched Rangi and Ru carry a bed into the whare. Betty showed them where she wanted it placed and had a few words with Ru to make her point. "It needs to be there, by the wall, not out in the middle." She looked ready to argue for what she wanted.

Jake was surprised that a little thing like that could be so stubborn. The wagon was now emptied of the few pieces of furniture when suddenly, Jake remembered he was supposed to invite them to join the family at the river. "Mother and Father said for you to come down to the river and have some tea with us, Rangi, all of you. Mother wants to meet you, Mrs Rewai. She'll be disappointed if you don't come." Jake wanted to go but knew he had to make sure they felt welcome. "Please come."

"I don't know Jake, Betty's a bit tired. What about it Betty, do you want to go and have a swim?" asked Ru.

"Swim be good, not sure about the rest," said Betty.

"Oh come on Betty. You'll like them."

Rangi knew what it was like to be shy. He'd suffered as a boy but, after going to the mission school, was able to meet anyone and not feel any shame. "Come on, Betty," he said. "We'll be with you and you don't need to stay long. I know you want to begin setting out your new home, unpack your kits and boxes eh? It's only a few yards away and you can come back when you like."

Jake turned Blueboy's head around and was ready to leave when there was a rustle through the bushes and Cathy came along, on Bonny. "Did you feel the quake?" she asked. "Mother sent me to get you." She looked at the girl standing next to Ru and smiled at her. "You must come too," she said. "Father's boiling the billy."

Rangi took Betty by the arm and began to walk towards the path through the bush, holding her firmly, but not unkindly. "It has to happen sooner or later," he said.

Betty looked back and called to Ru, "Bring Joseph."

Jake and Cathy cantered away ahead to tell the picnickers that Rangi and Ru were on their way and the whole party smiled welcome as the two Maori men, a young woman and a small child approached.

John greeted Rangi and Ru and introduced them to Arthur Peat while the girl stood back quietly. Kate was adding tealeaves to the boiling billy but, looking up, smiled at Betty and went over to her. "It's good to meet you at last," she said, holding out her hand. Betty returned the smile and pulled forward the child who had been hiding behind her skirt. "This is my son," she said. "He toru,"

"Hello Toru," said Kate, and wondered why Ru laughed.

"His name is Joseph, missy. Toru is his age. He is three."

"Hello Joseph," said Kate. "I didn't know you had children."

"Ru say it don't matter to him. He love me just the same," said Betty.

Kate looked at the strong young boy with a mop of gingery hair. Beautiful brown eyes shone from a light brown face. The lad was obviously a half caste. And who was the father? Harvey, or Major Martin, perhaps? "Come and have some tea and food," she said and motioned to Cathy to make room for Betty to sit with her.

———— ∞ ————

The men were deep in discussion and the women chatting when Dennis stumbled out of the bush carrying Polly. He was struggling with her weight, and would have dropped her if Tessa hadn't taken her from him. "Whatever is the matter with her?" she asked. "Polly Polly, wake up girl." Paddy stood up to take her.

Dennis sat down. Sweat was running down his face. "She found some berries down in the potatoes, and ate them. They were black and green. I tasted some but they were nasty. She said she felt sick and then she couldn't stand up."

Betty looked at the child and saw that she had telltale purple stains on her lips. "She been eatin' bully-bully berries," she said.

"What are they?" asked Mrs Kelly, alarmed. "Will she die?"

"You'd better get her to the doctor, John. Get him to look her over. She's very limp," Kate said. She put her hand on Polly's brow and felt the coldness there. "Jake, ride home and get Beauty, bring her back here as quick as you can." John said and watched as Jake untied his pony and went away up the track. "We should try and make her sick if we can."

Kate picked up the salt and poured it into a little water. "Here Polly, drink this," Kate urged, holding Polly's nose so she'd open her mouth as Kate poured the salty water in. "Try and be sick." She rubbed Polly's stomach, but nothing came up. "How long ago did she eat them Dennis?" she asked.

"About an hour," said the boy.

A quick movement through the trees revealed Jake leading Beauty by her bridle. John picked Polly up, wrapped her in a blanket, gave her to her father to pass up to him when he was mounted, then rode away down the track as fast as Beauty could go.

Kate looked at Mrs Kelly who was standing as if in a dream. "It'll be all right my dear. The doctor will know what to do and John will bring her back safe and sound. You'll see."

"The kids at the pa eat them, missy. Sometimes they get sick too, but they're always all right," said Rangi. Ru agreed and sat down to enjoy the cup of tea Kate had poured from the billy.

"It's called nightshade, and belongs to the potato family," said Arthur. "She'll be fine. The doctor will pump out her stomach if he thinks he needs to."

"Oh, that's horrible," said Kate. She'd heard of nightshade and knew it could kill. Arthur Peat hadn't used its full name. 'Deadly night-shade' was what she'd called it at home. "It must have come with the potato seed. Hopped a ride on the tubers, perhaps. I hope the doctor is home."

Paddy Kelly was just holding his cup, not drinking. His wife was still standing. Kate went to coax her to sit down and drink the tea she'd been given. "She'll be all right. Here Dennis, come and give your mother a hug."

Mrs Kelly came out of her reverie and took the mug of strong tea. "Why is it always us? I couldn't bear to lose Polly. Not after Patrick. It would kill my husband. Will she really get better?" She looked at Betty. She seemed to know the most about the effects. "Do they wake up properly? Or does it affect the mind?"

Betty thought about what was asked before she replied. "She'll be fine Mrs Kelly."

The Dicksons packed their picnic things and prepared to leave. It had been a lovely day until the events of the last half hour. "I think we'll head away home," said Johanna. "It's been a great change for me. I don't want to stay out too long with Catherine. Will you be all right?"

"Yes, yes we'll be fine. We'll clean up and Rangi will put the fire out. Mr Peat can drive the buggy while I look after William. You get away before it gets dark. Thank you for coming."

"You know how much we love seeing you, and you too Mrs Kelly. It'll be just a memory tomorrow, and we'll wonder what we worried about. You'll see," said Henry Dickson and he took Tessa Kelly's hand reassuringly before saying good-bye.

Cathy had been holding Catherine but now said to her mother, "Can I have one more swim please?"

Kate nodded and everyone watched the girl as she ran and jumped into the water.

Suddenly, Paddy Kelly came to life, "No, No, Cathy!" He ran to the edge of the bank as Cathy dived into the slow moving stream.

'What has got into him?' Kate asked herself. Cathy was a strong swimmer. John had seen to that. 'Is he just fearful after the death of his son?'

Cathy surfaced and swam to the bank. She climbed out and dived in again, but this time her head hit a boulder and she sank like a stone. Kate, who had been putting things into the buggy, looked up as Jane jumped into the water and dived down. Grabbing hold of Cathy's clothing, she pulled her up to the surface, gasping for air. Jake leapt into the water and dragged them out onto the river bank, then turned Cathy onto her back and pressed hard. Water ran from her mouth and she spluttered as she came to and he helped her to sit up. Mr Kelly was standing holding Jane, his arms around her.

"You'll be all right now Cathy," Kate said. "Jane, that was such a brave thing to do." She turned to Paddy Kelly. "Thank you. Did you see the boulder was in her way?"

"No Mrs Johnson, I just got this bad feeling. I can't explain. She'll be all right and so will Polly. I'm sure of that now," said Paddy while Arthur Peat looked on, wondering what Paddy had seen.

Tess was helping Jane get dressed when she asked, "Where's James? I haven't seen him for a while. Dennis, where is James? Was he with Polly when she ate those berries?" And she called in a loud voice. "Dennis!"

Dennis was pouring water on the remains of the fire. "No I don't think so," he said. "But he could've been there. I just saw Polly was sick and didn't see what James was doing." He looked around as he spoke. "I'll go and look for him."

"We'll all go," said Kate. "We've finished here." Kate looked at Paddy and Tessa Kelly who were standing with Jane. "We'll look for him. You go on home and we'll have him back to you in a little while. You'll see."

Paddy Kelly took his wife's arm and said, "I hope you're right. I'll get Mother and Jane home. He's most likely asleep somewhere. He gets tired swimming, I know."

Tessa Kelly looked at Kate with tears in her eyes. How could she bear it? Polly might recover but what if James had eaten them too? "I suppose you're right. It was a lovely thought to ask us but somehow we're just meant to have bad luck."

Rangi, Ru, Betty and Joseph, watched as Kate placed William in his box, and helped Cathy up to sit beside her. "You'll have to walk, Mr Peat, and lead Bonny," she said. "I can drive Bessie, and Cathy can mind William. We don't want any more accidents, do we?"

Bessie was glad to be going home, and so was Kate. The lovely afternoon had turned into a disaster. Every few minutes she called to Bessie to halt and called loudly for James while Dennis ran alongside, searching the bush close to the track, looking more and more anxious. Kate kept on calling. Suddenly, there was an answer. "Here I am," called James and he emerged blearily from behind a flax bush. "I was going home 'cos I wanted to finish a pen for my chooks but I was tired so I sat down for a rest. I went to sleep."

Greatly relieved, Kate decided not to berate the boy - she was sure his parents would do that - and drove on to tell Paddy and Tessa that all was well and the boys would be home shortly.

"I'll scalp the young monkey when he gets here," said his father. "Giving us a fright like that." Just then, John rode up with Polly sitting in front of him, brave as brass.

"I'll have a bit to say to you too," said her mother firmly.

Paddy Kelly took the girl from John and gave her a hug. "I don't think you'll do that again," he said, "will you my precious girl?"

"No Dada," said Polly in a small voice. "It was horrible."

"What did Doctor McDonald have to say?" asked Kate. "Did he mind that it was New Year's Day?"

"No. He made her vomit a couple of times, then drink a lot of water. He said the salty water you gave her was a good idea. He said it's usual for children to get very sleepy with those berries but they don't usually die."

———— ∞ ————

Paddy and Tessa sat at the table thinking about the events of the day. Polly seemed quite recovered from her ordeal. They were thankful Mr Johnson had taken her to see the doctor. Poor man, not even New Year's Day in peace! Then had come Cathy's accident. Tessa remembered Paddy's shout as she ran to the water. "What did you see, Paddy? What made you shout out to Cathy like that?"

"I don't know. I just felt she was in danger, as she was, wasn't she?" Paddy scratched his beard. Tessa looked at Paddy, waiting for more, but he stood up and said, "Leave it off woman. I just had an image of her laid out on the sand. I think Jane was with her. It was like a dream. I must be a bit fey."

"Maybe you are. Let's get to bed," said Tessa.

"What did you think about the little boy of Betty's?" asked Paddy as they undressed. "He's a cute little chap, but very shy. I wonder if Ru has done the right thing saddling himself with another man's child. Who do you think his father is?"

"Poor little chap, he'll be all right," said Tessa as she yawned. She'd no desire to discuss the matter any further tonight.

John and Kate were also discussing the day's events as they drank a last cup of tea together on the veranda. John had not seen Cathy's accident but had examined the bruise on her head, telling her she'd have a headache for a few days, and not to run around too much. He told Kate all the details of his visit to the doctor. Polly had twice been sick on the way in and had little left to bring up by the time they reached the doctor's surgery. She was still sleepy but not too distressed.

"Ru and Betty seemed happy to be settled in the cabin, didn't they?" said Kate. "And Joseph, what did you think of the little chap?"

"Oh, he'll be fine. Ru will look after him. Rangi told me that before Major Martin died he wanted to take Joseph to live with him, but Betty was very much against it. It's strange how events determine the shape of someone's life. I mean, Joseph could be living in Lower Hutt with all the benefits of life as a pakeha, instead of living in a whare in the back of beyond."

CHAPTER 74 New Homes

Rangi walked home with Ru and Betty, with Joseph looking at the trees and plants along the path as he followed them. Betty was not sure that she'd been accepted by the pakehas. She was used to the whanau treating her with scorn. They hadn't approved of her relationship with the old man at the farm and the baby resulting from it. Her mother would have taken her child to rear if he had been full blooded Maori but not the half caste he was. Ru was kind to her but she wasn't sure that he truly loved her, or whether he pitied her.

Betty pushed open the door of the whare and went inside. There was no need to cook tea. Kate had given them the leftover food. It would do for a couple of days.

Rangi turned his wagon for home. It had been good of the boss to include them in the picnic and he'd enjoyed listening to the men's discussions, especially the idea of setting up a building firm. Rangi didn't understand the ways of the business world, but knew the boss would explain things.

Rangi thought of Joseph's father and the sudden way his life had ended. Major Martin had wanted to take Betty's boy away from her to rear in Lower Hutt. He'd come up on the coach especially to make Betty give him up, saying he had the law on his side. Betty had been broken hearted at the thought.

Ru lay on the mattress on the floor of the hut with his arm around his wife. Joseph was sleeping peacefully with his thumb in his mouth. There'd not been time to see what the Johnsons had thought about Joseph because of the episode with Polly but they'd not seemed concerned at all.

Ru had heard the Major's widow was returning to live in the Wairarapa and was going to marry the vicar. Had she wanted Joseph too? They had no children. Perhaps she'd told Major Martin he could bring the child home. He hoped it all stayed buried with the Major.

He fell into a fitful sleep, but he wasn't used to having company in bed. Betty stirred beside him and Joseph rolled over in his sleep. Now he was responsible for them. Father Brady had explained what marriage was all about and what he was taking on. It was good of the boss to let them have this whare. It had been hard work building it but it was solid and warm.

Betty woke first and went to light the fire in the stove Mr Johnson had found for them. It was the one his wife had used when she first arrived. A good Dover stove which would serve them for now.

—⚬⚬⚬—

The wagon driver pulled up at Mrs Martin's house, ready to load the furniture she wished to take to the Wairarapa. There was not very much as the bank manager had offered her a good price for the heavy items. She'd been glad of that. Some of the memories these pieces brought back were very painful although their time in India had been happy.

She'd lived the life of an army wife, with servants to do all the work. Then her husband had been sent to the Sudan, where she'd been very ill. Finally they'd come to New Zealand where the Maoris were threatening war and she'd had to adjust to life with no servants or friends.

Now she was to begin a new life with the vicar. She hoped she'd make him a good wife. Moving from country to country with the Major had left her worn out. There had never been time to consider having children, but her husband had wanted to bring his illegitimate son to live with them, telling her she had no say in the matter.

The driver knocked at the parlour door, "I've got it all on board," he said. "Are going to ride with me?"

"No, no, I'll go over on the coach. Thank you though. Here's the address in Greytown where you can unload. I've written and asked for storage from the storekeeper there. I expect he'll have the letter by now but here is another for you to give him just in case. Here's the money we agreed on. Please take good care of my things."

"Right, I'll be on my way now," said the driver. "It'll take the rest of the day to get to Featherston even if the going's good. Are you sure you don't want me to take the load as far as Masterton?"

"No no, thank you. Just do as I asked please, and take care on the way." She smiled at the driver as she didn't want to offend him. His offer of a ride on the wagon had been made in a kindly manner. "I'll be up there as soon as I've settled things here," she said.

"Right you are Mrs Martin. I'll be on my way," he said as he placed his grubby hat firmly on his head and went to the door.

Mrs Martin watched as he drove away. It was another new beginning. 'Am I doing the right thing?' she wondered.

———— ∞∞∞ ————

The coach swayed and rocked up the incline as the horses found their feet on the rough road. There was little to see from the dusty window. Mrs Martin sat crammed in beside a large lady who talked non-stop to her husband across the way. 'If only she would hush, I might get some sleep and shorten the journey.' But that was not to be as the woman turned her attention to Mrs Martin. "Have you been over the hill before?"

"Yes," replied Mrs Martin. She didn't feel like telling this stranger her plans for the future but knew she'd get no peace if she didn't tell her a little about herself. "My husband had land in Greytown," she said. "He died a few months ago."

"Oh my dear, how sad. Hear that Richard? This lady's a widow. How sad."

"Yes indeed," agreed the husband.

"So what are you going to do?"

"I'm going to live in Masterton if I can find the right house."

"Hear that Richard? This lady is going to live in Masterton."

"I do indeed my dear, I hear you well," said Richard. And so the journey went on with the woman plying more and more questions until Mrs Martin felt like getting out and walking. Just when she was giving up hope of rescue the woman fell into a doze and snored loudly as the horses plodded on up the mountainside.

Featherston was reached without incident. Luckily, this was where the couple were headed. The other passengers were continuing on and it was a relieved foursome who took their seats to continue their journey to Greytown. Mrs Martin wondered if Amos would be there to greet her. If he'd received her letter she was sure he would be. 'What will I do if he's not?' she wondered.

The river crossings were made without trouble as the water was low and the horses could see the route through the pebbles and larger stones. Soon the driver was urging them on over the last few miles of good road to the township, where the horses would be fed and rested. They seemed to know they were nearly home and made good time on this leg of the journey. As the driver pulled them up at the stop the stable boys came out to take care of them while the passengers alighted. Mrs Martin looked hopefully around, but there was no sign of Amos. 'I hope he hasn't changed his mind', she thought.

Mary Smith came forward to greet her with a smile. "Mr Dickson sent me to tell you the vicar has been held up in Masterton but will be with you tonight. Where are your bags? Did you have a good trip?"

"Thank you Mrs Smith. I sent all my furniture and things over last week. They are to be stored here in Greytown, so this is all I have," said Mrs Martin as she received her travelling bag from the driver. "It's lovely to see you again. How are you all?"

"All well thank goodness. We've had a few upsets with the children and Mrs Dickson has had a daughter. The baby is lovely and her father is delighted. Also, my husband has returned from Australia, but that's another story," said Mary. "What about you? Did you sell your house? I suppose you must have since you're here."

"Yes, I was very lucky. A bank manager bought it and a lot of the heavy furniture too. Shall we walk to the hotel? I could do with a cup of tea or a drink of brandy. There was this awful woman on the coach." And Mrs Martin told Beth the story as they walked to the hotel.

Martha greeted her warmly, and asked if she was staying.

"I think I'll be here for a while if you have room. I don't know what Reverend Porter has arranged for me."

"That's quite all right Mrs Martin, I'll show you to your room. I suppose you'd like a drink."

"Indeed I would," replied Mrs Martin and the two women followed Martha down the hall to the parlour. "I'm worn out," she said. "Let's have a cup of tea and a chat then I'll rest until Reverend Porter arrives."

Later, Dulcie Martin and Amos Porter had a joyful reunion when he finally arrived at the hotel in time for dinner. They were given the use of the small salon where they could talk in private about where they should make their home and Dulcie was able to show Amos she was an astute woman with a mind of her own and enough capital to purchase a house in Masterton without help from him.

Reverend Porter was in no position to object. His living was dependent on the generosity of his parishioners who were scattered far and wide in the Wairarapa. They would marry soon and live in Masterton. This decided, they retired to their separate rooms for much needed rest.

Next morning Martha and Molly were pleased to see Mrs Martin had recovered from her journey and the disappointment of the vicar's absence when she arrived at the stables and, when she showed them the fine ring of his late mother's which Reverend Porter had given her, they admired it with just a little envy.

CHAPTER 75 Ellen Has a Visitor

Sunday had been uneventful for O'bie and Ellen. They'd done as little work as possible in the morning then spent the rest of the day in a relaxed way. O'bie had gone for an afternoon nap in the barn. Ellen did a little gardening before she made the evening meal. Pork, roast vegetables and apple sauce made a tasty change as things had been a bit tight lately.

The young pigs had grown quickly. Ellen would need to decide if they were to be sold as porkers or raised for bacon. Mr Dickson would always advise her and O'bie was learning more as time went on. But she was the one who made the decisions. She'd heard Widow Martin was returning and wondered what changes she would make.

"I'm off to bed," said Obie as he dried the last plate and hung the plate-rack on the wall. He looked longingly at Ellen, hoping she'd give him some sign that she was falling for him, but she just smiled and said goodnight.

After he'd gone she heard a noise outside and went to see what it was. She didn't want a cow eating her flowers. The cosmos were tall and so pretty by the door. There on her doorstep stood Constable Dan O'Reilly, large as life. "What are you doing way out here?" asked Ellen.

"Just came to see you're all right," he said. "Just wondered how you are."

"As you see, I'm perfectly all right," said Ellen, holding the door closed behind her. "It's been a long day and I'm ready to retire. Please don't worry about me. We're doing very well. I'm sorry you've had an unnecessary trip."

The constable leaned confidently against the doorpost. "I thought you might be a bit lonely and want some company. It can't be much fun out here with only that oaf O'Brien to talk to," he said and he tried to put his arm around her shoulders.

Ellen looked around for something to deliver a blow to ward him off but couldn't reach anything heavy enough. She decided to appeal to his better nature, hoping that he still had some. "Look here Constable," she said. "I'm not interested in you, or any man for that matter. Please leave me alone. You're a police officer and surely this behaviour is not acceptable. Please leave."

He took another step forward. "You don't mean that."

"Yes she does," said O'bie. "You'd better leave, or I'll give you a lesson in good manners and report you."

"I was just trying to cheer her up, no harm meant. I thought she might be miserable and lonely."

"Well she's not so go and visit one of the grass widows you take such good care of. Cheer them up and hope their husbands don't get wind of your activities," advised O'bie.

"Leave it O'bie. Just get out Constable, and don't come here again or I'll go to your superior officer, and make a complaint," said Ellen.

"Yes ma'am, I'll leave you two in peace. I apologise, I'm sure," he said as he stepped back off the veranda, nearly falling into the flower bed before making a hasty retreat.

"Man's an idiot," said O'bie. "Are you all right?" Ellen looked a bit shaken. O'bie wished he could comfort her but didn't want his actions misunderstood.

"I'm fine, I'll make up the fire and we can have a cup of cocoa together before you go back to the barn," she said. Soon they were sitting together watching the flames of the dying fire as they drank the sweet chocolate. Ellen put out her hand and took O'bie's in hers. Surprised, O'bie looked up to see Ellen's face. She was looking at him with a whimsical smile. "I need a minder," she said.

CHAPTER 76 Lifting the Potatoes

Ru rose early next morning and sat looking at Betty as she slept with one arm around Joseph, thinking about what a close run thing it had been with that Major bloke. He'd been pestering Betty to let him have the boy. Suspecting she was going to meet the Major, Ru had followed Betty one day into the bush near the pa and had overheard him going over the advantages of the education he could provide and how well Joseph would be looked after by his wife who wanted a child to care for. He'd said Betty could get on with her own life if she let him take the child, but Betty would not agree.

Next day, when he'd been doing some work for Harvey, Ru had watched from afar Jock Harvey and the Major talking. Even from a distance it was clear that the conversation was becoming very heated and tense so he'd gone close enough to hear what was being said. He could still remember the sound of the Major's head hitting the stump, and had watched Harvey feel for a pulse. Then, when Harvey ran to the shed near the house he saw his chance of getting rid of this man who had made Betty's life so difficult.

Creeping forward, he had dealt a blow to the head with his pounamu mere close to where the Major had hit the stump. He had dropped the mere down a nearby hollow cabbage tree then hurried back to complete the task he'd been working on as if nothing untoward had happened.

Ru had been having instruction from the old Irish priest, Father Brady. He was puzzled by the teaching he'd had at the mission school and wanted to learn more.

Father Brady had told him that no good purpose would be served by confessing his crime as there was no way of telling which blow had caused Maurice Martin's death. Later, when Betty agreed to marry him, Father Brady offered to give them his blessing and told Ru to forget about the matter altogether.

Ru had tried, but now and then he'd wake in a sweat after bad dreams. He hoped they'd go away. Father Brady said time heals all things and perhaps it was better to keep his own counsel.

However, he kept thinking that that man at the picnic had looked at him in a funny way, as if he could see into his mind. He looked like a down-and-out pakeha, but could find water under the ground. He must be an atua, god, and might be raru raru, trouble.

Ru lit the fire and put some water on to boil. Betty came to the kitchen and went to look at the weather. "You going to work today?" she asked.

"Yes. I think the boss wants to start digging the potatoes," he said. "Do you want to come and help?"

"Yes Ru. boss is good man. You're a good man too," Betty said as she ruffled Joseph's hair. "We have some kai then go pick up spuds, eh?"

They packed some food and made their way to the paddock where Rangi and John had begun to dig two of the rows, the long pronged forks tossing the tubers out of the soil on to the ground where they would dry. Betty filled her kit then tipped them into sacks lying ready. Joseph helped for a while but soon tired and sat down on a bag to nap.

"You lazy boy," said Ru, but he was laughing. Jake and Cathy also helped. Soon big sacks of potatoes stood at intervals down the long rows. It was a good crop, but not so heavy where the flood had been. John was well pleased though and was glad when Kate arrived with the lunch baskets and could see the result of their efforts.

When lunch was over, Ru loaded the sacks on to the wagon to take back to the barn where they'd be laid out to dry. 'Wellington will be glad to have the potatoes sent down there,' thought John. With the population growing and ships arriving daily, food was always in demand. Now that more wagons were making the trip over the hill, freight had become less expensive and so the profit from the farmers' crops had increased.

The afternoon progressed as row after row gave up their bounty. Kelly walked down to see how things were going and, impressed, told John that if spuds had grown as well in the old country, there'd be less Irishmen seeking a better life here. John could only agree. Soon it was time for Jake to take the cows up for milking, and Cathy breathed a sigh of relief when she was told to go and help her mother.

When the last of the day's diggings were loaded on the wagon Betty got up to sit on the sacks for a ride to the barn. She was used to working in the farms around the pa but only for short periods. Today had been hard and long. She'd be glad to get home and make the evening meal. 'No potatoes,' she thought, 'but then again what else is there?' so she was very pleased when Kate once again gave Betty and Ru some surplus food to take home.

Between the Johnsons' house and the barn Ru stopped the wagon by the track to their whare near the stream and lifted Joseph down to Betty.

"Now we need a wash," she said to the child and, holding hands, they waded into the stream, where she gave him a good wash-down to remove the dirt gathered during the day, especially on his knees. Then, not noticing the lonely figure of Arthur Peat watching from the bush, she removed her long skirt and shirt and washed herself as well as she could in the refreshing water.

CHAPTER 77 Back to Work Again

The month was flying by as January was wont to do and, after the excitement of Christmas and the New Year celebrations, life was back to normal.

Things were going well at the mill. Jim was handling the horses well and had become skilled in driving the teams. They were used to their tasks. He'd learnt to trust them to pull the heavy logs close to the rails from where men rolled them closer to the wooden track. Then another set of horses pulled the logs on low wheeled platforms along the rails to the mill. There was so much timber in the district of Greytown and Carterton there'd be work at the mill for years.

Jim found it hard to be separated from Mary and the children but, until they could find a house or get money to build, he'd have to put up with it. If he was not too tired, Jim would have the evening meal with Mary, Beth and the children then play card games and talk about the future, before returning to the hostel. They were sometimes joined by Peter Fairman but he spent a lot of time after a hard day's work in his blacksmith shop, finishing his house. There were only a few months left before the wedding in April. Sometimes Miss Goode would be out with her fiancé which allowed Mary and Jim time on their own. Jim would tell Mary about how the men worked, about the sound of cross-cut saws and cries of "Timber!" as huge logs fell in a tangled mass and the ground shook with the force of the blow as they hit the earth with a whump. Then about the ten men who chopped the branches from the trunks to prepare them for the trip to the mill.

Jim had become very friendly with Eddie Browne and told Mary how popular he was at the mill. He knew all the men by name, worked out their pay and kept their time sheets, as well as a neat set of books ready to be examined by the owner. Fairman had made him a clip to hold the pages firm and, though he sometimes had trouble with simple things, all in all he managed well. He was also known to forget if a man had been a few minutes late but would have something to say if it happened two days in a row, knowing the mill owner was always watching.

Meanwhile, discussion continued amongst some of the men in the village about a new project they wanted to start. Their plan was to form a company to construct more houses and shops in the township.

Henry Dickson wanted a larger store and increasing numbers of people were wanting houses. They'd not be doing the building themselves, but employ a manager and a gang of carpenters. John Johnson was keen and said they could all take shares in the company. Jim Smith hadn't been approached as he had no money. Fairman was all for the scheme, as was Dickson. Doctor McDonald would be invited to join them and John wanted Rangi included, as he felt he, as a Maori, should be involved, and Rangi was a good bloke.

They met on the last Sunday of January to decide if they should go ahead and, after a few hours of debate they'd got to the stage of needing advice about setting up the company. Henry Dickson suggested asking the new lawyer in town to draw up the contract as he seemed an honest man.

While the lawyer foresaw no difficulties he said the company would have to be registered in Wellington and he'd let them know when the papers would be ready for signing. John was disappointed that Rangi declined to join the scheme as he wasn't sure he could find the money to invest, but he was happy to work with the group.

———— ⌇⌇ ————

School had started again. The teachers were glad to see the children had enjoyed the holidays and were ready to work hard. "Write a story about some of the things you did during the holidays," Mrs Thompson told the older children, while Beth Goode asked her class to draw a picture about what they'd done.

They were both thinking about their coming weddings. Mrs Thompson planned a quiet affair as she and Paul Jones didn't want a fuss but Miss Goode and Peter Fairman had lots of friends and wanted to make theirs an occasion. Both thought April was a good month to choose. With the coming marriage of the vicar and Mrs Martin, and rumours of romance between O'bie O'Brien and Ellen Harvey it promised to be a busy time for the little community.

One morning, as they had a cup of tea during the playtime break, Beth Goode suddenly said, "I've had such a good idea! Why don't we all get married on the same day? It would be such fun and save all of us a lot of money. We could have separate services at our own churches and then meet at the hotel for a banquet with all our friends. What do you think?"

"Oh no, I don't think so," said Joan Thompson with a shudder. "I don't think Mr Jones would like that at all."

"Oh go on. Just suggest it and see what he says."

Surprisingly, when Paul Jones called in soon after and Mrs Thompson laughingly told him about Miss Goode's idea he said, "Well why not? You know how hard it is to get a preacher to marry you in these out-lying places. You'd have a captive one in the vicar."

"I want to have my own special day," said Joan. "I don't fancy us all together. I agree it would save money but is that a problem?"

"Not at all, my dear, you shall have just what you want. But it could be fun. We all have the same friends. Let's just see what the others think."

"I'll see what my fiancé thinks about a double wedding," said Miss Goode.

"All right, but we won't all go on honeymoon together will we?" Mrs Thompson said with a laugh. "Let's just think about it for a while. April is months away. I was thinking about the middle of the month and so were you Miss Goode. Let's just bide a while before we decide."

"I agree. Now, what do you need doing around the school grounds?" asked Paul Jones. "I've a spare hour or two if you want something done."

"The post and rail fence has been given a hard time by the ponies and could do with a tidy up," Mrs Thompson said. "That would be such a help as they get out on to the road and the children have to round them up. It's such a disruption."

<hr>

Once school was over Beth walked down to see Peter. Joan Thompson had come around to the idea of a combined wedding, or seemed to have, and Beth was sure Peter would be in favour too. The scent of manuka flowers in the bush and the dry grass-heads along the roadside hung in the air. April was not far away. There would be a lot to do if they all agreed.

Peter scooped her up and hugged her to him. It was good she didn't worry about causing gossip when she came on her own to see him. As a school teacher she had her reputation to consider, but young Peter was always there as a chaperone. He was used to seeing his parents kiss when they met at the boarding house after work so he took no notice of Auntie Beth and Big Peter hugging. As Beth anticipated, Peter Fairman was happy about her idea. "After all, we all have the same friends and it would make sense, wouldn't it?" said Beth. "We could have separate services and join together for a reception at the hotel."

"I'll go along with anything you plan, my love," said Peter. "It sounds a very good idea. Talk to the others and see what comes up. The house will be finished soon and we need to order some furniture. I've an advertisement we could study to see what we both like."

"Yes, let's do that later. When I see Mrs Martin and Reverend Porter I'll ask them. Perhaps I should write to her. She's gone to stay with Mrs Harvey's cousin in Masterton. I'll do that now, as soon as I get home." Beth made a move to leave. "Are you coming home now Peter, or do you want to stay longer?"

"Can I stay please, Auntie Beth? Peter needs me to hand him things, don't you Big Peter?" the young lad said. "I'm learning the trade."

"Yes you can stay, boy. It's true he's handy. I'm careful he doesn't get in the way. It can get hot around here," said the blacksmith with a twinkle in his eye as he put more coal in the forge, then used the bellows to pump up heat.

Beth was setting the table for the meal when Mary arrived home, and she had only just taken off her coat and hat when her friend burst out, "I want to ask you what you think about an idea I've had about the weddings. I wonder if we could all marry on the same day and have a combined celebration. I asked Mrs Thompson, but she wasn't keen. Paul Jones was though. What do you think?"

"I don't know. You're right there would be a lot of the same guests at both, so I suppose it could work," said Mary.

"There could be O'bie and Mrs Harvey too if what I've heard is true," said Beth.

"I saw Mrs Harvey at the store today, but there was no hint of anything." Mary tried to remember the conversation they'd had.

Just then Young Peter and Marie came running in, saying "What's for tea?"

"Go and wash your hands and you'll find out," said Mary. Jim knocked at the door, and got a welcoming smile from Mary. "Come in, tea's nearly ready. How was the mill today?"

"We were really lucky. Browne saw smoke coming from a heap of scrap timber and came to get help to put it out. We managed to pull the logs apart and bucket up water from the river. It was just luck he noticed it. It could've been the end of the mill. Browne had been looking around for tools that had got lost - axes and jemmys and things like that. He's a real hero now," Jim explained as he ate.

"Well, I hope the owner gives him a bonus," said Mary. "He must be worth his weight in gold now, after this."

"I wouldn't go that far, but the men were very happy with him, you can be sure of that," said Jim. "They'll take the hat around on pay-day. It would've meant looking for work if the mill had gone up and they know that."

After the unwelcome visit by Dan O'Reilly, Ellen and O'bie had made a commitment to each other to say nothing to their friends about the change in Ellen's feelings for O'bie, but to wait for a while and see how things went.

That day Ellen had had a hard time keeping quiet while chatting to Mary Smith and Mrs Dickson, but she never said a word, except to say that she and O'bie were happy working on the farm and were waiting for Mrs Martin to tell them of her plans.

The vexed question of when to sell the remaining pigs had come up over breakfast. O'bie was for keeping them for bacon, while Ellen wanted to ask Henry Dickson to look at them when he came past the next day.

"The cows still have a lot of milk and won't dry off for a few months. Then the mangolds will be big enough to feed them," said O'bie. He reached for his hat and went to leave. "Just see what Dickson thinks." He bent and kissed Ellen. "I'm going to cut down the last trees by the river."

"Be careful, I don't like you working on your own," said Ellen.

CHAPTER 78 House Hunting

Mrs Martin had been staying at the boarding house with Mrs Harvey's cousin Dora Davis for some days.

"We'll marry as soon as you like, my dear," Dulcie had told Amos. "I don't want a big wedding, just the two of us and a couple of witnesses. But first we must find a house."

When she had first arrived at the boarding house Dora Davis had brought some tea into the parlour and sat with them both to enjoy a cup, and some gossip. "How long have you been over here?" she asked. "In the Wairarapa I mean."

"As you know, I did live here on a farm some time ago with my late husband. I recently sold my house in Lower Hutt. Now I want to buy one in Masterton. Do you know of any for sale?"

"I don't know of any close by, but there were some for sale a bit out of town. You might have seen them, Reverend Porter - three cottages at the boundary of the town on Johnson Street. A man built them all to the same design. They're tidy little places, with a bit of land. Do you know them?"

"I do, but they're rather small. I've seen another on the west side of town. Perhaps we could go and look at that tomorrow," said Amos. "You'll be tired after the journey yesterday and then coming up here. Why don't you rest my dear, while I go around my flock? They know when I'm around and wait for me to call, so I'd better not disappoint them."

"I'll have a rest then look around the town. If I make my need for a home known something will turn up. I have faith in the Lord."

"And so do I, my dear," said Amos, with a smile. "After all, he brought me you."

Dora had stood up and removed the tea things. "I wish my cousin had stayed with me. I thought she'd have been a good help from what I saw of her, even though she was here was only a short time. How is she getting on with the farm? It was your farm wasn't it?"

"Miss Goode said she and O'bie, the manager, were fine. I'll catch up on them when I go back down to Greytown to collect my furniture."

Afterwards, Dulcie Martin had rested on her bed and wondered about the change she was to make in her life. It was a big step. Amos was rather staid most of the time, but that came with the training he'd had when studying for the ministry. When they were alone he seemed to unfold and become someone else. She smiled when she thought of him waylaying the coach as she was leaving Greytown and asking her to marry him. 'If we can only find a house,' she thought.

Later she went down the passage to the parlour to ask Dora if she knew of anyone who dealt in real estate. There seemed to be houses going up everywhere. Surely some were for sale. Dora was serving tea to two men and introduced Mrs Martin.

They greeted her politely but when they learnt she was to marry the vicar, had become quite friendly. Mrs Martin said she was looking for a home to purchase and wished to hear of any for sale and, when she indicated she was going for a walk to see how the town was progressing, the men offered to accompany her, an idea which Dora Davis supported. "There are some unruly types around, Mrs Martin."

They set off as soon as Mrs Martin collected her hat and put on stout boots. The roads were rough but some work had been put in on the main street to flatten out the deep ruts made by the carts and wagons. Shops were set back from the street with hitching posts for horses. Burnt stumps and miserable skeletons of trees, left standing when the good trees were logged, could be seen on the outskirts.

As well as substantial cottages, Mrs Martin was delighted to see some fine homes which were two-storied and modern in appearance with ornate decoration around the verandas. One of these would be admirable.

However, Dulcie and Amos had no luck finding the house they wanted in Masterton. All the fine buildings going up were for business people, or wealthier farmers wanting a house in the town.

"We might be better to return to Greytown, my dear," said Amos some time later. "Johnson is starting a company to build shops and houses. He asked me to join them when I saw him in Greytown yesterday. I said I had no capital to put into such a scheme, but I was all for the idea. Do you have to live up here?"

"No, I don't suppose so. Let's return to Greytown and see what comes up," said Dulcie with a smile. "As long as I have you, I can live anywhere."

"Tomorrow, we'll go down tomorrow?" said Amos. "I really think we'll have more luck there."

John and Kate were looking around the garden, admiring the little fruit trees that had grown tall after the rain. They even had a few fruit on them, but Kate said they should be pulled off so the trees weren't stressed trying to fruit at a young age. It was tempting though. It was, after all, time for bottling and preserving to begin.

"Where do you want to make the big orchard?" John asked. "We'll have to plant these out in the winter or they'll be too big to handle." Kate looked at the field near the house that was the pony's home paddock. It was flat and not too large an area.

"There, by the totara tree. That little paddock would be just right. What do you think ?"

"I suppose it would do. We can find somewhere else for the horses. The ground should be full of goodness after all the manure. Yes, it will do very well," said John. "Look, I have to go into town to see the lawyer about the company, and make a few changes to the contract for people to sign when they want us to build them a home. I've left work for Rangi and Ru, and will be as quick as I can." They walked to where John's horse was waiting

"You don't think you're taking too much on?" asked Kate.

"Not at all. We're only setting up the company and will find someone to run it. There are new people coming every day; some will know about building. I think we'll be up and running in a month," said John. "I must be off. I won't be long." He kissed Kate goodbye and rode away on Beauty.

The morning coach was arriving when John reached the stables. He was surprised to see Amos Porter and Dulcie Martin among the passengers. "Have you found a home then?" he asked.

"No," said Amos. "We've decided to look for one down here instead. We don't want a mansion but it must have at least two reception rooms. I'll have a lot of visits from clergy and people wanting advice, so don't want to tie up the sitting-room. Mrs Martin will need some space too."

"I don't know of any large homes for sale but when we get the company up and running we could build one just the way you want it," John said with a smile. "I'm not out for business but if we can help?"

Dulcie looked up at Amos for his reaction, and then said, "I think that we might well think about that option, Mr Johnson."

"We'll be at the hotel in the meantime, so come and see us there and we'll discuss it," said Amos. "It might be the answer."

CHAPTER 79 Moving Forward

A few days later John went to tell Fairman and Dickson they might have their first contract to build a home for the vicar and his bride and he wanted to have plans sent up from a firm of architects in Wellington. "We need to have something to show them. If we make a good job of this one, it would be a great start."

Peter Fairman smiled. "That's quick! Congratulations Johnson. You're really on to it."

"I know of a section that might be just the place for them, next to the doctor's. I'll find out if it's available. I'm going to see the lawyer now. The council will have the plan of Main Street, so I'll check there too," John said.

The lawyer had made good progress and told John he should call a meeting of the partners at his office to sign the papers. "I'll be down in Wellington this week but perhaps Monday next week would be suitable," he said.

John agreed and then asked if he'd do him a favour by going to the architects' in Willis Street and picking up some plans. He didn't want to brag, but was excited that they'd almost received their first contract. "The vicar and his wife may let us build a house for them in Greytown," John said, explaining the need for the plans.

"Well, don't go too fast. There's many a slip twixt cup and lip," the lawyer advised. "I'll get the plans for you. They'll know what you want?" He stood up and straightened his tall frame.

"I've written to them and they should have had the letter by now. I've asked for basic plans of one-storied houses." John rose to leave. "What time for the meeting on Monday?"

"About eleven, do you think? That will give you time to ride in and meet with the others. You'll be able to talk over the scheme before you sign. You'll tell them all?"

"I'm on my way to see them now," said John.

Henry Dickson was talking to Fairman when John rode up. They were pleased to see him and to hear about the meeting with the lawyer on Monday. "So we'll be in business soon enough if Mrs Martin has changed her mind about Masterton?"

"It would seem so, but only if we find the right design," said John. He went on to tell them of the vicar's needs for a large home with two parlours. "It will be quite imposing," he said.

Beauty grazed the grass along the verge close by the hitching post as she waited for John to finish talking. It looked like it was going to be a long session. She took a long drink from the trough and continued nibbling all the rough grass she could reach.

"I've had some replies to the notice in the window about a manager," said Dickson. "One man looks very promising. He's just arrived from Sydney and was building homes over there. Mostly in brick, but he has built in wood too. He's at the mill, waiting to hear. There are some others as well. I don't think we 'll have trouble getting enough men."

Peter Fairman added his news, saying, "I saw the owner of the mill too, and he's happy to supply us. There's matai, rimu and totara at a good price. The two men I had building my house are coming in with us too, so all we need is the work."

"Don't forget the meeting on Monday," said John as he rode away. Doctor McDonald was his next target.

Mrs McDonald came to the door, looking flustered as she wiped flour from her hands on her apron. "Oh Mr Johnson, it's only you," she said.

"Yes, it's me again. Is the doctor in?"

"He has a patient but will be finished soon. I've just been making scones. Come into the kitchen, and tell me all about this new scheme you're getting him into."

"It's a great opportunity. There's a need for shops and housing. We're starting a company to employ men to build them. We'll put in a certain amount each and have equal shares. It's all above board and we've a lawyer to see we're not getting into more than we can handle," John explained.

"Well, my husband has enough to do. I don't want him trying to run a building business on top of what he's doing already," said Annie with a sharp note in her voice John had never heard before.

"He won't need to do anything. You know Dickson and Fairman wouldn't rob anybody, and you trust me, don't you?" said John as he watched her put the tray of scones into the oven. "If we find enough men to work for us and a good overseer, it will run itself."

"Well, I just hope you're right. Some of these get rich schemes are nothing but trouble." Annie McDonald sat down and looked at John severely. "I don't want him tired out with worry. It's taken him years to save a little and he's not young anymore."

"Who's not young anymore?" asked the doctor as he came into the room.

"Mr Johnson was telling me about the firm of builders he's starting up and wants you to be involved in. I'm afraid you'll be doing too much."

"So you think I'm too old, do you?"

"No, but I think you have a long enough day now, my love." she said as she went to check on the oven and put the kettle on to boil.

Wanting her to understand his plans, John said, "The difference is that it's not a get rich scheme. It's a way of getting more houses built and more people to live here."

Doctor McDonald looked at John. "I believe in you Johnson, and that your motives are honourable. We're all good citizens, Annie, and not out to make thousands of pounds. Some people are living in slab huts with several children. I'm all for having better homes being built. Please don't worry. Mr Johnson has explained the way it will work. I'm not stupid enough to think it will all be plain sailing, but I'm happy to put in the little I have."

"There's to be a meeting at the lawyer's on Monday at eleven o'clock and we'll sign up then. Dickson has found some men and Fairman has sought supplies. Oh, by the way, the land next door to here, is that for sale?"

"I believe so," said the doctor. "Why?"

"It would be a good section for the vicar and his wife. They've decided to build down here. Couldn't find what they wanted in Masterton."

"It belongs to some man who lives in Australia. The council will have the details," the doctor said as he enjoyed a scone.

"What time on Monday?" asked his wife. "I need to remind the doctor these days. He's becoming forgetful."

"I'm not. It's just that I get busy with a patient and can't leave them halfway through some treatment. Hush woman," chided the doctor gruffly.

"I'll see you on Monday at eleven o'clock," John reminded him. " This lawyer is a stickler for punctuality. I must get home and catch up with some chores. Thank you for the tea. Please don't worry, Mrs McDonald. We know what we're doing."

Paul Jones was standing near the blacksmith's shop as John rode past so he stopped. "I hear you've a new project, Johnson, something about building houses."

"Yes that's right. We hope to begin soon."

"I've been looking at a farm out Waihakeke way. It's bigger than the forty acre blocks around here. I might want to put a house on that for when Mrs Thompson and I marry. There's just a cottage there."

"Well, we'll be up and running soon. I've one possible order already. Reverend Porter and Mrs Martin have decided to come down here. They're getting married soon too," said John. "April I believe."

"Mrs Thompson said Miss Goode wants us all to marry on the same day. What do you think about that for an idea? She said we all have the same friends and it would make sense to have one big celebration. I really think it would save a lot of time for people. Get it over in one go."

"She's right really, and I know the women are all friends. Mrs Martin might not be keen, but she seems to get on with everybody, so why not? Would Mrs Thompson go along with a triple wedding?"

"There may be another one as well. Ellen Harvey is very quiet about how things are between O'bie and her, but I've heard they're more than friends and fellow farmers now."

"My goodness! Well, I'd be happy to have one big party and let us get some work done. Now I'd better get home and see Rangi and Ru."

The meeting on Monday was in John's thoughts as he rode home. Annie McDonald's reservations had unsettled him. He hadn't said so to Paul Jones, but there was always an element of chance in any new venture. 'I can't see anything that can go wrong,' he told himself as he neared his gateway. 'Oh well, time will tell.' He took the mail from the saddle bag and went to find Kate. "Letters from home," he called.

"Oh, give them to me, please John. Don't tease," said Kate as John held the bag high above her head. She was holding William and couldn't catch John as he moved around the room. "You are a brute."

"Here you are, there's one from your mother. You go and have a read. I'll mind my boy," said John as he hugged William. "I saw Paul Jones in town. He tells me Miss Goode wants to have one big wedding for all the courting couples. What do you think of that?"

"It would be something different, wouldn't it?" said Kate. "All together, or one after the other?"

"I think that we can leave it to the brides to decide and just wait for the invitations to arrive."

Early on Monday John set off to meet with the others at Fairman's to interview some men from the mill who had seen the advertisement in Dickson's window and wanted to join the company. There was one man in particular who could make a good foreman. Dickson was there already and they set about asking the men what experience they had. The answers were mixed. Some wanted a new occupation and others were skilled craftsmen. John told the men to stay at the mill until they had notice they were needed. He didn't want them to give up their jobs in case the lawyer had found some flaw in their scheme. Five men from the group seemed particularly suitable and, pleased with the morning's work, the men set off for the lawyer's. The doctor would meet them there.

It was just eleven o'clock when they reached the lawyer's office where he announced he had attended to all the details requested and everything was in order; the company had been registered and he'd send a signed copy down to the Companies Office in Wellington as soon as they'd completed the deed. He showed them where they should sign and initial the document. Then he brought out the sheaf of house designs for them to see, spoke a little about the changes to housing in Wellington, wished them well in their venture and bade them good-bye.

The whole meeting had taken less than an hour. John said they should go to the hotel to celebrate, but the doctor said it would be better to come home with him and keep the celebrations quiet. "We can have a spot at my place," he said.

Peter Fairman agreed, pleased to see that Alex McDonald wanted to keep the company's affairs private. "We don't want the whole town knowing our business," he said.

"Home already?" Annie McDonald said as they walked into the parlour. "I thought you'd be hours."

"He's very efficient, our lawyer. A very good man," her husband told her as he poured their drinks. "Well gentlemen, cheers." They all drank and shook hands, as they considered what the day could mean to each of them.

"Good luck, good health, and good business to all of us," said Peter Fairman. "I'm off to work."

John raised his glass, "Let's drink to our wives and sweethearts, God bless 'em."

The lawyer sat alone in his office after his clients left rubbing his hands together to warm them up. Although it was a warm day, the office was chilly. 'What would the winter be like here?' he wondered. He'd heard stories of flooding and gale force winds that swept up from the south, but all in all it seemed to be a nice place to set up his practice. Yes, he would do very well if the parties he had just seen were an example of the business people here. He put the papers away in a safe place and went home to make some lunch. He was lonely on his own, but had to make what he could of his new life here in the colonies.

'Confound the woman,' he thought, his mind turning to his wife back in London. Perhaps in time, if he was successful, she'd join him. But for the moment, he'd have to fend for himself and pray that she'd see sense and come out to New Zealand. He'd sent her the money but he was getting impatient with her indecision.

He reached the door of his cottage and felt in his pocket for the key. If the men were able to start their building company there would be rich pickings for a useful lawyer.

CHAPTER 80 More Plans

Beth Goode had talked over the wedding arrangements with Mary Smith long into the night. Now it was Saturday and she was going to see Mrs Martin. Reverend Porter had gone down to Featherston to see some of his flock but Mrs Martin was staying at the hotel. Beth walked the short distance from the boarding house, thinking of what she'd say.

When she entered the parlour at the hotel she found Mrs Martin sitting near the window, admiring the view of the ranges. There were a few clouds gathered around the hilltops but otherwise the day was fine.

"Good morning, Mrs Martin." Beth greeted her. "It's so nice to see you again. I hear you might build a home here, instead of Masterton. Is that right?"

"That's what we think, if we find the right plans. Mr Johnson has loaned us some he had brought up from Wellington and there is one I especially like. It has a passage through the middle and rooms on each side with one large sitting room and a smaller one for the vicar to see his visitors in. Then there's a big kitchen at the end with room for a dining area, by the window. I think it would do very well."

"That sounds very nice. You must come and see the one my fiancé is building for us," said Beth. "It's not large but will be a good start. However, I've come to ask your opinion on our weddings," said Beth.

"Oh and why is that?" Mrs Martin.

"I have had this thought that all our weddings could be on the same day and we could celebrate together," said Beth in a rush. "Mrs Thompson is willing. I think it would be a wonderful way to enjoy all the weddings with all our friends together, what do you think?"

"I only know a few people here. Do you really want us to join in your special day?" asked Mrs Martin, conscious of her greying hair.

"I think it would be lovely if you were part of it. It would be a good way for you to get to know everyone, don't you think?"

"I'll wait to hear from the vicar before I decide, but it sounds sensible I admit. It's very, very kind of you to suggest it, my dear. But the vicar and I are older, and we wouldn't want to spoil your day. We don't intend to have a white wedding, either of us, you know. I'll give it some thought. What do you have in mind?"

"Mrs Thompson and Mr Jones, and Mr Fairman and I are to marry in the Anglican Church. The vicar will marry us, then you and Reverend Porter could say your vows before the magistrate at the church, as well. I'm hoping that then we can go to the Catholic Church to see Ellen Harvey and O'bie married by Father Brady. I'm going to drive out there later to try and convince her to agree. Then, on the day, we'll go to the hotel and enjoy a meal together with our friends. It would be wonderful, a boost to the community and be such fun." Beth smiled at Mrs Martin in an engaging way. She couldn't say no, could she?

"I'll see what the vicar says, but you seem to have it all arranged. Let's go and ask Martha for some tea," said Mrs Martin, smiling at Beth. They walked together down the passage to the kitchen where Martha was busy preparing dinner. "Can I make us some tea?"

"I'll have it ready in a jiffy, Mrs Martin." She wasn't going to let another woman loose in her kitchen. Only Molly was ever allowed to do any work there, and only if Martha had a big job on. "I'll bring it through in a minute. Just you go and sit down and I'll be there right away," said Martha with a sniff.

"Just as you please," said Dulcie. She was used to servant's ways. "I was only trying to save you the trouble."

"She's a bit funny, isn't she?" laughed Beth Goode back in the parlour. " Did you know she had an argument with Molly over the éclairs at the McDonald wedding. The poor doctor was so disappointed. I hope they don't come to blows over ours."

Mrs Martin didn't know the story, but shushed Beth as Martha came through the doorway with a tray and set it on the table. "Is there anything else, Mrs Martin?" she asked.

"No, that is lovely of you Martha. Thank you so much. We could have saved you the bother."

"No bother at all, but I must get on with dinner," said Martha.

"I must get on too if I'm going to drive out to see Mrs Harvey and O'bie O'Brien," said Beth. Would you like to come?"

"That would be lovely if it won't take long. The vicar won't be back until late. I'll leave him a message. So drink up and we'll go."

"It won't take long," said Beth. "Peter Fairman's lending me a gig."

Peter had the gig ready for Beth, and warned her to take care. The pony was good natured but could be easily frightened. "Just take it slowly," he said. They set off through the settlement and turned on to the road which ran past the pa. Beth had not been out this way for a while. It was lovely to see the paddocks looking green after the rain.

Mrs Martin could see big changes to the farms close to her own, and was pleased to see there were a few new houses being built near the road. She remembered how lonely she'd been the few years they'd lived on the farm; now there would be a lot more company for the women and children of farmers.

Ellen Harvey was in the garden and was surprised to see the gig stop at her gate. When she realised who her visitors were she was delighted and ran to help them down and tie the horse to a post where it could eat grass. She gave Beth a hug and smiled shyly at Mrs Martin. "Good afternoon, Mrs Martin. Do you want to see O'bie?"

"That would be nice," said Mrs Martin. "How is the farm going? Are you happy here?" She looked at the little cottage with its pretty curtains at the window, and the neat flower beds, with appreciation. "It looks very well cared for. Are you and O'bie getting along all right?"

"Do come inside, please," said Ellen, recovering from the surprise of the visit. "We're very happy. He's a good worker." She opened the door and they all went to sit at the table.

"I have heard that you're getting on very well," said Miss Goode. "There are rumours you know." She smiled at Ellen and added, "Nice happy rumours."

"I don't know what you have heard." Ellen Harvey said stiffly. "I hope you don't think he is taking advantage of me. I'm a lot older than he is, you know. I can handle myself."

"Oh, I know that. Perhaps we're just wishful that you can have the same happiness that we're enjoying, planning our special day. We're here on a little matter of weddings," said Beth Goode. "I've come to ask you to our wedding, which will be in April on the fifth, or eleventh. We haven't quite made up our minds."

"And that's not all," said Mrs Martin. "The vicar and I will probably be married on the same day."

Ellen Harvey looked surprised. "Really?" she said.

"Yes, that's right. And would you believe me when I tell you that Joan Thompson and Paul Jones are to marry on the same day too?" Beth watched Ellen's face to see her reaction, and laughed when she saw her disbelieving look. "What do you think of the idea of a combined service where we can take our vows together? Then we'll have all our friends gather at the hotel for a celebration. What do you think?"

"We don't want to offend you." Mrs Martin interjected hurriedly. "We've only come to ask you to be one of our maids if you don't want to join us as one of the brides." Then, thinking it was better to say no more, she changed the subject. "Everything going well on the farm?" she asked again.

"Yes, yes everything is fine," said Ellen. "O'bie will be in for his tea in a minute or two. So please don't say a word about your idea."

There was the sound of steps on the gravel path and O'bie came into the kitchen. He greeted the women warmly. "So what brings you out here?" he asked.

"Just a friendly visit, we must be going back before dark," said Beth. "The blacksmith will be worried if we don't turn up at home soon, and the vicar too." She stood up and kissed Ellen. "Think over what we said. It could be fun."

They all went out to the gig and O'bie helped the women up. They waved goodbye and set off up the road.

"Well, what was that about?" asked O'bie as he shut the gate.

"Oh, just a silly idea they have about all getting married on the same day in April. They think it would be fun," said Ellen.

"Sounds good to me," said O'bie, as he put his arm around Ellen's waist and pulled her close. "Did they want you to join in?"

"No, they asked me to be a maid of honour," said Ellen, worried that O'bie had put his finger on the spot so quickly.

"I've a better idea than that. Why don't we join them?" he said, and swung her around the room. "A man can only wait so long."

"Now, listen to me," said Ellen. "I know Mrs Martin is very nice and also our employer. I just don't like Reverend Porter that much. He wouldn't bury Jock, if you remember. Said he wasn't sure Jock could be buried in the Anglican part of the cemetery. He may have been going to Wellington but could have put off the trip if he had wanted to. I like Father Brady. He was very kind to me. If I was to get married again I would want him."

"I do understand, my dear, but it would be fun to join in, wouldn't it? I mean we all have the same friends. Think about it anyway. You're going to marry me soon aren't you?"

"I suppose so. But I'm so much older than you. You're only twenty-two just starting out in life, and I don't want to tie you to an old woman," said Ellen. "I've come to love you and long to be your wife, but there is the age gap. I mean, what will people say?"

"Who cares what people say? You're only twenty-nine. I love you for what you are, not for the years you lived before we met. So let's go and see the others tomorrow and tell them 'Yes'," said O'bie.

CHAPTER 81 Father Brady Visits

Arthur Peat had found work in the village, surveying some of the acre blocks into smaller sections for housing. There was a lot of activity now that a proper building firm was being established. He was also helping out at a neighbour's farm where he had a room, and could use some of the skills he had learnt as a boy.

It was good to be part of a community again after several years of moving around. He was sure he had controlled his appetite for young girls and was hopeful his past would not catch up with him. He still spent a lot of time at the Johnsons' where he was helping dig the well, helped by Rangi and Ru. Betty, Ru's young wife, was very attractive, but Arthur knew better than to venture there.

Betty brought tea for them each morning and sat with the men with Joseph on her knee. The digging was going well but the sides had to be shored up with wood to keep them from collapsing. Arthur admired from afar. Betty did not trust him and kept a safe distance, while she waited to take the tea- basket home to Kate who she was helping with the baby and to learn pakeha ways. Betty was a good pupil and they were putting down jars of fruit and salting beans almost every day.

———— ∞ ————

Father Brady whistled a happy Irish tune as he rode his mount along the road to the pa. He'd made a few converts among the Maori folk and wanted to keep in touch. He also had a mind to visit Ellen Harvey and Patrick O'Brien.

At the pa the young ones gathered around him while an older boy took charge of his horse. He'd sold his old pony as he was becoming too heavy for it. This new steed was full of life. Well broken in, but much livelier. "Watch out she doesn't kick you," he said.

The women came to greet him and, after a few words of prayer, he spent some time listening to any problems they had. May came forward with one concern. Betty had told her about the man at the Johnsons' who kept on watching her. She could not tell Ru in case he became angry and was violent towards him. "What can Betty do?" she asked. "I don't think she's making it up."

"I'll see Johnson and have the man sent on his way. We don't want any trouble, but I'm sure I can convince him to continue on his journey," said Father Brady. "Now I must go and visit Mrs Harvey, and see how she is. Do you see much of her?"

May shook her head as Father mounted his horse. "Not much, she's busy and so am I. But I do like her. I'll try and go to see her soon Father. Thank you for coming all the way out here. You boys get away from Father's horse, and don't ask for rides."

"Not at all my dear," he said. "I'm only too pleased to help." He looked at the boys' disappointed faces and said, "Perhaps next time."

Ellen was in the garden and was happy to see him. Ever since he'd buried Jock she had wanted to join his flock. Now she had something to ask him about that could change her life. "How do I become a Catholic, Father?"

"You only have to ask, my child. There are no big hurdles to jump. I have some books you could read that will tell all you need to know. Is there a special reason for asking?"

"Well O'bie is a Catholic. We've agreed to marry and he explained that he should marry a Catholic if possible. So I'd like to become a Catholic if you'll have me," said Ellen.

"I think that's wonderful news. When will this happy wedding take place?" asked Father Brady with a broad smile.

"That's the hard part," said Ellen. "I've been invited to be a maid at the big celebration Miss Goode is planning, or be a bride and join in. Have you heard about it?"

"Yes, I have heard. I think it's a grand idea. You won't have trouble with the guest list as it will be all the same people.When do you think it will be?"

"Sometime in April I think they said." Ellen looked at the old priest. "I think about the fifteenth, perhaps, but I'll have to fall in with the others."

"It will have to be after Easter. We don't marry anyone during Lent. It could be Easter Sunday, if you like, or the week after. As long as Lent is over it doesn't matter. This is wonderful news, I'm so pleased for you. What does O'bie think?"

"Oh, he's impatient to wed," said Ellen "I've been worried because I'm older. Do you think it's wrong of me to marry him?"

"Of course not, I think you're very suited. God bless you."

Early the next day Father Brady decided to ride out to Johnsons'. He was worried about what he'd been told about the man at the farm. There may be no truth in the story, but it was better to check up on these rumours and lay them to rest. He was sure Johnson would have a good idea what to do if they were true. It may be that the man was lonely and yearned for companionship. But if he had a reputation, and it became known, he'd be hounded out of the town.

Father decided it would be good to call into Kellys' as well since it was a while since he'd seen them at Mass. Tessa was hanging out the washing and was pleased to see him. "Come in for a cup of tea, Father," she said. "I've nearly finished here and my husband will be up soon. He's away down the paddock looking at a heifer."

"Thank you Mrs Kelly, I will. It's warm for this time of the year. I was feeling the heat as I rode along. It'll soon be autumn though," said Father.

"Yes summer will soon be over for another year, but we can still get some lovely days, even in the winter," said Tessa as she made the tea. "It's the best thing about the place. It can be raining in the morning and bright sunshine in the afternoon. Better than the old country where it seemed to rain for days on end. Perhaps it was because we were in poor spirits that made it seem so bleak."

"I agree with you there, Mrs Kelly. I've been out here for ten years now and have loved every minute of it. I miss my old mother, God rest her soul, but I don't wish to be transferred back home. I hope the Bishop isn't listening," said Father. "I have some news. You know the widow Mrs Harvey, I believe? Well, she wants to become a Catholic and get married in the church. Isn't that great news? She and O'bie have plans to marry when Easter is over. They may join the others and have one big celebration. You'll know about that?"

"But the others are all Anglican, aren't they?" said Tessa.

"I don't mean they will all marry in our church, just join together for the party. And what a party that will be. Half of Greytown will be there. Ah, I hear your husband coming," said Father.

"Good day to you, Father," said Paddy as he hung up his hat. "What brings you out here so early in the morning?"

"I have a delicate matter to discuss with you both," said Father "It's about Arthur Peat."

"What's he done?" asked Paddy. "I've found him to be quite a help."

"Nothing yet," said Father. "I'm sure he is a good worker, but we don't want him causing any trouble. Young Ru's wife has the feeling that he watches her all the time, so I was told by May. I'm just going to talk to Johnson to see what he thinks we should or not do. I only mention it because of Polly and Jane. You might want to have a talk with them in a quiet way. Don't frighten them though."

"He seems nice enough to me," said Tessa, "but yes, we should talk to the girls. There are lots of young men working around the bush, so a word about safety won't hurt."

"Well, I must get on," said Father. "I don't want to make a big thing of this, just to put you on your guard. He may never offend again. I hope he doesn't, but as Betty told May of her concerns, I think we should take it seriously. She is frightened Ru will notice his interest and deal with it in his own way. Extract utu as they say."

⸎

Kate welcomed Father Brady as she sat in the warm sunshine outside her door with William on her knee. "What brings you all the way our here?" she asked. "Can I make you a cup of tea?"

"No thank you Mrs Johnson, I just had one with the Kellys. I came to talk to your husband about the man you have helping here, the water diviner. It's nothing to worry about, but I'm going to ask your husband what he thinks we should do. If anything happened because we hadn't taken the matter in hand we'd never forgive ourselves."

"What is it he's supposed to have done?" asked Kate. She could hardly believe the man had been in trouble. He'd always been more than polite to her.

"It's a delicate matter Mrs Johnson, and I'd rather your husband told you after I've discussed it with him. I hope you don't mind," said Father.

"Of course not," said Kate. "I don't mind at all."

"Oh! On another subject," said Father. "Have you heard about the flurry of nuptials about to take place? There may be four couples if Ellen Harvey and O'bie join in. Won't that be a day to remember?"

John came up the path, swinging a billy of milk. "Hullo Father. Nice to see you. How do you like my son? Isn't he bonny?"

"It's a fine boy you have there for sure, Mr Johnson. I can see how proud you are. But I have a wee matter to ask your advice about," said Father. "It's about the man you have helping with the well."

"Oh - what about him?" asked John. "He seems a good worker and has been very helpful finding the stream of underground water. Not everyone can do that."

"It's not about his work. It's about his leisure time activities," said Father. "Ru's wife is frightened of the way he looks at her and told May about it. She asked me to have a word with you since you have him working here. It may be nothing, but we don't want Ru to hear about it in case he decides to do something about it."

"I can see what you mean. We don't want any trouble, and I have a young daughter too. What do you think, Kate?" asked John.

"It would be a shame if he is trying to stay out of trouble. Where did the story come from?"

"It was something Betty told May and she took a very dim view of it. I'm happy for you to ask the man about it on the quiet and if you find there is cause for worry, ask him to move on. I know it sounds unfair but you can't be too careful," said Father Brady.

"I can try, but he seems as if he is making the effort to have a better life here," said John. "I'll approach the subject very carefully."

"Well, I must be on my way. And thank you. I know you'll be diplomatic," said Father. "Good bye and may God bless you and your family."

"Good bye Father Brady and thank you for the blessing. I'll wait to hear more about the weddings from Mrs Dickson. She's always up to date with the news," said Kate. As the old priest went off down the track William began to cry so Kate went inside to change and feed him. John followed. "You be careful, John," she said. "We don't know Arthur Peat well and he might take umbrage. If word got back to Ru, he could take things into his own hands. We don't want him upset," said Kate.

"Surely you know me better than that," replied John huffily.

⌘

John thought long and hard about how to approach Peat. 'I don't want to accuse him of something I know nothing about, but we don't need anything like that happening around here.' He turned the options over and over and decided to confront the man straight out. After all, if Ru got to hear about this, he would stop at nothing to protect his wife.

The well was dug and lined and a frame to suspend a bucket on a rope had been designed by the blacksmith and put in place. A wall of boulders had been built around it for safety, and the water was clear with a pleasant taste. John was pleased with the outcome of the project and grateful to Peat for his help.

Rangi and Ru had returned to clearing bush on the second farm. The men from the mill had taken the best trees away. Jim had been with them and seemed happy with the work he was doing and not envious of John at all.

John rode down to where the men were working and was pleased to see Peat working alongside them. He would have a quiet word while Rangi and Ru were busy. He waited patiently until they were using the crosscut saw then called to Peat to come to look where rabbits had dug burrows. They were becoming a real nuisance. There was rabbit dirt everywhere.

Arthur Peat agreed that something should be done but had no suggestions. John asked him to sit with him on a fallen tree as there was something he wanted to discuss. "I feel embarrassed to speak about something that is only a rumour, but if it is true, and Ru sees you looking at Betty you wouldn't last long. He has a fine sense of decency towards women and is very protective of his own."

"I don't know what you mean at all, Johnson. I served my time for a mistake I made years ago and have put all such things behind me. I've no designs on Betty except I'd like to paint her portrait. I left all my paint and canvases in Napier so I can only draw pencil sketches. She fascinates me when she is with Joseph as the beauty in her face when she is looking at him is inspiring. I swear that's all I wish to do, to make a portrait of her with her son, but it's true that I've studied her when she's not looking. I've written to my sister in Napier to send my box of equipment down to Masterton. Where did you hear these stories?"

"I believe Father Brady was told that Betty was becoming very upset about your watching her, and he asked me to speak with you. If it's in the past, as you say, we'll take your word for it. I've had no cause to doubt you and no-one else has been told, so let's leave it be. Now, we'd better do some work. But I would urge you to be more than careful. Ru has a hasty temper, and is easily roused."

"I will, Johnson, and thank you. I'm happier here than I've been for years. You and your wife have been more than kind and I assure you that I only want to live a decent life and be a good citizen." Arthur Peat spoke with real feeling and John could only believe that he was sincere, but he'd keep a close eye on him all the same.

"Well now, what do you think about a fire to burn some of the rubbish? It's not as dry after that rain so we should be safe." John walked to a huge pile of dead branches and gathered some chips of wood and dry grass to make a start.

CHAPTER 82 Ellen Goes to Town

Ellen decided that if she and O'bie were to share a wedding party she should visit the other brides-to-be. She could hardly just turn up on the day. They'd have to get together and plan the event carefully. She drove into town in the buggy and stopped first at the store. Mrs Dickson was busy with the baby and Mary was helping a customer with her purchases.

She went looking for Johanna and found her upstairs laying the baby in her cradle. Almost three months old, she was growing so well. "I'll have to look for a cot soon, she's so strong and looks around at everything. I haven't seen you for a while. How are things on the farm? Mrs Martin's not causing you any problems?"

"Not at all. She came out to see us a while ago with Miss Goode. They had an idea O'bie and I would like to join with them in their wedding plans."

"So what did you say?" asked Johanna Dickson. "It sounds a splendid idea to me."

"At first I dismissed the idea as silly, but now I don't."

"Tell me more. Have you really decided to marry O'bie?" asked Johanna. earnestly. "I mean, has he asked you?"

"Many times, and I've thought about it and decided I'd be happy to be his wife. I'm a bit older but really, what does that matter?" said Ellen. "He's grown up a lot since we've been looking after the farm. Mrs Martin and Miss Goode were sure Mrs Thompson wanted us to be part of the celebrations so I've come to ask what you think."

"I think you're very sensible and you'll make a fine couple. I know the others have set their hearts on an April wedding and will marry after Easter. What about you and O'bie? Will Father Brady marry you?" asked Johanna. "I heard you have joined his church. Have you been to Mass?"

"Yes, two Sundays in a row, and I've been given some books to read. I find them quite fascinating. Father Brady had no problem with the idea at all. In fact, just the opposite. He's all for the first week after Easter. I'm going to talk with the others this afternoon if I can. I want to be sure they meant what they said. When I told O'bie of their plan, he was delighted and said how happy it would make him."

"I think it's wonderful. What a celebration for the town. I can hardly wait. Have you decided on who will stand by you?" asked Johanna.

"No, I will have to wait and see who the other ladies want. I don't want to poach any of the people they planned to have. I'd better go, school should be out soon and I want to see Mrs Thompson and Miss Goode. I just needed to let you know about it and get your reaction. You and your husband have been such good friends to me that I wanted you to be the first to hear." Ellen picked up her hat and smoothed her skirt. "I'll tell you what we decide as soon as I find out what the others want."

Mrs Thompson was cleaning the blackboard as Ellen arrived. "Nearly finished," she said. "Just sit you down and I'll make us a cup of tea."

"I can make it," said Ellen Harvey, happy to have something to do. She imagined teaching a large group of children could be very tiring, but knew Mrs Thompson loved her job. The old black kettle was singing away where it hung from a hook in the chimney and soon they were enjoying their tea.

"So what brings you into town this afternoon?" asked Mrs Thompson, "I've made some new biscuits. Ginger, do try them," she said as she passed the plate.

"I want to ask your advice, or permission," said Ellen. "Miss Goode and Mrs Martin came out to the farm the other day. They had the idea that O'bie O'Brien and I might be getting married soon, and asked us to join you and Mr Jones, and the others, at a combined wedding. We weren't engaged then so I just laughed at the idea. However, O'bie was very keen when he heard about it and talked me into it. What do you think?"

"I think that's wonderful. You've been through so much. It will be good for you to have something pleasant to look forward to."

"Are you sure you wouldn't mind?" Ellen said the words slowly, as she watched Mrs Thompson's face, but she could see she was sincere. "Have you set a date yet?"

"Just that it's to be in April. Towards the middle of the month we thought. Is there any day you want?"

"We have to wait until after Easter. Father Brady said Easter Sunday, or the week after. It doesn't have to be a Sunday, but we have no special date planned."

Just then Miss Goode came into the room. "Miss Goode," said Mrs Thompson, "did you know our wedding party is growing bigger and bigger? Mrs Harvey and O'bie have decided to join us after all. Isn't that wonderful?"

"Oh that's grand. I knew you were getting serious. I could see the way O'bie looked at you. I'm so pleased."

The women sat and talked about the plans for their big day until Ellen said she'd like to see Mrs Martin to make sure she was happy to have she and O'bie included. "I'll go to the hotel and see if she's there before I go home."

The two schoolmistresses decided they would accompany her and they walked off down the road, dodging the horse manure which peppered the ground. "It's very good for roses," said Joan Thompson as she avoided another pile.

"But not your shoes," laughed Beth.

Mrs Martin was sitting at the window of the hotel and, pleased to have a diversion, came to meet them. "It's so good to see you all," she said. "Are you on a mission?"

"In a way we are," said Joan Thompson. "We are to have Mrs Harvey and O'bie join us on the great day. They will marry at church house and then join us at the Anglican Church. Father Brady is giving special permission for them to come to our church for the weddings."

"Why do they have to have permission?" asked Beth Goode. "It sounds old fashioned to me."

"I was reading up on that," Ellen Harvey said. "We're not supposed to go to other churches. But Father Brady said these were special circumstances and he would be pleased to allow it."

"Sounds strange to me," remarked Beth Goode. " I know the Cattys and Proddys have been at each others' throats for centuries, but we don't want that sort of thing here. Do we?"

"No indeed. Let's just find the best day and time and get on with the plans. Come and sit in the parlour. I can see Doris Bell's curtains moving. She'll be all agog to see us all here together." Mrs Martin led them into the private salon where they could be comfortable.

Ellen explained about not being able to marry during Lent and Joan Thompson and Dulcie Martin said the same thing applied in their church as well. "We're not really so far apart in our beliefs as you think. We're happy to go along with any day you like. So you and Mrs Harvey decide, Miss Goode."

"We would have to marry in the early morning," said Ellen Harvey, "as we'll have nuptial mass and have to fast. What about nine?"

"So nine o'clock it is, and what day?" asked Mrs Thompson. "Easter Monday is the eighteenth; would that be a good idea, or the Sunday?"

"Sunday would be good for us," said Ellen. "We can have the service at the usual Mass time. Then go to the other church."

"So we'd have our service at about ten-thirty, or eleven?" asked Joan. They all agreed this sounded sensible, but they would have to ask their prospective spouses.

The discussion then turned to who they would have to stand with them as witnesses. Soon it was all settled to everyone's satisfaction. Only Beth was to dress as a new bride, as all the others had been married before and thought they should show some decorum.

They'd have their own special people alongside them at the altar. Mrs Martin was to ask Dora Davis to be her maid of honour, Joan Thompson wanted Mary Smith, and Ellen thought that Kate Johnson would be pleased. Beth said she wanted Polly and Olga to be flower girls, and Cathy Johnson and Jane Kelly to be maids. "Now we have to make a list of the guests," said Joan. "I think we should just write lists and compare them next time we meet, and talk to the men about who they want to stand with them."

"I'd better get away home. We still have a month to get it all sorted out, but I think we have done well to get this far," said Mrs Harvey.

CHAPTER 83 Progress is Made

Ru was worried. Betty didn't seem as happy as she was when they first moved to the cabin. Joseph was really enjoying being out with the men and Betty liked working with Mrs Johnson, but there was an undercurrent that Ru could see no reason for. He'd ask Betty straight out what the matter was. Perhaps she was missing living at the pa.

He wanted to return to the Harvey farm to recover his mere on the quiet if he could. He could go out there on Sunday when O'bie and Ellen Harvey might be going to church. The boss had told him about the weddings and how Ellen had become a Catholic so the chances were that they would be away from the farm for part of the day. He didn't want to be seen as the bush that had concealed him before was almost gone.

That night as they lay in bed, Ru asked Betty if she'd like to go out to see her family on Sunday. She was very pleased at the idea. For a moment she was tempted to mention her fear of Arthur Peat and his strange ways, but kept quiet.

On Sunday, they walked the miles back to the pa, arriving before lunch. O'bie and Ellen passed them on their way to the village, but waved without stopping to talk. Joseph had ridden on Ru's shoulders part of the time. It was a long way for his little legs to trot.

As soon as they'd eaten the food Rangi and May had ready for them, Ru excused himself, saying he wanted to see how O'bie was getting on with the bush felling. He set off down the road to Harvey's farm.

The cabbage trees were still standing. Ru knew which one had the axe hidden in its hollow trunk, but he couldn't reach it with his hand, no matter how he stretched down into the dark interior. He would have to cut the bowl down to the ground. If he could find O'bie's saw lying around he could do that. But there were no tools left out. He'd have to go to the shed and find something to do the job which made the chance of being found out much greater.

He ran for his life to the house, and soon returned with a sharp saw, then set about lowering the bowl to ground level. It only took a few minutes to have the trunk down and, when he reached into the cavity he felt huge relief when his hand clasped the handle of the mere. He took the cut part of the tree and added it to the heap of branches and stumps left by O'bie, ready for burning, and returned the saw to the shed. Then he fastened the mere securely to his waistband, covering it with his coat.

When Ru returned to the pa he was pleased to see how happy Betty was looking. To give time for she and Betty to talk, May had sent Joseph to see his cousins, then told Betty, now very relieved, about Father Brady's visit and that she mustn't worry any more.

Soon it was time to retrace their steps. Joseph wanted to stay with May, but Betty said she'd miss him too much. Away back down the road they went, laden with bags of food and some new clothes for Joseph that May had been given.

Back at their cabin, Ru wondered where he could safely hide the mere. It was old and valuable and had been his grandfather's who had been given it by an old tohunga many years ago.

———— ✦ ————

Jerry Jenkins studied the sign hanging above his doorway. It read 'J.C.Jenkins, Solicitor, At your Service.' Now he'd decided to stay in the district, he needed work that would give him a reputation for winning cases, and fighting battles for little people.

He was determined to keep his nose clean this time. He didn't want to go to prison again. He'd had a run-in with the law, but had managed to explain away the small discrepancy in the funds he'd been given to invest by an elderly lady who trusted him. He'd been able to convince the judge that he was not a thief, only a bit casual in his record-keeping. But that was all in the past.

The partners in the building firm were all honest people and you were judged by your associates, weren't you? It was a new beginning and he must be wary of any thoughts of straying from the straight and narrow.

The problem was that the building firm was doing well but was not enough to keep him employed full time. There were some cases of land being taken up by squatters, and the Maoris were trying to prove they had only leased the land and not sold it outright. This might be an opening for him. But he must not get offside with the townsfolk or Member of Parliament. No, he'd have to tread carefully and not step on any toes.

He reread the letter he'd received from his wife just this morning. She was still adamant that she'd not make the trip to New Zealand yet. He could only hope she would miss him and change her mind. He was tired of living alone but didn't want to make the mistake of setting up house with a local girl. That would not do his image any good at all.

He turned his mind to the papers he was drawing up for the mill owner who wanted to make sure his accounts were kept up to date and that the building firm paid up regularly. The bill should be paid by the twentieth of the following month, and a ten percent penalty would be added to any outstanding amount. There was a large workforce at his own business to be paid and he had no wish to carry the load for John Johnson and Co. The mill owner had spent some time setting out his wishes and demands, and Jenkins fully agreed with the soundness of his arguments. He set about writing the agreement, adding a clause that would ensure that once signed it would be binding on both parties. The mill owner was a hard man.

After lunch he walked down to the site of the house being built for Amos Porter and Dulcie Martin. He'd done the work on the sale of the section and wanted to see the progress. The frame was up and he was very impressed at the way the men were working. He chatted with the foreman for a while before he went to the store for some items of food for the larder.

Billy-the-broom was just setting out on the afternoon delivery and he watched as the wagon moved off with its heavy load. Dickson seemed to be doing well and was building a new store down the road, out of the way of the river.

Mrs Dickson greeted him in a friendly way, and asked how he liked living in Greytown. He replied he was feeling very settled and ready for business and left feeling happier and more part of the community.

CHAPTER 84 A New Beginning for Arthur

When the crate of goods arrived from Napier Arthur Peat was glad his sister had included his clothes. The ones he'd been given by Johnson were frayed and soiled and he was glad to be able to show a more presentable image to the world. He'd thought long and hard about what Johnson had said but was sure that if he kept his word nothing more would be mentioned. Keen to find a new place to live, he looked in the window of the store for notices of rooms to rent.

One that he liked the sound of was with a widow with two children, but he thought he'd be better to take another, a one-roomed cottage with a workroom. He could work at the mill, or for the builders, and then spend his spare time painting portraits of the locals. The gentry were always wanting studies of their children or themselves, to hang on the walls of their homes. His sister had included a letter for him from his mother. He must write to her and let her know that he was starting again and living the good life she had always wanted for him. He could only thank God that he had stumbled on the Johnsons when he was on his way to Wellington.

If only he could get Ru's wife to sit for him, he'd be satisfied. Every detail of the painting was set in his mind. He'd managed to become friendly with Ru and thought he wouldn't object, if he showed him some portraits to demonstrate what he could do.

Kate had tried to tell Betty why Mr Peat had watched her so closely but knew she wouldn't understand until she'd seen some of his work. She decided to drive into town and find out where he was living. She felt it would be somewhere close to town as he only had 'shank's pony' to get around. Mrs Dickson was sure to know. With William settled in his box at her side, she set off, stopping to tell John where she was going. Beauty stepped out smartly and it took no time at all to reach the village.

Mrs Dickson was pleased to see her and helped her down after taking William from his mother. "It's been ages since I've seen you, there's so much to talk about," said Joanna. "Aren't you getting a big boy?" She smiled at William and was rewarded with a huge grin. Kate was surprised as William was usually quite shy with strangers. "Come inside. It's so good to have company."

Settled over a cup of tea, the two women chatted. "I'm looking for the address of Arthur Peat," said Kate. "Have you met him? He found water for us and helped dig the well, but now he's come to live in town and I need to see him."

"He was going to rent a place, a bit out of town, I think, on the Masterton road," said Johanna, "but I don't know if he's moved there yet."

"Oh well, I'll try on the way home if you tell me where to look. Now tell me all the news. I've heard about the weddings. What else is new?"

"Do you know that O'bie and Ellen Harvey are to join the others?" Johanna smiled as Kate looked surprised. "It's all settled and you'll get an invitation soon. Mrs Martin's house is being built and Peter Fairman's will be ready to move into soon. The big day is to be Easter Sunday, but you'll soon hear all the details."

"I'm looking forward to it," said Kate. "Now, how is Catherine Agnes? Is she sleeping through the night yet?" She didn't want Johanna Dickson to ask about why she needed, or wanted, to see Arthur Peat. "Is she feeding well now?"

"Oh yes, she's a little glutton," laughed the new mother, "and she's growing out of her baby clothes. Just look at William rolling over!" The two friends spent a few more minutes discussing the weddings and what they'd wear, and then Kate made her excuses.

Driving along the Masterton road, Kate could see the improvements along the way and felt proud at the way the district was growing. The cottage she'd been told to look for soon came in view. However, the man who opened the door was very different to the Arthur Peat she'd become used to. He was dressed in a well cut suit and had been to the barber for a shave and haircut.

"Good day Mrs Johnson. Do come in. Would you like a cup of tea?" He was very pleased to see Kate, but couldn't help wondering if she knew about his past.

"I can't really stop, thank you Mr Peat. William will be needing his dinner. I just wanted to talk to you about Betty. My husband said you wished to do her portrait and I thought if you gave me a sketch or two to show her she might agree. She's seen you looking at her and misunderstood your motives."

"I'm just unpacking my trunk now. I'll see what's in there. My sister sent it down from Napier and I'm pleased to say she also sent some clothes. It's good to be decent again." He lifted the lid of the crate and shuffled through some paintings. "Here, these should do," he said.

He held up several unframed canvases for Kate to see. They were studies of young women and girls, all beautifully painted. Kate could see that he was a very competent artist indeed. As a girl she'd visited exhibitions in Devon and, while that was a long time ago, she could still recognise an artist with talent. "I'll give you some to show Betty and Ru. I'll only be able to paint at weekends though as I need to earn my living."

"I understand completely and I'll take these and show them with pleasure. I think you'll soon have enough work to keep you painting full time," said Kate. "I hope so anyway."

"You and Mr Johnson have been so good to me. I can never thank you enough. I had a talk with Father Brady and would like to go back to the faith. I've written to my mother as well. It's taken me a long time to find the words, but now I'm ready to begin again."

They walked to the buggy where Kate picked the baby out of his box. Arthur admired the scene. "I'd like to paint you and William too," he said. "You'd make a lovely study."

"Oh I don't know about that," laughed Kate. "Do Betty first, and then we'll see."

Kate drove home thinking about the events of the day. Arthur Peat seemed ready to make a new start. She went over in her mind the things he'd said and wondered if there was a way to persuade Betty to sit for him. She was a beautiful girl, with thick glossy black hair and the high cheekbones and flattened nose of her race. Joseph's features were in between, not Pakeha and not Maori. The paintings she'd seen showed real talent, but where would the work be done?

As she neared home she was still pondering the problem. William had gone to sleep in his box. John came to help lift him down and carry the sleeping baby into the house. Jake came out to take care of Beauty. There was time to have a quiet word with John.

"So how did you get on?" he asked as Kate went to feed the fire. "Here, I'll do that. Did you find Peat?"

"Oh yes, he's very well. You wouldn't recognise him. He's had his things sent down from Napier and showed me some of his art. I brought a few of them home. Jake will bring them in to show you when he settles Beauty. Now I'd better get on with dinner. What do you feel like?"

"Just whatever you like, my dear," said John.

Jake came in with the canvases in his hand and laid them on the table. He looked at them carefully. He didn't understand how anyone could paint like that. He'd seen pictures in the books of art at school, but when you saw the real thing, it's amazing. Kate could see his interest and wondered if this was the answer to her problem. She'd sound him out later.

Once the meal was eaten Kate told John about her visit with Mrs Dickson and the arrangements for the weddings. "It's so exciting," she said as she washed the dishes and handed them to Cathy to dry. "Cathy, Miss Goode wants you and Jane to be her maids, and Polly and Olga will be flower girls. I hope Olga's father will let her."

"Oh, he's good now. Olga is so much happier these days," said Cathy. "I'll have to have a new dress, won't I?"

"I'm sure you will. Miss Goode will have ideas about that. She'll tell us what she wants. She's a very modern young lady, and states her mind. Mr Fairman will have to watch out."

"Oh I don't know about that," said John. "Fairman's a strong chap and will make her toe the line."

"Like you do me?" said Kate, flicking the tea-towel at John.

That night as she lay in bed, Kate asked John how she could get Betty to sit for Arthur Peat and not be in danger of unwanted attention. "I saw how Jake was interested in the paintings and I know he loves to draw. I thought perhaps he could sit in on the sessions and learn some of the tricks. What do you think?"

"It could be all right I suppose, if Peat agrees. He may not want anyone there. Where will he do the work?" John asked. "I don't want Jake tied up for days when he should be helping on the farm."

"I don't know," said Kate. "I haven't even asked Betty yet, and Ru will have something to say as well. Let's just wait and see what happens. We'll have enough to think about with the weddings."

"Good idea, my love, now let's get some sleep before the monster wakes up," said John, looking at the cradle. "He's getting too big for that. I'll have to make him a new one. I saw a cot in an advertisement in the paper. It looked a good design. I'll have another look at it and see what I can do."

"That's a good idea. I don't want him to be falling out. He's very active now." Kate sighed, turned over and closed her eyes. "Good night, John."

CHAPTER 85 More Wedding Arrangements

The coach from Masterton arrived on time. Reverend Porter stepped down and collected his case. He'd been away for a few days seeing his flock and had been pleased with his reception from the people he met. They were all in favour of his marriage to Mrs Martin, but some would rather have had him build his home up in Masterton instead of Greytown. He assured them that he'd be visiting them often enough and asked one or two to attend the wedding.

As he walked along to the hotel he was pleased to see Mrs Martin coming towards him. He kissed her gently, aware their every move was being watched by somebody. "Let's go and see the house," she said. "You'll be amazed at the progress. I'll be able to get my furniture out of storage soon."

"I'm glad to hear that. It'll be good to have a home of our own and not be at the hotel. Bill Evans is a good host but I can't wait to move into our own place. We can have a garden, some fruit trees and a place for my horse." As they strolled along, he asked who he should ask to be his best man. "I'd like to ask Doctor McDonald. Do you think he would do it?"

"Well, here we are at his door," said Mrs Martin. "Let's go and ask."

Annie McDonald hurried to answer their knock, and was relieved to see it wasn't an emergency. "Come in, come in. My husband is in the sitting room. He's had a busy morning but a quiet afternoon. I think he's dozing. Wake up Alex, you have visitors."

The doctor rubbed his eyes and sat up. "I must have dropped off," he said. "Do sit down. It's nice to see you. The house is coming along nicely."

"We're just going to look it over and see when we might be able to move in," said the vicar. "It's not long 'til the wedding, and that's why I am here. I'd like you to be my best man. Would you do it?"

"I'd be delighted. What do you think of that, Annie?"

"I think it's a lovely idea," she said. "Who will be bridesmaid, do you know?"

"I'm writing to Dora Davis to ask her. She was so good when I stayed there. I don't know many people and I like her. I'm sure she could find someone to mind the boarding house."

The two men shook hands and the soon to be married couple left to go next door to see their house and check on progress with the foreman. He was a man of few words and didn't spend much time showing them around, only telling them to be careful where they walked and not to get in the way. They could see the layout and which room would be the sitting-room and which the kitchen. It was looking even larger now than it had when marked out on the ground. Mrs Martin was happy with it, and if she was, so was the vicar.

They walked down Main Street arm in arm, stopping to see Peter Fairman and chat for a moment or two. Amos Porter asked who would stand with him at the altar. "Have you made up your mind?"

"Yes, I've asked Henry Dickson and he agreed I 'm pleased to say. I had thought to ask Johnson, but O'bie wants him. What about you?"

"I've just asked Doctor McDonald and he said yes, so it's all arranged. The ladies will do the rest. We just need to turn up on the day," said Amos Porter with a smile, "and pay for the breakfast. I suppose."

"Split it four ways, do you think? We've put a lot of cash into the building scheme and there won't be any profit for a while, but we'll all get by."

"That sounds fair to me. I expect that Bill Evans will be able to provide a light luncheon for the guests. Have you got a list of those you wish to invite? There won't be a lot of room in the church-house," said Amos. "I think that most of the guests are the same for all of us, but don't worry if there are some special friends you and Miss Goode want to ask. I have only one or two. I'm sure there'll be room." He looked at Mrs Martin for her thoughts, but she just nodded her head. She had been considering the layout of her new kitchen and had lost track of what the men were saying.

"We'd better let you get on. We've held you up long enough," said Mrs Martin, shaking the blacksmith's hand. "You are fortunate to have found such a charming young lady as Miss Goode. I hope you'll be very happy together."

"I know I'm very lucky, and so are you both. I do wish you all the best. Thank you. I think we'll all do very well together. But it will be a busy three weeks if we are to get everything done on time." Peter picked up his hammer to begin work again.

CHAPTER 86 Memories of Home for Kate

Betty and Joseph arrived at Kate's door early next morning. John wanted an early start on ploughing the paddock where the potatoes had been. Kate was glad to see her and set Joseph a place at the table with Cathy and Jake. He was very fond of porridge, and loved the brown sugar and cream. Betty said she'd eaten, and would start the washing if that was what Mrs Johnson wanted her to do. She was learning all aspects of housework and in time could perhaps get a position as a housekeeper. Ru would provide for her and Joseph, Kate knew, but anything she could teach Betty would never go astray.

After the children left for school, over a cup of tea Kate approached the possibility of Betty sitting for her portrait. She showed her Mr Peat's paintings, explaining the reason he'd watched her as well as she could. Betty was not sure Ru would agree but was rather excited at the idea. May had told her about talking to Father Brady, but she still had some reservations. A girl in one of the paintings was holding a young baby, a sort of Maori 'Mother and Child' Madonna. It was very appealing.

"I thought that if you had someone with you, it would be easier. Jake is very keen to learn how to paint. He has a bit of talent, but none of the materials he'd need. If he sat in on some of the lessons he'd be company for you and you'd be quite safe. I haven't asked Mr Peat if he'd agree to that, but he is coming out this weekend. Perhaps we can talk about it then. What do you think?"

"I don't know. I'll have to ask Ru. He got on all right with Mr Peat when he was doing the well but Rangi might have told him about the other business. When he comes back, you show him pictures and see what he says."

"I think that will be all we can do. But it would be a great honour to have your portrait painted. You might be hung in a city gallery one day. Your picture on the wall I mean, not hung by the neck," laughed Kate as Betty looked scared.

"Well Missy Kate, I don't know why he wants me, but I hope Ru says yes. Now I better get on with making lunch for the men. What do you want to give them?"

The men were pleased to see Betty arriving with the lunch basket and tea billy. John started a fire and set the billy to boil. The work had gone well. The three men sat around on logs talking about the best way to sow the grass seed. Native grass was all right but better pasture came from better seed and cows could eat a large amount of pasture in a few days. Imported seed was expensive, but gave a good cover with a high proportion of white clover.

After a while, when there was a lull in the talk, John told Ru about the paintings he'd seen, and that Kate was going to ask Betty to sit for the artist. "Mr Peat has been watching Betty as he wants to paint her. He thinks he could do a great study of her with Joseph. What do you think?"

"I don't know boss, might give her high ideas eh?" Ru said.

"No, she's a sensible girl. It would give the man a real chance to stay around here and paint portraits, as well as some survey work. He's making a big effort to start a new life. My wife thinks she'll get him to give Jake some lessons. He's not bad with a pencil. When Peat comes out this weekend we'll ask him about that then," said John. He bent to lift the billy from the fire and throw in a handful of tea leaves. "Think it over."

Rangi looked at John, wondering how much he knew about Peat. Father Brady had told him Betty should be careful. He hadn't told Ru yet and decided to wait and see before he spoke up. Peat had better be sincere about his new start, or he would feel the mere hitting his head. Ru was a force to be reckoned with if he got angry.

Betty gathered up the lunch things and walked back up to the house. Jake's dog had come along for the walk. Betty was glad of his company, even when he rushed off down the path after a rabbit. She thought about Joseph's father. Poor old Maurice, she was glad he was no longer a threat. She didn't want to give up Joseph, even if it meant he could have a better life. Ru would look after them both, she was sure.

When she reached the house Joseph was asleep on Kate's couch. He'd had a busy morning playing with William, rolling around on the floor trying to teach him to crawl. Kate was out in the garden, planting out some winter vegetables. "Come and look at the fruit trees," called Kate. "They're doing so well. We're going to plant them out in the paddock when my husband puts up a fence. The cows would love to chew them up, and so would the ponies."

"They look pretty good Missy Kate," said Betty. "The men enjoyed their lunch. They pretty hungry, eh?" She looked at Kate, waiting for her to give her something to do, but Kate was too busy planning the orchard.

"You've done enough today, Betty. I can't work you to death," said Kate. She didn't want the girl to think she was a slave-driver. It was a help to have her take the men their lunch. She would've had to harness the buggy and take William with her if Betty wasn't around to do it. "I'm going to look through some boxes in the shed where I have some tea-cloths and tablecloths stored. I want to find something to give the brides. I don't have much use for that sort of thing here, but they'll all have nice new houses with proper dining rooms and sitting rooms and would find more use for them. Come and see." Kate led the way to the stables where John had given her space to store the tin trunk, safe from the mice and mildew.

Betty's eyes opened wide as Kate lifted some beautifully embroidered cloths from the trunk. They were wrapped in tissue paper for protection and the colours were still as bright as when they were packed. Kate thought of the hours of work that had gone into them. 'I'll never use them,' she thought. 'I might as well give them to the brides.' She'd already given a large tablecloth to Annie McDougal when she married Alex McDonald.

Betty watched with awe as layer after layer of paper was removed to reveal the contents of the trunk. The exquisite detail in the flowers, scenes and all manner of designs, were a credit to Kate. She had been taught by her mother and later, when she showed talent, had gone to the convent where nuns gave lessons to augment their meagre living. "The nuns were so strict. I remember how much unpicking I had to do," she explained to Betty. Even so, Kate had loved the time with them. Just looking at the contents of the trunk brought back happy memories of her youth, and she felt like weeping for the days gone by.

She gave herself a good mental shake, and laughed. "So what do you think, Betty? Will the brides like these?"

"Oh yes Missy Kate. They're beautiful. What are these red flowers? What is the grain?" asked Betty, pouncing on a small cloth with a design of poppies and corn in each corner. "And these birds?" she asked as she saw the bluebirds of happiness and pink ribbons decorating another. "They're beautiful."

"Why, thank you Betty. I love them too, but...."

"You made them all?" asked Betty.

"No, not all, my sister Maud and my Mother did some," said Kate as she sorted the items into piles. "See, some have napkins to go with them. Don't they look pretty?"

"I wish I could do something like that," said Betty. "Could you teach me?"

"I could try," said Kate. "Betty, you've given me an idea. Cathy might like to learn too. Maybe even her friend Jane. We could become a little sewing circle. Let's take these inside and I'll wash and press them up for the big day."

The two women found Joseph amusing William. Kate was surprised to see William was quite happy and not crying for her. "You're a good boy Joseph. William loves you," she said. Joseph hung his head. He was still shy, but he smiled broadly.

Just then, the children came clattering into the yard on their ponies and Dot set up a racket, wanting to be let off the chain. "Goodness, is it that late?" said Kate as Cathy came into the room, her eyes lighting on the piles of cloths.

"Oh Mother! Aren't they beautiful. Were they in the trunk?"

"Yes. I've just unpacked them. I'm going to give them to the brides as wedding presents," said Kate.

"No Mother, don't give them away. Did you make all of them?" asked Cathy putting her hand out to touch them.

"No touching with those paws, please. Wash your hands and I'll see," said

Kate, looking at the ink-stained fingers. "You should go home now Betty, and thanks for your help. See you tomorrow?"

"Yes Missy Kate. You remember, you gonna teach me eh?" said Betty, as she took Joseph by the hand. "You say good-bye Joseph," but Joseph just hung his head.

Cathy returned from washing her hands and looked at the embroidery carefully. She wished she could do work like that. Kate felt proud of them too. "Auntie Maud and Grandma did some of them for me. We would sit by the fire in the winter time and either knit or sew, or read books. How about I give you some lessons in the winter; Betty would like to learn too. Maybe Jane would as well. It's very satisfying. Now I must think about dinner and put these away. Set the table please, dear."

"Mother, Miss Goode told me she'd needs an adult in the wedding party because we're too young to sign the register. She asked me to ask you to be that person. She's sorry she hasn't been able to ask you herself," said Cathy.

"Well, I don't know. I'll have William to watch. I'll ask your father what he thinks. O'bie wants him for best man." Kate paused. "I'd like to do it for her. Surely someone will be able to watch William."

"Polly and Olga have tried on the frocks Miss Goode made for them. They're so excited. Jane and I are going to try ours on after school on Friday. I can't wait." Cathy placed the cutlery on the table and swirled around the room. "Miss Goode is making them all."

"I must get your father to give her the money for your dress," said Kate.

"Miss Goode said she'd pay for all of the material for them. I know she wants to pay for Polly and Olga's. We can keep them to wear," said Cathy, as she finished laying the table.

Once the meal was over Kate talked over the plans for the big day. John agreed that if Miss Goode wanted Kate to be in the party there should be no problem. "It'll all be over in a few minutes."

"How's the building going?" asked Kate. "Is anything completed yet?"

"Nearly. That Australian bloke is a fast worker and has the men working very well. Dickson's shop has the roof on now. I'm proud of the men. I saw Eddie Browne when I went to the mill to see about timber. He's been asked to be best man for Paul Jones. There'll be more wedding party than guests if any more join in," said John with a smile.

"Now, have you thought about Jake and Mr Peat? Will you let Jake sit in on the sessions?" asked Kate.

"So long as his work gets done I don't mind at all," said John.

CHAPTER 87 Betty Sits for Arthur

Arthur decided to hire a trap rather than a horse as it wasn't much dearer and would make transporting his materials out to the farm easier. He'd sorted through his stock of paper and canvases and had some brushes and pencils for Jake to use. It was quite exciting to be back in a tutoring role. He'd trained as a surveyor to please his father and had studied art at night. In his final year he had been a part time tutor as well. Now he was ready to start over again.

Kate had told Betty to ask Ru if she could come on Saturday to talk with Mr Peat about sitting for him, and here she was bright and early with Joseph still rubbing the sleep out of his eyes. When Mr Peat arrived he spoke to Ru and Rangi about his painting and they were quite happy for Betty to sit for him after they had seen the portraits. "You plurry good artist eh?" said Ru.

Ru and Rangi went off down to the bush to continue stumping with John. Jake quickly did his chores while Mr Peat set up in part of the stables with his easel, a bench for Jake to work on, and chairs for Betty and Joseph.

Mr Peat gave Jake some paper and charcoal to use and encouraged him to follow what he was doing on his canvas, giving him some instruction as he sketched Betty, but it was very hard. He wondered if he'd ever be able to make a picture like Mr Peat.

After some time of quiet work Mr Peat came to see what Jake had done. "You're doing well, Jake," he said. "Don't try to go so fast. Some famous artists take years to finish a portrait."

"I know," said Jake. "I've seen books on art at school. Mrs Thompson gives us lessons, but she doesn't have much time. We only have drawing once a week. I wish it was more." And he went to have another look at Mr Peat's work.

Meanwhile, Joseph had soon grown tired of siting still with Betty so Kate took him to play with William. He was delighted to go, and soon had William laughing as they rolled around the kitchen floor.

When Kate came to offer them a cup of tea Betty was pleased to stand and walk around. It was hard trying to keep in one position and she was pleased when Mr Peat told her he had enough to go on with and he'd see her again next Saturday.

Arthur Peat drove home and unloaded his materials, before taking the trap back. He was pleased at the progress made and decided to suggest Betty come and sit for him at his house when he was a bit further ahead with the portrait. He didn't mind having Jake there too. The boy was quite good but would need years of tuition before he could be considered an artist.

As he walked back from the stables along Main Street he saw the sign on the lawyer's office door. 'J. C. Jenkins.' Oh, that name is familiar. So this is where you've got to, Jerry. I wonder if you're up to your old tricks.

Arthur knocked at the door and went in. Jerry didn't look pleased to see him, but invited him to sit and offered a spot of whisky. "So what brings you down here? I thought you were in Napier."

"I was glad to leave the place after I got out. I did some work as a surveyor, but fell on hard times as they say. I happened to meet up with the Johnsons. They've been very good to me and, in case you think you can blackmail me, I've told them the truth about my past. What about you? Have you made a clean start?"

"I believe I have, Peat. I'm trying to stay on the straight and narrow. I want my wife to come out here, but so far she refuses. I'm working up a good clientele among the business people and don't want to go wrong. Perhaps it's the company of the people here that makes it easier to stay within the law. Somehow the thought of another jail sentence helps too," Jenkins said and he refilled their glasses.

As they talked the atmosphere became friendlier by the minute. Both were lonely, in need of company, and both wished to begin again. It was growing dark before Arthur Peat decided to go home. They shook hands, vowing to stay silent about their falls from grace. It was a new beginning for each of them and they needed to trust and depend on each other.

Jenkins thought of the money he'd deposited in the bank for Johnson and his mates, and of how close he'd been to using some to send to his wife. Peat would keep him from making any mistakes, as if the thought of a term in prison again was not enough. He wasn't sorry he'd seen Peat again. They'd suffered in prison, but had served their time. Now they had another chance, they must make the most of it.

CHAPTER 88 At Last!

Finally the big day arrived, sunny and warm. The church house was packed with the usual congregation as well as Ellen and O'bie's friends. Others stood outside, including Doris Bell who had told her neighbour she wasn't going to miss seeing Ellen Harvey and O'bie married. She'd known all along that something was going on. "It's time he made an honest woman of her," she said. "I mean...." But the neighbour didn't wait to hear what she meant.

Father Brady began by welcoming those present and began the Mass while Dennis, as altar boy, performed his duties very seriously. The service proceeded until, before the gospel reading, Father Brady asked the bridal group to come forward and blessed them before asking the old traditional questions.

"Who gives this woman in matrimony?"

"I do," replied John, and so the ceremony continued.

"Do you take this woman, Ellen Harvey, to be your lawful wedded wife?" asked Father.

"I do," said O'bie, smiling and handsome in his dark suit.

"And you, Ellen, do you take this man, Patrick O'Brien, to be your lawful wedded husband?"

"I do," replied Ellen looking prettily happy in her blue silk gown and matching bonnet.

"I now pronounce you man and wife. You may kiss the bride." And the congregation smiled and clapped. Father Brady then read the gospel from Corinthians about love and charity and instructed the couple to always love and respect each other and to carefully listen to what each said. He then gave communion to the faithful.

Afterwards, the congregation stood about outside giving the happy couple their good wishes, then buggies and traps, loaded with a merry mix of families, made their way along Main Street to Saint Luke's Anglican Church.

Meanwhile, the schoolroom was full of excitement as the school mistresses and their attendants prepared for their weddings.

Beth Goode had hurried away from the service at the church house to dress Polly and Olga with Tessa Kelly's help. Kate was helping Cathy and Jane with their frocks. Beth had made four delightful frocks of muslin in shades of pink and green with sprays of daisies and the children were so excited theycould hardly stand still as buttons and domes were done up and circlets of daisies were placed on their heads.

Then Beth Goode and Joan Thompson were helped to dress. Soon it was time to walk the short distance to the church where Paul Jones waited with Eddie Browne at his side.

Amos had thought it best to marry Paul Jones and Joan Thompson first, and then have Beth Goode arrive with her attendants, so she could make a grand entrance. After all, it was her special day. After she and Peter Fairman were married, he and Dulcie Martin would say their vows, with Doctor McDonald officiating as a Justice of the Peace since the magistrate was away.

Mrs Thompson looked lovely in a silk gown trimmed with pearls and a corsage of late roses, as Mary Smith followed her up the aisle to take their places beside the groom and best man. Dressed in cassock, surplice and stole, the vicar began the service in the time honoured manner, "Dearly beloved, we have come together...." and then spent a few minutes reminding the congregation of the sanctity of marriage. The answers were given with firm voices and once again a couple were pronounced man and wife to the applause of the congregation.

Now it was time for Beth Goode and her attendants to arrive. John went to the door to escort her to the altar and, to the sound of a piper playing a lively march, Beth and John proceeded down the aisle, the four girls taking care to look as solemn as the occasion demanded.

When Beth reached Peter Fairman's side he took her hand and gave it a little squeeze. She was so lovely. The veil covering her face did nothing to hide her beauty. There was a fresh country goodness there that nothing could disguise. He was so lucky.

Reverend Porter was ready to begin the service, and soon was asking the question that was being heard for the third time this morning.

"Who gives this woman in matrimony?"

Alex McDonald replied "I do" and the service proceeded with Peter promising to love, honour and cherish Beth, until "death do us part". Then Beth made the same vows, also agreeing to "obey" Peter and abide by his decisions. Eddie Browne produced the ring which Peter placed carefully on his bride's finger and the blessing concluded the ceremony.

It was then the turn of Amos Portrer himself. Dulcie Martin and Dora Davis took their places at the altar and Amos took his place beside his bride. Alex McDonald as celebrant wasted no time giving advice on how to live and love each other as they'd had three lessons on the sanctity of marriage already that morning. Instead, he began with "Who gives this woman in holy matrimony?" And when John replied, "I do" the service continued.

Dora Davis took Dulcie's bouquet while she removed her glove so she could receive the ring Amos Porter had been handed by Paul Jones. He'd agreed to fill the role of best man for Amos after Alex had agreed to marry them when the magistrate was unavailable. It was a merry mix up, but now it was all done.

After the register was signed in the side room by all three couples the piper lead them from the church with the children following them carefully down the aisle, and out into the sunshine of a lovely autumn day.

There a surprise awaited them as children from the school, lined up on each side along the pathway, showered them with rose petals as they passed. Even Ellen and O'bie, who had come to see the others wed.

The sun was quite hot for April and the children, their job done, were excitedly running around and chasing one another. As it had been his idea to have the line-up Jake tried to call them to order to tell them they could go home now but few took any notice. He looked at his father to back him up but he was in conversation with the doctor. Oh well, he had done what he could. Mrs Thompson would settle them down. Oops. She was Mrs Jones now. It sounded strange.

The Kellys, with William, stood with Johanna Dickson looking at the brides and their bridegrooms standing in the shade of the totara tree. "Isn't Beth Goode clever? The girls look so lovely," said Johanna, shifting Catherine on her arm. Just then Kate came up to reclaim her son and thank Tessa. "I think Miss Goode is just beautiful," Tessa said. "I always thought she was shy, and look at her now."

Kate agreed. "You're right, Mrs Kelly. I couldn't get a word out of her on the boat. She was so sad after her little charge died. But look at her now. They make a lovely couple."

"It's a beautiful day for beautiful weddings. I don't want it to end. The brides all look lovely and so happy. I wonder what life will bring for them?" said Johanna.

Tessa Kelly looked around for her husband and saw him talking to O'bie and Ellen. She wondered if everyone was ready to go to the hotel. She could do with a good cup of tea. A good big cup of tea was just what the doctor ordered. She wasn't going to say anything, but she'd missed a couple of months now and didn't think it was the change. Young William was a handful, but it had been lovely to hold a baby again, even just on loan. Oh well, time would tell. She hadn't told Paddy either. He might find it too hard to resist celebrating, and there was enough to celebrate today already.

When everyone arrived at the Rising Sun for the reception they found the publican, Martha and Molly had done them proud. The dining room looked lovely with white tablecloths and flowers. A cold buffet was set ready to be enjoyed. At one end a long table was set for Beth and Peter and their attendants. The others sat with their friends at round tables in groups of eight.

Mr and Mrs Petersen sat with the Dicksons. John and Kate joined them. "It's lovely to see you here," said Kate. "You must be proud of Olga."

"Ya ya. We very proud of her," said Mrs Petersen. "I not speak much English. You please excuse me for mistakes ya?"

"Not at all," said Kate. "You're doing very well." Tessa and Paddy Kelly came to sit with them too but when the men began to discuss the mill and the building work Kate and Johanna held up their hands. "Not today. No business today. Please."

"Quite right," said John. "Let's have a drink instead." So the men rose and went to the bar together.

"Whiskys all round?' said Petersen.

Paddy Kelly shook his head, saying "Ginger ale for me."

When the meal was eaten, John tapped a wine glass and called for attention. He said what a wonderful day it had been, and called for the guests to drink the health of the brides and grooms. A murmur of voices filled the room as each couple was toasted. Then he asked Peter and Beth Fairman to cut the wedding cake which had been made by Mrs Annie McDonald. They came forward shyly. Their hands together on the knife, they cut through the shiny coat of frosting. Martha came to take away the bottom layer to cut for the guests to taste.

There were three other cakes on a side table, ready for the ceremony to continue with the other couples. They also came forward and with much toasting and clapping carried out the tradition of sharing a piece. Kate looked around at all her friends and thought how lucky they all were. To all be friends and part of such a gathering.

After Martha returned with the plates of cake Polly and Olga took them around those gathered at the tables. They were enjoying the party atmosphere, feeling very important as they received many compliments. Olga had never seen her parents out at a gathering together, as her mother was very shy, but here she was, laughing and joking with the other ladies.

Soon it was time to go home. Gigs and buggies were brought around to the door and the newly married couples drove away with cheers and good wishes following them down the roadway.

CHAPTER 89 More New Beginnings

Ellen and O'bie made their way to the farm in a happy mood. Everything had gone to plan. They didn't feel like talking and were satisfied to let the horse plod along as they sat together holding the reins, an arm about each other. Their peace was not to last. As the horse turned in the gateway, Ellen let out a shriek. Her garden was a shambles. The pigs had got out of their paddock and rooted up the garden. "I asked you to fix the fence," she cried.

O'bie hung his head. "I'm so sorry Ellen," he said.

Dulcie and Amos Porter had booked rooms at a hotel in Carterton and made their way there as soon as they could get away from people wanting to shake their hands. Dora kissed Mrs Porter on both cheeks and wished her well. "Come and see me," she said, as Amos flicked the reins and clicked his tongue to start the horse. He'd not long owned the buggy but they were soon pointed in the right direction and bowling along on the road.

"Well Mrs Porter, how do you feel?" Amos asked.

"Very well indeed, sir. It all went very well, didn't it," said Dulcie. "Doctor McDonald did a good job, didn't he?"

"Yes he did. He's more than just a doctor. He's a true friend to all the people in the town. And Annie, she's so worried about his health. She won't let him overdo it if she can help it." Amos flicked the horse with his whip and they moved along faster. There was still plenty of daylight, but they had to negotiate the river bridge before they reached Carterton. He put his mind on the task in hand and went at a steady pace.

They clattered over the wooden planks of the bridge without bother. Sometimes horses would baulk at going across, and would have to be led. They reached their hotel, and were soon in the room Amos had requested, happy with each other.

———— ∞∞∞ ————

Paul drove the gig out into the countryside with a smile on his face, not saying where they were headed. His bride thought that perhaps he'd booked a room at the Gladstone hotel. It would be a long drive this late in the afternoon. But, once over the Waiohine bridge, he turned the horse down a narrow road to the east, Waihakeke Road. The road was just a gravel track, and she bounced along the seat until Paul put his arm around her to steady her and hold her tightly to him. A short while later he pulled the horse to a halt outside a farm gate, and pointed to a cottage set back from the road. A dog came down the driveway barking loudly, and ran around sniffing the wheels of the gig and the horse's legs, where he got a short shift.

"Well my darling," said Paul. "What do you think of our new home? I signed the deal last week and wanted to surprise you."

"It looks lovely dear," said Joan, trying to recover from the drive.

Paul opened the gate and drove into the yard. He helped her down and opened the door of their home. He went first and lit a lantern to show her the way in as she stood at the door. Once the lantern was lit, he picked her up and carried her over the doorstep. "Welcome to our home," he said.

Joan didn't know what to say. This was a real surprise. She knew Paul was looking for a farm to buy, but had no idea he'd found one to suit his needs. "When did you acquire this place?" she asked, a little annoyed that he hadn't told her.

"Just last week, I didn't tell you as I wanted to surprise you and I have," said Paul, laughing. "It's a nice wee place and it's not too far from town. I thought you could drive in to school if you want to stay teaching, or keep your home and come out here at the weekends and holidays. I do hope you're not cross with me."

She couldn't find words to answer him with. Even if it had been done with the best of intentions, she was not used to having decisions made for her. "I'm sure we will be able to come to an agreement when we've talked it over. You know I don't want to give up teaching, but I'll try to be a loving wife and do what you think is best. The children fill a big place in my life," said Joan.

"I know my dear. I don't want you to stay home and coddle me. I've other things on my mind now and it's been a long day." Paul held out his arms to Joan, who came willingly to his side. He kissed her tenderly as he led her to their room.

———— ∞∞∞ ————

The workmen laid down their tools and left for home as Peter and Beth walked up to the door of their new home. It had been a rush job to finish enough of the house to make it habitable. They were sensitive to the needs of the young couple, but could not refrain from giving Fairman a few nods and winks as they passed him while Beth looked away and pretended not to notice. The blacksmith was well thought of and had real standing in the community. They knew better than to upset him.

There were some nice pieces of furniture in place already, as Peter had ordered some from Wellington and bought some locally as well. The day was drawing in and there was a chill in the air. Peter went to light the fire and place the kettle to boil. Beth went into the bedroom to change out of her wedding frock. Peter followed her and somehow the kettle never boiled, and the tea was never made until breakfast next morning.

Beth woke first and looked at this man she had married. He was dark and swarthy in a clean countrified way. She traced her fingers around his face, feeling the stubble of a day's growth of beard. 'I truly love him,' she told herself. 'I know we'll be happy.'

CHAPTER 90 After the Weddings

John and Kate were up early next morning. They'd spent a few minutes with the Kellys on the way home and were glad that everything had gone so well. It would be a lovely day to look back on for years to come. Mrs Kelly hadconfided to Kate her suspicion she might be expecting. Kate was delighted for her.

Kate thought she'd write a long letter to her mother telling her all the wedding details. She'd not written much lately, as William took more of her time. He was eight months old and crawling around the kitchen. He loved her pot cupboard, and spent ages banging pot lids together.

Jake was keen to go in to see Arthur Peat, but Kate didn't want him to think he could just go to town anytime he wished. "Just work on your drawing here at home," she said. "Mr Peat may pay us a visit out here anyway."

Sure enough, by mid morning, there was a knock on the door. Arthur stood there, hat in hand, wanting to know if Betty was there. "I'd like to get on with the portrait," he said.

"No, I'm afraid she's having the day off. I think they're going to walk to the pa to see Rangi and May. But Jake is out in the barn working on his drawing."

"What about you and William?" Mr Peat asked. "Have you thought about my offer? I'd do it for nothing because you've been so kind. What did your husband think?"

"I'm not sure what John would think about it. I haven't talked to him about it and I'm too busy today anyway. I'm afraid I'm still getting over yesterday."

"Well, sometime soon I hope." Arthur turned to go. "I hope my past hasn't put you off," he said. "I'm a changed man."

"Not at all, I take people as I find them and judge them by what I find. I'd love to have you do a painting of the family, but not today." Kate brushed hair from her eyes in a sweeping motion. She was anxious to write her letter to her mother while William was asleep and it was all fresh in her mind. "Just go and see Jake."

Arthur Peat looked at the drawings Jake had done and pointed out a few changes that could enhance the shape of the figures. "Look past the head at what's in the background. If you include some of the scenery, it will give more meaning to the images."

They worked together on their projects. Jake could see what he meant and tried his best to use the idea. He looked at the portrait on the easel thinking it was a very good likeness of Betty. Young Joseph's face had a shy smile as he peeped from the cloak Betty wore. Even though it was just a picture Jake could feel a real presence when looking at the little boy.

Kate called them to the house for a cup of tea and took the opportunity to ask Mr Peat what his future plans were. "Are you going to stay around the district?"

"I'd like to. I've been made welcome here, and feel I could use my talents to teach drawing at the school, or work as an artist in my free time. What do you think?"

"I can't really advise you. Just remember you're here on trust. If you really think you can make a life here, do it."

Thanking Kate, he went back to the barn. John had told Jake he'd need his help after lunch. They needed meat, and there was a sheep to be killed and dressed. Jake wasn't sorry. He'd done all he could to his portrait of Betty. He took Dot and made his way to the paddock where the sheep were grazing peacefully. It seemed a shame to cut a life short, but that was the way of farming.

Dot had soon rounded them up and brought them closer to the house so that John could pick out the one for the pot. The cattle lifted their heads as the dog went past them but they were not his target, so continued to lie in the shade of the karaka trees.

There were three of these trees in a group. Jake always stopped to look at the carving of a Maori head on one of the trunks. 'The Maoris must have been here many years before the pakeha,' Jake thought as he examined the carving. There was a burial ground near the river, and skulls had been ploughed up on the land. He must ask Rangi about the carving, it might be important. He was always saying the pakeha must look after any Maori settlements and not destroy their remains.

Jake wandered back to the house with Dot who was racing ahead chasing a rabbit. 'Mmm, rabbit pie. And poor sheep.'

———— ⁂ ————

The day after their wedding, while O'bie and Ellen put a manuka fence around the garden to keep the pigs out, Ellen promised herself that these devils would soon be bacon. They fixed the rails and laced tea tree branches through them to secure the area. There wasn't much they could salvage from the flower beds. She'd just have to begin again.

The memory of the previous evening was painful to them both. They hadn't had a row exactly, but hurt pride kept them apart. O'bie had said how sorry he was and Ellen had said it was as much her fault, as she should have insisted that he fix the fence after one pig had got into the garden a few days ago.

Pig farming was a big part of their lives and gave them some income towards the rent, but Ellen was nearly ready to get rid of the lot of them, sows and all. They could concentrate on the cows. But... what would they do with the milk? No they must not make hasty decisions. "Let's have lunch," said Ellen "We've done enough for today."

O'bie could only agree, hoping they might spend some time 'resting' together. He'd said sorry as many times as he thought fit and now only waited for the word to pick up from where they had left off in the buggy. He went to boil the kettle.

CHAPTER 91 Lost

As the weeks went by things were very quiet after the excitement of the weddings. Life settled down for most of the farmers as cows dried off and the men began to look for things to do. This time of the year was a good time to attend to maintenance.

On their new farm, Joan Jones was getting used to living in the country, with roosters waking them at dawn, and having a few chores to attend to before school. They'd agreed that while the weather was good she should take the gig and drive in each day. Later she'd spend the night at the school-house if it was too wet or windy to drive home.

They were very happy with their lives, and, although they didn't always agree, spent the evenings discussing farming and education with vigour. Some days she wished she didn't have to leave him, but she loved the children too, so for the moment was content to do the best she could for both.

Paul Jones was lonely during the day and wondered if he should look for a boy to employ to help him. He wanted to start a stud farm and breed Romneys. He'd bought some at a sale in Masterton and already had some stock on another farm being grazed by a farmer. They'd need to be driven home now, and yes, a boy would be a big help. He'd go to the pa and see if the kaumatua could find one for him. Or he could ask the men at the mill if any had a son ready to leave school. Most boys were expected to leave after the age of twelve and would be glad of a job which gave them a few bob and board. He would go to see Joan first though. With these ideas going around in his head he caught his mare and rode to Greytown.

What he found there was worry and anxiety. A young girl from the pa was missing. She'd gone to school the previous morning but hadn't returned home in the afternoon. It was most unusual as she was keen to learn, and would have to be really sick before she missed a day. She was May's sister's girl, a sweet natured lass of ten years called Tui. The men from the pa had searched, but found no sign of her. None of the children had seen her leave the school grounds. Jane and Jake had seen her sitting there when the school bell rang at the end of lessons.

"We should tell Constable O'Reilly and get a search party going if she's been gone all night. There must be something wrong for her to stay away," said Paul Jones when he was told. "I'll go and get him?" he offered. The teachers both nodded their heads.

Dan O'Reilly was talking with the doctor who had called to ask about some minor matter but, when told of the missing child, they were on their feet in a moment asking questions about where and when. Gathering up their hats, they made for the schoolhouse where several men from the mill were already waiting for instructions. Ru and Rangi, who had been with the search at the pa the night before, were also there.

Constable O'Reilly soon took charge, allotting places for each group to look in buildings, the bush and along riverbanks. The men searching in the sheds and buildings made short work of the central part of town then went to look in outlying buildings. Only one thing of interest was found - a sketch of a Maori girl, about the right age, in a building which the policeman thought was unoccupied. He thought he knew all that was going on in the district and was surprised he hadn't heard that the building was let. There was no sign of life there so he returned to the schoolhouse to ask if anyone knew who rented it and to show the sketch. Perhaps this was the missing child.

Jake looked at the drawing and immediately knew who the artist was. He liked Mr Peat and didn't think he'd have had anything to do with Tui's absence. But he liked Tui too, so he gave Mr Peat's name to Constable O'Reilly, saying that he had been employed by his father to dig a well. He didn't say he'd been watching the man paint Betty's portrait at the stables at home. He thought the least said the better. It had nothing to do with the missing girl.

The search progressed until dusk fell, filling the bush with eerie shadows. The men were ready to concede defeat so Ru decided to go home and ask Betty if she'd any ideas where Peat might have gone - he may have said something to her when she was sitting for him at the stables. He'd finished that portrait, and had started on one of Kate and William, but hadn't got further than a rough outline as Kate was kept busy and couldn't spare the time. All that Betty could think of was that he'd said he needed to go to Wellington for more art supplies.

Meanwhile, Arthur Peat was making progress through the bush tracks. He'd hoped he'd be far enough away before they looked for him. When he heard that a child was missing he knew he'd get the blame. He'd seen her sitting on a bench in the school yard and stopped to talk. He wanted to paint her picture and had asked her to come to his shack.

She was a shy little thing, uncertain about the request. He'd told her it would only take a little time, and then she could return to the pa. He'd sat her down, quickly made the sketch, and had then sent her on her way with the promise that he'd see her mother at the pa to ask if she might sit for him there. This morning he'd gone to the store for supplies and heard that a child was missing. He knew that it was her.

He wanted to join in the search but thought the lawyer might put his weights up. No, he'd better try to get away. He couldn't use the Rimutaka hill road as everyone who drove or plodded that trail was well and truly noticed. Now he was at the foot of the western ranges and undecided as to where he should go. There was a good climb ahead of him. He tied some string around his trouser legs to stop himself from tripping over. To the south there was a trail around the coast but it was treacherous. There was always the Manawatu Gorge, ninety miles to the north, through heavy bush. Or should he just return and see what had happened. She might have been found by now. I should pray, he thought, and knelt down to ask God what he should do.

There was no sudden shaft of light, but through the trees there came a rider on a roan horse. He stopped briefly to ask if there was any news of the missing girl, and which part of the bush he had searched.

Startled, Arthur quickly told him he'd been looking everywhere but there was no sign of anybody and when the man said they should return to the base and see what was happening he had no answer and agreed.

It was a hard tramp back to the schoolhouse. All the way there he told himself he'd done nothing wrong so had nothing to fear. He shouldn't have taken the child to his shack, but she hadn't been harmed in any way by him. 'Dear God, please let her be found by now,' he prayed. But back at the base he heard there was still no sign of her.

Dan O'Reilly looked at the new searcher with interest. He'd not seen him around before. He usually looked up any recent arrivals and gave them the third degree. You couldn't be too careful. He looked around for Dickson to ask who the tall rangy man was.

"His name's Arthur Peat. He's been doing a bit of work for Johnson. He's an artist. Quite good, so they say," was the reply.

"Was it his shack where the men found the sketch?" asked the constable. "I'll have a word with him, I think."

Peat, who had his back to him, was drinking tea and talking to Fairman when the policeman tapped him on the shoulder. "I'd like a word," he said. Arthur dropped his tin mug and the tea soaked into the grass at his feet. "I'll get you another, Peat, and then you and I can have a talk."

"Yes, if you like. Talk about what?" Arthur Peat asked with a smile and a show of confidence he was far from feeling.

"I'd like to ask you a few questions, so we'll go to the station where it's more private," he said.

At the station, after Arthur was shown the sketch of Tui that had been found in his cabin, Arthur explained what had happened, that it had been stupid of him but he'd wanted to paint the girl. He swore that she had left his shack after about an hour. "That was the last I saw of her," he said, by now thoroughly frightened.

Dan O'Reilly was not convinced, but couldn't hold the man on just the evidence of the sketch. "I'll see you tomorrow," he said. "Don't leave town."

CHAPTER 92 Found

Away from the area of the search, Tui was hobbling along through the bush. She'd taken a short-cut through paddocks, and had tripped and fallen over a stump in the grass, hurting her ankle. She was hungry, thirsty and miserable. Her ankle was swollen but she'd been able to sleep a little. When darkness came the sounds of the bush kept her company with the ruru's call and, at dawn the big heavy kereru were flying about, and the tuis sang. All day she'd hoped for someone to find her and carry her home, but none had. Her ankle was throbbing. She'd found a branch to use as a crutch and hobbled her way closer to the post and rail fence on the road to the pa, wishing with all her heart she'd not been running home so that she could tell her mother about the man.

Tui sat down to rest and to try to think of how she could get someone to find her. If only someone would come before it got dark again. Perhaps one of the dogs from the pa would find her and go for help. Tears flowed, but she couldn't give in. Hopefully she tied her cardigan to a branch and waved it in the air above her head.

Rangi was on his way home. The search had been called off for the day. It was too dangerous to send people out in the dark. His horse was trotting along at a steady pace and Rangi was thinking of the reception he'd get when he told them that Tui had not been found. There'd be a lot of weeping and wailing.

There was a lot of talk about the sketch found at the cabin, but no-one was pointing the finger - yet. Rangi had become quite friendly with Arthur Peat when they were working on the well, and couldn't believe he was capable of hurting anybody. Jake liked him and Betty and Ru were very happy with the painting he'd done of Joseph and Betty. But did he have a dark past?

Suddenly, something close to the post and rail fence caught his eye, a movement in the bracken. What was it? Sure enough, there it was again, something red swaying above the ground. Rangi dismounted and tied the reins to the post. He peered through the dusk to see better and called out. "Tui, girl, is that you?" Tui lowered the branch and called back as loudly as her dry throat would permit.

"Uncle Rangi. Oh Uncle Rangi, I'm here!" she cried. She tried to stand up but the pain was too great. She didn't need to worry. Rangi was over the fence in an instant, gathering her in his arms.

"What you doin' here Tui? We've been lookin' for you all day." Tui cuddled into his chest and sighed. She didn't want to explain. "Come on, I'll get you home," said Rangi as he lifted her carefully through the rails and on to his horse. "You'll be all right."

May and Tui's mother were waiting at the entrance to the pa for news. Then Tui's mother saw what Rangi had in the folds of his jacket. "My baby!" she cried. "Where you been?" Tui hobbled forward, showing the women her ankle.

"Bring her inside Rangi," said May, "I'll have a look at her leg. She might need the doctor eh?"

"I just took a short cut home and fell over a stump and hurt my leg," said Tui. Her tears were drying up now she was safely at home. "Then it got dark."

"Well, you lucky I don't give you a plurry good hiding, eh?" said Tui's mother, but she smiled as she spoke.

"Do you think I should get Doctor McDonald, May?" asked Rangi. "I have to go in to tell them she's been found. Or shall I take her in?"

"No, you ask the doctor to come out here. She's had enough," said May firmly.

Rangi galloped away to give the good news to those still at the schoolhouse. It wasn't far from Papawai to Greytown, and he soon drew rein to dismount and shouted to anyone listening that Tui was safely at home, and he was going to get the doctor to look at her ankle.

Those still there with the teachers were very relieved and wanted to ask Rangi for the story of her rescue, but he was keen to get to the doctor, and gave only a few details before riding on.

Annie McDonald came to the door to see who was troubling the doctor at this late hour. She was so pleased to hear the news she went in to get him without protest. Doctor McDonald had been dozing in his favourite chair and rubbed his eyes as he asked Rangi what was wrong. "Do you think it's broken?" he asked as he gathered up his medicine bag. The portmanteau had seen better days, but was a valued friend. "I'll come as soon as I've put Daisy in the gig."

Rangi nodded and walked down the path to help if he could. Nags could be hard to catch if they thought that their working day was over, but the mare was no trouble and they were soon on their way to the pa.

The doctor examined Tui's ankle, which was very swollen, and did what he could to ease her pain, giving her a powder and binding the ankle firmly. "Now you must rest it and keep it up on a pillow." Suggesting to Rangi that he bring Tui to his surgery in the morning, he said good-night. A full moon was rising as he drove along the gravel road and he gave thanks their worst fears hadn't been realised.

Annie had a hot drink ready for her husband. He hadn't felt the cold as he drove along, but was now shivering as Annie took off his boots and stood them aside before fitting his warm slippers on to his feet. "You should have said you wouldn't go all the way out there this late at night," she said. "You'll catch your death-o-cold." He sipped the hot drink and smiled. He loved Annie so much and rued their wasted years, but oh well...

CHAPTER 93 Letters

The next day, while John was in the village, Jake and Cathy were at school and William was asleep, Kate sat down to write to her mother.

Now, where to start? There was so much to tell her. Rangi told them that morning that the little girl had been found. He'd taken Tui to see the doctor and she was the centre of attention at the pa. Already memories of the weddings were fading. Kate had to think about who did the honours for which bride, but gave a good account of them. She'd seen little of the brides after that day but Mrs

Dickson would be able to give her any news of them. Jake told her that Mrs Jones was driving the gig to school each day and they'd bought a farm near Carterton. I wonder if her Mr Jones is a relation of yours, Mother? His name is Paul and he came from Cornwall.

What else could she write about? Over the months, when she wrote, she'd mentioned many of the people she'd encountered in the settlement and knew that her mother would be pleased to have her assurance that all was well in Greytown. John and Jake had planted out the orchard under her direction and the trees were showing shoots swelling on the bare branches. There was a good crop of winter vegetables and everything was going well on the farm. An artist is painting my portrait holding William and it's progressing well now the poor man had been freed of suspicion of harming a child. The little girl had gone missing and started a huge hue and cry but was found, with just a twisted ankle.

John and the rest of the building company were pleased they had plenty of work for their workmen. Eddie Browne was doing a good job keeping the books. We've all become such good friends I can't believe we haven't known each other for years. They are such lovely people. I do wish you could meet them.

Later that day John returned from the village with a bag of mail - including a letter for Kate from her mother. She settled down to read it in the late autumn sunshine.

The wedding had been held in the church the family had attended for most of their lives and the reception at the hotel where they'd enjoyed dancing and meals together. Kate wished her mother had given more detail so she could imagine the scene but her mother was not one for lengthy descriptions and gave only the bare facts.

They'd gone away to the Lake District for a few days, and had loved the scenery. Keats, Coleridge, Shelley, Wordsworth and Constable were all held in high regard in the area. Places where they'd lived, or written poetry, or painted landscapes were all made much of. 'It was so interesting,' wrote her mother, 'to see the scenes that had inspired the artists and the poets. I'd have painted something myself if I'd any talent. Rhys did some sketches of the churches with the tall spires. We were sad when we had to leave, as we'd a lovely time.'

'Wonderful,' thought Kate.

Reference Books

Pirinoa; People and Pasture, Ann Aburn, Carterton, 1987

Goodly Heritage: Eketahuna and districts, 100 years, 1873-1973, Irene Adcock, Eketahuna, 1973

Old Greytown: the story of the first hundred years of Greytown settlement, 1854-1954, A. G. Bagnall, Greytown, 1953

Wairarapa: an historical excursion, A. G. Bagnall, Masterton, 1976

Tawa Flat and the Old Porirua Road 1840-1955, A. Carman, Wellington, 1956

Gateway to the Wairarapa: the story of the tribulations and triumphs of the settlement of Featherston and district over the past 100 years, 1857-1957, C. J. Carle, Featherston, 1957

Swagger Country, Jim Henderson, Auckland, 1978

A meeting of gentlemen on matters agricultural: The Masterton Show 1871-1986, Angus McCallum, Masterton, 1986

Fruits of Toil: a history of the Catholic Church in the district of the Wairarapa, NZ, 1845-1956, Vincent J. McGlone, Carterton, 1957

Waiohine: a river and its people, Stephen Oxenham. Carterton, 1993

The Look of Greytown, Chris Slater & Ian F. Grant, Masterton, 2004

The Look of Carterton, Gareth Winter, Masterton , 2004